MAGICIAN

RAYMOND E. FEIST

VOLUME ONE OF THE RIFTWAR SAGA

MAGICIAN

BARNES
&NOBLE
BOOKS
NEW YORK

This edition published by Barnes & Noble, Inc., by arrangement with
The Doubleday Broadway Publishing Group, a division of Random House, Inc.

2003 Barnes & Noble Books

ISBN 0-7607-4177-8

Printed and bound in the United States of America

03 04 05 06 M 9 8 7 6 5 4 3 2 1

BVG

This book is dedicated to the memory of my father,
Felix E. Feist,
in all ways, a magician

# ACKNOWLEDGMENTS

Many people have provided me with incalculable aid in bringing this novel into existence. I would like to offer my heartfelt thanks to:

The Friday Nighters: April and Stephen Abrams; Steve Barett; David Brin; Anita and Jon Everson; Dave Guinasso; Conan LaMotte; Tim LeSelle; Ethan Munson; Bob Potter; Rich Spahl; Alan Springer; and Lori and Jeff Velten, for their useful criticism, enthusiasm, support, belief, wise counsel, wonderful ideas, and most of all, their friendship.

Billie and Russ Blake, and Lilian and Mike Fessier, for always being willing to help.

Harold Matson, my agent, for taking a chance on me.

Adrian Zackheim, my editor, for asking rather than demanding, and for working so hard to build a good book.

Kate Cronin, assistant to the editor, for having a sense of humor and for so gracefully putting up with all my nonsense.

Elaine Chubb, copy editor, for having such a gentle touch and for caring so much about the words.

And Barbara A. Feist, my mother, for all of the above and more.

RAYMOND E. FEIST
San Diego, California
July 1982

ACKNOWLEDGMENT TO THE REVISED EDITION

On this occasion, the publication of the author's preferred edition, I would like to add the following names to the preceding list, people who, though not known to me at the time I made the foregoing acknowledgment, proved invaluable aid to me in bringing *Magician* to the public and contributed materially to my success:

Mary Ellen Curley, who took over from Katie and kept us all on course.

Peter Schneider, whose enthusiasm for the work gave me a valued ally within Doubleday and a close friend for the last decade.

Lou Aronica, who bought it even when he really didn't want to do reprints, and for giving me the chance to return to my first work and "rewrite it one more time."

Pat Lobrutto, who helped before it was his job, and who took over at a tough time, and whose friendship endures beyond our business relationship.

Janna Silverstein, who despite her short tenure as my editor has shown an uncanny knack for knowing when to leave me alone and when to stay in touch.

Nick Austin, John Booth, Jonathan Lloyd, Malcolm Edwards, and everyone at Granada, now HarperCollins Books, who made the work an international bestseller.

Abner Stein, my British agent, who sold it to Nick in the first place.

Janny Wurts, for being my friend, and who, by working with me on the

Empire Trilogy, gave me a completely different perspective on the Tsurani; she helped turn The Game of the Council from a vague concept to a murderously real arena of human conflict. Kelewan and Tsuranuanni are as much her inventions as mine. I drew the outlines and she colored in the details.

And Jonathan Matson, who received the torch from a great man's hand and continued without faltering, for wise counsel and friendship. The acorn fell very close to the tree.

And most of all, my wife Kathlyn S. Starbuck, who understands my pain and joy in this craft because she toils in the same vineyard, and who is always there even when I don't deserve to have her there, and who makes things make sense through her love.

RAYMOND E. FEIST
San Diego, California
April 1991

FOREWORD TO THE REVISED EDITION

It is with some hesitation and a great deal of trepidation that an author approaches the task of revising an earlier edition of fiction. This is especially true if the book was his first effort, judged successful by most standards, and continuously in print for a decade.

Magician was all this, and more. In late 1977 I decided to try my hand at writing, part-time, while I was an employee of the University of California, San Diego. It is now some fifteen years later, and I have been a full-time writer for the last fourteen years, successful in this craft beyond my wildest dreams. *Magician*, the first novel in what became known as *The Riftwar Saga*, was a book that quickly took on a life of its own. I hesitate to admit this publicly, but the truth is that part of the success of the book was my ignorance of what makes a commercially successful novel. My willingness to plunge blindly forward into a tale spanning two dissimilar worlds, covering twelve years in the lives of several major and dozens of minor characters, breaking numerous rules of plotting along the way, seemed to find kindred souls among readers the world over. After a decade in print, my best judgment is that the appeal of the book is based upon its being what was known once as a "ripping yarn." I had little ambition beyond spinning a good story, one that satisfied my sense of wonder, adventure, and whimsy. It turned out that several million readers—many of whom read translations in languages I can't even begin to comprehend—found it one that satisfied their tastes for such a yarn as well.

But insofar as it was a first effort, some pressures of the marketplace did manifest themselves during the creation of the final book. *Magician* is by anyone's measure a large book. When the penultimate manuscript version sat upon my editor's desk, I was informed that some fifty thousand words would have to be cut. And cut I did. Mostly line by line, but a few scenes were either truncated or excised.

While I could live out my life with the original manuscript as published being the only edition ever read, I have always felt that some of the material cut added a certain resonance, a counterpoint if you will, to key elements of the tale. The relationships between characters, the additional details of an alien world, the minor moments of reflection and mirth that act to balance the more frenetic activity of conflict and adventure, all these things were "close but not quite what I had in mind."

In any event, to celebrate the tenth anniversary of the original publication of *Magician*, I have been permitted to return to this work, to reconstruct and change, to add and cut as I see fit, to bring forth what is known in publishing as the "Author's Preferred Edition" of the work. So, with the old admonition, "If it ain't broke, don't fix it," ringing in my ears, I return to the first work I undertook, back when I had no pretensions of craft, no stature as a bestselling author, and basically no idea of what I was doing. My desire is to restore some of those excised bits, some of the minor detail that I felt added to the heft of the narrative, as well as the weight of the book. Other material was more directly related to the books that follow, setting some of the background for the mythic underpinning of the Riftwar. The slightly lengthy discussion of lore between Tully and Kulgan in Chapter Three, as well as some of the things revealed to Pug on the Tower of Testing were clearly in this area. My editor wasn't sold on the idea of a sequel, then, so some of this was cut. Returning it may be self-indulgent, but as this was material I felt belonged in the original book, it has been restored.

To those readers who have already discovered *Magician*, who wonder if it's in their interests to purchase this edition, I would like to reassure them that nothing profound has been changed. No characters previously dead are now alive, no battles lost are now won, and two boys still find the same destiny. I ask you to feel no compulsion to read this new volume, for your memory of the original work is as valid, perhaps more so, than mine. But if you wish to return to the world of Pug and Tomas, to rediscover old friends and forgotten adventure, then consider this edition your opportunity to see a bit more than the last time. And to the new reader, welcome. I trust you'll find this work to your satisfaction.

It is with profound gratitude I wish to thank you all, new readers and old acquaintances, for without your support and encouragement, ten years of "ripping yarns" could not have been possible. If I have the opportunity to provide you with a small part of the pleasure I feel in being able to share my fanciful adventures with you, we are equally rewarded, for by your embracing my works you have allowed me to fashion more. Without you there would have been no *Silverthorn, A Darkness at Sethanon, Faerie Tale,* and no *Empire Trilogy*. The letters get read, if not answered—even if they sometimes take months to reach me —and the kind remarks, in passing at public appearances, have enriched me beyond measure. But most of all, you gave me the freedom to practice a craft that was begun to "see if I could do it," while working at the Residence Halls of John Muir College at UCSD.

So, thank you. I guess "I did it." And with this work, I hope you'll agree that *this time* I did it a little more elegantly, with a little more color, weight, and resonance.

RAYMOND E. FEIST
San Diego, California
August 1991

MAGICIAN

NORTHLANDS
The Great Northern Mountains
Stone Mountain
The Lake of the Sky
Elvandar
Crydee
The Far Coast
The Green Heart
The Grey Towers
Walinor
Hush
Natal
Ylith
Questor's View
Tyr-Sog
Yabon
LaMut
Loriél
Zūn
Hawk's Hollow
The Kingdom
Carse
Jonril
Tulan
Bordon
Port Natal
The Free Cities
Margrave's Port
Lan
Palanque
Queg
The Kingdom of Queg
Calastius Mountains
Sarth
Sorcerer's Isle
Sethanon
Darkmoor
Krondor
Dorgin
The Endless Sea
The Straits of Darkness
LiMeth
The Bitter Sea
Land's End
Landreth
Sea of Dreams
Durbin
Shamata
Vale of Dreams (Disputed Border)
Elarial
Ranom
Caralyan
Trollhome Mountains
Jal-Pur Desert
The Pillars of the Stars
Midkemia

of the World
Ironpass
Northwarden
Highcastle
THE BLACKWOOD
N
W
E
S
Dolth
Rodez
Ran
Euper
Romney
Tiburn
Sadara
Bas-Tyra
Silden
Cheam
Rillanon
Timons
THE KINGDOM OF ROLDEM
THE KINGDOM SEA
Deep Taunton
GREEN REACHES
Mallow Haven
Pointer's Head
The Peaks of Tranquillity
OF GREAT KESH

BOOK I

PUG AND TOMAS

A boy's will is the wind's will,
And the thoughts of youth are
long, long thoughts.

—LONGFELLOW, *My Lost Youth*

1

▼▼

STORM

THE STORM HAD BROKEN.

Pug danced along the edge of the rocks, his feet finding scant purchase as he made his way among the tide pools. His dark eyes darted about as he peered into each pool under the cliff face, seeking the spiny creatures driven into the shallows by the recently passed storm. His boyish muscles bunched under his light shirt as he shifted the sack of sandcrawlers, rockclaws, and crabs plucked from this water garden.

The afternoon sun sent sparkles through the sea spray swirling around him, as the west wind blew his sun-streaked brown hair about. Pug set his sack down, checked to make sure it was securely tied, then squatted on a clear patch of sand. The sack was not quite full, but Pug relished the extra hour or so that he could relax. Megar the cook wouldn't trouble him about the time as long as the sack was almost full. Resting with his back against a large rock, Pug was soon dozing in the sun's warmth.

A cool wet spray woke him hours later. He opened his eyes with a start, knowing he had stayed much too long. Westward, over the sea, dark thunderheads were forming above the black outline of the Six Sisters, the small islands on the horizon. The roiling, surging clouds, with rain trailing below like some sooty veil, heralded another of the sudden storms common to this part of the coast in early summer. To the south, the high bluffs of Sailor's Grief reared up against the sky, as waves crashed against the base of that rocky pinnacle. Whitecaps started to form behind the breakers, a sure sign the storm would quickly strike. Pug knew he was in danger, for the storms of summer could drown anyone on the beaches, or if severe enough, on the low ground beyond.

He picked up his sack and started north, toward the castle. As he moved among the pools, he felt the coolness in the wind turn to a deeper, wetter cold. The day began to be broken by a patchwork of shadows as the first clouds passed before the sun, bright colors fading to shades of grey. Out to sea, lightning flashed against the blackness of the clouds, and the distant boom of thunder rode over the noise of the waves.

Pug picked up speed when he came to the first stretch of open beach. The storm was coming in faster than he would have thought possible, driving the rising tide before it. By the time he reached the second stretch of tide pools, there was barely ten feet of dry sand between water's edge and cliffs.

Pug hurried as fast as was safe across the rocks, twice nearly catching his foot. As he reached the next expanse of sand, he mistimed his jump from the last rock and landed poorly. He fell to the sand, grasping his ankle. As if waiting for the mishap, the tide surged forward, covering him for a moment. He reached out blindly and felt his sack carried away. Frantically grabbing at it, Pug lunged forward, only to have his ankle fail. He went under, gulping water. He raised his head, sputtering and coughing. He started to stand when a second wave, higher than the last, hit him in the chest, knocking him backward. Pug had grown up playing in the waves and was an experienced swimmer, but the pain of his ankle and the battering of the waves were bringing him to the edge of panic. He fought it off and came up for air as the wave receded. He half swam, half scrambled toward the cliff face, knowing the water would be only inches deep there.

Pug reached the cliffs and leaned against them, keeping as much weight off the injured ankle as possible. He inched along the rock wall, while each wave brought the water higher. When Pug finally reached a place where he could make his way upward, water was swirling at his waist. He had to use all his strength to pull himself up to the path. He lay panting a moment, then started to crawl up the pathway, unwilling to trust his balky ankle on this rocky footing.

The first drops of rain began to fall as he scrambled along, bruising knees and shins on the rocks, until he reached the grassy top of the bluffs. Pug fell forward exhausted, panting from the exertion of the climb. The scattered drops grew into a light but steady rain.

When he had caught his breath, Pug sat up and examined the swollen ankle. It was tender to the touch, but he was reassured when he could move it: it was not broken. He would have to limp the entire way back, but with the threat of drowning on the beach behind him, he felt relatively buoyant.

Pug would be a drenched, chilled wretch when he reached the town. He would have to find a lodging there, for the gates of the castle would be closed for the night, and with his tender ankle he would not attempt to climb the wall behind the stables. Besides, should he wait and slip into the keep the next day, only Megar would have words for him, but if he was caught coming over the wall, Swordmaster Fannon or Horsemaster Algon would surely have a lot worse in store for him than words.

While he rested, the rain took on an insistent quality and the sky darkened as the late-afternoon sun was completely engulfed in storm clouds. His momentary relief was replaced with anger at himself for losing the sack of sandcrawlers. His displeasure doubled when he considered his folly at falling asleep. Had he remained awake, he would have made the return trip unhurriedly, would not have sprained his ankle, and would have had time to explore the streambed above the bluffs for the smooth stones he prized so dearly for slinging. Now there would be no stones, and it would be at least another week before he could return. If Megar didn't send another boy instead, which was likely now that he was returning empty-handed.

Pug's attention shifted to the discomfort of sitting in the rain, and he decided it was time to move on. He stood and tested his ankle. It protested such treatment, but he could get along on it. He limped over the grass to where he had left his belongings and picked up his rucksack, staff, and sling. He swore an oath he had heard soldiers at the keep use when he found the rucksack ripped apart and his bread and cheese missing. Raccoons, or possibly sand lizards, he thought. He tossed the now useless sack aside and wondered at his misfortune.

Taking a deep breath, he leaned on his staff as he started across the low rolling hills that divided the bluffs from the road. Stands of small trees were scattered over the landscape, and Pug regretted there wasn't more substantial shelter nearby, for there was none upon the bluffs. He would be no wetter for trudging to town than for staying under a tree.

The wind picked up, and Pug felt the first cold bite against his wet back. He shivered and hurried his pace as well as he could. The small trees started to bend before the wind, and Pug felt as if a great hand were pushing at his back. Reaching the road, he turned north. He heard the eerie sound of the great forest off to the east, the wind whistling through the branches of the ancient oaks, adding to its already foreboding aspect. The dark glades of the forest were probably no more perilous than the King's road, but remembered tales of outlaws and other, less human, malefactors stirred the hairs on the boy's neck.

Cutting across the King's road, Pug gained a little shelter in the gully that ran alongside it. The wind intensified and rain stung his eyes, bringing tears to already wet cheeks. A gust caught him, and he stumbled off balance for a moment. Water was gathering in the roadside gully, and he had to step carefully to keep from losing his footing in unexpectedly deep puddles.

For nearly an hour he made his way through the ever growing storm. The road turned northwest, bringing him almost full face into the howling wind. Pug leaned into the wind, his shirt whipping out behind him. He swallowed hard, to force down the choking panic rising within him. He knew he was in danger now, for the storm was gaining in fury far beyond normal for this time of year. Great ragged bolts of lightning lit the dark landscape, briefly outlining the trees and road in harsh, brilliant white and opaque black. The dazzling afterimages, black and white reversed, stayed with him for a moment each time, confusing his senses. Enormous thunder peals sounding overhead felt like physical blows. Now his fear of the storm outweighed his fear of imagined brigands and goblins. He decided to walk among the trees near the road; the wind would be lessened somewhat by the boles of the oaks.

As Pug closed upon the forest, a crashing sound brought him to a halt. In the gloom of the storm he could barely make out the form of a black forest boar as it burst out of the undergrowth. The pig tumbled from the brush, lost its footing, then scrambled to its feet a few yards away. Pug could see it clearly as it stood there regarding him, swinging its head from side to side. Two large tusks seemed to glow in the dim light as they dripped rainwater. Fear made its eyes wide, and it pawed at the ground. The forest pigs were bad-tempered at best, but normally avoided humans. This one was panic-stricken by the storm, and Pug knew if it charged he could be badly gored, even killed.

Standing stock-still, Pug made ready to swing his staff, but hoped the pig would return to the woods. The boar's head raised, testing the boy's smell on the wind. Its pink eyes seemed to glow as it trembled with indecision. A sound made it turn toward the trees for a moment, then it dropped its head and charged.

Pug swung his staff, bringing it down in a glancing blow to the side of the pig's head, turning it. The pig slid sideways in the muddy footing, hitting Pug in the legs. He went down as the pig slipped past. Lying on the ground, Pug saw the boar skitter about as it turned to charge again.

Suddenly the pig was upon him, and Pug had no time to stand. He thrust the staff before him in a vain attempt to turn the animal again. The boar dodged the staff and Pug tried to roll away, but a weight fell across his body. Pug covered his face with his hands, keeping his arms close to his chest, expecting to be gored.

After a moment he realized the pig was still. Uncovering his face, he discovered the pig lying across his lower legs, a black-feathered, cloth-yard arrow protruding from its side. Pug looked toward the forest. A man garbed in brown leather was standing near the edge of the trees, quickly wrapping a yeoman's longbow with an oilcloth cover. Once the valuable weapon was protected from further abuse by the weather, the man crossed to stand over the boy and beast.

He was cloaked and hooded, his face hidden. He knelt next to Pug and shouted over the sound of the wind, "Are you 'right, boy?" as he lifted the dead boar easily from Pug's legs. "Bones broken?"

"I don't think so," Pug yelled back, taking account of himself. His right side smarted, and his legs felt equally bruised. With his ankle still tender, he was feeling ill-used today, but nothing seemed broken or permanently damaged.

Large, meaty hands lifted him to his feet. "Here," the man commanded, handing him his staff and the bow. Pug took them while the stranger quickly gutted the boar with a large hunter's knife. He completed his work and turned to Pug. "Come with me, boy. You had best lodge with my master and me. It's not far, but we'd best hurry. This storm'll get worse afore it's over. Can you walk?"

Taking an unsteady step, Pug nodded. Without a word the man shouldered the pig and took his bow. "Come," he said, as he turned toward the forest. He set off at a brisk pace, which Pug had to scramble to match.

The forest cut the fury of the storm so little that conversation was impossible. A lightning flash lit the scene for a moment, and Pug caught a glimpse of the man's face. Pug tried to remember if he had seen the stranger before. He had the look common to the hunters and foresters that lived in the forest of Crydee: large-shouldered, tall, and solidly built. He had dark hair and beard and the raw, weather-beaten appearance of one who spends most of his time outdoors.

For a few fanciful moments the boy wondered if he might be some member of an outlaw band, hiding in the heart of the forest. He gave up the notion, for no outlaw would trouble himself with an obviously penniless keep boy.

Remembering the man had mentioned having a master, Pug suspected he was a franklin, one who lived on the estate of a landholder.

He would be in the holder's service, but not bound to him as a bondsman. The franklins were freeborn, giving a share of crop or herd in exchange for the use of land. He must be freeborn. No bondsman would be allowed to carry a longbow, for they were much too valuable—and dangerous. Still, Pug couldn't remember any landholdings in the forest. It was a mystery to the boy, but the toll of the day's abuses was quickly driving away any curiosity.

AFTER WHAT SEEMED to be hours, the man walked into a thicket of trees. Pug nearly lost him in the darkness, for the sun had set some time before, taking with it what faint light the storm had allowed. He followed the man more from the sound of his footfalls and an awareness of his presence than from sight. Pug sensed he was on a path through the trees, for his footsteps met no resisting brush or detritus. From where they had been moments before, the path would be difficult to find in the daylight, impossible at night, unless it was already known. Soon they entered a clearing, in the midst of which sat a small stone cottage. Light shone through a single window, and smoke rose from the chimney. They crossed the clearing, and Pug wondered at the storm's relative mildness in this one spot in the forest.

Once before the door, the man stood to one side and said, "You go in, boy. I must dress the pig."

Nodding dumbly, Pug pushed open the wooden door and stepped in.

"Close that door, boy! You'll give me a chill and cause me my death."

Pug jumped to obey, slamming the door harder than he intended.

He turned, taking in the scene before him. The interior of the cottage was a small single room. Against one wall was the fireplace, with a good-size hearth before it. A bright, cheery fire burned, casting a warm glow. Next to the fireplace a table sat, behind which a heavyset, yellow-robed figure rested on a bench. His grey hair and beard nearly covered his entire head, except for a pair of vivid blue eyes that twinkled in the firelight. A long pipe emerged from the beard, producing heroic clouds of pale smoke.

Pug knew the man. "Master Kulgan . . . ," he began, for the man was the Duke's magician and adviser, a familiar face around the castle keep.

Kulgan leveled a gaze at Pug, then said in a deep voice, given to rich rolling sounds and powerful tones, "So you know me, then?"

"Yes, sir. From the castle."

"What is your name, boy from the keep?"

"Pug, Master Kulgan."

"Now I remember you." The magician absently waved his hand. "Do not call me 'Master,' Pug—though I am rightly called a master of my arts," he said with a merry crinkling around his eyes. "I am higher-born than you, it is true, but not by much. Come, there is a blanket hanging by the fire, and you are drenched. Hang your clothes to dry, then sit there." He pointed to a bench opposite him.

Pug did as he was bid, keeping an eye on the magician the entire time. He was a member of the Duke's court, but still a magician, an object of suspicion, generally held in low esteem by the common folk. If a farmer had a cow calve a monster, or blight strike the crops, villagers were apt to ascribe it to the work of some magician lurking in nearby shadows. In times not too far past they would have stoned Kulgan from Crydee as like as not. His position with the Duke earned him the tolerance of the townsfolk now, but old fears died slowly.

After his garments were hung, Pug sat down. He started when he saw a pair of red eyes regarding him from just beyond the magician's table. A scaled head rose up above the tabletop and studied the boy.

Kulgan laughed at the boy's discomfort. "Come, boy. Fantus will not eat you." He dropped his hand to the head of the creature, who sat next to him on his bench, and rubbed above its eye ridges. It closed its eyes and gave forth a soft crooning sound, not unlike the purring of a cat.

Pug shut his mouth, which had popped open with surprise, then asked, "Is he truly a dragon, sir?"

The magician laughed, a rich, good-natured sound. "Betimes he thinks he is, boy. Fantus is a firedrake, cousin to the dragon, though of smaller stature." The creature opened one eye and fastened it on the magician. "But of equal heart," Kulgan quickly added, and the drake closed his eye again. Kulgan spoke softly, in conspiratorial tones. "He is very clever, so mind what you say to him. He is a creature of finely fashioned sensibilities."

Pug nodded that he would. "Can he breathe fire?" he asked, eyes wide with wonder. To any boy of thirteen, even a cousin to a dragon was worthy of awe.

"When the mood suits him, he can belch out a flame or two, though he seems rarely in the mood. I think it is due to the rich diet I supply him with, boy. He has not had to hunt for years, so he is something out of practice in the ways of drakes. In truth, I spoil him shamelessly."

Pug found the notion somehow reassuring. If the magician cared enough to spoil this creature, no matter how outlandish, then he seemed somehow more human, less mysterious. Pug studied Fantus, admiring how the fire brought golden highlights to his emerald scales. About the size of a small hound, the drake possessed a long, sinuous neck atop which rested an alligatorlike head. His wings were folded across his back, and two clawed feet extended before him, aimlessly pawing the air, while Kulgan scratched behind bony eye ridges. His long tail swung back and forth, inches above the floor.

The door opened and the big bowman entered, holding a dressed and spitted loin of pork before him. Without a word he crossed to the fireplace and set the meat to cook. Fantus raised his head, using his long neck to good advantage to peek over the table. With a flick of his forked tongue, the drake jumped down and, in stately fashion, ambled over to the hearth. He selected a warm spot before the fire and curled up to doze away the wait before dinner.

The franklin unfastened his cloak and hung it on a peg by the door. "Storm will pass afore dawn, I'm thinking." He returned to the fire and prepared a basting of wine and herbs for the pig. Pug was startled to see a large scar that ran down the left side of the man's face, showing red and angry in the firelight.

Kulgan waved his pipe in the franklin's direction. "Knowing my tight-lipped man here, you'll not have made his proper acquaintance. Meecham, this boy is Pug, from the keep at Castle Crydee." Meecham gave a brief nod, then returned to tending the roasting loin.

Pug nodded back, though a bit late for Meecham to notice. "I never thought to thank you for saving me from the boar."

Meecham replied, "There's no need for thanks, boy. Had I not startled the beast, it's unlikely it would have charged you." He left the hearth and crossed over to another part of the room, took some brown dough from a cloth-covered bucket, and started kneading.

"Well, sir," said Pug to Kulgan, "it was his arrow that killed the pig. It was indeed fortunate that he was following the animal."

Kulgan laughed. "The poor creature, who is our most welcome guest for dinner, happened to be as much a victim of circumstance as yourself."

Pug looked perplexed. "I don't follow, sir."

Kulgan stood and took down an object from the topmost shelf on his bookcase and placed it on the table before the boy. It was wrapped in a cover of dark blue velvet, so Pug knew at once it must be a prize of great value for such an expensive material to be used for covering. Kulgan removed the velvet, revealing an orb of crystal that gleamed in the firelight. Pug gave an *ah* of pleasure at the beauty of it, for it was without apparent flaw and splendid in its simplicity of form.

Kulgan pointed to the sphere of glass. "This device was fashioned as a gift by Althafain of Carse, a most puissant artificer of magic, who thought me worthy of such a present, as I have done him a favor or two in the past—but that is of little matter. Having just this day returned from the company of Master Althafain, I was testing his token. Look deep into the orb, Pug."

Pug fixed his eyes on the ball and tried to follow the flicker of firelight that seemed to play deep within its structure. The reflections of the room, multiplied a hundredfold, merged and danced as his eyes tried to fasten upon each aspect within the orb. They flowed and blended, then grew cloudy and obscure. A soft white glow at the center of the ball replaced the red of firelight, and Pug felt his gaze become trapped by its pleasing warmth. Like the warmth of the kitchen at the keep, he thought absently.

Suddenly the milky white within the ball vanished, and Pug could see an image of the kitchen before his eyes. Fat Alfan the cook was making pastries, licking the sweet crumbs from his fingers. This brought the wrath of Megar, the head cook, down upon his head, for Megar considered it a disgusting habit. Pug laughed at the scene, one he had witnessed before many times, and it vanished. Suddenly he felt tired.

Kulgan wrapped the orb in the cloth and put it away. "You did well, boy," he said thoughtfully. He stood watching the boy for a moment, as if considering something, then sat down. "I would not have suspected you of being able to fashion such a clear image in one try, but you seem to be more than you first appear to be."

"Sir?"

"Never mind, Pug." He paused for a moment, then said, "I was using that toy for the first time, judging how far I could send my sight, when I spied you making for the road. From your limp and bruised condition, I judged that you would never reach the town, so I sent Meecham to fetch you."

Pug looked embarrassed by the unusual attention, color rising to his cheeks. He said, with a thirteen-year-old's high estimation of his own ability, "You needn't have done that, sir. I would have reached the town in due time."

Kulgan smiled. "Perhaps, but then again, perhaps not. The storm is unseasonably severe and perilous for traveling."

Pug listened to the soft tattoo of rain on the roof of the cottage. The storm seemed to have slackened, and Pug doubted the magician's words. As if reading the boy's thought, Kulgan said, "Doubt me not, Pug. This glade is protected by more than the great boles. Should you pass beyond the circle of oaks that marks the edge of my holding, you would feel the storm's fury. Meecham, how do you gauge this wind?"

Meecham put down the bread dough he was kneading and thought for a moment. "Near as bad as the storm that beached six ships three years back." He paused for a moment, as if reconsidering the estimate, then nodded his endorsement. "Yes, nearly as bad, though it won't blow so long."

Pug thought back three years to the storm that had blown a Quegan trading fleet bound for Crydee onto the rocks of Sailor's Grief. At its height, the guards on the castle walls were forced to stay in the towers, lest they be blown down. If this storm was that severe, then Kulgan's magic was impressive, for outside the cottage it sounded no worse than a spring rain.

Kulgan sat back on the bench, occupied with trying to light his extinguished pipe. As he produced a large cloud of sweet white smoke, Pug's attention wandered to a case of books standing behind the magician. His lips moved silently as he tried to discern what was written on the bindings, but could not.

Kulgan lifted an eyebrow and said, "So you can read, aye?"

Pug started, alarmed that he might have offended the magician by intruding on his domain. Kulgan, sensing his embarrassment, said, "It is all right, boy. It is no crime to know letters."

Pug felt his discomfort diminish. "I can read a little, sir. Megar the cook has shown me how to read the tallies on the stores laid away for the kitchen in the cellars. I know some numbers, as well."

"Numbers, too," the magician exclaimed good-naturedly. "Well, you are something of a rare bird." He reached behind himself and pulled out one volume, bound in red-brown leather, from the shelf. He opened it, squinting at one page, then another, and at last found a page that seemed to meet his requirements. He turned the open book around and lay it upon the table before Pug. Kulgan pointed to a page illuminated by a magnificent design of snakes, flowers, and twining vines in a colorful design around a large letter in the upper left corner. "Read this, boy."

Pug had never seen anything remotely like it. His lessons had been on plain parchment with letters fashioned in Megar's blunt script, using a charcoal stick. He sat, fascinated by the details of the work, then realized the magician was staring at him. Regaining his wits, he began to read.

"And then there came a sum . . . summons from . . ." He looked at the word, stumbling over the complex combinations that were new to him. ". . . Zacara." He paused, looking at Kulgan to see if he was correct. The magician nodded for him to continue. "For the north was to be forgot . . . forgotten, lest the heart of the empire lan . . . languish and all be lost. And though of Bosania from birth, those soldiers still were loyal to Great Kesh in their service. So for her great need, they took up their arms and put on their armor and quit Bosania, taking ship to the south, to save all from destruction."

Kulgan said, "That's enough," and gently closed the cover of the book. "You are well gifted with letters for a keep boy."

"This book, sir, what is it?" asked Pug, as Kulgan took it from him. "I have never seen anything like it."

Kulgan looked at Pug for a moment, with a gaze that made him uncomfortable again, then smiled, breaking the tension. As he put the book back, he said, "It is a history of this land, boy. It was given as a gift by the abbot of an Ishapian monastery. It is a translation of a Keshian text, over a hundred years old."

Pug nodded and said, "It all sounded very strange. What does it tell of?"

Kulgan once more looked at Pug as if trying to see something inside of the boy, then said, "A long time ago, Pug, all these lands, from the Endless Sea across the Grey Tower Mountains to the Bitter Sea, were part of the Empire of Great Kesh. Far to the east existed a small kingdom, on one small island called Rillanon. It grew to engulf its neighboring island kingdoms, and it became the Kingdom of the Isles. Later it expanded again to the mainland, and while it is still the Kingdom of Isles, most of us simply call it 'the Kingdom.' We, who live in Crydee, are part of the Kingdom, though we live as far from the capital city of Rillanon as one can and still be within its boundaries.

"Once, many long years ago, the Empire of Great Kesh abandoned these lands, for it was engaged in a long and bloody conflict with its neighbors to the south, the Keshian Confederacy."

Pug was caught up in the grandeur of lost empires, but hungry enough to notice Meecham was putting several small loaves of dark bread in hearth oven. He turned his attention back to the magician. "Who were the Keshian Con— . . . ?"

"The Keshian Confederacy," Kulgan finished for the boy. "It is a group of small nations who had existed as tributaries to Great Kesh for centuries. A dozen years before that book was written, they united against their oppressor. Each alone was insufficient to contest with Great Kesh, but united they proved its match. Too close a match, for the war dragged on year after year. The Empire was forced to strip its northern provinces of their legions and send them south, leaving the north open to the advances of the new, younger Kingdom.

"It was Duke Borric's grandfather, youngest son of the King, who brought the army westward, extending the Western Realm. Since then all of what was once the old imperial province of Bosania, except for the Free Cities of Natal, has been called the Duchy of Crydee."

Pug thought for a moment, then said, "I think I would like to travel to this Great Kesh someday."

Meecham snorted, something close to a laugh. "And what would you be traveling as, a freebooter?"

Pug felt his face flush. Freebooters were landless men, mercenaries who fought for pay, and who were regarded as being only one cut above outlaws.

Kulgan said, "Perhaps you might someday, Pug. The way is long and full of peril, but it is not unheard of for a brave and hearty soul to survive the journey. Stranger things have been known to happen."

The talk at the table turned to more common topics, for the magician had been at the southern keep at Carse for over a month and wanted the gossip of Crydee. When the bread was done baking, Meecham served it hot, carved the pork loin, and brought out plates of cheese and greens. Pug had never eaten so well in his life. Even when he had worked in the kitchen, his position as keep boy earned him only meager fare. Twice during dinner, Pug found the magician regarding him intently.

When the meal was over, Meecham cleared the table, then began washing the dishes with clean sand and fresh water, while Kulgan and Pug sat talking. A single scrap of meat remained on the table, which Kulgan tossed over to Fantus, who lay before the fire. The drake opened one eye to regard the morsel. He pondered the choice between his comfortable resting place and the juicy scrap for a moment, then moved the necessary six inches to gulp down the prize and closed his eye again.

Kulgan lit his pipe, and once he was satisfied with its production of smoke, he said, "What are your plans when you reach manhood, boy?"

Pug was fighting off sleep, but Kulgan's question brought him alert again. The time of Choosing, when the boys of the town and keep were taken into apprenticeship, was close, and Pug became excited as he said, "This Midsummer's Day I hope to take the Duke's service under Swordmaster Fannon."

Kulgan regarded his slight guest. "I would have thought you still a year or two away from apprenticeship, Pug."

Meecham gave out a sound somewhere between a laugh and a grunt. "Bit small to be lugging around sword and shield, aren't you, boy?"

Pug flushed. He was the smallest boy of his age in the castle. "Megar the cook said I may be late coming to my growth," he said with a faint note of defiance. "No one knows who my parents were, so they have no notion of what to expect."

"Orphan, is it?" asked Meecham, raising one eyebrow, his most expressive gesture yet.

Pug nodded. "I was left with the Priests of Dala, in the mountain abbey, by a woman who claimed she found me in the road. They brought me to the keep, for they had no way to care for me."

"Yes," injected Kulgan, "I remember when those who worship the Shield of the Weak first brought you to the castle. You were no more than a baby fresh from the teat. It is only through the Duke's kindness that you are a freeman today. He felt it a lesser evil to free a bondsman's son than to bond a freeman's. Without proof, it was his right to have you declared bondsman."

Meecham said in a noncommittal tone, "A good man, the Duke."

Pug had heard the story of his origin a hundred times before from Magya in the kitchen of the castle. He felt completely wrung out and could barely keep his eyes open. Kulgan noticed and signaled Meecham. The tall franklin took some blankets from a shelf and prepared a sleeping pallet. By the time he finished, Pug had fallen asleep with his head on the table. The large man's hands lifted him gently from the stool and placed him on the blankets, then covered him.

Fantus opened his eyes and regarded the sleeping boy. With a wolfish yawn, he scrambled over next to Pug and snuggled in close. Pug shifted his weight in his sleep and draped one arm over the drake's neck. The firedrake gave an approving rumble, deep in his throat, and closed his eyes again.

2

▾▾

APPRENTICE

THE FOREST WAS QUIET.

The slight afternoon breeze stirred the tall oaks and cut the day's heat, while rustling the leaves only slightly. Birds who would raise a raucous chorus at sunrise and sundown were mostly quiet at this time of morning. The faint tang of sea salt mixed with the sweet smell of flowers and pungency of decaying leaves.

Pug and Tomas walked slowly along the path, with the aimless weaving steps of boys who have no particular place to go and ample time to get there. Pug shied a small rock at an imagined target, then turned to look at his companion. "You don't think your mother was mad, do you?" he asked.

Tomas smiled. "No, she understands how things are. She's seen other boys the day of Choosing. And truthfully, we were more of hindrance than a help in the kitchen today."

Pug nodded. He had spilled a precious pot of honey as he carried it to Alfan, the pastrycook. Then he had dumped an entire tray of fresh bread loaves as he took them from the oven. "I made something of a fool of myself today, Tomas."

Tomas laughed. He was a tall boy, with sandy hair and bright blue eyes. With his quick smile, he was well liked in the keep, in spite of a boyish tendency to find trouble. He was Pug's closest friend, more brother than friend, and for that reason Pug earned some measure of acceptance from the other boys, for they all regarded Tomas as their unofficial leader.

Tomas said, "You were no more the fool than I. At least you didn't forget to hang the beef sides high." Pug grinned. "Anyway, the Duke's hounds are happy." He snickered, then laughed. "She is angry, isn't she?"

Tomas laughed along with his friend. "She's mad. Still, the dogs only ate a little before she shooed them off. Besides, she's mostly mad at Father. She claims the Choosing's only an excuse for all the Craftmasters to sit around smoking pipes, drinking ale, and swapping tales all day. She says they already know who will choose which boy."

Pug said, "From what the other women say, she's not alone in that opinion." Then he grinned at Tomas. "Probably not wrong, either."

Tomas lost his smile. "She truly doesn't like it when he's not in the kitchen to oversee things. I think she knows this, which is why she tossed us out of the keep for the morning, so she wouldn't take out her temper on us. Or at least you," he added with a questioning smile. "I swear you're her favorite."

Pug's grin returned and he laughed again. "Well, I do cause less trouble."

With a playful punch to the arm, Tomas said, "You mean you get caught less often."

Pug pulled his sling out from within his shirt. "If we came back with a brace of partridge or quail, she might regain some of her good temper."

Tomas smiled. "She might," he agreed, taking out his own sling. Both boys were excellent slingers, Tomas being undoubted champion among the boys, edging Pug by only a little. It was unlikely either could bring down a bird on the wing, but should they find one at rest, there was a fair chance they might hit it. Besides, it would give them something to do to pass the hours and perhaps for a time forget the Choosing.

With exaggerated stealth they crept along, playing the part of hunters. Tomas led the way as they left the footpath, heading for the watering pool they knew lay not too far distant. It was improbable they would spot game this time of the day unless they simply blundered across it, but if any were to be found, it most likely would be near the pool. The woods to the northeast of the town of Crydee were less forbidding than the great forest to the south. Many years of harvesting trees for lumber had given the green glades a sunlit airiness not found in the deep haunts of the southern forest. The keep boys had often played here over the years. With small imagination, the woods were transformed into a wondrous place, a green world of high adventure. Some of the greatest deeds known had taken place here. Daring escapes, dread quests, and mightily contested battles had been witnessed by the silent trees as the boys gave vent to their youthful dreams of coming manhood. Foul creatures, mighty monsters, and base outlaws had all been fought and vanquished, often accompanied by the death of a great hero, with appropriate last words to his mourning companions, all managed with just enough time left to return to the keep for supper.

Tomas reached a small rise that overlooked the pool, screened off by young beech saplings, and pulled aside some brush so they could mount a vigil. He stopped, awed, and softly said, "Pug, look!" Standing at the edge of the pool was a stag, head held high as he sought the source of something that disturbed his drinking. He was an old animal, the hair around his muzzle nearly all white, and his head crowned by magnificent antlers.

Pug counted quickly. "He has fourteen points."

Tomas nodded agreement. "He must be the oldest buck in the forest." The stag turned his attention in the boys' direction, flicking an ear nervously. They froze, not wishing to frighten off such a beautiful creature. For a long, silent minute the stag studied the rise, nostrils flaring, then slowly lowered his head to the pool and drank.

Tomas gripped Pug's shoulder and inclined his head to one side. Pug followed Tomas's motion and saw a figure walking silently into the clearing. He was a tall man dressed in leather clothing, dyed forest green. Across his back hung a longbow and at his belt a hunter's knife. His green cloak's hood was thrown back, and he walked toward the stag with a steady, even step. Tomas said, "It's Martin."

Pug also recognized the Duke's Huntmaster. An orphan like Pug, Martin had come to be known as Longbow by those in the castle, as he had few equals with that weapon. Something of a mystery, Martin Longbow was still well liked by the boys, for while he was aloof with the adults in the castle, he was always friendly and accessible to the boys. As Huntmaster, he was also the Duke's Forester. His duties absented him from the castle for days, even weeks at a time, as he kept his trackers busy looking for signs of poaching, possible fire dangers, migrating goblins, or outlaws camping in the woods. But when he was in the castle, and not organizing a hunt for the Duke, he always had time for the boys. His dark eyes were always merry when they pestered him with questions of woodlore or for tales of the lands near the boundaries of Crydee. He seemed to possess unending patience, which set him apart from most of the Craftmasters in the town and keep.

Martin came up to the stag, gently reached out, and touched his neck. The great head swung up, and the stag nuzzled Martin's arm.

Softly Martin said, "If you walk out slowly, without speaking, he might let you approach."

Pug and Tomas exchanged startled glances, then stepped into the clearing. They walked slowly around the edge of the pool, the stag following their movements with his head, trembling slightly. Martin patted him reassuringly and he quieted. Tomas and Pug came to stand beside the hunter, and Martin said, "Reach out and touch him, slowly so as not to frighten him."

Tomas reached out first, and the stag trembled beneath his fingers. Pug began to reach out, and the stag retreated a step. Martin crooned to the stag in a language Pug had never heard before, and the animal stood still. Pug touched him and marveled at the feel of his coat—so like the cured hides he had touched before, yet so different for the feel of life pulsing under his fingertips.

Suddenly the stag backed off and turned. Then, with a single bounding leap, he was gone among the trees. Martin Longbow chuckled and said, "Just as well. It wouldn't do to have him become too friendly with men. Those antlers would quickly end up over some poacher's fireplace."

Tomas whispered, "He's beautiful, Martin."

Longbow nodded, his eyes still fastened upon the spot where the stag had vanished into the woods. "That he is, Tomas."

Pug said, "I thought you hunted stags, Martin. How—"

Martin said, "Old Whitebeard and I have something of an understanding, Pug. I hunt only bachelor stags, without does, or does too old to calve. When Whitebeard loses his harem to some younger buck someday, I may take him. Now each leaves the other to his own way. The day will come when I will look at him down the shaft of an arrow." He smiled at the boys. "I won't know until then if I shall let the shaft fly. Perhaps I will, perhaps not." He fell silent for a time, as if the thought of Whitebeard's becoming old was saddening, then as a light breeze rustled the branches said, "Now, what brings two such bold hunters into the Duke's woods in the early morning? There must be a thousand things left undone with the Midsummer festival this afternoon."

Tomas answered. "My mother tossed us out of the kitchen. We were more trouble than not. With the Choosing today . . ." His voice died away, and he felt suddenly embarrassed. Much of Martin's mysterious reputation stemmed from when he first came to Crydee. At his time for the Choosing, he had been placed directly with the old Huntmaster by the Duke, rather than standing before the assembled Craftmasters with the other boys his age. This violation of one of the oldest traditions known had offended many people in town, though none would dare openly express such feelings to Lord Borric. As was natural, Martin became the object of their ire, rather than the Duke. Over the years Martin had more than justified Lord Borric's decision, but still most people were troubled by the Duke's special treatment of him that one day. Even after twelve years some people still regarded Martin Longbow as being different and, as such, worthy of distrust.

Tomas said, "I'm sorry, Martin."

Martin nodded in acknowledgment, but without humor. "I understand, Tomas. I may not have had to endure your uncertainty, but I have seen many others wait for the day of Choosing. And for four years I myself have stood with the other Masters, so I know a little of your worry."

A thought struck Pug and he blurted, "But you're not with the other Craftmasters."

Martin shook his head, a rueful expression playing across his even features. "I had thought that, in light of your worry, you might fail to observe the obvious. But you've a sharp wit about you, Pug."

Tomas didn't understand what they were saying for a moment, then comprehension dawned. "Then you'll select no apprentices!"

Martin raised a finger to his lips. "Not a word, lad. No, with young Garret chosen last year, I've a full company of trackers."

Tomas was disappointed. He wished more than anything to take service with Swordmaster Fannon, but should he not be chosen as a soldier, then he would prefer the life of a forester, under Martin. Now his second choice was denied him. After a moment of dark brooding, he brightened: perhaps Martin didn't choose him because Fannon already had.

Seeing his friend entering a cycle of elation and depression as he considered all the possibilities, Pug said, "You haven't been in the keep for nearly a month, Martin." He put away the sling he still held and asked, "Where have you kept yourself?"

Martin looked at Pug as the boy instantly regretted his question. As friendly as Martin could be, he was still Huntmaster, a member of the Duke's household, and keep boys did not make a habit of questioning the comings and goings of the Duke's staff.

Martin relieved Pug's embarrassment with a slight smile. "I've been to Elvandar. Queen Aglaranna has ended her twenty years of mourning the death of her husband, the Elf King. There was a great celebration."

Pug was surprised by the answer. To him, as to most people in Crydee, the elves were little more than legend. But Martin had spent his youth near the elven forests and was one of the few humans to come and go through those forests to the north at will. It was another thing that set Martin Longbow apart from others. While Martin had shared elvish lore with the boys before, this was the first time in Pug's memory he had spoken of his relationship to the elves. Pug stammered, "You feasted with the Elf Queen?"

Martin assumed a pose of modest inconsequence. "Well, I sat at the table farthest from the throne, but yes; I was there." Seeing the unasked questions in their eyes, he continued. "You know as a boy I was raised by the monks of Silban's Abbey, near the elven forest. I played with elven children, and before I came here, I hunted with Prince Calin and his cousin, Galain."

Tomas nearly jumped with excitement. Elves were a subject holding particular fascination for him. "Did you know King Aidan?"

Martin's expression clouded, and his eyes narrowed, his manner suddenly becoming stiff. Tomas saw Martin's reaction and said, "I'm sorry, Martin. Did I say something wrong?"

Martin waved away the apology. "No fault of yours, Tomas," he said, his manner softening somewhat. "The elves do not use the names of those who have gone to the Blessed Isles, especially those who have died untimely. They believe to do so recalls those spoken of from their journey there, denying them their final rest. I respect their beliefs.

"Well, to answer you, no, I never met him. He was killed when I was only a small boy. But I have heard the stories of his deeds, and he was a good and wise King by all accounts." Martin looked about. "It approaches noon. We should return to the keep."

He began to walk toward the path, and the boys fell in beside him.

"What was the feast like, Martin?" asked Tomas.

Pug sighed as the hunter began to speak of the marvels of Elvandar. He was also fascinated by tales of the elves, but to nowhere near the degree Tomas was. Tomas could endure hours of tales of the people of the elven forests, regardless of the speaker's credibility. At least, Pug considered, in the Huntmaster they had a dependable eye witness. Martin's voice droned on, and Pug's attention wandered, as he again found himself pondering the Choosing. No matter that he told himself worry was useless: he worried. He found he was facing the approaching of this afternoon with something akin to dread.

THE BOYS STOOD in the courtyard. It was Midsummer, the day that ended one year and marked the beginning of another. Today everyone in the castle would be counted one year older. For the milling boys this was significant, for today was the last day of their boyhood. Today was the Choosing.

Pug tugged at the collar of his new tunic. It wasn't really new, being one of Tomas's old ones, but it was the newest Pug had ever owned. Magya, Tomas's mother, had taken it in for the smaller boy, to ensure he was presentable before the Duke and his court. Magya and her husband, Megar the cook, were as close to being parents to the orphan as anyone in the keep. They tended his ills, saw that he was fed, and boxed his ears when he deserved it. They also loved him as if he were Tomas's brother.

Pug looked around. The other boys all wore their best, for this was one of the most important days of their young lives. Each would stand before the assembled Craftmasters and members of the Duke's staff, and each would be considered for an apprentice's post. It was a ritual, its origins lost in time, for the choices had already been made. The crafters and the Duke's staff had spent many hours discussing each boy's merits with one another and knew which boys they would call.

The practice of having the boys between eight and thirteen years of age work in the crafts and services had proved a wise course over the years in fitting the best suited to each craft. In addition, it provided a pool of semiskilled individuals for the other crafts should the need arise. The drawback to the system was that certain boys were not chosen for a craft or staff position. Occasionally there would be too many boys for a single position, or no lad judged fit even though there was an opening. Even when the number of boys and openings seemed well matched, as it did this year, there were no guarantees. For those who stood in doubt, it was an anxious time.

Pug scuffed his bare feet absently in the dust. Unlike Tomas, who seemed to do well at anything he tried, Pug was often guilty of trying too hard and bungling his tasks. He looked around and noticed that a few of the other boys also showed signs of tension. Some were joking roughly, pretending no concern over whether they were chosen or not. Others stood like Pug, lost in their thoughts, trying not to dwell on what they would do should they not be chosen.

If he was not chosen, Pug—like the others—would be free to leave Crydee to try to find a craft in another town or city. If he stayed, he would have to either farm the Duke's land as a franklin, or work one of the town's fishing boats. Both prospects were equally unattractive, but he couldn't imagine leaving Crydee.

Pug remembered what Megar had told him, the night before. The old cook had cautioned him about fretting too much over the Choosing. After all, he had pointed out, there were many apprentices who never advanced to the rank of journeyman, and when all things were taken into account, there were more men without craft in Crydee than with. Megar had glossed over the fact that many fishers' and farmers' sons forsook the choosing, electing to follow their fathers. Pug wondered if Megar was so removed from his own Choosing he couldn't remember that the boys who were not chosen would stand before the assembled company of Craftmasters, householders, and newly chosen apprentices, under their gaze until the last name was called and they were dismissed in shame.

Biting his lower lip, Pug tried to hide his nervousness. He was not the sort to jump from the heights of Sailor's Grief should he not be chosen, as some had done in the past, but he couldn't bear the idea of facing those who had been chosen.

Tomas, who stood next to his shorter friend, threw Pug a smile. He knew Pug was fretting, but could not feel entirely sympathetic as his own excitement mounted. His father had admitted that he would be the first called by Swordmaster Fannon. Moreover, the Swordmaster had confided that should Tomas do well in training, he might be found a place in the Duke's personal guard. It would be a signal honor and would improve Tomas's chance for advancement, even earning him an officer's rank after fifteen or twenty years in the guard.

He poked Pug in the ribs with an elbow, for the Duke's herald had come out upon the balcony overlooking the courtyard. The herald signaled to a guard, who opened the small door in the great gate, and the Craftmasters entered. They crossed to stand at the foot of the broad stairs of the keep. As was traditional, they stood with their backs to the boys, waiting upon the Duke.

The large oaken doors of the keep began to swing out ponderously, and several guards in the Duke's brown and gold darted through to take up their positions on the steps. Upon each tabard was emblazoned the golden gull of Crydee, and above that a small golden crown, marking the Duke a member of the royal family.

The herald shouted, "Hearken to me! His Grace, Borric conDoin, third Duke of Crydee, Prince of the Kingdom; Lord of Crydee, Carse, and Tulan; Warden of the West; Knight-General of the King's Armies; heir presumptive to the throne of Rillanon." The Duke stood patiently while the list of offices was completed, then stepped forward into the sunlight.

Past fifty, the Duke of Crydee still moved with the fluid grace and powerful step of a born warrior. Except for the grey at the temples of his dark brown hair, he looked younger than his age by twenty years. He was dressed from neck to boot in black, as he had been for the last seven years, for he still mourned the loss of his beloved wife, Catherine. At his side hung a black-scabbarded sword with a silver hilt, and upon his hand his ducal signet ring, the only ornamentation he permitted himself.

The herald raised his voice. "Their Royal Highnesses, the Princes Lyam conDoin and Arutha conDoin, heirs to the House of Crydee; Knight-Captains of the King's Army of the West; Princes of the royal house of Rillanon."

Both sons stepped forward to stand behind their father. The two young men were six and four years older than the apprentices, the Duke having wed late, but the difference between the awkward candidates for apprenticeship and the sons of the Duke was much more than a few years in age. Both Princes appeared calm and self-possessed.

Lyam, the older, stood on his father's right, a blond, powerfully built man. His open smile was the image of his mother's, and he looked always on the verge of laughter. He was dressed in a bright blue tunic and yellow leggings and wore a closely trimmed beard, as blond as his shoulder-length hair.

Arutha was to shadows and night as Lyam was to light and day. He stood nearly as tall as his brother and father, but while they were powerfully built, he was rangy to the point of gauntness. He wore a brown tunic and russet leggings. His hair was dark and his face clean-shaven. Everything about Arutha gave one the feeling of quickness. His strength was in his speed: speed with the rapier, speed with wit. His humor was dry and often sharp. While Lyam was openly loved by the Duke's subjects, Arutha was respected and admired for his ability, but not regarded with warmth by the people.

Together the two sons seemed to capture most of the complex nature of their sire, for the Duke was capable of both Lyam's robust humor and Arutha's dark moods. They were nearly opposites in temperament, but both capable men who would benefit the Duchy and Kingdom in years to come. The Duke loved both his sons.

The herald again spoke. "The Princess Carline, daughter of the royal house."

The slim and graceful girl who made her entrance was the same age as the boys who stood below, but already beginning to show the poise and grace of one born to rule and the beauty of her late mother. Her soft yellow gown contrasted strikingly with her nearly black hair. Her eyes were Lyam's blue, as their mother's had been, and Lyam beamed when his sister took their father's arm. Even Arutha ventured one of his rare half smiles, for his sister was dear to him also.

Many boys in the keep harbored a secret love for the Princess, a fact she often turned to her advantage when there was mischief afoot. But even her presence could not drive the day's business from their minds.

The Duke's court then entered. Pug and Tomas could see that all the members of the Duke's staff were present, including Kulgan. Pug had glimpsed him in the castle from time to time since the night of the storm, and they had exchanged words once, Kulgan inquiring as to his well-being, but mostly the magician was absent from sight. Pug was a little surprised to see the magician, for he was not properly considered a full member of the Duke's household, but rather a sometime adviser. Most of the time Kulgan was ensconced in his tower, hidden from view as he did whatever magicians do in such places.

The magician was deep in conversation with Father Tully, a priest of Astalon the Builder and one of the Duke's oldest aides. Tully had been adviser to the Duke's father and had seemed old then. He now appeared ancient—at least to Pug's youthful perspective—but his eyes betrayed no sign of senility. Many a keep boy had been impaled upon the pointed gaze of those clear grey eyes. His wit and tongue were equally youthful, and more than once a keep boy had wished for a session with Horsemaster Algon's leather strap rather than a tongue-lashing from Father Tully. The white-haired priest could nearly strip the skin from a miscreant's back with his caustic words.

Nearby stood one who had experienced Tully's wrath upon occasion, Squire Roland, son of Baron Tolburt of Tulan, one of the Duke's vassals. He was companion to both Princes, being the only other boy of noble birth in the keep. His father had sent him to Crydee the year before, to learn something of the management of the Duchy and the ways of the Duke's court. In the rather rough frontier court Roland discovered a home away from home. He was already something of a rogue when he arrived, but his infectious sense of humor and ready wit often eased much of the anger that resulted from his prankish ways. It was Roland, more often than not, who was Princess Carline's accomplice in whatever mischief she was embarked upon. With light brown hair and blue eyes, Roland stood tall for his age. He was a year older than the gathered boys and had played often with them over the last year, as Lyam and Arutha were frequently busy with court duties. Tomas and he had been boyish rivals at first, then fast friends, with Pug becoming his friend by default, because where Tomas was, Pug was certain to be nearby. Roland saw Pug fidgeting near the edge of the assembled boys and gave him a slight nod and wink. Pug grinned briefly, for while he was as often the butt of Roland's jokes as any other, he still found himself liking the wild young Squire.

After all his court was in attendance, the Duke spoke. "Yesterday was the last day of the eleventh year of the reign of our Lord King, Rodric the Fourth. Today is the Festival of Banapis. The following day will find these boys gathered here counted among the men of Crydee, boys no longer, but apprentices and freemen. At this time it is proper for me to inquire if any among you wishes to be released from service to the Duchy. Are there any among you who so wish?" The question was formal in nature and no response was expected, for few ever wished to leave Crydee. But one boy did step forward.

The herald asked, "Who seeks release of his service?"

The boy looked down, clearly nervous. Clearing his throat, he said, "I am Robert, son of Hugen." Pug knew him, but not well. He was a netmender's son, a town boy, and they rarely mixed with the keep boys. Pug had played with him upon a few occasions and had a sense the lad was well regarded. It was a rare thing to refuse service, and Pug was as curious as any to hear the reasons.

The Duke spoke kindly. "What is your purpose, Robert, son of Hugen?"

"Your grace, my father is unable to take me into his craft, for my four brothers are well able to ascend to the craft as journeymen and masters after him, as are many other netmender's sons. My eldest brother is now married and has a son of his own, so my family no longer has room for me in the house. If I may not stay with my family and practice my father's craft, I beg your grace's leave to take service as a sailor."

The Duke considered the matter. Robert was not the first village boy to be called by the lure of the sea. "Have you found a master willing to take you into his company?"

"Yes, Your Grace. Captain Gregson, master of the ship *Green Deep* from Margrave's Port is willing."

"I know this man," said the Duke. Smiling slightly he said, "He is a good and fair man. I recommend you into his service and wish you well in your travels. You will be welcomed at Crydee whenever you return with your ship."

Robert bowed, a little stiffly, and left the courtyard, his part in the Choosing done. Pug wondered at Robert's adventuresome choice. In less than a minute the boy had renounced his ties with his family and home and was now a citizen of a city he had never seen. It was custom that a sailor was considered to owe his loyalty to the city that was his ship's home port. Margrave's Port was one of the Free Cities of Natal, on the Bitter Sea, and was now Robert's home.

The Duke indicated the herald should continue.

The herald announced the first of the Craftmasters, Sailmaker Holm, who called the names of three boys. All three took service, and none seemed displeased. The Choosing went smoothly, as no boy refused service. Each boy went to stand next to his new master.

As the afternoon wore on and the number of boys diminished, Pug became more and more uncomfortable. Soon there were only two boys besides Pug and Tomas standing in the center of the court. All the Craftmasters had called their apprentices, and only two of the Duke's household staff beside the Swordmaster had not been heard from. Pug studied the group on the top of the steps, his heart pounding with anxiety. The two Princes regarded the boys, Lyam with a friendly smile, Arutha brooding on some thought or another. The Princess Carline was bored by the entire affair and took little pains to hide the fact, as she was whispering to Roland. This brought a disapproving look from Lady Marna, her governess.

Horsemaster Algon came forth, his brown-and-golden tabard bearing a small horsehead embroidered over his left breast. The Horsemaster called the name of Rulf, son of Dick, and the stocky son of the Duke's stableman walked over to stand behind the master. When he turned, he smiled condescendingly at Pug. The two boys had never gotten along, the pock-scarred boy spending many hours taunting and tormenting Pug. While they both worked in the stable under Dick, the stableman had looked the other way whenever his son sprang a trap on Pug, and the orphan was always held responsible for any difficulty that arose. It had been a terrible period for Pug, and the boy had vowed to refuse service rather than face the prospect of working next to Rulf the rest of his life.

Housecarl Samuel called the other boy, Geoffry, who would become a member of the castle's serving staff, leaving Pug and Tomas standing alone. Swordmaster Fannon then stepped forward, and Pug felt his heart stand still as the old soldier called, "Tomas, son of Megar."

There was a pause, and Pug waited to hear his own name called, but Fannon stepped back and Tomas crossed over to stand alongside him. Pug felt dwarfed by the gaze of all upon him. The courtyard was now larger than he had ever remembered it, and he felt ill fashioned and poorly dressed. His heart sank in his chest as he realized that there was no Craftmaster or staff member present who had not taken an apprentice. He would be the only boy uncalled. Fighting back tears, he waited for the Duke to dismiss the company.

As the Duke started to speak, sympathy for the boy showing clearly in his face, he was interrupted by another voice. "Your Grace, if you would be so kind."

All eyes turned to see Kulgan the magician step forward. "I have need of an apprentice and would call Pug, orphan of the keep, to service."

A wave of murmuring swept through the assembled Craftmasters. A few voices could be heard saying it wasn't proper for a magician to participate in the Choosing. The Duke silenced them with a sweep of his gaze, his face stern. No Craftmaster would challenge the Duke of Crydee, the third-ranking noble in the Kingdom, over the standing of one boy. Slowly all eyes returned to regard the boy.

The Duke said, "As Kulgan is a recognized master of his craft, it is his right to choose. Pug, orphan of the keep, will you take service?" Pug stood rigid. He had imagined himself leading the King's army into battle as a Knight-Lieutenant, or discovering someday he was the lost son of nobility. In his boyish imaginings he had sailed ships, hunted great monsters, and saved the nation. In quieter moments of reflection he had wondered if he would spend his life building ships, making pottery, or learning the trader's skill, and speculated on how well he would do in each of those crafts. But the one thing he never thought of, the one dream that had never captured his fantasies, was that of becoming a magician.

He snapped out of his shocked state, aware the Duke patiently awaited his response. He looked at the faces of those before him. Father Tully gave him one of his rare smiles, as did Prince Arutha. Prince Lyam nodded a slight yes, and Kulgan regarded him intently. There were signs of worry upon the magician's face, and suddenly Pug decided. It might not be an entirely proper calling, but any craft was better than none. He stepped forward and caught his own heel with his other foot, and landed face down in the dust. Picking himself up, he half scrambled, half ran to the magician's side. The misstep broke the tension, and the Duke's booming laughter filled the courtyard. Flushing with embarrassment, Pug stood behind Kulgan. He looked around the broad girth of his new master and found the Duke watching, his expression tempered by a kind nod at the blushing Pug. The Duke turned back to those who stood waiting for the Choosing to end.

"I declare that each boy present is now the charge of his master, to obey him in all matters within the laws of the Kingdom, and each shall be judged a true and proper man of Crydee. Let the apprentices attend their masters. Until the feasting, I bid you all good day." He turned and presented his left arm to his daughter. She placed her hand lightly upon it and they passed into the keep between the ranks of the courtiers, who drew aside. The two Princes followed, and the others of the court. Pug saw Tomas leave in the direction of the guard barracks, behind Master Fannon.

He turned his attention back to Kulgan, who was standing lost in thought. After a moment the magician said, "I trust neither of us has made a mistake this day."

"Sir?" Pug asked, not understanding the magician's meaning. Kulgan waved one hand absently, causing his pale yellow robe to move like waves rippling over the sea. "It is no matter, boy. What's done is done. Let us make the best of things."

He placed his hand on the boy's shoulder. "Come, let us retire to the tower where I reside. There is a small room below my own that should do for you. I had intended it for some project or another, but have never managed to find the time to prepare it."

Pug stood in awe. "A room of my own?" Such a thing for an apprentice was unheard of. Most apprentices slept in the workrooms of their master, or protected herds, or the like. Only when an apprentice became a journeyman was it usual for him to take private quarters.

Kulgan arched one bushy eyebrow. "Of course. Can't have you underfoot all the time. I would never get anything done. Besides, magic requires solitude for contemplation. You will need to be untroubled as much as or perhaps more than I will." He took out his long, thin pipe from a fold of his robe and started to stuff it full of tabac from a pouch that had also come from within the robe.

"Let's not bother with too much discussion of duties and such, boy. For in truth, I am not prepared for you. But in short order I will have things well in hand. Until then we can use the time by becoming acquainted with one another. Agreed?" Pug was startled. He had little notion of what a magician was about, in spite of the night spent with Kulgan weeks ago, but he readily knew what Craftmasters were like, and none would have thought to inquire whether or not an apprentice agreed with his plans. Not knowing what to say, Pug just nodded.

"Good, then," said Kulgan, "let us be off to the tower to find you some new clothes, and then we will spend the balance of the day feasting. Later there will be ample time to learn how to be master and apprentice." With a smile for the boy, the stout magician turned Pug around and led him away.

THE LATE AFTERNOON was clear and bright, with a gentle breeze from the sea cooling the summer heat. Throughout the keep of Castle Crydee, and the town below, preparations for the Festival of Banapis were in progress.

Banapis was the oldest known holiday, its origins lost in antiquity. It was held each Midsummer's Day, a day belonging to neither the past nor the coming year. Banapis, known by other names in other nations, was celebrated over the entire world of Midkemia according to legend. It was believed by some that the festival was borrowed from the elves and dwarves, for the long-lived races were said to have celebrated the feast of Midsummer as far back as the memory of both races could recall. Most authorities disputed this allegation, citing no reason other than the unlikelihood of humans borrowing anything from the elven or dwarven folk. It was rumored that even the denizens of the Northlands, the goblin tribes and the clans of the Brotherhood of the Dark Path, celebrated Banapis, though no one had ever reported seeing such a celebration.

The courtyard was busy. Huge tables had been erected to hold the myriad varieties of foods that had been in preparation for over a week. Giant barrels of dwarven ale, imported from Stone Mountain, had been hauled out of the cellars and were resting on protesting, overburdened wood frames. The workmen, alarmed at the fragile appearance of the barrel ricks, were quickly emptying some of the contents. Megar came out of the kitchen and angrily shooed them away. "Leave off, there will be none left for the evening meal at this rate! Back to the kitchen, dolts! There is much work to be done yet."

The workers went off, grumbling, and Megar filled a tankard to ensure the ale was at proper temperature. After he drained it dry and satisfied himself that all was as it should be, he returned to the kitchen.

There was no formal beginning to the feast. Traditionally, people and food, wine and ale, all accumulated until they reached a certain density, then all at once the festivities would be in full swing.

Pug ran from the kitchen. His room in the northmost tower, the magician's tower as it had become known, provided him with a shortcut through the kitchen, which he used rather than the main doors of the keep. He beamed as he sped across the courtyard in his new tunic and trousers. He had never worn such finery and was in a hurry to show his friend Tomas.

He found Tomas leaving the soldiers' commons, nearly as much in a hurry as Pug. When the two met, they both spoke at once.

"Look at the new tunic—" said Pug.

"Look at my soldier's tabard—" said Tomas.

Both stopped and broke into laughter.

Tomas regained his composure first. "Those are very fine clothes, Pug," he said, fingering the expensive material of Pug's red tunic. "And the color suits you."

Pug returned the compliment, for Tomas did cut a striking figure in his brown-and-gold tabard. It was of little consequence that he wore his regular homespun tunic and trouser underneath. He would not receive a soldier's uniform until Master Fannon was satisfied with his worthiness as a man-at-arms.

The two friends wandered from one heavily laden table to another. Pug's mouth watered from the rich fragrances in the air. They came to a table heaped with meat pies, steam rising from their hot crusts, pungent cheeses, and hot bread. At the table a young kitchen boy was stationed with a shoo-fly. His job was to keep pests from the food, whether of the insect variety or the chronically hungry apprentice variety. Like most other situations involving boys, the relationship between this guardian of the feast and the older apprentices was closely bound by tradition. It was considered ill-mannered and in poor taste merely to threaten or bully the smaller boy into parting with food before the start of the feast. But it was considered fair to use guile, stealth, or speed in gaining a prize from the table.

Pug and Tomas observed with interest as the boy, named Jon, delivered a wicked whack to the hand of one young apprentice seeking to snag a large pie. With a nod of his head, Tomas sent Pug to the far side of the table. Pug ambled across Jon's field of vision, and the boy watched him carefully. Pug moved abruptly, a feint toward the table, and Jon leaned in his direction. Then suddenly Tomas snatched a puff-pastry from the table and was gone before the shoo-fly lash began to descend. As they ran from the table, Pug and Tomas could hear the distressed cries of the boy whose table they had plundered.

Tomas gave Pug half the pie when they were safely away, and the smaller apprentice laughed. "You're the quickest hand in the castle, I bet."

"Or young Jon was slow of eye for keeping it on you."

They shared a laugh. Pug popped his half of the pie into his mouth. It was delicately seasoned, and the contrast between the salty pork filling and the sweet puff-pastry crust was delicious.

The sound of pipes and drums came from the side courtyard as the Duke's musicians approached the main courtyard. By the time they had emerged around the keep, a silent message seemed to pass through the crowd. Suddenly the kitchen boys were busy handing out wooden platters for the celebrants to heap food upon, and mugs of ale and wine were being drawn from the barrels.

The boys dashed to a place in line at the first table. Pug and Tomas used their size and quickness to good advantage, darting through the throng, snagging food of every description and a large mug of foamy ale each.

They found a relatively quiet corner and fell to with ravenous hunger. Pug tasted his first drink of ale and was surprised at the robust, slightly bitter taste. It seemed to warm him as it went down, and after another experimental taste he decided that he liked it.

Pug could see the Duke and his family mingling with the common folk. Other members of his court could also be seen standing in line before the tables. There was no ceremony, ritual, or rank observed this afternoon. Each was served as he arrived, for Midsummer's Day was the time when all would equally share in the bounties of the harvest.

Pug caught a glimpse of the Princess and felt his chest tighten a little. She looked radiant as many of the boys in the courtyard complimented her on her appearance. She wore a lovely gown of deep blue and a simple, broad-brimmed hat of the same color. She thanked each author of a flattering remark and used her dark eyelashes and bright smile to good advantage, leaving a wake of infatuated boys behind.

Jugglers and clowns made their appearance in the courtyard, the first of many groups of traveling performers who were in the town for the festival. The actors of another company had set up a stage in the town square and would give a performance in the evening. Until the early hours of the next morning the festivities would continue. Pug knew that many of the boys the year before had to be excused duty the day following Banapis, for their heads and stomachs were in no condition for honest work. He was sure that scene would be repeated tomorrow.

Pug looked forward to the evening, for it was the custom for new apprentices to visit many of the houses in the town, receiving congratulations and mugs of ale. It was also a ripe time for meeting the town girls. While dalliance was not unknown, it was frowned upon. But mothers tended to be less vigilant during Banapis. Now that the boys had crafts, they were viewed less as bothersome pests and more as potential sons-in-law, and there had been more than one case of a mother looking the other way while a daughter used her natural gifts to snare a young husband. Pug, being of small stature and youthful appearance, got little notice from the girls of the keep. Tomas, however, was more and more the object of girlish flirtation as he grew in size and good looks, and lately Pug had begun to be aware that his friend was being sized up by one or another of the castle girls. Pug was still young enough to think the whole thing silly, but old enough to be fascinated by it.

Pug chewed an improbable mouthful and looked around. People from the town and keep passed, offering congratulations on the boys' apprenticeship and wishing them a good new year. Pug felt a deep sense of rightness about everything. He was an apprentice, even if Kulgan seemed completely unsure of what to do with him. He was well fed, and on his way to being slightly intoxicated—which contributed to his sense of well-being. And, most important, he was among friends. There can't be much more to life than this, he thought.

3

▼▼

KEEP

PUG SAT SULKING ON HIS SLEEPING PALLET.

Fantus the firedrake pushed his head forward, inviting Pug to scratch him behind his eye ridges. Seeing that he would get little satisfaction, the drake made his way to the tower window and with a snort of displeasure, complete with a small puff of black smoke, launched himself in flight. Pug didn't notice the creature's leaving, so engrossed was he in his own world of troubles. Since he had taken on the position of Kulgan's apprentice fourteen months ago, everything he had done seemed to go wrong.

He lay back on the pallet, covering his eyes with a forearm; he could smell the salty sea breeze that blew in through his window and feel the sun's warmth across his legs. Everything in his life had taken a turn for the better since his apprenticeship, except the single most important thing, his studies.

For months Kulgan had been laboring to teach him the fundamentals of the magician's arts, but there was always something that caused his efforts to go awry. In the theories of spell casting, Pug was a quick study, grasping the basic concepts well. But each time he attempted to use his knowledge, something seemed to hold him back. It was as if a part of his mind refused to follow through with the magic, as if a block existed that prevented him from passing a certain point in the spell. Each time he tried he could feel himself approach that point, and like a rider of a balky horse, he couldn't seem to force himself over the hurdle.

Kulgan dismissed his worries, saying that it would all sort itself out in time. The stout magician was always sympathetic with the boy, never reprimanding him for not doing better, for he knew the boy was trying.

Pug was brought out of his reverie by someone's opening the door. Looking up, he saw Father Tully entering, a large book under his arm. The cleric's white robes rustled as he closed the door. Pug sat up.

"Pug, it's time for your writing lesson—" He stopped himself when he saw the downcast expression of the boy. "What's the matter, lad?"

Pug had come to like the old priest of Astalon. He was a strict master, but a fair one. He would praise the boy for his success as often as scold him for his failures. He had a quick mind and a sense of humor and was open to questions, no matter how stupid Pug thought they might sound.

Coming to his feet, Pug sighed. "I don't know, Father. It's just that things don't seem to be going right. Everything I try I manage to make a mess of."

"Pug, it can't be all black," the priest said, placing a hand on Pug's shoulder. "Why don't you tell me what is troubling you, and we can practice writing some other time." He moved to a stool by the window and adjusted his robes around him as he sat. As he placed the large book at his feet, he studied the boy.

Pug had grown over the last year, but was still small. His shoulders were beginning to broaden a bit, and his face was showing signs of the man he would someday be. He was a dejected figure in his homespun tunic and trousers, his mood as grey as the material he wore. His room, which was usually neat and orderly, was a mess of scrolls and books, reflecting the disorder in his mind.

Pug sat quietly for a moment, but when the priest said nothing, started to speak. "Do you remember my telling you that Kulgan was trying to teach me the three basic cantrips to calm the mind, so that the working of spells could be practiced without stress? Well, the truth is that I mastered those exercises months ago. I can bring my mind to a state of calm in moments now, with little effort. But that is as far as it goes. After that, everything seems to fall apart."

"What do you mean?"

"The next thing to learn is to discipline the mind to do things that are not natural for it, such as think on one thing to the exclusion of everything else, or not to think of something, which is quite hard once you've been told what it is. I can do those things most of the time, but now and again I feel like there are some forces inside my head, crashing about, demanding that I do things in a different way. It's like there was something else happening in my head than what Kulgan told me to expect.

"Each time I try one of the simple spells Kulgan has taught me, like making an object move, or lifting myself off the ground, these things in my head come flooding in on my concentration, and I lose my control. I can't even master the simplest spell." Pug felt himself tremble, for this was the first chance he had had to speak about this to anyone besides Kulgan. "Kulgan simply says to keep at it and not worry." Nearing tears, he continued. "I have talent. Kulgan said he knew it from the first time we met, when I used the crystal. You've told me that I have talent. But I just can't make the spells work the way they're supposed to. I get so confused by it all."

"Pug," said the priest, "magic has many properties, and we understand little of how it works, even those of us who practice it. In the temples we are taught that magic is a gift from the gods, and we accept that on faith. We do not understand how this can be so, but we do not question. Each order has its own province of magic, with no two quite alike. I am capable of magic that those who follow their orders are not. But none can say why.

"Magicians deal in a different sort of magic, and their practices are very different from our practices in the temples. Much of what they do, we cannot. It is they who study the art of magic, seeking its nature and workings, but even they cannot explain how magic works. They only know how to work it, and pass that knowledge along to their students, as Kulgan is doing with you."

"Trying to do with me, Father. I think he may have misjudged me."

"I think not, Pug. I have some knowledge of these things, and since you have become Kulgan's pupil, I have felt the power growing in you. Perhaps you will come to it late, as others have, but I am sure you will find the proper path."

Pug was not comforted. He didn't question the priest's wisdom or his opinion, but he did feel he could be mistaken. "I hope you're right, Father. I just don't understand what's wrong with me."

"I think I know what's wrong," came a voice from the door. Startled, Pug and Father Tully turned to see Kulgan standing in the doorway. His blue eyes were set in lines of concern, and his thick grey brows formed a V over the bridge of his nose. Neither Pug nor Tully had heard the door open. Kulgan hiked his long green robe and stepped into the room, leaving the door open.

"Come here, Pug," said the magician with a small wave of his hand.

Pug went over to the magician, who placed both hands on his shoulders. "Boys who sit in their rooms day after day worrying about why things don't work make things not work. I am giving you the day for yourself. As it is Sixthday, there should be plenty of other boys to help you in whatever sort of trouble boys can find." He smiled, and his pupil was filled with relief. "You need a rest from study. Now go." So saying, he fetched a playful cuff to the boy's head, sending him running down the stairs. Crossing over to the pallet, Kulgan lowered his heavy frame to it and looked at the priest. "Boys," said Kulgan, shaking his head. "You hold a festival, give them a badge of craft, and suddenly they expect to be men. But they're still boys, and no matter how hard they try, they still act like boys, not men." He took out his pipe and began filling it. "Magicians are considered young and inexperienced at thirty, but in all other crafts thirty would mark a man a journeyman or master, most likely readying his own son for the Choosing." He put a taper to the coals still smouldering in Pug's fire pot and lit his pipe.

Tully nodded. "I understand, Kulgan. The priesthood also is an old man's calling. At Pug's age I still had thirteen years of being an acolyte before me." The old priest leaned forward. "Kulgan, what of the boy's problem?"

"The boy's right, you know," Kulgan stated flatly. "There is no explanation for why he cannot perform the skills I've tried to teach. The things he can do with scrolls and devices amaze me. The boy has such gifts for these things, I would have wagered he had the makings of a magician of mighty arts. But this inability to use his inner powers . . ."

"Do you think you can find a solution?"

"I hope so. I would hate to have to release him from apprenticeship. It would go harder on him than had I never chosen him." His face showed his genuine concern. "It is confusing, Tully. I think you'll agree he has the potential for a great talent. As soon as I saw him use the crystal in my hut that night, I knew for the first time in years I might have at last found my apprentice. When no master chose him, I knew fate had set our paths to cross. But there is something else inside that boy's head, something I've never met before, something powerful. I don't know what it is, Tully, but it rejects my exercises, as if they were somehow . . . not correct, or . . . ill suited to him. I don't know if I can explain what I've encountered with Pug any better. There is no simple explanation for it."

"Have you thought about what the boy said?" asked the priest, a look of thoughtful concern on his face.

"You mean about my having been mistaken?"

Tully nodded. Kulgan dismissed the question with a wave of his hand.

"Tully, you know as much about the nature of magic as I do, perhaps more. Your god is not called the God Who Brought Order for nothing. Your sect unraveled much about what orders this universe. Do you for one moment doubt the boy has talent?"

"Talent, no. But his ability is the question for the moment."

"Well put, as usual. Well, then, have you any ideas? Should we make a cleric out of the boy, perhaps?"

Tully sat back, a disapproving expression upon his face. "You know the priesthood is a calling, Kulgan," he said stiffly.

"Put your back down, Tully. I was making a joke." He sighed. "Still, if he hasn't the calling of a priest, nor the knack of a magician's craft, what can we make of this natural ability of his?"

Tully pondered the question in silence for a moment, then said, "Have you thought of the lost art?"

Kulgan's eyes widened. "That old legend?" Tully nodded. "I doubt there is a magician alive who at one time or another hasn't reflected on the legend of the lost art. If it had existed, it would explain away many of the shortcomings of our craft." Then he fixed Tully with a narrowed eye, showing his disapproval. "But legends are common enough. Turn up any rock on the beach and you'll find one. I for one prefer to look for real answers to our shortcomings, not blame them on ancient superstitions."

Tully's expression became stern and his tone scolding. "We of the temple do not count it legend, Kulgan! It is considered part of the revealed truth, taught by the gods to the first men."

Nettled by Tully's tone, Kulgan snapped, "So was the notion the world was flat, until Rolendirk—a magician, I'll remind you—sent his magic sight high enough to disclose the curvature of the horizon, clearly demonstrating the world to be a sphere! It was a fact known by almost every sailor and fisherman who'd ever seen a sail appear upon the horizon before the rest of the ship since the beginning of time!" His voice rose to a near shout.

Seeing Tully was stung by the reference to ancient church canon long since abandoned, Kulgan softened his tone. "No disrespect to you, Tully. But don't try to teach an old thief to steal. I know your order chops logic with the best of them, and that half your brother clerics fall into laughing fits when they hear those deadly serious young acolytes debate theological issues set aside a century ago. Besides which, isn't the legend of the lost art an Ishapian dogma?"

Now it was Tully's turn to fix Kulgan with a disapproving eye. With a tone of amused exasperation, he said, "Your education in religion is still lacking, Kulgan, despite a somewhat unforgiving insight into the inner workings of my order." He smiled a little. "You're right about the moot gospel courts, though. Most of us find them so amusing because we remember how painfully grim we were about them when we were acolytes." Then turning serious, he said, "But I am serious when I say your education is lacking. The Ishapians have some strange beliefs, it's true, and they are an insular group, but they are also the oldest order known and are recognized as the senior church in questions pertaining to interdenominational differences."

"Religious wars, you mean," said Kulgan with an amused snort.

Tully ignored the comment. "The Ishapians are caretakers for the oldest lore and history in the Kingdom, and they have the most extensive library in the Kingdom. I have visited the library at their temple in Krondor, and it is most impressive."

Kulgan smiled and with a slight tone of condescension said, "As have I, Tully, and I have browsed the shelves at the Abbey of Sarth, which is ten times as large. What's the point?"

Leaning forward, Tully said, "The point is this: say what you will about the Ishapians, but when they put forth something as history, not lore, they can usually produce ancient tomes to support their claims."

"No," said Kulgan, waving aside Tully's comments with a dismissive wave. "I do not make light of your beliefs, or any other man's, but I cannot accept this nonsense about lost arts. I might be willing to believe Pug could be somehow more attuned to some aspect of magic I'm ignorant of, perhaps something involving spirit conjuration or illusion—areas I will happily admit I know little about—but I cannot accept that he will never learn to master his craft because the long-vanished god of magic died during the Chaos Wars! No, that there is unknown lore, I accept. There are too many shortcomings in our craft even to begin to think our understanding of magic is remotely complete. But if Pug can't learn magic, it is only because I have failed as a teacher."

Tully now glared at Kulgan, suddenly aware the magician was not pondering Pug's possible shortcomings but his own. "Now you are being foolish. You are a gifted man, and were I to have been the one to discover Pug's talent, I could not imagine a better teacher to place him with than yourself. But there can be no failing if you do not know what he needs to be taught." Kulgan began to sputter an objection, but Tully cut him off. "No, let me continue. What we lack is understanding. You seem to forget there have been others like Pug, wild talents who could not master their gifts, others who failed as priests and magicians."

Kulgan puffed on his pipe, his brow knitted in concentration. Suddenly he began to chuckle, then laugh. Tully looked sharply at the magician. Kulgan waved offhandedly with his pipe. "I was just struck by the thought that should a swineherd fail to teach his son the family calling, he could blame it upon the demise of the gods of pigs."

Tully's eyes went wide at the near-blasphemous thought, then he too laughed, a short bark. "That's one for the moot gospel courts!" Both men laughed a long, tension-releasing laugh at that. Tully sighed and stood up. "Still, do not close your mind entirely to what I've said, Kulgan. It may be Pug is one of those wild talents. And you may have to reconcile yourself for letting him go."

Kulgan shook his head sadly at the thought. "I refuse to believe there is any simple explanation for those other failures, Tully. Or for Pug's difficulties, as well. The fault was in each man or woman, not in the nature of the universe. I have often felt where we fail with Pug is in understanding how to reach him. Perhaps I would be well advised to seek another master for him, place him with one better able to harness his abilities."

Tully sighed. "I have spoken my mind of this question, Kulgan. Other than what I've said, I cannot advise you. Still, as they say, a poor master's better than no master at all. How would the boy have fared if no one had chosen to teach him?"

Kulgan bolted upright from his seat. "What did you say?"

"I said, how would the boy have fared if no one had chosen to teach him?"

Kulgan's eyes seemed to lose focus as he stared into space. He began puffing furiously upon his pipe. After watching for a moment, Tully said, "What is it, Kulgan?"

Kulgan said, "I'm not sure, Tully, but you may have given me an idea."

"What sort of idea?"

Kulgan waved off the question. "I'm not entirely sure. Give me time to ponder. But consider your question, and ask yourself this: how did the first magicians learn to use their power?"

Tully sat back down, and both men began to consider the question in silence. Through the window they could hear the sound of boys at play, filling the courtyard of the keep.

EVERY SIXTHDAY, the boys and girls who worked in the castle were allowed to spend the afternoon as they saw fit. The boys, apprentice age and younger, were a loud and boisterous lot. The girls worked in the service of the ladies of the castle, cleaning and sewing, as well as helping in the kitchen. They all gave a full week's work, dawn to dusk and more, each day, but—on the sixth day of the week they gathered in the courtyard of the castle, near the Princess's garden. Most of the boys played a rough game of tag, involving the capture of a ball of leather, stuffed hard with rags, by one side, amid shoves and shouts, kicks and occasional fistfights. All wore their oldest clothes, for rips, bloodstains, and mudstains were common.

The girls would sit along the low wall by the Princess's garden, occupying themselves with gossip about the ladies of the Duke's court. They nearly always put on their best skirts and blouses, and their hair shone from washing and brushing. Both groups made a great display of ignoring each other, and both were equally unconvincing.

Pug ran to where the game was in progress. As was usual, Tomas was in the thick of the fray, sandy hair flying like a banner, shouting and laughing above the noise. Amid elbows and kicks he sounded savagely joyous, as if the incidental pain made the contest all the more worthwhile. He ran through the pack, kicking the ball high in the air, trying to avoid the feet of those who sought to trip him. No one was quite sure how the game had come into existence, or exactly what the rules were, but the boys played with battlefield intensity, as their fathers had years before.

Pug ran onto the field and placed a foot before Rulf just as he was about to hit Tomas from behind. Rulf went down in a tangle of bodies, and Tomas broke free. He ran toward the goal and, dropping the ball in front of himself, kicked it into a large overturned barrel, scoring for his side. While other boys yelled in celebration, Rulf leaped to his feet and pushed aside another boy to place himself directly in front of Pug. Glaring out from under thick brows, he spat at Pug, "Try that again and I'll break your legs, sand squint!" The sand squint was a bird of notoriously foul habits—not the least of which was leaving eggs in other birds' nests so that its offspring were raised by other birds. Pug was not about to let any insult of Rulf's pass unchallenged. With the frustrations of the last few months only a little below the surface, Pug was feeling particularly thin-skinned this day.

With a leap he flew at Rulf's head, throwing his left arm around the stockier boy's neck. He drove his right fist into Rulf's face and could feel Rulf's nose squash under the first blow. Quickly both boys were rolling on the ground. Rulf's greater weight began to tell, and soon he sat astride Pug's chest, driving his fat fists into the smaller boy's face.

Tomas stood by helpless, for as much as he wanted to aid his friend, the boys' code of honor was as strict and inviolate as any noble's. Should he intervene on his friend's behalf, Pug would never live down the shame. Tomas jumped up and down, urging Pug on, grimacing each time Pug was struck, as if he felt the blows himself.

Pug tried to squirm out from under the larger boy, causing many of his blows to slip by, striking dirt instead of Pug's face. Enough of them were hitting the mark, however, so that Pug soon began to feel a queer detachment from the whole procedure. He thought it strange that everybody sounded so far away, and that Rulf's blows seemed not to hurt. His vision was beginning to fill with red and yellow colors, when he felt the weight lifted from his chest.

After a brief moment things came into focus, and Pug saw Prince Arutha standing over him, his hand firmly grasping Rulf's collar. While not as powerful a figure as his brother or father, the Prince was still able to hold Rulf high enough so that the stableboy's toes barely touched the ground. The Prince smiled, but without humor. "I think the boy has had enough," he said quietly, eyes glaring. "Don't you agree?" His cold tone made it clear he wasn't asking for an opinion. Blood still ran down Rulf's face from Pug's initial blow as he choked out a sound the Prince took to mean agreement. Arutha let go of Rulf's collar, and the stableboy fell backward, to the laughter of the onlookers. The Prince reached down and helped Pug to his feet.

Holding the wobbly boy steady, Arutha said, "I admire your courage, youngster, but we can't have the wits beaten out of the Duchy's finest young magician, can we?" His tone was only slightly mocking, and Pug was too numb to do more than stand and stare at the younger son of the Duke. The Prince gave him a slight smile and handed him over to Tomas, who had come up next to Pug, a wet cloth in hand.

Pug came out of his fog as Tomas scrubbed his face with the cloth, and felt even worse when he saw the Princess and Roland standing only a few feet away as Prince Arutha returned to their side. To take a beating before the girls of the keep was bad enough; to be punished by a lout like Rulf in front of the Princess was a catastrophe.

Emitting a groan that had little to do with his physical state, Pug tried to look as much like someone else as he could. Tomas grabbed him roughly. "Try not to squirm around so much. You're not all that bad off. Most of this blood is Rulf's anyway. By tomorrow his nose will look like an angry red cabbage."

"So will my head."

"Nothing so bad. A black eye, perhaps two, with a swollen cheek thrown in to the bargain. On the whole, you did rather well, but next time you want to tangle with Rulf, wait until you've put on a little more size, will you?" Pug watched as the Prince led his sister away from the site of battle. Roland gave him a wide grin, and Pug wished himself dead.

▼▼

PUG AND TOMAS walked out of the kitchen, dinner plates in hand. It was a warm night, and they preferred the cooling ocean breeze to the heat of the scullery. They sat on the porch, and Pug moved his jaw from side to side, feeling it pop in and out. He experimented with a bite of lamb and put his plate to one side.

Tomas watched him. "Can't eat?"

Pug nodded. "Jaw hurts too much." He leaned forward, resting his elbows on his knees and chin on his fists. "I should have kept my temper. Then I would have done better."

Tomas spoke from around a mouthful of food. "Master Fannon says a soldier must keep a cool head at all times or he'll lose it."

Pug sighed. "Kulgan said something like that. I have some drills I can do that make me relax. I should have used them."

Tomas gulped a heroic portion of his meal. "Practicing in your room is one thing. Putting that sort of business into use while someone is insulting you to your face is quite another. I would have done the same thing, I suppose."

"But you would have won."

"Probably. Which is why Rulf would never have come at me." His manner showed he wasn't being boastful, merely stating things as they were. "Still, you did all right. Old cabbage nose will think twice before picking on you again, I'm sure, and that's what the whole thing is about, anyway."

Pug said, "What do you mean?"

Tomas put down his plate and belched. With a satisfied look at the sound of it, he said, "With bullies it's always the same: whether or not you can best them doesn't matter. What is important is whether or not you'll stand up to them. Rulf may be big, but he's a coward under all the bluster. He'll turn his attention to the younger boys now and push them around a bit. I don't think he'll want any part of you again. He doesn't like the price." Tomas gave Pug a broad and warm smile. "That first punch you gave him was a beaut. Right square on the beak."

Pug felt a little better. Tomas eyed Pug's untouched dinner. "You going to eat that?"

Pug looked at his plate. It was fully laden with hot lamb, greens, and potatoes. In spite of the rich smell, Pug felt no appetite. "No, you can have it."

Tomas scooped up the platter and began shoving the food into his mouth. Pug smiled. Tomas had never been known to stint on food.

Pug returned his gaze to the castle wall. "I felt like such a fool."

Tomas stopped eating, with a handful of meat halfway to his mouth. He studied Pug for a moment. "You too?"

"Me too, what?"

Tomas laughed. "You're embarrassed because the Princess saw Rulf give you a thrashing."

Pug bridled. "It wasn't a thrashing. I gave as well as I got!"

Tomas whooped. "There! I knew it. It's the Princess."

Pug sat back in resignation. "I suppose it is."

Tomas said nothing, and Pug looked over at him. He was busy finishing off Pug's dinner. Finally Pug said, "And I suppose you don't like her?"

Tomas shrugged. Between bites he said, "Our Lady Carline is pretty enough, but I know my place. I have my eye on someone else, anyway."

Pug sat up. "Who?" he asked, his curiosity piqued.

"I'm not saying," Tomas said with a sly smile.

Pug laughed. "It's Neala, right?"

Tomas's jaw dropped. "How did you know?"

Pug tried to look mysterious. "We magicians have our ways."

Tomas snorted. "Some magician. You're no more a magician than I am a Knight-Captain of the King's army. Tell me, how did you know?"

Pug laughed. "It's no mystery. Every time you see her, you puff up in that tabard of yours and preen like a bantam rooster."

Tomas looked troubled. "You don't think she's on to me, do you?"

Pug smiled like a well-fed cat. "She's not on to you, I'm sure." He paused. "If she's blind, and all the other girls in the keep haven't pointed it out to her a hundred times already."

A woebegone look crossed Tomas's face. "What must the girl think?"

Pug said, "Who knows what girls think? From everything I can tell, she probably likes it."

Tomas looked thoughtfully at his plate. "Do you ever think about taking a wife?"

Pug blinked like an owl caught in a bright light. "I . . . I never thought about it. I don't know if magicians marry. I don't think they do."

"Nor soldiers, mostly. But Master Fannon says a soldier who thinks about his family is not thinking about his job." Tomas was silent for a minute.

Pug said, "It doesn't seem to hamper Sergeant Gardan or some of the other soldiers."

Tomas snorted, as if those exceptions merely proved his point. "I sometimes try to imagine what it would be like to have a family."

"You have a family, stupid. I'm the orphan here."

"I mean a wife, rock head." Tomas gave Pug his best "you're too stupid to live" look. "And children someday, not a mother and father."

Pug shrugged. The conversation was turning to provinces that disturbed him. He never thought about these things, being less anxious to grow up than Tomas. He said, "I expect we'll get married and have children if it's what we're supposed to do."

Tomas looked very seriously at Pug, so the younger boy didn't make light of the subject. "I've imagined a small room somewhere in the castle, and . . . I can't imagine who the girl would be." He chewed his food. "There's something wrong with it, I think."

"Wrong?"

"As if there's something else I'm not understanding . . . I don't know."

Pug said, "Well, if you don't, how am I supposed to?"

Tomas suddenly changed the topic of conversation. "We're friends, aren't we?"

Pug was taken by surprise. "Of course we're friends. You're like a brother. Your parents have treated me like their own son. Why would you ask something like that?"

Tomas put down his plate, troubled. "I don't know. It's just that sometimes I think this will all somehow change. You're going to be a magician, maybe travel over the world, seeing other magicians in faraway lands. I'm going to be a soldier, bound to follow my lord's orders. I'll probably never see more than a little part of the Kingdom, and that only as an escort in the Duke's personal guard, if I'm lucky."

Pug became alarmed. He had never seen Tomas so serious about anything. The older boy was always the first to laugh and seemed never to have a worry. "I don't care what you think, Tomas," said Pug. "Nothing will change. We will be friends no matter what."

Tomas smiled at that. "I hope you're right." He sat back, and the two boys watched the stars over the sea and the lights from the town, framed like a picture by the castle gate.

PUG TRIED to wash his face the next morning, but found the task too arduous to complete. His left eye was swollen completely shut, his right only half-open. Great bluish lumps decorated his visage, and his jaw popped when he moved it from side to side. Fantus lay on Pug's pallet, red eyes gleaming as the morning sun poured in through the tower window.

The door to the boy's room swung open, and Kulgan stepped through, his stout frame covered in a green robe. Pausing to regard the boy for a moment, he sat on the pallet and scratched the drake behind the eye ridges, bringing a pleased rumble from deep within Fantus's throat. "I see you didn't spend yesterday sitting about idly," he said.

"I had a bit of trouble, sir."

"Well, fighting is the province of boys as well as grown men, but I trust that the other boy looks at least as bad. It would be a shame to have had none of the pleasure of giving as well as receiving."

"You're making sport of me."

"Only a little, Pug. The truth is that in my own youth I had my share of scraps, but the time for boyish fighting is past. You must put your energies to better use."

"I know, Kulgan, but I have been so frustrated lately that when that clod Rulf said what he did about my being an orphan, all the anger came boiling up out of me."

"Well, knowing your own part in this is a good sign that you're becoming a man. Most boys would have tried to justify their actions, by shifting blame or by claiming some moral imperative to fight."

Pug pulled over the stool and sat down, facing the magician. Kulgan took out his pipe and started to fill it. "Pug, I think in your case we may have been going about the matter of your education in the wrong way." Searching for a taper to light in the small fire that burned in a night pot and finding none, Kulgan's face clouded as he concentrated for a minute; then a small flame erupted from the index finger of his right hand. Applying it to the pipe, he soon had the room half-filled with great clouds of white smoke. The flame disappeared with a wave of his hand. "A handy skill, if you like the pipe."

"I would give anything to be able to do even that much," Pug said in disgust.

"As I was saying, I think that we may have been going about this in the wrong way. Perhaps we should consider a different approach to your education."

"What do you mean?"

"Pug, the first magicians long ago had no teachers in the arts of magic. They evolved the skills that we've learned today. Some of the old skills, such as smelling the changes in the weather, or the ability to find water with a stick, go back to our earliest beginnings. I have been thinking that for a time I am going to leave you to your own devices. Study what you want in the books that I have. Keep up with your other work, learning the scribe's arts from Tully, but I will not trouble you with any lessons for a while. I will, of course, answer any question you have. But I think for the time being you need to sort yourself out."

Crestfallen, Pug asked, "Am I beyond help?"

Kulgan smiled reassuringly. "Not in the least. There have been cases of magicians having slow starts before. Your apprenticeship is for nine more years, remember. Don't be put off by the failures of the last few months.

"By the way, would you care to learn to ride?"

Pug's mood did a complete turnabout, and he cried, "Oh, yes! May I?"

"The Duke has decided that he would like a boy to ride with the Princess from time to time. His sons have many duties now that they are grown, and he feels you would be a good choice for when they are too busy to accompany her."

Pug's head was spinning. Not only was he to learn to ride, a skill limited to the nobility for the most part, but to be in the company of the Princess as well! "When do I start?"

"This very day. Morning chapel is almost done." Being Firstday, those inclined went to devotions either in the Keep's chapel, or in the small temple down in the town. The rest of the day was given to light work, only that needed to put food on the Duke's table. The boys and girls might get an extra half day on Sixthday, but their elders rested only on Firstday. "Go to Horsemaster Algon; he has been instructed by the Duke and will begin your lessons now."

Without a further word, Pug leaped up and sped for the stables.

4

▾▾

ASSAULT

PUG RODE IN SILENCE.

His horse ambled along the bluffs that overlooked the sea. The warm breeze carried the scent of flowers, and to the east the trees of the forest swayed slowly. The summer sun caused a heat shimmer over the ocean. Above the waves, gulls could be seen hanging in the air, then diving to the water as they sought food. Overhead, large white clouds drifted.

Pug remembered this morning, as he watched the back of the Princess on her fine white palfrey. He had been kept waiting in the stables for nearly two hours before the Princess appeared with her father. The Duke had lectured Pug at length on his responsibility toward the lady of the castle. Pug had stood mute throughout as the Duke repeated all of Horsemaster Algon's instructions of the night before. The master of the stables had been instructing him for a week and judged him ready to ride with the Princess—if barely.

Pug had followed her out of the gate, still marveling at his unexpected fortune. He was exuberant, in spite of having spent the night tossing and then skipping breakfast.

Now his mood was changing from boyish adulation to outright irritation. The Princess refused to respond to any of his polite attempts at conversation, except to order him about. Her tone was imperious and rude, and she insisted on calling him "boy," ignoring several courteous reminders that his name was Pug. She acted little like the poised young woman of the court now, and resembled nothing as much as a spoiled, petulant child.

He had felt awkward at first as he sat atop the old grey dray horse that had been judged sufficient for one of his skills. The mare had a calm nature and showed no inclination to move faster than absolutely necessary.

Pug wore his bright red tunic, the one that Kulgan had given to him, but still looked poorly attired next to the Princess. She was dressed in a simple but exquisite yellow riding dress trimmed in black, and a matching hat. Even sitting sidesaddle, Carline looked like one born to ride, while Pug felt as if he should be walking behind his mare with a plow between. Pug's horse had an irritating tendency to want to stop every dozen feet to crop grass or nibble at shrubbery, ignoring Pug's frantic kicks to the side, while the Princess's excellently trained horse responded instantly to the slightest touch of her crop. She rode along in silence, ignoring the grunts of exertion from the boy behind, who attempted by force of will as much as horsemanship to keep his recalcitrant mount moving.

Pug felt the first stirring of hunger, his dreams of romance surrendering to his normal, fifteen-year-old's appetite. As they rode, his thoughts turned more and more to the basket of lunch that hung from his saddle horn. After what seemed like an eternity to Pug, the Princess turned to him. "Boy, what is your craft?"

Startled by the question after the long silence, Pug stammered his reply. "I . . . I'm apprenticed to Master Kulgan."

She fixed him with a gaze that would have suited her had an insect been found crawling across a dinner plate. "Oh. You're that boy." Whatever brief spark of interest there had been went out, and she turned away from him. They rode awhile longer, then the Princess said, "Boy, we stop here."

Pug pulled up his mare, and before he could reach the Princess's side, she was nimbly down, not waiting for his hand as Master Algon had instructed him she would. She handed him the reins of her horse and walked to the edge of the cliffs.

She stared out to sea for a minute, then, without looking at Pug, said, "Do you think I am beautiful?"

Pug stood in silence, not knowing what to say. She turned and looked at him. "Well?"

Pug said, "Yes, Your Highness."

"Very beautiful?"

"Yes, Your Highness. Very beautiful."

The Princess seemed to consider this for a moment, then returned her attention to the vista below. "It is important for me to be beautiful, boy. Lady Marna says that I must be the most beautiful lady in the Kingdom, for I must find a powerful husband someday, and only the most beautiful ladies in the Kingdom can choose. The homely ones must take whoever will ask for them. She says that I will have many suitors, for Father is very important." She turned, and for a brief moment Pug thought he saw a look of apprehension pass over her lovely features. "Have you many friends, boy?"

Pug shrugged. "Some, Your Highness."

She studied him for a moment, then said, "That must be nice," absently brushing aside a wisp of hair that had come loose from under her broad-brimmed riding hat. Something in her seemed so wounded and alone that moment, that Pug found his heart in his throat again. Obviously his expression revealed something to the Princess, for suddenly her eyes narrowed and her mood shifted from thoughtful to regal. In her most commanding voice she announced, "We will have lunch now." Pug quickly staked the horses and unslung the basket. He placed it on the ground and opened it.

Carline stepped over and said, "I will prepare the meal, boy. I'll not have clumsy hands overturning dishes and spilling wine." Pug took a step back as she knelt and began unpacking the lunch. Rich odors of cheese and bread assailed Pug's nostrils, and his mouth watered.

The Princess looked up at him. "Walk the horses over the hill to the stream and water them. You may eat as we ride back. I'll call you when I have eaten." Suppressing a groan, Pug took the horses' reins and started walking. He kicked at some loose stones, emotions conflicting within him as he led the horses along. He knew he wasn't supposed to leave the girl, but he couldn't very well disobey her either. There was no one else in sight, and trouble was unlikely this far from the forest. Additionally he was glad to be away from Carline for a little while.

He reached the stream and unsaddled the mounts; he brushed away the damp saddle and girth marks, then left their reins upon the ground. The palfrey was trained to ground-tie, and the draft horse showed no inclination to wander far. They cropped grass while Pug found a comfortable spot to sit. He considered the situation and found himself perplexed. Carline was still the loveliest girl he had ever seen, but her manner was quickly taking the sheen off his fascination. For the moment his stomach was of larger concern than the girl of his dreams. He thought perhaps there was more to this love business than he had imagined.

He amused himself for a while by speculation on that. When he grew bored, he went to look for stones in the water. He hadn't had much opportunity to practice with his sling of late, and now was a good time. He found several smooth stones and took out his sling. He practiced by picking out targets among the small trees some distance off, startling the birds in residence there. He hit several clusters of bitter berries, missing only one target out of six. Satisfied his aim was still as good as always, he tucked his sling in his belt. He found several more stones that looked especially promising and put them in his pouch. He judged the girl must be nearly through, and he started toward the horses to saddle them so that when she called, he'd be ready.

As he reached the Princess's horse, a scream sounded from the other side of the hill. He dropped the Princess's saddle and raced to the crest and, when he cleared the ridge, stopped in shock. The hair on his neck and arms stood on end.

The Princess was running, and close in pursuit were a pair of trolls. Trolls usually didn't venture this far from the forest, and Pug was unprepared for the sight of them. They were humanlike, but short and broad, with long, thick arms that hung nearly to the ground. They ran on all fours as often as not, looking like some comic parody of an ape, their bodies covered by thick grey hide and their lips drawn back, revealing long fangs. The ugly creatures rarely troubled a group of humans, but they would attack a lone traveler from time to time.

Pug hesitated for a moment, pulling his sling from his belt and loading a stone; then he charged down the hill, whirling his sling above his head. The creatures had nearly overtaken the Princess when he let fly with a stone. It caught the foremost troll in the side of the head, knocking it for a full somersault. The second stumbled into it, and both went down in a tangle. Pug stopped as they regained their feet, their attention diverted from Carline to their attacker. They roared at Pug, then charged. Pug ran back up the hill. He knew that if he could reach the horses, he could outrun them, circle around for the girl, and be safely away. He looked over his shoulder and saw them coming—huge canine teeth bared, long foreclaws tearing up the ground. Downwind, he could smell their rank, rotting-meat odor.

He cleared the top of the hill, his breath coming in ragged gasps. His heart skipped as he saw that the horses had wandered across the stream and were twenty yards farther away than before. Plunging down the hill, he hoped the difference would not prove fatal.

He could hear the trolls behind him as he entered the stream at a full run. The water was shallow here, but still it slowed him down.

Splashing through the stream, he caught his foot on a stone and fell. He threw his arms forward and broke his fall with his hands, keeping his head above water. Shock ran up through his arms as he tried to regain his feet. He stumbled again and turned as the trolls approached the water's edge. They howled at the sight of their tormentor stumbling in the water and paused for a moment. Pug felt blind terror as he struggled with numb fingers to put a stone in his sling. He fumbled and dropped the sling, and the stream carried it away. Pug felt a scream building in his throat.

As the trolls entered the water, a flash of light exploded behind Pug's eyes. A searing pain ripped across his forehead as letters of grey seemed to appear in his mind. They were familiar to Pug, from a scroll that Kulgan had shown him several times. Without thinking, he mouthed the incantation, each word vanishing from his mind's eye as he spoke it.

When he reached the last word, the pain stopped, and a loud roar sounded from before him. He opened his eyes and saw the two trolls writhing in the water, their eyes wide with agony as they thrashed about helplessly, screaming and groaning.

Dragging himself out of the water, Pug watched while the creatures struggled. They were making choking and sputtering noises now as they flopped about. After a moment one shook and stopped moving, lying facedown in the water. The second took a few minutes longer to die, but like its companion, it also drowned, unable to keep its head above the shallow water.

Feeling light-headed and weak, Pug recrossed the stream. His mind was numb, and everything seemed hazy and disjointed. He stopped after he had taken a few steps, remembering the horses. He looked about and could see nothing of the animals. They must have run off when they caught wind of the trolls and would be on the way to safe pasture.

Pug resumed his walk to where the Princess had been. He topped the hillock and looked around. She was nowhere in sight, so he headed for the overturned basket of food. He was having trouble thinking, and he was ravenous. He knew he should be doing or thinking about something, but all he could sort out of the kaleidoscope of his thoughts was food.

Dropping to his knees, he picked up a wedge of cheese and stuffed it in his mouth. A half-spilled bottle of wine lay nearby, and he washed the cheese down with it. The rich cheese and piquant white wine revived him, and he felt his mind clearing. He ripped a large piece of bread from a loaf and chewed on it while trying to put his thoughts in order. As Pug recalled events, one thing stood out. Somehow he had managed to cast a magic spell. What's more, he had done so without the aid of a book, scroll, or device. He was not sure, but that seemed somehow strange. His thoughts turned hazy again. More than anything he wanted to lie down and sleep, but as he chewed his food, a thought pushed through the crazy quilt of his impressions. The Princess!

He jumped to his feet, and his head swam. Steadying himself, he grabbed up some bread and the wine and set off in the direction he had last seen her running. He pushed himself along, his feet scuffing as he tried to walk. After a few minutes he found his thinking improving and the exhaustion lifting. He started to call the Princess's name, then heard muted sobbing coming from a clump of bushes. Pushing his way through, he found Carline huddled behind the shrubs, her balled fists pulled up into her stomach. Her eyes were wide with terror, and her gown was soiled and torn. Startled when Pug stepped into view, she jumped to her feet and flew into his arms, burying her head in his chest. Great racking sobs shook her body as she clutched the fabric of his shirt. Standing with his arms still outstretched, wine and bread occupying his hands, Pug was totally confused over what to do. He awkwardly placed his arm around the terrified girl and said, "It's all right. They're gone. You're safe."

She hung on to him for a moment, then, when her tears subsided, she stepped away. With a sniffle she said, "I thought they had killed you and were coming back for me."

Pug found this situation more perplexing than any he had ever known. Just when he had come through the most harrowing experience of his young life, he was faced with one that sent his mind reeling with a different sort of confusion. Without thinking, he held the Princess in his arms, and now he was suddenly aware of the contact, and her soft, warm appeal. A protective, masculine feeling welled up inside him, and he started to step toward her.

As if sensing his mood change, Carline retreated. For all her courtly ways and education, she was still a girl of fifteen and was disturbed by the rush of emotions she had experienced when he had held her. She took refuge in the one thing she knew well, her role as Princess of the castle. Trying to sound commanding, she said, "I am glad to see you are unhurt, boy." Pug winced visibly at that. She struggled to regain her aristocratic bearing, but her red nose and tearstained face undermined her attempt. "Find my horse, and we shall return to the keep."

Pug felt as if his nerves were raw. Keeping tight control over his voice, he said, "I'm sorry, Your Highness, but the horses have run off. I'm afraid we'll have to walk."

Carline felt abused and mistreated. It was not Pug's fault any of the afternoon's events had taken place, but her often-indulged temper seized on the handiest available object. "Walk! I can't walk all the way to the keep," she snapped, looking at Pug as if he were supposed to do something about this matter at once and without question.

Pug felt all the anger, confusion, hurt, and frustration of the day surge up within him. "Then you can bloody well sit here until they notice you're missing and send someone to fetch you." He was now shouting. "I figure that will be about two hours after sunset."

Carline stepped back, her face ashen, looking as if she'd been slapped. Her lower lip trembled, and she seemed on the verge of tears again. "I will not be spoken to in that manner, boy."

Pug's eyes grew large, and he stepped toward her, gesturing with the wine bottle. "I nearly got myself killed trying to keep you alive," he shouted. "Do I hear one word of thanks? No! All I hear is a whining complaint that you can't walk back to the castle. We of the keep may be lowborn, but at least we have enough manners to thank someone when it's deserved." As he spoke, he could feel the anger flooding out of him. "You can stay here if you like, but I'm going. . . ." He suddenly realized that he was standing with the bottle raised high overhead, in a ridiculous pose. The Princess's eyes were on the loaf of bread, and he realized that he was holding it at his belt, thumb hooked in a loop, which only added to the awkward appearance. He sputtered for a moment, then felt his anger evaporate and lowered the bottle. The Princess looked at him, her large eyes peeking over her fists, which she held before her face. Pug started to say something, thinking she was afraid of him, when he saw she was laughing. It was a musical sound, warm and unmocking. "I'm sorry, Pug," she said, "but you look so silly standing there like that. You look like one of those awful statues they erect in Krondor, with bottle held high instead of a sword."

Pug shook his head. "I'm the one who's sorry, Your Highness. I had no right to yell at you that way. Please forgive me."

Her expression abruptly changed to one of concern. "No, Pug. You had every right to say what you did. I really do owe you my life, and I've acted horribly." She stepped closer to him and placed a hand on his arm. "Thank you."

Pug was overcome by the sight of her face. Any resolutions to rid himself of his boyhood fantasies about her were now carried away on the sea breeze. The marvelous fact of his using magic was replaced by more urgent and basic considerations. He started to reach for her; then the reality of her station intruded, and he presented the bottle to her. "Wine?"

She laughed, sensing his sudden shift in thought. They were both wrung out and a little giddy from the ordeal, but she still held on to her wits and understood the effect she was having on him. With a nod she took the bottle and sipped. Recovering a shred of poise, Pug said, "We'd better hurry. We might make the keep by nightfall."

She nodded, keeping her eyes upon him, and smiled. Pug was feeling uncomfortable under her gaze and turned toward the way to the keep. "Well, then. We'd best be off."

She fell into step beside him. After a moment she asked, "May I have some bread too, Pug?"

PUG HAD RUN the distance between the bluffs and the keep many times before, but the Princess was unused to walking such distances, and her soft riding boots were ill suited to such an undertaking. When they came into view of the castle, she had one arm draped over Pug's shoulder and was limping badly.

A shout went up from the gate tower, and guards came running toward them. After them came the Lady Marna, the girl's governess, her red dress pulled up before her as she sprinted toward the Princess. Although twice the size of court ladies—and a few of the guards as well—she outdistanced them all. She was coming on like a she-bear whose cub was being attacked. Her great bosom heaved with the effort as she reached the slight girl and grasped her in a hug that threatened to engulf Carline completely. Soon the ladies of the court were gathered around the Princess, overwhelming her with questions. Before the din subsided, Lady Marna turned and fell on Pug like the sow bear she resembled. "How *dare* you allow the Princess to come to such a state! Limping in, dress all torn and dirty. I'll see you whipped from one end of the keep to the other. Before I have done with you, you'll wish you'd never seen the light of day." Backing away before the onslaught, Pug was overwhelmed by confusion, unable to get a word in. Sensing that somehow Pug was responsible for the Princess's condition, one of the guards stepped up and seized him by the arm.

"Leave him alone!"

Silence descended as Carline forced her way between the governess and Pug. Small fists struck at the guard as he let go of Pug and fell back with a look of astonishment on his face. "He saved my life! He almost got killed saving me." Tears were running down her face. "He's done nothing wrong. And I won't have any of you bullying him." The crowd closed in around them, regarding Pug with newfound respect. Hushed voices sounded from all sides, and one of the guards ran to carry the news to the castle. The Princess placed her arm around Pug's shoulder once more and started toward the gate. The crowd parted, and the two weary travelers could see the torches and lanterns being lit on the wall.

By the time they had reached the courtyard gate, the Princess had consented to let two of her ladies help her, much to Pug's relief. He could not have believed that such a slight girl could become such a burden. The Duke hurried out to her, having been told of Carline's return. He embraced his daughter, then started to speak with her. Pug lost sight of them as curious, questioning onlookers surrounded him. He tried to push his way toward the magician's tower, but the press of people held him back.

"Is there no work to be done?" a voice roared.

Heads turned to see Swordmaster Fannon, followed closely by Tomas. All the keep folk quickly retired, leaving Pug standing before Fannon, Tomas, and those of the Duke's court with rank enough to ignore Fannon's remark. Pug could see the Princess talking to her father, Lyam, Arutha, and Squire Roland. Fannon said, "What happened, boy?"

Pug tried to speak, but stopped when he saw the Duke and his sons approaching. Kulgan came hurrying behind the Duke, having been alerted by the general commotion in the courtyard. All bowed to the Duke when he approached, and Pug saw Carline break free of Roland's solicitations and follow her father, to stand at Pug's side. Lady Marna threw a besieged look heavenward, and Roland followed the girl, an open expression of surprise upon his face. When the Princess took Pug's hand in her own, Roland's expression changed to one of black-humored jealousy.

The Duke said, "My daughter has said some very remarkable things about you, boy. I would like to hear your account." Pug felt suddenly self-conscious and gently disengaged his hand from Carline's. He recounted the events of the day, with Carline enthusiastically adding embellishments. Between the two of them, the Duke gained a nearly accurate account of things. When Pug finished, Lord Borric asked, "How is it the trolls drowned in the stream, Pug?"

Pug looked uncomfortable. "I cast a spell upon them, and they were unable to reach the shore," he said softly. He was still confused by this accomplishment and had not given much thought to it, as the Princess had pushed all other thoughts aside. He could see surprise registered on Kulgan's face. Pug began to say something, but was interrupted by the Duke's next remark.

"Pug, I can't begin to repay the service you've done my family. But I shall find a suitable reward for your courage." In a burst of enthusiasm Carline threw her arms around Pug's neck, hugging him fiercely. Pug stood in embarrassment, looking frantically about, as if trying to communicate that this familiarity was none of his doing.

Lady Marna looked ready to faint, and the Duke pointedly coughed, motioning with his head for his daughter to retire. As she left with the Lady Marna, Kulgan and Fannon simply let their amusement show, as did Lyam and Arutha. Roland shot Pug an angry, envious look, then turned and headed off toward his own quarters. Lord Borric said to Kulgan, "Take this boy to his room. He looks exhausted. I'll order food sent to him. Have him come to the great hall after tomorrow's morning meal." He turned to Pug. "Again, I thank you." The Duke motioned for his sons to follow and walked away. Fannon gripped Tomas by the elbow, for the sandy-haired boy had started to speak with his friend. The old Swordmaster motioned with his head that the boy should come with him, leaving Pug in peace. Tomas nodded, though he was burning with a thousand questions.

When they had all left, Kulgan placed his arm around the boy's shoulder. "Come, Pug. You're tired, and there is much to speak of."

PUG LAY BACK on his pallet, the remains of his meal lying on a platter next to him. He couldn't remember ever having been this tired before. Kulgan paced back and forth across the room. "It's absolutely incredible." He waved a hand in the air, his red robe surging over his heavy frame like water flowing over a boulder. "You close your eyes, and the image of a scroll you saw weeks before appears. You incant the spell, as if you were holding the scroll in your hand before you, and the trolls fall. Absolutely incredible." Sitting down on the stool near the window, he continued. "Pug, nothing like this has ever been done before. Do you know what you've done?"

Pug started from the edge of a warm, soft sleep and looked at the magician. "Only what I said I did, Kulgan."

"Yes, but do you have any idea what it means?"

"No."

"Neither do I." The magician seemed to collapse inside as his excitement left, replaced by complete uncertainty. "I don't have the slightest idea what it all means. Magicians don't toss spells off the top of their heads. Clerics can, but they have a different focus and different magic. Do you remember what I taught you about focuses, Pug?"

Pug winced, not being in the mood to recite a lesson, but forced himself to sit up. "Anyone who employs magic must have a focus for the power he uses. Priests have power to focus their magic through prayer; their incantations are a form of prayer. Magicians use their bodies, or devices, or books and scrolls."

"Correct," said Kulgan, "but you have just violated that truism." He took out his long pipe and absently stuffed tabac into the bowl. "The spell you incanted cannot use the caster's body as a focus. It has been developed to inflict great pain upon another. It can be a very terrible weapon. But it can be cast only by reading from a scroll that it is written upon, *at the time it's cast.* Why is this?"

Pug forced leaden eyelids open. "The scroll itself is magic."

"True. Some magic is intrinsic to the magician, such as taking on the shape of an animal or smelling weather. But casting spells outside the body, upon something else, needs an external focus. Trying to incant the spell you used from memory should have produced terrible pain in *you,* not the trolls, if it would have worked at all! *That* is why magicians developed scrolls, books, and other devices, to focus that sort of magic in a way that will not harm the caster. And until today, I would have sworn that no one alive could have made that spell work without the scroll in hand."

Leaning against the windowsill, Kulgan puffed on his pipe for a moment, gazing out into space. "It's as if you have discovered a completely new form of magic," he said softly. Hearing no response, Kulgan looked down at the boy, who was deeply asleep. Shaking his head in wonder, the magician pulled a cover over the exhausted boy. He put out the lantern that hung on the wall and let himself out. As he walked up the stairs to his own room, he shook his head. "Absolutely incredible."

PUG WAITED as the Duke held court in the great hall. Everyone in the keep and town who could contrive a way to gain entrance to the audience was there. Richly dressed Craftmasters, merchants, and minor nobles were in attendance. They stood regarding the boy with expressions ranging from wonder to disbelief. The rumor of his deed had spread through the town and had grown in the telling.

Pug wore new clothing, which had been in his room when he awoke. In his newfound splendor he felt self-conscious and awkward. The tunic was a bright yellow affair of the costliest silk, and the hose were a soft pastel blue. Pug tried to wiggle his toes in the new boots, the first he had ever worn. Walking in them seemed strange and uncomfortable. At his side a jeweled dagger hung from a black leather belt with a golden buckle in the form of a gull in flight. Pug suspected the clothing had once belonged to one of the Duke's sons, put aside when outgrown, but still looking new and beautiful.

The Duke was finishing the morning's business: a request from one of the shipwrights for guards to accompany a lumber expedition to the great forest. Borric was dressed, as usual in black, but his sons and daughter wore their finest court regalia. Lyam was listening closely to the business before his father. Roland stood behind him, as was the custom. Arutha was in rare good humor, laughing behind an upraised hand at some quip Father Tully had just made. Carline sat quietly, her face set in a warm smile, looking directly at Pug, which was adding to his discomfort—and Roland's irritation.

The Duke gave his permission for a company of guards to accompany the craftsmen into the forest. The Craftmaster gave thanks and bowed, then returned to the crowd, leaving Pug alone before the Duke. The boy stepped forward as Kulgan had told him to do and bowed properly, albeit a little stiffly, before the Lord of Crydee. Borric smiled at the boy and motioned to Father Tully. The priest removed a document from the sleeve of his voluminous robe and handed it to a herald. The herald stepped forward and unrolled the scroll.

In a loud voice he read: "To all within our demesne: Whereas the youth Pug, of the castle of Crydee, has shown exemplary courage in the act of risking life and limb in defense of the royal person of the Princess Carline, and; Whereas the youth, Pug of Crydee, is considered to hold us forever in his debt; It is my wish that he be known to all in the realm as our beloved and loyal servant, and it is furthermore wished that he be given a place in the court of Crydee, with the rank of Squire, with all rights and privileges pertaining thereunto. Furthermore let it be known that the title for the estate of Forest Deep is conferred upon him and his progeny as long as they shall live, to have and to hold, with servants and properties thereupon. Title to this estate shall be held by the crown until the day of his majority. Set this day by my hand and seal Borric conDoin, third Duke of Crydee; Prince of the Kingdom; Lord of Crydee, Carse, and Tulan; Warden of the West; Knight-General of the King's Armies; heir presumptive to the throne of Rillanon."

Pug felt his knees go slack but caught himself before he fell. The room erupted in cheers. People were pressing around him, offering their congratulations and slapping him on the back. He was a Squire and a landholder with franklins, a house, and stock. He was rich. Or at least he would be in three years when he reached his majority. While he was considered a man of the Kingdom at fourteen, grants of land and titles couldn't be conferred until he reached eighteen. The crowd backed away as the Duke approached, his family and Roland behind. Both Princes smiled at Pug, and the Princess seemed positively aglow. Roland gave Pug a rueful smile, as if in disbelief.

"I'm honored, Your Grace," Pug stammered. "I don't know what to say."

"Then say nothing, Pug. It makes you seem wise when everyone is babbling. Come, and we'll have a talk." The Duke motioned for a chair to be placed near his own, as he put an arm around the boy's shoulders and walked him through the crowd. Sitting down, he said, "You may all leave us now. I would speak with the Squire." The crowd pressing around muttered in disappointment, but began to drift out of the hall. "Except you two," the Duke added, pointing toward Kulgan and Tully.

Carline stood by her father's chair, a hesitant Roland at her side. "You as well, my child," said the Duke.

Carline began to protest, but was cut off by her father's stern admonition: "You may pester him later, Carline." The two Princes stood at the door, obviously amused at her outrage; Roland tried to offer his arm to the Princess, but she pulled away and swept by her grinning brothers. Lyam clapped Roland on the shoulder as the embarrassed Squire joined them. Roland glared at Pug, who felt the anger like a blow.

When the doors clanged closed and the hall was empty, the Duke said, "Pay no heed to Roland, Pug. My daughter has him firmly under her spell; he counts himself in love with her and wishes someday to petition for her hand." With a lingering look at the closed door, he added almost absently, "But he'll have to show me he's more than the rakehell he's growing into now if he ever hopes for my consent."

The Duke dismissed the topic with a wave of his hand. "Now, to other matters. Pug, I have an additional gift for you, but first I want to explain something to you.

"My family is among the oldest in the Kingdom. I myself am descended from a King, for my grandfather, the first Duke of Crydee, was third son to the King. Being of royal blood, we are much concerned with matters of duty and honor. You are now both a member of my court and apprentice of Kulgan. In matters of duty you are responsible to him. In matters of honor you are responsible to me. This room is hung with the trophies and banners of our triumphs. Whether we have been resisting the Dark Brotherhood in their ceaseless effort to destroy us, or fighting off pirates, we have ever fought bravely. Ours is a proud heritage that has never known the stain of dishonor. No member of our court has ever brought shame to this hall, and I will expect the same of you."

Pug nodded, tales of glory and honor remembered from his youth spinning in his mind. The Duke smiled. "Now to the business of your other gift. Father Tully has a document that I asked him to draw up last night. I am going to ask him to keep it, until such time as he deems fit to give it to you. I will say no more on the subject, except that when he gives it to you, I hope you will remember this day and consider long what it says."

"I will, Your Grace." Pug was sure the Duke was saying something very important, but with all the events of the last half hour, it did not register very well.

"I will expect you for supper, Pug. As a member of the court, you will not be eating meals in the kitchen anymore." The Duke smiled at him. "We'll make a young gentleman out of you, boy. And someday when you travel to the King's city of Rillanon, no one will fault the manners of those who come from the court of Crydee."

5

▾▾

SHIPWRECK

THE BREEZE WAS COOL.

The last days of summer had passed, and soon the rains of autumn would come. A few weeks later the first snows of winter would follow. Pug sat in his room, studying a book of ancient exercises designed to ready the mind for spell casting. He had fallen back into his old routine once the excitement of his elevation to the Duke's court had worn off.

His marvelous feat with the trolls continued to be the object of speculation by Kulgan and Father Tully. Pug found he still couldn't do many of the things expected of an apprentice, but other feats were beginning to come to him. Certain scrolls were easier to use now, and once, in secret, he had tried to duplicate his feat.

He had memorized a spell from a book, one designed to levitate objects. He had felt the familiar blocks in his mind when he tried to incant it from memory. He had failed to move the object, a candleholder, but it trembled for a few seconds and he felt a brief sensation, as if he had touched the holder with a part of his mind. Satisfied that some sort of progress was being made, he lost much of his former gloom and renewed his studies with vigor.

Kulgan still let him find his own pace. They had had many long discussions on the nature of magic, but mostly Pug worked in solitude.

Shouting came from the courtyard below. Pug walked to his window.

Seeing a familiar figure, he leaned out and cried, "Ho! Tomas! What is afoot?" Tomas looked up.

"Ho! Pug! A ship has foundered in the night. The wreck has beached beneath Sailor's Grief. Come and see."

"I'll be right down."

Pug ran to the door, pulling on a cloak, for while the day was clear, it would be cold near the water. Racing down the stairs, he cut through the kitchen, nearly knocking over Alfan, the pastry cook. As he bolted out the door, he heard the stout baker yell, "Squire or not, I'll box your ears if you don't watch where you're going, boy!" The kitchen staff had not changed their attitude toward the boy, whom they considered one of their own, beyond feeling proud of his achievement.

Pug shouted back with laughter in his voice, "My apologies, Mastercook!"

Alfan gave him a good-natured wave as Pug vanished through the outside door and around the corner to where Tomas was waiting. Tomas turned toward the gate as soon as he saw his friend.

Pug grabbed his arm. "Wait. Has anyone from the court been told?"

"I don't know. Word just came from the fishing village a moment ago," Tomas said impatiently. "Come on, or the villagers will pick the wreck clean." It was commonly held that salvage could be legally carried away before any of the Duke's court arrived. As a result, the villagers and townsfolk were less than timely in informing the authorities of such occurrences. There was also a risk of bloodshed, should the beached ship still be manned by sailors determined to keep their master's cargo intact so that they would get their fair sailing bonus. Violent confrontation, and even death, had been the result of such dispute. Only the presence of men-at-arms could guarantee no commoner would come to harm from lingering mariners.

"Oh, no," said Pug. "If there is any trouble down there and the Duke finds out I didn't tell someone else, I'll be in for it."

"Look, Pug. Do you think with all these people rushing about, the Duke will be long in hearing of it?" Tomas ran his hand through his hair. "Someone is probably in the great hall right now, telling him the news. Master Fannon is away on patrol, and Kulgan won't be back awhile yet." Kulgan was due back later that day from his cottage in the forest, where he and Meecham had spent the last week. "It may be our only chance to see a shipwreck." A look of sudden inspiration came over his face. "Pug, I have it! You're a member of the court now. Come along, and when we get there, you declare for the Duke." A calculating expression crossed his face. "And if we find a rich bauble or two, who's to know?"

"I would know." Pug thought a moment. "I can't properly declare for the Duke, then take something for myself . . ." He fixed Tomas with a disapproving expression. ". . . or let one of his men-at-arms take something either." As Tomas's face showed his embarrassment, Pug said, "But we can still see the wreck! Come one!"

Pug was suddenly taken with the idea of using his new office, and if he could get there before too much was carried away or someone was hurt, the Duke would be pleased with him. "All right," he said, "I'll saddle a horse and we can ride down there before everything is stolen." Pug turned and ran for the stable. Tomas caught up with him as he opened the large wooden doors. "But, Pug, I have never been on a horse in my life. I don't know how."

"It's simple," Pug said, taking a bridle and saddle from the tack room. He spied the large grey he had ridden the day he and the Princess had their adventure. "I'll ride and you sit behind me. Just keep your arms around my waist, and you won't fall off."

Tomas looked doubtful. "I'm to depend on you?" He shook his head. "After all, who has looked after you all these years?"

Pug threw him a wicked smile. "Your mother. Now fetch a sword from the armory in case there's trouble. You may get to play soldier yet."

Tomas looked pleased at the prospect and ran out the door. A few minutes later the large grey with the two boys mounted on her back lumbered out the main gate, heading down the road toward Sailor's Grief.

THE SURF was pounding as the boys came in sight of the wreckage. Only a few villagers were approaching the site, and they scattered as soon as a horse and rider appeared, for it could only be a noble from the court to declare the wreck's salvage for the Duke. By the time Pug reined in, no one was about.

Pug said, "Come on. We've got a few minutes to look around before anyone else gets here."

Dismounting, the boys left the mare to graze in a little stand of grass only fifty yards from the rocks. Running through the sand, the boys laughed, with Tomas raising the sword aloft, trying to sound fierce as he yelled old war cries learned from the sagas. Not that he had any delusions about his ability to use it, but it might make someone think twice about attacking them—at least long enough for castle guards to arrive.

As they neared the wreck, Tomas whistled a low note. "This ship didn't just run on the rocks, Pug. It looks like it was driven by a storm."

Pug said, "There certainly isn't much left, is there?"

Tomas scratched behind his right ear. "No, just a section of the bow. I don't understand. There wasn't any storm last night, just a strong wind. How could the ship be broken up so badly?"

"I don't know." Suddenly something registered on Pug. "Look at the bow. See how it's painted."

The bow rested on the rocks, held there until the tide rose. From the deck line down, the hull was painted a bright green, and it shone with reflected sunlight, as if it had been glazed over. Instead of a figurehead, intricate designs were painted in bright yellow, down to the waterline, which was a dull black. A large blue-and-white eye had been painted several feet behind the prow, and all the above-deck railing that they could see was painted white.

Pug grabbed Tomas's arm. "Look!" He pointed to the water behind the prow, and Tomas could see a shattered white mast extending a few feet above the surging foam.

Tomas took a step closer. "It's no Kingdom ship, for certain." He turned to Pug. "Maybe they were from Queg?"

"No," answered Pug. "You've seen as many Quegan ships as I have. This is nothing from Queg or the Free Cities. I don't think a ship like this has ever passed these waters before. Let's look around."

Tomas seemed suddenly timid. "Careful, Pug. There is something strange here, and I have an ill feeling. Someone may still be about."

Both boys looked around for a minute, before Pug concluded, "I think not; whatever snapped that mast and drove the ship ashore with enough force to wreck it this badly must have killed any who tried to ride her in."

Venturing closer, the boys found small articles lying about, tossed among the rocks by the waves. They saw broken crockery and boards, pieces of torn red sailcloth, and lengths of rope. Pug stopped and picked up a strange-looking dagger fashioned from some unfamiliar material. It was a dull grey and was lighter than steel, but still quite sharp.

Tomas tried to pull himself to the railing, but couldn't find a proper footing on the slippery rocks. Pug moved along the hull until he found himself in danger of having his boots washed by the tide; they could board the hulk if they waded into the sea, but Pug was unwilling to ruin his good clothing. He walked back to where Tomas stood studying the wreck.

Tomas pointed behind Pug. "If we climb up to that ledge, we could lower ourselves down to the deck."

Pug saw the ledge, a jutting single piece of stone that started twenty feet back on their left, extending upward and out to overhang the bow. It looked like an easy climb, and Pug agreed. They pulled themselves up and inched along the ledge, backs flat to the base of the bluffs. The path was narrow, but by stepping carefully, they ran little risk of falling. They reached a point above the hull; Tomas pointed. "Look. Bodies!"

Lying on the deck were two men, both dressed in bright blue armor of unfamiliar design. One had his head crushed by a fallen spar, but the other, lying facedown, didn't show any injuries, beyond his stillness. Strapped across that man's back was an alien-looking broadsword, with strange serrated edges. His head was covered by an equally alien-looking blue helmet, potlike, with an outward flaring edge on the sides and back. Tomas shouted over the sound of the surf, "I'm going to let myself down. After I get on the deck, hand me the sword, and then lower yourself so I can grab you."

Tomas handed Pug the sword, then turned around slowly. He knelt with his face against the cliff wall. Sliding backward, he let himself down until he was almost hanging free. With a shove he dropped the remaining four feet, landing safely. Pug reversed the sword and handed it down to Tomas, then followed his friend's lead, and in a moment they both stood on the deck. The foredeck slanted alarmingly down toward the water, and they could feel the ship move beneath their feet.

"The tide's rising," Tomas shouted. "It'll lift what's left of the ship and smash it on the rocks. Everything will be lost."

"Look around," Pug shouted back. "Anything that looks worth saving we can try to throw up on the ledge."

Tomas nodded, and the boys started to search the deck. Pug put as much space as he could between the bodies and himself when he passed them. All across the deck, debris created a confused spectacle for the eye. Trying to discern what might prove valuable and what might not was difficult. At the rear of the deck was a shattered rail, on either side of a ladder to what was left of the main deck below: about six feet of planking remaining above the water. Pug was sure that only a few feet more could be underwater, or else the ship would be higher on the rocks. The rear of the ship must have already been carried away on the tide.

Pug lay down on the deck and hung his head over the edge. He saw a door to the right of the ladder. Yelling for Tomas to join him, he made his way carefully down the ladder. The lower deck was sagging, the undersupports having been caved in. He grasped the handrail of the ladder for support. A moment later Tomas stood beside him, stepped around Pug, and moved to the door. It hung half-open, and he squeezed through with Pug a step behind. The cabin was dark, for there was only a single port on the bulkhead next to the door. In the gloom they could see many rich-looking pieces of fabric and the shattered remnants of a table. What looked like a cot or low bed lay upside down in a corner. Several small chests could be seen, with their contents spread around the room as if tossed about by some giant hand.

Tomas tried to search through the mess, but nothing was recognizable as important or valuable. He found one small bowl of unusual design glazed with bright colored figures on the sides, and he put it inside his tunic.

Pug stood quietly, for something in the cabin commanded his attention. A strange, urgent feeling had overtaken him as soon as he had stepped in.

The wreck lurched, throwing Tomas off balance. He caught himself on a chest, dropping the sword. "The ship's lifting. We'd better go."

Pug didn't answer, his attention focused on the strange sensations. Tomas grabbed his arm. "Come on. The ship'll break up in a minute."

Pug shook his hand off. "A moment. There is something . . ." His voice trailed off. Abruptly he crossed the disordered room and pulled open a drawer in a latched chest. It was empty. He yanked open another, then a third. In it was the object of his search. He drew out a rolled parchment with a black ribbon and black seal on it and thrust it into his shirt.

"Come on," he shouted as he passed Tomas. They raced up the ladder and scrambled over the deck. The tide had raised the ship high enough for them to pull themselves up to the ledge with ease, and they turned to sit.

The ship was now floating on the tide, rocking forward and back, while the waves sent a wet spray into the boys' faces. They watched as the bow slid off the rocks, timbers breaking with a loud and deep tearing sound, like a dying moan. The bow lifted high, and the boys were splashed by waves striking the cliffs below their ledge.

Out to sea the hulk floated, slowly leaning over to its port side, until the outward surging tide came to a halt.

Ponderously, it started back toward the rocks. Tomas grabbed at Pug's arm, signaling him to follow. They got up and made their way back to the beach. When they reached the place where the rock overhung the sand, they jumped down.

A loud grinding sound made them turn to see the hull driven onto the rocks. Timbers shattered, and separated with a shriek. The hull heaved to starboard, and debris started sliding off the deck into the sea.

Suddenly Tomas reached over and caught Pug's arm. "Look." He pointed at the wreck sliding backward on the tide.

Pug couldn't make out what he was pointing at. "What is it?"

"I thought for a moment there was only one body on deck."

Pug looked at him. Tomas's face was set in an expression of worry. Abruptly it changed to anger. "Damn!"

"What?"

"When I fell in the cabin, I dropped the sword. Fannon will have my ears."

A sound like an explosion of thunder marked the final destruction of the wreck as the tide smashed it against the cliff face. Now the shards of the once fine, if alien, ship would be swept out to sea, to drift back in along the coast for miles to the south over the next few days.

A low groan ending in a sharp cry made the boys turn. Standing behind them was the missing man from the ship, the strange broadsword held loosely in his left hand and dragging in the sand. His right arm was held tightly against his side; blood could be seen running from under his blue breastplate, and from under his helmet. He took a staggering step forward. His face was ashen, and his eyes wide with pain and confusion. He shouted something incomprehensible at the boys. They stepped back slowly, raising their hands to show they were unarmed.

He took another step toward them, and his knees sagged. He staggered erect and closed his eyes for a moment. He was short and stocky, with powerfully muscled arms and legs. Below the breastplate he wore a short skirt of blue cloth. On his forearms were bracers, and on his legs, greaves that looked like leather, above thonged sandals. He put his hand to his face and shook his head. His eyes opened, and he regarded the boys again. Once more he spoke in his alien tongue. When the boys said nothing, he appeared to grow angry and yelled another series of strange words, from the tone seemingly questions.

Pug gauged the distance necessary to run past the man, who blocked the narrow strip of beach. He decided it wasn't worth the risk of finding out if the man was in a condition to use that wicked-looking sword. As if sensing the boy's thoughts, the soldier staggered a few feet to his right, cutting off any escape. He closed his eyes again, and what little color there was in his face drained away. His gaze began to wander, and the sword slipped from limp fingers. Pug started to take a step toward him, for it was now obvious that he could do them no harm.

As he neared the man, shouts sounded up the beach. Pug and Tomas saw Prince Arutha riding before a troop of horsemen. The wounded soldier turned his head painfully at the sound of approaching horses, and his eyes widened. A look of pure horror crossed his face, and he tried to flee. He took three staggering steps toward the water and fell forward into the sand.

PUG STOOD near the door of the Duke's council chamber. Several feet away a concerned group sat at Duke Borric's round council table. Besides the Duke and his sons, Father Tully, Kulgan, who had returned only an hour before, Swordmaster Fannon, and Horsemaster Algon sat in assembly. The tone was serious, for the arrival of the alien ship was viewed as potentially dangerous to the Kingdom.

Pug threw a quick glance at Tomas, standing on the opposite side of the door. Tomas had never been in the presence of nobility, other than serving in the dining hall, and being in the Duke's council chamber was making him nervous. Master Fannon spoke, and Pug returned his attention to the table.

"Reviewing what we know," said the old Swordmaster, "it is obvious that these people are completely alien to us." He picked up the bowl Tomas had taken from the ship. "This bowl is fashioned in a way unknown to our Masterpotter. At first he thought it was simply a fired and glazed clay, but upon closer inspection it proved otherwise. It is fashioned from some sort of hide, parchment-thin strips being wound around a mold—perhaps wood—then laminated with resins of some type. It is much stronger than anything we know."

To demonstrate, he struck the bowl hard against the table. Instead of shattering, as a clay bowl would have, it made a dull sound. "Now, even more perplexing are these weapons and armor." He pointed to the blue breastplate, helmet, sword, and dagger. "They appear to be fashioned in a similar manner." He lifted the dagger and let it drop. It made the same dull sound as the bowl. "For all its lightness, it is nearly as strong as our best steel."

Borric nodded. "Tully, you've been around longer than any of us. Have you heard of any ship constructed like that?"

"No." Tully absently stroked his beardless chin. "Not from the Bitter Sea, the Kingdom Sea, or even from Great Kesh have I heard of such a ship. I might send word to the Temple of Ishap in Krondor. They have records that go further back than any others. Perhaps they have some knowledge of these people."

The Duke nodded. "Please do. Also we must send word to the elves and dwarves. They have abided here longer than we by ages, and we would do well to seek their wisdom."

Tully indicated agreement. "Queen Aglaranna might have knowledge of these people if they are travelers from across the Endless Sea. Perhaps they have visited these shores before."

"Preposterous," snorted Horsemaster Algon. "There are no nations across the Endless Sea. Otherwise it wouldn't be endless."

Kulgan took on an indulgent expression. "There are theories that other lands exist across the Endless Sea. It is only that we have no ships capable of making such a long journey."

"Theories," was all Algon said.

"Whoever these strangers are," said Arutha, "we had best make sure we can find out as much as possible about them."

Algon and Lyam gave him a questioning look, while Kulgan and Tully looked on without expression. Borric and Fannon nodded as Arutha continued. "From the boys' description, the ship was obviously a warship. The heavy prow with bowsprit is designed for ramming, and the high foredeck is a perfect place for bowmen, as the low middle deck is suitable for boarding other vessels when they have been grappled. I would imagine the rear deck was also high. If more of the hull had survived, I would guess we would have found rowers' benches as well."

"A war galley?" asked Algon.

Fannon looked impatient. "Of course, you simpleton." There was a friendly rivalry between the two masters, which at times degenerated to some unfriendly bickering. "Take a look at our guest's weapon." He indicated the broadsword. "How would you like to ride at a determined man wheeling that toy? He'd cut your horse right out from under you. That armor is light, and efficiently constructed for all its gaudy coloring. I would guess that he was infantry. As powerfully built as he is, he probably could run half a day and still fight." He stroked his mustache absently. "These people have some warriors among them."

Algon nodded slowly. Arutha sat back in his chair, making a tent of his hands, fingertips flexing. "What I can't understand," said the Duke's younger son, "is why he tried to run. We had no weapons drawn and were not charging. There was no reason for him to run."

Borric looked at the old priest. "Will we ever know?"

Tully looked concerned, his brow furrowed. "He had a long piece of wood embedded in his right side, under the breastplate, as well as a bad blow to the head. That helmet saved his skull. He has a high fever and has lost a great deal of blood. He may not survive. I may have to resort to a mind contact, if he regains enough consciousness to establish it." Pug knew of the mind contact; Tully had explained it to him before. It was a method only a few clerics could employ, and it was extremely dangerous for both the subject and the caster. The old priest must feel a strong need to gain information from the injured man to risk it.

Borric turned his attention to Kulgan. "What of the scroll the boys found?"

Kulgan waved a hand absently. "I have given a preliminary, and brief, inspection. It has magical properties without a doubt. That is why Pug felt some compulsion to inspect the cabin and that chest, I think. Anyone as sensitive to magic as he is would feel it." He looked directly at the Duke. "I am, however, unwilling to break the seal until I have made a more involved study of it, to better determine its purpose. Breaking enchanted seals can be dangerous if not handled properly. If the seal was tampered with, the scroll might destroy itself, or worse, those trying to break it. It wouldn't be the first such trap I've seen for a scroll of great power."

The Duke drummed his fingers on the table for a moment. "All right. We will adjourn this meeting. As soon as something new has been learned, either from the scroll or from the wounded man, we will reconvene." He turned to Tully. "See how the man is, and if he should wake, use your arts to glean whatever you can." He stood, and the others rose also. "Lyam, send word to the Elf Queen and the dwarves at Stone Mountain and the Grey Towers of what has happened. Ask for their counsel."

Pug opened the door. The Duke went through and the others followed. Pug and Tomas were the last to leave, and as they walked down the hall, Tomas leaned over toward Pug.

"We really started something."

Pug shook his head. "We were simply the first to find the man. If not us, then someone else."

Tomas looked relieved to be out of the chamber and the Duke's scrutiny. "If this turns out badly, I hope they remember that."

Kulgan went up the stairs to his tower room as Tully moved off toward his own quarters, where the wounded man was being tended by Tully's acolytes. The Duke and his sons turned through a door to their private quarters, leaving the boys alone in the hallway.

Pug and Tomas cut through a storage room, and into the kitchen. Megar stood supervising the kitchen workers, several of whom waved greetings to the boys. When he saw his son and fosterling, he smiled and said, "Well, what have you two gotten yourselves into, now?" Megar was a loose-jointed man, with sandy hair and an open countenance. He resembled Tomas, as a rough sketch resembled a finished drawing. He was a fair-looking man of middle years, but lacked the fine features that set Tomas apart.

Grinning, Megar said, "Everyone is hushed up about that man in Tully's quarters, and messengers are dashing from here to there, one place to another. I haven't seen such a to-do since the Prince of Krondor visited seven years ago!"

Tomas grabbed an apple from a platter and jumped up to sit on a table. Between bites he recounted to his father what had taken place.

Pug leaned on the counter while listening. Tomas told the story with a minimum of embellishment. When he was done, Megar shook his head. "Well, well. Aliens, is it? I hope they're not marauding pirates. We have had peaceful enough times lately. Ten years since the time the Brotherhood of the Dark Path"—he gestured spitting—"curse their murderous souls, stirred up that trouble with the goblins. Can't say as I'd welcome that sort of mess again, sending all those stores to the outlying villages. Having to cook based on what will spoil first and what will last longest. I couldn't make a decent meal for a month."

Pug smiled. Megar had the ability to take even the most difficult possibilities and break them down to basics: how much inconvenience they were likely to cause the scullery staff.

Tomas jumped down from the counter. "I had best return to the soldiers' commons and wait for Master Fannon. I'll see you soon." He ran from the kitchen.

Megar said, "Is it serious, Pug?"

Pug shook his head. "I really can't say. I don't know. I know that Tully and Kulgan are worried, and the Duke thinks enough of the problem to want to talk to the elves and dwarves. It could be."

Megar looked out the door that Tomas had used. "It would be a bad time for war and killing." Pug could see the poorly hidden worry in Megar's face and could think of nothing to say to a father of a son who had just become a soldier.

Pug pushed himself away from the counter. "I'd better be off, as well, Megar." He waved good-bye to the others in the kitchen and walked out of the kitchen and into the courtyard. He had little temper for study, being alarmed by the serious tone of the meeting in the Duke's chambers. No one had come out and said as much, but it was obvious they were considering the possibility that the alien ship was the vanguard of an invasion fleet.

Pug wandered around to the side of the keep and climbed the three steps to the Princess's small flower garden. He sat on a stone bench, the hedges and rows of rosebushes masking most of the courtyard from sight. He could still see the top of the high walks, with the guards patrolling the parapets. He wondered if it was his imagination, or were the guards looking especially watchful today?

The sound of a delicate cough made him turn. Standing on the other side of the garden was Princess Carline, with Squire Roland and two of her younger ladies-in-waiting. The girls hid their smiles, for Pug was still something of a celebrity in the keep. Carline shooed them off, saying, "I would like to speak with Squire Pug in private." Roland hesitated, then bowed stiffly. Pug was irritated by the dark look Roland gave him as he left with the young ladies.

The two young ladies looked over their shoulder at Pug and Carline, giggling, which seemed only to add to Roland's irritation.

Pug stood as Carline approached and made an awkward bow. She said, in short tones, "Oh, sit down. I find that rubbish tiring and get all I need from Roland."

Pug sat. The girl took her place next to him, and they were both silent for a moment. Finally she said, "I haven't seen you for more than a week. Have you been busy?

Pug felt uncomfortable, still confused by the girl and her mercurial moods. She had been only warm to him since the day, three weeks ago, when he had saved her from the trolls, stirring up a storm of gossip among the staff of the castle. She remained short-tempered with others, however, especially Squire Roland.

"I have been busy with my studies."

"Oh, pooh. You spend too much time in that awful tower."

Pug didn't consider the tower room the least bit awful—except for being a bit drafty. It was his own, and he felt comfortable there.

"We could go riding, Your Highness, if you would like."

The girl smiled. "I would like that. But I'm afraid Lady Marna won't allow it."

Pug was surprised. He thought that after the way he had protected the Princess, even the girl's surrogate mother would allow that he was proper company. "Why not?"

Carline sighed. "She says that when you were a commoner, you would keep your place. Now that you are a courtier, she suspects you of having aspirations." A slight smile played across her lips.

"Aspirations?" Pug said, not understanding.

Carline said shyly, "She thinks that you have ambitions to rise to higher station. She thinks you seek to influence me in certain ways."

Pug stared at Carline. Abruptly comprehension dawned on him, and he said, "Oh," then, "*Oh!* Your Highness." He stood up. "I never would do such a thing. I mean, I would never think to . . . I mean . . ."

Carline abruptly stood and threw Pug an exasperated look. "Boys! You're all idiots." Lifting the hem of her long green gown, she stormed off.

Pug sat down, more perplexed than before by the girl. It was almost as if . . . He let the thought trail away. The more it seemed possible that she could care for him, the more anxious the prospect made him. Carline was quite a bit more than the fairy-tale Princess he had imagined a short time back. With the stamp of one little foot, she could raise a storm in a saltcellar, one that could shake the keep. A girl of complex mind was the Princess, with a contradictory nature tossed into the bargain.

Further musing was interrupted by Tomas, dashing by. Catching a glimpse of his friend, he leapt up the three steps and halted breathlessly before him. "The Duke wants us. The man from the ship has died."

THEY HASTILY ASSEMBLED in the Duke's council chamber, except Kulgan, who had not answered when a messenger knocked at his door. It was supposed he was too deeply engrossed in the problem of the magic scroll.

Father Tully looked pale and drawn. Pug was shocked by his appearance. Only a little more than an hour had passed, yet the old cleric looked as if he had spent several sleepless nights. His eyes were red-rimmed and deep-set in dark circles. His face was ashen, and a light sheen of perspiration showed across his brow.

Borric poured the priest a goblet of wine from a decanter on a sideboard and handed it to him. Tully hesitated, for he was an abstemious man, then drank deeply. The others resumed their former positions around the table.

Borric looked at Tully and said, simply, "Well?"

"The soldier from the beach regained consciousness for only a few minutes, a final rally before the end. During that time I had the opportunity to enter into a mind contact with him. I stayed with him through his last feverish dreams, trying to learn as much about him as I could. I nearly didn't remove the contact in time."

Pug paled. During the mind contact, the priest's mind and the subject become as one. If Tully had not broken contact with the man when he died, the priest could have died or been rendered mad, for the two men shared feelings, fears, and sensations as well as thought. He now understood Tully's exhausted state: the old priest had spent a great deal of energy maintaining the link with an uncooperative subject and had been party to the dying man's pain and terror.

Tully took another drink of wine, then continued. "If this man's dying dreams were not the product of fevered imaginings, then I fear his appearance heralds a grave situation." Tully took another sip of wine and pushed the goblet aside. "The man's name was Xomich. He was a simple soldier of a nation, Honshoni, in something called the Empire of Tsuranuanni."

Borric said, "I have never heard of this nation, nor of that Empire."

Tully nodded and said, "I would have been surprised if you had. That man's ship came from no sea of Midkemia." Pug and Tomas looked at each other, and Pug felt a chilling sensation, as, apparently, did Tomas, whose face had turned pale.

Tully went on. "We can only speculate on how the feat was managed, but I am certain that this ship comes from another world, removed from our own in time and space." Before questions could be asked, he said, "Let me explain."

"This man was sick with fever, and his mind wandered." Tully's face flickered with remembered pain. "He was part of an honor guard for someone he thought of only as 'Great One.' There were conflicting images, and I can't be sure, but it seems that the journey they were on was considered strange, both for the presence of this Great One and for the nature of the mission. The only concrete thought I gained was that this Great One had no need to travel by ship. Beyond that, I have little but quick and disjointed impressions. There was a city he knew as Yankora, then a terrible storm, and a sudden blinding brilliance, which may have been lightning striking the ship, but I think not. There was a thought of his captain and comrades being washed overboard. Then a crash on the rocks." He paused for a moment. "I am not sure if those images are in order, for I think it likely that the crew was lost before the blinding light."

"Why?" asked Borric.

"I'm ahead of myself," said Tully. "First I'd like to explain why I think this man is from another world.

"This Xomich grew to manhood in a land ruled by great armies. They are a warrior race, whose ships control the seas. But what seas? Never, to my knowledge, has there been mention of contact with these people. And there are other visions that are even more convincing. Great cities, far larger than those in the heart of Kesh, the largest known to us. Armies on parade during high holiday, marching past a review stand; city garrisons larger than the King's Army of the West."

Algon said, "Still, there is nothing to say they are not from"—he paused, as if the admission were difficult—"across the Endless Sea." That prospect seemed to trouble him less than the notion of some place not of this world.

Tully looked irritated at the interruption. "There is more, much more. I followed him through his dreams, many of his homeland. He remembers creatures unlike any I have heard of or seen, things with six legs that pull wagons like oxen, and other creatures, some that look like insects or reptiles, but speak like men. His land was hot, and his memory of the sun was of one larger than ours and more green in color. This man was not of our world." The last was said flatly, removing from all in the room any lingering doubts. Tully would never make a pronouncement like that unless he was certain.

The room was silent as each person reflected on what had been said. The boys watched and shared the feeling. It was as if no one were willing to speak, as if to do so would seal the priest's information forever in fact, while to stay silent might let it pass like a bad dream. Borric stood and paced over to the window. It looked out upon a blank rear wall of the castle, but he stared as if seeking something there, something that would provide an answer for the questions that spun in his mind. He turned quickly and said, "How did they get here, Tully?"

The priest shrugged. "Perhaps Kulgan can offer a theory as to the means. What I construct as being the most likely series of events is this: the ship foundered in the storm; the captain of the ship and most of its crew were lost. As a last resort this Great One, whoever he is, invoked a spell to remove the ship from the storm, or change the weather, or some other mighty feat. As a result, the ship was cast from its own world into this, appearing off the coast at Sailor's Grief. With the ship moving at great speed on its own world, it may have appeared here with the same movement, and with the westerly blowing strong, and little or no crew, the ship was driven straight onto the rocks. Or it simply may have appeared upon the rocks, smashed at the instant it came into being here."

Fannon shook his head. "From another world. How can that be possible?"

The old priest raised his hands in a gesture of mystification. "One can only speculate. The Ishapians have old scrolls in their temples. Some are reputed to be copies of older works, which in turn are copies of still older scrolls. They claim the originals date back, in unbroken line, to the time of the Chaos Wars. Among them is mention of 'other planes' and 'other dimensions,' and of concepts lost to us. One thing is clear, however. They speak of lands and peoples unknown and suggest that once mankind traveled to other worlds, or to Midkemia from other worlds. These notions have been the center of religious debate for centuries, and no one could say with certainty what truth there was in any of them." He paused, then said, "Until now. If I had not seen what was in Xomich's mind, I would not have accepted such a theory to explain this day's occurrences. But now . . ."

Borric crossed to his chair to stand behind it, his hands gripping each side of the high back. "It seems impossible."

"That the ship and man were here is fact, Father," said Lyam.

Arutha followed his brother's comment with another. "And we must decide what the chances are that this feat may be duplicated."

Borric said to Tully, "You were right when you said this may herald a grave situation. Should a great Empire be turning its attention toward Crydee and the Kingdom . . ."

Tully shook his head. "Borric, have you so long been removed from my tutelage that you miss the point entirely?" He held up a bony hand as the Duke started to protest. "Forgive me, my lord. I am old and tired and forget my manners. But the truth is still the truth. A mighty nation they are, or rather an empire of nations, and if they have the means to reach us, it could prove dire, but most important is the possibility that this Great One is a magician or priest of high art. For if he is not one alone, if there are more within this Empire, and if they did indeed try to reach this world with magic, then grave times are truly in store for us."

When everyone at the table still appeared not to comprehend what he was alluding to, Tully continued, like a patient teacher lecturing a group of promising but occasionally slow students. "The ship's appearance may be the product of chance and, if so, is only a cause for curiosity. But if it was by design that it came here, then we may be in peril, for to move a ship to another world is an order of magic beyond my imagining. If these people, the Tsurani as they call themselves, know we are here, and if they possess the means to reach us, then not only must we fear armies that rival Great Kesh at the height of its power, when its reach extended to even this remote corner of the world, we must also face magic far greater than any we have known."

Borric nodded, for the conclusion was obvious, once pointed out. "We must have Kulgan's counsel on this at once."

"One thing, Arutha," said Tully. The Prince looked up from his chair, for he had been lost in thought. "I know why Xomich tried to run from you and your men. He thought you were creatures he knew in his own world, centaurlike creatures, called Thūn, feared by the Tsurani."

"Why would he think that?" asked Lyam, looking puzzled.

"He had never seen a horse, or any creature remotely like it. I expect these people have none."

The Duke sat down again. Drumming his fingers on the table, he said, "If what Father Tully says is true, then we must make some decisions, and quickly. If this is but an accident that has brought these people to our shores, then there may be little to fear. If, however, there is some design to their coming, then we should expect a serious threat.

Here we are the fewest in number of all the Kingdom's garrisons, and it would be a hard thing should they come here in force."

The others murmured agreement, and the Duke said, "We would do well to try to understand that what has been said here is still only speculation, though I am inclined to agree with Tully on most points. We should have Kulgan's thoughts upon the matter of these people." He turned to Pug. "Lad, see if your master is free to join us."

Pug nodded and opened the door, then raced through the keep. He ran to the tower steps and took them two at a time. He raised his hand to knock and felt a strange sensation, as if he were near a lightning strike, causing the hair on his arms and scalp to stand up. A sudden sense of wrongness swept over him, and he pounded on the door. "Kulgan! Kulgan! Are you all right?" he shouted, but no answer was forthcoming. He tried the door latch and found it locked. He placed his shoulder against the door and tried to force it, but it held fast. The feeling of strangeness had passed, but fear rose in him at Kulgan's silence. He looked about for something to force the door and, finding nothing, ran back down the stairs.

He hurried into the long hall. Here guards in Crydee livery stood at their post. He shouted at the two nearest, "You two, come with me. My master is in trouble." Without hesitation they followed the boy up the stairs, their boots pounding on the stone steps.

When they reached the magician's door, Pug said, "Break it down!" They quickly put aside spear and shield and leaned their shoulders against the door. Once, twice, three times they heaved, and with a protesting groan the timbers cracked around the lock plate. One last shove and the door flew open. The guards stopped themselves from falling through the door and stepped back, amazement and confusion on their faces. Pug shouldered between them and looked into the room.

On the floor lay Kulgan, unconscious. His blue robes were disheveled, and one arm was thrown across his face, as if in protection. Two feet from him, where his study table should have stood, hung a shimmering void. Pug stared at the place in the air. A large sphere of grey that was not quite grey shimmered with traces of a broken spectrum. He could not see through it, but there was nothing solid there. Coming out of the grey space was a pair of human arms, reaching toward the magician. When they touched the material of his robe, they stopped and fingered the cloth. As if a decision had been made, they traveled over his body, until they identified Kulgan's arm. The hands took hold of him and tried to lift his arm into the void. Pug stood in horror, for whoever or whatever was on the other side of the void was trying to pull the stout magician up and through. Another pair of hands reached through and picked up the magician's arm next to where the first held him, and Kulgan was being pulled toward the void.

Pug turned and grabbed one of the spears from against the wall where the shocked guards had placed them. Before either of the men-at-arms could act, he leveled it at the grey spot and threw.

The spear flew across the ten feet that separated them from Kulgan and disappeared into the void. A brief second after, the arms dropped Kulgan and withdrew. Suddenly the grey void blinked out of existence, with a clap of air rushing in to fill it. Pug ran to Kulgan's side and knelt by his master.

The magician was breathing, but his face was white and beaded with sweat. His skin felt cold and clammy. Pug ran to Kulgan's sleeping pallet and pulled off a blanket. As he was covering the magician, he shouted at the guards, "Get Father Tully."

PUG AND TOMAS sat up that night, unable to sleep. Tully had tended to the magician, giving a favorable prognosis. Kulgan was in shock but would recover in a day or two.

Duke Borric had questioned Pug and the guards on what they had witnessed, and now the castle was in an uproar. All the guards had been turned out, and patrols to the outlying areas of the Duchy had been doubled. The Duke still did not know what the connection between the appearance of the ship and the strange manifestation in the magician's quarters was, but he was taking no chances with the safety of his realm. All along the walls of the castle, torches burned, and guards had been sent to Longpoint lighthouse and the town below.

Tomas sat next to Pug on a bench in Princess Carline's garden, one of the few quiet places in the castle. Tomas looked thoughtfully at Pug. "I expect that these Tsurani people are coming."

Pub ran a hand through his hair. "We don't know that."

Tomas sounded tired. "I just have a feeling."

Pug nodded. "We'll know tomorrow when Kulgan can tell us what happened."

Tomas looked out toward the wall. "I've never seen it so strange around here. Not even when the Dark Brotherhood and the goblins attacked back when we were little, remember?"

Pug nodded, silent for a moment, then said, "We knew what we were facing then. The dark elves have been attacking castles on and off as far back as anyone can remember. And goblins . . . well, they're goblins."

They sat in silence for a long time; then the sound of boots on the pavement announced someone coming. Swordmaster Fannon, in chain mail and tabard, halted before them. "What? Up so late? You should both be abed." The old fighter turned to survey the castle walls. "There are many who find themselves unable to sleep this night." He turned his attention back to the boys. "Tomas, a soldier needs to learn the knack of taking sleep whenever he can find it, for there are many long days when there is none. And you, Squire Pug, should be asleep as well. Now, why don't you try to rest yourselves?"

The boys nodded, bade the Swordmaster good night, and left. The grey-haired commander of the Duke's guard watched them go and stood quietly in the little garden for a time, alone with his own disquieting thoughts.

PUG WAS AWAKENED by the sound of footsteps passing his door. He quickly pulled on trousers and tunic and hurried up the steps to Kulgan's room. Passing the hastily replaced door, he found the Duke and Father Tully standing over Kulgan's sleeping pallet. Pug heard his master's voice, sounding feeble, as he complained about being kept abed. "I tell you, I'm fine," Kulgan insisted. "Just let me walk about a bit, and I'll be back to normal in no time."

Tully, still sounding weary, said, "Back on your back, you mean. You sustained a nasty jolt, Kulgan. Whatever it was that knocked you unconscious packed no small wallop. You were lucky, it could have been much worse."

Kulgan noticed Pug, who stood quietly at the door, not wishing to disturb anyone. "Ha, Pug," he said, his voice regaining some of its usual volume. "Come in, come in. I understand I have you to thank for not taking an unexpected journey with unknown companions."

Pug smiled, for Kulgan seemed his old, jovial self, in spite of his wan appearance. "I really did nothing, sir. I just felt that something was not right, and acted."

"Acted quickly and well," said the Duke with a smile. "The boy is again responsible for the well-being of one of my household. At this rate I may have to grant him the title Defender of the Ducal Household."

Pug smiled, pleased with the Duke's praise. Borric turned to the magician. "Well, seeing as you are full of fire, I think we should have a talk about yesterday. Are you well enough?"

The question brought an irritated look from Kulgan. "Of course I'm well enough. That's what I've been trying to tell you for the last ten minutes." Kulgan started to rise from the bed, but as dizziness overtook him, Tully put a restraining hand on his shoulder, guiding him back to the large pile of pillows he had been resting on.

"You can talk here quite well enough, thank you. Now, stay in bed."

Kulgan made no protest. He shortly felt better and said, "Fine, but hand me my pipe, will you, please?"

Pug fetched Kulgan's pipe and pouch of tabac and, as the magician tamped down the bowl, a long burning taper from the fire pot. Kulgan lit his pipe and, when it was burning to his satisfaction, lay back with a contented look on his face. "Now," he said, "where do we begin?"

The Duke quickly filled him in on what Tully had revealed, with the priest adding a few details the Duke overlooked. When they were done, Kulgan nodded. "Your assumption about the origin of these people is likely. I suspected the possibility when I saw the artifacts brought from the ship, and the events in this room yesterday bear me out." He paused for a moment, organizing his thoughts. "The scroll was a personal letter from a magician of these people, the Tsurani, to his wife, but it was also more. The seal was magically endowed to force the reader to incant a spell contained at the end of the message. It is a remarkable spell enabling anyone, whether or not they can normally read, to read the scroll."

The Duke said, "This is a strange thing."

Tully said, "It's astonishing."

"The concepts involved are completely new to me," agreed Kulgan. "Anyway, I had neutralized that spell so I could read the letter without fear of magical traps, common to private messages written by magicians. The language was of course strange, and I employed a spell from another scroll to translate it. Even understanding the language through that spell, I don't fully understand everything discussed.

"A magician named Fanatha was traveling by ship to a city on his homeworld. Several days out to sea, they were struck by a severe storm. The ship lost its mast, and many of the crew were washed overboard. The magician took a brief time to pen the scroll—it was written in a hasty hand—and cast the spells upon it. It seems this man could have left the ship at any time and returned to his home or some other place of safety, but was enjoined from doing so by his concern for the ship and its cargo. I am not clear on this point, but the tone of the letter suggested that risking his life for the others on the ship was somehow unusual. Another puzzling thing was a mention of his duty to someone he called the 'Warlord.' I may be reaching for straws, but the tone leads me to think this was a matter of honor or a promise, not some personal duty. In any event he penned the note, sealed it, and was then going to undertake to move the ship magically."

Tully shook his head in disbelief. "Incredible."

"And as we understand magic, impossible," Kulgan added excitedly.

Pug noticed that the magician's professional interest was not shared by the Duke, who looked openly troubled. The boy remembered Tully's comments on what magic of that magnitude meant if these people were to invade the Kingdom. The magician continued, "These people possess powers about which we can only speculate. The magician was very clear on a number of points—his ability to compress so many ideas into so short a message shows an unusually organized mind.

"He took great pains to reassure his wife he would do everything in his power to return. He referred to opening a rift to the 'new world,' because—and I don't fully understand this—a bridge was already established, and some device he possessed lacked . . . some capacity or another to move the ship on his own world. From all indications, it was a most desperate gamble. He placed a second spell on the scroll—and this is what caught me in the end. I thought by neutralizing the first spell I had countered the second also, but I was in error. The second spell was designed to activate as soon as someone had finished reading the scroll aloud, another unheard-of piece of magical art. The spell caused another of these rifts to open, so the message would be transported to a place called 'the Assembly' and from there to his wife. I was nearly caught in the rift with the message."

Pug stepped forward. Without thinking, he blurted, "Then those hands might have been his friends trying to find him."

Kulgan looked at his apprentice and nodded. "A possibility. In any event, we can derive much from this episode. These Tsurani have the ability to control magic that we can only hint at in our speculation. We know a little about the occurrences of rifts, and nothing of their nature."

The Duke looked surprised. "Please explain."

Kulgan drew deep on his pipe, then said, "Magic, by its nature, is unstable. Occasionally a spell will become warped—why, we don't know—to such a degree, it . . . tears at the very fabric of the world. For a brief time a rift occurs, and a passage is formed, going . . . somewhere. Little else is known about such occurrences, except that they involve tremendous releases of energy."

Tully said, "There are theories, but no one understands why every so often a spell, or magic device, suddenly explodes in this fashion and why this instability in reality is created. There have been several occurrences like this, but we have only secondhand observations to go on. Those who witnessed the creation of these rifts died or vanished."

Kulgan picked up the narrative again. "It's considered axiomatic that they were destroyed along with anything within several feet of the rift."

He looked thoughtful for a moment. "By rights I should have been killed when that rift appeared in my study."

The Duke interrupted. "From your description, these rifts, as you call them, are dangerous."

Kulgan nodded. "Unpredictable, as well. They are one of the most uncontrollable forces ever discovered. If these people know how to manufacture them and control them as well, to act as a gate between worlds, and can pass through them safely, then they have arts of the most powerful sort."

Tully said, "We've suspected something of the nature of rifts before, but this is the first time we've had anything remotely like hard evidence."

Kulgan said, "Bah! Strange people and unknown objects have appeared suddenly from time to time over the years, Tully. This would certainly explain where they came from."

Tully appeared unwilling to concede the point. "Theory only, Kulgan; not proof. The people have all been dead, and the devices . . . no one understands the two or three that were not burned and twisted beyond recognition."

Kulgan smiled. "Really? What about the man who appeared twenty years ago in Salador?" To the Duke he said, "This man spoke no language known and was dressed in the strangest fashion."

Tully looked down his nose at Kulgan. "He was also hopelessly mad and never could speak a word that could be understood. The temples invested much time on him—"

Borric paled. "Gods! A nation of warriors, with armies many times the size of our own, who have access to our world at will. Let us hope they have not turned their eyes toward the Kingdom."

Kulgan nodded and blew a puff of smoke. "As yet, we have not heard of any other appearances of these people, and we may not have to fear them, but I have a feeling . . ." He left the thought unfinished for a moment. He turned a little to one side, easing some minor discomfort, then said, "It may be nothing, but a reference to a bridge in the message troubles me. It smacks of a permanent way between the worlds already in existence. I hope I'm wrong." The sound of feet pounding up the stairs made them turn. A guard hurried in and came to attention before the Duke, handing him a small paper.

The Duke dismissed the man and opened the folded paper. He read it quickly, then handed it to Tully. "I sent fast riders to the elves and the dwarves, with pigeons to carry replies. The Elf Queen sends word that she is already riding to Crydee and will be here in two days' time."

Tully shook his head. "As long as I have lived, I have never heard of the Lady Aglaranna leaving Elvandar. This sets my bones cold."

Kulgan said, "Things must be approaching a serious turn for her to come here. I hope I am wrong, but think that we are not the only ones to have news of these Tsurani."

Silence descended over the room, and Pug was struck by a feeling of hopelessness. He shook it off, but its echoes followed him for days.

6

▼▼

ELFCOUNSEL

PUG LEANED OUT THE WINDOW.

Despite the driving rain that had come in early morning, the courtyard was in an uproar. Besides the necessary preparations for any important visit, there was the added novelty of these visitors being elves. Even the infrequent elf messenger from Queen Aglaranna was the object of much curiosity when one appeared at the castle, for rarely did the elves venture south of the river Crydee. The elves lived apart from the society of men, and their ways were thought strange and magical. They had lived in these lands long before the coming of men to the West, and there was an unvoiced agreement that, in spite of any claims made by the Kingdom, they were a free people.

A cough caused Pug to turn and see Kulgan sitting over a large tome. The magician indicated with a glance that the boy should return to his studies. Pug closed the window shutters and sat on his pallet. Kulgan said, "There will be ample time for you to gawk at elves, boy, in a few hours. Then there will be little time for studies. You must learn to make the best use of what time you have."

Fantus scrambled over to place his head in the boy's lap. Pug scratched absently behind an eye ridge as he picked up a book and started to read. Kulgan had given Pug the task of formulating shared qualities of spells as described by different magicians, in the hope it would deepen his understanding of the nature of magic.

Kulgan was of the opinion that Pug's spells with the trolls had been the result of the tremendous stress of the moment. He hoped the study of other magicians' research might help the boy break through the barriers that held him back in his studies. The book work also proved fascinating to Pug, and his reading had improved greatly.

Pug glanced at his master, who was reading while puffing great clouds of smoke from his long pipe. Kulgan showed no signs of the weakness of the day before and had insisted the boy use these hours to study, rather than sit idly by waiting for the arrival of the Elf Queen and her court.

A few minutes later, Pug's eyes began to sting from the pungent smoke, and he turned back to the window and pushed open the shutters. "Kulgan?"

"Yes, Pug?"

"It would be much nicer working with you if we could somehow keep the fire going for warmth but move the smoke outside." Between the smoking fire pot and the magician's pipe, the room was thick with a blue-white haze.

The magician laughed loudly. "Right you are." He closed his eyes for a moment, his hands flew in a furious motion, and he softly mouthed a series of incantations. Soon he was holding a large sphere of white and grey smoke, which he took to the window and tossed outside, leaving the room fresh and clear.

Pug shook his head, laughing. "Thank you, Kulgan. But I had a more mundane solution in mind. What do you think of making a chimney for the fire pot?"

"Not possible, Pug," Kulgan said, sitting down. He pointed to the wall. "If one had been installed when the tower was built, fine. But to try to remove the stones from the tower, from here past my room, and up to the roof would be difficult, not to mention costly."

"I wasn't thinking of a chimney in the wall, Kulgan. You know how the forge in the smithy has a stone hood taking the heat and smoke through the roof?" The magician nodded. "Well, if I could have a metal one fashioned by the smith, and a metal chimney coming from the hood to carry the smoke away, it would work the same way, wouldn't it?"

Kulgan pondered this for a moment. "I don't see why it wouldn't. But where would you put this chimney?"

"There." Pug pointed to two stones above and to the left of the window. They had been ill fitted when the tower was built, and now there was a large crack between them that allowed the wind to come howling into the room. "This stone could be taken out," he said, indicating the leftmost one. "I checked it and it's loose. The chimney could come from above the fire pot, bend here"—he pointed to a spot in the air above the pot and level with the stone—"and come out here. If we covered the space around it, it would keep the wind out."

Kulgan looked impressed. "It's a novel idea, Pug. It might work. I'll speak to the smith in the morning and get his opinion on the matter. I wonder that no one thought of it before."

Feeling pleased with himself for having thought of the chimney, Pug resumed his studies. He reread a passage that had caught his eye before, puzzling over an ambiguity. Finally he looked up at the magician and said, "Kulgan."

"Yes, Pug?" he answered, looking up from his book.

"Here it is again. Magician Lewton uses the same cantrip here as Marsus did, to baffle the effects of the spell upon the caster, directing it to an external target." Placing the large tome down so as not to lose his place, he picked up another. "But here Dorcas writes that the use of this cantrip blunts the spell, increasing the chance that it will not work. How can there be so much disagreement over the nature of this single construction?"

Kulgan narrowed his gaze a moment as he regarded his student. Then he sat back, taking a long pull on his pipe, sending forth a cloud of blue smoke. "It shows what I've said before, lad. Despite any vanity we magicians might feel about our craft, there's really very little order or science involved. Magic is a collection of folk arts and skills passed along from master to apprentice since the beginning of time. Trial and error, trial and error is the way. There has never been an attempt to create a system for magic, with laws and rules and axioms that are well understood and widely accepted." He looked thoughtfully at Pug. "Each of us is like a carpenter, making a table, but each of us choosing different woods, different types of saws, some using pegs and dowel, others using nails, another dovetailing joints, some staining, others not . . . in the end there's a table, but the means for making it are not the same in each case.

"What we have here is most likely an insight about the limits of each of these venerable sages you study, rather than any sort of prescription for magic. For Lewton and Marsus, the cantrip aided the construction of the spell; for Dorcas, it hindered."

"I understand your example, Kulgan, but I'll never understand how these magicians all could do the *same* thing, but in so many different ways. I understand that each of them wanted to achieve his end and found a different means, but there is something missing in the manner they did it."

Kulgan looked intrigued. "What is missing, Pug?"

The boy looked thoughtful. "I . . . I don't know. It's as if I expect to find something that will tell me, 'This is the way it must be done, the only way,' or something like that. Does that make any sense?"

Kulgan nodded. "I think I know you well enough to understand. You have a very well-ordered mind, Pug. You understand logic far better than most, even those much older than yourself. You see things as a system, rather than as a haphazard collection of events. Perhaps that is part of your trouble."

Pug's expression showed his interest in what the magician was saying. Kulgan continued. "Much of what I am trying to teach is based on a system of logic, cause and effect, but much is not. It is like trying to teach someone to play the lute. You can show them the fingering of the strings, but that knowledge alone will not make a great troubadour. It is the art, not the scholarship, that troubles you."

"I think I understand, Kulgan." He sounded dispirited.

Kulgan stood up. "Don't dwell on it; you are still young, and I have hope for you yet." His tone was light, and Pug felt the humor in it.

"Then I am not a complete loss?" he said with a smile.

"Indeed not." Kulgan looked thoughtfully at his pupil. "In fact, I have the feeling that someday you may use that logical mind of yours for the betterment of magic."

Pug was a little startled. He did not think of himself as one to accomplish great things.

Shouts came through the window, and Pug hurried to look out. A troop of guards was running toward the front gate. Pug turned to Kulgan. "The elves must be coming! The guard is out."

Kulgan said, "Very well. We are done with study for this day. There will be no holding you until you get a look at the elves. Run along."

Pug raced out the door and down the stairs. He took them two at a time, jumping to the bottom of the tower landing over the last four and hitting the floor at a full run. He dashed through the kitchen and out the door. As he rounded the keep to the front courtyard, he found Tomas standing atop a hay wagon. Pug climbed up next to him, to be better able to see the arrival over the heads of the curious keep folk gathered around.

Tomas said, "I thought you weren't coming, thought you'd be locked away with your books all day."

Pug said, "I wouldn't miss this. Elves!"

Tomas playfully dug his elbow into Pug's side. "Haven't you had your fill of excitement for this week?"

Pug threw him a black look. "If you're so indifferent, why are you standing in the rain on this wagon?"

Tomas didn't answer. Instead he pointed. "Look!"

Pug turned to see the guard company snap to attention as riders in green cloaks entered through the gate. They rode to the main doors of the keep, where the Duke waited. Pug and Tomas watched in awe, for they rode the most perfect white horses the boys had ever seen, using no saddle or bridle. The horses seemed untouched by wetness, and their coats glowed faintly; whether by some magic, or a trick of the grey afternoon light, Pug couldn't tell. The leader rode on an especially grand animal, full seventeen hands in height, with a long flowing mane and a tail like a plume. The riders reared the mounts in salute, and an audible intake of breath could be heard from those in the crowd.

"Elf steeds," said Tomas, in hushed tones. The horses were the legendary mounts of the elves. Martin Longbow had once told the boys they lived in hidden, deep glades near Elvandar. It was said they possessed intelligence and a magic nature, and no human could sit their backs. It was also said that only one with royal elvish blood could command them to carry riders.

Grooms rushed forward to take the horses, but a musical voice said, "There is no need." It came from the first rider, the one mounted on the greatest steed. She jumped nimbly down, without aid, landing lightly on her feet, and threw back her hood, revealing a mane of thick reddish hair. Even in the gloom of the afternoon rain it appeared to be shot through with golden highlights. She was tall, nearly a match for Borric. She mounted the steps as the Duke came forward to meet her.

Borric held out his hands and took hers in greeting. "Welcome, my lady; you do me and my house a great honor."

The Elf Queen said, "You are most gracious, Lord Borric." Her voice was rich and surprisingly clear, able to carry over the crowd so that all in the courtyard could hear. Pug felt Tomas's hand clutching his shoulder. He turned to see a rapt expression on Tomas's face. "She's beautiful," said the taller boy.

Pug returned his attention to the welcome. He was forced to agree that the Queen of the elves was indeed beautiful, if not in entirely human terms. Her eyes were large and a pale blue, nearly luminous in the gloom. Her face was finely chiseled, with high cheekbones and a strong but not masculine jaw. Her smile was full, and her teeth shone white between almost-red lips. She wore a simple circlet of gold around her brow, which held back her hair, revealing the lobeless, upswept ears that were the hallmark of her race.

The others in her company dismounted, all dressed in rich clothing. Each tunic was bright with contrasting leggings below. One wore a tunic of deep russet, another pale yellow with a surcoat of bright green. Some wore purple sashes, and others crimson hose. Despite the bright colors, these were elegant and finely made garments, with nothing loud or gaudy about them. There were eleven riders with the Queen, all similar in appearance, tall, youthful, and lithe in movement.

The Queen turned from the Duke and said something in her musical language. The elf steeds reared in salute, then ran through the gate, past the surprised onlookers. The Duke ushered his guests inside, and soon the crowd drifted away. Tomas and Pug sat quietly in the rain.

Tomas said, "If I live to be a hundred, I don't think that I'll ever see her like."

Pug was surprised, for his friend rarely showed such feelings. He had a brief impulse to chide Tomas over his boyish infatuation, but something about his companion's expression made that seem inappropriate. "Come on," he said, "we're getting drenched."

Tomas followed Pug from the wagon. Pug said, "You had better change into some dry clothing, and see if you can borrow a dry tabard."

Tomas said, "Why?"

With an evil grin, Pug said, "Oh? Didn't I tell you? The Duke wants you to dine with the court. He wants you to tell the Elf Queen what you saw on the ship."

Tomas looked as if he were going to break down and run. "Me? Dine in the great hall?" His face went white. "Talk? To the Queen?"

Pug laughed with glee. "It's easy. You open your mouth and words come out."

Tomas swung a roundhouse at Pug, who ducked under the blow, grabbing his friend from behind when he spun completely around. Pug had strength in his arms even if he lacked Tomas's size, and he easily picked his larger friend off the ground. Tomas struggled, and soon they were laughing uncontrollably. "Pug, put me down."

"Not until you calm down."

"I'm all right."

Pug put him down. "What brought that on?"

"Your smug manner, and not telling me until the last minute."

"All right. So I'm sorry I waited to tell you. Now what's the rest of it?"

Tomas looked uncomfortable, more than was reasonable from the rain. "I don't know how to eat with quality folk. I'm afraid I'll do something stupid."

"It's easy. Just watch me and do what I do. Hold the fork in your left hand and cut with the knife. Don't drink from the bowls of water; they're to wash with, and use them a lot, because your hands will get greasy from the rib bones. And make sure you toss the bones over your shoulder to the dogs, and not on the floor in front of the Duke's table.

And don't wipe your mouth on your sleeves, use the tablecloth, that's what it's for."

They walked toward the soldiers' commons, with Pug giving his friend instruction on the finer points of court manners. Tomas was impressed at the wealth of Pug's knowledge.

TOMAS VACILLATED between looking sick and pained. Each time someone regarded him, he felt as if he had been found guilty of the most grievous breach of etiquette and looked sick. Whenever his gaze wandered to the head table and he caught sight of the Elf Queen, his stomach tied up in knots and he looked pained.

Pug had arranged for Tomas to sit next to him at one of the more removed tables from the Duke's. Pug's usual place was at Lord Borric's table, next to the Princess. He was glad for this chance to be away from her, for she still showed displeasure with him. Usually she chatted with him about the thousand little bits of gossip the ladies of the court found so interesting, but last night she had pointedly ignored him, lavishing all her attention on a surprised and obviously pleased Roland. Pug found his own reaction puzzling, relief mixed with a large dose of irritation. While he felt relieved to be free of her wrath, he found Roland's fawning upon her a bothersome itch he couldn't scratch.

Pug had been troubled by Roland's hostility toward him of late, poorly hidden behind stiff manners. He had never been as close to Roland as Tomas had, but they had never before had cause to be angry with one another. Roland had always been one of the crowd of boys Pug's age. He had never hidden behind his rank when he had cause to be at odds with the common boys, always standing ready to settle the matter in whatever way proved necessary. And already being an experienced fighter when he arrived in Crydee, his differences soon were settled peacefully as often as not. Now there was this dark tension between Pug and Roland, and Pug found himself wishing he was Tomas's equal in fighting; Tomas was the only boy Roland was unable to best with fists, their one encounter ending quickly with Roland receiving a sound thumping. For as certain as the sun was rising in the morning, Pug knew a confrontation with the hotheaded young Squire was quickly approaching. He dreaded it, but knew once it came, he'd feel relief.

Pug glanced at Tomas, finding his friend lost in his own discomfort. Pug returned his attention to Carline. He felt overwhelmed by the Princess, but her allure was tempered by a strange discomfort he felt whenever she was near. As beautiful as he found her—her black locks and blue eyes igniting some very uncomfortable flames of imagination—the images were always somehow hollow, colorless at heart, lacking the amber-and-rose glow such daydreams had possessed when Carline had been a distant, unapproachable, and unknown figure. Observing her closely for even as short a time as he had recently made such idealized musing impossible. She was proving herself to be just too complicated to fit into simple daydreams. On the whole he found the question of the Princess troublesome, but seeing her with Roland made him forget his internal conflicts over her, as a less intellectual, more basic emotion came to the fore. He was becoming jealous.

Pug sighed, shaking his head as he thought about his own misery at this moment, ignoring Tomas's. At least, thought Pug, I'm not alone. To Roland's obvious discomfort, Carline was deeply involved at the moment in conversation with Prince Calin of Elvandar, son of Aglaranna. The Prince seemed to be the same age as Arutha, or Lyam, but then so did his mother, who appeared to be in her early twenties. All the elves, except the Queen's seniormost adviser, Tathar, were quite young looking, and Tathar looked no older than the Duke.

When the meal was over, most of the Duke's court retired. The Duke rose and offered his arm to Aglaranna and led those who had been ordered to attend them to his council chamber.

For the third time in two days, the boys found themselves in the Duke's council chamber. Pug was more relaxed about being there than before, thanks in part to the large meal, but Tomas seemed more disturbed than ever. If the taller boy had spent the hour before dinner staring at the Elf Queen, in these close quarters he seemed to be looking everywhere but in her direction. Pug thought Aglaranna noticed Tomas's behavior and smiled slightly, but he couldn't be sure.

The two elves who came with the Queen, Calin and Tathar, went at once to the side table that held the bowl and the artifacts taken from the Tsurani soldier. They examined them closely, fascinated by every detail.

The Duke called the meeting to order, and the two elves came to chairs on either side of the Queen. Pug and Tomas stood by the door as usual.

The Duke said, "We have told you what has occurred as well as we know, and now you have seen proof with your own eyes. If you think it would be helpful, the boys can recount the events on the ship."

The Queen inclined her head, but it was Tathar who spoke. "I would like to hear the story firsthand, Your Grace."

Borric motioned for the boys to approach. They stepped forward, and Tathar said, "Which of you found this outworlder?"

Tomas threw Pug a look that indicated the shorter boy should do the talking. Pug said, "We both did, sir," not knowing the proper address for the elf. Tathar seemed content with the general honorific. Pug recounted the events of that day, leaving out nothing he could remember. When he had done, Tathar asked a series of questions, each jogging Pug's memory, bringing out small details he had forgotten.

When he was done, Pug stepped back, and Tathar repeated the process with Tomas. Tomas began haltingly, obviously discomfited, and the Elf Queen bestowed a reassuring smile on him. That only served to make him more unsettled, and he was soon dismissed.

Tathar's questions provided more details about the ship, small things forgotten by the boys: fire buckets filled with sand tossed about the deck, empty spear-racks, substantiating Arutha's surmise that it had been, indeed, a warship.

Tathar leaned back. "We have never heard of such a ship. It is in many ways like other ships, but not in all ways. We are convinced."

As if by silent signal, Calin spoke. "Since the death of my Father-King, I serve as Warleader of Elvandar. It is my duty to supervise the scouts and patrols that guard our glades. For some time we have been aware that there were strange occurrences in the great forest, south of the river Crydee. Several times our runners have found tracks made by men, in isolated parts of the forest. They have been found as near as the borders of Elvandar, and as far as the North Pass near Stone Mountain.

"Our scouts have tried for weeks to find these men, but only tracks could be seen. There were none of the usual things that would be expected of a scouting or raiding party. These people were taking great care to disguise their presence. Had they not passed so close to Elvandar, they might have remained undetected, but no one may intrude near our home and go unnoticed.

"Several days ago, one of our scouts sighted a band of strangers passing the river, near the edge of our forests heading in the direction of the North Pass. He followed for a half day's march, then lost them."

Fannon raised his eyebrows. "An elven tracker lost them?"

Calin inclined his head slightly. "Not by his lack of skill. They simply entered a thick glade and never appeared on the other side. He followed their tracks up to the point where they vanished."

Lyam said, "I think we know now where they went." He looked uncommonly somber, resembling his father more than usual.

Calin continued. "Four days before your message arrived, I led a patrol that sighted a band near the place of last sighting. They were short and stocky men, without beards. Some were fair and others dark. There were ten of them, and they moved through the forest with little ease; the slightest sound put them on guard. But with all their caution, they still had no idea they were being tracked.

"They all wore armor of bright colors, reds and blues, some green, others yellow, save one in black robes. They carried swords like the one on the table and others without the serration, round shields, and strange bows, short and curved in an odd doubled-back way."

Algon sat forward. "They're recurved bows, like the ones used by Keshian dog-soldiers."

Calin spread his hands. "Kesh has long been gone from these lands, and when we knew the Empire, they used simple bows of yew or ash."

Algon interrupted in excited tones. "They have a way, secret to them, of fashioning such bows from wood and animal horn. They are small, but possess great power, though not as much as the longbow. Their range is surprisingly—"

Borric cleared his throat pointedly, being unwilling to let the Horsemaster indulge himself in his preoccupation with weaponry. "If His Highness will please continue?"

Algon sat back, blushing furiously, and Calin said, "I tracked them for two days. They stopped and made cold camp at night and took great care not to leave signs of their passing. All food scraps and body wastes were gathered together in a sack and carried by one of their band. They moved carefully, but were easy for us to follow.

"When they came to the edge of the forest, near the mouth of North Pass, they made marks upon a parchment as they had several times during their trek. Then the one in black activated some strange device, and they vanished." There was a stir from the Duke's company. Kulgan especially looked disturbed.

Calin paused. "The thing that was most strange, however, was their language, for their speech was unlike any we know. They spoke in hushed tones, but we could hear them, and their words were without meaning."

The Queen then spoke. "Hearing this, I became alarmed, for these outworlders are clearly mapping the West, ranging freely through the great forest, the hills of Stone Mountain, and now the coasts of the Kingdom. Even as we prepared to send you word, the reports of these outworlders became more frequent. Several more bands were seen in the area of the North Pass."

Arutha sat forward, resting his arms on the table. "If they cross the North Pass, they will discover the way to Yabon, and the Free Cities.

The snows will have started to fall in the mountains, and they may discover we are effectively isolated from aid during the winter."

For a moment alarm flickered on the Duke's face, betraying his stoic demeanor. He regained his composure and said, "There is still the South Pass, and they may not have mapped that far. If they were in that area, the dwarves would most likely have seen signs of them, as the villages of the Grey Towers are more widely scattered than those of Stone Mountain."

"Lord Borric," said Aglaranna, "I would never have ventured from Elvandar if I had not thought the situation critical. From what you have told us of the outworld Empire, if they are as powerful as you say, then I fear for all the free peoples of the West. While the elves have little love for the Kingdom as such, we respect those of the Crydee, for you have ever been honorable men and have never sought to extend your realm into our lands. We would ally with you should these outworlders come for conquest."

Borric sat quietly for a moment. "I thank the Lady of Elvandar for the aid of the elven folk should war come. We are also in your debt for your counsel, for now we can act. Had we not known of these happenings in the great forests, we would likely have given the aliens more time for whatever trouble they are preparing." He paused again, as if considering his next words. "And I am convinced that these Tsurani plan us ill. Scouting an alien and strange land I could see, trying to determine the nature and temper of the people who live there, but extensive mapping by warriors can only be a prelude to invasion."

Kulgan sounded fatigued as he said, "They most likely will come with a mighty host."

Tully shook his head. "Perhaps not." All eyes turned to him as he said, "I am not so certain. Much of what I read in Xomich's mind was confused, but there is something about this Empire of Tsuranuanni that makes it unlike any nation we know of; there is something very alien about their sense of duty and alliances. I can't tell you how I know, but I suspect they may choose to test us first, with but a small part of their might. It's as if their attentions are elsewhere, and we're an afterthought." He shook his head in admitted confusion. "I have this sense, nothing more."

The Duke sat upright, a commanding tone coming into his voice. "We will act. I will send messages to Duke Brucal of Yabon, and again to Stone Mountain and the Grey Towers."

Aglaranna said, "It would be good to hear what the dwarven folk know."

Borric said, "I had hoped for word by now, but our messengers have not returned, nor have the pigeons they carry."

Lyam said, "Hawks, perhaps. The pigeons are not always reliable, or perhaps the messengers never reached the dwarves."

Borric turned to Calin. "It has been forty years since the siege of Carse, and we have had little traffic with the dwarves since. Who commands the dwarven clans now?"

The Elf Prince said, "As then. Stone Mountain is under the banner of Harthorn, of Hogar's line, at village Delmoria. The Grey Towers rally to the banner of Dolgan, of Tholin's line, at village Caldara."

"Both are known to me, though I was but a boy when they raised the Dark Brothers' siege at Carse," said Borric. "They will prove fierce allies if trouble comes."

Arutha said, "What of the Free Cities, and the Prince in Krondor?"

Borric sat back. "I must think on that, for there are problems in the East, or so I have word. I will give thought to the matter this night." He stood. "I thank you all for this counsel. Return to your quarters and avail yourselves of rest and refreshments. I will ask you to consider plans for dealing with the invaders, should they come, and we will meet again tomorrow."

As the Elf Queen rose, he offered her his arm, then escorted her through the doors that Tomas and Pug held open. The boys were the last to exit. Fannon took Tomas in tow, leading him to the soldiers' commons, while Kulgan stood outside the hall with Tully and the two elven advisers.

The magician turned to his apprentice. "Pug, Prince Calin expressed an interest in your small library of magic books. Would you please show them to him?"

Pug said he would and led the Prince up the stairs to his door and opened it for him. Calin stepped through, and Pug followed. Fantus was asleep and woke with a start. He threw the elf a distrustful look.

Calin slowly crossed over to the drake and spoke a few soft words in a language that Pug didn't understand. Fantus lost his nervousness and stretched forth his neck to allow the Prince to scratch his head.

After a moment the drake looked expectantly to Pug. Pug said, "Yes, dinner is over. The kitchen will be full of scraps." Fantus moved to the window with a wolfish grin and used his snout to push it open. With a snap of his wings he was out, gliding toward the kitchen.

Pug offered Calin a stool, but the Prince said, "Thank you, but your chairs and stools are of little comfort to my kind. I will just sit on the floor, with your leave. You have a most unusual pet, Squire Pug." He gave Pug a small smile. Pug was a little uncomfortable hosting the Elf Prince in his poor room, but the elf's manner was such that the boy started to relax.

"Fantus is less a pet than a permanent guest. He has a mind of his own. It is not unusual for him to disappear for weeks at a time, now and again, but mostly he stays here. He must eat outside the kitchen now that Meecham has gone."

Calin inquired who Meecham was. Pug explained, adding, "Kulgan has sent him over the mountains to Bordon, with some of the Duke's guards, before the North Pass is snowed in. He didn't say why he was going, Highness."

Calin looked at one of the boy's books. "I prefer to be called Calin, Pug."

Pug nodded, pleased. "Calin, what do you think the Duke has in mind?"

The elf gave him an enigmatic smile. "The Duke will reveal his own plans, I think. My guess is that Meecham is preparing the way should the Duke choose to journey east. You will most probably know on the morrow." He held up the book he had glanced at. "Did you find this interesting?"

Pug leaned over and read the title. "Dorcas's *Treatise on the Animation of Objects?* Yes, though it seemed a little unclear."

"A fair judgment. Dorcas was an unclear man, or at least I found him so."

Pug started. "But Dorcas died thirty years ago."

Calin smiled broadly, showing even white teeth. His pale eyes shone in the lantern light. "Then you know little of elven lore?"

"Little," Pug agreed. "You are the first elf I have ever spoken with, though I may have seen another elf once, when I was very little. I'm not sure." Calin tossed aside the book. "I know only what Martin Longbow has told me, that you can somehow speak with animals, and some spirits. That you live in Elvandar and the surrounding elven forests, and that you stay among your own kind mostly."

The elf laughed, a soft, melodic sound. "Nearly all true. Knowing friend Longbow, I wager some of the tales were colorful, for while he is not a deceiving man, he has an elf's humor." Pug's expression showed he did not understand. "We live a very long time by your standards. We learn to appreciate the humor in the world, often finding amusement in places where men find little. Or you can call it simply a different way of looking at life. Martin has learned this from us, I think."

Pug nodded. "Mocking eyes."

Calin raised an eyebrow in question. Pug explained, "Many people here find Martin difficult to be with. Different, somehow. I once heard a soldier say he had mocking eyes."

Calin sighed. "Life has been difficult for Martin. He was left on his own at an early age. The Monks of Silban are good, kindly men, but ill equipped to raise a boy. Martin lived in the woods like a wild thing when he could flee his tutors. I found him one day, fighting with two of our children—we are not very much different from men when very young. Over the years he has grown to be one of the few humans who is free to come to Elvandar at will. He is a valued friend. But I think he bears a special burden of loneliness, not being fully in the world of elves nor of men, but partially in both."

Pug saw Martin in a new light and resolved to attempt to know the Huntmaster better. Returning to the original topic, he said, "Is what he said true?"

Calin nodded. "In some respects. We can speak to animals only as men do, in tones to make them easy, though we are better at it than most humans, for we read the moods of wild things more readily. Martin has some of this knack. We do not, however, speak with spirits. There are creatures we know whom humans consider spirits—dryads, sprites, pixies—but they are natural beings who live near our magic."

Pug's interest was piqued. "Your magic?"

"Ours is a magic that is part of our being, strongest in Elvandar. It is a heritage ages old, allowing us to live at peace within our forests. There we work as others do, hunting, tending our gardens, celebrating our joys, teaching our young. Time passes slowly in Elvandar, for it is an ageless place. That is why I can remember speaking with Dorcas, for in spite of my youthful appearance, I am over a hundred years old."

"A hundred . . ." Pug shook his head. "Poor Tomas, he was distressed to hear you were the Queen's son. Now he will be desolate."

Calin inclined his head, a half-smile playing across his face. "The lad who was with us in the council hall?"

Pug nodded. Calin said, "It is not the first time my Mother-Queen has had such an effect upon a human, though older men can mask the effect with more ease."

"You don't mind?" asked Pug, feeling protective toward his friend.

"No, Pug, of course not. All in Elvandar love the Queen, and it is acknowledged her beauty is unsurpassed. I find it not surprising your friend is smitten. Since my Father-King passed, more than one bold noble of your race has come to press his suit for Aglaranna's hand. Now her mourning is at an end, and she may take another should she wish. That it would be one of your race is unlikely, for while a few such marriages have been made, they are very rare, and tend to be sad things at the end for our kind. She will live many more human life spans, the gods willing."

Calin looked around the room, then added, "It is likely our friend Tomas will outgrow his feelings for the great lady of the elves. Much as your Princess will change her feelings toward you, I would think."

Pug felt embarrassed. He had been curious as to what Carline and the Elf Prince had spoken about during dinner, but had been uncomfortable asking. "I noticed you spoke with her at great length."

"I had expected to meet a hero of seven feet in height, with lightning dancing around his shoulders. It seems you slew a score of trolls with a cast of your hand."

Pug blushed. "It was only two, and mostly by accident."

Calin's eyebrows shot up. "Even two is an accomplishment. I had thought the girl guilty of a flight of fancy. I would like to hear the story."

Pug told him what had happened. When he was done, Calin said, "It is an unusual tale, Pug. I know little of human magic, but I do know enough to think that what you did was as strange as Kulgan said. Elf magic is far different from human, but we understand ours better than you understand your own. Never have I heard of such an occurrence, but I can share this with you. Occasionally, at times of great need, an inner call can be made, bringing forth powers that lay dormant, deep within."

Pug said, "I have thought as much, though it would be nice to understand a little better what happened."

"That may come in time."

Pug looked at his guest and sighed deeply. "I wish I could understand Carline, as well."

Calin shrugged and smiled. "Who can understand another's mind? I think for some time to come you will be the object of her attention. Then, it may be, another will distract her, perhaps young Squire Roland. He seems held in thrall by her."

Pug snorted. "Roland! That . . . bother."

Calin smiled appreciatively. "Then you are fond of the Princess?"

Pug looked upward, as if seeking guidance from some higher source. "I do like her," he admitted with a heavy sigh. "But I don't know if I care for her that special way. Sometimes I think I do—especially when I see Roland fawning over her—but other times I don't. She makes it *very* hard for me to think clearly, and I always seem to say the wrong things to her."

"Unlike Squire Roland," prompted Calin.

Pug nodded. "He's court born and bred. He knows all the right things to say." Pug leaned back on his elbows and sighed wistfully. "I guess I'm just bothered by him out of envy as much as anything. He makes me feel like an ill-mannered clod with great lumps of stone for hands and tree stumps for feet."

Calin nodded understandingly. "I don't count myself an expert in all the ways of your people, Pug, but I've spent enough time with humans to know that you choose how you feel; Roland makes you feel clumsy only because you let him.

"I would hazard a guess young Roland might feel much the same way when your positions are reversed. The faults we see in others never seem as dreadful as those we see in ourselves. Roland might envy your direct speech and honest manner.

"In any event, what you or Roland do will have little effect on the Princess so long as she's determined to have her own way. She has romanticized you in much the same manner your friend has our Queen. Short of you becoming a hopeless boor, she will not be shaken from this attitude until she is ready. I think she has you in mind as her future consort."

Pug gaped for a moment, then said, "Consort?"

Calin smiled. "The young are often overly concerned with matters to be settled in later years. I suspect her determination in the matter is as much a result of your reluctance as from a true appreciation of your worth. She, like many children, simply wants what she can't have." In a friendly tone he added, "Time will decide the issue."

Pug leaned forward, a worried expression on his face. "Oh, my, I have made a hash of things. Half the keep boys think themselves in love with the Princess. If they only knew how terrifying the real thing can be." He closed his eyes, squeezing them tightly shut a moment. "My head aches. I thought she and Roland . . ."

Calin said, "He may be but a tool to provoke your interest. Sadly, that seems to have resulted in bad feelings between you."

Pug nodded slowly. "I think so. Roland is a good enough sort on the whole; we've been friends for the most part. But since I was elevated in rank, he's been openly hostile. I try to ignore it, but it gets under my skin after a while. Maybe I should try to talk to him."

"That would prove wise, I think. But don't be surprised if he is not receptive to your words. He is most certainly caught up in her spell."

Pug was getting a headache from the topic, and the mention of spells made him ask, "Would you tell me more about elven magic?"

"Our magic is ancient. It is part of what we are and in what we create. Elven boots can make even a human silent when walking, and elven bows are better able to strike the mark, for that is the nature of our magic. It is vested in ourselves, our forests, our creations. It can sometimes be managed, subtly by those who fully understand it . . . Spellweavers, such as Tathar. But this is not easily done, for out magic resists manipulation. It is more like air than anything, always surrounding us, yet unseen. But like air, which can be felt when the wind blows, it has substance. Our forests are called enchanted by men, for so long have we dwelled there, our magic has created the mystery of Elvandar. All who dwell there are at peace. No one may enter Elvandar uninvited, save by mighty arts, and even the distant boundaries of the elven forests cause unease in those who enter with evil intent. It has not always been so; in ages past we shared our lot with others, the moredhel, those you call the Brotherhood of the Dark Path. Since the great break, when we drove them from our forests, Elvandar has been changing, becoming more our place, our home, our essence."

Pug said, "Are the Brothers of the Dark Path truly cousin to the elves?"

Calin's eyes grew hooded. He paused for a moment, then said, "We speak little of such things, for there is much we wish were not true. I can tell you this: there is a bond between the moredhel, whom you call the Brotherhood, and my people, though ancient and long strained. We wish it were not so, but they are true cousins to us. Once in a great while one comes back to us, what we call Returning." He looked as if the topic were making him very uncomfortable.

Pug said, "I'm sorry if—"

Calin waved away the apology. "Curiosity is nothing to apologize for in a student, Pug. I just would rather not say more on this subject."

They spoke late into the night, of many things. Pug was fascinated by the Elf Prince and was flattered so many things he said seemed to be of interest to Calin.

At last Calin said, "I should retire. Though I need little rest, I do need some. And I think you do as well."

Pug rose and said, "Thank you for telling me so much." Then he smiled, half in embarrassment. "And for talking to me about the Princess."

"You needed to talk."

Pug led Calin to the long hall, where a servant showed him to his quarters. Pug returned to his room and lay down for sleep, rejoined by a damp Fantus, who snorted in indignation at having to fly through the rain. Fantus was soon asleep. Pug, however, lay staring at the flickering light from his fire pot that danced on the ceiling, unable to call up sleep. He tried to put the tales of strange warriors out of his mind, but images of brightly clad fighters stalking through the forests of the westlands made sleep impossible.

THERE WAS a somber mood throughout Castle Crydee the next morning. The servants' gossip had spread the news about the Tsurani, though the details were lacking. Everyone went about his duties with one ear open for a tidbit of speculation on what the Duke was going to do. Everyone was agreed to one thing: Borric conDoin, Duke of Crydee, was not a man to sit idly by waiting. Something would be done, and soon.

Pug sat atop a bale of hay, watching Tomas practice with a sword, swinging at a pell post, hacking backhand, then forehand, over and over. His blows were halfhearted, and finally he threw his sword down with disgust. "I'm not accomplishing a thing." He walked over and sat next to Pug. "I wonder what they're talking about."

Pug shrugged. "They" were the Duke's council; today the boys had not been asked to attend, and the last four hours had passed slowly.

Abruptly the courtyard became busy as servants began to rush toward the front gate. "Come on," said Tomas. Pug jumped off the bale and followed his friend.

They rounded the keep in time to see the guards turning out as they had the day before. It was colder than yesterday, but there was no rain. The boys climbed on the same wagon, and Tomas shivered. "I think the snows will come early this year. Maybe tomorrow."

"If they do, it will be the earliest snowfall in memory. You should have worn your cloak. Now you're all sweaty from the drill, and the air is chilling you."

Tomas looked pained. "Gods, you sound like my mother."

Pug mimicked an exasperated manner. In a tone that was high-pitched and nasal, he said, "And don't come running to me when you're all blue with chill, and coughing and sneezing, looking for comfort, for you'll find none here, Tomas Megarson."

Tomas grinned. "Now you sound exactly like her."

They turned at the sound of the great doors opening. The Duke and Elf Queen led the other guests from the central keep, the Duke holding the Queen's hand in a parting gesture of friendship. Then the Queen placed her hand to her mouth and sang out a musical series of words, not loud, but carrying over the noise of the crowd. The servants who were standing in the court became silent, and soon the sound of hoof-beats could be heard outside the castle.

Twelve white horses ran through the gates and reared up in greeting to the Elf Queen. The elves quickly mounted, each springing up on an elf steed's back without assistance. They raised their hands in salute to the Duke, then turned and raced out the gate.

For a few minutes after they were gone, the crowd stood around, as if loath to admit that they had seen their last of the elves, probably their last in this lifetime. Slowly they began to drift back to work.

Tomas looked far away, and Pug turned toward him. "What is it?"

Tomas said softly, "I wish I could see Elvandar, someday."

Pug understood. "Maybe you will." Then he added, in lighter tones, "But I doubt it. For I will be a magician, and you will be a soldier, and the Queen will reign in Elvandar long after we are dead."

Tomas playfully jumped atop his friend, wrestling him down in the straw. "Oh! Is that so. Well, I will too go to Elvandar someday." He pinned Pug under him, sitting atop his chest. "And when I do, I'll be a great hero, with victories over the Tsurani by the score. She'll welcome me as an honored guest. What do you think of that?"

Pug laughed, trying to push his friend off. "And I'll be the greatest magician in the land."

They both laughed. A voice broke through their play. "Pug! There you are."

Tomas got off, and Pug sat up. Approaching them was the stocky figure of Gardell the smith. He was a barrel-chested man, with little hair but a thick black beard. His arms were grimy with smoke, and his apron was burned through with many small holes. He came to the side of the wagon and placed fists on hips. "I've been looking all over for you. I have that hood Kulgan asked me to fashion for your fire pot."

Pug scrambled out of the wagon, with Tomas close behind. They walked after Gardell toward the smithy behind the central keep. The burly smith said, "Damned clever idea, that hood. I've worked the forge for nearly thirty years and never thought of using a hood for a fire pot. Had to make one as soon as Kulgan told me of the plan."

They entered the smithy, a large shed with a large and small forge and several different-sized anvils. All manner of things lay about waiting for repair: armor, stirrup irons, and kitchen utensils. Gardell walked to the larger forge and picked up the hood. It was about three feet to a side, about three feet high, and formed a cone with a hole at the top. Lengths of round metal pipe lay nearby, fashioned especially thin.

Gardell held out his creation for them to study. "I made it fairly thin, using a lot of tin for lightness, for were it too heavy, it would collapse." With his toe he pointed to several lengths of metal rods. "We'll knock some little holes in the floor and use these for support. It may take a bit of time to get it right, but I think this thing of yours is going to work."

Pug smiled broadly. He found great pleasure in seeing an idea of his taking concrete form. It was a novel and gratifying sensation. "When can we install it?"

"Now if you like. I would like to see it work, I must confess."

Pug gathered up some of the pipe, and Tomas the rest, as well as the rods. Juggling the awkward load, they set out toward the magician's tower, with the chuckling smith following.

KULGAN WAS DEEP in thought as he started to mount the stairs to his room. Suddenly a shout from above sounded: "Watch out!" Kulgan glanced up in time to see a block of stone come tumbling down the stairs, bounding over the steps as if in some fit of drunken craziness. He leapt aside as it struck against the wall where he had stood and came to rest at the bottom of the stairs. Mortar dust filled the air, and Kulgan sneezed.

Tomas and Pug came running down the stairs, expressions of worry on their faces. When they saw no one was hurt, they both looked relieved.

Kulgan leveled a baleful gaze upon the pair and said, "What is all this?"

Pug appeared sheepish, while Tomas tried to blend in with the wall. Pug spoke first. "We were trying to carry the stone down to the yard, and it sort of slipped."

"Sort of slipped? It looked more like a mad dash for freedom. Now, why were you carrying the stone, and where did it come from?"

"It's the loose one from my wall," answered Pug. "We took it out so that Gardell could put the last pipe in place." When Kulgan still appeared uncomprehending, Pug said, "It's for my fire pot hood, remember?"

"Ah," said Kulgan, "yes. Now I do." A servant arrived to investigate the noise, and Kulgan asked him to fetch a couple of workmen from the yard to carry the block away. He left, and Kulgan said to the boys, "I think it would be better to let someone a little larger tote that stone out. Now let us see this marvel."

They climbed the stairs to the boy's room and found Gardell installing the last length of pipe. The smith turned when they entered and said, "Well, what do you think?"

The pot had been moved a little closer to the wall, and the hood sat on four metal rods of equal length over it. All of the smoke was trapped by the hood and carried away through the light metal pipe. Unfortunately, the hole where the stone was missing was considerably larger than the pipe, so most of the smoke was blown back into the room by the wind.

"Kulgan, what do you think?" said Pug.

"Well, boy. It looks rather impressive, but I can't see much improvement in the atmosphere here."

Gardell gave the hood a solid whack with his hand, causing it to ring out with a tinny sound. His thick calluses kept his hand from being burned by the hot metal. "She'll do, soon as I plug up that hole, magician. I'll fetch some bull hide that I use for making shields for the horsemen and cut a hole in a piece, slip it around the pipe, and nail it to the wall. A few slaps of tanning agent on it, and the heat will dry it out all stiff and hard. It will take the heat and keep the rain and wind out of the room, as well as the smoke." The smith looked pleased with his handiwork. "Well, I'll fetch the hide. Back in a moment."

Pug looked as if he would burst from pride, seeing his invention before him, and Tomas reflected Pug's glory. Kulgan chuckled softly to himself for a moment. Suddenly Pug turned to the magician, remembering where he had spent the day. "What is the news from the council?"

"The Duke sends messages to all the nobles of the West, explaining what has occurred in great detail, and asking that the Armies of the West be made ready. I am afraid Tully's scribes have some rigorous days ahead of them, since the Duke wants them all finished as soon as possible. Tully's in a state, for he has been commanded to stay and act as Lyam's adviser, along with Fannon and Algon, during the Duke's absence."

"Lyam's adviser? Absence?" asked Pug, uncomprehendingly.

"Yes, the Duke, Arutha, and I are going to journey to the Free Cities, and on to Krondor, to speak with Prince Erland. I am going to send a dream message to a colleague of mine tonight, if I can. Belgan lives north of Bordon. He will send word to Meecham, who should be there by now, to find us a ship. The Duke feels it best that he should carry the word in person."

Pug and Tomas looked excited. Kulgan knew they both wanted to come along. To visit Krondor would be the greatest adventure of their young lives. Kulgan stroked his grey beard. "It will be difficult to continue your lessons, but Tully can brush you up on a trick or two."

Pug looked as if he were going to burst. "Please, Kulgan, may I come too?"

Kulgan feigned surprise. "You come? I never thought of that." He paused for a moment while the suspense built. "Well . . ." Pug's eyes pleaded. ". . . I guess it would be all right." Pug let out a yelp and jumped in the air.

Tomas struggled to hide his disappointment. He forced a thin smile and tried to look happy for Pug.

Kulgan walked to the door. Pug noticed Tomas's dejected expression. "Kulgan?" Pug said. The magician turned, a faint smile on his lips.

"Yes, Pug?"

"Tomas, too?"

Tomas shook his head, for he was neither a member of the court nor the magician's charge, but his eyes looked at Kulgan imploringly.

Kulgan smiled broadly. "I guess we're better off keeping you together, so we need look for trouble in only one place. Tomas, too. I'll arrange things with Fannon."

Tomas shouted, and the two boys slapped each other on the back.

Pug said, "When do we leave?"

Kulgan laughed. "In five days' time. Or sooner, if the Duke hears from the dwarves. Runners are being sent to the North Pass to see if it is clear. If not, we ride by the South Pass."

Kulgan departed, leaving the two boys dancing arm in arm and whooping with excitement.

7

▼▼

UNDERSTANDING

PUG HURRIED ACROSS THE COURTYARD.

Princess Carline had sent him a note asking him to meet her in her flower garden. It was the first word from the girl since she had stormed away from their last meeting, and Pug was anxious. He did not want to be on bad terms with Carline, regardless of any conflicts he might be feeling. After his brief discussion with Calin, two days earlier, he had sought out Father Tully and talked with him at length.

The old priest had been willing to take time out to speak with the boy, in spite of the demands the Duke was placing upon his staff. It had been a good talk for Pug, leaving him with a surer sense of himself. The final message from the old cleric had been: Stop worrying about what the Princess feels and thinks, and start discovering what Pug feels and thinks.

He had taken the cleric's advice and was now sure of what he would say should Carline start referring to any sort of "understanding" between them. For the first time in weeks he felt something like a sense of direction—even if he was not sure what destination he would eventually reach, holding to such a course.

Reaching the Princess's garden, he rounded a corner, then stopped, for instead of Carline, Squire Roland stood by the steps. With a slight smile, Roland nodded. "Good day, Pug."

"Good day, Roland." Pug looked around.

"Expecting someone?" said Roland, forcing a note of lightness that did little to hide a belligerent tone. He casually rested his left hand on the pommel of his sword. Apart from his sword, he was dressed as usual, in colorful breeches and tunic of green and gold, with tall riding boots.

"Well, actually, I was expecting to see the Princess," Pug said, with a small note of defiance in his manner.

Roland feigned surprise. "Really? Lady Glynis mentioned something about a note, but I had come to understand things were strained between the two of you . . ."

While Pug had tried to sympathize with Roland's situation over the last few days, his offhanded, superior attitude and his chronic antagonism conspired to irritate Pug. Letting his exasperation get the better of him, he snapped, "As *one squire to another,* Roland, let me put it this way: how things stand between Carline and myself is *none of your business!*"

Roland's face took on an expression of open anger. He stepped forward, looking down at the shorter boy. "Be damned it's none of my business! I don't know what you're playing at, Pug, but if you do anything to hurt her, I'll—"

"Me hurt her!" Pug interrupted. He was shocked by the intensity of Roland's anger and infuriated by the threat. "She's the one playing us one against the other—"

Abruptly Pug felt the ground tilt under him, rising up to strike him from behind. Lights exploded before his eyes and a bell-like clanging sounded in his ears. It was a long moment before he realized Roland had just hit him. Pug shook his head and his eyes refocused. He saw the older, larger squire standing over him, both hands balled into fists. Through tightly clenched teeth, Roland spat his words. "If you ever say ill of her again, I'll beat you senseless."

Pug's anger fired within him, rising each second. He got carefully to his feet, his eyes upon Roland, who stood ready to fight. Feeling the bitter taste of anger in his mouth, Pug said, "You've had two years and more to win her, Roland. Leave it alone."

Roland's face grew livid and he charged, bowling Pug off his feet. They went down in a tangle, Roland striking Pug harmlessly on the shoulders and arms. Rolling and grappling, neither could inflict much damage. Pug got his arm around Roland's neck and hung on as the older squire thrashed in a frenzy. Suddenly Roland wedged a knee against Pug's chest and shoved him away. Pug rolled and came to his feet. Roland was up an instant later, and they squared off. Roland's expression had changed from rage to cold, calculating anger as he measured the distance between them. He advanced carefully, his left arm bent and extended, his right fist held ready before his face. Pug had no experience with this form of fighting, called fist-boxing, though he had seen it practiced for money in traveling shows. Roland had demonstrated on several occasions that he had more than a passing acquaintance with the sport.

Pug sought to take the advantage and swung a wild, roundhouse blow at Roland's head. Roland dodged back as Pug swung completely around; then the squire jumped forward, his left hand snapping out, catching Pug on the cheek, rocking his head back with a stinging blow. Pug stumbled away, and Roland's right hand missed Pug's chin by a fraction.

Pug held up his hands to ward off another blow and shook his head, clearing it of the dancing lights that obscured his vision, barely managing to duck beneath Roland's next blow. Under Roland's guard, Pug lunged, catching the other boy in the stomach with his shoulder, knocking him down again. Pug fell on top of him and struggled to pin the larger boy's arms to his side. Roland struck out, catching Pug's temple with an elbow, and the dazed magician's apprentice fell away, momentarily confused.

As he rose to his feet again, pain exploded in Pug's face, and the world tilted once more. Disoriented, unable to defend himself, Pug felt Roland's blows as distant events, somehow muted and not fully recognized by his reeling senses. A faint note of alarm sounded in part of Pug's mind. Without warning, processes began to occur under the level of pain-dimmed consciousness. Basic, more animal instincts took hold, and in a disjointed, hardly understood awareness, a new force emerged. As in the encounter with the trolls, blinding letters of light and flame appeared in his mind's eye, and he silently incanted.

Pug's being became primitive. In his remaining consciousness he was a primal creature fighting for survival with murderous intent. All he could envision was choking the very life from his adversary.

Suddenly an alarm rang within Pug's mind. A deep sense of wrongness, of evil, struck him. Months of training came to the fore, and it was as if he could hear Kulgan's voice crying, "This is not how the power is to be used!" Ripping aside the mental shroud that covered him, Pug opened his eyes.

Through blurred vision and sparkling lights, Pug saw Roland kneeling a mere yard before him, eyes enlarged, vainly struggling with the invisible fingers around his neck. Pug felt no sense of contact with what he saw, and with returning clarity of mind knew at once what had occurred. Leaning forward, he seized Roland's wrists. "Stop it, Roland! Stop it! It isn't real. There are no hands but your own at your throat." Roland, blind with panic, seemed unable to hear Pug's shouts. Mustering what remaining strength he possessed, Pug yanked Roland's hands away, then struck him a stinging slap to the face. Roland's eyes teared and suddenly he breathed in, a gasping, ragged sound.

Still panting, Pug said, "It's an illusion. You were choking yourself."

Roland gasped and pushed himself back from Pug, fear evident on his face. He struggled weakly to pull his sword. Pug leaned forward and firmly gripped Roland's wrist. Barely able to speak, he shook his head and said, "There's no reason."

Roland looked into Pug's eyes, and the fear in his own began to subside. Something inside the older squire seemed to break, and there was only a fatigued, drained young man sitting on the ground. Breathing heavily, Roland sat back, tears forming in his eyes, and asked, "Why?"

Pug's own fatigue made him lean back, supporting himself on his hands. He studied the handsome young face before him, twisted by doubt. "Because you're held under a spell more compelling than any I could fashion." He looked Roland in the eyes. "You truly love her, don't you?"

The last vestige of Roland's anger slowly evaporated and his eyes showed some slight fear remaining, but also Pug saw deep pain and anguish as a tear fell to his cheek. His shoulders slumped and he nodded, his breath ragged as he tried to speak. For a moment he was on the verge of crying, but he fought off his pain and regained his poise. Taking a deep breath, Roland wiped away the tears and took another deep breath. He looked directly at Pug, then guardedly asked, "And you?"

Pug sprawled on the ground, feeling some strength returning. "I . . . I'm not sure. She makes me doubt myself. I don't know. Sometimes I think of no one else, and other times I wish I were as far from her as I could be."

Roland indicated understanding, the last residue of fear draining away. "Where she's concerned, I don't have a whit of wit."

Pug giggled. Roland looked at him, then also began to laugh. "I don't know why," said Pug, "but for some reason, I find what you said terribly funny." Roland nodded and began to laugh too. Soon they were both sitting with tears running down their faces as the emotional vacuum left by the fleeing anger was replaced by giddiness.

Roland recovered slightly, holding back the laughter, when Pug looked at him and said, "A whit of wit!" which sent both of them off on another jag of laughter.

"Well!" a voice said sharply. They turned and found Carline, flanked by two ladies-in-waiting, surveying the scene before her. Instantly both boys became silent. Casting a disapproving look upon the pair as they sprawled upon the ground, she said, "Since you two seem so taken with each other, I'll not intrude."

Pug and Roland exchanged looks and suddenly erupted into uproarious laughter. Roland fell over backward, while Pug sat, legs stretched before him, laughing into his cupped hands. Carline flushed angrily and her eyes widened. With cold fury in her voice she said "Excuse me!" and turned, sweeping by her ladies. As she left, they could hear her loudly exclaim, "Boys!"

Pug and Roland sat for a minute until the near-hysterical fit passed; then Roland rose and extended his hand to Pug. Pug took it and Roland helped him to his feet. "Sorry, Pug. I had no right to be angry with you." His voice softened. "I can't sleep nights thinking of her. I wait for the few moments we're together each day. But since you saved her, all I ever hear is your name." Touching his sore neck, Roland said, "I got so angry, I thought I'd kill you. Damn near got myself killed instead."

Pug looked at the corner where the Princess had disappeared, nodding agreement. "I'm sorry, too, Roland. I'm not very good at controlling magic yet, and when I lose my temper, it seems all sorts of terrible things can happen. Like with the trolls." Pug wanted Roland to understand he was still Pug, even though he was now a magician's apprentice. "I would never do something like that on purpose—especially to a friend."

Roland studied Pug's face a moment and grinned, half-wryly, half-apologetically. "I understand. I acted badly. You were right: she's only setting us one against the other. I am the fool. It's you she cares for."

Pug seemed to wilt. "Believe me, Roland, I'm not so sure I'm to be envied."

Roland's grin widened. "She is a strong-willed girl, that's clear." Caught halfway between an open display of self-pity and mock-bravado, Roland selected mock-bravado.

Pug shook his head. "What's to be done, Roland?"

Roland looked surprised, then laughed loudly. "Don't look to me for advice, Pug. I dance to her tune more than any. But 'there are as many changes in a young girl's heart as in the fickle winds,' as the old saying goes. I'll not blame you for Carline's actions." He winked at Pug conspiratorially. "Still, you won't mind if I keep an eye out for a change in the weather?"

Pug laughed in spite of his exhaustion. "I thought you seemed a little too gracious in your concessions." A thoughtful look came over his face. "You know, it would be simpler—not better, but simpler—if she'd ignore me forever, Roland. I don't know what to think about all this. I've got my apprenticeship to complete. Someday I'll have estates to manage. Then there's this business with the Tsurani. It's all come so quickly, I don't know what to do."

Roland regarded Pug with some sympathy. He put his hand upon the younger boy's shoulder. "I forget this business of being apprentice and noble is all rather new to you. Still, I can't say I've given too much time to such weighty considerations myself, even though my lot was decided before I was born. This worrying about the future is a dry sort of work. I think it would be benefited by a mug of strong ale."

Feeling his aches and bruises, Pug nodded agreement. "Would that we could. But Megar will be of a different mind, I'm afraid."

Roland placed his finger alongside his nose. "We shan't let the Mastercook smell us out, then. Come on, I know a place where the boards of the ale shed are loose. We can quaff a cup or two in private."

Roland began to walk away, but Pug halted him by saying, "Roland, I am sorry we came to blows."

Roland stopped, studied Pug a moment, and grinned. "And I." He extended his hand. "A peace."

Pug gripped it. "A peace."

They turned the corner, leaving the Princess's garden behind, then stopped. Before them was a scene of unalloyed misery. Tomas was walking the length of the court, from the soldiers' commons to the side gate, in full armor—old chain mail over gambeson, full helm, and heavy metal greaves over knee boots. On one arm he bore a heater shield, and in the other hand he held a heavy spear, twelve feet long and iron-tipped, which bore down cruelly upon his right shoulder. It also gave him a comic appearance, as it caused him to lean a little to the right and wobble slightly as he struggled to keep it balanced while he marched.

The sergeant of the Duke's Guard stood counting out cadence for him. Pug knew the sergeant, a tall, friendly man named Gardan. He was Keshian by ancestry, evident in his dark skin. His white teeth split his dark, nappy beard in a grin at the sight of Pug and Roland. He stood nearly as broad in the shoulders as Meecham, with the same loose-gaited movement of a hunter or fighter. Though his black hair was lightly dusted with grey, his face was young-looking and unlined, despite thirty years' service. With a wink at Pug and Roland, he barked, "Halt!" and Tomas stopped in his tracks.

As Pug and Roland closed the distance between them, Gardan snapped, "Right turn!" Tomas obeyed. "Members of the court approaching. Present arms!" Tomas extended his right arm, and his spear dipped in salute. He let the tip drop slightly too low, and nearly broke from attention to pull it back.

Pug and Roland came up to stand next to Gardan, and the large soldier gave them a casual salute and a warm smile. "Good day, Squires." He turned to Tomas for a moment. "Shoulder arms! March post . . . march!" Tomas set off, marching the "post" assigned to him, in this case the length of the yard before the soldiers' commons.

With a laugh, Roland said, "What is this? Special drills?"

Gardan stood with one hand on his sword, the other pointed at Tomas. "Swordmaster Fannon felt it might prove beneficial to our young warrior if someone was here to see his drilling didn't become sloppy from exhaustion or some other petty inconvenience." Dropping his voice a bit, he added, "He's a tough lad; he'll be fine, if a little footsore."

"Why the special drilling?" asked Roland. Pug shook his head as Gardan told them.

"Our young hero lost two swords. The first was understandable, for the matter of the ship was vital, and in the excitement of the moment such an oversight could be forgiven. But the second was found lying on the wet ground near the pell the afternoon the Elf Queen and her party left, and young Tomas was nowhere in sight." Pug knew Tomas had forgotten all about returning to his drilling when Gardell had come with the hood for his fire pot.

Tomas reached the end of his appointed route, did an about-face, and began his return. Gardan regarded the two bruised and dirty boys and said, "What have you two young gentlemen been up to?"

Roland cleared his throat in a theatrical fashion and said, "Ah . . . I was giving Pug a fist-boxing lesson."

Gardan reached out and took Pug's chin in his hand, turning the boy's face for inspection. Evaluating the damage, he said, "Roland, remind me never to ask you to instruct my men in swordplay—we couldn't withstand the casualty rate." Releasing his hold upon Pug's face, he said, "You'll have a beautiful eye in the morning, Squire."

Changing the topic, Pug said, "How are your sons, Gardan?"

"Well enough, Pug. They learn their craft and dream of making themselves rich, save for the youngest, Faxon, who is still intent on becoming a soldier next Choosing. The rest are becoming expert cartwrights under my brother Jeheil's tutelage." He smiled sadly. "With only Faxon at home the house is very empty, though my wife seems glad for the peace." Then he grinned, an infectious smile that rarely could be viewed and not answered. "Still, it won't be too long before the elder boys marry, and then there'll be grandchildren under foot and plenty of merry noise again, from time to time."

As Tomas drew near, Pug asked, "May I speak with the condemned?"

Gardan laughed, stroking his short beard. "I guess I might look the other way for a moment, but be brief, Squire." Pug left Gardan talking with Roland and fell into step beside Tomas as he passed on his way to the opposite end of the court. "How goes it?" Pug asked.

Out of the side of his mouth, Tomas said, "Oh, just fine. Two more hours of this and I'll be ready for burial."

"Can't you rest?"

"On the half hour I get five minutes to stand at attention." He reached the terminus of his post and did a reasonably sharp about-face, then resumed walking back toward Gardan and Roland. "After the fire-pot cover was finished, I came back to the pell and found the sword missing. I thought my heart would stop. I looked everywhere. I almost thrashed Rulf, thinking he had hidden it to spite me. When I returned to the commons, Fannon was sitting on my bunk, oiling down the blade. I thought the other soldiers would hurt themselves holding in the laughter when he said, 'If you judge yourself skilled enough with the sword, perhaps you'd care to spend your time learning the proper way to walk post with a poll arm.' All day walking punishment," he added woefully. "I'll die."

They passed Roland and Gardan, and Pug struggled to feel sympathy. Like the others, he found the situation comical. Hiding his amusement, he lowered his voice to a conspiratorial tone and said, "I'd better get along. Should the Swordmaster come along, he might tack on an extra day's marching."

Tomas groaned at the thought. "Gods preserve me. Get away, Pug."

Pug whispered, "When you're done, join us in the ale shed if you're able." Pug left Tomas's side and rejoined Gardan and Roland. To the sergeant he said, "Thank you, Gardan."

"You are welcome, Pug. Our young knight-in-the-making will be fine, though he feels set upon now. He also chafes at having an audience."

Roland nodded. "Well, I expect he'll not be losing a sword again soon."

Gardan laughed. "Too true. Master Fannon could forgive the first, but not the second. He thought it wise to see Tomas didn't make a habit of it. Your friend is the finest student the Swordmaster has known since Prince Arutha, but don't tell Tomas that. Fannon's always hardest on those with the most potential. Well, good day to you both, Squires. And, boys,"—they paused—"I won't mention the 'fist-boxing lesson.' "

They thank the sergeant for his discretion and walked toward the ale shed, with the measured cadence of Gardan's voice filling the court.

▼▼

PUG WAS WELL into his second mug of ale and Roland finishing his fourth when Tomas appeared through the loose boards. Dirty and sweating, he was rid of his armor and weapons. With a great display of fatigue, he said, "The world must be coming to an end; Fannon excused me from punishment early."

"Why?" asked Pug.

Roland lazily reached over to a storage shelf, next to where he sat upon a sack of grain soon to be used for making ale, and got a cup from a stack. He tossed it to Tomas, who caught it, then filled it from the hogshead of ale that Roland rested his feet upon.

Taking a deep drink, Tomas wiped his mouth with the back of his hand and said, "Something's afoot. Fannon swooped down, told me to put away my toys, and nearly dragged Gardan off, he was in such a hurry."

Pug said, "Maybe the Duke is getting ready to ride east?"

Tomas said, "Maybe." He studied his two friends, taking note of their freshly bruised countenances. "All right. What happened?"

Pug regarded Roland, indicating he should explain the sad state of their appearance. Roland gave Tomas a lopsided grin and said, "We had a practice bout in preparation for the Duke's fist-boxing tourney."

Pug nearly choked on his ale, then laughed. Tomas shook his head. "If you two don't look a pair. Fighting over the Princess?"

Pug and Roland exchanged glances; then as one they leaped at Tomas and bore him to the floor under their combined weight. Roland pinned Tomas to the floor, then, while Pug held him in place, took a half-filled cup of ale and held it high. With mock solemnity Roland said, "I hearby anoint thee, Tomas, First Seer of Crydee!" So saying, he poured the contents of the cup over the struggling boy's face.

Pug belched, then said, "As do I." He poured what remained in his cup over his friend.

Tomas spat ale, laughing as he said, "Right! I was right!" Struggling against the weight upon him, he said, "Now get off! Or need I remind you, Roland, of who gave you your last bloody nose?"

Roland moved off very slowly, intoxicated dignity forcing him to move with glacial precision. "Quite right." Turning toward Pug, who had also rolled off Tomas, he said, "Still, it must be made clear that at the time, the *only reason* Tomas managed to bloody my nose is that during our fight he had an unfair advantage."

Pug looked at Roland through bleary eyes and said, "What unfair advantage?"

Roland put his finger to his lips indicating secrecy, then said, "He was winning."

Roland collapsed back upon the grain sack and Pug and Tomas dissolved into laughter. Pug found the remark so funny, he couldn't stop, and hearing Tomas's laughter only caused his own to redouble. At last he sat up, gasping, with his sides hurting.

Catching his breath, Pug said, "I missed that set-to. I was doing something else, but I don't remember what."

"You were down in the village learning to mend nets, if I remember rightly, when Roland first came here from Tulan."

With a crooked grin Roland said, "I got into an argument with someone or another—do you remember who?" Tomas shook his head no. "Anyway, I got into an argument, and Tomas came over and tried to break it up. I couldn't believe this skinny boy—" Tomas began to voice an objection, but Roland cut him off, holding a finger upright and wiggling it. "Yes, you were. Very skinny. I couldn't believe this skinny boy—skinny *common* boy—would *presume* to tell me—a newly appointed member of the Duke's court *and a gentleman,* I must add—the way to behave. So I did the only thing a proper gentleman could do under the circumstances."

"What?" asked Pug.

"I hit him in the mouth." The three laughed again.

Tomas shook his head at the recollection, while Roland said, "Then he proceeded to give me the worst beating I had since the last time my father caught me out at something.

"That's when I got serious about fist-boxing."

With an air of mock gravity, Tomas said, "Well, we were younger then."

Pug refilled the cups. Moving his jaw in discomfort, he said, "Well, right now I feel about a hundred years old."

Tomas studied them both a moment. "Seriously, what was the fight about?"

With a mixture of humor and regret, Roland said, "Our liege lord's daughter, a girl of ineffable charm . . ."

"What's ineffable?" Tomas asked.

Roland looked at him with intoxicated disdain. "Indescribable, dolt!"

Tomas shook his head. "I don't think the Princess is an indescribable dolt—" He ducked as Roland's cup sailed through the space occupied by his head an instant before. Pug fell over backward laughing again.

Tomas grinned as Roland, in a display of great ceremony, fetched down another cup from the shelf. "As I was saying," he began, filling the cup from the hogshead, "our lady, a girl of ineffable charms—if somewhat questionable judgment—has taken it into her head—for reasons only the gods may fully comprehend—to favor our young magician here with her attentions. *Why*—when she could spend time with me—I can't imagine." He paused to belch. "In any event, we were discussing the proper manner in which to accept such largess."

Tomas looked at Pug, a huge grin on his face. "You have my sympathy, Pug. You most certainly have your hands full."

Pug felt himself flush. Then with a wicked leer, he said, "Do I? And what about a certain young apprentice soldier, well-known hereabouts, who has been seen sneaking into the larder with a certain kitchen girl?" He leaned back and with a look of mock concern etched upon his face added, "I'd hate to think what would happen to him should Neala find out. . . ."

Tomas's mouth fell open. "You wouldn't . . . you couldn't!"

Roland lay back, holding his sides. "Never have I seen such a fair impersonation of a freshly landed fish!" He sat up, crossed his eyes, and opened and shut his mouth rapidly. All three degenerated into helpless mirth again.

Another round was poured, and Roland held up his cup. "Gentlemen, a toast!"

Pug and Tomas held up their cups.

Roland's voice turned serious, and he said, "No matter what differences we have had in the past, you are two fellows I gladly count friends." He held his cup higher and said, "To friendship!"

The three drained their cups and refilled them. Roland said, "Your hand upon it."

The three boys joined hands, and Roland said, "No matter where we go, no matter how many years pass, never again shall we be without friends."

Pug was stuck by the sudden solemnity of the pledge and said, "Friends!"

Tomas echoed Pug's words, and the three shook hands in a gesture of affirmation.

Again the cups were drained, and the afternoon sun quickly fled beyond the horizon as the three boys lost time in the rosy glow of camaraderie and ale.

PUG CAME AWAKE, groggy and disoriented. The faint glow from his nearly extinguished fire pot cast the room into halftones of rose and black. A faint but persistent knocking sounded on his door. He slowly stood, then nearly fell, still intoxicated from his drinking bout. He had stayed with Tomas and Roland in the storage room all evening and into the night, missing supper entirely. "Putting a considerable dent" in the castle's ale supply, as Roland had described it. They hadn't partaken of any great amount, but as their capacity was slight, it seemed a heroic undertaking.

Pug drew on his trousers and wobbled over to the door. His eyelids felt gritty, and his mouth was cotton dry. Wondering who could be demanding entrance in the middle of the night, he threw aside the door.

A blur of motion passed him, and he turned to find Carline standing in the room, a heavy cloak wrapped around her. "Close the door!" she hissed. "Someone might pass the base of the tower and see light upon the stairway."

Pug obeyed, still disoriented. The only thing that penetrated his numb mind was the thought that it was unlikely the faint light from the coals would cast much brightness down the stairwell. He shook his head, gathering his wits about him, and crossed to the fire pot. He lit a taper from the coals and lit his lantern. The room sprang into cheery brightness.

Pug's thinking began to pick up a little as Carline looked about the room, taking stock of the disorderly pile of books and scrolls next to the pallet. She peered into every corner of the room, then said, "Where is that dragon thing you keep about?"

Pug's eyes focused a little, and marshaling his balky tongue, he said, "Fantus? He's off somewhere, doing whatever it is firedrakes do."

Removing her cloak, she said, "Good. He frightens me." She sat on Pug's unmade pallet and looked sternly at him. "I want to speak with you." Pug's eyes went wide, and he stared, for Carline was wearing only a light cotton sleeping gown. While covering her from neck to ankles, it was thin and clung to her figure with alarming tenacity. Pug suddenly realized he was dressed only in trousers and hurriedly grabbed up his tunic from where he had dropped it onto the floor and pulled it over his head. As he struggled with the shirt, the last shreds of alcoholic fog evaporated. "Gods!" he said, in a pained whisper. "Should your father learn of this, he'd have my head."

"Not if you've wits enough to keep your voice lowered," she answered with a petulant look.

Pug crossed to the stool near his pallet, freed of his drunken wobble by newly arrived terror. She studied his rumpled appearance and with a note of disapproval in her voice said, "You've been drinking." When he didn't deny it, she added, "When you and Roland didn't appear at supper, I wondered where you'd gotten yourselves off to. It's a good thing Father also skipped the meal with the court, otherwise he'd have sent someone to find you."

Pug's discomfort was growing at an alarming rate as every tale of what horrible fate awaits lowborn lovers of noblewomen rushed back into his memory. That Carline was an uninvited guest and that nothing untoward had occurred were niceties he didn't think the Duke would find particularly mitigating. Gulping down panic, Pug said, "Carline, you can't stay here. You'll get us both into more trouble than I can imagine."

Her expression became determined. "I'm not leaving until I tell you what I came to say."

Pug knew it was futile to argue. He had seen that look too many times in the past. With a resigned sigh, he said, "All right, then, what is it?"

Carline's eyes widened at his tone. "Well, if that's how you're going to be, I won't tell you!"

Pug suppressed a groan and sat back with his eyes closed. Slowly shaking his head, he said, "Very well. I'm sorry. Please, what do you want me to do?"

She patted the pallet next to her. "Come, sit here."

He complied, trying to ignore the feeling that his fate—an abruptly short life—was being decided by this capricious girl. He landed rather than sat beside her. She giggled at the groan he made. "You got drunk! What's it like?"

"At this moment, not terribly entertaining. I feel like a used kitchen rag."

She tried to look sympathetic, but her blue eyes sparkled with mirth. With a theatrical pout, she said, "You boys get to do all the interesting things, like sword work and archery. Being a proper lady can be such a bore. Father would have a fit if I should ever drink more than a cup of watered wine with supper."

With rising desperation in his voice, Pug said, "Nothing compared to the fit he will have if you're found here. Carline, why did you come here?"

She ignored the question. "What were you and Roland doing this afternoon, fighting?" He nodded. "Over me?" she asked, a glimmer in her eyes.

Pug sighed. "Yes, over you." Her pleased look at the reply nettled him, and irritation crept into his voice. "Carline, you've used him rather badly."

"He's a spineless idiot!" she snapped back. "If I asked him to jump off the wall, he'd do it."

"Carline," Pug nearly whined, "why have—"

His question was cut off as she leaned forward and covered his mouth with her own. The kiss was one-sided, for Pug was too stunned to respond. She quickly sat back, leaving him agape, and she said, "Well?"

Lacking any original response, Pug said, "What?"

Her eyes flashed. "The kiss, you simpleton."

"Oh!" said Pug, still in shock. "It was . . . nice."

She rose and looked down on him, her eyes widening with mixed anger and embarrassment. She crossed her arms and stood tapping her foot, making a sound like summer hail striking the window shutters. Her tone was low and harsh. "Nice! Is that all you have to say?"

Pug watched her, a variety of conflicting emotions surging inside. At this moment panic was contesting with a nearly painful awareness of how lovely she looked in the dim lantern light, her features alive and animated, her dark hair loose around her face, and the thin shift pulled tight across her bosom by her crossed arms. His own confusion made his pose seem unintentionally casual, which further fueled her petulance. "You're the first man—not counting Father and my brothers—I've ever kissed, and all you can say is 'nice.' "

Pug was unable to recover. Still awash with tumultuous emotions, he blurted, "Very nice."

She placed her hands upon her hips—which pulled her nightdress in disturbing new directions and stood looking down on him with an expression of open disbelief. In controlled tones she said, "I come here and throw myself at you. I risk getting myself banished to a convent for life!" Pug noticed she failed to mention his possible fate. "Every other boy—and not a slight number of the older nobles—in the West fall over themselves to get my attention. And all you do is treat me like some common kitchen drudge, a passing amusement for the young lord."

Pug's wits returned, less of their own accord than from the realization that Carline was arguing her case a little more emphatically than was warranted. Suddenly struck with the insight that there was a fair bit of dramatics mixed in with her genuine irritation, he said, "Carline, wait. Give me a moment."

"A moment! I've given you weeks. I thought . . . well, I thought we had an understanding."

Pug tried to look sympathetic, as his mind raced. "Sit down, please. Let me try to explain."

She hesitated, then returned to sit next to him. Somewhat clumsily he took her hands in his own. Instantly he was struck by the nearness of the girl, her warmth, the smell of her hair and skin. The feelings of desire he had felt on the bluffs returned with stunning impact, and he had to fight to keep his mind upon what he wished to say.

Forcing his thoughts away from the hot surge he experienced, he said,

"Carline, I do care for you. A great deal. Sometimes I even think I love you as much as Roland does, but most of the time I only get confused when you're around. That's the problem: there's so much confusion inside of me. I don't understand what it is I feel most of the time."

Her eyes narrowed, for this obviously wasn't the answer she expected. Her tone was sharp as she said, "I don't know what you mean. I've never known a boy so caught up in understanding things."

Pug managed to force a smile. "Magicians are trained to seek explanations. Understanding things is very important to us." He saw a flicker of comprehension in her eyes at this and pressed on. "I have two offices now, both new to me. I may not become a magician, in spite of Kulgan's attempts to make me one, for I have trouble with a lot of my work. I don't really avoid you, you see, but with this trouble I have, I must spend as much time with my studies as I can."

Seeing his explanation was gaining little sympathy, he changed tactics. "In any event, I have little time to consider my other office. I may end up another noble of your father's court, running my estates—small though they might be—caring for my tenants, answering calls to arms, and the rest. But I can't even think of that until I resolve this other matter, my studies of magic. I must keep trying until I'm satisfied I made the wrong choice. Or until Kulgan dismisses me," he added quietly.

He stopped and studied her face. Her large blue eyes watched him intently. "Magicians are of little consequence in the Kingdom. I mean, should I become a master magician . . . Well, could you see yourself married to a magician, whatever his rank?"

She looked slightly alarmed. Quickly she leaned over and kissed him again, rupturing his already frayed composure. "Poor Pug," she said, pulling away a little. Her soft voice rang sweetly to his ears. "You don't have to be. A magician, I mean. You have land and title, and I know Father could arrange others when the time was right."

"It's not a question of what I want, don't you see? It's a question of what I am. Part of the problem may be I haven't truly given myself over to my work. Kulgan took me for his apprentice as much from pity as need, you know. And in spite of what he and Tully have said, I've never been really convinced I was especially talented. But perhaps I need to dedicate myself, commit myself to becoming a magician." He took a breath. "How can I do that if I'm concerning myself with my estates and offices? Or gaining new ones?" He paused. "Or you?"

Carline bit her lower lip slightly, and Pug fought down the urge to take her in his arms and tell her everything would be all right. He had no doubt that once he did that, matters would quickly be beyond his control. No girl in his limited experience, even the prettier ones in the town, aroused such strong feelings in him.

Lowering her lashes a little as she looked down, she softly said, "I'll do whatever you say, Pug." Pug felt relief for a moment, then the full impact of what she had just said hit him. Oh, gods! he thought. No magician's trick could keep him focused in the face of youthful passion. He frantically sought some way to drive desire from him and then thought of her father. Instantly an image of a scowling Duke of Crydee standing before the hangman's gibbet banished most of his lust.

Taking a deep breath, Pug said, "In my own way, I do love you, Carline." Her face came aglow, and forfending disaster, he plunged on. "But I think I should try to find out about myself before I try to make up my mind about the rest." His concentration was sorely tested as the girl seemed to ignore his remarks, being busy kissing his face.

Then she stopped and sat back. Her happy expression faded into one of thoughtfulness as her natural intelligence overrode her childish need to get everything she wanted. Comprehension came into her eyes as he said, "If I chose now, Carline, I might always doubt the choice. Would you want to face the possibility I would come to resent you for the choice I made?"

She said nothing for a while, then quietly said, "No. I don't think I could stand that, Pug."

He breathed a sigh of relief as he felt tension drain away. Suddenly the room seemed cold, and both of them shivered. Carline gripped his hands tight, with surprising strength. She mustered a smile and said, with forced calm, "I understand, Pug." She took a long breath, then softly added, "That's why I think I love you. You could never be false with anyone. Least of all with yourself."

"Or you, Carline." Her eyes grew moist, but she maintained her smile. "This isn't easy," Pug said, assaulted by feelings for the girl. "Please, please, believe me, this is not easy."

Suddenly the tension broke, and Carline laughed softly, sweet music to Pug. Caught halfway between tears and laughter, she said, "Poor Pug. I've upset you."

Pug's face showed his relief at her understanding. He felt buoyant with his affection for the girl. Shaking his head slowly, with a smile of released tension that gave him a somewhat silly expression, he said, "You've no idea, Carline. No idea." He reached out and touched her face tenderly. "We have time. I'm not going anywhere."

From under lowered lashes, blue eyes regarded him with worry. "You'll be leaving with Father soon."

"I mean when I return. I'll be here for years." Gently he kissed her cheek. Forcing a lighter tone, he said, "I can't inherit for three more years, that's the law. And I doubt your father would part with you for as many years yet." Attempting a wry smile, he added, "In three years you might not be able to stand the sight of me."

She came softly into his arms, holding him tightly, her face resting on his shoulder. "Never, Pug. I could never care for another." Pug could only marvel at the feel of her. Her body trembled as she said, "I don't have words, Pug. You're the only one who tried to . . . understand me. You see more than anyone else." Gently he pulled back a little and raised up her face with his hand. Again he kissed her, tasting salty tears upon her lips. She suddenly responded, holding him tighter and kissing him with passion. He could feel the heat of her body through the thin fabric of her gown, and heard soft sighing sounds in his ear as he felt himself drifting back into mindless passion, his own body beginning to respond. Steeling his resolve, he gently disengaged himself from Carline's embrace. Slowly he forced himself away from her and, with regret in his voice, said, "I think you should return to your rooms, Carline."

Carline looked up at Pug, her cheeks flushed and her lips slightly parted. Her breathing was husky, and Pug fought a mighty struggle to control himself and the situation. More firmly, he said, "You had best return to your rooms, *now*."

They rose slowly from the sleeping pallet, each intensely aware of the other. Pug held her hand a moment longer, then released it. He bent and retrieved her cloak, holding it for her as she slipped into it. Guiding her to the door, he pulled it open and peered down the steps of the tower. With no hint of anyone nearby, he opened the door fully. She stepped through, then turned. Softly she said, "I know you think me a sometimes silly and vain girl, and there are times when I am, Pug. But I do love you."

Before he could say a word, she vanished down the stairs, the faint rustling of her cloak echoing in the darkness. Pug quietly closed the door and then put out the lamp. He lay upon his pallet, staring up into the darkness. He could still smell her fresh scent in the air around him, and the remembered touch of her soft body under his hands made them tingle. Now that she was gone and the need for self-control gone with her, he let longing rush through himself. He could see her face alive with desire for him. Covering his eyes with his forearm, he groaned softly to himself and said, "I'm going to hate myself tomorrow."

PUG AWOKE to pounding on the door. His first thought as he scrambled toward the door was of the Duke having learned of Carline's visit. He's here to hang me! was all he could think. It was still dark outside, so Pug opened the door expecting the worst. Instead of the girl's angry father leading a company of castle guards, a castle porter stood outside the door.

"Sorry to wake you, Squire, but Master Kulgan wishes you to join him at once," he said, pointing up toward Kulgan's room. "At once," he repeated, mistaking Pug's expression of relief for one of sleepy confusion. Pug nodded and shut the door.

He took stock. He was still dressed, having fallen asleep again without undressing. He stood quietly as his pounding heart stilled. His eyes felt as if they were packed with sand, and his stomach was upset, leaving a foul taste in his mouth. He went to his small table and splashed cold water on his face, muttering that he would never have another cup of ale again.

Pug reached Kulgan's room and found the magician standing over a pile of personal belongings and books. Sitting on a stool by the magician's sleeping pallet was Father Tully. The priest watched the magician adding to the steadily growing pile and said, "Kulgan, you can't take all those books along. You would need two pack mules for them, and where you would keep them aboard ship where they would do you any good is beyond me."

Kulgan looked at two books he held, like a mother regarding her young. "But I must take them along to further the boy's education."

"Pah! So you'll have something to mull over around the campfires and aboard ship, more likely. Spare me excuses. You will be riding hard to clear the South Pass before it is snowed in. And who can read in a ship crossing the Bitter Sea in winter? The boy will only be away from his studies a month or two. He'll have over eight years more study after that. Give him a rest."

Pug was perplexed by the conversation and tried to ask a question, but was ignored by the two old companions as they bickered. After several more remonstrations from Tully, Kulgan surrendered. "I suppose you're right," he said, tossing the books onto his pallet. He saw Pug waiting by the door and said, "What? Still here?"

Pug said, "You haven't told me why you sent for me yet, Kulgan."

"Oh?" Kulgan said, eyes blinking wide like those of a barn owl caught in a bright light. "I haven't?" Pug nodded. "Well, then. The Duke orders us ready to ride at first light. The dwarves have not answered, but he will not wait. The North Pass is almost certain to be closed, and he fears snow in the South Pass." Kulgan said as an aside, "Which he should. My weather nose tells me snow is nearly here. We are in for an early and hard winter."

Tully shook his head as he stood up. "This from the man who predicted drought seven years ago, when we had the worst flooding in memory. Magicians! Charlatans, all of you." He walked slowly to the door, then stopped to look at Kulgan, his mock irritation replaced by genuine concern. "Though you are right this time, Kulgan. My bones ache deeply. Winter is upon us."

Tully left and Pug asked, "We're leaving?"

With exasperation, Kulgan said, "Yes! I just said so, didn't I? Get your things together and quickly. Dawn's less than an hour away."

Pug turned to leave, when Kulgan said, "Oh, a moment, Pug."

The magician crossed to the door and glanced through it, ensuring Tully was down the stairs and out of earshot. Kulgan turned to Pug and said, "I have no fault to find with your behavior . . . but should you in the future find yourself with another late-night caller, I suggest you not subject yourself to further . . . testing. I'm not so sure you would do as well a second time."

Pug blanched. "You heard?"

Kulgan pointed to a spot where the floor and wall met. "That fire-pot thing of yours exits the wall a foot below there, and it seems a marvelous conduit for sound." Absently he said, "I'll have to look to see how it conducts sound so well when we return." Returning to the boy, he said, "In any event, I was working late and didn't mean to eavesdrop, but I heard every word." Pug flushed. Kulgan said, "I don't mean to embarrass you, Pug. You acted rightly and showed surprising wisdom." Putting his hand upon Pug's shoulder, he said, "I'm not one to advise you in such matters, I fear, as I've had scant experience with women, of any age, let alone such young and headstrong ones." Looking Pug in the eyes, he said, "But this much I do know, it is almost impossible in the heat of the moment to understand long-term consequences. I am proud you were able to do this."

Pug smiled self-consciously. "It was easy enough, Kulgan, I just kept my mind focused on something."

"What?"

"Capital punishment."

Kulgan laughed, a sharp barking sound, then said, "Very well, but the potential for disaster would be as high for the Princess, too, Pug. A city-bred noblewoman of the eastern court may indulge herself in as many lovers of any rank that she can enjoy while maintaining discretion, but the only daughter of a frontier duke who is so closely related to the king has no such luxury. She must be above suspicion in all things. Even suspicion could harm Carline. One who cares for her would take that into consideration. Do you understand?"

Pug nodded, fully relieved now that he had resisted temptation the night before.

"Good, I know you'll be careful in the future." Kulgan smiled. "And don't mind old Tully. He's just cross because the Duke ordered him to stay behind. He still thinks he's as young as his acolytes. Now run along and get ready. Dawn's less than an hour away."

Pug nodded and hurried off, leaving Kulgan to regard the piles of books before him. With regret he picked the nearest one up and placed it on a nearby shelf. After a moment he grabbed another and stuffed it into a sack. "Just one won't cause any harm," he said to the invisible specter of Tully shaking his head in disapproval. He put the rest of the books back on the shelf, save the last volume, which he shoved into the sack. "All right, then," he said defiantly, "two!"

8

▼▼

JOURNEY

A LIGHT WET SNOW WAS FALLING.

Pug shivered under his greatcloak, sitting astride his horse. He had been in the saddle for the last ten minutes, waiting as the rest of the Duke's company made ready.

The courtyard filled with hurrying, shouting men, lashing supplies onto the balky mules of the baggage train. Dawn was just commencing, giving the courtyard a little color instead of the blacks and grey that had greeted Pug when he came from the tower. Porters had already carried his baggage down and were securing it among the other items being brought along.

A panicked "Whoa!" erupted behind Pug, and he turned to see Tomas pulling frantically at the reins of a spirited bay, his head tossing high. Like Pug's own sleek, light war-horse, he was a far cry from the old draft animal they had ridden to the site of the shipwreck. "Don't pull so hard," Pug shouted. "You'll saw at his mouth and make him mad. Pull back gently and release a couple of times."

Tomas did, and the horse quieted down, moving alongside Pug's own. Tomas sat as if the saddle had nails sticking through it. His face was a study in concentration as he tried to guess what the horse would do next.

"If you hadn't been walking post yesterday, you could have gone riding, getting in some practice. Now I'll have to teach you as we go."

Tomas looked thankful for the promise of aid. Pug smiled. "By the time we reach Bordon, you'll be riding like the King's Lancers."

"And walking like a ruptured spinster." Tomas shifted in the saddle. "Already I feel like I've been sitting on a stone block for hours. After just a little way from the saddling post."

Pug jumped down from his horse and looked over Tomas's saddle, making Tomas move his leg so he could examine under the saddle flap, then asked, "Who saddled this horse for you?"

"Rulf. Why?"

"I thought so. He's paying you back for threatening him about that sword, or because we're friends. He doesn't dare threaten me anymore, now that I'm a Squire, but he thinks nothing of knotting your stirrup leathers. A couple of hours riding like this, and you'd be standing at meals for a month, if you didn't get pitched on your head and killed. Here, get down and I'll show you."

Tomas dismounted, halfway between a leap and a fall. Pug showed him the knots. "They would have rubbed the inside of your thighs raw by the end of the day. And they're not long enough." Pug took out the knots and adjusted the leathers to the proper length. "It's going to feel very strange for a while, but you've got to keep your heels down. I'll remind you until you're sick of hearing it, but it'll keep you out of trouble when you do it without thought. And *don't* try to grip with your knees; that's wrong, and it'll make your legs so sore, you'll hardly be able to walk by tomorrow." He went on with a few basic instructions and inspected the cinch, which was loose. He tried tightening it, and the horse sucked air. Pug struck the gelding a blow in the side, and the animal exhaled sharply. Pug quickly pulled the cinch strap and said, "Sometime today, you most likely would have found yourself listing to one side, a most discomforting position."

"That Rulf!" Tomas turned toward the stable. "I'll thrash him within an inch of death!"

Pug grabbed his friend's arm. "Wait. We don't have time for brawling."

Tomas stood with fists clenched, then relaxed with a relieved sigh. "I'm in no condition for fighting, anyway." He turned to see Pug inspecting the horse.

Pug shook his head, then winced. "Me too." He finished inspecting the saddle and bridle, and the horse shied. Pug gentled the horse. "Rulf's also given you a temperamental mount. This fellow would have probably thrown you before noon, and be halfway back to the stable before you hit the ground. With sore legs and shortened stirrup leathers, you never would have stood a chance. I'll trade with you."

Tomas looked relieved and struggled into the saddle of the other horse. Pug readjusted the stirrups for both riders. "We can swap our travel rolls when we take our noon meal." Pug then soothed the high-strung warhorse and climbed nimbly into the saddle. Feeling surer hands at the reins, and a firm leg on either side, the gelding quieted.

"Ho! Martin," shouted Tomas as the Duke's Huntmaster walked into view. "Are you traveling with us?"

A wry grin split the face of the hunter, who was wearing his heavy green cloak over his forester's leathers. "For a short while, Tomas. I'm to lead some trackers around the boundaries of Crydee. I'll be heading due eastward when we come to the south branch of the river. Two of my trackers were on their way an hour ago, breaking trail for the Duke."

"What do you think of this Tsurani business, Martin?" Pug asked.

The still-youthful Huntmaster's face clouded. "If elves are given to worry, there is something to worry over." He turned toward the front of the assembling line. "Excuse me, I must instruct my men." He left the boys sitting alone.

Pug asked Tomas, "How's your head this morning?"

Tomas made a face. "About two sizes smaller than when I awoke." His face brightened a bit. "Still, the excitement seems to have stopped the banging inside. I feel almost good."

Pug gazed at the keep. Memories of his encounter last night kept tugging at his mind, and suddenly he regretted the need to travel with the Duke.

Tomas noticed his friend's pensive mood and said, "Why so glum? Aren't you excited about going?"

"It's nothing. Just thinking."

Tomas studied Pug for a moment. "I think I understand." With a deep sigh, he sat back in the saddle, and his horse stamped and nickered. "I, for one, am glad to be leaving. I think Neala has tumbled to that little matter we spoke of yesterday."

Pug laughed. "That will teach you to be mindful of who you escort into pantries."

Tomas smiled sheepishly.

The doors to the keep opened, and the Duke and Arutha came out, accompanied by Kulgan, Tully, Lyam, and Roland. Carline followed, with Lady Marna behind. The Duke and his companions made their way to the head of the column, but Carline hurried down to where Pug and Tomas sat. As she passed, guardsmen saluted her, but she paid them no heed. She reached Pug's side, and when he bowed politely, she said, "Oh, get off that stupid horse."

Pug climbed down, and Carline threw her arms around his neck, holding him closely for a moment. "Take care and stay well," she said. "Don't let anything happen to you." She pulled away, then kissed him briefly. "And come home." Holding back tears, she hurried to the head of the line, where her father and brother waited to say good-bye.

Tomas let out a theatrical whoop and laughed, while Pug remounted; the soldiers nearby attempted to restrain their own amusement. "It seems the Princess has made plans for you, m'lord," Tomas gibed. He ducked as Pug stirred to give him a backhanded cuff. The motion caused his horse to start forward, and suddenly Tomas was fighting to bring his horse back into line. The horse seemed determined to go in any direction except the one Tomas wished; now it was Pug's turn to laugh. He finally moved his own horse alongside Tomas's and herded the fractious mare back into line. She flattened her ears and turned to nip at Pug's horse, and the short boy said, "We both have accounts to settle with Rulf; he gave us two horses that don't like each other, too. We'll trade your mount off with one of the soldiers."

With relief Tomas half dismounted, half fell to the ground, and Pug directed the exchange with a soldier down the line. The exchange was made, and as Tomas returned to his place, Roland came down to where they stood and offered them both his hand. "You two watch yourselves, now. There's plenty of trouble waiting out there without your looking for it."

They acknowledged they would, and Roland said to Pug, "I'll keep an eye on things for you."

Pug noticed his wry smile, glanced back to where Carline stood with her father, and said, "No doubt," then added, "Roland, whatever happens, good luck to you, too."

Roland said, "Thank you. I'll take that as it's meant." To Tomas he said, "And things are certainly going to be dull without you around."

Tomas said, "Given what's going on, dull would be welcome."

Roland said, "As long as it's not too dull, right? Take good care! You're a bothersome pair, but I'd hate to lose you."

Tomas laughed as Roland walked off with a friendly wave. Watching the Squire go up to the Duke's party, and seeing Carline standing next to her father, Pug turned to Tomas. "That decides it. I am glad to be going. I need a rest."

Sergeant Gardan came riding back with orders to move the column, and they set off. The Duke and Arutha rode in the van, with Kulgan and Gardan behind. Martin Longbow and his trackers set off at a run beside the Duke's horse. Twenty pair of mounted guards followed, with Tomas and Pug nestled between them and the baggage train at the rear with its five pair of guards. Slowly at first, then with increasing speed, they moved through the gates of the castle and down the south road.

THEY HAD BEEN riding for three days, the last two through dense woodlands. Martin Longbow and his men had turned east that morning as they crossed the southern branch of the river Crydee, called river Boundary. It marked the border between Crydee and the Barony of Carse, one of Lord Borric's vassal provinces.

The sudden snows of early winter had come and draped the autumn landscape in white. Many of the denizens of the forest had been caught unaware by the sudden winter, rabbits whose coats were still more brown than white, and ducks and geese who scampered across half-frozen ponds, resting as they migrated south. The snow fell in flurries of heavy wet flakes, melting slightly during the day, to refreeze at night, making a thin crust of ice. As the horses' and mules' hooves cracked through the ice, the crunching of leaves underneath could be heard in the still winter air.

In the afternoon Kulgan observed a flight of firedrakes circling in the distance, barely visible through the trees. The colorful beasts, red, gold, green, and blue in color, raced over the treetops and dipped out of sight, then reappeared as they spiraled upward, with cries and small bursts of flame. Kulgan reined in as the train passed and waited for Pug and Tomas to overtake him. When they were alongside, he pointed out the display, saying, "It has the appearance of a mating flight. See, the more aggressively the males act, the more responsive the females. Oh, I wish we had time to study this more closely."

Pug followed the creatures with his eyes as they rode through a clearing, then, somewhat startled, said, "Kulgan, isn't that Fantus there, hovering near the edge?"

Kulgan's eyes widened. "By the gods! I think it is."

Pug asked, "Shall I call him?"

The magician chuckled. "Given the attention he's receiving from those females, I think it would do little good." They lost sight of the congregation of drakes as they rode after the Duke's train. Kulgan said, "Unlike most creatures, drakes mate at first snow. The females will lay eggs in nests, then sleep the winter, warming them with their bodies. In the spring the young hatch and are cared for by their mothers. Fantus will most likely spend the next few days . . . ahem, fathering a clutch of young. Then he'll be back at the keep, annoying Megar and the kitchen staff for the rest of the winter."

Tomas and Pug laughed. Tomas's father made a great show of considering the playful drake a plague from the gods visited upon his well-ordered kitchen, but on several occasions both boys had spied Megar lavishing some of the choicest dinner scraps upon the beast. In the fifteen months since Pug had become Kulgan's apprentice, Fantus had become a winged, scaled house pet to most of the Duke's staff, though a few, like the Princess, found Fantus's dragonlike appearance disquieting.

They continued to move east by south, as quickly as the terrain would permit. The Duke was concerned about reaching the South Pass before the snows made it impassable, cutting them off from the east until spring. Kulgan's weather sense had allowed they had a fair chance of making it before any big storms struck. Soon they came to the edge of the deepest part of the great southern forests, the Green Heart.

Deep within the glades, at prearranged locations, two troops of guards from the keep at Carse were waiting for them with fresh horses. Duke Borric had sent pigeons south with instructions for Baron Bellamy, who sent a reply the same way that horses would be waiting. The remounts and guards would be hurrying to the meeting places from the Jonril garrison, maintained by Bellamy and Tolburt of Tulan near the edge of the great forests. By changing mounts, the Duke would save three, perhaps four days of travel to Bordon. Longbow's trackers had left clear blazes for the Duke to follow, and they were due to reach the first meeting place later that day.

Pug turned to Tomas. The taller boy was sitting his horse somewhat better, though he still flapped his arms like a chicken trying to fly when they were forced to a fast trot. Gardan came riding back down the line, to where the boys rode before the baggage guards. "Be wary," he shouted. "From here to the Grey Towers is the darkest part of the Green Heart. Even the elves pass through here quickly and in numbers." The sergeant of the Duke's Guard turned his horse and galloped back to the head of the line.

They traveled the balance of the day, every eye searching the forest for signs of trouble. Tomas and Pug made light conversation, with Tomas remarking on the chance of a good fight. Both boys' banter sounded hollow to the soldiers around them, who sat silent and vigilant. They reached the place of meeting just before sundown. It was a clearing of considerable size, with several tree stumps grown over with ground cover that peeked through the snow, showing that the trees had been harvested long ago.

The fresh horses stood in a picket, each tied to a long line, while six guards stood careful watch around them. When the Duke's party had ridden up, they had weapons ready. They lowered their weapons when they saw the familiar banner of Crydee. These were men of Carse, who wore the scarlet tabard of Baron Bellamy quartered by a gold cross, a golden griffin rampant over their hearts. The shield of each man bore the same device.

The sergeant of the six guards saluted. "Well met, my lord."

Borric acknowledged the salute. "The horses?" he asked simply.

"They are fit, lord, and restless from waiting. As are the men."

Borric dismounted; another soldier of Carse took his horse's reins. "Trouble?"

"None, my lord, but this place is suited for other than honest men. All last night we stood watches by twos and felt the crawl of eyes upon us." The sergeant was a scarred veteran, who had fought goblins and bandits in his day. He was not the type to give in to flights of imagination, and the Duke acknowledged this. "Double the watch this night. You will escort the horses back to your garrison tomorrow. I would rather have them rested a day, but this is a poor place."

Prince Arutha came forward. "I have also felt eyes upon us for the last few hours, Father."

Borric turned to the sergeant. "It may be that we have been shadowed by a band of brigands, seeking to judge our mission. I will send two men back with you, for fifty men or forty-eight is of little difference, but eight is a far better number than six." If the sergeant felt any relief at this, he did not show it, simply saying, "I thank my lord."

Borric dismissed the man and with Arutha walked toward the center of the camp, where a large fire was burning. The soldiers were erecting rude shelters against the night wind, as they had each night of the journey. Borric saw two mules with the horses and noted that bales of hay had been brought along. Arutha followed his gaze. "Bellamy is a prudent man; he serves Your Grace well."

Kulgan, Gardan, and the boys approached the two nobles, who stood warming themselves before the fire. Darkness was descending quickly; even at noon there was little light in the snow-shrouded forest. Borric looked around and shivered from more than the cold. "This is an ill-omened place. We will do well to be away as soon as possible."

They ate a quick meal and turned in. Pug and Tomas lay close, starting at every strange sound until fatigue lulled them to sleep.

THE DUKE'S COMPANY passed deep into the forest, through glades so thick that often the trackers had had to change their course, doubling back to find another way for the horses, marking the trail as they went. Much of this forest was dark and twisted, with choking underbrush that impeded travel.

Pug said to Tomas, "I doubt the sun ever shines here." He spoke in soft tones. Tomas slowly nodded, his eyes watching the trees. Since leaving the men from Carse three days ago, they had felt more tension each passing day. The noises of the forest had lessened as they moved deeper into the trees, until they now rode in silence. It was as if the animals and birds themselves shunned this part of the forest. Pug knew it was only because there were few animals that hadn't migrated south or gone into hibernation, but that knowledge didn't lessen his and Tomas's dread.

Tomas slowed down. "I feel something terrible is about to happen."

Pug said, "You've been saying that for two days now." After a minute he added, "I hope we don't have to fight. I don't know how to use this sword, in spite of what you've tried to show me."

"Here," said Tomas, holding something out. Pug took it and found a small pouch inside of which was a collection of small, smooth rocks and a sling. "I thought you might feel better with a sling. I brought one, too."

They rode for another hour, then stopped to rest the horses and eat a cold meal. It was midmorning, and Gardan inspected each horse, ensuring it was fit. No soldier was given a chance to overlook the slightest possible injury or illness. Should a horse falter, its rider would have to double up with another, and those two would have to return as best they could, for the Duke could not wait for such a delay. This far from any safe haven, it was something no one wished to think about or discuss aloud.

They were due to meet the second detachment of horses at midafternoon. The breakneck pace of the first four days had given way to a careful walk, for to rush through the trees would be dangerous. At the rate they were progressing, they would be on time. Still, the Duke was chafing at the slow pace.

On and on they rode, at times having to stop while guards drew swords and cut at the brush before them, their sword blows echoing through the stillness of the forest as they followed the narrow path left by the trackers.

Pug was lost in thoughts of Carline when, later, a shout erupted from the front of the column, out of sight of the boys. Suddenly the horsemen near Pug and Tomas were charging forward, oblivious to the thicket around them, dodging low-hanging branches by instinct.

Pug and Tomas spurred their horses after the others, and soon their senses recorded a blur of brown and white, as snow-spotted trees seemed to fly past. They stayed low, close to the necks of their mounts, avoiding most tree branches, while they struggled to stay aboard. Pug looked over his shoulder and saw Tomas falling behind. Branches and twigs caught at Pug's cloak as he crashed through the forest into a clearing. The sounds of battle assaulted his ears, and the boy saw fighting in progress. The remount horses were trying to pull up their stakes, while fighting exploded around them. Pug could only vaguely make out the form of combatants, dark shrouded shapes slashing upward with swords at the horsemen.

A figure broke away and came running toward him, avoiding the blow of a guard a few yards ahead of Pug. The strange warrior grinned wickedly at Pug, seeing only the boy before him. Raising his sword for a blow, the fighter screamed and clawed at his face as blood ran between his fingers. Tomas had reined in behind Pug and with a yell let fly with another stone. "I thought you'd get yourself into trouble," he shouted. He spurred his horse forward and rode over the fallen figure. Pug sat rooted for a moment, then spurred his own horse. Pulling out his sling, he let fly at a couple of targets, but couldn't be sure if the stones struck.

Suddenly Pug was in a place of calm in the fighting. On all sides he could see figures in dark grey cloaks and leather armor pouring out from the forest. They looked like elves, save their hair was darker, and they shouted in a language unpleasant to Pug's ears. Arrows flew from the trees, emptying saddles of Crydee horsemen.

Lying about were bodies of both attackers and soldiers. Pug saw the lifeless bodies of a dozen men of Carse, as well as Longbow's two lead trackers, tied to stakes in lifelike poses around the campfire. Scarlet bloodstains spotted the white snow beside them. The ruse had worked, for the Duke had ridden straight into the clearing, and now the trap was sprung.

Lord Borric's voice rang out over the fray. "To me! To me! We are surrounded."

Pug looked about for Tomas as he frantically kicked his mount toward the Duke and his gathering men. Arrows filled the air, and the screams of the dying echoed in the glade. Borric shouted, "This way!" and the survivors followed him. They crashed into the forest, riding over attacking bowmen. Shouts followed them while they galloped away from the ambush, keeping low over the necks of their mounts, avoiding arrows and low-hanging branches.

Pug frantically pulled his horse aside, avoiding a large tree. He looked about, but could not see Tomas. Fixing his gaze upon the back of another horseman, Pug determined to concentrate on one thing only, not losing sight of the man's back. Strange loud cries could be heard from behind, and other voices answered from one side. Pug's mouth was dry and his hands sweating in the heavy gloves he wore.

They sped through the forest, shouts and cries echoing around them. Pug lost track of the distance covered, but he thought it surely a mile or more. Still the voices shouted in the forest, calling to others the course of the Duke's flight.

Suddenly Pug was crashing through the thick underbrush, forcing his lathered, panting horse up a small but steep rise. All around him was a gloom of grey and greens, broken only by patches of white. Atop the rise the Duke waited, his sword drawn, as others pulled up around him. Arutha sat by his father, his face covered with perspiration in spite of the cold. Panting horses and exhausted guards gathered around. Pug was relieved to see Tomas beside Kulgan and Gardan.

When the last rider approached, Lord Borric said, "How many?"

Gardan surveyed the survivors and said, "We've lost eighteen men, have six wounded, and all the mules and baggage were taken."

Borric nodded. "Rest the horses a moment. They'll come."

Arutha said, "Are we to stand, Father?"

Borric shook his head. "There are too many of them. At least a hundred struck the clearing." He spat. "We rode into that ambush like a rabbit into a snare." He glanced about. "We've lost nearly half our company."

Pug asked a soldier sitting beside him, "Who were they?"

The soldier looked at Pug. "The Brotherhood of the Dark Path, Squire, may Ka-hooli visit every one of the bastards with piles," he answered, invoking the vengeance god. The soldier indicated a circle around them with his hand. "Small bands of them travel through the Green Heart, though they mostly live in the mountains east of here, and way up in the Northlands. That was more than I'd have bargained was around, curse the luck."

Voices shouted from behind, and the Duke said, "They come. Ride!"

The survivors wheeled and rode off, again racing through the trees ahead of their pursuers. Time became suspended for Pug as he negotiated the dangerous course through the dense forest. Twice men nearby screamed, whether from striking branches or from arrows Pug didn't know.

Again they came to a clearing, and the Duke signaled a halt. Gardan said, "Your grace, the horses can't endure much more of this."

Borric struck his saddle horn in frustration, his face dark with anger. "Damn them! And where are we?"

Pug looked about. He had no idea of where they stood in relationship to the original site of attack, and from the looks on the faces around him, no one else did either.

Arutha said, "We must strike eastward, Father, and make for the mountains."

Borric nodded. "But which way lies east?" The tall trees and overcast sky with its defused sunlight conspired to deny them any point of reference.

Kulgan said, "One moment, your grace," and closed his eyes. Again shouts of pursuit echoed through the trees, as Kulgan opened his eyes and pointed. "That way. There lies the east." Without question or comment, the Duke spurred his horse in the indicated direction, motioning for the others to follow. Pug felt a strong urge to be near someone familiar and tried to rejoin Tomas, but couldn't make his way through the press of riders. He swallowed hard and admitted to himself he was badly scared. The grim faces of the nearby soldiers told him he was not alone in that feeling.

More time passed as they raced through the dark corridors of the Green Heart. Every advance along the escape route was accompanied by the echoing cries of Dark Brothers as they alerted others of the fugitives' route. Occasionally Pug would spy a shape loping along in the distance, quickly lost in the darkness of the trees as it ran a parallel course. The accompanying runners did not seek to hinder them, but always they were near.

Once more the Duke ordered a halt. Turning to Gardan, he said, "Skirmishers! Find out how close they follow. We must have rest." Gardan indicated three men, who quickly leapt from their horses and ran back along the route of their retreat. A single clash of steel and a strangled cry heralded their encounter with the closest Dark Brother tracker.

"Damn them!" said the Duke. "They're herding us in a circle, seeking to bring us back into their main strength. Already we're moving more north than east."

Pug took the opportunity to move next to Tomas. The horses were panting and shivering as perspiration steamed off them in the cold. Tomas managed a feeble smile, but said nothing.

Men moved quickly among the horses, checking for injury. In a few minutes the skirmishers returned at a run. Panting, one said, "Lord, they are close behind, fifty, sixty at least."

"How long?"

The man stood with perspiration pouring down his face as he answered, "Five minutes, my lord." With grim humor he said, "The two we killed will make them pause, but no more time than that."

Borric said to the company, "We rest a moment, then we ride."

Arutha said, "A moment or an hour, what does it matter? The horses are done. We should stand before more Brothers come to the call."

Borric shook his head. "I must get through to Erland. He must know of the coming of the Tsurani."

An arrow, quickly followed by a second, flew from the nearby trees, and another rider fell. Borric shouted, "Ride!"

They cantered the exhausted horses deeper into the woods, then slowed to a walk, while they kept watch for the coming attack. The Duke used hand signals to deploy the line of soldiers so they might swing to either flank and charge on command. Horses blew foam as their nostrils distended, and Pug knew they were close to dropping.

"Why don't they attack?" whispered Tomas.

"I don't know," answered Pug. "They just harry us from the sides and behind."

The Duke raised his hand and the column halted. No sounds of pursuit could be heard. He turned and spoke in a low tone. "They may have lost us. Pass the word to inspect your mounts—" An arrow sped past his head, missing him by inches. "Forward!" he shouted, and they began a ragged trot along the path they had been following.

Gardan shouted, "My lord, it seems they wish us to keep moving."

In a harsh whisper Borric swore, then asked, "Kulgan, which way lies east?"

The magician closed his eyes again, and Pug knew he was tiring himself with this particular spell. Not difficult if one was standing calmly, it had to be fatiguing him under these conditions. Kulgan's eyes opened and he pointed to the right. The column was heading northward.

Arutha said, "Again they slowly turn us, Father, back into their main strength."

Raising his voice, Borric said, "Only fools or children would keep to this route. On my command, wheel to the right and charge." He waited as every man readied weapons and made silent prayers to their gods that the horses could withstand one more gallop. Then the Duke shouted, "Now!" As a body, the column wheeled to the right, and riders spurred their flagging mounts. Arrows came pouring from the trees, and men and horses screamed.

Pug ducked under a branch, desperately holding on to the reins while he fumbled with sword and shield. He felt the shield slipping and, as he struggled with it, sensed his horse slowing. He couldn't exercise the needed control over the animal and manage the weapons at the same time.

Pug reined in, risking a momentary stop to put his equipment right. A noise made him look to the right. Standing less than five yards away was a bowman of the Brotherhood of the Dark Path. Pug stayed rooted for a moment, as did the bowman. Pug was struck by his resemblance to the Elf Prince, Calin. There was little to distinguish the two races, nearly the same in height and build, save hair and eyes. The creature's bowstring had snapped, and he stood with dark eyes fixed upon Pug while calmly setting about restringing his bow.

Pug's astonishment at finding the Dark Brother standing so close to him momentarily caused him to forget the reason he had halted. He sat numbly watching the bowman repairing his weapon, entranced by the dark elf's coolly efficient manner.

Then he was pulling an arrow from his quiver in a fluid motion and fitting the shaft to the bowstring. Sudden alarm made Pug act. His staggering horse answered his frantic kicks and was off again. He didn't see the bowman's arrow, but heard and felt it speed past his ear, then he was back to a gallop, the bowman lost behind as Pug overtook the Duke's company.

Noise from ahead made Pug urge his horse on, though the poor animal was giving every indication it was moving as fast as possible. Pug wove through the forest, the gloom making it difficult to negotiate.

Abruptly he was behind a rider wearing the Duke's colors and then passing the man as Pug's horse proved fresher for carrying a lighter rider. The terrain became more hilly, and Pug wondered if they were entering the foothills of the Grey Towers.

A horse's scream caused Pug to glance behind. He saw the soldier he had passed thrown as his mount collapsed, foaming blood spurting from the animal's nose. Pug and another rider halted, and the soldier turned back, riding over to where the first man stood. He extended his hand to offer the fallen man a double ride. The fallen soldier just shook his head, as he struck the standing horse on the rump, sending it ahead again. Pug knew the second man's horse could barely carry one rider, never two. The fallen rider pulled his sword and put down the injured horse, then turned to wait for the pursuing Dark Brothers. Pug found his eyes tearing as he contemplated the man's courage. The other soldier shouted something over his shoulder that was lost to the boy, then suddenly he was riding by. He shouted, "Move, Squire!"

Pug put heels to the sides of his horse, and the animal picked up a staggering trot.

The fleeing column continued on its stumbling, exhausted flight, Pug moving up through the company of riders to a place near the Duke. After a few minutes Lord Borric signaled for them to slow. They entered another clearing. Borric surveyed his company. A look of helpless rage crossed his face, to be replaced by surprise. He held his hand aloft, and the riders stopped their milling about. Shouts sounded in the forest, but from some distance away.

Arutha, eyes wide with wonder, said, "Have we lost them?"

Slowly the Duke nodded, his attention focused on the distant shouts. "For the moment. When we broke through the archers, we must have slipped behind their pursuit. They'll discover that fact shortly and double back. We have ten, fifteen minutes at best." He looked over his ragged company. "If only we could find a place to hide."

Kulgan moved his staggering horse alongside the Duke. "My lord, I might have a solution, though it is risky and might prove fatal."

Borric said, "No more fatal than waiting for them to come for us. What is your plan?"

"I have an amulet, which can control weather. I had planned to save it against possible storms at sea, for its use is limited. I may be able to mask our whereabouts with it. Let every man gather his horse at the far end of the clearing, near that outcropping of rock. Have them silence the animals."

Borric ordered it done, and the animals were moved to the opposite end of the clearing. Reassuring hands gentled exhausted and excited horses, quieting the mounts after their long flight.

They had gathered at the highest end of a narrow clearing, their backs to an outcropping of granite that rose overhead like a grey fist. On three sides the ground sloped away gently. Kulgan began to walk along the perimeter of the compact company.

He chanted in a low voice, waving the amulet in an intricate pattern. Slowly the grey afternoon light faded, and a mist began to gather around him. At first only light wisps appeared nearby, then other, more substantial patches of moisture formed, becoming light fog.

Soon the air between the Duke's company and the tree line grew hazy. Kulgan moved more quickly and the fog deepened, filling the clearing with whiteness, moving outward from the magician into the trees on all sides. Within a few minutes it was impossible to see beyond a few yards.

On and on paced Kulgan, sending thicker blankets of haze to obscure the already grey light in the trees. The clearing slowly became darker as the gloomy fog deepened with every incantation made by the magician.

Then Kulgan stopped and turned to the Duke, whispering, "All must remain quiet. Should the dark elves wander blindly into the fog, the sloping terrain will, I hope, guide them past on one side or the other as they come around the rocks. But let no man move. Any sound will defeat us."

Each man nodded, understanding the danger coming fast. They would stand in the center of this deep fog in the hope the Dark Brothers would walk past, putting the Duke and his men once more behind them. It was an all-or-nothing gambit, for should they win free, there was a good chance they would be far removed from this spot when the Brotherhood once more backtracked.

Pug looked at Tomas and whispered, "It's a good thing it's rocky here, else we'd leave some pretty tracks."

Tomas nodded, too frightened to speak. A nearby guard motioned for Pug to be silent, and the young Squire nodded.

Gardan and several guards, with the Duke and Arutha, took up position near the front of the company, weapons ready should the ploy fail. Shouts grew louder as the Dark Brotherhood returned along their trail. Kulgan stood near the Duke, enchanting quietly, gathering more mist around him, then sending it forth. Pug knew the mist would be expanding rapidly, shrouding a continuously larger area as long as Kulgan continued to incant. Every extra minute would encompass more of the Green Heart in fog, making it increasingly more difficult for the attackers to find them.

Pug felt wetness on his cheek and looked up. Snow was beginning to fall. With apprehension he looked to the mist, to see if the newly arriving snow was affecting it. He watched a tense minute, then silently sighed with relief, for if anything, the snow was adding to the masking effects of the fog.

A soft footfall could be heard nearby. Pug froze, as did every man near him. A voice rang out in the Brotherhood's strange language.

Pug felt an itch between his shoulders, but refused to move, fighting to ignore the nagging sensation on his back. He glanced sideways at Tomas. Tomas stood stock-still, his hand on his horse's muzzle, looking like a statue in the haze. Like every other remaining horse, Tomas's mount knew the hand upon his face was a command for quiet.

Another voice rang out in the mist, and Pug nearly jumped. It sounded as if the caller were standing directly in front of him. Again the answering call came, sounding farther away.

Gardan stood directly before Pug, who saw the sergeant's back twitch. Gardan slowly knelt, silently laying his sword and shield on the ground. He rose up, still moving slowly, pulling his belt knife. Then suddenly he stepped into the mist, his movements as quick and fluid as a cat disappearing into the night. There was a faint sound, and Gardan reappeared.

Before him struggled the form of a Dark Brother, one of Gardan's huge black hands clamped tightly over the creature's mouth. The other arm was choking its throat. Pug could see the sergeant couldn't risk letting go for the brief instant needed to plunge the knife in its back. Gardan gritted his teeth in pain as the creature raked the sergeant's arm with clawlike nails. Its eyes bulged as it fought to breathe. Gardan stood rooted to the spot, holding the Dark Brother off the ground by main force as it struggled to get free. The creature's face turned red, then purple, as Gardan choked the life from it. Blood from the creature's raking nails flowed freely down Gardan's arm; but the powerful soldier barely moved at all. Then the Dark Brother went limp, and Gardan gave it a final, throat-crushing jerk of his arm and let the creature slide silently to the ground.

Gardan's eyes were wide with exertion, and he panted quietly as he regained his breath. Slowly he turned, knelt, and replaced his knife. Recovering his sword and shield, he stood, resuming his watch in the mist.

Pug felt nothing but awe and admiration for the sergeant, but like the others he could only silently watch. Time passed, and the voices grew more faint as they sounded their angry inquiries to one another, seeking the fugitives' hiding place. The voices moved off, and then, like a long sigh of relief heaved by all in the clearing, it was silent. The Duke whispered, "They are past us. Lead the horses. We go east."

Pug looked about in the gloom. Ahead, Duke Borric and Prince Arutha led the way. Gardan stayed beside Kulgan, who was still exhausted from his magical undertaking. Tomas walked silently beside his friend. Of the fifty guardsmen who had set out with the Duke from Crydee, thirteen remained. Only six horses had survived the day. As they had faltered, the others had been quickly put down by silent, tight-lipped riders.

They trudged upward, climbing higher into the foothills. The sun had set, but the Duke ordered them onward, fearful of the return of their pursuers. The men stepped cautiously forward, tentative in the rough terrain at night. The darkness was punctuated by softly uttered oaths as men lost their footing on the icy rocks time and again.

Pug plodded along, his body numb with fatigue and cold. The day had seemed an eternity, and he could not remember when he had last stopped or eaten. Once he had been handed a waterskin by a soldier, but the lone drink was a dim memory. He grabbed a handful of snow and put it in his mouth, but the melting iciness gave him little relief.

The snow was falling more heavily, or at least it seemed so to Pug; he couldn't see it fall, but it struck his face with more frequency and force. It was bitterly cold, and he shivered inside his cloak.

Like a booming call, the Duke's whisper sounded in the murk. "Stop. I doubt they are wandering about in the dark. We'll rest here."

Arutha's whisper could be heard from somewhere ahead: "The falling snow should cover our tracks by morning."

Pug dropped to his knees and pulled his cloak about himself. Tomas's voice sounded nearby. "Pug?"

Softly he answered, "Here."

Tomas dropped heavily beside him. "I think . . . ," he said between panting breaths, "I'll never . . . move again."

Pug could only nod. The Duke's voice came from a short distance away. "No fires."

Gardan answered, "It's a bitter night for a cold camp, Your Grace."

Borric said, "Agreed, but if those sons of hell are nearby, a fire would bring them howling down upon us. Huddle together for warmth, so no one will freeze. Post guards and tell the others to sleep. When dawn breaks, I want to put as much distance between ourselves and them as possible." Pug felt bodies begin to press around him and didn't mind the discomfort for the warmth. Soon he drifted off into a fitful doze, starting awake often during the night. Then suddenly it was dawn.

THREE MORE HORSES died during the night, their frozen bodies lying uncovered in the snow. Pug came to his feet, feeling light-headed and stiff. He shivered uncontrollably as he stamped his feet, trying to stir some life into his chilled, aching body. Tomas stirred, then awoke with a start, looking to see what was occurring. He climbed awkwardly to his feet, then joined Pug in stamping feet and swinging arms. "I've never been so cold in my life," he said through chattering teeth.

Pug looked around. They were in a hollow between large outcroppings of granite, still bare and grey in patches, which rose up behind them thirty feet into the air, joining a ridge above. The ground sloped away along the path of their march, and Pug noticed the trees were thinner here. "Come along," he said to Tomas as he began to scramble up the rocks.

"Damn!" sounded from behind, and Pug and Tomas looked back to see Gardan kneeling over the still form of a guard. The sergeant looked at the Duke and said, "Died in the night, Your Grace." He shook his head as he added, "He took a wound and never spoke of it."

Pug counted; besides himself, Tomas, Kulgan, the Duke, and his son, there were now just twelve soldiers. Tomas looked up at Pug, who had climbed ahead, and said, "Where are we going?"

Pug noticed he whispered. He inclined his head upward and said, "To see what's over there."

Tomas nodded, and they continued their climb. Stiff fingers protested against the need to grip hard rock, but soon Pug found himself warm again as exertion heated his body. He reached up and gripped the edge of the ridge above. He pulled himself up and over and waited for Tomas.

Tomas came over the ridge, panting for breath, looked past Pug, and said, "Oh, glory!"

Rising up majestically before them were the tall peaks of the Grey Towers. The sun rose behind, casting rose and golden highlights on the north faces of the mountains, while the western faces were still veiled in indigo darkness. The sky was clear, the snowfall over. Everywhere they looked, the scenery was draped in white.

Pug waved toward Gardan. The sergeant walked up to the base of the rocks, climbed a short way, and said, "What is it?" Pug said, "The Grey Towers! No more than five miles away."

Gardan waved for the boys to return, and they scrambled down, falling the last few feet to land with a thump. With their destination in sight, they felt revived. They came to where Gardan stood in conference with the Duke, Arutha, and Kulgan. Borric spoke softly, his words carrying clearly in the crisp morning air. "Take whatever is left on the dead animals and divide it among the men. Bring the remaining horses, but no one rides. No use covering the animals, for we'll make broad tracks anyway."

Gardan saluted and began circulating among the soldiers. They stood about in pairs or singly, eyes watching for signs of possible pursuit.

Borric said to Kulgan, "Have you an idea where the South Pass lies?"

"I will try to use my magic sight, my lord." Kulgan concentrated, and Pug watched closely, for seeing with the mind's eye was another of the feats that had eluded him in his studies. It was akin to using the crystal, but less pictorial, more an impression of where something was in relation to the spellcaster. After a few minutes of silence, Kulgan said, "I cannot tell, Sire. If I had been there before, then perhaps, but I get no impression of where the pass may lie."

Borric nodded. "I wish Longbow were here. He knows the landmarks of the area." He turned to the east, as if seeing the Grey Towers through the intervening ridge. "One mountain looks much like another to me."

Arutha said, "Father, to the north?"

Borric smiled a little at Arutha's logic. "Yes. If the pass lies northward, we still might chance across it before it is impassable. Once across the mountains, the weather will prove milder in the east—at least that is the rule this time of year. We should be able to walk to Bordon. If we are already north of the pass, then we will eventually reach the dwarves. They will shelter us and perhaps know another route to the east." He inspected his exhausted company. "With three horses and snow melted for drinking water, we should last another week." He looked around, studying the sky. "If the weather holds."

Kulgan said, "We should be free of bad weather in two, perhaps three days. Farther into the future I cannot judge." A distant shout echoed over the trees, from deep within the forest below. Instantly everyone was still. Borric looked to Gardan. "Sergeant, how far away do you judge them?"

Gardan listened. "It is hard to say, my lord. One mile, two, maybe more. Sound carries oddly in the forest, more so when it is this cold." Borric nodded. "Gather the men. We leave now."

PUG'S FINGERTIPS BLED through his torn gloves. At every opportunity during the day, the Duke had kept the men traveling over rock, to prevent Dark Brotherhood trackers from following. Every hour guards had been sent back to cut false trails over their own, pulling blankets taken from the dead horses behind, obscuring the tracks as best they could.

They stood at the edge of a clearing, a circle of bare rock surrounded on all sides by scattered pines and aspens. The trees had grown progressively thinner as they moved up into the mountains, staying on the rougher, higher terrain rather than risk being followed. Since dawn they had moved northeast, following a ridge of rugged hills toward the Grey Towers, but to Pug's dismay the mountains seemed no closer.

The sun stood high overhead, but Pug felt little of its warmth, for a cold wind blew down from the heights of the Grey Towers. Pug heard Kulgan's voice some distance behind. "As long as the wind is from the northeast, we'll have no snow, as any moisture will have fallen on the peaks. Should the wind shift and come from the west, or northwest, from off the Endless Sea, we'll have more snow."

Pug panted as he scrambled along the rocks, balancing on the slippery surface. "Kulgan, must we have lessons, too?"

Several men laughed, and momentarily the grim tension of the last two days lessened. They reached a large flat, before another upward rise, and the Duke ordered a halt. "Build a fire and slaughter an animal. We'll wait here for the last rear guard."

Gardan quickly sent men to gather wood in the trees, and one was given two of the horses to lead away. The high-strung mounts were footsore, tired, and unfed, and in spite of their training, Gardan wanted them removed from the smell of blood.

The chosen horse screamed, then was suddenly silent, and when the fires were ready, the soldiers placed spits over the flames. Soon the aroma of roasting meat filled the air. In spite of his anticipated distaste, Pug found his mouth watering at the smell. In a while he was handed a stick, with a large piece of roasted liver on it, which he wolfed down. Nearby, Tomas was doing equal justice to a portion of sizzling haunch.

When they were done eating, the still-hot meat left over was wrapped with strips from horse blankets and torn tabards, then divided among the men.

Pug and Tomas sat by Kulgan as men broke camp, putting out fires, covering signs of passing, and readying for the resumption of the march.

Gardan came to the Duke. "My lord, the rear guard is overdue."

Borric nodded. "I know. They should have returned a half hour ago." He peered down the hillside, toward the huge forest, mist shrouded in the distance. "We'll wait five more minutes, then we will go."

They waited in silence, but the guards didn't return. Finally Gardan gave the order. "All right, lads. Off we go."

The men formed up behind the Duke and Kulgan, and the boys fell in at the rear. Pug counted. There were only ten soldiers left.

TWO DAYS LATER the howling winds came, icy knives ripping at exposed flesh. Cloaks were gathered around each figure tramping slowly northward, leaning into the wind. Rags had been torn and tied around boots in a feeble attempt to hold off frostbite. Pug tried vainly to keep his eyelashes free of ice, but the harsh wind made his eyes tear, and the drops quickly froze, blurring his vision.

Pug heard Kulgan's voice above the wind. "My lord, a storm comes. We must find shelter or perish." The Duke nodded and waved two men ahead to seek shelter. The two set off at a stumbling run, moving only slightly faster than the others, but valiantly putting their remaining meager strength into the task.

Clouds began to roll in from the northwest, and the skies darkened. "How much time, Kulgan?" shouted the Duke over the shrieking wind.

The magician waved his hand above his head, as the wind blew his hair and beard back from his face, exposing his high forehead. "An hour at most." The Duke nodded again and exhorted his men to move along.

A sad sound, a neighing cry, pierced the wind, and a soldier called out that the last horse was down. Borric stopped and with a curse ordered it slaughtered as quickly as possible. Soldiers butchered the animal, steaming hunks of meat being cut away, to chill in the snow where they were cast before they could be wrapped. When they were done, the meat was divided among the men.

"If we can find shelter, we will build a fire and cook the meat," the Duke shouted.

Silently Pug added that if they couldn't find shelter, they'd have little use for the meat. They resumed their march.

A short time later the two guards returned with the news of a cave less than a quarter mile distant. The Duke ordered them to show the way.

Snow began to fall, whipped by the driving wind. The sky was now dark, limiting visibility to only a few hundred feet. Pug felt light-headed and had to struggle to pull his feet from the resisting snow. Both hands were numb, and he wondered if he was frostbitten.

Tomas looked slightly better, being somewhat hardier by nature, but he also was too exhausted to speak. He just plodded along beside his friend.

Suddenly Pug was lying face down in the snow feeling surprisingly warm and sleepy. Tomas knelt beside the fallen magician's apprentice. He shook Pug, and the nearly unconscious boy groaned.

"Get up," Tomas shouted. "It's only a little way farther."

Pug struggled upright, aided by Tomas and one of the soldiers. When he was standing, Tomas indicated to the soldier he could take care of his friend. The soldier nodded, but stayed near. Tomas loosened one of the many strips of blanket tied around him for warmth, knotted one end to Pug's belt, and half guided, half pulled the smaller boy along.

The boys followed the guard who had helped them around an outcropping of rock and found themselves at the mouth of a cave. They staggered forward a few steps into the sheltering darkness, then fell to the stone floor. In contrast to the biting wind outside, the cave seemed warm, and they lapsed into an exhausted sleep.

PUG AWOKE to the smell of cooking horse meat. He roused himself and saw it was dark outside, beyond the fire. Piles of branches and deadwood were heaped nearby, and men were carefully feeding the fire. Others stood by, roasting pieces of meat. Pug flexed his fingers and found them painfully sore, but as he peeled off his tattered gloves, he saw no signs of frostbite. He nudged Tomas awake, and the other boy raised himself up on his elbows, blinking at the firelight.

Gardan stood on the other side of the fire, speaking with a guard. The Duke sat nearby, in quiet conversation with his son and Kulgan. Beyond Gardan and the guard, Pug could see only blackness. He couldn't remember what time of day it had been when they found the cave, but he and Tomas must have slept for hours.

Kulgan saw them stirring and came over. "How do you feel?" he asked, a look of concern on his face. The boys indicated they felt all right, considering the circumstances. Pug and Tomas doffed their boots at Kulgan's orders, and he was pleased to report they had suffered no frostbite, though one of the soldiers, he said, hadn't been as lucky.

"How long were we asleep?" asked Pug.

"Throughout last night and all this day," said the magician with a sigh.

Then Pug noticed signs that a lot of work had been done. Besides the brush being cut, he and Tomas had been covered by some of the blankets. A pair of snared rabbits hung near the cave mouth with a row of freshly filled waterskins stacked near the fire. "You could have woken us," Pug said, a note of worry in his voice.

Kulgan shook his head. "The Duke wouldn't have moved until the storm had passed, and that was only a few hours ago. In any event, you and Tomas weren't the only tired ones here. I doubt even the hearty sergeant there could have gone more than another few miles with only one night's rest. The Duke will see how things stand tomorrow. I expect we shall leave then, if the weather holds."

Kulgan stood and, with a small gesture indicating the boys should return to sleep if possible, went to stand beside the Duke. Pug was surprised that, for someone who had slept the day around, he was again tired, though he thought he would fill his stomach before seeking more sleep. Tomas nodded at his unspoken question, and the two scooted over by the fire. One of the soldiers was busy cooking meat and handed them hot portions.

The boys wolfed down the food and after they were done sat back against one wall of the large cave. Pug started to speak to Tomas but was distracted when he caught sight of the guard by the cave's mouth. A queer look passed over the man's face as he stood talking to Sergeant Gardan, then his knees buckled. Gardan reached out to catch him, lowering him to the floor. The big sergeant's eyes widened as he saw the arrow protruding from the man's side.

Time seemed suspended for an instant, then Gardan shouted, "Attack!"

A howling cry sounded from outside the cave's mouth, and a figure came bounding into the light, jumping over the low brush, then again bounding over the fire, knocking down the soldier cooking meat. It landed a short way from the boys and spun to face those it had leapt past. It was wrapped in a coat and trousers of animal furs. On one arm it bore a battle-scarred buckler-size shield, and in the other a curved sword was held high.

Pug stayed motionless as the creature regarded the company in the cave, a snarl on inhuman lips, eyes glowing with reflected firelight and fangs bared. Tomas's training asserted itself, and the sword he had clung to over the long march was out of its scabbard in an instant. With a show the creature swung downward at Pug, who rolled sideways, avoiding the blow. The blade rang out as it struck the ground, and Tomas made an off-balance lunge, awkwardly taking the creature low in the chest. It fell to its knees and gurgled as blood filled its lungs, then fell forward.

Other attackers were leaping into the cave and were quickly engaged by the men from Crydee. Curses and oaths sounded, and swords rang out in the close confines of the cave. Guards and attackers stood face-to-face, unable to move more than a few feet. Several of the Duke's men dropped swords and pulled daggers from their belts, better for close fighting.

Pug grabbed his sword and looked for an attacker, but found none. In the dancing light of the fire, he could see the attackers were outnumbered by the remaining guards, and as two or three men of Crydee grappled with each attacker, it was quickly down and killed.

Suddenly the cave was quiet, save for the heavy breathing of the soldiers. Pug looked and saw only one man down, the one who had taken the arrow. A few others sported light wounds. Kulgan hurried among the men, checking the wounds, then said to the Duke, "My lord, we have no other serious injuries."

Pug looked at the dead creatures. Six of them lay sprawled upon the cave floor. They were smaller than men, but not by much. Above thick browridges, their sloping foreheads were topped by thick black hair. Their blue-green tinged skins were smooth, save for one who had something like a youth's beard upon his cheeks. Their eyes, open in death, were huge and round, with black irises on yellow. All died with snarls upon their hideous faces, showing long teeth that came close to being fangs.

Pug crossed to Gardan, peering into the gloom of the night for signs of more of the creatures. "What are they, Sergeant?"

"Goblins, Pug. Though I can't fathom what they are doing this far from their normal range."

The Duke came to stand next to him and said, "Only a half dozen, Gardan. I have never heard of goblins attacking armed men except when the advantage was theirs. This was suicide."

"My lord, look here," came Kulgan's call, as he knelt over the body of a goblin. He had pulled away the dirty fur jacket worn by the creature and pointed to a poorly bandaged long, jagged wound on its chest. "This was not made by us. It is three, four days old and healing badly."

Guards inspected the other bodies and reported three others also bore recent wounds, not caused by this fight. One had a broken arm and had fought without a shield.

Gardan said, "Sire, they wear no armor. Only the weapons in their hands." He pointed to a dead goblin with a bow slung over its back, and an empty quiver at its belt. "They had but the one arrow they used to wound Daniel."

Arutha glanced at the carnage. "This was madness. Hopeless madness."

Kulgan said, "Yes, Highness; madness. They were battle weary, freezing, and starved. The smell of cooking meat must have driven them mad. From their appearance I'd say they've not eaten in some time. They preferred to gamble all on one last, frantic assault than to watch us eat while they froze to death."

Borric looked at the goblins again, then ordered his men to take the bodies outside the cave. To no one in particular, he said, "But who have they been fighting?"

Pug said, "The Brotherhood?"

Borric shook his head. "They are the Brotherhood's creatures, or when not allied against us, they leave one another alone. No, it was someone else."

Tomas looked around as he joined those by the entrance. He wasn't as comfortable speaking to the Duke as Pug, but finally he said, "My lord, the dwarves?"

Borric nodded. "If there's been a dwarven raid on a nearby goblin village, it would explain why they were unarmored and unprovisioned. They would have grabbed the nearest weapons and fought their way free, fleeing at first chance. Yes, perhaps it was the dwarves."

The guards who had carried the bodies off into the snow ran back into the cave. "Your Grace," one of them said, "we hear movement in the trees."

Borric turned to the others. "Get ready!"

Every man in the cave quickly readied his weapons. Soon all could hear the tread of feet crunching through the icy snow. It grew louder as they waited, getting closer. Pug stood tensely, holding his sword, pushing down a churning feeling inside.

Suddenly the sounds of footfalls stopped, as those outside halted. Then the sound of a single pair of boots could be heard coming closer. Appearing out of the dark came a figure directly toward the cave. Pug craned his neck to see past the soldiers, and the Duke said, "Who passes this night?"

A short figure, no more than five feet tall, pulled back the hood of his cloak, revealing a metal helm sitting over a shock of thick brown hair. Two sparkling green eyes reflected the firelight. Heavy brows of brown-red hair came together at a point above a large hooked nose. The figure stood regarding the party, then signaled behind. More figures appeared from out of the night, and Pug pressed forward to get a better view, Tomas at his side. At the rear they could see several of the arrivals leading mules.

The Duke and soldiers visibly relaxed, and Tomas said, "They're dwarves!"

Several of the guards laughed, as did the closest dwarf. The dwarf fixed Tomas with a wry gaze, saying, "What were you expecting, boy? Some pretty dryad come to fetch you away?"

The lead dwarf walked into the firelight. He stopped before the Duke and said, "From your tabard, I see you to be men of Crydee." He struck himself upon the chest and said, formally, "I hight Dolgan, chief of village Caldara, and Warleader of the Grey Towers dwarven people." Pulling a pipe out of his cloak, from under a long beard that fell below his belt, he filled his pipe as he looked at the others in the cave. Then in less formal language he said, "Now, what in the name of the gods brings such a sorry-looking party of tall folk to this cold and forlorn place?"

9

▾▾

MAC MORDAIN CADAL

THE DWARVES STOOD GUARD.

Pug and the others from Crydee sat around the campfire as they hungrily ate the meal prepared by Dolgan's men. A pot of stew bubbled near the fire. Hot loaves of trail bread, thick hard crust broken to reveal dark sweet dough thick with honey, were quickly being devoured. Smoked fish, from the dwarves' pack animals, provided a welcome change from the diet of horse meat of the last few days.

Pug looked from where he sat beside Tomas, who was hard at work consuming his third portion of bread and stew. Pug watched as the dwarves worked efficiently about the camp. Most were outside the cave's mouth, for they seemed less inconvenienced by the cold than the humans. Two tended the injured man, who would live, while two others served the hot meal to the Duke's men, and another filled ale cups from a large skin filled with the bubbling brown liquid.

There were forty dwarves with Dolgan. The dwarven chief was flanked by his sons, Weylin, the older, and Udell. Both showed a striking resemblance to their father, though Udell tended to darkness, having black hair rather than red-brown. Both seemed quiet compared to their father, who gestured expansively with a pipe in one hand and a cup of ale in the other as he spoke with the Duke.

The dwarves had been on some sort of patrol along the edge of the forest, though Pug gained the impression a patrol this far from their villages was unusual. They had come across the tracks of the goblins who had attacked a few minutes before and were following closely behind, otherwise they would have missed the Duke's party as the night's storm obliterated all tracks of the men from Crydee's passage.

"I remember you, Lord Borric," said Dolgan, sipping at his ale cup, "though you were scarcely more than a baby when I was last at Crydee. I dined with your father. He set a fine table."

"And should you come again to Crydee, Dolgan, I hope you'll find my table equally satisfactory." They had spoken of the Duke's mission, and Dolgan had remained mostly silent during the preparation of the meal, lost in thought. Suddenly he regarded his pipe, which had gone out. He sighed forlornly, putting it away, until he noticed Kulgan had pulled out his own and was producing respectable clouds of smoke. Brightening visibly, he said, "Would you be having the requirement of an extra pipe upon you, master magician?" He spoke with the deep, rolling burr the dwarves made when speaking the King's Tongue.

Kulgan fetched out his tabac pouch and handed it across to the dwarf. "Providentially," said Kulgan, "my pipe and pouch are two items always kept upon my person at all times. I can withstand the loss of my other goods—though the loss of my two books troubles me deeply—but to endure any circumstance without the comfort of my pipe is unthinkable."

"Aye," agreed the dwarf as he lit up his own, "you have the right of it there. Except for autumn's ale—and my loving wife's company or a good fight, of course—there's little to match the pipe for pure pleasure." He drew forth a long pull and blew out a large cloud of smoke to emphasize his point. A thoughtful look crossed his rugged face, and he said, "Now to the matter of the news you carry. They are strange tidings, but explain away some mysteries we have been tussling with for some time now."

Borric said, "What mysteries?"

Dolgan pointed out of the cave mouth. "As we told you, we've had to patrol the area hereabouts. This is a new thing, for in years past the lands along the borders of our mines and farms have been free from trouble." He smiled. "Occasionally a band of especially bold bandits or moredhel—the Dark Brothers you call them—or a more than usually stupid tribe of goblins troubles us for a time. But for the most part things remain pretty peaceful.

"But of late, everything's gone agley. About a month ago, or a bit more, we began to see signs of large movements of moredhel and goblins from their villages to the north of ours. We sent some lads to investigate. They found entire villages abandoned, both goblin and moredhel. Some were sacked, but others stood empty without sign of trouble.

"Needless to say, the displacement of those miscreants caused an increase in problems for us. Our villages are in the higher meadows and plateaus, so they dare not attack, but they do raid our herds in the lower valleys as they pass—which is why we now mount patrols down the mountainside. With the winter upon us, our herds are in our lowest meadows, and we must keep vigilant.

"Most likely your messengers didn't reach our villages because of the large number of moredhel and goblins fleeing the mountains down into the forests. Now at least we've some gleaning of what's causing this migration."

The Duke nodded. "The Tsurani."

Dolgan was thoughtful for a moment, while Arutha said, "Then they're up there in strength."

Borric gave his son a questioning look, while Dolgan chuckled and said, "That's a bright lad you've got, Lord Borric." He nodded thoughtfully, then said, "Aye, Prince. They're up there, and in strength. Despite their other grievous faults, the moredhel are not without skill in warcraft." He fell silent again, lost in thought for a few minutes. Then, tapping out the dottle of his pipe, he said, "The dwarven folk are not counted the finest warriors in the West for naught, but we lack the numbers to dispose of our more troublesome neighbors. To dislodge such a host as have been passing would require a great force of men, well armed and provisioned."

Kulgan said, "I would give anything to know how they reached these mountains."

"I would rather know how many there are," said the Duke.

Dolgan refilled his pipe and, after it was lit, stared thoughtfully into the fire. Weylin and Udell nodded at each other, and Weylin said, "Lord Borric, there may be as many as five thousand."

Before the startled Duke could respond, Dolgan came out of his reverie. Swearing an oath, he said, "Closer to ten thousand!" He turned to look at the Duke, whose expression showed he clearly didn't understand what was being said. Dolgan added, "We've given every reason for this migration save invasion. Plague, internal warfare between bands, pests in their crops causing famine, but an invading army of aliens was not one of them.

"From the number of towns empty, we guess a few thousand goblins and moredhel have descended into the Green Heart. Some of those villages are a clutch of huts my two boys could overcome unaided. But others are walled hill forts, with a hundred, two hundred warriors to man the palisade. They've swept away a dozen such in little over a month. How many men do you judge you'd need to accomplish such a deed, Lord Borric?"

For the first time in his memory, Pug saw fear clearly etched upon the Duke's face. Borric leaned forward, his arm resting across his knee, as he said, "I've fifteen hundred men in Crydee, counting those in the frontier garrisons along the boundary. I can call another eight hundred or a thousand each from the garrisons at Carse and Tulan, though to do so would strip them fully. The levies from the villages and towns number at best a thousand, and most would be old veterans from the siege at Carse or young boys without skills."

Arutha looked as grim as his father as he said, "Forty-five hundred at the outside, a full third unproved, against an army of ten thousand."

Udell looked at his father, then at Lord Borric. "My father makes no boast of our skills, nor of the moredhel's, Your Grace. Whether there be five thousand or ten thousand, they'll be hard, experienced fighters to drive out the enemies of our blood so quickly."

"Then I'm thinking," said Dolgan, "you'd best send word to your older son and your vassal barons, telling them to stay safely behind the walls of your castles, and hie yourself to Krondor. It will take all the Armies of the West to withstand these newcomers this spring."

Tomas suddenly said, "Is it really that bad?" then looked embarrassed for interrupting the council. "I'm sorry, my lord."

Borric waved away the apology. "It may be we are weaving many threads of fear together into a larger tapestry than exists, but a good soldier prepares for the worst, Tomas. Dolgan is right. I must enlist the Prince's aid." He looked at Dolgan. "But to call the Armies of the West to arms, I must reach Krondor."

Dolgan said, "The South Pass is closed, and your human ships' masters have too much sense to brave the Straits of Darkness in winter. But there is another way, though it is a difficult path. There are mines throughout these mountains, ancient tunnels under the Grey Towers. Many were carved by my people as we dug for iron and gold. Some are natural, fashioned when the mountains were born. And still others were here when my people first came to these mountains, dug by only the gods know whom. There is one mine that passes completely under the mountains, coming out on the other side of the range, only a day's march from the road to Bordon. It will take two days to pass through, and there may be dangers."

The dwarven brothers looked at their father, and Weylin said, "Father, the Mac Mordain Cadal?"

Dolgan nodded his head. "Aye, the abandoned mine of my grandfather, and his father before him." He said to the Duke, "We have dug many miles of tunnels under the mountain, and some connect with the ancient passages I have spoken of. There are dark and queer tales about Mac Mordain Cadal, for it is connected with these old passages. Not a few dwarves have ventured deep into the old mines, seeking legendary riches, and most have returned. But a few have vanished. Once upon a path, a dwarf can never lose his way back, so they were not lost in their searching. Something must have befallen them. I tell you this so there will be no misunderstandings, but if we keep to the passages dug by my ancestors, we should have small risk."

" 'We,' friend dwarf?" said the Duke.

Dolgan grinned. "Should I simply place your feet upon the path, you'd be hopelessly lost within an hour. No, I'd care not for traveling to Rillanon to explain to your King how I'd managed to lose one of his better Dukes. I will guide you willingly, Lord Borric, for a small price." He winked at Pug and Tomas as he spoke the last. "Say, a pouch of tabac and a fine dinner at Crydee."

The Duke's mood lightened a little. With a smile he said, "Done, and our thanks, Dolgan."

The dwarf turned to his sons. "Udell, you take half the company and one of the mules, and the Duke's men too ill or wounded to continue. Make for the castle at Crydee. There's an ink horn and quill, wrapped in parchment, somewhere in our baggage; find it for his lordship, so he may instruct his men. Weylin, take the others of our kin back to Caldara, then send word to the other villages before the winter blizzards strike. Come spring, the dwarves of the Grey Towers go to war."

Dolgan looked at Borric. "No one has ever conquered our highland villages, not in the longest memory of the dwarven folk. But it would prove an irritation for someone to try. The dwarves will stand with the Kingdom, Your Lordship. You have long been a friend to us, trading fairly and giving aid when asked. And we have never run from battle when we were called."

Arutha said, "And what of Stone Mountain?"

Dolgan laughed. "I thank His Highness for the jog to my memory. Old Harthorn and his clans would be sorely troubled should a good fight come and they were not invited. I'll send runners to Stone Mountain as well."

Pug and Tomas watched while the Duke wrote messages to Lyam and Fannon, then full stomachs and fatigue began to lull them, despite their long sleep. The dwarves gave them the loan of heavy cloaks, which they wrapped about pine boughs to make comfortable mattresses. Occasionally Pug would turn in the night, coming out of his deep sleep, and hear voices speaking low. More than once he heard the name Mac Mordain Cadal.

DOLGAN LED the Duke's party along the rocky foothills of the Grey Towers. They had left at first light, the dwarven chieftain's sons departing for their own destinations with their men. Dolgan walked before the Duke and his son, followed by the puffing Kulgan and the boys. Five soldiers of Crydee, those still able to continue, under the supervision of Sergeant Gardan followed behind, leading two mules. Walking behind the struggling magician, Pug said, "Kulgan, ask for a rest. You're all done in."

The magician said, "No, boy, I'll be all right. Once into the mines, the pace will slow, and we should be there soon."

Tomas regarded the stocky figure of Dolgan, marching along at the head of the party, short legs striding along, setting a rugged pace. "Doesn't he ever tire?"

Kulgan shook his head. "The dwarven folk are renowned for their strong constitutions. At the Battle of Carse Keep, when the castle was nearly taken by the Dark Brotherhood, the dwarves of Stone Mountain and the Grey Towers were on the march to aid the besieged. A messenger carried the news of the castle's imminent fall, and the dwarves ran for a day and a night and half a day again to fall on the Brotherhood from behind without any lessening of their fighting ability. The Brotherhood was broken, never again organizing under a single leader." He panted a bit. "There was no idle boasting in Dolgan's appraisal of the aid forthcoming from the dwarves, for they are undoubtedly the finest fighters in the West. While they have few numbers compared to men, only the Hadati hillmen come close to their equal as mountain fighters."

Pug and Tomas looked with newfound respect upon the dwarf as he strode along. While the pace was brisk, the meal of the night before and another this morning had restored the flagging energies of the boys, and they were not pushed to keep up.

They came to the mine entrance, overgrown with brush. The soldiers cleared it away, revealing a wide, low tunnel. Dolgan turned to the company. "You might have to duck a bit here and there, but many a mule has been led through here by dwarven miners. There should be ample room."

Pug smiled. The dwarves proved taller than tales had led him to expect, averaging about four and a half to five feet tall. Except for being short-legged and broad-shouldered, they looked much like other people.

It was going to be a tight fit for the Duke and Gardan, but Pug was only a few inches taller than the dwarf, so he'd manage.

Gardan ordered torches lit, and when the party was ready, Dolgan led them into the mine. As they entered the gloom of the tunnel, the dwarf said, "Keep alert, for only the gods know what is living in these tunnels. We should not be troubled, but it is best to be cautious."

Pug entered and, as the gloom enveloped him, looked over his shoulder. He saw Gardan outlined against the receding light. For a brief instant he thought of Carline, and Roland, then wondered how she could seem so far removed so quickly, or how indifferent he was to his rival's attentions. He shook his head, and his gaze returned to the dark tunnel ahead.

THE TUNNELS were damp. Every once in a while they would pass a tunnel branching off to one side or the other. Pug peered down each as he passed, but they were quickly swallowed up in gloom. The torches sent flickering shadows dancing on the walls, expanding and contracting as they moved closer or farther from each other, or as the ceiling rose or fell. At several places they had to pull the mules' heads down, but for most of their passage there was ample room.

Pug heard Tomas, who walked in front of him, mutter, "I'd not want to stray down here; I've lost all sense of direction." Pug said nothing, for the mines had an oppressive feeling to him.

After some time they came to a large cavern with several tunnels leading out. The column halted, and the Duke ordered watches to be posted. Torches were wedged in the rocks and the mules watered. Pug and Tomas stood with the last watch, and Pug thought a hundred times that shapes moved just outside the fire's glow. Soon guards came to replace them, and the boys joined the others, who were eating. They were given dried meat and biscuits to eat. Tomas asked Dolgan, "What place is this?"

The dwarf puffed on his pipe. "It is a glory hole, laddie. When my people mined this area, we fashioned many such places. When great runs of iron, gold, silver, and other metals would come together, many tunnels would be joined. And as the metals were taken out, these caverns would be formed. There are natural ones down here as large, but the look of them is different. They have great spires of stone rising from the floor, and others hanging from the ceiling, unlike this one. You'll see one as we pass through."

Tomas looked above him. "How high does it go?"

Dolgan looked up. "I can't rightly say. Perhaps a hundred feet, perhaps two or three times as much. These mountains are rich with metals still, but when my grandfather's grandfather first mined here, the metal was rich beyond imagining. There are hundreds of tunnels throughout these mountains, with many levels upward and downward from here. Through that tunnel there"—he pointed to another on the same level as the floor of the glory hole—"lies a tunnel that will join with another tunnel, then yet another. Follow that one, and you'll end up in the Mac Bronin Alroth, another abandoned mine. Beyond that you could make your way to the Mac Owyn Dur, where several of my people would be inquiring how you managed entrance into their gold mine." He laughed. "Though I doubt you could find the way, unless you were dwarven born."

He puffed at his pipe, and the balance of the guards came over to eat. Dolgan said, "Well, we had best be on our way."

Tomas looked startled. "I thought we were stopping for the night."

"The sun is yet high in the sky, laddie. There's half the day left before we sleep."

"But I thought . . ."

"I know. It is easy to lose track of time down here, unless you have the knack of it."

They gathered together their gear and started off again. After more walking they entered a series of twisting, turning passages that seemed to slant down. Dolgan explained that the entrance on the east side of the mountains was several hundred feet lower than on the west, and they would be moving downward most of the journey.

Later they passed through another of the glory holes, smaller than the last, but still impressive for the number of tunnels leading from it. Dolgan picked one with no hesitation and led them through.

Soon they could hear the sound of water, coming from ahead. Dolgan said, over his shoulder, "You'll soon see a sight that no man living and few dwarves have ever seen."

As they walked, the sound of rushing water became louder. They entered another cavern, this one natural and larger than the first by several times. The tunnel they had been walking in became a ledge, twenty feet wide, that ran along the right side of the cavern. They all peered over the edge and could see nothing but darkness stretching away below.

The path rounded a curve in the wall, and when they passed around it, they were greeted with a sight that made them all gasp. Across the cavern, a mighty waterfall spilled over a huge outcropping of stone. From fully three hundred feet above where they stood, it poured into the cavern, crashing down the stone face of the opposite wall to disappear into the darkness below. It filled the cavern with reverberations that made it impossible to hear it striking bottom, confounding any attempt to judge the fall's height. Throughout the cascade luminous colors danced, aglow with an inner light. Reds, golds, greens, blues, and yellows played among the white foam, falling along the wall, blazing with brief flashes of intense luminosity where the water struck the wall, painting a fairy picture in the darkness.

Dolgan shouted over the roar, "Ages ago the river Wynn-Ula ran from the Grey Towers to the Bitter Sea. A great quake opened a fissure under the river, and now it falls into a mighty underground lake below. As it runs through the rocks, it picks up the minerals that give it its glowing colors." They stood quietly for a while, marveling at the sight of the falls of Mac Mordain Cadal.

The Duke signaled for the march to resume, and they moved on. Besides the spectacle of the falls, they had been refreshed by spray and cool wind off them, for the caverns were dank and musty. Onward they went, deeper into the mines, past numberless tunnels and passages. After a time, Gardan asked the boys how they fared. Pug and Tomas both answered that they were fine, though tired.

Later they came to yet another cavern, and Dolgan said it was time to rest the night. More torches were lit, and the Duke said, "I hope we have enough brands to last the journey. They burn quickly."

Dolgan said, "Give me a few men, and I will fetch some old timbers for a fire. There are many lying about if you know where to find them without bringing the ceiling down upon your head."

Gardan and two other men followed the dwarf into a side tunnel, while the others unloaded the mules and staked them out. They were given water from the waterskins and a small portion of grain carried for the times when they could not graze.

Borric sat next to Kulgan. "I have had an ill feeling for the last few hours. Is it my imagining, or does something about this place bode evil?"

Kulgan nodded as Arutha joined them. "I have felt something also, but it comes and goes. It is nothing I can put a name to."

Arutha hunkered down and used his dagger to draw aimlessly in the dirt. "This place would give anyone a case of the jumping fits and starts. Perhaps we all feel the same thing: dread at being where men do not belong."

The Duke said, "I hope that is all it is. This would be a poor place to fight"—he paused—"or flee from." The boys stood watch, but could overhear the conversation, as could the other men, for no one else was speaking in the cavern and the sound carried well. Pug said in a hushed voice, "I will also be glad to be done with this mine."

Tomas grinned in the torchlight, his face set in an evil leer. "Afraid of the dark, little boy?"

Pug snorted. "No more than you, should you but admit it. Do you think you could find your way out?"

Tomas lost his smile. Further conversation was interrupted by the return of Dolgan and the others. They carried a good supply of broken timbers, used to shore up the passages in days gone by. A fire was quickly made from the old, dry wood, and soon the cavern was brightly lit.

The boys were relieved of guard duty and ate. As soon as they were done eating, they spread their cloaks. Pug found the hard dirt floor uncomfortable, but he was very tired, and sleep soon overtook him.

THEY LED the mules deeper into the mines, the animal's hooves clattering on the stone, the sound echoing down the dark tunnels. They had walked the entire day, taking only a short rest to eat at noon. Now they were approaching the cavern where Dolgan said they were to spend their second night. Pug felt a strange sensation, as if remembering a cold chill. It had touched him several times over the last hour, and he was worried. Each time he had turned to look behind him. This time Gardan said, "I feel it too, boy, as if something is near."

They entered another large glory hole, and Dolgan stood with his hand upraised. All movement ceased as the dwarf listened for something. Pug and Tomas strained to hear as well, but no sounds came to them. Finally the dwarf said, "For a time I thought I heard . . . but then I guess not. We will camp here." They had carried spare timber with them and used it to make a fire.

When Pug and Tomas left their watch, they found a subdued party around the fire. Dolgan was saying, "This part of Mac Mordain Cadal is closest to the deeper, ancient tunnels. The next cavern we come to will have several that lead directly to the old mines. Once past that cavern, we will have a speedy passage to the surface. We should be out of the mine by midday tomorrow."

Borric looked around. "This place may suit your nature, dwarf, but I will be glad to have it behind."

Dolgan laughed, the rich, hearty sound echoing off the cavern walls. "It is not that the place suits my nature, Lord Borric, but rather that my nature suits the place. I can travel easily under the mountains, and my folk have ever been miners. But as to choice, I would rather spend my time in the high pastures of Caldara tending my herd, or sit in the long hall with my brethren, drinking ale and singing ballads."

Pug asked, "Do you spend much time singing ballads?"

Dolgan fixed him with a friendly smile, his eyes shining in the firelight. "Aye. For winters are long and hard in the mountains. Once the herds are safely in winter pasture, there is little to do, so we sing our songs and drink autumn ale, and wait for spring. It is a good life."

Pug nodded. "I would like to see your village sometime, Dolgan."

Dolgan puffed on his ever-present pipe. "Perhaps you will someday, laddie."

They turned in for the night, and Pug drifted off to sleep. Once in the dead of night, when the fire had burned low, he awoke, feeling the chilling sensation that had plagued him earlier. He sat up, cold sweat dripping down his body, and looked around. He could see the guards who were on duty, standing near their torches. Around him he saw the forms of sleeping bodies. The feeling grew stronger for a moment, as if something dreadful was approaching, and he was about to wake Tomas when it passed, leaving him tired and wrung out. He lay back down and soon was lost in dreamless sleep.

HE AWOKE COLD and stiff. The guards were readying the mules, and soon they would all leave. Pug roused Tomas, who protested at being pulled from his dream. "I was in the kitchen at home, and Mother was preparing a large platter of sausages and corn cakes dripping with honey," he said sleepily.

Pug threw a biscuit at him. "This will have to do until Bordon. Then we shall eat."

They gathered together their meager provisions, loaded them on the mules, and set off. As they made their way along, Pug began to experience the icy feeling of the night before. Several times it came and went. Hours passed, and they came to the last great cave. Here Dolgan stopped them while he looked into the gloom. Pug could hear him saying, "For a moment I thought . . ."

Suddenly the hairs on Pug's neck stood up, and the feeling of icy terror swept over him, more horrible than before. "Dolgan, Lord Borric!" he cried. "Something terrible is happening!"

Dolgan stood stock-still, listening. A faint moan echoed from down another tunnel.

Kulgan shouted, "I feel something also."

Suddenly the sound repeated, closer, a chilling moan that echoed off the vaulted ceiling, making its origins uncertain.

"By the gods!" shouted the dwarf. "'Tis a wraith! Hurry! Form a circle, or it will be upon us and we'll be lost."

Gardan pushed the boys forward, and the guards moved the mules to the center of the cavern. They quickly staked the two mules down and formed a circle around the frantic animals. Weapons were drawn. Gardan placed himself before the two boys, forcing them back near the mules. Both had swords out, but held them uncertainly. Tomas could feel his heart pound, and Pug was bathed in cold sweat. The terror that gripped him had not increased since Dolgan had put a name to it, but it had not lessened either.

They heard the sharp hiss of intaken breath and looked to the right. Before the soldier who had made the sound, a figure loomed out of the darkness: a shifting man-shape, darker blackness against the black, with two glowing, red-coal lights where eyes should be.

Dolgan shouted, "Keep close, and guard your neighbor. You can't kill it, but they like not the feel of cold iron. Don't let it touch you, for it'll draw your life from your body. It is how they feed."

It approached them slowly as if having no need to hurry. It stopped for a moment, as if inspecting the defense before it.

The wraith let out another low, long moan, sounding like all the terror and hopelessness of the world given voice. Suddenly one of the guards struck downward, slashing at the wraith. A shrill moan erupted from the creature when the sword hit, and cold blue fire danced along the blade for a moment. The creature shrank away, then with sudden speed struck out at the guard. An armlike shadow extended from its body, and the guard shrieked as he crumpled to the ground.

The mules broke, pulling up stakes, terrified by the presence of the wraith. Guards were knocked to the ground, and confusion reigned. Pug lost sight of the wraith for a moment, being more concerned with flying hooves. As the mules kicked, Pug found himself dodging through the melee. He heard Kulgan's voice behind him and saw the magician standing next to Prince Arutha. "Stand close, all of you," the magician commanded. Obeying, Pug closed to Kulgan with the others as the scream of another guard echoed through the gallery. Within a moment a great cloud of white smoke began to appear around them, issuing from Kulgan's body. "We must leave the mules," said the magician. "The undead will not enter the smoke, but I cannot keep it together long or walk far. We must escape now!"

Dolgan pointed to a tunnel, on the other side of the cavern from where they had entered. "That's the way we must go." Keeping close together, the group started toward the tunnel while a terrified bray sounded. Bodies lay on the floor: the two mules as well as the fallen guards. Dropped torches flickered, giving the scene a nightmarish quality, as the black shape closed upon the party. Reaching the edge of the smoke, it recoiled from its touch. It ranged about the edge, unable or unwilling to enter the white smoke.

Pug looked past the creature, and the pit of his stomach churned.

Clearly standing in the light of a torch held in his hand was Tomas, behind the creature. Tomas looked helplessly past the wraith at Pug and the escaping party. "Tomas!" ripped from Pug's throat, followed by a sob.

The party halted for a brief second, and Dolgan said, "We can't stop. We'd all perish for the sake of the boy. We must press on." A firm hand clutched at Pug's shoulder as he started forward to aid his friend. He looked back and saw that it was Gardan holding him. "We must leave him, Pug," he said, a grim expression on his ebony face. "Tomas is a soldier. He understands." Pug was pulled along helplessly. He saw the wraith follow along for a moment, then stop and turn toward Tomas.

Whether alerted by Pug's cries or by some evil sense, the undead creature started toward Tomas, slowly stalking him. The boy hesitated, then spun and ran to another tunnel. The wraith shrieked and started after him. Pug saw the glow of Tomas's torch disappear down the tunnel, then flicker into blackness.

Tomas saw the pained expression on Pug's face as Gardan pulled his friend away. When the mules had broken, he had dodged away from the others and now found himself separated from them. He looked for a way to circle around the wraith, but it was too close to the passage his companions were taking. As Kulgan and the others escaped up the tunnel, Tomas saw the wraith turn toward him. It started to approach, and he hesitated a moment, then ran toward a different tunnel.

Shadows and light danced madly on the walls as Tomas fled down the passage, his footfalls echoing in the gloom. His torch was held tightly in his left hand, the sword clutched in his right. He looked over his shoulder and saw the two glowing red eyes pursuing him, though they seemed not to be gaining. With grim determination he thought, if it catches me, it will catch the fastest runner in all of Crydee. He lengthened his strides into a long, easy lope, saving strength and wind. He knew that if he had to turn and face the creature, he would surely die. The initial fear lessened, and now he felt a cold clarity holding his mind, the cunning reason of a prey knowing it is hopeless to fight. All his energy was turned toward fleeing. He would try to lose the creature any way possible.

He ducked into a side corridor and hurried along it, checking to see if the wraith would follow. The glowing red eyes appeared at the entrance to the tunnel he had turned into, following him. The distance between them seemed to have increased. The thought that many might have died at the thing's hand because they were too frightened to run crossed his mind. The wraith's strength lay in the numbing terror it caused.

Another corridor and another turn. Still the wraith followed. Ahead lay a large cavern, and Tomas found himself entering the same hall in which the wraith had attacked the party. He had circled around and entered through another tunnel. Racing across the floor, he saw the bodies of mules and guards lying in his path. He paused long enough to grab a fresh torch, for his was nearly spent, and transferred the flame.

He looked backward to see the undead creature closing on him and started off again. Hope briefly flickered in his breast, for if he could pick the proper corridor, he might catch up to the others. Dolgan had said that from this cavern it was a straight journey to the surface. He picked what he thought was the proper one, though he was disoriented and couldn't be sure.

The wraith let out a howl of rage at its prey's eluding it again, and followed. Tomas felt terror bordering on elation as his long legs stretched out, eating up the distance ahead of him. He gained his second wind and set a steady pace for himself. Never had he run so well, but then never had he possessed such a reason.

After what seemed an endless time of running, he found himself coming to a series of side tunnels, set closely together. He felt hope die, for this was not the straight path the dwarf had mentioned. Picking one at random, he turned into a passage and found more tunnels close by. Cutting through several more, he turned as quickly as possible, weaving his way through a maze of passages. Ducking around a wall formed between two such tunnels, he stopped briefly and caught his breath. He listened for a moment and heard only the sound of his pounding heart. He had been too busy to look behind and was unsure of the wraith's whereabouts.

Suddenly a shriek of rage echoed faintly down the corridors, sounding far off. Tomas sank to the floor of the tunnel and felt his body go limp. Another shriek echoed more faintly, and Tomas felt certain that the wraith had lost his trail and was moving off in another direction.

A sense of relief flooded through him, nearly causing him to laugh giddily. It was closely followed by the sudden realization of his situation. He sat up and took stock. If he could find his way back to the dead animals, he would at least have food and water. But as he stood up, he realized that he had no notion which way the cavern lay. Cursing himself for not counting the turns as he had made them, he tried to remember the general pattern he had followed. He had turned mostly to the right, he reminded himself, so if he retraced his steps mostly to the left, he should be able to find one of the many tunnels that led to the glory hole. Looking cautiously around the first corner, Tomas set off, searching his way through the maze of passages.

After an unknown time had passed, Tomas stopped and looked around in the second large cavern he had come to since he had fled the wraith. Like the first, this cavern was devoid of mules and men—and the hoped-for food and water. Tomas opened his pouch and took out the small biscuit he had hoarded to nibble while walking. It gave him little relief from his hunger.

When he was done, he set off again, trying to find some clue to the way out. He knew he had only a short time before his torch died, but he refused to simply sit and wait for a nameless death in the dark.

After some time Tomas could hear the sound of water echoing through the tunnel. Hurrying forward, his thirst spurring him on, he entered a large cavern, the biggest yet, as far as he could tell. Far away he could hear the faint roar of the Mac Mordain Cadal falls, but in which direction he couldn't be sure. Somewhere high in the darkness lay the path that they had taken two days earlier. Tomas felt his heart sink, he had moved deeper into the earth than he had thought.

The tunnel widened to a landing of some sort and disappeared beneath what appeared to be a large lake, constantly lapping against the sides of the cavern, filling it with muted echoes. Quickly he fell to his knees and drank. The water tasted rich with minerals, but was clear and fresh.

Sitting back on his haunches, he looked about. The landing was packed earth and sand and appeared to be fashioned rather than natural. Tomas guessed the dwarves might have used boats to cross the underground lake, but could only wonder what lay on the other side. Then the thought hit him that perhaps someone other than the dwarves had used boats to cross the lake, and he felt fear again.

To his left he spied a pile of wood, nestled against a junction of the landing and the cavern wall. Crossing to it, he pulled out several pieces and started a small fire. The wood was mostly timber pieces, used to shore up the tunnels, but mixed in were several branches and twigs. They must have been brought down by the falls from above, where the river enters the mountain, he thought. Underneath the pile he found some fibrous weeds growing. Wondering at the plants' ability to grow without sunlight, the boy was nevertheless thankful, for after cutting them with his sword, he was able to fashion some rude torches with the weeds wrapped around some driftwood. He tied them in a bundle, using his sword belt, forcing him to give up his scabbard. At least, he thought, I'll have a little more light. Some extra time to see where he was going was comforting.

He threw some bigger timber pieces on his small fire, and soon it was roaring into brightness. Abruptly the cavern seemed to light up, and Tomas spun around. The entire cavern was glowing with sparkling light, as some sort of mineral, or crystal, caught the light and reflected it to be caught and reflected again. It was a glittering, sparkling rainbow of colors cascading over walls and ceiling, giving the entire cavern a fairy-like quality as far as the eye could follow.

Tomas stood in awe for a minute, drinking in the sight, for he knew he would never be able to explain in words what he was seeing. The thought struck him that he might be the only human ever to have witnessed the display.

It was hard to tear his eyes from the glory of the vision, but Tomas forced himself. He used the extra illumination to examine the area he was in. There was nothing beyond the landing, but he did spy another tunnel off to the left, leaving the cavern at the far end of the sand.

He gathered together his torches and walked along the landing. As he reached the tunnel, his fire died down, the dry timber being quickly consumed. Another glorious vision assaulted his senses, for the gemlike walls and ceiling continued to glimmer and glow. Again he stood silently watching the display. Slowly the sparkling dimmed, until the cavern was again dark, except for his torch and the quickly dying fire's red glow.

He had to stretch to reach the other tunnel, but made it without dropping his sword or torches, or getting his boots wet. Turning away from the cavern, he resumed his journey.

He made his way for hours, the torch burning lower. He lit one of the new ones and found that it gave a satisfactory light. He was still frightened, but felt good about keeping his head under these conditions and was sure Swordmaster Fannon would approve of his actions.

After walking for a while, he came to an intersection. He found the bones of a creature in the dust, its fate unknowable. He spotted the tracks of some other small creature leading away, but they were faint with age. With no other notion than the need for a clear path, Tomas followed them. Soon they also vanished in the dust.

He had no means to reckon time, but thought that it must be well into night by now. There was a timeless feeling to these passages, and he felt lost beyond recovery. Fighting down what he recognized as budding panic, he continued to walk. He kept his mind on pleasant memories of home, and dreams of the future. He would find a way out, and he would become a great hero in the coming war. And most cherished dream of all, he would journey to Elvandar and see the beautiful lady of the elves again.

He followed the tunnel downward. This area seemed different from the other caverns and tunnels, its manner of fashioning unlike the others. He thought that Dolgan could tell if this was so, and who had done the work.

He entered another cavern and looked around. Some of the tunnels that entered the cavern were barely tall enough for a man to walk through upright. Others were broad enough for a company of men to walk through ten abreast, with long spears upon their shoulders. He hoped this meant the dwarves had fashioned the smaller tunnels and he could follow one upward, back to the surface.

Looking around, he spied a likely ledge to rest upon, within jumping distance. He crossed to it and tossed up his sword and the bundle of torches. He then gently tossed up his torch, so as not to put it out, and pulled himself up. It was large enough to sleep upon without rolling off. Four feet up the wall was a small hole, about three feet in diameter. Looking down it, Tomas could see that it opened up quickly to a size large enough to stand in and stretched away into blackness.

Satisfied that nothing lurked immediately above him, and that anything coming from below would awaken him, Tomas pulled his cloak around him, rested his head on his hand, and put out the torch. He was frightened, but the exhaustion of the day lulled him quickly to sleep. He lay in fitful dreams of red glowing eyes chasing him down endless black corridors, terror washing over him. He ran until he came to a green place where he could rest, feeling safe, under the gaze of a beautiful woman with red-gold hair and pale blue eyes.

He started awake to some nameless call. He had no idea of how long he had slept, but he felt as if it had been long enough for his body to run again, if need be. He felt in the dark for his torch and took flint and steel from out of his pouch. He struck sparks into the wadding of the torch and started a glow. Quickly bringing the torch close, he blew the spark into flame. Looking about, he found the cavern unchanged. A faint echoing of his own movements was all he heard.

He realized he could have a chance of survival only if he kept moving and found a way up. He stood and was about to climb down from the ledge when a faint noise sounded from the hole above.

He peered down it but could see nothing. Again there came a faint sound, and Tomas strained to hear what it was. It was almost like the tread of footfalls, but he could not be sure. He nearly shouted, but held off, for there was no assurance it was his friends returned to find him. His imagination provided many other possibilities, all of them unpleasant.

He thought for a moment, then decided. Whatever was making the noise might lead him out of the mines, even if only by providing a trail to follow. With no other option appearing more attractive, he pulled himself up through the small hole, entering the new tunnel.

10

▾▾

RESCUE

IT WAS A DISPIRITED GROUP THAT EMERGED FROM THE MINE.

The survivors sank to the ground, near exhaustion. Pug had fought tears for hours after Tomas had fled, and now he lay on the wet ground staring upward at the grey sky, feeling numb. Kulgan had fared worst of all, being completely drained of energy by the spell used to repel the wraith. He had been carried on the shoulders of the others most of the way, and they showed the price of their burden. All fell into an exhausted sleep, except Dolgan, who lit a fire and stood watch.

Pug awoke to the sound of voices and a clear, starry night. The smell of food cooking greeted him. When Gardan and the three remaining guards awakened, Dolgan had left them to watch over the others and had snared a brace of rabbits. These were roasting over a fire. The others awoke, except Kulgan, who snored deeply.

Arutha and the Duke saw the boy wake, and the Prince came to where he sat. The younger son of the Duke, ignoring the snow, sat on the ground next to Pug, who had his cloak wrapped around him. "How do you feel, Pug?" Arutha asked, concern showing in his eyes.

This was the first time Pug had seen Arutha's gentler nature. Pug tried to speak and found tears coming to his eyes. Tomas had been his friend as long as he could remember, more a brother than a friend. As he tried to speak, great racking sobs broke from his throat, and he felt hot, salty tears run down into his mouth.

Arutha placed his arm around Pug, letting the boy cry on his shoulder. When the initial flood of grief had passed, the Prince said, "There is nothing shameful in mourning the loss of a friend, Pug. My father and I share your pain."

Dolgan came to stand behind the Prince. "I also, Pug, for he was a likable lad. We all share your loss." The dwarf seemed to consider something and spoke to the Duke.

Kulgan had just awakened, sitting up like a bear waking from winter's sleep. He regained his bearings and, seeing Arutha with Pug, quickly forgot his own aching joints and joined them.

There was little they could say, but Pug found comfort in their closeness. He finally regained his composure and pulled away from the Prince. "Thank you, Your Highness," he said, sniffing. "I will be all right."

They joined Dolgan, Gardan, and the Duke near the fire. Borric was shaking his head at something the dwarf had said. "I thank you for your bravery, Dolgan, but I can't allow it."

Dolgan puffed on his pipe, a friendly smile splitting his beard. "And how do you intend to stop me, Your Grace? Surely not by force?"

Borric shook his head. "No, of course not. But to go would be the sheerest folly."

Kulgan and Arutha exchanged questioning looks. Pug paid little attention, being lost in a cold, numb world. In spite of having just awakened, he felt ready for sleep again, welcoming its warm, soft relief.

Borric told them, "This mad dwarf means to return to the mines."

Before Kulgan and Arutha could voice a protest, Dolgan said, "I know it is only a slim hope, but if the boy has eluded the foul spirit, he'll be wandering lost and alone. There are tunnels down there that have never known the tread of a dwarf's foot, let alone a boy's. Once down a passage, I have no trouble making my way back, but Tomas has no such natural sense. If I can find his trail, I can find him. If he is to have any chance of escaping the mines, he'll be needing my guidance. I'll bring home the boy if he lives, on this you have the word of Dolgan Tagarson, chief of village Caldara. I could not rest in my long hall this winter if I did not try."

Pug was roused from his lethargy by the dwarf's words. "Do you think you can find him, Dolgan?"

"If any can, I can," he said. He leaned close to Pug. "Do not get your hopes too high, for it is unlikely that Tomas eluded the wraith. I would do you a disservice if I said otherwise, boy." Seeing the tears brimming in Pug's eyes again, he quickly added, "But if there is a way, I shall find it."

Pug nodded, seeking a middle path between desolation and renewed hope. He understood the admonition, but still could not give up the faint flicker of comfort Dolgan's undertaking would provide.

Dolgan crossed over to where his shield and ax lay and picked them up. "When the dawn comes, quickly follow the trail down the hills through the woodlands. While not the Green Heart, this place has menace aplenty for so small a band. If you lose your way, head due east. You'll find your way to the road to Bordon. From there it is a matter of three days' walk. May the gods protect you."

Borric nodded, and Kulgan walked over to where the dwarf made ready to leave. He handed Dolgan a pouch. "I can get more tabac in the town, friend dwarf. Please take this."

Dolgan took it and smiled at Kulgan. "Thank you, magician. I am in your debt."

Borric came to stand before the dwarf and place a hand on his shoulder. "It is we who are in your debt, Dolgan. If you come to Crydee, we will have that meal you were promised. That, and more. May good fortune go with you."

"Thank you, Your Lordship. I'll look forward to it." Without another word, Dolgan walked into the blackness of Mac Mordain Cadal.

DOLGAN STOPPED by the dead mules, pausing only long enough to pick up food, water, and a lantern. The dwarf needed no light to make his way underground—his people had long ago adapted other senses for the darkness. But, he thought, it will increase the chances of finding Tomas if the boy can see the light, no matter the risk of attracting unwelcome attention. Assuming he is still alive, he added grimly.

Entering the tunnel where he had last seen Tomas, Dolgan searched about for signs of the boy's passing. The dust was thin, but here and there he could make out a slight disturbance, perhaps a footprint. Following, the dwarf came to even dustier passages, where the boy's footfalls were clearly marked. Hurrying, he followed them.

Dolgan came back to the same cavern, after a few minutes, and cursed.

He felt little hope of finding the boy's tracks again among all the disturbance caused by the fight with the wraith. Pausing briefly, he set out to examine each tunnel leading out of the cavern for signs. After an hour he found a single footprint heading away from the cavern, through a tunnel to the right of where he had entered the first time. Moving up it, he found several more prints, set wide apart, and decided the boy must have been running. Hurrying on, he saw more tracks, as the passage became dustier.

Dolgan came to the cavern on the lake and nearly lost the trail again, until he saw the tunnel near the edge of the landing. He slogged through the water, pulling himself up into the passage, and saw Tomas's tracks. His faint lantern light was insufficient to illuminate the crystals in the cavern. But even if it had, he would not have paused to admire the sight, so intent was he on finding the boy.

Downward he followed, never resting. He knew that Tomas had long before outdistanced the wraith. There were signs that most of his journey was at a slower pace: footprints in the dust showed he had been walking, and the cold campfire showed he had stopped. But there were other terrors besides the wraith down here, just as dreadful.

Dolgan again lost the trail in the last cavern, finding it only when he spied the ledge above where the tracks ended. He had difficulty climbing to it, but when he did, he saw the blackened spot where the boy had snuffed out his torch. Here Tomas must have rested. Dolgan looked around the empty cavern. The air did not move this deep below the mountains. Even the dwarf, who was used to such things, found this an unnerving place. He looked down at the black mark on the ledge. But how long did Tomas stay, and where did he go?

Dolgan saw the hole in the wall and, since no tracks led away from the ledge, decided that was the way Tomas must have gone. He climbed through and followed the passage until it came to a larger one, heading downward, into the bowels of the mountain.

Dolgan followed what seemed to be a group of tracks, as if a band of men had come this way. Tomas's tracks were mixed in, and he was worried, for the boy could have been along this way before or after the others, or could have been with them. If the boy was held prisoner by someone, then Dolgan knew every moment was critical.

The tunnel wound downward and soon changed into a hall fashioned from great stone blocks fitted closely together and polished smooth. In all his years he had never seen its like. The passage leveled out, and Dolgan walked along quietly. The tracks had vanished, for the stone was hard and free of dust. High overhead, Dolgan could make out the first of several crystal chandeliers hung from the ceiling by chains. They could be lowered by means of a pulley, so the candles might be lit. The sound of his boots echoed hollowly off the high ceiling.

At the far end of the passage he spied large doors, fashioned from wood, with bands of iron and a great lock. They were ajar, and light could be seen coming through.

Without a sound, Dolgan crept close to the doors and peered in. He gaped at what he saw, his shield and ax coming up instinctively.

Sitting on a pile of gold coins, and gems the size of a man's fist, was Tomas, eating what looked to be a fish. Opposite him crouched a figure that caused Dolgan to doubt his eyes.

A head the size of a small wagon rested on the floor. Shield-size scales of a deep golden color covered it, and the long, supple neck led back to a huge body extending into the gloom of the giant hall. Enormous wings were folded across its back, their drooping tips touching the floor. Two pointed ears sat atop its head, separated by a delicate-looking crest, flecked with silver. Its long muzzle was set in a wolflike grin, showing fangs as long as broadswords, and a long forked tongue flicked out for a moment.

Dolgan fought down the overwhelming and rare urge to run, for Tomas was sitting, and to all appearances sharing a meal, with the dwarven folk's most feared hereditary enemy: a great dragon. He stepped forward, and his boots clacked on the stone floor.

Tomas turned at the sound, and the dragon's great head came up. Giant ruby eyes regarded the small intruder. Tomas jumped to his feet, an expression of joy upon his face. "Dolgan!" He scrambled down from the pile of wealth and rushed to the dwarf.

The dragon's voice rumbled through the great hall, echoing like thunder through a valley. "Welcome, dwarf. Thy friend hath told me that thou wouldst not forsake him."

Tomas stood before the dwarf, asking a dozen questions, while Dolgan's senses reeled. Behind the boy, the Prince of all dragons sat quietly observing the exchange, and the dwarf was having trouble maintaining the equanimity that was normally his. Making little sense of Tomas's questions, Dolgan gently pushed him to one side to better see the dragon. "I came alone," he said softly to the boy. "The others were loath to leave the search to me, but they had to press on, so vital was the mission."

Tomas said, "I understand."

"What manner of wizardry is this?" asked Dolgan softly.

The dragon chuckled, and the room rumbled with the sound. "Come into my home, dwarf, and I will tell thee." The great dragon's head returned to the floor, his eyes still resting above Dolgan's head. The dwarf approached slowly, shield and ax unconsciously at the ready. The dragon laughed, a deep, echoing sound, like water cascading down a canyon. "Stay thy hand, small warrior, I'll not harm thee or thy friend."

Dolgan let his shield down and hung his ax on his belt. He looked around and saw that they were standing in a vast hall, fashioned out of the living rock of the mountain. On all its walls could be seen large tapestries and banners, faded and torn; something about their look set Dolgan's teeth on edge, for they were as alien as they were ancient—no creature he knew of, human, elf, or goblin fashioned those pennants. More of the giant crystal chandeliers hung from timbers across the ceiling. At the far end of the hall, a throne could be seen on a dais, and long tables with chairs for many diners stood before it. Upon the tables were flagons of crystal and plates of gold. And all was covered with the dust of ages.

Elsewhere in the hall lay piles of wealth: gold, gems, crowns, silver, rich armor, bolts of rare cloth, and carved chests of precious woods, fitted with inlaid enamels of great craft.

Dolgan sat upon a lifetime's riches of gold, absently moving it around to make as comfortable a seat as was possible. Tomas sat next to him as the dwarf pulled out his pipe. He didn't show it, but he felt the need to calm himself, and his pipe always soothed his nerves. He lit a taper from his lantern and struck it to his pipe. The dragon watched him, then said, "Canst thou now breathe fire and smoke, dwarf? Art thou the new dragon? Hath ever a dragon been so small?"

Dolgan shook his head. "'Tis but my pipe." He explained the use of tabac.

The dragon said, "This is a strange thing, but thine are a strange folk, in truth."

Dolgan cocked a brow at this but said nothing. "Tomas, how did you come to this place?"

Tomas seemed unmindful of the dragon, and Dolgan found this reassuring. If the great beast had wished to harm them, he could have done so with little effort. Dragons were undisputedly the mightiest creatures on Midkemia. And this was the mightiest dragon Dolgan had heard of, half again the size of those he had fought in his youth.

Tomas finished the fish he had been eating and said, "I wandered for a long time and came to a place where I could sleep."

"Aye, I found it."

"I awoke at the sound of something and found tracks that led here."

"Those I saw also. I was afraid you had been taken."

"I wasn't. It was a party of goblins and a few Dark Brothers, coming to this place. They were very concerned about what was ahead and didn't pay attention to what was behind, so I could follow fairly close."

"That was a dangerous thing to do."

"I know, but I was desperate for a way out. I thought they might lead me to the surface, and I could wait while they went on ahead, then slip out. If I could get out of the mines, I could have headed north toward your village."

"A bold plan, Tomas," said Dolgan, an approving look in his eyes.

"They came to this place, and I followed."

"What happened to them?"

The dragon spoke. "I sent them far away, dwarf, for they were not company I would choose."

"Sent them away? How?"

The dragon raised his head a little, and Dolgan could see that his scales were faded and dull in places. The red eyes were filmed over slightly, and suddenly Dolgan knew the dragon was blind.

"The dragons have long had magic, though it is unlike any other. It is by my arts that I can see thee, dwarf, for the light hath long been denied me. I took the foul creatures and sent them far to the north. They do not know how they came to that place, nor remember this place."

Dolgan puffed on his pipe, thinking of what he was hearing. "In the tales of my people, there are legends of dragon magicians, though you are the first I have seen."

The dragon lowered his head to the floor slowly, as if tired. "For I am one of the last of the golden dragons, dwarf, and none of the lesser dragons have the art of sorcery. I have sworn never to take a life, but I would not have their kind invade my resting place."

Tomas spoke up. "Rhuagh has been kind to me, Dolgan. He let me stay until you found me, for he knew that someone was coming."

Dolgan looked at the dragon, wondering at his foretelling.

Tomas continued, "He gave me some smoked fish to eat, and a place to rest."

"Smoked fish?"

The dragon said, "The kobolds, those thou knowest as gnomes, worship me as a god and bring me offerings, fish caught in the deep lake and smoked, and treasure gleaned from deeper halls."

"Aye," said Dolgan, "gnomes have never been known for being overly bright."

The dragon chuckled. "True. The kobolds are shy and harm only those who trouble them in their deep tunnels. They are a simple folk, and it pleaseth them to have a god. As I am not able to hunt, it is an agreeable arrangement."

Dolgan considered his next question. "I mean no disrespect, Rhuagh, but it has ever been my experience with dragons that you have little love for others not your own kind. Why have you aided the boy?"

The dragon closed his eyes for a moment, then opened them again to stare blankly toward the dwarf. "Know this, dwarf, that such was not always the way of it. Thy people are old, but mine are the oldest of all, save one. We were here before the elves and the moredhel. We served those whose names may not be spoken, and were a happy people."

"The Dragon Lords?"

"So your legends call them. They were our masters, and we were their servants, as were the elves and the moredhel. When they left this land, on a journey beyond imagining, we became the most powerful of the free people, in a time before the dwarves or men came to these lands. Ours was a dominion over the skies and all things, for we were mighty beyond any other.

"Ages ago, men and dwarves came to our mountains, and for a time we lived in peace. But ways change, and soon strife came. The elves drove the moredhel from the forest now called Elvandar, and men and dwarves warred with dragons.

"We were strong, but humans are like the trees of the forest, their numbers uncountable. Slowly my people fled to the south, and I am the last in these mountains. I have lived here for ages, for I would not forsake my home.

"By magic I could turn away those who sought this treasure, and kill those whose arts foiled my clouding of their minds. I sickened of the killing and vowed to take no more lives, even those as hateful as the moredhel. That is why I sent them far, and why I aided the boy, for he is undeserving of harm."

Dolgan studied the dragon. "I thank you, Rhuagh."

"Thy thanks are welcome, Dolgan of the Grey Towers. I am glad of thy coming also. It is only a little longer that I could shelter the boy, for I summoned Tomas to my side by magic arts, so he might sit my death-watch."

"What?" exclaimed Tomas.

"It is given to dragons to know the hour of their death, Tomas, and mine is close. I am old, even by the measure of my people, and have led a full life. I am content for it to be so. It is our way."

Dolgan looked troubled. "Still, I find it strange to sit here hearing you speak of this."

"Why, dwarf? Is it not true with thine own people that when one dieth, it is accounted how well he lived, rather than how long?"

"You have the truth of that."

"Then why should it matter if the death hour is known or not? It is still the same. I have had all that one of my kind could hope for: health, mates, young, riches, and rest. These are all I have ever wanted, and I have had them."

"'Tis a wise thing to know what is wanted, and wiser still to know when 'tis achieved," said Dolgan.

"True. And still wiser to know when it is unachievable, for then striving is folly. It is the way of my people to sit the deathwatch, but there are none of my kind near enough to call. I would ask thee to wait for my passing before thy leaving. Wilt thou?"

Dolgan looked at Tomas, who bobbed his head in agreement. "Aye, dragon, we will, though it is not a thing to gladden our hearts."

The dragon closed his eyes; Tomas and Dolgan could see they were beginning to swell shut. "Thanks to thee, Dolgan, and to thee, Tomas."

The dragon lay there and spoke to them of his life, flying the skies of Midkemia, of far lands where tigers lived in cities, and mountains where eagles could speak. Tales of wonder and awe were told, long into the night.

When his voice began to falter, Rhuagh said, "Once a man came to this place, a magician of mighty arts. He could not be turned from this place by my magic, nor could I slay him. For three days we battled, his arts against mine, and when done, he had bested me. I thought he would slay me and carry off my riches, but instead he stayed, for his only thought was to learn my magic, so that it would not be lost when I passed."

Tomas sat in wonder, for as little as he knew about magic from Pug, he thought this a marvelous thing. In his mind's eye he could see the titanic struggle and the great powers working.

"With him he had a strange creature, much like a goblin, though upright, and with features of finer aspect. For three years he stayed with me, while his servant came and went. He learned all I could teach, for I could deny him not. But he taught as well, and his wisdom gave me great comfort. It was because of him that I learned to respect life, no matter how mean of character, and vowed to spare any that came to me. He also had suffered at the hands of others, as I had in the wars with men, for much that I cherished was lost. This man had the art of healing the wounds of the heart and mind, and when he left, I felt the victor, not the vanquished." He paused and swallowed, and Tomas could see that speech was coming to him with more difficulty. "If a dragon could not have attended my deathwatch, I would as soon have him sit here, for he was the first of thy kind, boy, that I would count a friend."

"Who was he, Rhuagh?" Tomas asked.

"He was called Macros."

Dolgan looked thoughtful. "I've heard his name, a magician of most puissant arts. He is nearly a myth, having lived somewhere to the east."

"A myth he is not, Dolgan," said Rhuagh, thickly. "Still, it may be that he is dead, for he dwelt with me ages ago." The dragon paused. "My time is now close, so I must finish. I would ask a boon of thee, dwarf." He moved his head slightly and said, "In yon box is a gift from the mage, to be used at this time. It is a rod fashioned of magic. Macros left it so that when I die no bones will be left for scavengers to pick over. Wilt thou bring it here?"

Dolgan went to the indicated chest. He opened it to discover a black metal rod lying upon a blue velvet cloth. He picked up the rod and found it surprisingly heavy for its size. He carried it over to the dragon.

The dragon spoke, his words nearly unintelligible, for his tongue was swollen. "In a moment, touch the rod to me, Dolgan, for then will I end."

"Aye," said Dolgan, "though it will give me scant pleasure to see your end, dragon."

"Before that I have one last thing to tell. In a box next to the other is a gift for thee, dwarf. Thou mayest take whatever else here pleaseth thee, for I will have no use for any of it. But of all in this hall, that in the box is what I wish thee to have." He tried to move his head toward Tomas, but could not. "Tomas, thanks to thee, for spending my last with me. In the box with the dwarf's gift is one for you. Take whatever else pleaseth thee, also, for thy heart is good." He drew a deep breath, and Tomas could hear it rattle in his throat. "Now, Dolgan."

Dolgan extended the rod and lightly touched the dragon on the head with it. At first nothing happened. Rhuagh said softly, "It was Macros's last gift."

Suddenly a soft golden light began to form around the dragon. A faint humming could be heard, as if the walls of the hall reverberated with fey music. The sound increased as the light grew brighter and began to pulse with energy. Tomas and Dolgan watched as the discolored patches faded from Rhuagh's scales. His hide shone with golden sparkle, and the film started to lift from his eyes. He slowly raised his head, and they knew he could again see the hall around him. His crest stood erect, and his wings lifted, showing the rich silver sheen underneath. The yellowed teeth became brilliant white, and his faded black claws shone like polished ebony as he stood upright, lifting his head high.

Dolgan said softly, "'Tis the grandest sight I've ever beheld."

Slowly the light grew in intensity as Rhuagh returned to the image of his youthful power. He pulled himself to his full, impressive height, his crest dancing with silver lights. The dragon threw back his head, a youthful, vigorous motion, and with a shout of joy sent a powerful blast of flame up to the high vaulted ceiling. With a roar like a hundred trumpets he shouted, "I thank thee, Macros. It is a princely gift indeed."

Then the strangely harmonic thrumming changed in tone, becoming more insistent, louder. For a brief instant both Dolgan and Tomas thought a voice could be heard among the pulsing tones, a deep, hollow echo saying, "You are welcome, friend."

Tomas felt wetness on his face, and touched it. Tears of joy from the dragon's sheer beauty were running down his cheeks. The dragon's great golden wings unfolded, as if he were about to launch himself in flight. The shimmering light became so bright, Tomas and Dolgan could barely stand to look, though they could not pull their eyes from the spectacle. The sound in the room grew to a pitch so loud, dust fell from the ceiling upon their heads, and they could feel the floor shake. The dragon launched himself upward, wings extended, then vanished in a blinding flash of cold white light. Suddenly the room was as it had been and the sound was gone.

The emptiness in the cavern felt oppressive after the dragon vanished, and Tomas looked at the dwarf. "Let's leave, Dolgan. I have little wish to stay."

Dolgan looked thoughtful. "Aye, Tomas, I also have little desire to stay. Still, there is the matter of the dragon's gifts." He crossed over to the box the dragon had identified and opened it.

Dolgan's eyes became round as he reached in and pulled out a dwarven hammer. He held it out before himself and looked upon it with reverence. The head was made from a silver metal that shone in the lantern light with bluish highlights. Across the side were carved dwarven symbols. The haft was carved oak, with scrollwork running the length. It was polished, and the deep rich grain showed through the finish. Dolgan said, faintly, "'Tis the Hammer of Tholin. Long removed from my people. Its return will cause rejoicing in every dwarven long hall throughout the West. It is the symbol of our last king, lost ages ago."

Tomas came over to watch and saw something else in the box. He reached past Dolgan and pulled out a large bundle of white cloth. He unrolled it and found that the cloth was a tabard of white, with a golden dragon emblazoned on the front. Inside were a shield with the same device and a golden helm. Most marvelous of all was a golden sword with a white hilt. Its scabbard was fashioned from a smooth white material like ivory, but stronger, like metal. Beneath the bundle lay a coat of golden chain mail, which he removed with an "Oh!" of wonder.

Dolgan watched him and said, "Take them, boy. The dragon said it was your gift."

"They are much too fine for me, Dolgan. They belong to a prince or a king."

"I'm thinking the previous owner has scant use for them, laddie. They were freely given, and you may do what you will, but I think that there is something special to them, or else they wouldn't have been placed in the box with the hammer. Tholin's hammer is a weapon of power, forged in the ancient hearths of the Mac Cadman Alair, the oldest mine in these mountains. In it rests magic unsurpassed in the history of the dwarves. It is likely the gilded armor and sword are also such. It may be there is a purpose in their coming to you."

Tomas thought for a moment, then quickly pulled off his great cloak. His tunic was no gambeson, but the golden mail went over it easily enough, being fashioned for someone of larger stature. He pulled the tabard over it and put the helm upon his head. Picking up the sword and shield, he stood before Dolgan. "Do I look foolish?"

The dwarf regarded him closely. "They are a bit large, but you'll grow into them, no doubt." He thought he saw something in the way the boy stood and held the sword in one hand and the shield in the other. "No, Tomas, you do not look foolish. Perhaps not at ease, but not foolish. They are grand, and you will come to wear them as they were meant to be worn, I think."

Tomas nodded, picked up his cloak, and turned toward the door, putting up his sword. The armor was surprisingly light, much lighter than what he had worn at Crydee. The boy said, "I don't feel like taking anything else, Dolgan. I suppose that sounds strange."

Dolgan walked over to him. "No, boy, for I also wish nothing of the dragon's riches." With a backward glance at the hall, he added, "Though there will be nights to come when I will wonder at the wisdom of that. I may return someday, but I doubt it. Now let us find a way home." They set off and soon were in tunnels Dolgan knew well, taking them to the surface.

Dolgan gripped Tomas's arm in silent warning. The boy knew enough not to speak. He also felt the same alarm he had experienced just before the wraith had attacked the day before. But this time it was almost physically felt. The undead creature was near. Putting down the lantern, Tomas shuttered it. His eyes widened in sudden astonishment, for instead of the expected blackness, he saw faintly the figure of the dwarf moving slowly forward. Without thought he said, "Dolgan—"

The dwarf turned, and suddenly a black form loomed up at his back. "Behind you!" shouted Tomas.

Dolgan spun to confront the wraith, instinctively bringing up his shield and Tholin's hammer. The undead creature struck at the dwarf, and only Dolgan's battle-trained reflexes and dwarven ability to sense movement in the inky darkness saved him, for he took the contact on his iron-bosked shield. The creature howled in rage at the contact with iron. Then Dolgan lashed out with the legendary weapon of his ancestors, and the creature screamed as the hammer struck its form. Blue-green light sprang about the head of the hammer, and the creature retreated, wailing in agony.

"Stay behind me," shouted Dolgan. "If iron irritates it, then Tholin's hammer pains it. I may be able to drive it off."

Tomas began to obey the dwarf, then found his right hand crossing to pull the golden sword free of the scabbard on his left hip. Suddenly the ill-fitting armor seemed to settle more comfortably around his shoulders, and the shield balanced upon his arm as if he had carried it for years. Without volition of his own, Tomas moved behind Dolgan, then stepped past, bringing the golden sword to the ready.

The creature seemed to hesitate, then moved toward Tomas. Tomas raised his sword, readying to strike. With a sound of utter terror, the wraith turned and fled. Dolgan glanced at Tomas, and something he saw made him hesitate as Tomas seemed to come to an awareness of himself and put up his sword.

Dolgan returned to the lantern and said, "Why did you do that, lad?"

Tomas said, "I . . . don't know." Feeling suddenly self-conscious at having disobeyed the dwarf's instructions, he said, "But it worked. The thing left."

"Aye, it worked," agreed Dolgan, removing the shutter from the lantern. In the light he studied the boy.

Tomas said, "I think your ancestor's hammer was too much for it."

Dolgan said nothing, but he knew that wasn't the case. The creature had fled in fear from the sight of Tomas in his armor of white and gold. Then another thought struck the dwarf. "Boy, how did you know to warn me the creature was behind me?"

"I saw it."

Dolgan turned to look at Tomas with open astonishment. "You *saw* it? How? You had shuttered the lantern."

"I don't know how. I just did."

Dolgan closed the shutter on the lantern again and stood up. Moving a few feet away, he said, "Where am I now, lad?"

Without hesitation Tomas came to stand before him, placing a hand upon his shoulder. "Here."

"What—?" said the dwarf.

Tomas touched the helm, then the shield. "You said they were special."

"Aye, lad. But I didn't think they were *that* special."

"Should I take them off?" asked the worried boy.

"No, no." Leaving the lantern upon the floor, Dolgan said, "We can move more quickly if I don't have to worry about what you can and can't see." He forced a note of cheeriness into his voice. "And despite there being no two finer warriors in the land, it's best if we don't announce our presence with that light. The dragon's telling of the moredhel being down in our mines gives me no comfort. If one band was brave enough to risk my people's wrath, there may be others. Yon wraith may be terrified of your golden sword and my ancient hammer, but twenty or so moredhel might not be so easily impressed."

Tomas could find nothing to say, so they started moving off into the darkness.

THREE TIMES they stopped and hid while hurrying groups of goblins and Dark Brothers passed near by. From their dark vantage point they could see that many of those who passed harbored wounds or were aided by their kinsmen as they limped along. After the last group was gone, Dolgan turned to Tomas and said, "Never in history have the goblins and moredhel dared to enter our mines in such numbers. Too much do they fear my people to risk it."

Tomas said, "They look pretty beat up, Dolgan, and they have females and young with them, and carry great bundles, too. They are fleeing something."

The dwarf nodded. "They are all moving from the direction of the northern valley in the Grey Towers, heading toward the Green Heart. Something still drives them south."

"The Tsurani?"

Dolgan nodded. "My thought also. Come. We had best return to Caldara as quickly as we can." They set off and soon were in tunnels Dolgan knew well, taking them to the surface and home.

THEY WERE BOTH exhausted when they reached Caldara five days later. The snows in the mountains were heavy, and the going was slow. As they approached the village, they were sighted by guards, and soon the entire village turned out to greet them.

They were taken to the village long hall, and Tomas was given a room. He was so tired that he fell asleep at once, and even the stout dwarf was fatigued. The dwarves agreed to call the village elders together the next day in council and discuss the latest news to reach the valley.

Tomas awoke feeling ravenous. He stretched as he stood up and was surprised to find no stiffness. He had fallen asleep in the golden mail and should have wakened to protesting joints and muscles. Instead he felt rested and well. He opened the door and stepped into a hall. He saw no one until he came to the central room of the long hall. There were several dwarves seated along the great table, with Dolgan at the head. Tomas saw one was Weylin, Dolgan's son. Dolgan motioned the boy to a chair and introduced him to the company.

The dwarves all greeted Tomas, who made polite responses. Mostly he stared at the great feast of food on the table.

Dolgan laughed and said, "Help yourself, laddie; there is little cause for you to be hungry with the board full." Tomas heaped a plate with beef, cheese, and bread and took a flagon of ale, though he had little head for it and it was early in the day. He quickly consumed what was on the platter and helped himself to another portion, looking to see if anyone disapproved. Most of the dwarves were involved in a complicated discussion of an unknown nature to Tomas, having to do with the allocation of winter stores to various villages in the area.

Dolgan called a halt to the discussion and said, "Now that Tomas is with us, I think we had best speak of these Tsurani."

Tomas's ears pricked up at that, and he turned his attention fully to what was being said. Dolgan continued, "Since I left on patrol, we have had runners from Elvandar and Stone Mountain. There have been many sightings of these aliens near the North Pass. They have made camp in the hills south of Stone Mountain."

One of the dwarves said, "That is Stone Mountain's business, unless they call us to arms."

Dolgan said, "True, Orwin, but there is also the news they have been seen moving in and out of the valley just south of the pass. They have intruded on lands traditionally ours, and that is the business of the Grey Towers."

The dwarf addressed as Orwin nodded. "Indeed it is, but there is naught we can do until spring."

Dolgan put his feet up on the table, lighting a pipe. "And that is true also. But we can be thankful the Tsurani can do naught until spring, as well."

Tomas put down a joint of beef he was holding. "Has the blizzard struck?"

Dolgan looked at him. "Aye, laddie, the passes are all solid with snow, for the first winter blizzard came upon us last night. There will be nothing that can move out there, least of all an army."

Tomas looked at Dolgan. "Then . . ."

"Aye. You'll guest with us this winter, for not even our hardiest runner could make his way out of these mountains to Crydee."

Tomas sat back, for in spite of the comforts of the dwarven long hall, he wished for more familiar surroundings. Still, there was nothing that could be done. He resigned himself to that and returned his attention to his meal.

11

▾▾

SORCERER'S ISLE

THE WEARY GROUP TRUDGED INTO BORDON.

Around them rode a company of Natalese Rangers, dressed in their traditional grey tunics, trousers, and cloaks. They had been on patrol, had encountered the travelers a mile out of town, and were now escorting them. Borric was irritated that the rangers had not offered to let the exhausted travelers ride double, but he hid it well. They had little reason to recognize this group of ragamuffins as the Duke of Crydee and his party, and even if he should have arrived in state, there was little warmth between the Free Cities of Natal and the Kingdom.

Pug looked at Bordon with wonder. It was a small city by Kingdom standards, little more than a seaport town, but far larger than Crydee. Everywhere he looked, people were hurrying about on unknown tasks, busy and preoccupied. Little attention was paid the travelers except for an occasional glance from a shopkeeper or a woman at market. Never had the boy seen so many people, horses, mules, and wagons all in one place. It was a confusion of colors and sounds, overwhelming his senses. Barking dogs ran behind the rangers' horses, nimbly avoiding kicks by the irritated mounts. A few street boys shouted obscenities at the party, all obviously outlanders from their look, and most likely prisoners from the escort. Pug was vaguely troubled by this rudeness, but his attention was quickly distracted by the newness of the city.

Bordon, like the other cities in the area, had no standing army, but instead supported a garrison of Natalese Rangers, descendants of the legendary Imperial Keshian Guides and counted among the best horse soldiers and trackers in the west. They could provide ample warning of approaching trouble and allow the local militia time to turn out. Nominally independent, the rangers were free to dispose of outlaws and renegades on the spot, but after hearing the Duke's story, and at mention of the name Martin Longbow—whom they knew well—the leader of the patrol decided this matter should be turned over to the local prefects.

They were taken to the office of the local prefect, located in a small building near the city square. The rangers appeared pleased to be shed of the prisoners and return to their patrol as they gave over custody to the prefect.

The prefect was a short, swarthy man given to brightly colored sashes about his ample girth and large golden rings upon his fingers. He smoothed his dark, oiled beard as the ranger captain explained his company's meeting with the Duke's party. As the rangers rode off, the prefect greeted Borric coolly. When the Duke made it clear they were expected by Talbott Kilrane, the largest ships' broker in the city and Borric's trading agent in the Free Cities, the prefect's manner changed abruptly. They were taken from the office to the prefect's private quarters and offered hot, dark coffee. The prefect sent one of his servants with a message to the house of Kilrane and waited quietly, only occasionally making noncommittal small talk with the Duke.

Kulgan leaned over to Pug and said, "Our host is the sort who sees which way the wind blows before making up his mind; he waits word from the merchant before deciding if we're prisoners or guests." The magician chuckled. "You'll find as you grow older that minor functionaries are the same the world over."

An angry storm in the person of Meecham appeared suddenly in the door of the prefect's home a short time later, one of Kilrane's senior clerks at his elbow. The clerk quickly made it clear that this was indeed the Duke of Crydee and, yes, he was expected by Talbott Kilrane. The prefect was abjectly apologetic and hopeful the Duke would forgive the inconvenience, but under the present conditions, in these troubled times, he could understand? His manner was fawning and his smile unctuous.

Borric indicated that, yes, he did understand, all too well. Without any further delay, they left the prefect and went outside, where a group of grooms waited with horses. Quickly they mounted up, and Meecham and the clerk led them through the town, toward a hillside community of large, imposing houses.

The house of Talbott Kilrane stood topmost upon the highest hill overlooking the city. From the road Pug could see ships standing at anchor. Dozens of them were sitting with masts removed, obviously out of service during the harsh weather. A few coast-huggers bound for Ylith in the north or the other Free Cities were making their way cautiously in and out of the harbor, but for the most part the harbor was quiet.

They reached the house and entered an open gate in a low wall, where servants ran to take their horses. As they dismounted, their host came through the large entrance to the house.

"Welcome, Lord Borric, welcome," he said, a warm smile splitting his gaunt face. Talbott Kilrane looked like a vulture reincarnated into human form, with a balding head, sharp features, and small, dark eyes. His expensive robes did little to hide his gauntness, but there was an ease to his manner, and a concern in his eyes, that softened the unattractive aspect.

In spite of the man's appearance, Pug found him likable. He shooed servants off, to make ready rooms and hot meals for the party. He would not listen as the Duke tried to explain the mission. Raising a hand, he said, "Later, Your Grace. We can speak at length, after you have had rest and food. I will expect you for dinner tonight, but for now there are hot baths and clean beds for your party. I will have warm meals delivered to your quarters. Good food, rest, and clean clothes, and you'll feel like a new man. Then we can speak."

He clapped his hands, and a housecarl came to show them their rooms. The Duke and his son were given separate quarters, while Pug and Kulgan shared another. Gardan was shown to Meecham's room, and the Duke's soldiers were taken to the servants' quarters.

Kulgan told Pug to take the first bath while the magician spoke with his servant for a while. Meecham and Kulgan went off to the franklin's room, and Pug stripped off his dirty clothes. In the center of the room was a large metal tub, filled with scented water, hot and steaming. He stepped into it and pulled his foot out quickly. After three days of walking through snow, the water felt as if it were boiling. Gently he placed his foot back in and, when he had become used to the heat, slowly entered the water.

He sat back in the tub, the sloping back providing support. The inside of the tub was enameled, and Pug found the slick, smooth feeling strange after the wooden tubs of home. He lathered himself over with a sweet soap and washed the dirt from his hair, then stood in the tub and poured a bucket of cold water over his head to rinse off.

He dried himself and put on the clean nightshirt that had been left for him. In spite of the early hour he fell into the warm bed. His last thought was of the sandy-haired boy with the ready grin. As Pug slipped into sleep, he wondered if Dolgan had found his friend.

He awoke once during the day, hearing a nameless tune being hummed, while water was being splashed about with great zeal as Kulgan soaped his large body. Pug closed his eyes and was quickly asleep again.

He was hard asleep when Kulgan roused him for dinner. His tunic and trousers had been cleaned and a small rent in the shirt mended. His boots were polished and shone with a black gleam. As he stood inspecting himself in a mirror, he noticed for the first time a soft black shadow on his cheeks. He leaned closer and saw the early signs of a beard.

Kulgan watched him and said, "Well, Pug. Shall I have them fetch you a razor so you can keep your chin bare like Prince Arutha? Or do you wish to cultivate a magnificent beard?" He exaggeratedly brushed his own grey beard.

Pug smiled for the first time since leaving Mac Mordain Cadal. "I think I can leave off worrying about it for a time."

Kulgan laughed, glad to see the boy's spirits returning. The magician had been troubled at the depth of Pug's mourning for Tomas and was relieved to see the boy's resilient nature assert itself. Kulgan held the door open. "Shall we?"

Pug inclined his head, imitating a courtly bow, and said, "Certes, master magician. After you?" and broke into a laugh.

They made their way to the dining room, a large and well-lit hall, though nothing as large as in the castle of Crydee. The Duke and Prince Arutha were already seated, and Kulgan and Pug quickly took their places at the table.

Borric was just finishing his account of the events at Crydee and in the great forest when Pug and Kulgan sat. "So," he said, "I chose to carry this news myself, so important I believe it to be."

The merchant leaned back in his chair as servants brought a wide variety of dishes for the diners. "Lord Borric," said Talbott, "when your man Meecham first approached me, his request on your behalf was somewhat vague, due, I believe, to the manner in which the information was transmitted." He referred to the magic employed by Kulgan to contact Belgan, who had in turn sent the message to Meecham. "I never expected your desire to reach Krondor would prove as vital to my own people as I now see it to be." He paused, then continued, "I am, of course, alarmed by the news you bear. I was willing to act as a broker to find you a ship, but now I will undertake to send you in one of my own vessels." He picked up a small bell that sat near his hand and rang. In a moment a servant was standing at his shoulder. "Send word to Captain Abram to ready the *Storm Queen.* He leaves on tomorrow's afternoon tide for Krondor. I will send more detailed instructions later."

The servant bowed and left. The Duke said, "I thank you, Master Kilrane. I had hoped that you would understand, but I did not expect to find a ship so quickly."

The merchant looked directly at Borric. "Duke Borric, let me be frank. There is little love lost between the Free Cities and the Kingdom. And, to be franker still, less love for the name conDoin. It was your grandfather who laid waste to Walinor and siege to Natal. He was stopped only ten miles north of this very city, and that memory still rankles many of us. We are Keshian by ancestry, but freemen by birth, and have little affection for conquerors." Kilrane continued as the Duke sat stiffly in his chair, "Still, we are forced to admit that your father later, and yourself now, have been good neighbors, treating fairly with the Free Cities, even generously at times. I believe you to be a man of honor and realize these Tsurani people are likely all you say they are. You are not the sort of man given to exaggeration, I think."

The Duke relaxed a little at this. Talbott took a sip of wine, then resumed his conversation. "We would be foolish not to recognize that our best interests lie with those of the Kingdom, for alone we are helpless. When you have departed, I will summon a meeting of the Council of Guilds and Merchants and will argue for support of the Kingdom in this." He smiled, and all at the table could see that here was a man as confident in his influence and authority as the Duke was in his. "I think I will have little difficulty in making the council see the wisdom of this. A brief mention of that Tsurani war galley and a little conjecture on how our ships would fare against a fleet of such ships should convince them."

Borric laughed and slapped his hand upon the table. "Master merchant, I can see your wealth was not acquired by a lucky cast of fate's knucklebones. Your shrewd mind is a match for my own Father Tully's. As is your wisdom. I give you my thanks."

The Duke and the merchant continued to talk late into the night, but Pug was still tired and returned to his bed. When Kulgan came in hours later, he found the boy lying restfully, a peaceful expression on his face.

THE *STORM QUEEN* ran before the wind, her topgallants and sky sails slamming her through the raging sea. The swirling, stinging icy rain made the night so black that the tops of her tall masts were lost in hazy darkness to those who stood on her decks.

On the quarterdeck, figures huddled under great fur-lined oilcloth cloaks, trying to stay warm and dry in the bitterly cold wetness. Twice during the last two weeks they had run through high seas, but this was by far the worst weather they had encountered. A cry went up from the rigging, and word was carried to the captain that two men had fallen from the yards. Duke Borric shouted to Captain Abram, "Can nothing be done?"

"Nay, my lord. They are dead men, and to search would be folly, even if possible, which it is not," the captain shouted back, his voice carrying over the storm's roar.

A full watch was above in the treacherous rigging, knocking away the ice that was forming on the spars, threatening to crack them with additional weight, disabling the ship. Captain Abram held the rail with one hand, watching for signs of trouble, his whole body in tune with his ship. Next to him stood the Duke and Kulgan, less sure of their footing on the pitching deck. A loud groaning, cracking sound came from below, and the captain swore.

Moments later a sailor appeared before them. "Captain, we've cracked a timber and she's taking water."

The captain waved to one of his mates who stood on the main deck. "Take a crew below and shore up the damage, then report."

The mate quickly picked four men to accompany him below. Kulgan seemed to go into a trance for a minute before he said, "Captain, this storm will blow another three days."

The captain cursed the luck the gods had sent him and said to the Duke, "I can't run her before the storm for three days taking water. I must find a place to heave to and repair the hull."

The Duke nodded, shouting over the storm, "Are you turning for Queg?"

The captain shook his head, dislodging snow and water dripping from his black beard. "I cannot turn her into the wind for Queg. We will have to lie off Sorcerer's Isle."

Kulgan shook his head, though the gesture was not noticed by the others. The magician asked, "Is there nowhere else we can put in?"

The captain looked at the magician and the Duke. "Not as close. We would risk the loss of a mast. Then, if we didn't founder and sink, we'd lose six days rather than three. The seas run higher, and I fear I may lose more men." He shouted orders aloft and to the steersman, and they took a more southerly course, heading for Sorcerer's Isle.

Kulgan went below with the Duke. The rocking, surging motion of the ship made the ladder and narrow passageway difficult to negotiate, and the stout magician was tossed from one side to the other as they made their way to their cabins. The Duke went into his cabin, shared with his son, and Kulgan entered his own. Gardan, Meecham, and Pug were trying to rest on their respective bunks during the buffeting. The boy was having a difficult time, for he had been sick the first two days. He had gained sea legs of a sort, but still couldn't bring himself to eat the salty pork and hardtack they were forced to consume. Because of the rough seas, the ship's cook had been unable to perform his usual duties.

The ship's timbers groaned in protest at the pounding the waves were giving, and from ahead they could hear the sound of hammers as the work crew struggled to repair the breached hull.

Pug rolled over and looked at Kulgan. "What about the storm?"

Meecham came up on one elbow and looked at his master. Gardan did likewise. Kulgan said, "It will blow three days longer. We will put in to the lee of an island and hold there until it slackens."

"What island?" asked Pug.

"Sorcerer's Isle."

Meecham shot up out of his bunk, hitting his head on the low ceiling. Cursing and rubbing his head, while Gardan stifled a laugh, he exclaimed, "The island of Macros the Black?"

Kulgan nodded, while using one hand to steady himself as the ship nosed over a high crest and forward into a deep trough. "The same. I have little liking for the idea, but the captain fears for the ship." As if to punctuate the point, the hull creaked and groaned alarmingly for a moment.

"Who is Macros?" asked Pug.

Kulgan looked thoughtful for a moment, as much from listening to the work crew in the hold as from the boy's question, then said, "Macros is a great sorcerer, Pug. Perhaps the greatest the world has ever known."

"Aye," added Meecham, "and the spawn of some demon from the deepest circle of hell. His arts are the blackest, and even the bloody Priests of Lims-Kragma fear to set foot on his island."

Gardan laughed. "I have yet to see a wizard who could cow the death goddess's priests. He must be a powerful mage."

"Those are only stories, Pug," Kulgan said. "What we do know about him is that when the persecution of magicians reached its height in the Kingdom, Macros fled to this island. No one has since traveled to or from it."

Pug sat up on his bunk, interested in what he was hearing, oblivious to the terrible noise of the storm. He watched as Kulgan's face was bathed in moving half lights and shadows by the crazily swinging lantern that danced with every lurch of the ship.

"Macros is very old," Kulgan continued. "By what arts he keeps alive, only he knows, but he has lived there over three hundred years."

Gardan scoffed, "Or several men by the same name have lived there."

Kulgan nodded. "Perhaps. In any event, there is nothing truly known about him, except terrible tales told by sailors. I suspect that even if Macros does practice the darker side of magic, his reputation is greatly inflated, perhaps as a means of securing privacy."

A loud cracking noise, as if another timber in the hull had split, quieted them. The cabin rolled with the storm, and Meecham spoke all their minds: "And I'm hoping we'll all be able to stand upon Sorcerer's Isle."

THE SHIP LIMPED into the southern bay of the island. They would have to wait until the storm subsided before they could put divers over the side to inspect the damage to the hull.

Kulgan, Pug, Gardan, and Meecham came out on deck. The weather was slightly kinder with the cliffs cutting the fury of the storm. Pug walked to where the captain and Kulgan were standing. He followed their gaze up to the top of the cliffs.

High above the bay sat a castle, its tall towers outlined against the sky by the grey light of day. It was a strange place, with spires and turrets pointing upward like some clawed hand. The castle was dark save for one window in a high tower that shone with blue, pulsating light, as if lightning had been captured and put to work by the inhabitant.

Pug heard Meecham say, "There, upon the bluff. Macros."

THREE DAYS LATER the divers broke the surface and yelled to the captain their appraisal of the damage. Pug was on the main deck with Meecham, Gardan, and Kulgan. Prince Arutha and his father stood near the captain, awaiting the verdict on the ship's condition. Above, the seabirds wheeled, looking for the scraps and garbage heralded by a ship in these waters. The storms of winter did little to supplement the meager feeding of the birds, and a ship was a welcome source of fare.

Arutha came down to the main deck where the others waited. "It will take all of this day and half tomorrow to repair the damage, but the captain thinks it will hold fair until we reach Krondor. We should have little trouble from here."

Meecham and Gardan threw each other meaningful glances. Not wanting to let the opportunity pass, Kulgan said, "Will we be able to put ashore, Your Highness?"

Arutha rubbed his clean-shaven chin with a gloved hand. "Aye, though not one sailor will put out a boat to carry us."

"Us?" asked the magician.

Arutha smiled his crooked smile. "I have had my fill of cabins, Kulgan. I feel the need to stretch my legs on firm ground. Besides, without supervision, you'd spend the day wandering about places where you've no business." Pug looked up toward the castle, his glance noted by the magician.

"We'll keep clear of that castle and the road up from the beach, to be sure. The tales of this island only speak of ill coming to those who seek to enter the sorcerer's halls."

Arutha signaled a seaman. A boat was readied, and the four men and the boy got aboard. The boat was hauled over the side and lowered by a crew sweating despite the cold wind that still blew after the storm. By the glances they kept throwing toward the crest of the bluffs, Pug knew they were not sweating because of work or weather.

As if reading his thoughts, Arutha said, "There may be a more superstitious breed on Midkemia than sailors, but who they are I could not tell you."

When the boat was in the water, Meecham and Gardan cast off the lines that hung suspended from the davits. The two men awkwardly took oars and began to row toward the beach. It was a broken, stuttering rhythm at first, but with disapproving looks from the Prince, along with several comments about how men could spend their lives in a sea town and not know how to row, they finally got the boat moving in good order.

They put in at a sandy stretch of beach, a little cove that broke the bluffs of the bay. Upward toward the castle ran a path, which joined another leading away across the island.

Pug leaped out of the boat and helped pull it ashore. When it was fast aground, the others got out and stretched their legs.

Pug felt as if they were being watched, but each time he looked around, there was nothing in sight but the rocks, and the few seabirds that lived the winter in clefts of the cliff face.

Kulgan and the Prince studied the two paths up from the beach. The magician looked at the other path, away from the sorcerer's castle, and said, "There should be little harm in exploring the other trail. Shall we?"

Days of boredom and confinement outweighed whatever anxiety they felt. With a brusque nod, Arutha led the way up the trail.

Pug followed last, behind Meecham. The big-shouldered franklin was armed with a broadsword, upon which his hand rested. Pug kept his sling handy, for he still didn't feel comfortable with a sword, though Gardan was giving him lessons when possible. The boy fingered the sling absently, his eyes taking in the scene before them.

Along the trail they startled several colonies of turnstones and plovers, which took flight when the party came near. The birds squawked their protests and hovered near their roosts until the hikers passed, then returned to the scant comfort of the hillside.

They crested the first of a series of hills, and the path away from the castle could be seen to dip behind another crest. Kulgan said, "It must lead somewhere. Shall we continue?" Arutha nodded, and the others said nothing. They continued their journey until they came to a small valley, little more than a dell, between two ranges of low hills. On the floor of the valley sat some buildings.

Arutha said softly, "What do you think, Kulgan? Are they inhabited?"

Kulgan studied them for a moment, then turned to Meecham, who stepped forward. The franklin inspected the vista below, his gaze traveling from the floor of the vale to the hills around. "I think not. There is no sign of smoke from cook fires, nor sound of people working."

Arutha resumed his march down toward the floor of the valley, and the others followed. Meecham turned to watch Pug for a moment, then noticed the boy was unarmed except for his sling. The franklin pulled a long hunting knife from his belt and handed it to the boy without comment. Pug bobbed his head once in acknowledgment and took the knife in silence.

They reached a plateau above the buildings, and Pug could see an alien-looking house, the central building circled by a large court and several outbuildings. The entire property was surrounded by a low wall, no more than four feet tall.

They worked their way down the hillside to a gate in the wall. There were several barren fruit trees in the courtyard, and a garden area overgrown with weeds. Near the front of the central building a fountain stood, topped with a statue of three dolphins. They approached the fountain and saw that the interior of the low pool surrounding the statue was covered in blue tiles, faded and discolored with age. Kulgan examined the construction of the fountain. "This is fashioned in a clever manner. I believe that water should issue from the mouths of the dolphins."

Arutha agreed. "I have seen the King's fountains in Rillanon, and they are similar, though lacking the grace of this."

There was little snow on the ground, for it seemed the sheltered valley and the entire island received little even in the most severe winters. But it was still cold. Pug wandered a little way off and studied the house. It had a single story, with windows every ten feet along the wall. There was but one opening for a double door in the wall he stood facing, though the doors were long off their hinges.

"Whoever lived here expected no trouble."

Pug turned to see Gardan standing behind him, staring at the house as well. "There is no tower for lookout," continued the Sergeant. "And the low wall seems more likely to keep livestock out of the gardens than for defense."

Meecham joined them, hearing Gardan's last remark. "Aye, there is little concern for defense here. This is the lowest spot on the island, save for that small stream you could see behind the house when we came down the hill." He turned to stare up at the castle, the highest spires of which could still be seen from the valley. "There is where you build for trouble. This place," he said, indicating the low buildings with a sweep of his hand, "was fashioned by those who knew little of strife."

Pug nodded as he moved away. Gardan and Meecham headed in a different direction, toward an abandoned stable.

Pug moved around to the back of the house and found several smaller buildings. He clutched his knife in his right hand and entered the closest. It was open to the sky, for the roof had collapsed. Red roof tiles, shattered and faded, lay about the floor, in what seemed to be a storeroom, with large wooden shelves along three walls. Pug investigated the other rooms in the building, finding them to be of similar configuration. The entire building was some sort of storage area.

He moved to the next building and found a large kitchen. A stone stove stood against one wall, big enough for several kettles to cook upon it simultaneously, while a spit hung over a back opening above the fire was large enough for a beef side or whole lamb. A mammoth butcher's block stood in the center of the room, scarred from countless blows of cleaver and knife.

Pug examined a strange-looking bronze pot in the corner, overlaid with dust and cobwebs. He turned it over and found a wooden spoon. As he looked up, he thought he saw a glimpse of someone outside the door of the cookhouse.

"Meecham? Gardan?" he asked, as he slowly approached the door. When he stepped outside, there was no one in sight, but he did catch another glimpse of movement at the rear door of the main house.

He hurried toward that door, assuming his companions had already entered the building. As he entered the main house, he caught a hint of movement down a side corridor. He stopped for a moment to survey this strange house.

The door before him stood open, a sliding door fallen from railings that had once held it in place. Through the door he could see a large central courtyard, open to the sky above. The house was actually a hollow square, with pillars holding up the interior of the partial roof. Another fountain and a small garden occupied the very center of the courtyard. Like the one outside, the fountain was in disrepair, and this garden was also choked with weeds.

Pug turned toward the hall down which he had seen movement. He passed through a low side door into a shadowy corridor. In places the roof had lost several tiles, so that occasionally light shone down from above, making it easy for the boy to find his way. He passed two empty rooms; he suspected they might be sleeping quarters.

He turned a corner to find himself before the door of an odd-looking room and entered. The walls were tile mosaics, of sea creatures sporting in the foam with scantily dressed men and women. The style of art was new to Pug. The few tapestries and fewer paintings on display in the Duke's halls were all very lifelike, with muted colors and detailed execution in the finish. These mosaics were suggestive of people and animals without capturing details.

In the floor was a large depression, like a pool, with steps leading down before him. Out of the wall opposite obtruded a brass fish head, hanging over the pool. The nature of the room was beyond Pug.

As if someone had read his thoughts, a voice from behind said, "It is a tepidarium."

Pug turned and saw a man standing behind him. He was of average height, with a high forehead and deep-set black eyes. There were streaks of grey at the temples of his dark hair, but his beard was black as night. He wore a brown robe of simple material, a whipcord belt around the waist. In his left hand he held a sturdy oak staff. Pug came on guard, holding the long hunting knife before him.

"Nay, lad. Put up your scramasax, I mean you no harm." He smiled in a way that made Pug relax.

Pug lowered his knife and said, "What did you call this room?"

"A tepidarium," he said, entering the room. "Here warm water was piped into the pool, and bathers would remove their clothing and place them on those shelves." He pointed to some shelves against the rear wall.

"Servants would clean and dry the clothing of dinner guests while they bathed here."

Pug thought the idea of dinner guests bathing at someone's home in a group a novel one, but he said nothing. The man continued, "Through that door"—he pointed to a door next to the pool—"was another pool with very hot water, in a room called a calidarium. Beyond was another pool with cold water in a room called a frigidarium. There was a fourth room called the unctorium, where servants would rub down the bathers with scented oils. And they scraped their skins with wooden sticks. They didn't use soap then."

Pug was confused by all the different bathing rooms. "That sounds like a lot of time spent getting clean. This is all very odd."

The man leaned on his staff. "So it must seem to you, Pug. Still, I expect those that built this house would consider your keep halls strange as well."

Pug started. "How did you know my name?"

The man smiled again. "I heard the tall soldier call you by name as you approached the building. I was watching you, keeping out of sight until I was sure you were not pirates come to seek ancient loot. Few pirates come so young, so I thought it would be safe to talk to you."

Pug studied the man. There was something about him that suggested hidden meanings in his words. "Why would you speak with me?"

The man sat on the edge of the empty pool. The hem of his robe was pulled back, revealing cross-gartered sandals of sturdy construction. "I am alone mostly, and the chance to speak with strangers is a rare thing. So I thought to see if you would visit with me awhile, for a few moments at least, until you return to your ship."

Pug sat down also, but kept a comfortable distance between himself and the stranger. "Do you live here?"

The man looked around the room. "No, though I once did, long ago." There was a contemplative note in his voice, as if the admission were calling up long-buried memories.

"Who are you?"

The man smiled again, and Pug felt his nervousness vanish. There was something reassuring about his manner, and Pug could see that he intended no harm. "Mostly I am called the traveler, for many lands have I seen. Here I am sometimes known as the hermit, for so I live. You may call me what you like. It is all the same."

Pug looked at him closely. "Have you no proper name?"

"Many, so many that I have forgotten a few. At the time of my birth I was given a name, as you were, but among those of my tribe it is a name known only to the father and the mage-priest."

Pug considered this. "It is all very strange, much like this house. Who are your people?"

The man called the traveler laughed, a good-natured chuckle. "You have a curious mind, Pug, full of questions. That is good." He paused for a moment, then said, "Where are you and your companions from? The ship in the bay flies the Natalese banner of Bordon, but your accent and dress are of the Kingdom."

Pug said, "We are of Crydee," and gave the man a brief description of the journey. The man asked a few simple questions, and without being aware of it, Pug found that soon he had given a full accounting of the events that had brought them to the island, and the plans for the rest of the journey.

When he had finished, the traveler said, "That is a wondrous story indeed. I should think there will be many more wonders before this strange meeting of worlds is finished."

Pug questioned him with a look. "I don't understand."

The traveler shook his head. "I don't expect you to, Pug. Let us say that things are occurring that can be understood only by examination after the fact, with a distance of time separating the participants from the participating."

Pug scratched his knee. "You sound like Kulgan, trying to explain how magic works."

The traveler nodded. "An apt comparison. Though sometimes the only way to understand the workings of magic is to work magic."

Pug brightened. "Are you also a magician?"

The traveler stroked his long black beard. "Some have thought me one, but I doubt that Kulgan and I share the same understanding of such things."

Pug's expression showed he considered this an unsatisfactory explanation even if he didn't say so. The traveler leaned forward. "I can effect a spell or two, if that answers your question, young Pug."

Pug heard his name shouted from the courtyard. "Come," said the traveler. "Your friends call. We had best go and reassure them that you are all right."

They left the bathing room and crossed the open court of the inner garden. A large anteroom separated the garden from the front of the house, and they passed through to the outside. When the others saw Pug in the company of the traveler, they looked around quickly, their weapons drawn. Kulgan and the Prince crossed the court to stand before them. The traveler put up his hands in the universal sign that he was unarmed.

The Prince was the first to speak. "Who is your companion, Pug?"

Pug introduced the traveler. "He means no harm. He hid until he could see that we were not pirates." He handed the knife to Meecham.

If the explanation was unsatisfactory, Arutha gave no sign. "What is your business here?"

The traveler spread his hands, with the staff in the crook of his left arm. "I abide here, Prince of Crydee. I should think that the question better serves me."

The Prince stiffened at being addressed so, but after a tense moment relaxed. "If that is so, then you are correct, for we are the intruders. We came seeking relief from the solitary confines of the ship. Nothing more."

The traveler nodded. "Then you are welcome at Villa Beata."

Kulgan said, "What is Villa Beata?"

The traveler made a sweeping motion with his right hand. "This home is Villa Beata. In the language of the builders, it means 'blessed home,' and so it was for many years. As you can see, it has known better days."

Everyone was relaxing with the traveler, for they also felt a reassurance in his easy manner and friendly smile. Kulgan said, "What of those who built this strange place?"

"Dead . . . or gone. They thought this the Insula Beata, or Blessed Isle, when they first came here. They fled a terrible war, which changed the history of their world." His dark eyes misted over, as if the pain of remembering was great. "A great king died . . . or is thought to have died, for some say he may return. It was a terrible and sad time. Here they sought to live in peace."

"What happened to them?" asked Pug.

The traveler shrugged. "Pirates, or goblins? Sickness, or madness? Who can tell? I saw this home as you see it now, and those who lived here were gone."

Arutha said, "You speak of strange things, friend traveler. I know little of such, but it seems that this place has been deserted for ages. How is it you knew those who lived here?"

The traveler smiled. "It is not so long ago as you would imagine, Prince of Crydee. And I am older than I look. It comes from eating well and bathing regularly."

Meecham had been studying the stranger the entire time, for of all those who had come ashore, his was the most suspicious nature. "And what of the Black One? Does he not trouble you?"

The traveler looked over his shoulder at the top of the castle. "Macros the Black? The magician and I have little cause to be at odds.

He suffers me the run of the island, as long as I don't interfere with his work."

A suspicion crossed Pug's mind, but he said nothing, as the traveler continued. "Such a powerful and terrible sorcerer has little to fear from a simple hermit, I'm sure you'll agree." He leaned forward and added in conspiratorial tones, "Besides, I think much of his reputation is inflated and overboasted, to keep intruders away. I doubt he is capable of the feats attributed to him."

Arutha said, "Then perhaps we should visit this sorcerer."

The hermit looked at the Prince. "I don't think you would find a welcome at the castle. The sorcerer is oftentimes preoccupied with his work and suffers interruption with poor grace. He may not be the mythical author of all the world's ills that some imagine him to be, but he could still cause more trouble than it is worth to visit him. On the whole he is often poor company." There was a faint, wry hint of humor in his words.

Arutha looked around and said, "I think we have seen all of interest we are likely to. Perhaps we should return to the ship."

When none disagreed, the Prince said, "What of you, friend traveler?"

The stranger spread his hands in a general gesture. "I continue my habit of solitude, Your Highness. I have enjoyed this small visit, and the boy's news of the occurrences of the world outside, but I doubt that you would find me tomorrow if you were to seek me."

It was evident he was unlikely to provide any more information, and Arutha found himself growing irritated with the man's obscure answers. "Then we bid you farewell, traveler. May the gods watch over you."

"And you as well, Prince of Crydee."

As they turned to leave, Pug felt something trip his ankle, and he fell hard against Kulgan. Both went down in a tangle of bodies, and the traveler helped the boy up. Meecham and Gardan assisted the stout mage to his feet. Kulgan put weight upon his foot and started to fall. Arutha and Meecham grabbed him. The traveler said, "It appears your ankle is turned, friend magician. Here." He held out his staff. "My staff is stout oak and will bear your weight as you return to the ship."

Kulgan took the offered staff and put his weight on it. He took an experimental step and found that he could negotiate the path with the aid of the staff. "Thank you, but what of yourself?"

The stranger shrugged. "A simple staff, easily replaced, friend magician. Perhaps I shall have the opportunity of reclaiming it someday."

"I will keep it against that day."

The traveler turned away, saying, "Good. Then until that day, again farewell."

They watched as he walked back into the building, and then turned to face each other, expressions of wonder upon their faces. Arutha was the first to speak. "A strange man, this traveler."

Kulgan nodded. "More strange than you know, Prince. At his leaving I feel the lifting of some enchantment, as if he carries a spell about him, one that makes all near him trusting."

Pug turned to Kulgan. "I wanted to ask him so many questions, but I didn't seem to be able to make myself."

Meecham said, "Aye, I felt that also."

Gardan said, "There is a thought in my mind. I think we have been speaking to the sorcerer himself."

Pug said, "That is my thought."

Kulgan leaned on the staff and said, "Perhaps. If it is so, then he has his own reasons for masking his identity." They talked about this as they walked slowly up the path from the villa.

As they reached the cove where the boat was beached, Pug felt something brush against his chest. He reached inside his tunic and found a small folded piece of parchment. He withdrew it, startled by his find. He had not picked it up, as well as he could remember. The traveler must have slipped it inside his shirt when he had helped Pug to his feet.

Kulgan looked back as he started for the boat and, seeing Pug's expression, said, "What have you there?"

Pug handed the parchment over, while the others gathered around the magician. Kulgan unfolded the parchment. He read it, and a surprised expression crossed his face. He read it again, aloud. "I welcome those who come with no malice in their hearts. You will know in days to come that our meeting was not by chance. Until we meet again, keep the hermit's staff as a sign of friendship and goodwill. Seek me not until the appointed time, for that too is foreordained. Macros."

Kulgan handed the message back to Pug, who read it. "Then the hermit was Macros!"

Meecham rubbed his beard. "This is something beyond my understanding."

Kulgan looked up to the castle, where the lights still flashed in the single window. "As it is beyond mine, old friend. But whatever it means, I think the sorcerer wishes us well, and I find that a good thing."

They returned to the ship and retired to their cabins. After a night of rest, they found the ship ready to leave on the midday tide. As they raised sail, they were greeted with unseasonably light breezes, blowing them directly for Krondor.

12

▾▾

COUNCILS

PUG WAS RESTLESS.

He sat looking out a window of the Prince's palace in Krondor. Outside, the snow was falling, as it had been for the last three days. The Duke and Arutha had been meeting with the Prince of Krondor daily. On the first day Pug had told his story about finding the Tsurani ship, then had been dismissed. He remembered that awkward interview.

He had been surprised to find the Prince to be young, in his thirties, if not a vigorous and well man. Pug had been startled during their interview when the Prince's remarks were interrupted by a violent attack of coughing. His pale face, drenched with sweat, showed him to be in worse health than his manner indicated.

He had waved off Pug's suggestion that he should leave and come back when more convenient for him. Erland of Krondor was a reflective person, who listened patiently to Pug's narration, lessening the boy's discomfort at being before the heir apparent to the throne of the Kingdom. His eyes regarded Pug with reassurance and understanding, as if it were a common thing to have awkward boys standing before him. After listening to Pug's narration, he had spent a short time talking with Pug about small things, such as his studies and his fortuitous rise to the nobility, as if these were important matters to his realm.

Pug decided he liked Prince Erland. The second most powerful man in the Kingdom, and the single most powerful man in the West, was warm and friendly and cared for the comfort of his least-important guest.

Pug looked around the room, still not used to the splendor of the palace. Even this small room was richly appointed, with a canopied bed instead of a sleeping pallet. It was the first time Pug had ever slept in one, and he found it difficult to get comfortable on the deep, soft, feather-stuffed mattress. In the corner of the room stood a closet with more clothing in it than he thought he could wear in his lifetime, all of costly weave and fine cut, and all seemingly in his size. Kulgan had said it was a gift from the Prince.

The quiet of his room reminded Pug how little he had seen of Kulgan and the others. Gardan and his soldiers had left that morning with a bundle of dispatches for Prince Lyam from his father, and Meecham was housed with the palace guard. Kulgan was involved in the meetings as often as not, so Pug had a lot of time to himself. He wished he had his books with him, for then at least the time could be put to some good use. Since his arrival in Krondor there had been little for him to do.

More than once Pug had thought of how much Tomas would have loved the newness of this place—seemingly fashioned from glass and magic more than stone—and the people in it. He thought about his lost friend, hoping Dolgan had somehow found him, but not believing he had. The pain of loss was now a dull ache, but still tender. Even after the last month, he would find himself turning, expecting to see Tomas close by.

Not wishing to sit idle any longer, Pug opened the door and looked down the hallway that ran the length of the east wing of the Prince's palace. He hurried down the hall, looking for any familiar face to break the monotony.

A guard passed him by, going the other way, and saluted. Pug still couldn't get used to the idea of being saluted every time a guard passed, but as a member of the Duke's party he was given full honors due his Squire's rank by the household staff.

Reaching a smaller hallway, he decided to explore. One way was the same as another, he thought. The Prince had personally told him he had the run of the palace, but Pug had been shy about overstepping himself. Now boredom drove him to adventuring, or at least as much adventuring as possible under the circumstances.

Pug found a small alcove with a window, providing a different view of the palace grounds. Pug sat upon the window seat. Beyond the palace walls he could see the port of Krondor lying below like a white-shrouded toy village. Smoke was coming from many of the buildings, the only sign of life in the city. The ships in the harbor looked like miniatures, lying at anchor, waiting for more propitious conditions under which to sail.

A small voice behind him brought Pug out of his reverie. "Are you Prince Arutha?"

A girl was standing behind him, about six or seven years old, with big green eyes and dark reddish brown hair done up in silver netting. Her dress was simple but fine looking, of red cloth with white lace at the sleeves. Her face was pretty, but was set in an expression of deep concentration that gave it a comic gravity.

Pug hesitated for a moment, then said, "No, I'm Pug. I came with the Prince."

The girl made no attempt to hide her disappointment. With a shrug she came over and sat next to Pug. She looked up at him with the same grave expression and said, "I was so hoping that you might be the Prince, for I wanted to catch a glimpse of him before you leave for Salador."

"Salador," Pug said flatly. He had hoped the journey would end with the visit to the Prince. Lately he had been thinking of Carline.

"Yes. Father says you are all to leave at once for Salador, then take a ship for Rillanon to see the King."

"Who's your father?"

"The Prince, silly. Don't you know anything?"

"I guess not." Pug looked at the girl, seeing another Carline in the making. "You must be Princess Anita."

"Of course. And I'm a real princess too. Not the daughter of a duke, but the daughter of a prince. My father would have been King if he had wanted, but he didn't want to. If he had, I would be Queen someday. But I won't be. What do you do?"

The question, coming so suddenly without preamble, caught Pug off guard. The child's prattling wasn't very irksome, and he wasn't following closely, being more intent on the scene through the window.

He hesitated, then said, "I'm apprenticed to the Duke's magician."

The Princess's eyes grew round, and she said, "A real magician?"

"Real enough."

Her little face lit up with delight. "Can he turn people into toads? Mummy said magicians turn people into toads if they are bad."

"I don't know. I'll ask him when I see him—if I see him again," he added under his breath.

"Oh, would you? I would so very much like to know." She seemed utterly fascinated by the prospect of finding out if the tale was true. "And could you please tell me where I might see Prince Arutha?"

"I don't know. I haven't seen him myself in two days. What do you want to see him for?"

"Mummy says I may marry him someday. I want to see if he is a nice man."

The prospect of this tiny child's being married to the Duke's younger son confounded Pug for a moment. It was not an uncommon practice for nobles to pledge their children in marriage years before their coming of age. In ten years she would be a woman, and the Prince would still be a young man, the Earl of some minor keep in the Kingdom. Still, Pug found the prospect fascinating.

"Do you think you would like living with an earl?" Pug asked, realizing at once it was a stupid question. The Princess confirmed the opinion with a glance that would have done Father Tully credit.

She said, "Silly! How could I possibly know that when I don't even know who Mummy and Father will have me marry?"

The child jumped up. "Well, I must go back. I'm not supposed to be here. If they find me out of my rooms, I'll be punished. I hope you have a nice journey to Salador and Rillanon."

"Thank you."

With a sudden expression of worry, she said, "You won't tell anyone that I was here, will you?"

Pug gave her a conspiratorial smile. "No. Your secret's safe." With a look of relief, she smiled and peeked both ways down the hallway. As she started to leave, Pug said, "He's a nice man."

The Princess stopped. "Who?"

"The Prince. He's a nice man. Given to brooding and moods, but on the whole a nice person."

The Princess frowned for a moment as she digested the information. Then, with a bright smile, she said, "That's good. I'd not want to marry a man who's not nice." With a giggle she turned the corner and was gone.

Pug sat awhile longer, watching the snow fall, musing over the fact of children being concerned about matters of state, and over a child with big, serious green eyes.

THAT NIGHT the entire party was feted by the Prince. The whole population of nobles at court and most of the rich commoners of Krondor were attending the gala. Over four hundred people sat to dine, and Pug found himself at a table with strangers who, out of respect for the quality of his clothing and the simple fact of his being there in the first place, politely ignored him. The Duke and Prince Arutha were seated at the head table with Prince Erland and his wife, Princess Alicia, along with Duke Dulanic, Chancellor of the Principality and Knight-Marshal of Krondor. Owing to Erland's ill health, the business of running Krondor's military fell to Dulanic and the man he was deep in conversation with, Lord Barry, Erland's Lord-Admiral of the Krondorian fleet. Other royal ministers were seated nearby, while the rest of the guests were at smaller tables. Pug was seated at the one farthest removed from the royal table.

Servants were bustling in and out of the hall, carrying large platters of food and decanters of wine. Jongleurs strolled the hall, singing the newest ballads and ditties. Jugglers and acrobats performed between the tables, mostly ignored by the dinner guests, but giving their best, for the Master of Ceremony would not call them back again should he judge their efforts lacking.

The walls were covered with giant banners and rich tapestries. The banners were of every major household in the Kingdom, from the gold and brown of Crydee in the far west, to the white and green of far Ran, in the east. Behind the royal table hung the banner of the Kingdom, a golden lion rampant holding a sword, with a crown above his head, upon a field of purple, the ancient crest of the conDoin kings. Next to it hung Krondor's banner, an eagle flying above a mountain peak, silver upon the royal purple. Only the Prince, and the King in Rillanon, could wear the royal color. Borric and Arutha wore red mantles over their tunics, signifying they were princes of the realm, related to the royal family. It was the first time Pug had ever seen the two wearing the formal marks of their station.

Everywhere were sights and sounds of gaiety, but even from across the room Pug could tell that the talk at the Prince's table was subdued. Borric and Erland spent most of the dinner with their heads close together, speaking privately.

Pug was startled by a touch on his shoulder and turned to see a doll-like face peering through the large curtains not two feet behind him. Princess Anita put her finger to her lips and beckoned for him to step through. Pug saw the others at the table were looking at the great and near-great in the room and would scarcely notice the departure of a nameless boy. He rose and moved through the curtain, finding himself in a small servants' alcove. Before him was another curtain, leading to the kitchen, Pug supposed, through which peeked the tiny fugitive from bed. Pug moved to where Anita waited, discovering it was, indeed, a long connecting corridor between the kitchen and the great hall. A lengthy table covered with dishware and goblets ran along the wall.

Pug said, "What are you doing here?"

"Shush!" she said in a loud whisper. "I'm not supposed to be here."

Pug smiled at the child. "I don't think you have to worry about being heard, there's too much noise for that."

"I came to see the Prince. Which one is he?"

Pug motioned for her to step into the small alcove, then drew aside the curtain a little. Pointing at the head table, he said, "He's two removed from your father, in the black-and-silver tunic and red mantle."

The child stretched up on tiptoe and said, "I can't see."

Pug held the girl up for a moment. She smiled at him. "I am in your debt."

"Not at all," Pug intoned with mock gravity. They both giggled.

The Princess started as a voice spoke close to the curtain. "I must fly!" She darted through the alcove, passed through the second curtain, and disappeared from sight heading toward the kitchen and her getaway.

The curtain into the banquet hall parted, and a startled servant stared at Pug. Uncertain what to say, the servingman nodded. The boy by rights shouldn't be there, but by his dress he was certainly someone.

Pug looked about and, without much conviction, finally said, "I was looking for the way to my room. I must be going the wrong way."

"The guest wing is through the first door on the left in the dining hall, young sir. Ah . . . this way lies the kitchen. Would you care to have me show you the way?" The servant obviously didn't care to do so, and Pug was equally lacking any desire for a guide. "No, thank you, I can find it," he said.

Pug rejoined his table, unnoticed by the other guests. The balance of the meal passed without incident, except for an occasional strange glance by a servingman.

PUG PASSED the time after dinner talking with the son of a merchant. The two young men found each other in the crowded room where the Prince's after-dinner reception was being held. They spent a fitful hour being polite to one another, before the boy's father came and took him in tow. Pug stood around being ignored by the Prince's other dinner guests for a while, then decided he could slip back to his own quarters without affronting anyone—he wouldn't be missed. Besides he hadn't seen the Prince, Lord Borric, or Kulgan since they left the dinner table. Most of the reception seemed under the supervision of a score of household officials and Princess Alicia, a charming woman who had spoken politely with Pug for a moment as he passed through the reception line.

Pug found Kulgan waiting for him in his room when he returned.

Kulgan said, without preamble, "We leave at first light, Pug. Prince Erland is sending us on to Rillanon to see the King."

Pug said, "Why is the Prince sending *us?*" His tone was cross, for he was deeply homesick.

Before Kulgan could answer, the door flew open and Prince Arutha came storming in. Pug was surprised by Arutha's expression of unconfined anger.

"Kulgan! There you are," Arutha said, slamming the door. "Do you know what our royal cousin is doing about the Tsurani invasion?"

Before Kulgan could speak, the Prince supplied the answer. "Nothing! He won't lift a finger to send aid to Crydee until Father has seen the King. That will take another two months at least."

Kulgan raised his hand. Instead of an adviser to the Duke, Arutha saw one of his boyhood instructors. Kulgan, like Tully, could still command both sons of the Duke when the need arose. "Quietly, Arutha."

Arutha shook his head as he pulled over a chair. "I am sorry, Kulgan. I should have mastered my temper." He noticed Pug's confusion. "I apologize to you also, Pug. There is much involved here that you don't know of. Perhaps . . ." He looked questioningly at Kulgan.

Kulgan took out his pipe. "You might as well tell him, he's going along for the journey. He'll find out soon enough."

Arutha drummed his fingers on the arm of the chair for a moment, then sitting forward, said, "My father and Erland have been conferring for days on the best way to meet these outworlders should they come. The Prince even agrees it is likely they will come." He paused. "But he will do nothing to call the Armies of the West together until he has been given permission by the King."

"I don't understand," said Pug. "Aren't the Armies of the West the Prince's to command as he sees fit?"

"No longer," said Arutha with a near-grimace. "The King sent word, less than a year ago, that the armies may not be mustered without his permission." Arutha sat back in his chair as Kulgan blew a cloud of smoke. "It is in violation of tradition. Never have the Armies of the West had another commander than the Prince of Krondor, as the Armies of the East are the King's."

Pug was still unclear about the significance of all this. Kulgan said, "The Prince is the King's Lord-Marshal in the West, the only man besides the King who may command Duke Borric and the other Knight-Generals. Should he call, every Duke from Malac's Cross to Crydee would respond, with their garrisons and levies. King Rodric, for his own reasons, has decided that none may gather the armies without his authority."

Arutha said, "Father would come to the Prince's call, regardless, as would the other Dukes."

Kulgan nodded. "That may be what the King fears, for the Armies of the West have long been more the Prince's armies than the King's. If your father called, most would gather, for they revere him nearly as much as they revere Erland. And if the King should say not . . ." He let the sentence slip away.

Arutha nodded. "Strife within the Kingdom."

Kulgan looked at his pipe. "Even to civil war, perhaps."

Pug was troubled by the discussion. He was a keep boy, in spite of his newly acquired title. "Even if it is in defense of the Kingdom?"

Kulgan shook his head slowly. "Even then. For some men, kings also, there is as much importance in the manner in which things are done as the doing." Kulgan paused. "Duke Borric will not speak of it, but there has long been trouble between himself and certain eastern dukes, especially his cousin, Guy du Bas-Tyra. This trouble between the Prince and the King will only add to the strain between West and East."

Pug sat back. He knew that this was somehow more important than what he was understanding, but there were blank places in his picturings of the way things were. How could the King resent the Prince's summoning the armies in defense of the Kingdom? It didn't make sense to him, in spite of Kulgan's explanation. And what sort of trouble in the East was Duke Borric unwilling to speak of?

The magician stood. "We have an early day tomorrow, so we had best get some sleep. It will be a long ride to Salador, then another long passage by ship to Rillanon. By the time we reach the King, the first thaw will have come to Crydee."

Prince Erland bade the party a good journey as they sat upon their horses in the courtyard of the palace. He looked pale and deeply troubled as he wished them well.

The little Princess stood at an upstairs window and waved at Pug with a tiny handkerchief. Pug was reminded of another Princess and wondered if Anita would grow to be like Carline or be more even-tempered.

They rode out of the courtyard, where an escort of Royal Krondorian Lancers stood ready to accompany them to Salador. It would be a three weeks' ride over the mountains and past the marshes of Darkmoor, past Malac's Cross—the dividing point between the western and eastern realms—and on to Salador. There they would take ship, and after another two weeks they would reach Rillanon.

The lancers were shrouded in heavy cloaks of grey, but the purple-

and-silver tabards of Krondor's Prince could be seen underneath, and their shields bore the device of the royal Krondorian household. The Duke was being honored by an escort of the Prince's own household guard, rather than a detachment from the city garrison.

As they left the city, the snow began to fall once more, and Pug wondered if he would ever see spring in Crydee again. He sat quietly on his horse as it plodded along the road east, trying to sort out the impressions of the last few weeks, then gave up, resigning himself to whatever was to happen.

THE RIDE to Salador took four weeks instead of three, for there had been a storm of unusual intensity in the mountains west of Darkmoor. They had been forced to take lodging at an inn outside the village that took its name from the marshes. It had been a small inn, and they had all been forced to crowd together regardless of rank for several days. The food had been simple and the ale indifferent, and by the time the storm passed, they were all glad to leave Darkmoor behind.

Another day had been lost when they chanced upon a village being troubled by bandits. The sight of approaching cavalry had driven the brigands away, but the Duke had ordered a sweep of the area to insure that they didn't return as soon as the soldiers rode off. The villagers had opened their doors to the Duke's party, welcoming them and offering their best food and warmest beds. Poor offerings by the Duke's standards, yet he received their hospitality with graciousness, for he knew it was all they had. Pug enjoyed the simple food and company, the closest yet to home since he had left Crydee.

When they were a half day's ride short of Salador, they encountered a patrol of city guards. The guard captain rode forward. Pulling up his horse, he shouted, "What business brings the Prince's guard to the lands of Salador?" There was little love lost between the two cities, and the Krondorians rode without a heraldic banner. His tone left no doubt that he regarded their presence as an infringement upon his territory.

Duke Borric threw back his cloak, revealing his tabard. "Carry word to your master that Borric, Duke of Crydee, approaches the city and would avail himself of Lord Kerus's hospitality."

The guard captain was taken aback. He stammered, "My apologies, Your Grace. I had no idea . . . there was no banner. . . ."

Arutha said dryly, "We mislaid it in a forest sometime back."

The captain looked confused. "My lord?"

Borric said, "Never mind, Captain. Just send word to your master."

The captain saluted. "At once, Your Grace." He wheeled his horse and signaled for a rider to come forward. He gave him instructions, and the soldier spurred his horse toward the city and soon galloped out of sight.

The captain returned to the Duke. "If Your Grace will permit, my men are at your disposal."

The Duke looked at the travel-weary Krondorians, all of whom seemed to be enjoying the captain's discomfort. "I think thirty men-at-arms are sufficient, Captain. The Salador city guard is renowned for keeping the environs near the city free of brigands."

The captain, not realizing he was being made sport of, seemed to puff up at this. "Thank you, Your Grace."

The Duke said, "You and your men may continue your patrol."

The captain saluted again and returned to his men. He shouted the order to move out, and the guard column moved past the Duke's party. As they passed, the captain ordered a salute, and lances were dipped toward the Duke. Borric returned the salute with a lazy wave of his hand, then when the guards had passed, said, "Enough of this foolishness, let us to Salador."

Arutha laughed and said, "Father, we have need of men like that in the West."

Borric turned and said, "Oh? How so?"

As the horses moved forward, Arutha said, "To polish shields and boots."

The Duke smiled and the Krondorians laughed. The western soldiers held those of the East in low regard. The East had been pacified long before the West had been opened to Kingdom expansion, and there was little trouble in the Eastern Realm requiring real skill in warcraft. The Prince of Krondor's guards were battle-proved veterans, while those of Salador were considered by the guardsmen from the West to do their best soldiering on the parade ground.

Soon they saw signs that they were nearing the city: cultivated farmland, villages, roadside taverns, and wagons laden with trade goods. By sundown they could see the walls of distant Salador.

As they entered the city, a full company of Duke Kerus's own household guards lined the streets to the palace. As in Krondor, there was no castle, for the need for a small, easily defensible keep had passed as the lands around became civilized.

Riding through the city, Pug realized how much of a frontier town Crydee was. In spite of Lord Borric's political power, he was still Lord of a frontier province.

Along the streets, citizens stood gawking at the western Duke from the wild frontier of the Far Coast. Some cheered, for it seemed like a parade, but most stood quietly, disappointed that the Duke and his party looked like other men, rather than blood-drenched barbarians.

When they reached the courtyard of the palace, household servants ran to take their horses. A household guard showed the soldiers from Krondor to the soldiers' commons, where they would rest before returning to the Prince's city. Another, with a captain's badge of rank on his tunic, led Borric's party up the steps of the building.

Pug looked with wonder, for this palace was even larger than the Prince's in Krondor. They walked through several outer rooms, then reached an inner courtyard. Here fountains and trees decorated a garden, beyond which stood the central palace. Pug realized that the building they had passed through was simply one of the buildings surrounding the Duke's living quarters. He wondered what use Lord Kerus could possibly have for so many buildings and such a large staff.

They crossed the garden courtyard and mounted another series of steps toward a reception committee that stood in the door of the central palace. Once this building might have been a citadel, protecting the surrounding town, but Pug couldn't bring himself to imagine it as it might have been ages ago, for numerous renovations over the years had transformed an ancient keep into a glittering thing of glass and marble.

Duke Kerus's chamberlain, an old dried-up stick of a man with a quick eye, knew every noble worth noting—from the borders of Kesh in the south to Tyr-Sog in the north—by sight. His memory for faces and facts had often saved Duke Kerus from embarrassment. By the time Borric had made his way up the broad stairway from the courtyard, the chamberlain had provided Kerus with a few personal facts and a quick evaluation of the right amount of flattery required.

Duke Kerus took Borric's hand. "Ah, Lord Borric, you do me great honor by this unexpected visit. If you had only sent word of your arrival, I would have prepared a more fitting welcome."

They entered the antechamber of the palace, the Dukes in front. Borric said, "I am sorry to put you to any trouble, Lord Kerus, but I am afraid our mission is dependent on speed, and that the formal courtesies will have to be put aside. I bear messages for the King and must put to sea for Rillanon as soon as is possible."

"Of course, Lord Borric, but you will surely be able to stay for a short while, say a week or two?"

"I regret not. I would put to sea tonight if I could."

"That is indeed sorry news. I so hoped that you could guest with us for a time."

The party reached the Duke's audience hall, where the chamberlain gave instructions to a company of household servants, who jumped to the task of readying rooms for the guests. Entering the vast hall, with its high vaulted ceiling, gigantic chandeliers, and great arched glass windows, Pug felt dwarfed. The room was the largest he had ever seen, greater than the hall of the Prince of Krondor.

A huge table was set with fruits and wine, and the travelers fell to with vigor. Pug sat down with little grace, his whole body one mass of aches. He was turning into a skilled horseman simply from long hours in the saddle, but that fact didn't ease his tired muscles.

Lord Kerus pressed the Duke for the cause of his hurried journey, and between mouthfuls of fruit and drinks of wine, Borric filled him in on the events of the last three months. After he was done, Kerus looked distressed. "This is grave news indeed, Lord Borric. Things are unsettled in the Kingdom. I am sure the Prince has told you of some of the trouble that has occurred since last you came to the East."

"Yes, he did. But reluctantly and in only the most cursory manner. Remember, it has been thirteen years since I journeyed to the capital, at Rodric's coronation when I came to renew my vassalage. He seemed a bright enough young man then, able enough to learn to govern. But from what I've heard in Krondor, there seems to have been a change."

Kerus glanced around the room, then waved away his servants. Looking pointedly at Borric's companions, he raised one eyebrow questioningly.

Lord Borric said, "These have my trust and will not betray a confidence."

Kerus nodded. Loudly he said, "If you would like to stretch your legs before retiring, perhaps you'd care to see my garden?"

Borric frowned and was about to speak when Arutha put his hand upon his father's arm, nodding agreement.

Borric said, "That sounds interesting. Despite the cold I could use a short walk."

The Duke motioned for Kulgan, Meecham, and Gardan to remain, but Lord Kerus indicated Pug should join them. Borric looked surprised, but nodded agreement. They left through a small set of doors to the garden, and once outside, Kerus whispered, "It will look less suspicious if the boy comes with us. I can't even trust my own servants anymore. The King has agents everywhere."

Borric seemed infuriated. "The King has placed agents in your *household?*"

"Yes, Lord Borric, there has been a great change in our King. I know Erland has not told you the entire story, but it is one you must know."

The Duke and his companions watched Duke Kerus, who looked uncomfortable. He cleared his throat as he glanced around the snow-covered garden. Between the light from the palace windows and the large moon above, the gardan was a winterscape of white and blue crystals, undisturbed by footprints.

Kerus pointed to a set of tracks in the snow and said, "I made those this afternoon when I came here to think about what I could safely tell you." He glanced around one more time, seeing if anyone could overhear the conversation, then continued. "When Rodric the Third died, everyone expected Erland would take the crown. After the official mourning, the Priests of Ishap called all the possible heirs forward to present their claims. You were expected to be one of them."

Borric nodded. "I know the custom. I was late getting to the city. I would have renounced the claim in any event, so there was no importance in my absence."

Kerus nodded. "History might have been different had you been here, Borric." He lowered his voice. "I risk my neck by saying this, but many, even those of us here in the East, would have urged you to take the crown."

Borric's expression showed he did not like hearing this, but Kerus pressed on. "By the time you got here, all the back-hallway politics had been done—with most lords content to give the crown to Erland—but it was a tense day and a half while the issue was in doubt. Why the elder Rodric didn't name an heir I don't know. But when the priests had chased away all the distant kin with no real claim, three men stood before them, Erland, young Rodric, and Guy du Bas-Tyra. The priests asked for their declarations, and each gave them in turn. Rodric and Erland both had solid claims, while Guy was there as a matter of form, as you would have been had you arrived in time."

Arutha interjected dryly, "The time of mourning ensures no western Lord will be King."

Borric threw a disapproving glance at his son, but Kerus said, "Not entirely. If there had been any doubt to the rights of succession, the priest would have held off the ceremony until your father arrived, Arutha. It has been done before."

He looked at Borric and lowered his voice. "As I said, it was expected Erland would take the crown. But when the crown was presented to him, he refused, conceding the claim to Rodric. No one at that time knew of Erland's ill health, so most lords judged the decision a generous affirmation of Rodric's claim, as the only son of the King. With Guy du Bas-Tyra's backing the boy, the assembled Congress of Lords ratified his succession. Then the real infighting began, until at last your late wife's uncle was named as King's Regent."

Borric nodded. He remembered the battle over who would be named the then boy King's Regent. His despised cousin Guy had nearly won the position, but Borric's timely arrival and his support of Caldric of Rillanon, along with the support of Duke Brucal of Yabon and Prince Erland, had swung the majority of votes in the congress away from Guy.

"For the next five years there was only an occasional border clash with Kesh. Things were quiet. Eight years ago"—Kerus paused to glance around again—"Rodric embarked upon a program of public improvements, as he calls them, upgrading roads and bridges, building dams, and the like. At first they were of little burden, but the taxes have been increased yearly until now the peasants and freemen, even the minor nobles, are being bled white. The King has expanded his programs until now he is rebuilding the entire capital, to make it the greatest city known in the history of man, he says.

"Two years ago a small delegation of nobles came to the King and asked him to abjure this excessive spending and ease the burden upon the people. The King flew into a rage, accused the nobles of being traitors, and had them summarily executed."

Borric's eyes widened. The snow under his boot crunched dryly as he turned suddenly. "We've heard nothing of this in the West!"

"When Erland heard the news, he went immediately to the King and demanded reparation for the families of the nobles who were executed, and a lessening of the taxes. The King—or so it is rumored—was ready to seize his uncle, but was restrained by the few counselors he still trusted. They advised His Majesty that such an act, unheard of in the history of the Kingdom, would surely cause the western lords to rise up against the King."

Borric's expression darkened. "They were right. Had that boy hanged Erland, the Kingdom would have been irretrievably split."

"Since that time the Prince has not set foot in Rillanon, and the business of the Kingdom is handled by aides, for the two men will not speak to one another."

The Duke looked skyward, and his voice became troubled. "This is much worse than I had heard. Erland told me of the taxes and his refusal to impose them in the West. He said that the King was agreed, for he understood the need of maintaining the garrisons of the North and West."

Kerus slowly shook his head no. "The King agreed only when his aides painted pictures of goblin armies pouring down from the Northlands and plundering the cities of his Kingdom."

"Erland spoke of the strain between himself and his nephew, but even in light of the news I carry, said nothing about His Majesty's actions."

Kerus drew a deep breath and started walking once more. "Borric, I spend so much time with the sycophants of the King's court, I forget that you of the West are given to plain speech." Kerus was silent a moment, then said, "Our King is not the man he once was. Sometimes he seems his old self, laughing and open, filled with grand plans for the Kingdom; other times he is . . . someone else, as if a dark spirit has taken possession of his heart.

"Take care, Borric, for only Erland stands closer to the throne than yourself. Our King is well aware of that fact—even if you never think of it—and sees daggers and poison where none exists."

Silence descended over the group, and Pug saw Borric look openly troubled. Kerus continued. "Rodric fears others covet his crown. That may be, but not those the King suspects. There are only four conDoin males besides the King, all of whom are men of honor." Borric inclined his head at the compliment. "But there are perhaps a dozen more who can claim ties to the throne, through the King's mother and her people. All are eastern lords, and many would not flinch from the opportunity to press their claim to the throne before the Congress of Lords."

Borric looked incensed. "You speak of treason."

"Treason in men's hearts, if not in deeds . . . yet."

"Have things come to such a pass in the East, without us of the West knowing?"

Kerus nodded as they reached the far end of the garden. "Erland is an honorable man, and as such would keep unfounded rumors from his subjects, even yourself. As you have said, it is thirteen years since you last were at Rillanon. All warrants and missives from the King still pass through the Prince's court. How would you know?

"I fear it is only a matter of time before one or other of the King's advisers positions himself over the fallen heads of those of us who hold to our beliefs that the nobility are wardens of the nation's welfare."

Borric said, "Then you risk much with your frank speech."

Duke Kerus shrugged, indicating they should begin their return to the palace. "I have not always been a man to speak my mind, Lord Borric, but these are difficult times. Should anyone else have passed through, there would have been only polite conversation. You are unique, for with the Prince estranged from his nephew, you are the only man in the Kingdom with the strength and rank to possibly influence the King. I do not envy your weighty position, my friend.

"When Rodric the Third was king, I was among the most powerful nobles in the East, but I might as well be a landless freebooter for all the influence I now hold in Rodric the Fourth's court." Kerus paused. "Your black-hearted cousin Guy is now closest to the King, and the Duke of

Bas-Tyra and I have little love between us. Our reasons for disliking one another are not as personal as yours. But as his star rises, mine falls even more."

Kerus slapped his hands as the cold was beginning to bite. "But one bit of good news. Guy is wintering at his estate near Pointer's Head, so the King is free of his plotting for the present." Kerus gripped Borric's arm. "Use whatever influence you can muster to stem the King's impulsive nature, Lord Borric, for with this invasion you bring word of, we need to stand united. A lengthy war would drain us of what little reserves we possess, and should the Kingdom be put to the test, I do not know whether it would endure."

Borric said nothing, for even his worst fears since leaving the Prince were surpassed by Kerus's remarks. The Duke of Salador said, "One last thing, Borric. With Erland having refused the crown thirteen years ago, and the rumors of his health failing, many of the Congress of Lords will be looking to you for guidance. Where you lead, many will follow, even some of us in the East."

Borric said coldly, "Are you speaking of civil war?"

Kerus waved a hand, a pained expression crossing his face. His eyes seemed moist, as if near tears. "I am ever loyal to the crown, Borric, but if it comes to the right of things, the Kingdom must prevail. No one man is more important than the Kingdom."

Borric said through clenched jaws, "The King *is* the Kingdom."

Kerus said, "You would not be the man you are and say otherwise. I hope you are able to direct the King's energies toward this trouble in the West, for should the Kingdom be imperiled, others will not hold to such lofty beliefs."

Borric's tone softened a little as they walked up the steps leading from the garden. "I know you mean well, Lord Kerus, and there is only love of the realm in your heart. Have faith and pray, for I will do whatever I can to ensure the survival of the Kingdom."

Kerus stood before the door back into the palace. "I fear we will all be in deep water soon, my lord Borric. I pray that this invasion you speak of will not be the wave that drowns us. In whatever way I can aid you, I will." He turned toward the door, which was opened by a servant. Loudly he said, "I will bid you a good night, for I can see you're all tired."

The tension in the room was heavy as Borric, Arutha, and Pug reentered, and the Duke's mood one of dark reflection. Servants came to show the guests to their rooms, and Pug followed a boy near his own age, dressed in the Duke's livery. Pug looked over his shoulder as they left the hall to see the Duke and his son standing together, speaking quietly to Kulgan.

Pug was shown to a small but elegant room and, ignoring the richness of the bed covers, fell across them still fully clothed. The servant boy said, "Do you need aid in undressing, Squire?"

Pug sat up and looked at the boy with such a frank expression of wonder that the servant backed away a step. "If that will be all, Squire?" he asked, obviously uncomfortable.

Pug just laughed. The boy stood uncertainly for an instant, then bowed and hurriedly left the room. Pug pulled off his clothing, wondering at the eastern nobles and servants who had to help them undress. He was too tired to fold his garments, simply letting them fall to the floor in a heap.

After blowing out the bedside candle, Pug lay for a time in the darkness, troubled by the evening's discussion. He knew little of court intrigue, but knew that Kerus must have been deeply worried to speak as he did before strangers, in spite of Borric's reputation as a man of high honor.

Pug thought of all the things that had taken place in the last months and knew that his dreams of the King answering the call of Crydee with banners flying were another boyish fancy shattered upon the hard rock of reality.

13

▼▼

RILLANON

THE SHIP SAILED INTO THE HARBOR.

The climate of the Kingdom Sea was more clement than that of the Bitter Sea, and the journey from Salador had proven uneventful. They'd had to beat a tack much of the way against a steady northeast wind, so three weeks had passed instead of two.

Pug stood on the foredeck of the ship, his cloak pulled tightly around him. The winter wind's bitterness had given way to a softer cool, as if spring were but a few days in coming.

Rillanon was called the Jewel of the Kingdom, and Pug judged the name richly deserved. Unlike the squat cities of the West, Rillanon stood a mass of tall spires, gracefully arched bridges, and gently twisting roadways, scattered atop rolling hills in delightful confusion. Upon heroic towers, banners and pennons fluttered in the wind, as if the city celebrated the simple fact of its own existence. To Pug, even the ferrymen who worked the barges going to and from the ships at anchor in the harbor were more colorful for being within the enchantment of Rillanon.

The Duke of Salador had ordered a ducal banner sewn for Borric, and it now flew from the top of the ship's mainmast, informing the officials of the royal city that the Duke of Crydee had arrived. Borric's ship was given priority in docking by the city's harbor pilot, and quickly the ship was being secured at the royal quay. The party disembarked and were met by a company of the Royal Household Guard. At the head of the guards was an old, grey-haired, but still erect man, who greeted Borric warmly.

The two men embraced, and the older man, dressed in the royal purple and gold of the guard but with a ducal signet over his heart, said, "Borric, it is good to see you once more. What has it been? Ten . . . eleven years?"

"Caldric, old friend. It has been thirteen." Borric regarded him fondly. He had clear blue eyes and a short salt-and-pepper beard.

The man shook his head and smiled. "It has been much too long." He looked at the others. Spying Pug, he said, "Is this your younger boy?"

Borric laughed. "No, though he would be no shame to me if he were." He pointed out the lanky figure of Arutha. "This is my son. Arutha, come and greet your great-uncle."

Arutha stepped forward, and the two embraced. Duke Caldric, Lord of Rillanon, Knight-General of the King's Royal Household Guard, and Royal Chancellor, pushed Arutha back and regarded him at arm's length. "You were but a boy when I last saw you. I should have known you, for though you have some of your father's looks, you also resemble my dear brother—your mother's father—greatly. You do honor to my family."

Borric said, "Well, old war-horse, how is your city?"

Caldric said, "There is much to speak of, but not here. We shall bring you to the King's palace and quarter you in comfort. We shall have much time to visit. What brings you here to Rillanon?"

"I have pressing business with His Majesty, but it is not something to be spoken of in the streets. Let us go to the palace."

The Duke and his party were given mounts, and the escort cleared away the crowds as they rode through the city. If Krondor and Salador had impressed Pug with their splendor, Rillanon left him speechless.

The island city was built upon many hills, with several small rivers running down to the sea. It seemed to be a city of bridges and canals, as much as towers and spires. Many of the buildings seemed new, and Pug thought that this must be part of the King's plan for rebuilding the city. At several points along the way he saw workers removing old stones from a building, or erecting new walls and roofs. The newer buildings were faced with colorful stonework, many of marble and quartz, giving them a soft white, blue, or pink color. The cobblestones in the streets were clean, and gutters ran free of the clogs and debris Pug had seen in the other cities. Whatever else he might be doing, the boy thought, the King is maintaining a marvelous city.

A river ran before the palace, so that entrance was made over a high bridge that arched across the water into the main courtyard. The palace was a collection of great buildings connected by long halls that sprawled atop a hillside in the center of the city. It was faced with many-colored stone, giving it a rainbow aspect.

As they entered the courtyard, trumpets sounded from the walls, and guards stood to attention. Porters stepped forward to take the mounts, while a collection of palace nobles and officials stood near the palace entrance in welcome.

Approaching, Pug noticed that the greeting given by these men was formal and lacked the personal warmth of Duke Caldric's welcome. As he stood behind Kulgan and Meecham, he could hear Caldric's voice. "My lord Borric, Duke of Crydee, may I present Baron Gray, His Majesty's Steward of the Royal Household." This was a short, plump man in a tight-fitting tunic of red silk, and pale grey hose that bagged at the knees. "Earl Selvec, First Lord of the Royal Navies." A tall, gaunt man with a thin, waxed mustache bowed stiffly. And so on through the entire company. Each made a short statement of pleasure at Lord Borric's arrival, but Pug felt there was little sincerity in their remarks.

They were taken to their quarters. Kulgan had to raise a fuss to have Meecham near him, for Baron Gray had wanted to send him to the distant servants' wing of the palace, but he relented when Caldric asserted himself as Royal Chancellor.

The room that Pug was shown to far surpassed in splendor anything he had yet seen. The floors were polished marble, and the walls were made from the same material but flecked with what looked to be gold. A great mirror hung in a small room to one side of the sleeping quarters, where a large, gilded bathing tub sat. A steward put his few belongings —what they had picked up along the way since their own baggage had been lost in the forest—in a gigantic closet that could have held a dozen times all that Pug owned. After the man had finished, he inquired, "Shall I ready your bath, sir?"

Pug nodded, for three weeks aboard ship had made his clothes feel as if they were sticking to him. When the bath was ready, the steward said, "Lord Caldric will expect the Duke's party for dinner in four hours' time, sir. Shall I return then?"

Pug said yes, impressed with the man's diplomacy. He knew only that Pug had arrived with the Duke, and left it to Pug to decide whether or not he was included in the dinner invitation.

As he slipped into the warm water, Pug let out a long sigh of relief. He had never been one for baths when he had been a keep boy, preferring to wash away dirt in the sea and the streams near the castle. Now he could learn to enjoy them. He mused about what Tomas would have thought of that. He drifted off in a warm haze of memories, one very pleasant, of a dark-haired, lovely princess, and one sad, of a sandy-haired boy.

THE DINNER of the night before had been an informal occasion, with Duke Caldric hosting Lord Borric's party. Now they stood in the royal throne room waiting to be presented to the King. The hall was vast, a high vaulted affair, with the entire southern wall fashioned of floor-to-ceiling windows overlooking the city. Hundreds of nobles stood around as the Duke's party was led down a central aisle between the onlookers.

Pug had not thought it possible to consider Duke Borric poorly dressed, for he had always worn the finest clothing in Crydee, as had his children. But among the finery in evidence around the room, Borric looked like a raven amid a flock of peacocks. Here a pearl-studded doublet, there a gold-thread-embroidered tunic—each noble seemed to be outdoing the next. Every lady wore the costliest silks and brocades, but only slightly outshone the men.

They halted before the throne, and Caldric announced the Duke. The King smiled, and Pug was struck by a faint resemblance to Arutha, though the King's manner was more relaxed. He leaned forward on his throne and said, "Welcome to our city, cousin. It is good to see Crydee in this hall after so many years."

Borric stepped forward and knelt before Rodric the Fourth, King of the Kingdom of the Isles. "I am gladdened to see Your Majesty well."

A brief shadow passed over the monarch's face, then he smiled again. "Present to us your companions."

The Duke presented his son, and the King said, "Well, it is true that one of the conDoin line carries the blood of our mother's kin besides ourself." Arutha bowed and backed away. Kulgan was next as one of the Duke's advisers. Meecham, who had no rank in the Duke's court, had stayed in his room. The King said something polite, and Pug was introduced. "Squire Pug of Crydee, Your Majesty, Master of Forest Deep, and member of my court."

The King clapped his hands together and laughed. "The boy who kills trolls. How wonderful. Travelers have carried the tale from the far shores of Crydee, and we would hear it spoken by the author of the brave deed. We must meet later so that you may tell us of this marvel."

Pug bowed awkwardly, feeling a thousand eyes upon him. There had been times before when he had wished the troll story had not been spread, but never so much as now.

He backed away, and the King said, "Tonight we will hold a ball to honor the arrival of our cousin Borric."

He stood, arranging his purple robes around him, and pulled his golden chain of office over his head. A page placed the chain on a purple velvet cushion. The King then lifted his golden crown from his black-tressed head and handed it to another page.

The crowd bowed as he stepped down from his throne. "Come, cousin," he said to Borric, "let us retire to my private balcony, where we can speak without all the rigors of office. I grow weary of the pomp."

Borric nodded and fell in next to the King, motioning Pug and the others to wait. Duke Caldric announced that the day's audience was at an end, and that those with petitions for the King should return the next day.

Slowly the crowd moved out the two great doors at the end of the hall, while Arutha, Kulgan, and Pug stood by. Caldric approached and said, "I will show you to a room where you may wait. It would be well for you to stay close, should His Majesty call for your attendance."

A steward of the court took them through a small door near the one the King had escorted Borric through. They entered a large, comfortable room with a long table in the center laden with fruit, cheese, bread, and wine. At the table were many chairs, and around the edge of the room were several divans, with plump cushions piled upon them.

Arutha crossed over to large glass doors and peered through them. "I can see Father and the King sitting on the royal balcony."

Kulgan and Pug joined him and looked to where Arutha indicated. The two men were at a table, overlooking the city and the sea beyond. The King was speaking with expansive gestures, and Borric nodded as he listened.

Pug said, "I had not expected that His Majesty would look like you, Your Highness."

Arutha replied with a wry smile, "It is not so surprising when you consider that, as my father was cousin to his father, so my mother was cousin to his mother."

Kulgan put his hand on Pug's shoulder. "Many of the noble families have more than one tie between them, Pug. Cousins who are four and five times removed will marry for reasons of politics and bring the families closer again. I doubt there is one noble family in the East that can't claim some relationship to the crown, though it may be distant and follow along a twisted route."

They returned to the table, and Pug nibbled at a piece of cheese. "The King seems in good humor," he said, cautiously approaching the subject all had on their minds.

Kulgan looked pleased at the circumspect manner of the boy's comment, for after leaving Salador, Borric had cautioned them all regarding Duke Kerus's remarks. He had ended his admonition with the old adage, "In the halls of power, there are no secrets, and even the deaf can hear."

Arutha said, "Our monarch is a man of moods; let us hope he stays in a good one after he hears Father's tidings."

The afternoon slowly passed as they awaited word from the Duke. When the shadows outside had grown long, Borric suddenly appeared at a door. He crossed over to stand before them, a troubled expression on his face. "His Majesty spent most of the afternoon explaining his plans for the rebirth of the Kingdom."

Arutha said, "Did you tell him of the Tsurani?"

The Duke nodded. "He listened and then calmly informed me that he would consider the matter. We will speak again in a day or so was all he said."

Kulgan said, "At least he seemed in good humor."

Borric regarded his old adviser. "I fear too good. I expected some sign of alarm. I do not ride across the Kingdom for minor cause, but he seemed unmoved by what I had to tell him."

Kulgan looked worried. "We are overlong on this journey as it is. Let us hope that His Majesty will not take long in deciding upon a course of action."

Borric sat heavily in a chair and reached for a glass of wine. "Let us hope."

PUG WALKED THROUGH the door to the King's private quarters, his mouth dry with anticipation. He was to have his interview with King Rodric in a few minutes, and he was unsettled to be alone with the ruler of the Kingdom. Each time he had been close to other powerful nobles, he had hidden in the shadow of the Duke or his son, coming forward to tell briefly what he knew of the Tsurani, then able to disappear quickly back into the background. Now he was to be the only guest of the most powerful man north of the Empire of Great Kesh.

A house steward showed him through the door to the King's private balcony. Several servants stood around the edge of the large open veranda, and the King occupied the lone table, a carved marble affair under a large canopy.

The day was clear. Spring was coming early, as winter had before it, and there was a hint of warmth in the gusting air. Below the balcony, past the hedges and stone walls that marked its edge, Pug could see the city of Rillanon and the sea beyond. The colorful rooftops shone brightly in the midday sun, as the last snows had melted completely over the last four days. Ships sailed in and out of the harbor, and the streets teemed with citizens. The faint cries of merchants and hawkers, shouting over the noise of the streets, floated up to become a soft buzzing where the King took his midday meal.

As Pug approached the table, a servant pulled out a chair. The King turned and said, "Ah! Squire Pug, please take a seat." Pug began a bow, and the King said, "Enough. I don't stand on formality when I dine with a friend."

Pug hesitated, then said, "Your Majesty honors me," as he sat.

Rodric waved the comment way. "I remember what it is to be a boy in the company of men. When I was but a little older than you, I took the crown. Until then I was only my father's son." His eyes got a distant look for a moment. "The Prince, it's true, but still only a boy. My opinion counted for nothing, and I never seemed to satisfy my father's expectations, in hunting, riding, sailing, or swordplay. I took many a hiding from my tutors, Caldric among them. That all changed when I became King, but I still remember what it was like." He turned toward Pug, and the distant expression vanished as he smiled. "And I do wish us to be friends." He glanced away and again his expression turned distant. "One can't have too many friends, now, can one? And since I'm the King, there are so many who claim to be my friend, but aren't." He was silent a moment, then again came out of his revery. "What do you think of my city?"

Pug said, "I have never seen anything like it, Majesty. It's wonderful."

Rodric looked out across the vista before them. "Yes, it is, isn't it?" He waved a hand, and a servant poured wine into crystal goblets. Pug sipped at his; he still hadn't developed a taste for wine, but found this very good, light and fruity with a hint of spices. Rodric said, "I have tried very hard to make Rillanon a wonderful place for those who live here. I would have the day come when all the cities of the Kingdom are as fine as this, where everywhere the eye travels, there is beauty. It would take a hundred lifetimes to do that, so I can only set the pattern, building an example for those who follow to imitate. But where I find brick, I leave marble. And those who see it will know it for what it is—my legacy."

The King seemed to ramble a bit, and Pug wasn't sure of all that he was saying as he continued to talk about buildings and gardens and removing ugliness from view. Abruptly the King changed topics. "Tell me how you killed the trolls."

Pug told him, and the King seemed to hang on every word. When the boy had finished, the King said, "That is a wonderful tale. It is better than the versions that have reached the court, for while it is not half so heroic, it is twice as impressive for being true. You have a stout heart, Squire Pug."

Pug said, "Thank you, Majesty."

Rodric said, "In your tale you mentioned the Princess Carline."

"Yes, Majesty?"

"I have not seen her since she was a baby in her mother's arms. What sort of woman has she become?"

Pug found the shift in topic surprising, but said, "She has become a beautiful woman, Majesty, much like her mother. She is bright and quick, if given to a little temper."

The King nodded. "Her mother was a beautiful woman. If the daughter is half as lovely, she is lovely indeed. Can she reason?"

Pug looked confused. "Majesty?"

"Has she a good head for reason, logic? Can she argue?"

Pug nodded vigorously. "Yes, Your Majesty. The Princess is very good at that."

The King rubbed his hands together. "Good. I must have Borric send her for a visit. Most of these eastern ladies are vapid, without substance. I was hoping Borric gave the girl an education. I would like to meet a young woman who knew logic and philosophy, and could argue and declaim."

Pug suddenly realized what the King had meant by arguing wasn't what he had thought. He decided it best not to mention the discrepancy.

The King continued. "My ministers dun me to seek a wife and give the Kingdom an heir. I have been busy, and frankly, have found little to interest me in the court ladies—oh, they're fine for a moonlight walk and . . . other things. But as the mother of my heirs? I hardly think so. But I should become serious in my search for a queen. Perhaps the only conDoin daughter would be the logical place to start."

Pug began to mention another conDoin daughter, then stifled the impulse, remembering the tension between the King and Anita's father. Besides, the girl was only seven.

The King shifted topics again. "For four days cousin Borric has regaled me with tales of these aliens, these Tsurani. What do you think of all this business?"

Pug looked startled. He had not thought the King might ask him for an opinion on anything, let alone a matter as important as the security of the Kingdom. He thought for a long moment, trying to frame his answer as best he could, then said, "From everything I have seen and heard, Your Majesty, I think these Tsurani people not only are planning to invade, but are already here."

The King raised an eyebrow. "Oh? I would like to hear your reasoning."

Pug considered his words carefully. "If there have been as many sightings as we are aware of, Majesty, considering the stealth these people are employing, wouldn't it be logical that there are many more occurrences of their coming and going than we know of?"

The King nodded. "A good proposition. Continue."

"Then might it also not be true that once the snows have fallen, we are less likely to find signs of them, as they are holding to remote areas?"

Rodric nodded and Pug continued. "If they are as warlike as the Duke and the others have said them to be, I think they have mapped out the West to find a good place to bring their soldiers in during the winter so they can launch their offensive this spring."

The King slapped the table with his hand. "A good exercise in logic, Pug." Motioning for the servants to bring food, he said, "Now, let us eat."

Food of an amazing variety and amount for just the two of them was produced, and Pug picked small amounts of many things, so as not to appear indifferent to the King's generosity. Rodric asked him a few questions as they dined, and Pug answered as well as he could.

As Pug was finishing his meal, the King put his elbow on the table and stroked his beardless chin. He stared out into space for a long time, and Pug began to feel self-conscious, not knowing the proper courtesy toward a king who is lost in thought. He elected to sit quietly.

After a time Rodric came out of his revery. There was a troubled note in his voice as he looked at Pug and said, "Why do these people come to plague us now? There is so much to be done. I can't have war disrupting my plans." He stood and paced around the balcony for a while, leaving Pug standing, for he had risen when the King had. Rodric turned to Pug. "I must send for Duke Guy. He will advise me. He has a good head for such things."

The King paced, looking at the city for a few minutes more, while Pug stood by his chair. He heard the monarch mutter to himself about the great works that must not be interrupted, then felt a tug on his sleeve. He turned and saw a palace steward standing quietly at his side. With a smile and a gesture toward the door, the steward indicated the interview was at an end. Pug followed the man to the door, wondering at the staff's ability to recognize the moods of the King.

Pug was shown the way back to his room, and he asked the servant to carry word to Lord Borric that Pug wished to see him if he was not busy.

He went into his room and sat down to think. A short time later he was brought out of his musing by a knock at the door. He gave permission for the caller to enter, and the same steward who had carried the message to the Duke entered, with the message that Borric would see Pug at once.

Pug followed the man from his room and sent him away, saying he could find the Duke's room without guidance. He walked slowly, thinking of what he was going to tell the Duke. Two things were abundantly clear to the boy: the King was not pleased to hear that the Tsurani were a potential threat to his kingdom, and Lord Borric would be equally displeased to hear that Guy du Bas-Tyra was being called to Rillanon.

AS WITH EVERY dinner over the last few days, there was a hushed mood at the table. The five men of Crydee sat eating in the Duke's quarters, with palace servants, all wearing the King's purple-and-gold badge on their dark tunics, hovering nearby.

The Duke was chafing to leave Rillanon for the West. Nearly four months had passed since they left Crydee: the entire winter. Spring was upon them, and if the Tsurani were going to attack, as they all believed, it was only a matter of days now. Arutha's restlessness matched his father's. Even Kulgan showed signs that the waiting was telling upon him. Only Meecham, who revealed nothing of his feelings, seemed content to wait.

Pug also longed for home. He had grown bored in the palace. He wished to be back in his tower with his studies. He also wished to see Carline again, though he didn't speak of this to anyone. Lately he found himself remembering her in a softer light, forgiving those qualities that had once irritated him. He also knew, with mixed feelings of anticipation, that he might discover the fate of Tomas. Dolgan should soon send word to Crydee, if the thaw came early to the mountains.

Borric had endured several more meetings with the King over the last week, each ending unsatisfactorily as far as he was concerned. The last had been hours ago, but he would say nothing about it until the room was emptied of servants.

As the last dishes were being cleared away, and the servants were pouring the King's finest Keshian brandy, a knock came at the door and Duke Caldric entered, waving the servants outside. When the room was cleared, he turned to the Duke.

"Borric, I am sorry to interrupt your dining, but I have news."

Borric stood, as did the others. "Please join us. Here, take a glass."

Caldric took the offered brandy and sat in Pug's chair, while the boy pulled another over. The Duke of Rillanon sipped his brandy and said, "Messengers arrived less than an hour ago from the Duke of Bas-Tyra. Guy expresses alarm over the possibility that the King might be 'unduly' distressed by these 'rumors' of trouble in the West."

Borric stood and threw his glass across the room, shattering it. Amber fluid dripped down the wall as the Duke of Crydee nearly roared with anger. "What game does Guy play at? What is this talk of rumors and undue distress!"

Caldric raised a hand and Borric calmed a little, sitting again. The old Duke said, "I myself penned the King's call to Guy. Everything you had told, every piece of information and every surmise, was included. I can only think Guy is ensuring that the King reaches no decision until he arrives at the palace."

Borric drummed his fingers on the table and looked at Caldric with anger flashing in his eyes. "What is Bas-Tyra doing? If war comes, it comes to Crydee and Yabon. My people will suffer. My lands will be ravaged."

Caldric shook his head slowly. "I will speak plainly, old friend. Since the estrangement between the King and his uncle, Erland, Guy plays to advance his own banner to primacy in the Kingdom. I think that, should Erland's health fail, Guy sees himself wearing the purple of Krondor."

Through clenched teeth Borric said, "Then hear me clearly, Caldric. I would not put that burden on myself or mine for any but the highest purpose. But if Erland is as ill as I think, in spite of his claims otherwise, it will be Anita who sits the throne in Krondor, not Black Guy. If I have to march the Armies of the West into Krondor and assume the regency myself, that is what shall be, even should Rodric wish it otherwise. Only if the King has issue will another take the western throne."

Caldric looked at Borric calmly. "And will you be branded traitor to the crown?"

Borric slapped the table with his hand. "Curse the day that villain was born. I regret that I must acknowledge him kinsman."

Caldric waited for a minute until Borric calmed down, then said, "I know you better than you know yourself, Borric. You would not raise the war banner of the West against the King, though you might happily strangle your cousin Guy. It was always a sad thing for me that the Kingdom's two finest generals could hate each other so."

"Aye, and with cause. Every time there is a call to aid the West, it is cousin Guy who opposes. Every time there is intrigue and a title is lost, it is one of Guy's favorites who gains. How can you not see? It was only because you, Brucal of Yabon, and I myself held firm that the congress did not name Guy regent for Rodric's first three years. He stood before every Duke in the Kingdom and called you a tired old man who was not fit to rule in the King's name. How can you forget?"

Caldric did look tired and old as he sat in the chair, one hand shading his eyes, as if the room light were too bright. Softly he said, "I do see, and I haven't forgotten. But he also is my kinsman by marriage, and if I were not here, how much more influence do you think he would have with Rodric? As a boy the King idolized him, seeing in him a dashing hero, a fighter of the first rank, a defender of the Kingdom."

Borric leaned back in his chair. "I am sorry, Caldric," he said, his voice losing its harsh edge. "I know you act for the good of us all. And Guy did play the hero, rolling the Keshian Army back at Deep Taunton, all those years ago. I should not speak of things I have not seen first-hand."

Arutha sat passively through all this, but his eyes showed he felt the same anger as his father. He moved forward in his chair, and the dukes looked at him. Borric said, "You have something to say, my son?"

Arutha spread his hands wide before him. "In all this the thought has bothered me: should the Tsurani come, how would it profit Guy to see the King hesitate?"

Borric drummed his fingers on the table. "That is the puzzle, for in spite of his scheming, Guy would not peril the Kingdom, not to spite me."

"Would it not serve him," said Arutha, "to let the West suffer a little, until the issue was in doubt, then to come at the head of the Armies of the East, the conquering hero, as he was at Deep Taunton?"

Caldric considered this. "Even Guy could not think so little of these aliens, I would hope."

Arutha paced the room. "But consider what he knows. The ramblings of a dying man. Surmise on the nature of a ship that only Pug, here, has seen, and I caught but a glimpse of as it slid into the sea. Conjecture by a priest and a magician, both callings Guy holds in little regard. Some migrating Dark Brothers. He might discount such news."

"But it is all there for the seeing," protested Borric.

Caldric watched the young Prince pace the room. "Perhaps you are right. What may be lacking is the urgency of your words, an urgency lacking in the dry message of ink and parchment. When he arrives, we must convince him."

Borric nearly spat his words. "It is for the King to decide, not Guy!"

Caldric said, "But the King has given much weight to Guy's counsel. If you are to gain command of the Armies of the West, it is Guy who must be convinced."

Borric looked shocked. "I? I do not want the banner of the armies. I only wish for Erland to be free to aid me, should there be need."

Caldric placed both hands upon the table. "Borric, for all your wisdom, you are much the rustic noble. Erland cannot lead the armies. He is not well. Even if he could, the King would not allow it. Nor would he give leave for Erland's Marshal, Dulanic. You have seen Rodric at his best, of late. When the black moods are upon him, he fears for his life. None dare say it, but the King suspects his uncle of plotting for the crown."

"Ridiculous!" exclaimed Borric. "The crown was Erland's for the asking thirteen years ago. There was no clear succession. Rodric's father had not yet named him heir apparent, and Erland's claim was as clear as the King's, perhaps more so. Only Guy and those who sought to use the boy pressed Rodric's claim. Most of the congress would have sustained Erland as King."

"I know, but times are different, and the boy is a boy no longer. He is now a frightened young man who is sick from fear. Whether it is due to Guy's and the others' influence or from some illness of the mind, I do not know. The King does not think as other men do. No king does, and Rodric less than most. Ridiculous as it may seem, he will not give the Armies of the West to his uncle. I am also afraid that once Guy has his ear, he will not give them to you either."

Borric opened his mouth to say something, but Kulgan interrupted. "Excuse me, Your Graces, but may I suggest something?"

Caldric looked at Borric, who nodded. Kulgan cleared his throat and said, "Would the King give the Armies of the West to Duke Brucal of Yabon?"

Comprehension slowly dawned on Borric's and Caldric's faces, until the Duke of Crydee threw back his head and laughed. Slamming his fist on the table, he nearly shouted, "Kulgan! If you had not served me well in all the years I have known you, tonight you have." He turned to Caldric. "What do you think?"

Caldric smiled for the first time since entering the room. "Brucal? That old war dog? There is no more honest man in the Kingdom. And he is not in the line of succession. He would be beyond even Guy's attempts to discredit. Should he receive the command of the armies . . ."

Arutha finished the thought. "He would call Father to be his chief adviser. He knows Father is the finest commander in the West."

Caldric sat up straight in his chair, excitement on his face. "You would even have command of the armies of Yabon."

"Yes," said Arutha, "and LaMut, Zūn, Ylith, and the rest."

Caldric stood. "I think it will work. Say nothing to the King tomorrow. I will find the proper time to make the 'suggestion.' Pray that His Majesty approves."

Caldric took his leave, and Pug could see that for the first time there was hope for a good ending to this journey. Even Arutha, who had fumed like black thunder all week, looked nearly happy.

PUG WAS AWAKENED by a pounding on his door. He sleepily called out for whoever was out there to enter, and the door opened. A royal steward peeked in. "Sir, the King commands all in the Duke's party to join him in the throne room. At once." He held a lantern for Pug's convenience.

Pug said he would come straight away and hurriedly got dressed. Outside it was still dark, and he felt anxious about what had caused this surprise summons. The hopeful feeling of the night before, after Caldric had left, was replaced by a gnawing worry that the unpredictable King had somehow learned of the plan to circumvent the arrival of the Duke of Bas-Tyra.

He was still buckling his belt about his tunic when he left his room. He hurried down the hall, with the steward beside him holding a lantern against the dark, as the torches and candles usually lit in the evening had all been extinguished.

When they reached the throne room, the Duke, Arutha, and Kulgan were arriving, all looking apprehensively toward Rodric, who paced by his throne, still in his night-robes. Duke Caldric stood to one side, a grave expression on his face. The room was dark, save for the lanterns carried by the stewards.

As soon as they were gathered before the throne, Rodric flew into a rage. "Cousin! Do you know what I have here?" he screamed, holding out a sheaf of parchment.

Borric said he didn't. Rodric's voice lowered only a little. "It is a message from Yabon! That old fool Brucal has let those Tsurani aliens attack and destroy one of his garrisons. Look at these!" he nearly shrieked, throwing the parchments toward Borric. Kulgan picked them up and handed them to the Duke. "Never mind," said the King, his voice returning to near-normalcy. "I'll tell you what they say.

"These invaders have attacked into the Free Cities, near Walinor. They have attacked into the elven forests. They have attacked Stone Mountain. They have attacked Crydee."

Without thinking, Borric said, "What news from Crydee?"

The King stopped his pacing. He looked at Borric, and for a moment Pug saw madness in his eyes. He closed them briefly, then opened them, and Pug could see the King was himself again. He shook his head slightly and raised his hand to his temple. "I have only secondhand news from Brucal. When those messages left six weeks ago, there had only been one attack at Crydee. Your son Lyam reports the victory was total, driving the aliens deep into the forest."

Caldric stepped forward. "All reports say the same thing. Heavily armed companies of foot soldiers attacked during the night, before the snows had melted, taking the garrisons by surprise. Little is known save that a garrison of LaMutians near Stone Mountain was overrun. All other attacks seem to have been driven back." He looked at Borric meaningfully. "There is no word of the Tsurani's using cavalry."

Borric said, "Then perhaps Tully was right, and they have no horses."

The King seemed to be dizzy, for he took a staggering step backward and sat on his throne. Again he placed a hand to his temple, then said, "What is this talk of horses? My Kingdom is invaded. These creatures dare to attack my soldiers."

Borric looked at the King. "What would Your Majesty have me do?"

The King's voice rose. "Do? I was going to wait for my loyal Duke of Bas-Tyra to arrive before I made any decision. But now I must act."

He paused, and his face took on a vulpine look, as his dark eyes gleamed in the lantern light. "I was considering giving the Armies of the West to Brucal, but the doddering old fool can't even protect his own garrisons."

Borric was about to protest on Brucal's behalf, but Arutha, knowing his father, gripped his arm, and the Duke remained silent.

The King said, "Borric, you must leave Crydee to your son. He is capable enough, I should think. He's given us our only victory so far." His eyes wandered and he giggled. He shook his head for a moment, and his voice lost its frantic edge. "Oh, gods, these pains. I think my head will burst." He closed his eyes briefly. "Borric, leave Crydee to Lyam and Arutha; I'm giving you the banner of the Armies of the West; go to Yabon. Brucal is sorely pressed, for most of the alien army strikes toward LaMut and Zūn. When you are there, request what you need. These invaders must be driven from our lands."

The King's face was pale, and perspiration gleamed on his forehead. "This is a poor hour to start, but I have sent word to the harbor to ready a ship. You must leave at once. Go now."

The Duke bowed and turned. Caldric said, "I will see His Majesty to his room. I will accompany you to the docks when you are ready."

The old Chancellor helped the King from the throne, and the Duke's party left the hall. They rushed back to their rooms to find stewards already packing their belongings. Pug stood around excitedly, for at last he was returning to his home.

THEY STOOD at dockside, bidding farewell to Caldric. Pug and Meecham waited, and the tall franklin said, "Well, lad. It will be some time before we see home again, now that war is joined."

Pug looked up into the scarred face of the man who had found him in the storm, so long ago. "Why? Aren't we going home?"

Meecham shook his head. "The Prince will ship from Krondor through the Straits of Darkness to join his brother, but the Duke will ship for Ylith, then to Brucal's camp somewhere near LaMut. Where Lord Borric goes, Kulgan goes. And where my master goes, I go. And you?"

Pug felt a sinking in his stomach. What the franklin said was true. He belonged with Kulgan, not with the folk at Crydee, though he knew if he asked, he would be allowed to go home with the Prince. He resigned himself to another sign that his boyhood was ending. "Where Kulgan goes, I go."

Meecham clapped him on the shoulder and said, "Well, at least I can teach you to use that bloody sword you swing like a fishwife's broom."

Feeling little cheer at the prospect, Pug smiled weakly. They soon boarded the ship and were under way toward Salador, and the first leg of the long journey west.

14

▾▾

INVASION

THE SPRING RAINS WERE HEAVY THAT YEAR.

The business of war was hampered by the ever-present mud. It would stay wet and cold for nearly another month before the brief, hot summer came.

Duke Brucal of Yabon and Lord Borric stood looking over a table laden with maps. The rain hammered on the roof of the tent, the central part of the commander's pavilion. On either side of the tent two others were attached, providing sleeping quarters for the two nobles. The tent was filled with smoke, from lanterns and from Kulgan's pipe. The magician had proven an able adviser to the dukes, and his magical aid helpful. He could detect trends in the weather, and his wizard's sight could detect some of the Tsurani's troop movements, though not often. And over the years his reading of every book he encountered, including narratives of warfare, had made him a fair student of tactics and strategy.

Brucal pointed to the newest map on the table. "They have taken this point here, and another here. They hold this point"—he indicated another spot on the map—"in spite of our every effort to dislodge them. They also seem to be moving along a line from here, to here." His finger swept down a line along the eastern face of the Grey Towers. "There is a coordinated pattern here, but I'm damned if I can anticipate where it's going next." The old Duke looked weary. The fighting had been going on sporadically for over two months now, and no distinct advantage could be seen on either side.

Borric studied the map. Red spots marked known Tsurani strongholds: hand-dug, earthen breastworks, with a minimum of two hundred men defending. There were also suspected reinforcement companies, their approximate location indicated with yellow spots. It was known that any position attacked was quick to get reinforcements, sometimes in a matter of minutes. Blue spots indicated the location of Kingdom pickets, though most of Brucal's forces were billeted around the hill upon which the commander's tent sat.

Until the heavy foot soldiers and engineers from Ylith and Tyr-Sog arrived to man and create permanent fortifications, the Kingdom was fighting a principally mobile war, for most of the troops assembled were cavalry. The Duke of Crydee agreed with the other man's assessment. "It seems their tactics remain the same: bring in a small force, dig in, and hold. They prevent our troops from entering, but refuse to follow when we withdraw. There is a pattern. But for the life of me, I can't see it either."

A guard entered. "My lords, an elf stands without, seeking entrance."

Brucal said, "Show him in."

The guard held aside the tent flap, and an elf entered. His red-brown hair was plastered to his head, and his cloak dripped water on the floor of the tent. He made a slight bow to the dukes.

"What news from Elvandar?" Borric asked.

"My Queen sends you greetings." He quickly turned to the map. He pointed at the pass between the Grey Towers on the south and Stone Mountain on the north, the same pass Borric's forces now bottled up at its east end. "The outworlders move many soldiers through this pass. They have advanced to the edge of the elven forests, but seek not to enter. They have made it difficult to get through." He grinned. "I led several a merry chase for half a day. They run nearly as well as the dwarves. But they could not keep up in the forest." He returned his attention to the map. "There is word from Crydee that skirmishes have been fought by outriding patrols, but nothing close to the castle itself. There is no word of activity from the Grey Towers, Carse, or Tulan. They seem content to dig in along this pass. Your forces to the west will not be able to join you, for they could not break through now."

"How strong do the aliens appear to be?" asked Brucal.

"It is not known, but I saw several thousand along this route." His finger indicated a route along the northern edge of the pass, from the elven forests to the Kingdom camp. "The dwarves of Stone Mountain are left alone, so long as they do not venture south. The outworlders deny them the pass also."

Borric asked the elf, "Has there been any report of the Tsurani's having cavalry?"

"None. Every report refers only to infantry."

Kulgan said, "Father Tully's speculation on their being horseless seems to be borne out."

Brucal took brush and ink in hand and entered the information on the map. Kulgan stood looking over his shoulder.

Borric said to the elf, "After you've rested, carry my greetings to your mistress, and my wish for her good health and prosperity. If you should send runners to the west, please carry the same message to my sons."

The elf bowed. "As my lord wishes. I shall return to Elvandar at once." He turned and left the tent.

Kulgan said, "I think I see it." He pointed to the new red spots on the map. They formed a rough half circle, through the pass. "The Tsurani are trying to hold this area here. That valley is the center of the circle. I would guess they are attempting to keep anyone from getting close."

Both the dukes looked puzzled. Borric said, "But to what purpose? There is nothing there of any value militarily. It is as if they are inviting us to bottle them up in that valley."

Suddenly Brucal gasped. "It's a bridgehead. Think of it in terms of crossing a river. They have a foothold on this side of the rift, as the magician calls it. They have only as many supplies as their men can carry through. They don't have enough control of the area for foraging, so they need to expand the area under their control and build up supplies before they launch an offensive."

Brucal turned to the magician. "Kulgan, what do you think? This is more in your province."

The magician looked at the map as if trying to divine information hidden in it. "We know nothing of the magic involved. We don't know how fast they can pass supplies and men through, for no one has ever witnessed an appearance. They may require a large area, which this valley provides them. Or they may have some limit on the amount of time available to pass troops through."

Duke Borric considered this. "Then there is only one thing to do. We must send a party into the valley to see what they are doing."

Kulgan smiled. "I will go too, if Your Grace permits. Your soldiers might not have the faintest idea of what they are seeing if it involves magic."

Brucal started to object, his gaze taking in the magician's ample size. Borric cut him off. "Don't let his look fool you. He rides like a trooper."

He turned to Kulgan. "You had best take Pug, for if one should fall, then the other can carry the news."

Kulgan looked unhappy at that, but saw the wisdom in it. The Duke of Yabon said, "If we strike at the North Pass, then into this valley and draw their forces there, a small, fast company might break through here." He pointed at a small pass that entered the south end of the valley from the east.

Borric said, "It is a bold enough plan. We have danced with the Tsurani so long, holding a stable front, I doubt they will expect it." The magician suggested they retire for the rest of the evening, for it would be a long day on the morrow. He closed his eyes briefly, then informed the two leaders that the rain would stop and the next day would be sunny.

PUG LAY WRAPPED in a blanket, trying to nap, when Kulgan entered their tent. Meecham sat before the cook fire, preparing the evening meal and attempting to keep it from the greedy maw of Fantus. The firedrake had sought out his master a week before, eliciting startled cries from the soldiers as he swooped over the tents. Only Meecham's commanding shouts had kept a bowman from putting a cloth-yard arrow into the playful drake. Kulgan had been pleased to see his pet, but at a loss to explain how the creature had found them. The drake had moved right into the magician's tent, content to sleep next to Pug and steal food from under Meecham's watchful eye.

Pug sat up as the magician pulled off his sopping cloak. "There is an expedition going deep within Tsurani-held territory, to break the circle they've thrown up around a small valley and find out what they are up to. You and Meecham will be going with me on this trip, I would have friends at my back and side."

Pug felt excited by the news. Meecham had spent long hours schooling him in use of sword and shield, and the old dream of soldiering had returned. "I have kept my blade sharp, Kulgan."

Meecham gave forth a snort that passed for laughter, and the magician threw him a black look. "Good, Pug. But with any luck we'll not be fighting. We are to go in a smaller force attached to a larger one that will draw off the Tsurani. We will drive quickly into their territory and discover what they are hiding. We will then ride as fast as possible to bring back the news. I thank the gods they are without horses, or we could never hope to accomplish so bold a stroke. We shall ride through them before they know we have struck."

"Perhaps we may take a prisoner," the boy said hopefully.

"It would be a change," said Meecham. The Tsurani had proved to be fierce fighters, preferring to die rather than be captured.

"Maybe then we'd discover why they've come to Midkemia," ventured Pug.

Kulgan looked thoughtful. "There is little we understand about these Tsurani. Where is this place they come from? How do they cross between their world and ours? And as you've pointed out, the most vexing question of all, why do they come? Why invade our lands?"

"Metal."

Kulgan and Pug looked over at Meecham, who was spooning up stew, keeping one eye on Fantus. "They don't have any metal and they want ours." When Kulgan and Pug regarded him with blank expressions, he shook his head. "I'd thought you puzzled it out by now, so I didn't think to bring it up." He put aside the bowls of stew, reached behind himself, and drew a bright red arrow out from under his bedding. "Souvenir," he said, holding it out for inspection. "Look at the head. It's the same stuff their swords are made from, some kind of wood, hardened like steel. I picked over a lot of things fetched in by the soldiers, and I haven't seen one thing these Tsurani make with any metal in it."

Kulgan looked flabbergasted. "Of course! It's all so simple. They found a way to pass between their world and ours, sent through scouts, and found a land rich in metals they lack. So they sent in an invading army. It also explains why they marshal in a high valley of the mountains, rather than in the lower forests. It gives them free access to . . . the dwarven mines!" He jumped up. "I'd better inform the dukes at once. We must send word to the dwarves to be alert for incursions into the mines."

Pug sat thoughtfully as Kulgan vanished through the tent entrance. After a moment he said, "Meecham, why didn't they try trading?"

Meecham shook his head. "The Tsurani? From what I've seen, boy, it's a good bet trading never entered their minds. They are one very warlike bunch. Those bastards fight like six hundred kinds of demons. If they had cavalry, they would have chased this whole lot back to LaMut, then probably burned the city down around them. But if we can wear them down, like a bulldog does, just keep hanging on until they tire, we might settle this after a time. Look what happened to Kesh. Lost half of Bosania to the Kingdom in the north 'cause the Confederacy just plain wore the Empire out with one rebellion after another in the south."

After a time, Pug gave up on Kulgan's returning soon, ate supper alone, and made ready for bed. Meecham quit trying to keep the magician's meal away from the drake, and also turned in.

In the dark, Pug lay staring up at the tent roof, listening to the sound of the rain and the drake's joyous chewing. Soon he drifted off into sleep, where he dreamed of a dark tunnel and a flickering light vanishing down it.

THE TREES were thick and the air hung heavy with mist as the column moved slowly through the forest. Outriders came and went every few minutes, checking for signs that the Tsurani were preparing an ambush. The sun was lost high in the trees overhead, and the entire scene had a greyish-green quality to it, making it difficult to see more than a few yards ahead.

At the head of the column rode a young captain of the LaMutian army, Vandros, son of the old Earl of LaMut. He was also one of the more level-headed and capable young officers in Brucal's army.

They rode in pairs, with Pug sitting next to a soldier, behind Kulgan and Meecham. The order to halt came down the line, and Pug reined in his horse and dismounted. Over a light gambeson, he wore a well-oiled suit of chain mail. Over that was a tabard of the LaMutian forces, with the grey wolf's head on a circle of blue in the center. Heavy woolen trousers were tucked into his high boots. He had a shield on his left arm, and his sword hung from his belt; he felt truly a soldier. The only discordant note was his helm, which was a little too large and gave him a slightly comic appearance.

Captain Vandros came back to where Kulgan stood waiting, and dismounted. "The scouts have spotted a camp about half a mile ahead. They think they were not seen by the guards."

The captain pulled out a map. "We are about here. I will lead my men and attack the enemy position. Cavalry from Zūn will support us on either side. Lieutenant Garth will command the column you will ride with. You will pass the enemy camp and continue on toward the mountains. We will try to follow if we can, but if we haven't rejoined you by sundown, you must continue alone.

"Keep moving, if only at a slow walk. Push the horses, but try to keep them alive. On horseback you can always outrun these aliens, but on foot I wouldn't give you much chance of getting back. They run like fiends.

"Once in the mountains, move through the pass. Ride into the valley one hour after sunrise. The North Pass will be attacked at dawn, so if you get safely into the valley you should, I hope, find little between you and the North Pass. Once in the valley, don't stop for anything. If a man falls, he is to be left. The mission is to get information back to the commanders. Now try to rest. It may be your last chance for some time. We attack in an hour."

He walked his horse back to the head of the line. Kulgan, Meecham, and Pug sat without speaking. The magician wore no armor because he claimed it would interfere with his magic. Pug was more inclined to believe it would interfere with his considerable girth. Meecham had a sword at his side, like the others, but held a horse bow. He preferred archery to close fighting, though Pug knew, from long hours of instruction at his hands, that he was no stranger to the blade.

The hour passed slowly, and Pug felt mounting excitement, for he was still possessed by boyish notions of glory. He had forgotten the terror of the fighting with the Dark Brothers before they reached the Grey Towers.

Word was passed and they remounted. They rode slowly at first, until the Tsurani were in sight. As the trees thinned, they picked up speed, and when they reached the clearing, they galloped the horses. Large breastworks of earth had been thrown up as a defense against the charge of horsemen. Pug could see the brightly colored helmets of the Tsurani rushing to defend their camp. As the riders charged, the sounds of fighting could be heard echoing through the trees as the Zūnese troops engaged other Tsurani camps.

The ground shook under the horses as they rode straight at the camp, sounding like a rolling wave of thunder. The Tsurani soldiers stayed behind the earthworks, shooting arrows, most of which fell short. As the first element of the column hit the earthworks, the second element turned to the left, riding off at an angle past the camp. A few Tsurani soldiers were outside the breastworks here, and were ridden down like wheat before a scythe. Two came close to hitting the riders with the great two-handed swords they wielded, but their blows went wide. Meecham, guiding his horse with his legs, dropped both with two quick arrows.

Pug heard a horse scream among the sounds of the fighting behind, then suddenly found himself crashing through the brush as they entered the forest. They rode as hard as possible, cutting through the trees, ducking under low branches, the scene a passing kaleidoscope of greens and browns.

The column rode for nearly a half hour, then slackened pace as the horses began to tire. Kulgan called to Lieutenant Garth, and they halted to check their position against the map. If they moved slowly for the balance of the day and night, they would reach the mouth of the pass near daybreak.

Meecham peered over the heads of the lieutenant and Kulgan as they knelt on the ground. "I know this place. I hunted it as a boy, when I lived near Hūsh."

Pug was startled. This was the first time Meecham had ever mentioned anything about his past. Pug had supposed that Meecham was from Crydee, and was surprised to find he had been a youth in the Free Cities. But then he found it difficult to imagine Meecham as a boy.

The franklin continued. "There is a way over the crest of the mountains, a path that leads between two smaller peaks. It is little more than a goat trail, but if we led the horses all night, we could be in the valley by sunrise. This way is difficult to find on this side if you don't know where to seek it. From the valley side, it is nearly impossible. I would bet the Tsurani know nothing about it."

The lieutenant regarded Kulgan with a question in his eyes. The magician looked at Meecham, then said, "It might be worth a try. We can mark our trail for Vandros. If we move slowly, he might catch up before we reach the valley."

"All right," said the lieutenant, "our biggest advantage is mobility, so let's keep moving. Meecham, where will we come out?"

The large man leaned over the lieutenant's shoulder to point at a spot on the map near the south end of the valley. "Here. If we come out straight west for a half mile or so, then swing north, we can cut down the heart of the valley." He motioned with his finger as he spoke. "This valley's mostly woods at the north and south end, with a big meadow in the middle. That's where they'd be if they have a big camp. It's mostly open there, so if the aliens haven't come up with anything surprising, we should be able to ride right by them afore they can organize to stop us. The dicey part will be getting through the northern woods if they've garrisoned soldiers there. But if we get through them, we'll be free to the North Pass."

"All agreed?" asked the lieutenant. When no one said anything, he gave orders for the men to walk their horses, and Meecham took the lead as guide.

They reached the entrance to the pass, or what Pug thought Meecham had correctly called a goat trail, an hour before sundown. The lieutenant posted guards and ordered the horses unsaddled. Pug rubbed down his horse with handfuls of long grass, then staked it out. The thirty soldiers were busy tending to their horses and armor. Pug could feel the tension in the air. The run around the Tsurani camp had set the soldiers on edge, and they were anxious for a fight.

Meecham showed Pug how to muffle his sword and shield with rags torn from the soldiers' blankets. "We're not going to be using these bed rolls this night, and nothing will ring through the hills like the sound of metal striking metal, boy. Except maybe the clopping of hooves on the rock." Pug watched as he muffled the horses' hooves with leather stockings designed for just this purpose and carried in the saddlebags. Pug rested as the sun began to set. Through the short spring twilight, he waited until he heard the order to resaddle. The soldiers were beginning to pull their horses into a line when he finished.

Meecham and the lieutenant were walking down the line repeating instructions to the men. They would move in single file, Meecham taking the lead, the lieutenant second, down the line to the last soldier. They tied a series of ropes through the left stirrup of each horse, and each man gripped it tightly as he led his own horse. After everyone was in position, Meecham started off.

The path rose steeply, and the horses had to scramble in places. In the darkness they moved slowly, taking great care not to stray from the path. Occasionally Meecham stopped the line, to check ahead. After several such stops, the trail crested through a deep, narrow pass and started downward. An hour later it widened, and they stopped to rest. Two soldiers were sent ahead with Meecham to scout the way, while the rest of the tired line dropped to the ground to ease cramped legs. Pug realized the fatigue was as much the result of the tension created by the silent passage as of the climbing, but it didn't make his legs feel any better.

After what seemed to be much too short a rest they were moving again. Pug stumbled along, fatigue numbing his mind to the point where the world became an endless series of picking up one foot and placing it before the other. Several times the horse before him was literally towing him as he grasped the rope tied to its stirrup.

Suddenly Pug was aware that the line had stopped and that they were standing in a gap between two small hills, looking down at the valley floor. From here it would take only a few minutes to ride down the slope.

Kulgan walked back to where the boy stood next to his animal. The stout wizard seemed little troubled by the climb, and Pug wondered at the muscle that must lie hidden beneath the layers of fat. "How are you feeling, Pug?"

"I'll live, I expect, but I think next time I'll ride, if it's all the same to you." They were keeping their voices low, but the magician gave out with a soft chuckle anyway.

"I understand completely. We'll be staying here until first light. That will be slightly less than two hours. I suggest you get some sleep, for we have a great deal of hard riding ahead."

Pug nodded and lay down without a word. He used his shield for a pillow and, before the magician had taken a step away, was fast asleep. He never stirred as Meecham came and removed the leather muffles from his horse.

A GENTLE SHAKING brought Pug awake. He felt as if he had just closed his eyes a moment before. Meecham was squatting before him, holding something out. "Here, boy. Eat this."

Pug took the offered food. It was soft bread, with a nutty flavor. After two bites he began to feel better.

Meecham said, "Eat quickly, we're off in a few minutes." He moved forward to where the lieutenant and the magician stood by their horses. Pug finished the bread and remounted. The soreness had left his legs, and by the time he was astride his mount, he felt anxious to be off.

The lieutenant turned his horse and faced the men. "We will ride west—then, on my command, north. Fight only if attacked. Our mission is to return with information about the Tsurani. If any man falls, we cannot stop. If you are separated from the others, get back as best you can. Remember as much of what you see as possible, for you may be the only one to carry the news to the dukes. May the gods protect us all."

Several of the soldiers uttered quick prayers to various deities, chiefly Tith, the war god, then they were off. The column came down the hillside and reached the flat of the valley. The sun was cresting the hills behind, and a rosy glow bathed the landscape. At the foot of the hills they crossed a small creek and entered a plain of tall grass. Far ahead was a stand of trees, and another could be seen off to the north. At the north end of the valley the haze of campfire smoke hung in the air. The enemy was there all right, thought Pug, and from the volume of smoke there must be a large concentration of them. He hoped Meecham was right and they were all garrisoned out in the open, where the Kingdom soldiers stood a fair chance of outrunning them.

After a while the lieutenant passed the word, and the column turned north. They trotted along, saving the horses for when they would be sure to need the speed.

Pug thought he saw glimpses of color in the trees ahead, as they descended into the southern woods of the valley, but couldn't be sure. As they reached the woods, a shout went up from within the trees. The lieutenant cried, "All right, they've seen us. Ride hard and stay close." He spurred his horse forward, and soon the entire company was thundering through the woods. Pug saw the horses in front bear to the left and turned his to follow, seeing a clearing in the trees. The sound of voices grew louder as the first trees went flying past, and his eyes tried to adjust to the darkness of the woods. He hoped his horse could see more clearly than he could, or he might find himself inside a tree.

The horse, battle trained and quick, darted between the trunks, and Pug could begin to see flashes of color among the branches. Tsurani soldiers were rushing to intercept the horsemen, but were forced to weave through the trees, making it impossible. They were speeding through the woods faster than the Tsurani could pass the word and react. Pug knew that this advantage of surprise couldn't last much longer; they were making too great a commotion for the enemy not to realize what was happening.

After a mad dash through the trees, they broke into another clear area where a few Tsurani soldiers stood waiting for them. The horsemen charged, and most of the defenders scattered to avoid being run down. One, however, stood his ground, in spite of the terror written on his face, and swung the blue two-handed sword he carried. A horse screamed, and the rider was thrown as the blade cut the horse's right leg from under him. Pug lost sight of the fight as he sped quickly past.

An arrow shot over Pug's shoulder, buzzing like an angry bee. He hunched over the withers of his mount, trying to give the archers behind him as small a target as possible. Ahead, a soldier fell backward out of his saddle, a red arrow through his neck.

Soon they were out of bow range and riding toward a breastwork thrown across an old road from the mines in the south. Hundreds of brightly colored figures scurried behind it. The lieutenant signaled for the riders to pass around it, to the west.

As soon as it was apparent they would pass the earthwork and not charge it, several Tsurani bowmen came tumbling over the top of the redoubt and ran to intercept the riders. As soon as they came within bowshot, the air filled with red and blue shafts. Pug heard a horse scream, but he couldn't see the stricken animal or its rider.

Riding quickly beyond the range of the bowmen, they entered another thick stand of trees. The lieutenant pulled up his mount for a moment and yelled, "From here on, make straight north. We're almost to the meadow, so there'll be no cover, and speed is your only ally. Then once you're in the woods to the north, keep moving. Our forces should have broken through up there, and if we can get past those woods, we should be all right." Meecham had described the woods as being about two or three miles across. From there it was three miles of open ground until the North Pass through the hills began.

They slowed to a walk, trying to rest the horses as much as possible.

They could see the tiny figures of the Tsurani coming from behind, but they would never catch up before the horses were running again. Ahead Pug could see the trees of the forest, looming larger with each passing minute. He could feel the eyes that must be there, watching them, waiting.

"As soon as we are within bowshot, ride as fast as you can," shouted the lieutenant. Pug saw the soldiers pull their swords and bows out, and drew his own sword. Feeling uncomfortable with the weapon clutched in his right hand, he rode at a trot toward the trees.

Suddenly the air was filled with arrows. Pug felt one glance off his helm, but it still snapped his head back and brought tears to his eyes. He urged his horse ahead blindly, trying to blink his eyes clear. He had the shield in his left hand and a sword in his right, so that by the time he blinked enough to be able to see clearly, he found himself in the woods. His war-horse responded to leg pressure as he moved into the forest.

A yellow-garbed soldier burst from behind a tree and aimed a swing at the boy. He caught the sword blow on his shield, which sent a numbing shock up his left arm. He swung overhand and down at the soldier, who leaped away, and the blow missed. Pug spurred his horse on, before the soldier could get in position to swing again. All around, the forest rang with the sounds of battle. He could barely make out the other horsemen among the trees.

Several times he rode down Tsurani soldiers as they tried to block his passage. Once one tried to grab at the reins of the horse, but Pug sent him reeling with a blow on the potlike helmet. To Pug it seemed as if they were all engaged in some mad game of hide-and-go-seek, with foot soldiers jumping out from behind every other tree.

A sharp pain stung Pug on the right cheek. Feeling with the back of his sword hand as he bounded through the wood, he felt a wetness, and when he pulled his hand away, he could see blood on his knuckles. He felt a detached curiosity. He hadn't even heard the arrow that had stung him.

Twice more he rode down soldiers, the war-horse knocking them aside. Suddenly he burst out of the forest and was assaulted by a kaleidoscope of images. He pulled up for a moment and let the scene register. Less than a hundred yards to the west of where he exited the woodlands, a great device, some hundred feet in length, with twenty-foot-high poles at each end, stood. Around it were clustered several men, the first Tsurani Pug had seen who weren't wearing armor. These men wore long black robes and were completely unarmed. Between the poles a shimmering grey haze like the one they had seen in Kulgan's room filled the air, blocking out the view of the area directly behind. From out of the haze a wagon was being pulled by two grey, squat, six-legged beasts, who were prodded by two soldiers in red armor. Several more wagons were standing beyond the machines, and a few of the strange beasts could be seen grazing beyond the wagons.

Beyond the strange device, a mighty camp sprawled across the meadow, with more tents than Pug could count. Banners of strange design and gaudy colors fluttered in the wind above them, and the rising smoke of the campfires stung his nose with acrid pungency as it was carried off in the breeze.

More riders were coming through the trees, and Pug spurred his horse forward, angling away from the strange device. The six-legged beasts raised their heads and ambled away from the oncoming horses, seeming to move with little more than the minimum effort required to take them out of the path of the riders.

One of the black-robed men ran toward the riders. He stopped and stood off to one side as they sped past. Pug got a glimpse of his face, clean shaven, his lips moving and eyes fixed on something behind the boy. Pug heard a yell and, looking back, saw a rider on the ground, his horse rooted in place, like a statue. Several guards were rushing over to subdue the man when the boy turned away. Once beyond the strange device, he could see a series of large, brightly colored tents off to the left. Ahead, the way was clear.

Pug caught sight of Kulgan and reined his horse to bring himself closer to the magician. Thirty yards to the right, Pug could see other riders. As they dashed away, Kulgan shouted something at the boy that he couldn't make out. The magician pointed at the side of his face, then at Pug, who realized the mage was asking if he was all right. Pug waved his sword and smiled, and the magician smiled back.

Suddenly, about a hundred yards in front, a loud buzzing noise filled the air, and a black-robed man appeared, as if from thin air. Kulgan's horse bore straight for him, but the man had a queer-looking device in his hand that he pointed at the magician.

The air sizzled with energy. Kulgan's horse screamed and fell as if poleaxed. The fat magician was tossed over the horse's head and tucked his shoulder under as he hit the ground. With an amazing display of agility he rolled up onto his feet and bowled over the black-robed man.

Pug pulled up in spite of the order to keep going. He reined his horse around and charged back to find the magician sitting astride the chest of the smaller man, each grasping the left wrist of the other with his right hand. Pug could see that they were locked eye to eye in a contest of wills. Kulgan had explained this strange mental power to Pug before.

It was a way in which a magician could bend the will of another to his own. It took great concentration and was very dangerous. Pug leaped from his own mount and rushed over to where the two men were locked in struggle. With the flat of his sword, he struck the black-robed figure on the temple. The man slumped unconscious.

Kulgan staggered to his feet. "Thank you, Pug. I don't think I could have bettered him. I've never encountered such mental strength." Kulgan looked to where his horse lay quivering on the ground. "It's useless." Turning to Pug, he said, "Listen well, for you'll have to carry word to Lord Borric. From the speed that wagon was coming through the rift, I estimate they can bring in several hundred men a day, perhaps a great deal more. Tell the Duke it would be suicide to try to take the machine. Their magicians are too powerful. I don't think we can destroy the machine they use to hold the rift open. If I had time to study it . . . He must call for reinforcements from Krondor, perhaps from the East."

Pug grabbed Kulgan by the arm. "I can't remember all that. We'll ride double."

Kulgan began to protest but was too weak to prevent the boy's pulling him to where his horse stood. Ignoring Kulgan's objections, he bullied his master up into the saddle. Pug hesitated a moment, noting the animal's fatigue, then came to a decision. "With both of us to carry, he'll never make it, Kulgan," he shouted as he struck the animal on the flank. "I'll find another."

Pug scanned the area as the horse bearing Kulgan sped away. A riderless mount was wandering about, less than twenty feet away, but as he approached, the animal bolted. Cursing, Pug turned and was confronted by the sight of the black-robed Tsurani regaining his feet. The man appeared confused and weak, and Pug charged him. Only one thought was in Pug's mind: to capture a prisoner, and, from his appearance, a Tsurani magician in the bargain. Pug took the magician by surprise, knocking him down.

The man scrambled backward in alarm as Pug raised his sword threateningly. The man put forth his hand in what Pug took as a sign of submission, and the boy hesitated. Suddenly a wave of pain passed through him, and he had to fight to keep his feet. He staggered about and through the agony saw a familiar figure riding toward him, shouting his name.

Pug shook his head, and suddenly the pain vanished. Meecham sped toward him, and Pug knew the franklin could carry the Tsurani to the Duke's camp if Pug could keep him from fleeing. So he spun, all pain forgotten, and closed upon the still-supine Tsurani. A look of shock crossed the magician's face when he saw the boy again advancing on him. Pug heard Meecham's voice calling his name from behind but didn't take his eyes from the Tsurani.

Several Tsurani soldiers ran across the meadow, seeking to aid their fallen magician, but Pug stood only a few feet away, and Meecham would reach them in a few more moments.

The magician jumped to his feet and reached into his robe. He pulled out a small device and activated it. A loud humming came from the object. Pug rushed the man, determined to knock the device from his hand, whatever it might be. The device hummed louder, and Pug could hear Meecham again shouting his name as he struck the magician, burying his shoulder in the man's stomach.

Suddenly the world exploded with white and blue lights, and Pug felt himself falling through a rainbow of colors into a pit of darkness.

PUG OPENED his eyes. For a moment he struggled to bring them into focus, for everything in his field of vision seemed to be flickering. He then came fully awake and realized it was still night and the flickering came from campfires a short distance from where he lay. He tried to sit up and found his hands tied behind him. A groan sounded next to him. In the dim light he could make out the features of a LaMutian horse soldier lying a few feet away. He was also bound. His face was drawn, and there was a nasty-looking cut running down from his hairline to his cheekbone, all crusted over with dried blood.

Pug's attention was distracted by the sound of voices speaking low, behind him. He rolled over and saw two Tsurani guards in blue armor standing watch. Several more tied prisoners lay about between the boy and the two aliens, who were speaking together in their strange, musical-sounding language. One noticed Pug's movement and said something to the other, who nodded and quickly hurried off.

In a moment he was back with another soldier, this one in red-and-yellow armor, with a large crest on his helm, who ordered the two guards to stand Pug up. He was pulled roughly to his feet, and the newcomer stood before him and took stock. This man was dark-haired and had the uptilted, wide-set eyes that Pug had seen before in the field among the Tsurani dead. His cheekbones were flat, and he had a broad brow, topped by thick dark hair. In the dim firelight, his skin looked nearly golden in color.

Except for their short stature, most of the Tsurani soldiers could pass for citizens of many of the nations of Midkemia, but these golden men, as Pug thought of them, resembled some Keshian traders Pug had seen in Crydee years before, from the distant trading city of Shing Lai.

The officer inspected the boy's clothing. Next he knelt and inspected the boots on Pug's feet. He stood and barked an order at the soldier who had fetched him, who saluted and turned to Pug. He seized the bound boy and led him away, on a winding course through the Tsurani camp.

At the center of the camp, large banners hung from the cross pieces of standards, all set in a circle around a large tent. All bore strange designs, creatures of outlandish configuration, depicted in bold colors. Several had glyphs of an unknown language on them. It was to this place Pug was half pulled, half dragged, through the hundreds of Tsurani soldiers who sat quietly polishing their leather armor and making repairs on weapons. Several watched as he passed, but the camp was free of the usual noise and bustle Pug was used to in the camp of his own army. There was more than just the strange and colorful banners to give this place an otherworld feeling. Pug tried to note the details, so if he could escape and report, he could tell Duke Borric something useful, but he found his senses betrayed by so many unfamiliar images. He didn't know what was important in all he saw.

At the entrance of the large tent, the guard who pulled Pug along was challenged by two others, wearing black-and-orange armor. A quick exchange of words resulted in the tent flap being held aside while Pug was thrust through. He fell forward onto a thick pile of furs and woven mats. From where he lay, Pug could see more banners hanging on the tent walls. The tent was richly fashioned, with silklike hangings and thick rugs and pillows.

Hands roughly pulled him upright, and he could see several men regarding him. All stood dressed in the gaudy armor and crested helms of the Tsurani officers except for two. They sat upon a raised dais covered with cushions. The first wore a simple black robe with cowl pulled back, revealing a thin, pale face and bald pate: a Tsurani magician. The other wore a rich-looking robe of orange with black trim, cut below knees and elbows, so that it gave the look of something worn for comfort. From his wiry, muscled appearance and several visible scars, Pug assumed that this man was a warrior who had put aside his armor for the night.

The man in black said something in a high-pitched, singsong language to the others. None of the other men said anything, but the one in the orange robe nodded. The great tent was lit by a single brazier near where the two robed men sat. The lean, black-robed one sat forward, and the light from the brazier cast upward on his face, giving him a decidedly demonic look. His words came haltingly, and thick with accent.

"I know only . . . little . . . of your speech. You understand?"

Pug nodded, his heart pounding while his mind worked furiously. Kulgan's training was coming into play. First he calmed himself, clearing the fog that had gripped his mind. Then he extended every sense, automatically, taking in every scrap of information available, seeking any useful bit of knowledge that might improve his chances of survival. The soldier nearest the door seemed to be relaxing, his left arm behind his head as he lay back on a pile of cushions, his attention only half focused on the captive. But Pug noticed that his other hand was never more than an inch from the hilt of a wicked-looking dagger at his belt. A brief gleam of light on lacquer revealed the presence of another dagger hilt, half protruding from a pillow at the right elbow of the man in orange.

The man in black said slowly, "Listen, for I tell you something. Then you asked questions. If you lie, you die. Slowly. Understand?" Pug nodded. There was no doubt in his mind.

"This man," said the black-robed one, pointing to the man in the short orange robe, "is a . . . great man. He is . . . high man. He is . . ." The man used a word Pug didn't understand. When Pug shook his head, the magician said, "He family great . . . Minwanabi. He second to . . ." He fumbled for a term, then moved his hand in a circle, as if indicating all the men in the tent, officers from their proud plumes. ". . . man who lead."

Pug nodded and softly said, "Your lord?"

The magician's eyes narrowed, as if he were about to object to Pug's speaking out of turn, but instead he paused, then said, "Yes. Lord of War. It is that one's will that we are here. This one is second to Lord of War." He pointed to the man in orange, who looked on impassively. "You are nothing to this man." It was obvious the man was feeling frustration in his inability to convey what he wished. It was plain this lord was something special by the lights of his own people, and the man translating was trying to impress this upon Pug.

The lord cut the translator off and said several things, then nodded toward Pug. The bald magician bobbed his head in agreement, then turned his attention toward Pug. "You are lord?"

Pug looked startled, then stammered out a negative. The magician nodded, translated, and was given instruction by the lord. He turned back to Pug. "You wear cloth like lord, true?"

Pug nodded. His tunic was of a finer fabric than the homespun of the common soldiers. He tried to explain his position as a member in the Duke's court. After several attempts he resigned himself to the presumption they made of his being some sort of highly placed servant.

The magician picked up a small device and held it out to Pug. Hesitating for a moment, the boy reached out and took it. It was a cube of some crystallike material, with veins of pink running throughout. After a moment in his hand, it took on a glow, softly pink. The man in orange gave an order, and the magician translated. "This lord says, how many men along pass to . . ." He faltered and pointed.

Pug had no idea of where he was, or what direction was being pointed to. "I don't know where I am," he said. "I was unconscious when I was brought here."

The magician sat in thought for a moment, then stood. "That way," he said, pointing at a right angle to the direction he had just indicated, "is tall mountain, larger than others. That way," he moved his hand a little, "in sky, is five fires, like so." His hands traced a pattern. After a moment Pug understood. The man had pointed to where Stone Mountain lay and where the constellation called the Five Jewels hung in the sky. He was in the valley they had raided. The pass indicated was the one used as an escape route.

"I . . . really, I don't know how many."

The magician looked closely at the cube in Pug's hand. It continued to glow in soft pink tones. "Good, you tell truth."

Pug then understood that he held some sort of device that would inform his captives if he tried to deceive them. He felt black despair wash over him. He knew that any survival hopes he entertained were going to involve some manner of betraying his homeland.

The magician asked several questions about the nature of the force outside the valley. When most went unanswered, for Pug had not been privy to meetings on strategy matters, the question changed to a more general nature, about common things in Midkemia, but which seemed to hold a fascination for the Tsurani.

The interview continued for several hours. Pug began to feel faint on several occasions as the pressure of the situation combined with his general exhaustion. He was given a strong drink one of these times, which restored his energy for a while but left him light-headed.

He answered every question. Several times he got around the truth device by telling only some of the information requested, not volunteering anything. On several of these occasions, he could tell both the lord and magician were nettled by their inability to deal with answers that were incomplete or complex. Finally the lord indicated the interview was over, and Pug was dragged outside. The magician followed.

Outside the tent the magician stood before Pug. "My lord says, 'I think this servant' "—he pointed at Pug's chest—" 'he is . . .' " He groped for a word. " 'He is clever.' My lord does not mind clever servants, for they work well. But he thinks you are too clever. He says to tell you to be careful, for you are now slave. Clever slave may live long time. Too clever slave, dies quickly if . . ." Again the pause. Then a broad smile crossed the magician's face. "If he is fortun . . . fortunate. Yes . . . that is the word." He rolled the word around his mouth one more time, as if savoring the taste of it. "Fortunate."

Pug was led back to the holding area and left with his own thoughts. He looked around and saw that a few other captives were awake. Most looked confused and dispirited. One openly wept. Pug turned his eyes skyward and saw the pink edge along the mountains in the east, heralding the coming dawn.

15

CONFLICTS

THE RAIN WAS UNCEASING.

Huddled near the mouth of the cave, a group of dwarves sat around a small cook fire, the gloom of the day reflected upon their faces. Dolgan puffed upon his pipe, and the others were working on their armor, repairing cuts and breaks in leather, cleaning and oiling metal. A pot of stew simmered on the fire.

Tomas sat at the back of the cave, his sword set across his knees. He looked blankly past the others, his eyes focused on some point far beyond them.

Seven times the dwarves of the Grey Towers had ventured out against the invaders, and seven times they had inflicted heavy losses. But each time it was clear that the Tsurani's numbers were undiminished. Many dwarves were missing now, their lives bought at a dear price to the enemy, but dearer to the families of the Grey Towers. The long-lived dwarves had fewer children, years further apart, than did humans. Each loss diminished dwarvenkind at a much more damaging cost than could have been imagined by the humans.

Each time the dwarves had gathered and attacked through the mines into the valley, Tomas had been in the van. His golden helm would be a signal beacon for the dwarves. His golden broadsword would arc above the fray, then swing down to take its toll from the enemy. In battle the keep boy was transformed into a figure of power, a fighting hero whose presence on the field struck awe and fear into the Tsurani. Had he possessed any doubt about the magical nature of his arms and armor after driving off the wraith, they were dispelled the first time he wore them into battle.

They had gathered thirty fighting dwarves from Caldara and ventured through the mines to an entrance in the south portion of the captured valley. They surprised a Tsurani patrol not far from the mines and slew them. But during the course of the fighting, Tomas had been cut off from the dwarves by three Tsurani warriors. As they bore down on him, their swords raised high overhead, he felt something take hold of him. Darting between two of them, like some maddened acrobat, he had slain both with a single stroke from one side to the other. The third had been taken quickly from behind before he could recover from the sudden move.

After the fray, Tomas had been filled with an elation new to him, and somehow frightening as well. All the way back from the battle, he had felt suffused with an unknown energy.

Each subsequent battle had gained him the same power and skill of arms. But the elation had become something more urgent, and the last two times the visions had begun. Now for the first time the visions were coming unbidden. They were transparent, like an image laid upon another.

He could see the dwarves through it, as well as the forest beyond. But upon them played a scene of people long dead and places vanished from the memories of the living. Halls decked with golden trappings were lit with torches that threw dancing light from crystal set upon tables. Goblets that never knew human touch were raised to lips that curved in unfamiliar smiles. Great lords of some long-dead race supped at banquet before his eyes. Strange they were, yet also familiar. Humanlike, but with elven ears and eyes. Tall like the elvenfolk, but broader of shoulder and thicker of arm. The women were beautiful, but in alien ways.

The dream took shape and substance, more vivid than any he had experienced so far. Tomas strained to hear the faint laughter, the sound of alien music, and the spoken words of these people.

He was ripped from his reverie by Dolgan's voice. "Will you take some food, laddie?" He could answer with only a part of his awareness, as he rose and crossed the space between them to take the offered bowl of meat stew. When his hand touched the bowl, the vision vanished, and he shook his head to clear it.

"Are you all right, Tomas?"

Slowly sitting, Tomas looked at his friend for a moment. "I'm not sure," he said hesitantly. "There is something. I . . . I'm not really sure. Just tired, I guess."

Dolgan looked at the boy. The ravages of battle were showing on his young face. Already he looked less the boy and more the man. But beyond the normal hardening of character expected from battle, something else was occurring in Tomas. Dolgan had not as yet decided if the change was fully for good or ill—or if it could even be considered in those terms. Six months of watching Tomas was not long enough to come to any sort of conclusion.

Since donning the dragon's gift armor, Tomas had become a fighter of legendary capabilities. And the boy . . . no, the young man, was taking on weight, even though food was often scarce. It was as if something were acting to bring him to a growth sufficient to fit the cut of the armor. And his features were gaining a strange cast. His nose had taken on a slightly more angular shape, more finely chiseled than before. His brows had become more arched, his eyes deeper set. He was still Tomas, but Tomas with a slight change in appearance, as if wearing someone else's expression.

Dolgan pulled long on his pipe and looked at the white tabard Tomas wore. Seven times in battle, and free from stain. Dirt, blood, and all other manner of contamination were refused purchase in its fabric. And the device of the golden dragon gleamed as brightly as when they had first found it. So it was also with the shield he wore in battle. Many times struck, still it was free of any scar. The dwarves were circumspect in this matter, for their race had long ago used magic in the fashioning of weapons of power. But this was something else. They would wait and see what it brought before they would judge.

As they finished their meager meal, one of the guards on the edge of camp came into the clearing before the cave. "Someone comes."

The dwarves quickly armed themselves and stood ready. Instead of the strangely armored Tsurani soldiers, a single man dressed in the dark grey cloak and tunic of a Natalese Ranger appeared. He walked directly into the center of the clearing and announced in a voice hoarse from days running through wet forests, "Hail, Dolgan of the Grey Towers."

Dolgan stepped forward. "Hail, Grimsworth of Natal."

The rangers were serving as scouts and runners since the invaders had taken the Free City of Walinor. The man walked into the cave mouth and sat down. He was given a bowl of stew, and Dolgan asked, "What news?"

"None good, I'm afraid," he said, between mouthfuls of stew. "The invaders hold a hard front from out of the valley, northeast toward LaMut. Walinor has been reinforced with fresh troops from their homeland and stands like a knife between the Free Cities and the Kingdom. They had thrice raided the main camp of the Kingdom's host when I left two weeks ago, probably again since. They harry patrols from Crydee. I am to tell you that it is believed they will start a drive into your area soon."

Dolgan looked perplexed. "Why do the dukes think that? Our lookouts have seen no increase in the aliens' activity in these parts. Every patrol they send out we attack. If anything, they seem to be leaving us alone."

"I am not sure. I heard that the magician Kulgan thinks the Tsurani seek metals from your mines, though why I do not know. In any event, this is what the dukes have said. They think there will be an assault on the mine entrances in the valley. I am to tell you that new Tsurani troops may be coming into the southern end of the valley, for there has been no new major assault in the north, only the small raids.

"Now you must do what you think is best." So saying, he turned his full attention to the stew.

Dolgan thought. "Tell me, Grimsworth, what news of the elvenfolk?"

"Little. Since the aliens have invaded the southern part of the elven forests, we are cut off. The last elven runner came through over a week before I left. At last word, they had stopped the barbarians at the fords of the river Crydee where it passes through the forest.

"There are also rumors of alien creatures fighting with the invaders. But as far as I know, only a few burned-out village folk have seen these creatures, so I wouldn't place too much stock in what they say.

"There is one interesting piece of news, though. It seems a patrol from Yabon made an unusually broad sweep to the edge of the Lake of the Sky. On the shore they found what was left of some Tsurani and a band of goblins raiding south from the Northlands. At least we don't have to worry about the northern borders. Perhaps we could arrange for them to battle each other for a while and leave us alone."

"Or take up common cause against us," said Dolgan. "Still, I think that unlikely, as the goblins tend to kill first and negotiate later."

Grimsworth chuckled deeply. "It is somehow meet that these two bloody-handed folk should run across one another."

Dolgan nodded. He hoped Grimsworth correct, but was disquieted by the thought of the Nations of the North—as the dwarves thought of the Northlands—joining the fray.

Grimsworth wiped his mouth with the back of his hand. "I will stay this night only, for if I am to pass safely through their lines, I must move quickly. They step up their patrols to the coast, cutting off

Crydee for days at a time. I will spend some time there, then start the long run for the dukes' camp."

"Will you return?" asked Dolgan.

The ranger smiled, his grin showing up brightly against his dark skin. "Perhaps, if the gods are obliging. If not I, then one of my brothers. It might be that you'll see Long Leon, for he was sent to Elvandar and, if he is a'right, may be bound here with missives from the Lady Aglaranna. It would be good to know how the elvenfolk fare." Tomas's head came up from his musing at the mention of the Elf Queen's name.

Dolgan puffed on his pipe and nodded. Grimsworth turned to Tomas and spoke directly to him for the first time. "I bring you a message from Lord Borric, Tomas." It had been Grimsworth who carried the first messages from the dwarves along with the news that Tomas was alive and well. Tomas had wanted to return to the Kingdom forces with Grimsworth, but the Natalese Ranger had refused to have him along, citing his need to travel fast and quietly. Grimsworth continued his message. "The Duke rejoices at your good fortune and your good health. But he sends grave news as well. Your friend Pug fell in the first raid into the Tsurani camp and was taken by them. Lord Borric shares your loss."

Tomas stood without a word and moved deep into the cave. He sat in the rear, for a few moments as still as the rock around him, then a faint trembling started in his shoulders. It grew in severity until he shook violently, teeth chattering as if from bitter cold. Then tears came unbidden to his cheeks, and he felt a hot pain rush up from his bowels to his throat, constricting his chest. Without a sound he gasped for breath, and great silent sobs shook him. As the pain grew near-unbearable, a seed of cold fury formed in the center of his being, pushing upward, displacing the hot pain of grief.

Dolgan, Grimsworth, and the rest looked up when Tomas reentered the light of the fire. "Would you please tell the Duke that I thank him for thinking of me?" he asked the ranger.

Grimsworth nodded. "Yes, I will, lad. I think it would be a'right for you to make the run to Crydee, if you wish to return home. I'm sure Prince Lyam could use your sword."

Tomas thought. It would be good to see home again, but at the keep he would be just another apprentice, even if he did bear arms. They would let him fight if the keep was attacked, but they certainly wouldn't let him participate in raids.

"Thank you, Grimsworth, but I will remain. There is much yet to be done here, and I would be a part of it. I would ask you to give word to my mother and father that I am well enough and think of them." Sitting down, he added, "If it is my destiny to return to Crydee, I shall."

Grimsworth looked hard at Tomas, seemed about to speak, then noticed a slight shake of Dolgan's head. More than any other humans in the West, the Rangers of Natal were sensitive to the ways of the elves and dwarves. Something was occurring here that Dolgan thought best left unexplored for the time being, and Grimsworth would bow before the dwarven chief's wisdom.

As soon as the meal was finished, guards were posted, and the rest made ready for sleep. As the fire died down, Tomas could hear the faint sounds of inhuman music and again saw the shadows dance. Before sleep claimed him, he plainly saw one figure stand apart from the rest, a tall warrior, cruel of face and powerful in countenance, dressed in a white tabard emblazoned with a golden dragon.

TOMAS STOOD with his back pressed against the wall of the passage. He smiled, a cruel and terrible smile. His eyes were wide, whites vivid around pale blue irises. His body was nearly rigid as he stood motionless. His fingers clenched and unclenched on the hilt of his sword of white and gold.

Images shimmered before his eyes: tall, graceful people who rode on the backs of dragons and lived in halls deep in the earth. Music could be faintly heard in his mind's ear, and strange tongues. The long-dead race called to him, a mighty race who had fashioned this armor, never meant for human use.

More and more the visions came. He could keep his mind free of them most times, but when he felt the battle lust rise, as it did now, the images took on dimension, color, and sound. He would strain to hear the words. They came faintly, and he could almost understand them.

He shook his head, bringing himself back to the present. He looked around the dark passage, no longer surprised at his ability to see in the dark. He signaled across the intersecting tunnel to Dolgan, who stood quietly waiting in position with his men forty feet away and acknowledged him with a wave. On each side of the large tunnel sixty dwarves waited to spring the trap. They waited for the handful of dwarves who were running before a Tsurani force, leading the enemy into the trap.

The sound of footfalls pounding down the tunnel alerted them. In a moment it was joined by the sounds of clashing arms. Tomas tensed. Several dwarves came into view, moving backward as they fought a rearward action. Passing the side tunnels, the fighting dwarves gave no indication they were aware of their brethren waiting on either side.

As soon as the first Tsurani warriors were past, Tomas cried, "Now!" and leaped forward. Suddenly the tunnel was filled with turning, slashing bodies. The Tsurani were mostly armed with broadswords, ill fitted for close quarters, and the dwarves wielded hand axes and hammers with expertise. Tomas laid about himself, and several bodies fell. The flickering Tsurani torches threw mad, dancing shadows high on the passage walls, creating confusion for the eye.

A shout from the rear of the Tsurani force sounded, and the aliens began to back down the tunnel. Those with shields came to the fore, forming a wall over which the swordsmen could strike. The dwarves were unable to reach far enough to do any damage. Each time a dwarf attacked, the shield wall would stand, and the attacker would be answered by sword blows from behind the shield. In short spurts the enemy backed away.

Tomas moved to the fore, since his reach was long enough to strike at the shield holders. He felled two, but as quickly as each dropped, another took his place. Still the dwarves pressed them and they retreated.

They reached a glory hole, entering it at the lowest level, and the Tsurani rapidly took position in the center of the great cavern, forming a rough circle of shields. The dwarves paused for a moment, then charged the position.

A faint flicker of movement caught Tomas's eye, and he looked up to one of the ledges above. In the darkness of the mine it was impossible to see anything clearly, but a sudden feeling alerted him. "Look to the rear!" he shouted.

Most of the dwarves had broken through the shield wall and were too busy to heed him, but a few close by stopped their attack and looked up. One standing next to Tomas cried, "From above!"

Black shapes came pouring from above, seeming to crawl down the face of the rock. Other, human, shapes came running down the paths from the higher levels. Lights appeared above as Tsurani warriors on the upper levels opened shuttered lamps and lit torches.

Tomas stopped in shock. Directly behind the few surviving Tsurani in the center of the cavern he could see creatures entering from every opening above, like a herd of ants, which they closely resembled. Unlike ants, though, they were upright from the center of their bodies, with humanlike arms bearing weapons. Their faces, insectlike, had large multifaceted eyes but very humanlike mouths. They moved with incredible speed, dodging forward to strike at the dwarves, who, surprised though they were, responded without hesitation, and the battle was joined.

The fray increased in intensity, and several times Tomas faced two opponents, Tsurani, or monster, or both. The creatures were obviously intelligent, for they fought in an organized manner, and their inhuman voices could be heard crying out in the Tsurani tongue.

Tomas looked up after dispatching one of the creatures and saw a new influx of warriors from above. "To me! To me!" he shouted, and the dwarves started fighting toward him. When most were close by, Dolgan could be heard shouting, "Back, fall back! They are too many."

The dwarves slowly began to move toward the tunnel they had entered from, with its relative safety. There they could face a smaller number of creatures and Tsurani and, they hoped, lose them in the mines. Seeing the dwarves moving back, the Tsurani and their allies pressed the attack. Tomas saw a large number of the creatures interpose themselves between the dwarves and the escape route. He sprang forward and heard a strange war cry escape from his lips, words he didn't understand. His golden sword flashed, and with a shriek one of the strange creatures fell. Another wielded a broadsword at him, and he caught it on his shield. A lesser being's arm would have been broken, but the blow rang out on the white shield and the creature backed away, then struck again.

Again he blocked it, and with a looping overhand swing struck through its neck, severing head from body. It stiffened for a moment, then collapsed at his feet. He leaped over its fallen body and landed before three startled Tsurani warriors. One held two lanterns and the others were armed. Before the man with the lanterns could drop them, Tomas jumped forward and struck down the other two men. The third died trying to draw his sword.

Letting his shield hang on his arm, Tomas reached down and grabbed a lantern. He turned and saw the dwarves scrambling over the bodies of the fallen creatures he had killed. Several carried wounded comrades. A handful of dwarves, with Dolgan at their head, held their enemies at bay while the others made good their escape. The dwarves who carried wounded hurried past Tomas.

One, who had stayed behind in the tunnel during the fighting, hastened forward when his comrades were obviously in retreat. Instead of weapons he carried two bulging skins filled with liquid.

The rear guard was pressed back toward the escape tunnel, and twice soldiers tried to circle to cut them off. Both times Tomas struck out, and they fell. When Dolgan and his fighters stood atop the bodies of the fallen monsters, Tomas yelled, "Be ready to jump."

He took the two heavy skins from the dwarf. "Now!" he shouted. Dolgan and the others leaped back, and the Tsurani were left standing on the other side of the corpses. Without hesitation, the dwarves sped up the tunnel while Tomas threw the skins at the bodies. They had been carried carefully, for they were fashioned to rupture on impact. Both contained naphtha, which the dwarves had gathered from deep black pools under the mountain. It would burn without a wick, as oil would not.

Tomas raised the lantern and smashed it in the midst of the pools of volatile liquid. The Tsurani, hesitating only briefly, were moving forward as the lantern burst. White heat exploded in the tunnel as the naphtha burst into flame. The dwarves, blinded, could hear the screams of the Tsurani who had been caught. When their vision recovered, they could see a single figure striding down the tunnel. Tomas appeared black, outlined against the near-white flames.

When he reached them, Dolgan said, "They'll be upon us when the flames die."

They quickly made their way through a series of tunnels and headed back toward the exit on the western side of the mountains. After they had traveled a short distance, Dolgan halted the party. He and several others stood still, listening to the silence in the tunnels. One dropped to the floor and placed his ear on the ground, but immediately jumped to his feet. "They come! By the sound, hundreds of them, and the creatures too. They must be mounting a major offensive."

Dolgan took stock. Of the hundred and fifty dwarves who had begun the ambush, only seventy or so stood here, and of these, twelve were injured. It could be hoped that others had escaped through other passages, but for the moment they were all in danger.

Dolgan acted quickly. "We must make for the forest." He started to trot along with the others following behind.

Tomas ran easily, but his mind reeled with images. In the heat of battle they assaulted him, more vivid and clear than before. He could see the bodies of his fallen enemies, yet they looked nothing like the Tsurani. He could taste the blood of the fallen, the magic energies that came with him as he drank from their open wounds in the ceremony of victory. He shook his head to clear the images. What ceremony? he wondered.

Dolgan spoke, and Tomas forced his attention to the dwarf's words. "We must find another stronghold," he said as they ran. "Perhaps it would be best to try for Stone Mountain. Our villages here are safe, but we have no base to fight from, for I think the Tsurani will have control of these mines soon. Those creatures of theirs fight well in the dark, and if they have many of them, they can ferret us out of the deeper passages."

Tomas nodded, unable to speak. He was burning inside, a cold fire of hatred for these Tsurani. They had savaged his homeland and taken his brother in all but name, and now many dwarven friends lay dead under the mountain because of them. His face was grim as he made a silent vow to destroy these invaders, whatever the cost.

THEY MOVED CAUTIOUSLY through the trees, watching for signs of the Tsurani. Three times in six days they had skirmished, and now the dwarves numbered fifty-two. The more seriously wounded had been carried to the relative safety of the high villages, where the Tsurani were unlikely to follow.

Now they approached the southern part of the elven forests. At first they had tried to turn eastward toward the pass, seeking a way toward Stone Mountain. The route was thick with Tsurani camps and patrols, and they had been constantly turned northward. Finally it had been decided to try for Elvandar, where they could find rest from the constant flight.

A scout returned from his position twenty yards ahead and said softly, "A camp, at the ford."

Dolgan considered. The dwarves were not swimmers, and they would need to cross at a ford. It was likely the Tsurani would hold all the fords on this side. They would have to find a place free of guards, if one existed.

Tomas looked around. It was nearly nightfall, and if they were to sneak across the river this close to the Tsurani lines, it would best be done in the dark. Tomas whispered this to Dolgan, who nodded. He signaled the guard to head off to the west of the espied camp, to find a likely looking place to hole up.

After a short wait the guide returned with word of a thicket facing a hollowed rock, where they could wait for nightfall. They hurried to the place and found a boulder of granite extruding from the ground, twelve feet tall, and broadening to a base twenty-five or thirty feet across. When they pulled back the brush, they found a hollow in which they could tightly fit. It was only twenty feet across, but it reached back under the rock shelf for over forty feet, angling down. When they were all safely tucked in, Dolgan observed, "This must have been under the river at one time—see how it is worn smooth on the underside. It is cramped, but we should be safe for a bit."

Tomas barely heard, for he was once again fighting his battle against the images, the waking dreams, as he thought of them. He closed his eyes, and again the visions came, and the faint music.

▾▾

THE VICTORY had been swift, but Ashen-Shugar brooded. Something troubled the Ruler of the Eagles' Reaches. The blood of Algon-Kokoon, Tyrant of Wind Valley, was still salty upon his lips, and his consorts were now Ashen-Shugar's. Still there was something lacking.

He studied the moredhel dancers, moving in perfect time with the music for his amusement. That was as it should be. No, the lack was felt deep within Ashen-Shugar.

Alengwan, one whom the elves called their Princess, and his latest favorite, sat on the floor beside his throne, awaiting his pleasure. He barely noticed her lovely face and her supple body, clothed in silken garments that served to accent her beauty rather than conceal it.

"Art thou troubled, master?" she asked faintly, her terror of him as thinly veiled as her body.

He glanced away. She had glimpsed his uncertainty; that earned her death, but he would kill her later. Appetites of the flesh had fled lately, both the pleasure of the bed and that of killing. Now he thought upon his nameless feeling, that phantom emotion so strange within. Ashen-Shugar raised his hand, and the dancers were on the floor, foreheads pressed to the stone. The musicians had ceased playing in midnote, it seemed, and the cavern was silent. With a flickering of his hand he dismissed them, and they fled out of the great hall, past the mighty golden dragon, Shuruga, who patiently awaited his master. . . .

"TOMAS," CAME the voice.

Tomas's eyes opened with a snap. Dolgan had his hand upon the young man's arm. "It is time. Night has fallen. You've been asleep, laddie."

Tomas shook his head to clear it, and the lingering images fled. He felt a churning in his stomach as the last flickering vision of a warrior in white and gold standing over the bloody body of an elven princess vanished.

With the others, he crawled out from under the overhanging rock, and they set out once more toward the river. The forest was silent, even the night birds seemingly cautious about revealing their whereabouts.

They reached the river without incident, save that they had to lie hidden while a patrol of Tsurani passed. They followed the river, with a scout in front. After a few minutes, the scout returned. "A sandbar crosses the river."

Dolgan nodded; the dwarves moved quietly forward and entered the water in single file. Tomas waited with Dolgan while the others crossed.

When the last dwarf entered the water, an inquiring shout sounded from farther up the bank. The dwarves froze. Tomas moved quickly forward and surprised a Tsurani guard who was trying to peer through the gloom. The man cried out as he was felled, and shouting erupted a short way off.

Tomas saw lantern light rapidly approaching him, turned, and ran. He found Dolgan waiting on the bank and shouted, "Fly! They are upon us."

Several dwarves stood indecisively as Tomas and Dolgan splashed into the river. The water was cold, moving rapidly over the sandbar. Tomas had to steady himself as he waded through. The water was only waist deep for him, but the dwarves were covered nearly to their chins. They would never be able to fight in the river.

As the first Tsurani guards leaped into the water, Tomas turned to hold them off while the dwarves made good their escape. Two Tsurani attacked, and he struck them both down. Several more jumped into the river, and he had only a brief moment to see to the dwarves. They were almost at the opposite bank, and he caught sight of Dolgan, helpless frustration clearly marked on his face in the Tsurani lamplight.

Tomas struck out again at the Tsurani soldiers. Four or five were trying to surround him, and the best he could manage was to keep them at bay. Each time he tried for a kill, he would leave himself open from a different quarter.

The sound of new voices told him it was only a matter of moments before he would be overwhelmed. He vowed to make them pay dearly and lashed out at one man, splitting his shield and breaking his arm. The man went down with a cry.

Tomas barely caught an answering blow on his shield when a whistling sound sped past his ear, and a Tsurani guard fell screaming, a long arrow protruding from his chest. The air was at once full of arrows. Several more Tsurani fell, and the rest pulled back. Every soldier in the water died before he could reach the shore.

A voice called out, "Quickly, man. They will answer in kind." As if to demonstrate the truth of the warning, an arrow sped past Tomas's face from the other direction. He hurried toward the safety of the opposite bank. A Tsurani arrow struck him in the helm, and he stumbled. As he righted himself, another took him in the leg. He pitched forward and felt the sandy soil of the riverbank below him. Hands reached down and pulled him unceremoniously along.

A dizzy, swimming sensation swept over him, and he heard a voice say, "They poison their arrows. We must . . ." The rest trailed away into blackness.

▼▼

TOMAS OPENED his eyes. For a moment he had no idea of where he was. He felt light-headed and his mouth was dry. A face loomed over him, and a hand lifted his head as water was placed at his lips. He drank deeply, feeling better afterward. He turned his head a little and saw two men sitting close by. For a moment he feared he had been captured, but then he saw that these men wore dark green leather tunics.

"You have been very ill," said the one who had given him water. Tomas then realized these men were elves.

"Dolgan?" he croaked.

"The dwarves have been taken to council with our mistress. We could not chance moving you, for fear of the poison. The outworlders have a venom unknown to us, which kills rapidly. We treat it as best we can, but those wounded die as often as not."

He felt his strength returning slowly. "How long?"

"Three days. You have hovered near death since we fished you from the river. We carried you as far as we dared."

Tomas looked around and saw that he had been undressed and was lying under a shelter fashioned from tree branches, a blanket over him. He smelled food cooking over a fire and saw the pot the savory aroma came from. His host noticed and signaled for a bowl to be brought over.

Tomas sat up, and his head swam for a moment. He was given a large piece of bread and used it in place of a spoon. The food was delicious, and every bite seemed to fill him with increasing strength. As he ate, he took stock of the others sitting nearby. The two silent elves regarded him with blank expressions. Only the speaker showed any signs of hospitality.

Tomas looked at him and said, "What of the enemy?"

The elf smiled. "The outworlders still fear to cross the river. Here our magic is stronger, and they find themselves lost and confused. No outworlder has reached our shore and returned to the other side."

Tomas nodded. When he finished eating, he felt surprisingly well. He tried to stand and found he was only a little shaky. After a few steps, he could feel the strength returning to his limbs, and that his leg was already healed. He spent a few minutes stretching and working out the stiffness of three days sleeping on the ground, then dressed.

"You're Prince Calin. I remember you from the Duke's court."

Calin smiled in return. "And I you, Tomas of Crydee, though you have changed much in a year's time. These others are Galain and Algavins. If you feel up to it, we can rejoin your friends at the court of the Queen."

Tomas smiled. "Let's go."

They broke camp and set out. At first they moved slowly, giving Tomas plenty of time to gain his wind, but after a while it was evident he was remarkably fit in light of his recent brush with death.

Soon the four figures were running through the trees. Tomas, in spite of his armor, kept pace. His hosts glanced questioningly at each other.

They ran most of the afternoon before stopping. Tomas looked around the forest and said, "What a wonderful place."

Galain said, "Most of your race would disagree, man. They find the forest frightening, full of strange shapes and fearful sounds."

Tomas laughed. "Most men lack imagination, or possess too much. The forest is quiet and peaceful. It is the most peaceful place I think I have known."

The elves said nothing, but a look of mild surprise crossed Calin's face. "We had best continue, if we are to reach Elvandar before dark."

As night fell, they reached a giant clearing. Tomas stopped and stood rooted by the sight before him. Across the clearing a huge city of trees rose upward. Gigantic trees, dwarfing any oaks imagined, stood together. They were linked by gracefully arching bridges of branches, flat across the tops, on which elves could be seen crossing from bole to bole. Tomas looked up and saw the trunks rise until they were lost in a sea of leaves and branches. The leaves were deep green, but here and there a tree with golden, silver, or even white foliage could be seen, sparkling with lights. A soft glow permeated the entire area, and Tomas wondered if it ever became truly dark here.

Calin placed his hand on Tomas's shoulder and simply said, "Elvandar."

They hurried across the clearing, and Tomas could see the elven tree city was even larger than he had first imagined. It spread away on all sides and must have been over a mile across. Tomas felt a thrill of wonder at this magic place, a singular exaltation.

They reached a stairway, carved into the side of a tree, that wound its way upward, into the branches. They started up the steps, and Tomas again felt a sensation of joy, as if the mad frenzy that filled him during a battle had a harmonious aspect of gentler nature.

Upward they climbed, and as they passed the large branches that served as roadways for the elves, Tomas could see elven men and women on all sides. Many of the men wore fighting leather like his guides, but many others wore long, graceful robes or tunics of bright and rich colors. The women were all beautiful, with their hair worn long and down, unlike the ladies of the Duke's court. Many had jewels woven into their tresses that sparkled when they passed. All were tall and graceful.

They reached a gigantic branch and left the stairs. Calin began to warn him about not looking down, for he knew humans had difficulty on the high pathways, but Tomas stood near the edge, looking down with no sign of discomfort or vertigo.

"This is a marvelous place," he said. The three elves exchanged questioning glances, but no words were spoken.

They set off again, and when they came to an intersection of branches, the two elves turned off the path, leaving Tomas and Calin to travel alone. Deeper and deeper they moved, Tomas as surefooted on the branch road as the elf, until they reached a large opening. Here a circle of trees formed a central court for the Elf Queen. A hundred branches met and merged into a huge platform. Aglaranna was sitting upon a wooden throne, surrounded by her court. A single human, in the grey of a Natalese Ranger, stood near the Queen, his black skin gleaming in the night glow. He was the tallest man Tomas had ever seen, and the young man from Crydee knew this must be Long Leon, the ranger Grimsworth had spoken of.

Calin led Tomas into the center of the clearing and presented him to Queen Aglaranna. She showed slight surprise as she saw the figure of the young man in white and gold, but quickly composed her features. In her rich voice she welcomed Tomas to Elvandar, and bade him stay as long as he wished.

The court adjourned, and Dolgan came to where Tomas stood. "Well, laddie, I am glad to see you recovered. It was an undecided issue when we left you. I hated to do so, but I think you understand. I was in need of getting word on the fighting near Stone Mountain."

Tomas nodded. "I understand. What news?"

Dolgan shook his head. "Bad, I fear. We are cut off from our brethren. I think we will be staying with the elvenfolk for a while, and I have little love for these heights."

Tomas broke into open laughter at that. Dolgan smiled, for it was the first time since the boy had donned the dragon's armor he had heard the sound.

16

▾▾

RAID

WAGONS GROANED UNDER HEAVY LOADS.

Whips cracked and wheels creaked as lumbering oxen pulled their burdens down the road toward the beach. Arutha, Fannon, and Lyam rode before soldiers protecting the wagons traveling between the castle and the shore. Behind the wagons a ragged crowd of townspeople followed. Many carried bundles or pulled carts, following the Duke's sons toward the waiting ships.

They turned down the road that split off from the town road, and Arutha's gaze swept over the signs of destruction. The once-thriving town of Crydee was now covered in an acrid blue haze. The sounds of hammering and sawing rang through the morning air as workmen labored to repair what they could of the damage.

The Tsurani had raided at sundown two days before, racing through the town, overwhelming the few guards at their posts before an alarm was raised by terrified women, old men, and children. The aliens had run riot through the town, not pausing until they reached dockside, where they had fired three ships, heavily damaging two. The damaged ships were already limping toward Carse, while the undamaged ships in the harbor had moved down the coast to their present location, north of Sailor's Grief.

The Tsurani had put most of the buildings near the quay to the torch, but while heavily damaged, they were reparable. The fire had spread into the heart of town, resulting in the heaviest loss there. The Hall of the Craftmasters, the two inns, and dozens of lesser buildings were now only smoldering ruins. Blackened timbers, cracked roof tiles, and scorched stones marked their locations. Fully one third of Crydee had burned before the fire had been brought under control.

Arutha had stood on the wall, watching the hellish glow reflected on the clouds above the town as the flames spread. Then at first light he had led the garrison out, finding the Tsurani already vanished into the forests.

Arutha still chafed at the memory. Fannon had advised Lyam not to allow the garrison out until dawn—fearing it was a ruse to get the castle gates open or to lure the garrison into the woods where a larger force waited in ambush—and Lyam had acceded to the old Swordmaster's request. Arutha was sure he could have prevented much of the damage had he been allowed to rout the Tsurani at once.

As he rode down the coast road, Arutha was lost in thought. Orders arrived the day before instructing Lyam to leave Crydee. The Duke's aide-de-camp had been killed, and with the war beginning its third year this spring, he wished Lyam to join him at his camp in Yabon. For reasons Arutha didn't understand, Duke Borric had not given command to him as expected; instead Borric had named the Swordmaster garrison commander. But, thought the younger Prince, at least Fannon will be less ready to order me about without Lyam's backing. He shook his head slightly in an attempt to dislodge his irritation. He loved his brother, but wished Lyam had shown more willingness to assert himself. Since the beginning of the war, Lyam had commanded in Crydee, but it had been Fannon making all the decisions. Now Fannon had the office as well as the influence.

"Thoughtful, brother?"

Lyam had pulled his own horse up and was now beside Arutha, who shook his head and smiled faintly. "Just envious of you."

Lyam smiled his warmest at his younger brother. "I know you wish to be going, but Father's orders were clear. You're needed here."

"How needed can I be where every suggestion I make has been ignored?"

Lyam's expression was conciliatory. "You're still disturbed by Father's decision to name Fannon commander of the garrison."

Arutha looked hard at his brother. "I am now the age you were when Father named you commander at Crydee. Father was full commander and second Knight-General in the West at my age, only four years shy of being named King's Warden of the West. Grandfather trusted him enough to give him full command."

"Father's not Grandfather, Arutha. Remember, Grandfather grew up in a time when we were still warring in Crydee, pacifying newly conquered lands. He grew up in war. Father did not. He learned all his warcraft down in the Vale of Dreams, against Kesh, not defending his own home as Grandfather had. Times change."

"How they change, brother," Arutha said dryly. "Grandfather, like his father before him, would not have sat behind safe walls. In the two years since the war began, we have not mounted one major offensive against the Tsurani. We cannot continue letting them dictate the course of the war, or surely they will prevail."

Lyam regarded his brother with concern mirrored in his eyes. "Arutha, I know you are restless to harry the enemy, but Fannon is right in saying we dare not risk the garrison. We must hold here and protect what we have."

Arutha cast a quick glance at the ragged townspeople behind. "I'll tell those who follow how well they're protected."

Lyam saw the bitterness in Arutha. "I know you blame me, brother. Had I taken your advice, rather than Fannon's . . ."

Arutha lost his harsh manner. "It is not your doing," he conceded. "Old Fannon is simply cautious. He also is of the opinion a soldier's worth is measured by the grey in his beard. I am still only the Duke's boy. I fear my opinions from now on will receive short shrift."

"Curb thy impatience, youngster," he said in mock seriousness. "Perhaps between your boldness and Fannon's caution, a safe middle course will be followed." Lyam laughed.

Arutha had always found his brother's laughter infectious and couldn't repress a grin. "Perhaps, Lyam," he said with a laugh.

They came to the beach where longboats waited to haul the refugees out to the ships anchored offshore. The captains would not return to the quayside until they were assured their ships would not again come under attack, so the fleeing townspeople were forced to walk through the surf to board the boats. Men and women began to wade to the boats, bundles of belongings and small children held safely overhead. Older children swam playfully, turning the event into sport. There were many tearful partings, for most of the townsmen were remaining to rebuild their burned homes and serve as levies in the dukes' army. The women, children, and old men who were leaving would be carried down the coast to Tulan, the southernmost town in the Duchy, as yet untroubled by either the Tsurani or the rampaging Dark Brothers in the Green Heart.

Lyam and Arutha dismounted, and a soldier took their horses. The brothers watched as soldiers carefully loaded crates of messenger pigeons onto the sole longboat pulled up on shore. The birds would be shipped through the Straits of Darkness to the dukes' camp. Pigeons trained to fly to the camp were now on their way to Crydee, and with their arrival some of the responsibility for carrying information to and from the dukes' camp would be lifted from Martin Longbow's trackers and the Natalese Rangers. This was the first year mature pigeons raised in the camp—necessary for them to develop the homing instinct—were available.

Soon the baggage and refugees were loaded, and it was time for Lyam to depart. Fannon bid him a stiff and formal farewell, but it was apparent from his controlled manner that the old Swordmaster felt concern for the Duke's older son. With no family of his own, Fannon had been something of an uncle to the boys when they were growing, personally instructing them in swordsmanship, the maintenance of armor, and the theories of warcraft. He maintained his formal pose, but both brothers could see the genuine affection there.

When Fannon left, the brothers embraced. Lyam said, "Take care of Fannon." Arutha looked surprised. Lyam grinned and said, "I'd not care to think what would happen here should Father pass you over once more and name Algon commander of the garrison."

Arutha groaned, then laughed with his brother. As Horsemaster, Algon was technically second-in-command behind Fannon. All in the castle shared genuine affection for the man, and deep respect for his vast knowledge of horses, but everyone conceded his general lack of knowledge about anything *besides* horses. After two years of warfare, he still resisted the idea the invaders came from another world, an attitude that caused Tully no end of irritation.

Lyam moved into the water, where two sailors held the longboat for him. Over his shoulder he shouted, "And take care of our sister, Arutha."

Arutha said he would. Lyam leaped into the longboat, next to the precious pigeons, and the boat was pushed away from shore. Arutha watched as the boat dwindled into the distance.

Arutha walked slowly back to where a soldier held his mount. He paused to stare down the beach. To the south, the high bluffs reared, dominated by Sailor's Grief, which stood upthrust against the morning sky. Arutha silently cursed the day the Tsurani ship crashed against those rocks.

CARLINE STOOD ATOP the southern tower of the keep, watching the horizon, gathering her cloak around her against the sea breeze. She had stayed at the castle, bidding Lyam good-bye earlier, not wishing to ride to the beach. She preferred that her fears not becloud Lyam's happiness at joining their father in the dukes' camp. Many times over the last two years she had chided herself over such feelings. Her men were soldiers, all trained since boyhood for war. But since word had reached Crydee of Pug's capture, she had remained afraid for them.

A feminine clearing of the throat made Carline turn. Lady Glynis, the Princess's companion for the last four years, smiled slightly and indicated with a nod of her head the newcomer who appeared at the trapdoor leading down into the tower.

Roland emerged from the doorway in the floor. The last two years had added to his growth, and now he stood as tall as Arutha. He was still thin, but his boyish features were resolving into those of a man.

He bowed and said, "Highness."

Carline acknowledged the greeting with a nod and gestured that Lady Glynis should leave them alone. Glynis fled down the stairway into the tower.

Softly Carline said, "You did not ride to the beach with Lyam?"

"No, Highness."

"You spoke with him before he left?"

Roland turned his gaze to the far horizon. "Yes, Highness, though I must confess to a foul humor at his going."

Carline nodded understanding. "Because you have to stay."

He spoke with bitterness, "Yes, Highness."

Carline said gently, "Why so formal, Roland?"

Roland looked at the Princess, seventeen years old just this last Midsummer's Day. No longer a petulant little girl given to outbursts of temper, she was changing into a beautiful young woman of thoughtful introspection. Few in the castle were unaware of the many nights' sobbing that issued from Carline's suite after news of Pug had reached the castle. After nearly a week of solitude, Carline had emerged a changed person, more subdued, less willful. There was little outward to show how Carline felt, but Roland knew she carried a scar.

After a moment of silence, Roland said, "Highness, when . . ." He halted, then said, "It is of no consequence."

Carline placed her hand upon his arm. "Roland, whatever else, we have always been friends."

"It pleases me to think that is true."

"Then tell me, why has a wall grown between us?"

Roland sighed, and there was none of his usual roguish humor in his answer. "If there has, Carline, it is not of my fashioning."

A spark of the girl's former self sprang into being, and with a temperamental edge to her voice she said, "Am I, then, the architect of this estrangement?"

Anger erupted in Roland's voice. "Aye, Carline!" He ran his hand through his wavy brown hair and said, "Do you remember the day I fought with Pug? The very day before he left."

At the mention of Pug's name she tensed. Stiffly she said, "Yes, I remember."

"Well, it was a silly thing, a boys' thing, that fight. I told him should he ever cause you any hurt, I'd thrash him. Did he tell you that?"

Moisture came unbidden to her eyes. Softly she said, "No, he never mentioned it."

Roland looked at the beautiful face he had loved for years and said, "At least then I knew my rival." He lowered his voice, the anger slipping away. "I like to think then, near the end, he and I were fast friends. Still, I vowed I'd never stop my attempts to change your heart."

Shivering, Carline drew her cloak about her, though the day was not that cool. She felt conflicting emotions within, confusing emotions. Trembling, she said, "Why did you stop, Roland?"

Sudden harsh anger burst within Roland. For the first time he lost his mask of wit and manners before the Princess. "Because I can't contend with a memory, Carline." Her eyes opened wide, and tears welled up and ran down her cheeks. "Another man of flesh I can face, but this shade from the past I cannot grapple with." Hot anger exploded into words. "He's dead, Carline. I wish it were not so; he was my friend and I miss him, but I've let him go. Pug is dead. Until you grant that this is true, you are living with a false hope."

She put her hand to her mouth, palm outward, her eyes regarding him in wordless denial. Abruptly she turned and fled down the stairs.

Alone, Roland leaned his elbows on the cold stones of the tower wall. Holding his head in his hands, he said, "Oh, what a fool I have become!"

"PATROL!" SHOUTED the guard from the wall of the castle. Arutha and Roland turned from where they watched soldiers giving instructions to levies from the outlying villages.

They reached the gate, and the patrol came riding slowly in, a dozen dirty, weary riders, with Martin Longbow and two other trackers walking beside. Arutha greeted the Huntmaster and then said, "What have you there?"

He indicated the three men in short grey robes who stood between the line of horsemen. "Prisoners, Highness," answered the hunter, leaning on his bow.

Arutha dismissed the tired riders as other guards came to take position around the prisoners. Arutha walked to where they waited, and when he came within touching distance, all three fell to their knees, putting their foreheads to the dirt.

Arutha raised his eyebrows in surprise at the display. "I have never seen such as these."

Longbow nodded in agreement. "They wear no armor, and they didn't give fight or run when we found them in the woods. They did as you see now, only then they babbled like fishwives."

Arutha said to Roland, "Fetch Father Tully. He may be able to make something of their tongue." Roland hurried off to find the priest. Longbow dismissed his two trackers, who headed for the kitchen. A guard was dispatched to find Swordmaster Fannon and inform him of the captives.

A few minutes later Roland returned with Father Tully. The old priest of Astalon was dressed in a deep blue, nearly black, robe, and upon catching a glimpse of him, the three prisoners set up a babble of whispers. When Tully glanced in their direction, they fell completely silent. Arutha looked at Longbow in surprise.

Tully said, "What have we here?"

"Prisoners," said Arutha. "As you are the only man here to have had some dealings with their language, I thought you might get something out of them."

"I remember little from my mind contact with the Tsurani Xomich, but I can try." The priest spoke a few halting words, which resulted in a confusion as all three prisoners spoke at once. The centermost snapped at his companions, who fell silent. He was short, as were the others, but powerfully built. His hair was brown, and his skin swarthy, but his eyes were a startling green. He spoke slowly to Tully, his manner somehow less deferential than his companions'.

Tully shook his head. "I can't be certain, but I think he wishes to know if I am a Great One of this world."

"Great One?" asked Arutha.

"The dying soldier was in awe of the man aboard ship he called 'Great One.' I think it was a title rather than a specific individual. Perhaps Kulgan was correct in his suspicion these people hold their magicians or priests in awe."

"Who are these men?" asked the Prince.

Tully spoke to them again in halting words. The man in the center spoke slowly, but after a moment Tully cut him off with a wave of his hand. To Arutha he said, "These are slaves."

"Slaves?" Until now there had been no contact with any Tsurani except warriors. It was something of a revelation to find they practiced slavery. While not unknown in the Kingdom, slavery was not widespread and was limited to convicted felons. Along the Far Coast, it was nearly nonexistent. Arutha found the idea strange and repugnant. Men might be born to low station, but even the lowliest serf had rights the nobility were obligated to respect and protect. Slaves were property. With a sudden disgust, Arutha said, "Tell them to get up, for mercy's sake."

Tully spoke and the men slowly rose, the two on the flanks looking about like frightened children. The other stood calmly, eyes only slightly downcast. Again Tully questioned the man, finding his understanding of their language returning.

The centermost man spoke at length, and when he was done Tully said, "They were assigned to work in the enclaves near the river. They say their camp was overrun by the forest people—he refers to the elves, I think—and the short ones."

"Dwarves, no doubt," added Longbow with a grin.

Tully threw him a withering look. The rangy forester simply continued to smile. Martin was one of the few young men of the castle never intimidated by the old cleric, even before becoming one of the Duke's staff.

"As I was saying," continued the priest, "the elves and dwarves overran their camp. They fled, fearing they would be killed. They wandered in the woods for days until the patrol picked them up this morning."

Arutha said, "This fellow in the center seems a bit different from the others. Ask why this is so."

Tully spoke slowly to the man, who answered with little inflection in his tones. When he was done, Tully spoke with some surprise. "He says his name is Tchakachakalla. He was once a Tsurani officer!"

Arutha said, "This may prove most fortunate. If he'll cooperate, we may finally learn some things about the enemy."

Swordmaster Fannon appeared from the keep and hurried to where Arutha was questioning the prisoners. The commander of the Crydee garrison said, "What have you here?"

Arutha explained as much as he knew about the prisoners, and when he was finished, Fannon said, "Good, continue with the questioning."

Arutha said to Tully, "Ask him how he came to be a slave."

Without sign of embarrassment, Tchakachakalla told his story. When he was done, Tully stood shaking his head. "He was a Strike Leader. It may take some time to puzzle out what his rank was equivalent to in our armies, but I gather he was at least a Knight-Lieutenant. He says his men broke in one of the early battles and his 'house' lost much honor. He wasn't given permission to take his own life by someone he calls the Warchief. Instead he was made a slave to expiate the shame of his command."

Roland whistled low. "His men fled and he was held responsible."

Longbow said, "There's been more than one earl who's bollixed a command and found himself ordered by his Duke to serve with one of the Border Barons along the Northern Marches."

Tully shot Martin and Roland a black look. "If you are finished?" He addressed Arutha and Fannon: "From what he said, it is clear he was stripped of everything. He may prove of use to us."

Fannon said, "This may be some trick. I don't like his looks."

The man's head came up, and he fixed Fannon with a narrow gaze. Martin's mouth fell open. "By Kilian! I think he understands what you said."

Fannon stood directly before Tchakachakalla. "Do you understand me?"

"Little, master." His accent was thick, and he spoke with a slow singsong tone alien to the King's Tongue. "Many Kingdom slaves on Kelewan. Know little King's Tongue."

Fannon said, "Why didn't you speak before?"

Again without any show of emotion, he answered, "Not ordered. Slave obey. Not . . ." He turned to Tully and spoke a few words.

Tully said, "He says it isn't a slave's place to show initiative."

Arutha said, "Tully, do you think he can be trusted?"

"I don't know. His story is strange, but they are a strange people by our standards. My mind contact with the dying soldier showed me much I still don't understand." Tully spoke to the man.

To Arutha the Tsurani said, "Tchakachakalla tell." Fighting for words, he said, "I Wedewayo. My house, family. My clan Hunzan. Old, much honor. Now slave. No house, no clan, no Tsuranuanni. No honor. Slave obey."

Arutha said, "I think I understand. If you go back to the Tsurani, what would happen to you?"

Tchakachakalla said, "Be slave, maybe. Be killed, maybe. All same."

"And if you stay here?"

"Be slave, be killed?" He shrugged, showing little concern.

Arutha said, slowly, "We keep no slaves. What would you do if we set you free?"

A flicker of some emotion passed over the slave's face, and he turned to Tully and spoke rapidly. Tully translated. "He says such a thing is not possible on his world. He asks if you can do such a thing."

Arutha nodded. Tchakachakalla pointed to his companions. "They work. They always slaves."

"And you?" said Arutha.

Tchakachakalla looked hard at the Prince and spoke to Tully, never taking his eyes from Arutha. Tully said, "He's recounting his lineage. He says he is Tchakachakalla, Strike Leader of the Wedewayo, of the Hunzan Clan. His father was a Force Leader, and his great-grandfather Warchief of the Hunzan Clan. He has fought honorably, and only once has he failed in his duty. Now he is only a slave, with no family, no clan, no nation, and no honor. He asks if you mean to give him back his honor."

Arutha said, "If the Tsurani come, what will you do?"

Tchakachakalla indicated his companions. "These men slaves. Tsurani come, they do nothing. Wait. Go with . . ." He and Tully exchanged brief remarks and Tully supplied him with the word he wished. ". . . victors. They go with victors." He looked at Arutha, and his eyes came alive. "You make Tchakachakalla free. Tchakachakalla be your man, lord. Your honor is Tchakachakalla's honor. Give life if you say. Fight Tsurani if you say."

Fannon spoke. "Likely story that. More's the odds he's a spy."

The barrel-chested Tsurani looked hard at Fannon, then with a sudden motion stepped before the Swordmaster, and before anyone could react, pulled Fannon's knife from his belt.

Longbow had his own knife out an instant later, as Arutha's sword was clearing its scabbard. Roland and the other soldiers were only a moment behind. The Tsurani made no threatening gesture, but simply flipped the knife, reversing it and handing it to Fannon hilt first. "Master think Tchakachakalla enemy? Master kill. Give warrior's death, return honor."

Arutha returned his sword to his scabbard and took the knife from Tchakachakalla's hand. Returning the knife to Fannon, he said, "No, we will not kill you." To Tully he said, "I think this man may prove useful. For now, my inclination is to believe him."

Fannon looked less than pleased. "He may be a very clever spy, but you're right. There's no harm if we keep a close watch on him. Father Tully, why don't you take these men to soldiers' commons and see what you can learn from them. I'll be along shortly."

Tully spoke to the three slaves and indicated they should follow. The two timid slaves moved at once, but Tchakachakalla bent his knee before Arutha. He spoke rapidly in the Tsurani tongue; Tully translated.

"He's just demanded you either kill him or make him your man. He asked how a man can be free with no house, clan, or honor. On his world such men are called grey warriors and have no honor."

Arutha said, "Our ways are not your ways. Here a man can be free with no family or clan and still have honor."

Tchakachakalla bent his head slightly while listening, then nodded. He rose and said, "Tchakachakalla understand." Then with a grin he added, "Soon, I be your man. Good lord need good warrior. Tchakachakalla good warrior."

"Tully, take them along, and find out how much Tchak . . . Tchakal . . ." Arutha laughed. "I can't pronounce that mouthful." To the slave he said, "If you're to serve here, you need a Kingdom name."

The slave looked about and then gave a curt nod.

Longbow said, "Call him Charles. It's as close a name as I can imagine."

Arutha said, "As good a name as any. From now on, you will be called Charles."

The newly named slave said, "Tcharles?" He shrugged and nodded. Without another word he fell in beside Father Tully, who led the slaves toward the soldiers' commons.

Roland said, "What do you make of that?" as the three slaves vanished around the corner.

Fannon said, "Time will tell if we've been duped."

Longbow laughed. "I'll keep an eye on Charles, Swordmaster. He's a tough little fellow. He traveled at a good pace when we brought them in. Maybe I'll turn him into a tracker."

Arutha interrupted. "It will be some time before I'll be comfortable letting him outside the castle walls."

Fannon let the matter drop. To Longbow he said, "Where did you find them?"

"To the north, along the Clearbrook branch of the river. We were following the signs of a large party of warriors heading for the coast."

Fannon considered this. "Gardan leads another patrol near there. Perhaps he'll catch sight of them and we'll find out what the bastards are up to this year." Without another word he walked back toward the keep.

Martin laughed; Arutha was surprised to hear him. "What in this strikes you as funny, Huntmaster?"

Martin shook his head. "A little thing, Highness. It's the Swordmaster himself. He'll not speak of it to anyone, but I wager he would give all he owns to have your father back in command. He's a good soldier, but he dislikes the responsibility."

Arutha regarded the retreating back of the Swordmaster, then said, "I think you are right, Martin." His voice carried a thoughtful note. "I have been at odds with Fannon so much of late, I lost sight of the fact he never requested this commission."

Lowering his voice, Martin said, "A suggestion, Arutha."

Arutha nodded. Martin pointed to Fannon. "Should anything happen to Fannon, name another Swordmaster quickly; do not wait for your father's consent. For if you wait, Algon will assume command, and he is a fool."

Arutha stiffened at the Huntmaster's presumption, while Roland tried to silence Martin with a warning look. Arutha coldly said, "I thought you a friend of the Horsemaster."

Martin smiled, his eyes hinting at strange humor. "Aye, I am, as are all in the castle. But anyone you ask will tell you the same: take his horses away, and Algon is an indifferent thinker."

Nettled by Martin's manner, Arutha said, "And who should take his place? The Huntmaster?"

Martin laughed, a sound of such open, clear amusement at the thought, Arutha found himself less angry at his suggestion.

"I?" said the Huntmaster. "Heaven forfend, Highness. I am a simple hunter, no more. No, should the need come, name Gardan. He is by far the most able soldier in Crydee."

Arutha knew Martin was correct, but gave in to impatience. "Enough. Fannon is well, and I trust will remain so."

Martin nodded. "May the gods preserve him . . . and us all. Please excuse me, it was but a passing concern. Now, with Your Highness's leave, I've not had a hot meal in a week."

Arutha indicated he could leave, and Martin walked away toward the kitchen. Roland said, "He is wrong on one account, Arutha."

Arutha stood with his arms folded across his chest, watching Longbow as he vanished around the corner. "What is that, Roland?"

"That man is much more than the simple hunter he pretends."

Arutha was silent for a moment. "He is. Something about Martin Longbow has always made me uneasy, though I have never found fault with him."

Roland laughed, and Arutha said, "Now something strikes you as funny, Roland?"

Roland shrugged. "Only that many think you and he are much alike."

Arutha turned a black gaze upon Roland, who shook his head. "It's often said we take offense most in what we see of ourselves in others. It's true, Arutha. You both have that same cutting edge to your humor, almost mocking, and neither of you suffers foolishness." Roland's voice became serious. "There's no mystery to it, I should think. You're a great deal like your father, and with Martin having no family, it follows he would pattern himself after the Duke."

Arutha became thoughtful. "Perhaps you're right. But something else troubles me about that man." He left the thought unfinished and turned toward the keep.

Roland fell into step beside the thoughtful Prince and wondered if he had overstepped himself.

THE NIGHT THUNDERED. Ragged bolts of lightning shattered the darkness as clouds rolled in from the west. Roland stood on the southern tower watching the display. Since dinner his mood had been as dark as the western sky. The day had not gone well. First he had felt troubled by his conversation with Arutha by the gate. Then Carline had treated him at dinner with the same stony silence he had endured since their meeting on this very tower two weeks earlier. Carline had seemed more subdued than usual, but Roland felt a stab of anger at himself each time he chanced a glance in her direction. Roland could still see the pain in the Princess's eyes. "What a witless fool I am," he said aloud.

"Not a fool, Roland."

Carline was standing a few paces away, looking toward the coming storm. She clutched a shawl around her shoulders, though the air was temperate. The thunder had masked her footfalls, and Roland said, "It is a poor night to be upon the tower, my lady."

She came to stand beside him and said, "Will it rain? These hot nights bring thunder and lightning, but usually little rain."

"It will rain. Where are your ladies?"

She indicated the tower door. "Upon the stairs. They fear the lightning, and besides, I wished to speak with you alone."

Roland said nothing, and Carline remained silent for a time. The night was sundered with violent displays of energy tearing across the heavens, followed by cracking booms of thunder. "When I was young," she said at last, "Father used to say on nights such as this the gods were sporting in the sky."

Roland looked at her face, illuminated by the single lantern hanging on the wall. "My father told me they made war."

She smiled. "Roland, you spoke rightly on the day Lyam left. I have been lost in my own grief, unable to see the truth. Pug would have been the first to tell me that nothing is forever. That living in the past is foolish and robs us of the future." She lowered her head a little. "Perhaps it has something to do with Father. When Mother died, he never fully recovered. I was very young, but I can still remember how he was. He used to laugh a great deal before she died. He was more like Lyam then. After . . . well, he became more like Arutha. He'd laugh, but there'd be a hard edge to it, a bitterness."

"As if somehow mocking?"

She nodded thoughtfully. "Yes, mocking. Why did you say that?"

"Something I noticed . . . something I pointed out to your brother today. About Martin Longbow."

She sighed. "Yes, I understand. Longbow is also like that."

Softly Roland said, "Nevertheless, you did not come to speak of your brother or Martin."

"No, I came to tell you how sorry I am for the way I've acted. I've been angry with you for two weeks, but I'd no right. You only said what was true. I've treated you badly."

Roland was surprised. "You've not treated me badly, Carline. I acted the boor."

"No, you have done nothing but be a friend to me, Roland. You told me the truth, not what I wanted to hear. It must have been hard . . . considering how you feel." She looked out at the approaching storm. "When I first heard of Pug's capture, I thought the world ended."

Trying to be understanding, Roland quoted, " 'The first love is the difficult love.' "

Carline smiled at the aphorism. "That is what they say. And with you?"

Roland mustered a carefree stance. "So it seems, Princess."

She placed her hand upon his arm. "Neither of us is free to feel other than as we do, Roland."

His smile became sadder. "That is the truth, Carline."

"Will you always be my good friend?"

There was a genuine note of concern in her voice that touched the young Squire. She was trying to put matters right between them, but without the guile she'd used when younger. Her honest attempt turned aside any frustration he felt at her not returning his affections fully. "I will, Carline. I'll always be your good friend."

She came into his arms and he held her close, her head against his chest. Softly she said, "Father Tully says that some loves come unbidden like winds from the sea, and others grow from the seeds of friendship."

"I will hope for such a harvest, Carline. But should it not come, still I will remain your good friend."

They stood quietly together for a time, comforting each other for different causes, but sharing a tenderness each had been denied for two years. Each of them was lost in the comfort of the other's nearness, and neither saw what the lightning flashes revealed for brief instants. On the horizon, beating for the harbor, came a ship.

THE WINDS WHIPPED the banners on the palisades of the castle walls as rain began to fall. As water gathered in small pools, the lanterns cast yellow reflections upward off the puddles to give an otherworldly look to the two men standing on the wall.

A flash of lightning illuminated the sea, and a soldier said, "There! Highness, did you see? Three points south of the Guardian Rocks." He extended his arm, pointing the way.

Arutha peered into the gloom, his brow furrowed in concentration. "I can see nothing in this darkness. It's blacker than a Guis-wan priest's soul out there." The soldier absently made a protective sign at the mention of the killer god. "Any signal from the beacon tower?"

"None, Highness. Not by beacon, nor by messenger."

Another flash of lightning illuminated the night, and Arutha saw the ship outlined in the distance. He swore. "It will need the beacon at Longpoint to reach the harbor safely." Without another word, he ran down the stairs leading to the courtyard. Near the gate he instructed a soldier to get his horse and two riders to accompany him. As he stood there waiting, the rain passed, leaving the night with a clean but warm, moist feeling. A few minutes later, Fannon appeared from the direction of the soldiers' commons. "What's this? Riding?"

Arutha said, "A ship makes for the harbor, and there is no beacon at Longpoint."

As a groom brought Arutha's horse, followed by two mounted soldiers, Fannon said, "You'd best be off, then. And tell those stone-crowned layabouts at the lighthouse I'll have words for them when they finish duty."

Arutha had expected an argument from Fannon and felt relieved there would be none. He mounted and the gates were opened. They rode through and headed down the road toward town.

The brief rain had made the night rich with fresh odors: the flowers along the road, and the scent of salt from the sea, soon masked by the acrid odor of burned wood from the charred remnants of gutted buildings as they neared town.

They sped past the quiet town, taking the road along the harbor. A pair of guards stationed by the quayside hastily saluted when they saw the Prince fly past. The shuttered buildings near the docks bore mute testimony to those who had fled after the raid.

They left the town and rode out to the lighthouse, following a bend in the road. Beyond the town they gained their first glimpse of the lighthouse, upon a natural island of rock joined to the mainland by a long causeway of stone, topped by a compacted dirt road. The horses' hooves beat a dull tattoo upon the dirt as they approached the tall tower. A lightning flash lit up the sky, and the three riders could see the ship running under full sail toward the harbor.

Shouting to the others, Arutha said, "They'll pile upon the rocks without a beacon."

One of the guards shouted back, "Look, Highness. Someone signals!"

They reined in and saw figures near the base of the tower. A man dressed in black stood swinging a shuttered lantern back and forth. It could be clearly seen by those on the ship, but not by anyone upon the castle walls. In the dim light, Arutha saw the still forms of Crydee soldiers lying on the ground. Four men, also attired in black with head coverings that masked their faces, ran toward the horsemen. Three drew long swords from back scabbards, while the fourth aimed a bow. The soldier to Arutha's right cried out as an arrow struck him in the chest. Arutha charged his horse among the three who closed, knocking over two while his sword slashed out, taking the third across the face. The man fell without a sound.

The Prince wheeled around and saw his other companion also engaged, hacking downward at the bowman. More men in black dashed from within the tower, rushing forward silently.

Arutha's horse screamed. He could see an arrow protruding from its neck. As it collapsed beneath him, he freed his feet from the stirrups and lifted his left leg over the dying animal's neck, jumping free as it struck the ground. He hit and rolled, coming to his feet before a short figure in black with a long sword held high overhead with both hands. The long blade flashed down, and Arutha jumped to his left, thrusting with his own sword. He took the man in the chest, then yanked his sword free. Like the others before, the man in black fell without uttering a cry.

Another flash of lightning showed men rushing toward Arutha from the tower. Arutha turned to order the remaining rider back to warn the castle, but the shouted command died aborning when he saw the man pulled from his saddle by swarming figures in black. Arutha dodged a blow from the first man to reach him and ran past three startled figures. He smashed at the face of a fourth man with his sword hilt, trying to knock the man aside. His only thought was to open a pathway so he might flee to warn the castle. The struck man reeled back, and Arutha attempted to jump past him. The falling man reached out with one hand, catching Arutha's leg as he sprang.

Arutha struck hard stone and felt hands frantically grab at his right foot. He kicked backward with his left and took the man in the throat with his boot. The sound of the man's windpipe being crushed was followed by a convulsion of movement.

Arutha came to his feet as another attacker reached him, others only a step behind. Arutha sprang backward, trying to gain some distance. His boot heel caught on a rock, and suddenly the world tilted crazily. He found himself suspended in space for an instant, then his shoulders met rock as he bounced down the side of the causeway. He hit several more rocks, and icy water closed over him.

The shock of the water kept him from passing into unconsciousness. Dazed, he reflexively held his breath, but had little wind. Without thinking, he pushed upward and broke the surface with a loud, ragged gasp. Still groggy, he nevertheless possessed enough wits to duck below the surface when arrows struck the water near him. He couldn't see a thing in the murky darkness of the harbor, but clung to the rocks, pulling himself along more than swimming. He moved back toward the tower end of the causeway, hoping the raiders would think him headed in the other direction.

He quietly surfaced and blinked the salt water from his eyes. Peering around the shelter of a large rock, he saw black figures searching the darkness of the water. Arutha moved quietly, nestling himself into the rocks. Bruised muscles and joints made him wince as he moved, but nothing seemed broken.

Another flash of lightning lit the harbor. Arutha could see the ship speeding safely into Crydee harbor. It was a trader, but rigged for speed and outfitted for war. Whoever piloted the ship was a mad genius, for he cleared the rocks by a scant margin, heading straight for the quayside around the bend of the causeway. Arutha could see men in the rigging, frantically reefing in sails. Upon the deck a company of black-clad warriors stood with weapons ready.

Arutha turned his attention to the men on the causeway and saw one motion silently to the others. They ran off in the direction of the town. Ignoring the pain in his body, Arutha pulled himself up, negotiating the slippery rocks to regain the dirt road of the causeway. Staggering a bit, he came to his feet and looked off toward the town. There was still no sign of trouble, but he knew it would erupt shortly.

Arutha half staggered, half ran to the lighthouse tower and forced himself to climb the stairs. Twice he came close to blacking out, but he reached the top of the tower. He saw the lookout lying dead near the signal fire. The oil-soaked wood was protected from the elements by a hood that hung suspended over it. The cold wind blew through the open windows on all sides of the building.

Arutha found the dead sentry's pouch and removed flint, steel, and tinder. He opened the small door in the side of the metal hood, using his body to shield the wood from the wind. The second spark he fired caught in the wood, and a small flame sprang into existence. It quickly spread, and when it was burning fully, Arutha pulled on the chain hoist that elevated the hood. With an audible whoosh, the flames sprang fully to the ceiling as the wind struck the fire.

Against one wall stood a jar of powder mixed by Kulgan against such an emergency. Arutha fought down dizziness as he bent again to pull the knife from the dead sentry's belt. He used it to pry the lid off the jar and then tossed the entire contents into the fire.

Instantly the flames turned bright crimson, a warning beacon none could confuse with a normal light. Arutha turned toward the castle, standing away from the window so as not to block the light. Brighter and brighter the flames burned as Arutha found his mind going vague again. For a long moment there was silence in the night, then suddenly an alarm sounded from the castle. Arutha felt relief. The red beacon was the signal for reavers in the harbor, and the castle garrison had been well drilled to meet such raids. Fannon might be cautious with chasing Tsurani raiders into the woods at night, but a pirate ship in his harbor was something he would not hesitate to answer.

Arutha staggered down the stairs, stopping to support himself at the door. His entire body hurt, and he was nearly overcome by dizziness. He drew a deep breath and headed for the town. When he came to where his dead horse lay, he looked about for his sword, then remembered he had carried it with him into the harbor. He stumbled to where one of his riders lay, next to a black-clad bowman. Arutha bent down to pick up the fallen soldier's sword, nearly blacking out as he stood. He held himself erect for a moment, fearing he might lose consciousness if he moved, and waited as the ringing in his head subsided. He slowly reached up and touched his head. One particularly sore spot, with an angry lump forming, told him he had struck his head hard at least once as he fell down the causeway. His fingers came away sticky with clotting blood.

Arutha began to walk to town, and as he moved, the ringing in his head resumed. For a time he staggered, then he tried to force himself to run, but after only three wobbly strides he resumed his clumsy walk. He hurried as much as he could, rounding the bend in the road to come in sight of town. He heard faint sounds of fighting. In the distance he could see the red light of fires springing heavenward as buildings were put to the torch. Screams of men and women sounded strangely remote and muted to Arutha's ears.

He forced himself into a trot, and as he closed upon the town, anticipation of fighting forced away much of the fog clouding his mind. He turned along the harborside; with the dockside buildings burning, it was bright as day, but no one was in sight. Against the quayside the raiders' ship rested, a gangway leading down to the dock. Arutha approached quietly, fearing guards had been left to protect it. When he reached the gangway, all was quiet. The sounds of fighting were distant, as if all the raiders had attacked deeply into the town.

As he began to move away, a voice cried out from the ship, "Gods of mercy! Is anyone there?" The voice was deep and powerful, but with a controlled note of terror.

Arutha hurried up the gangway, sword ready. He stopped when he reached the top. From the forward hatch cover he could see fire glowing brightly belowdecks. He looked about: everywhere his eyes traveled he saw seamen lying dead in their own blood. From the rear of the ship the voice cried out, "You, man. If you're a godsfearing man of the Kingdom, come help me."

Arutha made his way amid the carnage and found a man sitting against the starboard rail. He was large, broad-shouldered, and barrel-chested. He could have been any age between twenty and forty. He held the side of an ample stomach with his right hand, blood seeping through his fingers. Curly dark hair swept back from a receding hairline, and he wore his black beard cut short. He managed a weak smile as he pointed to a black-clothed figure lying nearby. "The bastards killed my crew and fired my ship. That one made the mistake of not killing me with the first blow." He pointed at the section of a fallen yard pinning his legs. "I can't manage to budge that damned yard and hold my guts in at the same time. If you'd lift it a bit, I think I can pull myself free."

Arutha saw the problem: the man was pinned down at the short end of the yard, tangled in a mass of ropes and blocks. He gripped the long end and heaved upward, moving it only a few inches, but enough. With a half grunt, half groan, the wounded man pulled his legs out. "I don't think my legs are broken, lad. Give me a hand up and we'll see."

Arutha gave him a hand and nearly lost his footing pulling the bulky seaman to his feet. "Here, now," said the wounded man. "You're not in much of a fighting trim yourself, are you?"

"I'll be all right," said Arutha, steadying the man while fighting off an attack of nausea.

The seaman leaned upon Arutha. "We'd better hurry, then. The fire is spreading." With Arutha's help, he negotiated the gangway. When they reached the quayside, gasping for breath, the heat was becoming intense. The wounded seaman gasped, "Keep going!"

Arutha nodded and slung the man's arm over his shoulder. They set off down the quay, staggering like a pair of drunken sailors on the town.

Suddenly there came a roar, and both men were slammed to the ground. Arutha shook his dazed head and turned over. Behind him a great tower of flames leaped skyward. The ship was a faintly seen black silhouette in the heart of the blinding yellow-and-white column of fire. Waves of heat washed over them, as if they were standing at the door of a giant oven.

Arutha managed to croak, "What was that?"

His companion gave out with an equally feeble reply: "Two hundred barrels of Quegan fire oil."

Arutha spoke in disbelief. "You didn't say anything about fire oil back aboard ship."

"I didn't want you getting excited. You looked half-gone already. I figured we'd either get clear or we wouldn't."

Arutha tried to rise, but fell back. Suddenly he felt very comfortable resting on the cool stone of the quay. He saw the fire begin to dim before his eyes, then all went dark.

ARUTHA OPENED his eyes and saw blurred shapes over him. He blinked and the images cleared. Carline hovered over his sleeping pallet, looking anxiously on as Father Tully examined him. Behind Carline, Fannon watched, and next to him stood an unfamiliar man. Then Arutha remembered him. "The man from the ship."

The man grinned. "Amos Trask, lately master of the *Sidonie* until those bast—begging the Princess's pardon—those cursed land rats put her to the torch. Standing here thanks to Your Highness."

Tully interrupted. "How do you feel?"

Arutha sat up, finding his body a mass of dull aches. Carline placed cushions behind her brother. "Battered, but I'll survive." His head swam a little. "I'm a bit dizzy."

Tully looked down his nose at Arutha's head. "Small wonder. You took a nasty crack. You may find yourself occasionally dizzy for a few days, but I don't think it is serious."

Arutha looked at the Swordmaster. "How long?"

Fannon said, "A patrol brought you in last night. It's morning."

"The raid?"

Fannon shook his head sadly. "The town's gutted. We managed to kill them all, but there's not a whole building left standing in Crydee. The fishing village at the south end of the harbor is untouched, but otherwise everything was lost."

Carline fussed around near Arutha, tucking in covers and fluffing his cushions. "You should rest."

He said, "Right now, I'm hungry."

She brought over a bowl of hot broth. He submitted to the light broth in place of solid food, but refused to let her spoon-feed him. Between mouthfuls he said, "Tell me what happened."

Fannon looked disturbed. "It was the Tsurani."

Arutha's hand stopped, his spoon poised halfway between bowl and mouth. "Tsurani? I thought they were reavers, from the Sunset Islands."

"At first so did we, but after talking to Captain Trask here, and the Tsurani slaves who are with us, we've pieced together a picture of what's happened."

Tully picked up the narrative. "From the slaves' story, these men were specially chosen. They called it a death raid. They were selected to enter the town, destroy as much as possible, then die without fleeing. They burned the ship as much as a symbol of their commitment as to deny it to us. I gather from what they say it's considered something of a great honor."

Arutha looked at Amos Trask. "How is it they managed to seize your ship, Captain?"

"Ah, that is a bitter story, Highness." He leaned to his right a little, and Arutha remembered his wound.

"How is your side?"

Trask grinned, his dark eyes merry. "A messy wound, but not a serious one. The good father put it right as new, Highness."

Tully made a derisive sound. "That man should be in bed. He is more seriously injured than you. He would not leave until he saw you were all right."

Trask ignored the comment. "I've had worse. We once had a fight with a Quegan war galley turned rogue pirate and—well, that's another story. You asked about my ship." He limped over closer to Arutha's pallet. "We were outward bound from Palanque with a load of weapons and fire oil. Considering the situation here, I thought to find a ready market. We braved the straits early in the season, stealing the march on other ships, or so we hoped.

"But while we made the passage early, we paid the price. A monstrous storm blew up from the south, and we were driven for a week. When it was over, we headed east, striking for the coast. I thought we'd have no trouble plotting our position from landmarks. When we sighted land, not one aboard recognized a single feature. As none of us had ever been north of Crydee, we judged rightly we had gone farther than we had thought.

"We coasted by day, heaving to at night, for I'd not risk unknown shoals and reefs. On the third night the Tsurani came swimming out from shore like a pod of dolphins. Dived right under the ship, and came up on both sides. By the time I was awake from the commotion on deck, there was a full half dozen of the bast—begging the Princess's pardon—them Tsurani swarming over me. It took them only minutes to take my ship." His shoulders sagged a bit. "It's a hard thing to lose one's ship, Highness."

He grimaced and Tully stood, making Trask sit on the stool next to Arutha. Trask continued his story. "We couldn't understand what they said; their tongue is more suited for monkeys than men—I myself speak five civilized languages and can do 'talk-see' in a dozen more. But as I was saying, we couldn't understand their gibberish, but they made their intentions clear enough.

"They pored over my charts." He grimaced in remembering. "I purchased them legal and aboveboard from a retired captain down in Durbin. Fifty years of experience in those charts, there were, from here in Crydee to the farthest eastern shores of the Keshian Confederacy, and they were tossing them around my cabin like so much old canvas until they found the ones they wanted. They had some sailors among them, for as soon as they recognized the charts, they made their plans known to me.

"Curse me for a freshwater fisherman, but we had heaved to only a few miles north of the headlands above your lighthouse. If we'd sailed a little longer, we would have been safely in Crydee harbor two days ago."

Arutha and the others said nothing. Trask continued, "They went through my cargo holds and started tossing things overboard, no matter what. Over five hundred fine Quegan broadswords, over the side. Pikes, lances, longbows, everything—I guess to keep any of it from reaching Crydee somehow. They didn't know what to do with the Quegan fire oil —the barrels would've needed a dock hoist to get them out of the hold —so they left it alone. But they made sure there wasn't a weapon aboard that wasn't in their hands. Then some of the little land rats got dressed up in those black rags, swam ashore, and started down the coast toward the lighthouse. While they were going, the rest were praying, on their knees rocking back and forth, except for a few with bows watching my crew. Then all of a sudden, about three hours after sundown, they're up and kicking my men around, pointing to the harbor on the map.

"We set sail and headed down the coast. The rest you know. I guess they judged you would not expect an attack from seaward."

Fannon said, "They judged correctly. Since their last raid we've patrolled the forests heavily. They couldn't get within a day's march of Crydee without our knowing. This way they caught us unawares." The old Swordmaster sounded tired and bitter. "Now the town is destroyed, and we've a courtyard filled with terrified townsmen."

Trask also sounded bitter. "They put most of their men ashore quickly, but left two dozen to slaughter my men." An expression of pain crossed his face. "They were a hard lot, my lads, but on the whole good enough men. We didn't know what was happening until the first of my boys began to fall from the spars with Tsurani arrows in them, waving like little flags as they hit the water. We thought they were going to have us take them out again. My boys put up a struggle then, you can bet. But they didn't start soon enough. Marlinspikes and belayin' pins can't stand up to men with swords and bows."

Trask sighed deeply, the pain on his face as much from his story as from his injury. "Thirty-five men. Dock rats, cutthroats, and murderers all, but they were *my* crew. I was the only one allowed to go killing them. I cracked the skull of the first Tsurani who came at me, took his sword, and killed another. But the third one knocked it from my hand and ran me through." He barked a short, harsh-sounding laugh. "I broke his neck. I passed out for a time. They must have thought me dead. The next I knew, the fires were going and I started yelling. Then I saw you come up the gangway."

Arutha said, "You're a bold man, Amos Trask."

A look of deep pain crossed the large man's face. "Not bold enough to keep my ship, Highness. Now I'm nothing more than another beached sailor."

Tully said, "Enough for now. Arutha, you need rest." He put his hand on Amos Trask's shoulder. "Captain, you'd do well to follow his example. Your wound is more serious than you admit. I'll take you to a room where you can rest."

The captain rose, and Arutha said, "Captain Trask."

"Yes, Highness?"

"We have need of good men here in Crydee."

A glimmer of humor crossed the seaman's face. "I thank you, Highness. Without a ship, though, I don't know what use I could be."

Arutha said, "Between Fannon and myself, we'll find enough to keep you busy."

The man bowed slightly, restricted by his wounded side. He left with Tully. Carline kissed Arutha on the cheek, saying, "Rest now." She took away the broth and was escorted from the room by Fannon. Arutha was asleep before the door closed.

17

▼▼

ATTACK

CARLINE LUNGED.

She thrust the point of her sword in a low line, aiming a killing blow for the stomach. Roland barely avoided the thrust by a strong beat of his blade, knocking hers out of line. He sprang back and for a moment was off balance. Carline saw the hesitation and lunged forward again.

Roland laughed as he suddenly leaped away, knocking her blade aside once more, then stepping outside her guard. Quickly tossing his sword from right hand to left, he reached out and caught her sword arm at the wrist, pulling her, in turn, off balance. He swung her about, stepping behind her. He wrapped his left arm around her waist, being careful of his sword edge, and pulled her tightly to him. She struggled against his superior strength, but while he was behind her, she could inflict no more than angry curses on him. "It was a trick! A loathsome trick," she spat.

She kicked helplessly as he laughed. "Don't overextend yourself that way, even when it looks like a clean kill. You've good speed, but you press too much. Learn patience. Wait for a clear opening, then attack. You overbalance that much and you're dead." He gave her a quick kiss on the cheek and pushed her unceremoniously away.

Carline stumbled forward, regained her balance, and turned. "Rogue! Make free with the royal person, will you?" She advanced on him, sword at the ready, slowly circling to the left. With her father away, Carline had pestered Arutha into allowing Roland to teach her swordplay. Her final argument had been, "What do I do if the Tsurani enter the castle? Attack them with embroidery needles?" Arutha had relented more from tiring of the constant nagging than from any conviction she would have to use the weapon.

Suddenly Carline launched a furious attack in high line, forcing Roland to retreat across the small court behind the keep. He found himself backed against a low wall and waited. She lunged again, and he nimbly stepped aside, the padded point of her rapier striking the wall an instant after he vacated the spot. He jumped past her, playfully swatting her across the rump with the flat of his blade as he took up position behind her. "And don't lose your temper, or you'll lose your head as well."

"Oh!" she cried, spinning to face him. Her expression was caught halfway between anger and amusement. "You monster!"

Roland stood ready, a look of mock contrition on his face. She measured the distance between them and began to advance slowly. She was wearing tight-fitting men's trousers—to the despair of Lady Marna—and a man's tunic cinched at the waist by her sword belt. In the last year her figure had filled out, and the snug costume bordered on the scandalous. Now eighteen years of age, there was nothing about Carline that was girlish. The specially crafted boots she wore, black, ankle-high, carefully beat upon the ground as she stepped the distance between them, and her long, lustrous dark hair was tied into a single braid that swung freely about her shoulders.

Roland welcomed these sessions with her. They had rediscovered much of their former playful fun in them, and Roland held the guarded hope her feelings for him might be developing into something more than friendship. In the year since Lyam's departure they had practiced together, or had gone riding when it was considered safe, near the castle. The time with her had nourished a sense of companionship between them he had previously been unable to bring about. While more serious than before, she had regained her spark and sense of humor.

Roland stood lost in reflection a moment. The little-girl Princess, spoiled and indulged, was gone. The child grown petulant and demanding from the boredom of her role was now a thing of the past. In her stead was a young woman of strong mind and will, tempered by harsh lessons.

Roland blinked and found himself with her sword's point at his throat. He playfully threw down his own weapon and said, "Lady, I yield!"

She laughed. "What were you daydreaming about, Roland?"

He gently pushed aside the tip of her sword. "I was remembering how distraught Lady Marna became when you first went riding in those clothes and came back all dirty and very unladylike."

Carline smiled at the memory. "I thought she would stay abed for a week." She put up her sword. "I wish I could find reasons to wear these clothes more often. They are so comfortable."

Roland nodded, grinning widely. "And very fetching." He made a display of leering at the way they hugged Carline's curvaceous body. "Though I expect that is due to the wearer."

She tilted her nose upward in a show of disapproval. "You are a rogue and a flatterer, sir. And a lecher."

With a chuckle, he picked up his sword. "I think that is enough for today, Carline. I could endure only one defeat this afternoon. Another, and I shall have to quit the castle in shame."

Her eyes widened as she drew her weapon, and he saw the dig had struck home. "Oh! Shamed by a mere girl, is it?" she said, advancing with her sword ready.

Laughing, he brought his own to the ready, backing away. "Now, Lady. This is most unseemly."

Leveling her sword, she fixed him with an angry gaze. "I have Lady Marna to be concerned with my manners, Roland. I don't need a buffoon like you to instruct me."

"Buffoon!" he cried, leaping forward. She caught his blade and riposted, nearly striking. He took the thrust on his blade, sliding his own along hers until they stood *corps a corps*. He seized her sword wrist with his free hand and smiled. "You never want to find yourself in this position." She struggled to free herself, but he held her fast. "Unless the Tsurani start sending their women after us, most anyone you fight will prove stronger than yourself, and from here have his way with you." So saying, he jerked her closer and kissed her.

She pulled back, an expression of surprise on her face. Suddenly the sword fell from her fingers and she grabbed him. Pulling him with surprising force, she kissed him with a passion that answered his.

When he pulled back, she regarded him with a look of surprise mixed with longing. A smile spread on her face, as her eyes sparkled. Quietly she said, "Roland, I—"

Alarm sounded throughout the castle, and the shout of "Attack!" could be heard from the walls on the other side of the keep.

Roland swore softly and stepped back. "Of all the gods-cursed, ill-timed luck." He headed into the hall that led to the main courtyard. With a grin he turned and said, "Remember what you were going to say, Lady." His humor vanished when he saw her following after, sword in hand. "Where are you going?" he asked, all lightness absent from his voice.

Defiantly she said, "To the walls. I'm not going to sit in the cellars any longer."

Firmly he said, "No. You've never experienced true fighting. As a sport, you do well enough with a sword, but I'll not risk your freezing the first time you smell blood. You'll go to the cellars with the other ladies and lock yourself safely in."

Roland had never spoken to her in this manner before, and she was amazed. Always before he had been the teasing rogue, or the gentle friend. Now he was suddenly a different man. She began to protest, but he cut her off. Taking her by the arm, half leading, half dragging her, he walked in the direction of the cellar doors. "Roland!" she cried. "Let me go!"

Quietly he said, "You'll go where you were ordered. And I'll go where I'm ordered. There will be no argument."

She pulled against his hold, but the grip was unyielding. "Roland! Take your hand from me this instant!" she commanded.

He continued to ignore her protests and dragged her along the hall. At the cellar door a startled guard watched the approaching pair. Roland came to a stop and propelled Carline toward the door with a less than gentle shove. Her eyes wide in outrage, Carline turned to the guard. "Arrest him! At once! He"—anger elevated her voice to a most unladylike volume—"laid *hands* on me!"

The guard hesitated, looking from one to another, then tentatively began to step toward the Squire. Roland raised a warning finger and pointed it at the guard, less than an inch from his nose. "You will see Her Highness to her appointed place of safety. You will ignore her objections, and should she try to leave, you will restrain her. Do you understand?" His voice left no doubt he was deadly serious.

The guard nodded, but still was reluctant to place hands upon the Princess. Without taking his eyes from the soldier's face, Roland pushed Carline gently toward the door and said, "If I find she has left the cellar before the signal that all is safe has sounded, I will ensure that the Prince and the Swordmaster are informed you allowed the Princess to step in harm's way."

That was enough for the guard. He might not understand who had right of rank between Princess and Squire during attacks, but there was no doubt at all in his mind of what the Swordmaster would do to him under such circumstances. He turned to the cellar door before Carline could return and said, "Highness, this way," forcing her down the steps.

Carline backed down the stairs, fuming. Roland closed the door behind them. She turned after another backward step, then haughtily walked down. When they reached the room set aside for the women of the castle and town in time of attack, Carline found the other women waiting, huddled together, terrified.

The guard hazarded an apologetic salute and said, "Begging the Princess's pardon, but the Squire seemed most determined."

Suddenly Carline's scowl vanished, and in its place a small smile appeared. She said, "Yes, he did, didn't he?"

RIDERS SPED INTO the courtyard, the massive gates swinging shut behind. Arutha watched from the walls and turned to Fannon.

Fannon said, "Of all the worst possible luck."

Arutha said, "Luck has nothing to do with it. The Tsurani would certainly not be attacking when the advantage is ours." Everything looked peaceful, except the burned town standing as a constant reminder of the war. But he also knew that beyond the town, in the forests to the north and northeast, an army was gathering. And by all reports as many as two thousand more Tsurani were on the march toward Crydee.

"Get back inside, you rat-bitten, motherless dog."

Arutha looked downward into the courtyard and saw Amos Trask kicking at the panic-stricken figure of a fisherman, who dashed back into one of the many rude huts erected inside the wall of the castle to house the last of the displaced townsfolk who had not gone south. Most of the townspeople had shipped for Carse after the death raid, but a few had stayed the winter. Except for some fishermen who were to stay to help feed the garrison, the rest were due to be shipped south to Carse and Tulan this spring. But the first ships of the coming season were not due in for weeks. Amos had been put in charge of these folk since his ship had been burned the year before, keeping them from getting underfoot and from causing too much disruption in the castle. The former sea captain had proved a gift during the first weeks after the burning of the town. Amos had the necessary talent for command and kept the tough, ill-mannered, and individualistic fisherfolk in line. Arutha judged him a braggart, a liar, and most probably, a pirate, but generally likable.

Gardan came up the stairs from the court, Roland following. Gardan saluted the Prince and Swordmaster, and said, "That's the last patrol, sir."

"Then we must only wait for Longbow," said Fannon.

Gardan shook his head. "Not one patrol caught sight of him, sir."

"That's because Longbow is undoubtedly closer to the Tsurani than any soldier of sound judgment is likely to get," ventured Arutha. "How soon, do you think, before the rest of the Tsurani arrive?"

Pointing to the northeast, Gardan said, "Less than an hour, if they push straight through." He looked skyward. "They have less than four hours of light. We might expect one attack before nightfall. Most likely they'll take position, rest their men, and attack at first light."

Arutha glanced at Roland. "Are the women safe?"

Roland grinned. "All, though your sister might have a few harsh words about me when this is over."

Arutha returned the grin. "When this is over, I'll deal with it." He looked around. "Now we wait."

Swordmaster Fannon's eyes swept the deceptively peaceful scene before them. There was a note of worry mixed with determination in his voice as he said, "Yes, now we wait."

MARTIN RAISED HIS hand. His three trackers stopped moving. The woods were quiet as far as they could tell, but the three knew Martin possessed more acute senses than they. After a moment he moved along, scouting ahead.

For ten hours, since before dawn, they had been marking the Tsurani line of march. As well as he could judge, the Tsurani had been repulsed once more from Elvandar at the fords along the river Crydee and were now turning their attention to the castle at Crydee. For three years the Tsurani had been occupied along four fronts: against the Duke's armies in the east, the elves and dwarves along the north, the hold at Crydee in the west, and the Brotherhood of the Dark Path and the goblins in the south.

The trackers had stayed close to the Tsurani trailbreakers, occasionally too close. Twice they had been forced to run from attackers, Tsurani warriors tenaciously willing to follow the Huntmaster of Crydee and his men. Once they had been overtaken, and Martin had lost one of his men in the fighting.

Martin gave the raucous caw of a crow, and in a few minutes his three remaining trackers joined him. One, a long-faced young man named Garret, said, "They move far west of where I thought they would turn."

Longbow considered. "Aye, it seems they may be planning to encircle all of the lands around the castle. Or they may simply wish to strike from an unexpected quarter." Then with a wry grin he said, "But most likely, they simply sweep the area before the attack begins, ensuring they have no harrying forces at their backs."

Another tracker said, "Surely they know we mark their passing."

Longbow's crooked grin widened. "No doubt. I judge them unconcerned with our comings and goings." He shook his head. "These Tsurani are an arrogant crew." Pointing, he said, "Garret will come with me. You two will make straight for the castle. Inform the Swordmaster some two thousand more Tsurani march on Crydee." Without a word the two men set off at a brisk pace toward the castle.

To his remaining companion he spoke lightly. "Come, let us return to the advancing enemy and see what he is about now."

Garret shook his head. "Your cheerful manner does little to ease my worrisome mind, Huntmaster."

Turning back the way they had come, Longbow said, "One time is much like another to death. She comes when she will. So why give over your mind to worry?"

"Aye," said Garret, his long face showing he was unconvinced. "Why, indeed? It's not death arriving when she will that worries me; it's your inviting her to visit that gets me shivering."

Martin laughed softly. He motioned for Garret to follow. They set off at a trot, covering ground with long, loose strides. The forest was bright with sunlight, but between the thick boles were many dark places wherein a watchful enemy could lurk. Garret left it to Longbow's able judgment whether these hiding places were safe to pass. Then, as one, both men stopped in their tracks at the sound of movement ahead. Noiselessly they melted into a shadowy thicket. A minute passed slowly with neither man speaking. Then a faint whispering came to them, the words unclear.

Into their field of vision came two figures, moving cautiously along a north-south path that intersected the one Martin followed. Both were dressed in dark grey cloaks, with bows held ready. They stopped, and one kneeled down to study the signs left by Longbow and his trackers. He pointed down the trail and spoke to his companion, who nodded and returned the way they had come.

Longbow heard Garret hiss as he drew in his breath. Peering around the area was a tracker of the Brotherhood of the Dark Path. After a moment of searching he followed his companion.

Garret began to stir and Martin gripped his arm. "Not yet," Longbow whispered.

Garret whispered back, "What are they doing this far north?"

Martin shook his head. "They've slipped in behind our patrols along the foothills. We've grown lax in the south, Garret. We never thought they'd move north this far west of the mountains." He waited silently for a moment, then whispered, "Perhaps they tire of the Green Heart and are trying for the Northlands to join their brothers."

Garret started to speak, but stopped when another Dark Brother entered the spot vacated by the others a moment before. He looked around, then raised his hand in signal. Other figures appeared along the trail intersecting the one Martin's men had traveled. In ones, twos, and threes, Dark Brothers crossed the path, disappearing into the trees.

Garret sat holding his breath. He could hear Martin counting faintly as the figures crossed their field of vision: ". . . ten, twelve, fifteen, sixteen, eighteen . . ."

The stream of dark-cloaked figures continued, seemingly unending to Garret. ". . . thirty-one, thirty-two, thirty-four . . ."

As the crossing continued, larger numbers of Brothers appeared, and after a time Martin whispered, "There are more than a hundred."

Still they came, some now carrying bundles on their backs and shoulders. Many wore the dark grey mountain cloaks, but others were dressed in green, brown, or black clothing. Garret leaned close to Martin and whispered, "You are right. It is a migration north. I mark over two hundred."

Martin nodded. "And still they come."

For many more minutes the Dark Brothers crossed the trail, until the flood of warriors was replaced by ragged-looking females and young. When they had passed, a company of twenty fighters crossed the trail, and then the area was quiet.

They waited a moment in silence. Garret said, "They are elven-kin to move so large a number through the forest undetected so long."

Martin smiled. "I'd advise you not mention that fact to the next elf you encounter." He stood slowly, unbending cramped muscles from the long sitting in the brush. A faint sound echoed from the east, and Martin got a thoughtful look on his face. "How far along the trail do you judge the Dark Brothers' march?"

Garret said, "At their rear, a hundred yards; at the van, perhaps a quarter mile or less. Why?"

Martin grinned, and Garret became discomforted by the mocking humor in his eyes. "Come, I think I know where we can have some fun."

Garret groaned softly, "Ah, Huntmaster, my skin gets a poxy feeling when you mention fun."

Martin struck the man a friendly blow to the chest with the back of his hand. "Come, stout fellow." The Huntmaster broke trail, with Garret behind. They loped along through the woods, easily avoiding obstacles that would have hindered less experienced woodsmen.

They came to a break in the trail, and both men halted. Just down the trail, at the edge of their vision in the gloom of the forest, came a company of Tsurani trailbreakers. Martin and Garret faded into the trees, and the Huntmaster said, "The main column is close behind. When they reach the crossing where the Dark Brothers passed, they might chance to follow."

Garret shook his head. "Or they might not, so we will make certain they do." Taking a deep breath, he added, "Oh well," then made a short silent prayer to Kilian, the Singer of Green Silences, Goddess of Foresters, as they unshouldered their bows.

Martin stepped out onto the trail and took aim, and Garret followed his example. The Tsurani trailbreakers came into view, cutting away the thick underbrush along the trail so the main body could more easily follow. Martin waited until the Tsurani were uncomfortably close, then he let fly, just as the first trailbreaker took notice of them. The first two men fell, and before they hit the ground, two more arrows were loosed. Martin and Garret pulled arrows from back quivers in fluid motions, set arrow to bowstring, and let fly with uncommon quickness and accuracy. It was not from any act of kindness Martin had selected Garret five years before. In the eye of the storm, he would stand calmly, do as ordered, and do it with skill.

Ten stunned Tsurani fell before they could raise an alarm. Calmly Martin and Garret shouldered their bows and waited. Then along the trail appeared a veritable wall of colored armor. The Tsurani officers in the van stopped in shocked silence as they regarded the dead trailbreakers. Then they saw the two foresters standing quietly down the trail and shouted something. The entire front of the column sprang forward, weapons drawn.

Martin leaped into the thicket on the north side of the trail, Garret a step behind. They dashed through the trees, the Tsurani in close pursuit.

Martin's voice filled the forest with a wild hunter's call. Garret shouted as much from some nameless, crazy exhilaration as from fear. The noise behind was tremendous as a horde of Tsurani pursued them through the trees.

Martin led them northward, paralleling the course taken by the Dark Brotherhood. After a time he stopped and between gasping breaths said, "Slowly, we don't want to lose them."

Garret looked back and saw the Tsurani were out of sight. They leaned against a tree and waited. A moment later the first Tsurani came into view, hurrying along on a course that angled off to the northwest.

With a disgusted look, Martin said, "We must have killed the only skilled trackers on their whole bloody world." He took his hunter's horn from his belt and let forth with such a loud blast the Tsurani soldier froze, an expression of shock clearly evident on his face even from where Martin and Garret stood.

The Tsurani looked around and caught sight of the two huntsmen. Martin waved for the man to follow, and he and Garret were off again. The Tsurani shouted for those behind and gave chase. For a quarter mile they led the Tsurani through the woods, then they angled westward. Garret shouted, between heaving breaths, "The Dark Brothers . . . they'll know . . . we come."

Martin shouted back, "Unless they've . . . suddenly all . . . gone deaf." He managed a smile. "The Tsurani . . . hold a six-to-one . . . advantage. I . . . think it . . . only fair to let . . . the Brotherhood . . . have the . . . ambush."

Garret spared enough breath for a low groan and continued to follow his master's lead. They crashed out of a thicket and Martin stopped, grabbing Garret by the tunic. He cocked his head and said, "They're up ahead."

Garret said, "I don't know . . . how you can hear a thing with . . . all that cursed racket behind." It sounded as if most of the Tsurani column had followed, though the forest amplified the noise and confused its source.

Martin said, "Do you still wear that . . . ridiculous red undertunic?"

"Yes, why?"

"Tear off a strip." Garret pulled his knife without question and lifted up his green forester's tunic. Underneath was a garish red cotton undertunic. He cut a long strip off the bottom, then hastily tucked the undertunic in. While Garret ordered himself, Martin tied the strip to an arrow. He looked back to where the Tsurani thrashed in the brush. "It must be those stubby legs. They may be able to run all day, but they can't keep up in the woods." He handed the arrow to Garret. "See that large elm across that small clearing?"

Garret nodded. "See the small birch behind, off to the left?" Again Garret nodded. "Think you can hit it with that rag dragging at your arrow?"

Garret grinned as he unslung his bow, notched the arrow, and let fly. The arrow sped true, striking the tree. Martin said, "When our bandy-legged friends get here, they'll see that flicker of color over there and go charging across. Unless I'm sadly mistaken, the Brothers are about fifty feet the other side of your arrow." He pulled his horn as Garret shouldered his bow again. "Once more we're off," he said, blowing a long, loud call.

Like hornets the Tsurani descended, but Longbow and Garret were off to the southwest before the note from the hunter's horn had died in the air. They dashed to be gone before the Tsurani caught sight of them, aborting the hoax. Suddenly they broke through a thicket and ran into a group of women and children milling about. One young woman of the Brotherhood was placing a bundle upon the ground. She stopped at the sight of the two men. Garret had to slide to a halt to keep from bowling her over.

Her large brown eyes studied him for an instant as he stepped sideways to get around her. Without thinking, Garret said, "Excuse me, ma'am," and raised his hand to his forelock. Then he was off after the Huntmaster as shouts of surprise and anger erupted behind them.

Martin called a halt after they had covered another quarter mile and listened. To the northeast came the sounds of battle, shouts and screams, and the ring of weapons. Martin grinned. "They'll both be busy for a while."

Garret sank wearily to the ground and said, "Next time send me to the castle, will you, Huntmaster?"

Martin kneeled beside the tracker. "That should prevent the Tsurani from reaching Crydee until sundown or after. They won't be able to mount an attack until tomorrow. Four hundred Dark Brothers are not something they can safely leave at their rear. We'll rest a bit, then make for Crydee."

Garret leaned back against a tree. "Welcome news." He let out a long sigh of relief. "That was a close thing, Huntmaster."

Martin smiled enigmatically. "All life is a close thing, Garret."

Garret shook his head slowly. "Did you see that girl?"

Martin nodded. "What of her?"

Garret looked perplexed. "She was pretty . . . no, closer to being beautiful, in a strange sort of way, I mean. But she had long black hair, and her eyes were the color of otter's fur. And she had a pouty mouth and pert look. Enough to warrant a second glance from most men. It's not what I would have expected from the Brotherhood."

Martin nodded. "The moredhel are a pretty people, in truth, as are the elves. But remember, Garret," he said with a smile, "should you chance to find yourself exchanging pleasantries with a moredhel woman again, she'd as soon cut your heart out as kiss you."

They rested for a while as cries and shouts echoed from the northeast. Then slowly they stood and began the return to Crydee.

▼▼

SINCE THE START of the war, the Tsurani had confined their activities to those areas immediately adjacent the valley in the Grey Towers. Reports from the dwarves and the elves revealed mining activities were taking place in the Grey Towers. Enclaves had been thrown up outside the valley, from which they raided Kingdom positions. Once or twice during the year they would mount an offensive against the Dukes' Armies of the West, the elves in Elvandar, or Crydee, but for the most part they were content to hold what they had already taken.

And each year they would expand their holdings, building more enclaves, expanding the area under their control, and gaining themselves a stronger position from which to conduct the next year's campaign. Since the fall of Walinor, the expected thrust toward the coast of the Bitter Sea had not materialized, nor had the Tsurani again tried for the LaMutian fortresses near Stone Mountain. Walinor and Crydee town were sacked and abandoned, more to deny them to the Kingdom and Free Cities than for any Tsurani gain. By the spring of the third year of the war, the leaders of the Kingdom forces despaired of a major attack, one that might break the stalemate. Now it came. And it came at the logical place, the allies' weakest front, the garrison at Crydee.

Arutha looked out over the walls at the Tsurani army. He stood next to Gardan and Fannon, with Martin Longbow behind. "How many?" he asked, not taking his eyes from the gathering host.

Martin spoke. "Fifteen hundred, two thousand, it is hard to judge. There were two thousand more coming yesterday, less whatever the Dark Brotherhood took with them."

From the distant woods the sounds of workmen felling trees rang out. The Swordmaster and Huntmaster judged the Tsurani were cutting trees to build scaling ladders.

Martin said, "I'd never thought to hear myself say such, but I wish there'd been four thousand Dark Brothers in the forest yesterday."

Gardan spat over the wall. "Still, you did well, Huntmaster. It is only fitting they should run afoul of each other."

Martin chuckled humorlessly. "It is also a good thing the Dark Brothers kill on sight. Though I am sure they do it out of no love for us, they do guard our southern flank."

Arutha said, "Unless yesterday's band was not an isolated case. If the Brotherhood is abandoning the Green Heart, we may soon have to fear for Tulan, Jonril, and Carse."

"I'm glad they've not parleyed," said Fannon. "If they should truce . . ."

Martin shook his head. "The moredhel will traffic only with weapons runners and renegades who will serve them for gold. Otherwise they have no use for us. And by all evidence, the Tsurani are bent on conquest. The moredhel are no more spared their ambition than we are."

Fannon looked back at the mounting Tsurani force. Brightly colored standards with symbols and designs strange to behold were placed at various positions along the leading edge of the army. Hundreds of warriors in different-colored armor stood in groups under each banner.

A horn sounded, and the Tsurani soldiers faced the walls. Each standard was brought forward a dozen paces and planted in the ground. A handful of soldiers wearing the high-crested helmets that the Kingdom forces took to denote officers walked forward and stood halfway between the army and the standard-bearers. One, wearing bright blue armor, called something and pointed at the castle. A shout went up from the assembled Tsurani host, and then another officer, this one in bright red armor, began to walk slowly up to the castle.

Arutha and the others watched in silence while the man crossed the distance to the gate. He looked neither right nor left, nor up at the people on the walls, but marched with eyes straight ahead until he reached the gate. There he took out a large hand ax and banged three times upon it with the haft.

"What is he doing?" asked Roland, just come up the stairs.

Again the Tsurani pounded on the gates of the castle. "I think," said Longbow, "he's ordering us to open up and quit the castle."

Then the Tsurani reached back and slammed his ax into the gate, leaving it quivering in the wood. Without hurrying, he turned and began walking away to cheers from the watching Tsurani.

"What now?" asked Fannon.

"I think I know," said Martin, unshouldering his bow. He drew out an arrow and fitted it to the bowstring. With a sudden pull, he let fly. The shaft struck the ground between the Tsurani officer's legs and the man halted.

"The Hadati hillmen of Yabon have rituals like this," said Martin. "They put great store by showing bravery in the face of an enemy. To touch one and live is more honorable than killing him." He pointed toward the officer, who stood motionless. "If I kill him, I have no honor, because he's showing us all how brave he is. But we can show we know how to play this game."

The Tsurani officer turned and picked up the arrow and snapped it in two. He faced the castle, holding the broken arrow high as he shouted defiance at those on the walls. Longbow sighted another arrow and let fly. The second arrow sped down and sliced the plume from the officer's helmet. The Tsurani fell silent as feathers began drifting down around his face.

Roland whooped at the shot, and then the walls of the castle erupted with cheers. The Tsurani slowly removed his helm.

Martin said, "Now he's inviting one of us either to kill him, showing we are without honor, or to come out of the castle and dare to face him."

Fannon said, "I will not allow the gates open over some childish contest!"

Longbow grinned as he said, "Then we'll change the rules." He leaned over the edge of the walkway and shouted down to the courtyard below. "Garret; fowling blunt!"

Garret, in the court below, drew a fowling arrow from his quiver and tossed it up to Longbow. Martin showed the others the heavy iron ball that served as the tip, used to stun game birds where a sharp arrow would destroy them, and then fitted it to his bow. Sighting the officer, he let fly.

The arrow took the Tsurani officer in the stomach, knocking him backward. All on the wall could imagine the sound made as the man had his breath knocked from him. The Tsurani soldiers shouted in outrage, then quieted as the man stood up, obviously stunned but otherwise showing no injury. Then he doubled over, his hands on his knees, and vomited.

Arutha said dryly, "So much for an officer's dignity."

"Well," said Fannon, "I think it is time to give them another lesson in Kingdom warfare." He raised his arm high above his head. "Catapults!" he cried.

Answering flags waved from the tops of the towers along the walls and atop the keep. He dropped his arm, and the mighty engines were fired. On the smaller towers, ballistae, looking like giant crossbows, shot spearlike missiles, while atop the keep, huge mangonels flung buckets of heavy stones. The rain of stones and missiles landed amid the Tsurani, crushing heads and limbs, tearing ragged holes in their lines. The screams of wounded men could be heard by the defenders, while the catapult crew quickly rewound and loaded their deadly engines.

The Tsurani milled about in confusion and, when the second flight of stones and missiles struck, broke and ran. A cheer went up from the defenders on the wall, then died when the Tsurani regrouped beyond the range of the engines.

Gardan said, "Swordmaster, I think they mean to wait us out."

"I think you're wrong," said Arutha, pointing. The other looked: a large number of Tsurani detached themselves from the main body, moving forward to stop just outside missile range.

"They look to be readying an attack," said Fannon, "but why with only a part of their force?"

A soldier appeared and said, "Highness, there are no signs of Tsurani along any of the other positions."

Arutha looked to Fannon. "And why attack only one wall?" After a few minutes, Arutha said, "I'd judge a thousand."

"More likely twelve hundred," said Fannon. He saw scaling ladders appearing at the rear of the attackers, moving forward. "Anytime now."

A thousand defenders waited inside the walls. Other men of Crydee still manned outlying garrisons and lookout positions, but the bulk of the Duchy's strength was here. Fannon said, "We can withstand this force as long as the walls remain unbreached. Less than a ten-to-one advantage we can deal with."

More messengers came from the other walls. "They still mount nothing along the east, north, and south, Swordmaster," one reported.

"They seem determined to do this the hard way." Fannon looked thoughtful for a moment. "Little of what we've seen is understandable. Death raids, marshaling within catapult range, wasting time with games of honor. Still, they are not without skill, and we can take nothing for granted." To the guard he said, "Pass the word to keep alert on the other walls, and be ready to move to defend should this prove a feint."

The messengers left, and the waiting continued. The sun moved across the sky, until an hour before sunset, when it sat at the backs of the attackers. Suddenly horns blew and drums beat, and in a rush the Tsurani broke toward the walls. The catapults sang, and great holes appeared in the lines of attackers. Still they came, until they moved within bow range of the patiently waiting defenders. A storm of arrows fell upon the attackers, and to a man the front rank collapsed, but those behind came on, large brightly colored shields held overhead as they rushed the walls. A half-dozen times men fell, dropping scaling ladders, only to have others grab them up and continue.

Tsurani bowmen answered the bowmen from the walls with their own shower of arrows, and men of Crydee fell from the battlements. Arutha ducked behind the walls of the castle as the arrows sped overhead, then he risked a glance between the merlons of the wall. A horde of attackers filled his field of vision, and a ladder top suddenly appeared before him. A soldier near the Prince grabbed the ladder top and pushed it away, aided by a second using a pole arm. Arutha could hear the screams of the Tsurani as they fell from the ladder. The first soldier to the ladder then fell backward, a Tsurani arrow protruding from his eye, and disappeared into the courtyard.

A sudden shout went up from below, and Arutha sprang to his feet, risking a bowshaft by looking down. All along the base of the wall, Tsurani warriors were withdrawing, running back to the safety of their own lines.

"What are they doing?" wondered Fannon.

The Tsurani ran until they were safe from the catapults, then stopped, turned, and formed up ranks. Officers were walking up and down before the men, exhorting them. After a moment the assembled Tsurani cheered.

"Damn me!" came from Arutha's left, and he glimpsed Amos Trask at his shoulder, a seaman's cutlass in his hand. "The maniacs are congratulating themselves on getting slaughtered."

The scene below was grisly. Tsurani soldiers lay scattered around like toys thrown by a careless giant child. A few moved feebly and moaned, but most were dead.

Fannon said, "I'd wager they lost a hundred or more. This makes no sense." He said to Roland and Martin, "Check the other walls." They both hurried off. "What are they doing now?" he said as he watched the Tsurani. In the red glow of sunset, he could see them still in lines, while men lit torches and passed them around. "Surely they don't intend to attack after sunset? They'll fall over themselves in the dark."

"Who knows what they plan?" said Arutha. "I've never heard of an attack being staged this badly."

Amos said, "Beggin' the Prince's pardon, but I know a thing or two about warcraft—from my younger days—and I've also never heard of this like before. Even the Keshians, who'll throw away dog soldiers like a drunken seaman throws away his money, even they wouldn't try a frontal assault like this. I'd keep a weather eye out for trickery."

"Yes," answered Arutha. "But of what sort?"

THROUGHOUT THE NIGHT the Tsurani attacked, rushing headlong against the walls, to die at the base. Once a few made the top of the walls, but they were quickly killed and the ladders thrown back. With dawn the Tsurani withdrew.

Arutha, Fannon, and Gardan watched as the Tsurani reached the safety of their own lines, beyond catapult and bow range. With the sunrise a sea of colorful tents appeared, and the Tsurani retired to their campsites. The defenders were astonished at the number of Tsurani dead along the base of the castle walls.

After a few hours the stink of the dead became overpowering. Fannon consulted with an exhausted Arutha as the Prince was readying for an overdue sleep. "The Tsurani have made no attempt to reclaim their fallen."

Arutha said, "We have no common language in which to parley, unless you mean to send Tully out under a flag of truce."

Fannon said, "He'd go, of course, but I'd not risk him. Still, the bodies could be trouble in a day or two. Besides the stink and flies, with unburied dead comes disease. It's the gods' way of showing their displeasure over not honoring the dead."

"Then," said Arutha, pulling on the boot he had just taken off, "we had best see what can be done."

He returned to the gate and found Gardan already making plans to remove the bodies. A dozen volunteers were waiting by the gate to go and gather the dead for a funeral pyre.

Arutha and Fannon reached the walls as Gardan led the men through the gate. Archers lined the walls to cover the retreat of the men outside the walls if necessary, but it soon became evident the Tsurani were not going to trouble the party. Several came to the edge of their lines, to sit and watch the Kingdom soldiers working.

After a half hour it was clear the men of Crydee would not be able to complete the work before they were exhausted. Arutha considered sending more men outside, but Fannon refused, thinking it what the Tsurani were waiting for. "If we have to move a large party back through the gate, it might prove disastrous. If we close the gate, we lose men outside, and if we leave it open too long, the Tsurani breach the castle." Arutha was forced to agree, and they settled down to watch Gardan's men working in the hot morning.

Then, near midday, a dozen Tsurani warriors, unarmed, walked casually across their lines and approached the work party. Those on the wall watched tensely, but when the Tsurani reached the spot where Crydee men worked, they silently began picking up bodies and carrying them to where the pyre was being erected.

With the help of the Tsurani, the bodies were stacked upon the huge pyre. Torches were set, and soon the bodies of the slain were consumed in fire. The Tsurani who had helped place the bodies upon the pyre watched as the soldier who led the volunteers stood away from the mounting flames. Then one Tsurani soldier spoke a word, and he and his companions bowed in respect to those upon the fire. The soldier who led the Crydee soldiers said, "Honors to the dead!" The twelve men of Crydee assumed a posture of attention and saluted. Then the Tsurani turned to face the Kingdom soldiers and again they bowed. The commanding soldier called out, "Return salute!" and the twelve men of Crydee saluted the Tsurani.

Arutha shook his head, watching men who had tried to kill one another working side by side as if it were the most natural thing in the world, then saluting one another. "Father used to say that, among man's strange undertakings, war stood clearly forth as the strangest."

AT SUNDOWN they came again, wave after wave of attackers, rushing the west wall, to die at the base. Four times during the night they struck, and four times they were repulsed.

Now they came again, and Arutha shrugged off his fatigue to fight once more. They could see more Tsurani joining those before the castle, long snakes of torchlight coming from the forest to the north. After the last assault, it was clear the situation was shifting to the Tsurani's favor. The defenders were exhausted from two nights of fighting, and the Tsurani were still throwing fresh troops into the fray.

"They mean to grind us down, no matter what the cost," said a fatigued Fannon. He began to say something to a guard when a strange expression crossed his face. He closed his eyes and collapsed. Arutha caught him. An arrow protruded from his back. A panicky-looking soldier kneeling on the other side looked at Arutha, clearly asking: What do we do?

Arutha shouted, "Get him into the keep, to Father Tully," and the man and another soldier picked up the unconscious Swordmaster and carried him down. A third soldier asked, "What orders, Highness?"

Arutha spun around, seeing the worried faces of Crydee's soldiers nearby, and said, "As before. Defend the wall."

The fighting went hard. A half-dozen times Arutha found himself dueling with Tsurani warriors who topped the wall. Then, after a timeless battling, the Tsurani withdrew.

Arutha stood panting, his clothing drenched with perspiration beneath his chest armor. He shouted for water, and a castle porter arrived with a bucket. He drank, as did the others around, and turned to watch the Tsurani host.

Again they stood just beyond catapult range, and their torchlights seemed undiminished. "Prince Arutha," came a voice behind. He spun around. Horsemaster Algon was standing before him. "I just heard of Fannon's wound."

Arutha said, "How is he?"

"A close thing. The wound is serious, but not yet fatal. Tully thinks should he live another day, he will recover. But he will not be able to command for weeks, perhaps longer."

Arutha knew Algon was waiting for a decision from him. The Prince was Knight-Captain of the King's army and, without Fannon, the commander of the garrison. He was also untried and could turn over command to the Horsemaster. Arutha looked around. "Where is Gardan?"

"Here, Highness," came a shout from a short way down the wall. Arutha was surprised at the sergeant's appearance. His dark skin was nearly grey from the dust that stuck to it, held fast by the sheen of perspiration. His tunic and tabard were soaked with blood, which also covered his arms to the elbows.

Arutha looked down at his own hands and arms and found them likewise covered. He shouted, "More water!" and said to Algon, "Gardan will act as my second commander. Should anything happen to me, he will take command of the garrison. Gardan is acting Swordmaster."

Algon hesitated as if about to say something, then a look of relief crossed his face. "Yes, Highness. Orders?"

Arutha looked back toward the Tsurani lines, then to the east. The first light of the false dawn was coming, and the sun would rise over the mountains in less than two hours. He seemed to weigh facts for a time, as he washed away the blood on his arms and face. Finally he said, "Get Longbow."

The Huntmaster was called for and arrived a few minutes later, followed by Amos Trask, who wore a wide grin. "Damn me, but they can fight," said the seaman.

Arutha ignored the comment. "It is clear to me they plan to keep constant pressure upon us. With as little regard as they show for their own lives, they can wear us down in a few weeks. This is one thing we didn't count upon, this willingness of their men to go to certain death. I want the north, south, and east walls stripped. Leave enough men to keep watch, and hold any attackers until reinforcements can arrive. Bring the men from the other walls here, and order those here to stand down. I want six-hour watches rotated throughout the rest of the day. Martin, has there been any more word of Dark Brother migration?"

Longbow shrugged. "We've been a little busy, Highness. My men have all been in the north woods the last few weeks."

Arutha said, "Could you slip a few trackers over the walls before first light?"

Longbow considered. "If they leave at once, and if the Tsurani aren't watching the east wall too closely, yes."

"Do so. The Dark Brothers aren't foolish enough to attack this force, but if you could find a few bands the size of the one you spotted three days ago and repeat your trap . . ."

Martin grinned. "I'll lead them out myself. We'd best leave now, before it gets much lighter." Arutha dismissed him, and Martin ran down the stairs. "Garret!" he shouted. "Come on, lad. We're off for some fun." A groan could be heard by those on the wall as Martin gathered his trackers around him.

Arutha said to Gardan, "I want messages sent to Carse and Tulan. Use five pigeons for each. Order Barons Bellamy and Tolburt to strip their garrisons and take ship for Crydee at once."

Gardan said, "Highness, that will leave those garrisons nearly undefended."

Algon joined in the objection. "If the Dark Brotherhood moves toward the Northlands, the Tsurani will have an open path to the southern keeps next year."

Arutha said, "If the Dark Brothers are moving en masse, which they may not be, and if the Tsurani learn they have abandoned the Green Heart, which they may not. I am concerned by this known threat, not a possible one next year. If they keep this constant pressure upon us, how long can we withstand?"

Gardan said, "A few weeks, perhaps a month. No longer."

Arutha once more studied the Tsurani camp. "They boldly pitch their tents near the edge of town. They range through our forests, building ladders and siege engines no doubt. They know we cannot sally forth in strength. But with eighteen hundred fresh soldiers from the southern keeps attacking up the coast road from the beaches and the garrison sallying forth, we can rout them from Crydee. Once the siege is broken, they will have to withdraw to their eastern enclaves. We can harry them continuously with horsemen, keep them from regrouping. Then we can return those forces to the southern keeps, and they'll be ready for any Tsurani attacks against Carse or Tulan next spring."

Gardan said, "A bold enough plan, Highness." He saluted and left the wall, followed by Algon.

Amos Trask said, "Your commanders are cautious men, Highness."

Arutha said, "You agree with my plan?"

"Should Crydee fall, what matters when Carse or Tulan falls? If not this year, then next for certain. It might as well be in one fight as two or three. As the sergeant said, it is a bold plan. Still, a ship was never taken without getting close enough to board. You have the makings of a fine corsair should you ever grow tired of being a Prince, Highness."

Arutha regarded Amos Trask with a skeptical smile. "Corsair, is it? I thought you claimed to be an honest trader."

Amos looked slightly discomposed. Then he broke out in a hearty laugh. "I only said I had a cargo for Crydee, Highness. I never said how I came by it."

"Well, we have no time for your piratical past now."

Amos looked stung. "No pirate, Sire. The *Sidonie* was carrying letters of marque from Great Kesh, given by the governor of Durbin."

Arutha laughed. "Of course! And everyone knows there is no finer, more law-abiding group upon the high seas than the captains of the Durbin coast."

Amos shrugged. "They tend to be a crusty lot, it's true. And they sometimes make free with the concept of free passage on the high seas, but we prefer the term *privateer.*"

Horns blew and drums beat, and with shrieking war cries the Tsurani came. The defenders waited, then as the attacking host crossed the invisible line marking the outer range of the castle's war engines, death rained down upon the Tsurani. Still they came.

The Tsurani crossed the second invisible line marking the outer range of the castle's bowmen, and scores more died. Still they came.

The attackers reached the walls, and defenders dropped stones and pushed over scaling ladders, dealing out death to those below. Still they came.

Arutha quickly ordered a redeployment of his reserves, directing them to be ready near the points of heaviest attack. Men hurried to carry out his orders.

Standing atop the west wall, in the thick of the fight, Arutha answered attack with attack, repulsing warrior after warrior as they reached the top of the wall. Even in the midst of battle, Arutha was aware of the scene around him, shouting orders, hearing replies, catching glimpses of what others were doing. He saw Amos Trask, disarmed, strike a Tsurani full in the face with his fist, knocking the man from the wall. Trask then carefully bent down and picked up his cutlass as if he had simply dropped it while strolling along the wall. Gardan moved among the men, exhorting the defenders, bolstering sagging spirits, and driving the men beyond the point where they would normally have given in to exhaustion.

Arutha helped two soldiers push away another scaling ladder, then stared in momentary confusion as one of the men slowly turned and sat at his feet, surprise on his face as he looked down at the Tsurani bowshaft in his chest. The man leaned back against the wall and closed his eyes as if deciding to sleep for a time.

Arutha heard someone shout his name. Gardan stood a few feet away, pointing to the north section of the west wall. "They've crested the wall!"

Arutha ran past Gardan, shouting, "Order the reserves to follow!" He raced along the wall until he reached the breach in the defenses. A dozen Tsurani held each end of a section of the wall, pushing forward to clear room for their comrades to follow. Arutha hurled himself into the front rank, past weary and surprised guards who were being forced back along the battlement. Arutha thrust over the first Tsurani shield, taking the man in the throat. The Tsurani's face registered shock, then he keeled over and fell into the courtyard below. Arutha attacked the man next to the first and shouted, "For Crydee! For the Kingdom!"

Then Gardan was among them, like a towering black giant, dealing blows to all who stood before. Suddenly the men of Crydee pressed forward, a wave of flesh and steel along the narrow rampart. The Tsurani stood their ground, refusing to yield the hard-won breach, and to a man were killed.

Arutha struck a Tsurani warrior with the bell guard of his rapier, knocking him to the ground below, and turned to find the wall once more in the possession of the defenders. Horns blew from the Tsurani lines, and the attackers withdrew.

Arutha became aware the sun had cleared the mountains to the east. The morning had finally come. He surveyed the scene below and felt suddenly more fatigued than he could ever remember. Turning slowly, he saw every man on the wall was watching him. Then one of the soldiers shouted, "Hail, Arutha! Hail, Prince of Crydee!"

Suddenly the castle was ringing with shouts as men chanted, "Arutha! Arutha!"

To Gardan, Arutha asked, "Why?"

With a satisfied look the sergeant replied, "They saw you personally take the fight to the Tsurani, Highness, or heard from others. They are soldiers and expect certain things from a commander. They are now truly your men, Highness."

Arutha stood quietly as the cheers filled the castle. Then he raised his hand and the courtyard fell silent. "You have done well. Crydee is served aright by her soldiers." He spoke to Gardan. "Change the watch upon the walls. We may have little time to enjoy the victory."

As if his words were an omen, a shout came from a guard atop the nearest tower. "Highness, 'ware the field."

Arutha saw the Tsurani lines had been re-formed. Wearily he said, "Have they no limit?"

Instead of the expected attack, a single man walked from the Tsurani line, apparently an officer by his crested helm. He pointed to the walls, and the entire Tsurani line erupted in cheers. He walked farther, within bow range, stopping several times to point at the wall. His blue armor glinted in the morning sun as the attackers cheered with his gestures toward the castle.

"A challenge?" said Gardan, watching the strange display as the man showed his back, unmindful of personal danger, and walked back to his own lines.

"No," said Amos Trask, who came to stand next to Gardan. "I think they salute a brave enemy." Amos shook his head slightly. "A strange people."

Arutha said, "Shall we ever understand such men?"

Gardan put his hand upon Arutha's shoulder. "I doubt it. Look, they quit the field."

The Tsurani were marching back toward their tents before the remains of Crydee town. A few watchmen were left to observe the castle, but it was clear the main force was being ordered to stand down again. Gardan said, "I would have ordered another assault." His voice betrayed his disbelief. "They have to know we are near exhaustion. Why not press the attack?"

Amos said, "Who can say. Perhaps they, too, are tired."

Arutha said, "This attacking through the night has some meaning I do not understand." He shook his head. "In time we will know what they plot. Leave a watch upon the walls, but have the men retire to the courtyard. It is becoming clear they prefer not to attack during the day. Order food brought from the kitchen, and water to bathe with." Orders were passed, and men left their posts, some sitting on the walks below the wall, too tired to trudge down the steps. Others reached the courtyard and tossed aside their weapons, sitting in the shade of the battlements while castle porters hurried among them with buckets of fresh water. Arutha leaned against the wall. He spoke silently to himself. "They'll be back."

They came again that night.

18

▾▾

SIEGE

WOUNDED MEN GROANED AT SUNRISE.

For the twelfth straight night the Tsurani had assaulted the castle, only to retire at dawn. Gardan could not see any clear reason for the dangerous night attacks. As he watched the Tsurani gathering up their dead, then returning to their tents, he said, "They are strange. Their archers cannot fire at the walls once the ladders are up for fear of hitting their own men. We have no such problem, knowing everyone below is the enemy. I don't understand these men."

Arutha sat numbly washing the blood and dirt from his face, oblivious to the scene about him. He was too tired even to answer Gardan. "Here," a voice nearby said, and he pulled the damp cloth from his face to see a proffered drinking cup. He took the cup and drained it in one long pull, savoring the taste of strong wine.

Carline stood before him, wearing tunic and trousers, her sword hanging at her side. "What are you doing here?" Arutha asked, fatigue making his voice sound harsh in his own ears.

Carline's manner was brisk. "Someone must carry water and food. With every man on the walls all night long, who do you think is fit for duty in the morning? Not that pitiful handful of porters who are too old for fighting, that is certain."

Arutha looked about and saw other women, ladies of the castle as well as servants and fishwives, walking among the men, who thankfully took the offered food and drink. He smiled his crooked smile. "How fare you?"

"Well enough. Still, sitting in the cellar is as difficult in its own way as being on the wall, I judge. Each sound of battle that reaches us brings one or another of the ladies to tears." Her voice carried a tone of mild disapproval. "They huddle like rabbits. Oh, it is so tiresome." She stood quietly for a moment, then asked, "Have you seen Roland?"

He looked about. "Last night for a time." He covered his face in the soothing wetness of the cloth. Pulling it away after a moment, he added, "Or perhaps it was two nights past. I've lost track." He pointed toward the wall nearest the keep. "He should be over there somewhere. I put him in charge of the off watch. He is responsible for guarding against a flank attack."

Carline smiled. She knew Roland would be chafing to get into the fight, but with his responsibilities it would be unlikely unless the Tsurani attacked on all sides. "Thank you, Arutha."

Arutha feigned ignorance. "For what?"

She kneeled and kissed his wet cheek. "For knowing me better than I know myself sometimes." She stood and walked away.

ROLAND WALKED ALONG the battlements, watching the distant forest beyond the broad clearing that ran along the eastern wall of the castle. He approached a guard standing next to an alarm bell and said, "Anything?"

"Nothing, Squire."

Roland nodded. "Keep a watchful eye. This is the narrowest open area before the wall. If they come against a second flank, this is where I would expect the assault."

The soldier said, "In truth, Squire. Why do they come only against one wall, and why the strongest?"

Roland shrugged. "I don't pretend to know. Perhaps to show contempt, or bravery. Or for some alien reason."

The guard came to attention and saluted. Carline had come silently up behind them. Roland took her by the arm and hurried her along. "What do you think you're doing up here?" he said in ungentle tones.

Her look of relief at finding him alive and unhurt turned to one of anger. "I came to see if you were all right," she said defiantly.

Guiding her down the stairs to the courtyard below, he answered, "We're not so far removed from the forest a Tsurani bowman could not reduce the Duke's household by one. I'll not explain to your father and brothers what my reasons were for allowing you up there."

"Oh! Is that your only reason? You don't want to face Father."

He smiled and his voice softened. "No. Of course not."

She returned the smile. "I was worried."

Roland sat upon the lower steps and plucked at some weeds growing near the base of the stones, pulling them out and tossing them aside. "Little reason for that. Arutha has seen I'll not risk much."

Placatingly, Carline said, "Still, this is an important post. If they attack here, you'll have to hold with a small number until reinforcements come."

"If they attack. Gardan came by yesterday, and he thinks they may tire of this soon and dig in for a long siege, waiting for us to starve."

She said, "More's their hard luck, then. We've stores through the winter, and they'll find little to forage out there once the snows come."

Playfully mocking, he said, "What have we here? A student of tactics?"

She regarded him like an overtaxed teacher confronted with a particularly slow student. "I listen, and I have my wits about me. Do you think I do nothing but sit around waiting for you men to tell me what is occurring? If I did, I'd know nothing."

He put up his hands in sign of supplication. "I'm sorry, Carline. You are most definitely no one's fool." He stood and took her hand. "But you have made me your fool."

She squeezed his hand. "No, Roland, I have been the fool. It has taken me almost three years to understand just how good a man you are. And how good a friend." She leaned over and kissed him lightly. He returned the kiss with tenderness. "And more," she added quietly.

"When this is over . . ." he began.

She placed her free hand over his lips. "Not now, Roland. Not now."

He smiled his understanding. "I'd best be back to the walls, Carline."

She kissed him again and left for the main courtyard and the work to be done. He climbed back to the wall and resumed his vigil.

IT WAS LATE afternoon when a guard shouted, "Squire! In the forest!" Roland looked in the indicated direction and saw two figures sprinting across the open ground. From the trees the shouts of men came, and the clamor of battle.

Crydee bowmen raised their weapons, then Roland shouted, "Hold! It's Longbow!" To the guard next to him he said, "Bring ropes, quickly."

Longbow and Garret reached the wall as the ropes were being lowered and, as soon as they were secured, scrambled upward. When they were safely over the walls, they sank exhaustedly behind the battlements. Waterskins were handed the two foresters, who drank deeply.

"What now?" asked Roland.

Longbow gave him a lopsided smile. "We found another band of travelers heading northward about thirty miles southeast of here and arranged for them to visit with the Tsurani."

Garret looked up at Roland with eyes darkly circled from fatigue. "A band he calls it. Damn near five hundred moredhel moving in strength. Must have been a full hundred chasing us through the woods the last two days."

Roland said, "Arutha will be pleased. The Tsurani have hit us each night since you left. We could do with a little diverting of their attentions."

Longbow nodded. "Where's the Prince?"

"At the west wall, where all the fighting's been."

Longbow stood and pulled the exhausted Garret to his feet. "Come along. We'd better report."

Roland instructed the guards to keep a sharp watch and followed the two huntsmen. They found Arutha supervising the distribution of weapons to those in need of replacing broken or dulled ones. Gardell, the smith, and his apprentices gathered up those that were reparable and dumped them into a cart, heading for the forge to begin work.

Longbow said, "Highness, another band of moredhel have come north. I led them here, so the Tsurani could be too busy to attack tonight."

Arutha said, "That is welcome news. Come, we'll have a cup of wine, and you can tell of what you saw."

Longbow sent Garret off to the kitchen and followed Arutha and Roland into the keep. The Prince sent word asking Gardan to join them in the council room and, when they were all there, asked Longbow to recount his travels.

Longbow drank deeply from the wine cup placed before him. "It was touch and go for a while. The woods are thick with both Tsurani and moredhel. And there are many signs they have little affection for one another. We counted at least a hundred dead on both sides."

Arutha looked at the other three men. "We know little of their ways, but it seems foolish for them to travel so close to Crydee."

Longbow shook his head. "They have little choice, Highness. The Green Heart must be foraged clean, and they cannot return to their mountains because of the Tsurani. The moredhel are making for the Northlands and won't risk passing near Elvandar. With the rest of the way blocked by the Tsurani strength, their only path is through the forests nearby, then westward along the river toward the coast. Once they reach the sea, they can turn northward again. They must gain the Great Northern Mountains before winter to reach their brothers in the Northlands safely."

He drank the rest of his cup and waited while a servant refilled it. "From all signs, nearly every moredhel in the south is making for the Northlands. It looks as if over a thousand have already safely been by here. How many more will come this way through the summer and fall, we cannot guess." He drank again. "The Tsurani will have to watch their eastern flank and would do well to watch the south as well. The moredhel are starved and might chance a raid into the Tsurani camp while the bulk of the army is thrown against the walls of the castle. Should a three-way fight occur, it could get messy."

"For the Tsurani," said Gardan.

Martin hoisted his cup in salute. "For the Tsurani."

Arutha said, "You've done well, Huntmaster."

"Thank you, Highness." He laughed. "I'd never thought to see the day I'd welcome sight of the Dark Brotherhood in the forests of Crydee."

Arutha drummed his fingers upon the table. "It will be another two to three weeks before we can expect the armies from Tulan and Carse. If the Dark Brothers harry the Tsurani enough, we might have some respite." He looked at Martin. "What occurs to the east?"

Longbow spread his hands upon the table. "We couldn't get close enough to see much as we hurried past, but they are up to something. They've a good number of men scattered throughout the woods from the edge of the clearing back about a half mile. If it hadn't been for the moredhel hot on our heels, Garret and I might not have made it back to the walls."

"I wish I knew what they were doing out there," said Arutha. "This attacking only at night, it surely masks some trickery."

Gardan said, "We'll know soon enough, I fear."

Arutha stood, and the others rose as well. "We have much to do in any event. But if they do not come this night, we should all take advantage of the rest. Order watches posted, and send the men back to the commons for sleep. If I'm needed, I'll be in my room."

The others followed him from the council hall, and Arutha walked slowly to his room, his fatigued mind trying to grasp what he knew were important matters, but failing. He threw off only his armor and fell fully clothed across his pallet. He was quickly asleep, but it was a troubled, dream-filled slumber.

For a week no attacks came, as the Tsurani were cautious of the migrating Brotherhood of the Dark Path. As Martin had foretold, the moredhel were emboldened by hunger and had twice struck into the heart of the Tsurani camp.

On the eighth afternoon after the first moredhel attack, the Tsurani were again gathering on the field before the castle, their ranks once more swelled by reinforcements from the east. Messages carried by pigeon between Arutha and his father told of increased fighting along the eastern front as well. Lord Borric speculated Crydee was being attacked by troops fresh from the Tsurani homeworld, as there had been no reports of any troop movements along his front. Other messages arrived with word of relief from Carse and Tulan. Baron Tolburt's soldiers had departed Tulan within two days of receiving Arutha's message, and his fleet would join with Baron Bellamy's at Carse. Depending upon the prevailing winds, it would be from one to two weeks before the relief fleet arrived.

Arutha stood at his usual place upon the west wall, Martin Longbow at his side. They watched the Tsurani taking position as the sun sank in the west, a red beacon bathing the landscape in crimson.

"It seems," said Arutha, "they mount a full attack tonight."

Longbow said, "They've cleared the area of troublesome neighbors by all appearances, at least for a time. The moredhel gained us a little time, Highness, but no more."

"I wonder how many will reach the Northlands?"

Longbow shrugged. "One in five perhaps. From the Green Heart to the Northlands is a long, difficult journey under the best of circumstances. Now . . ." He let his words trail off.

Gardan came up the stairs from the courtyard. "Highness, the tower watch reports the Tsurani are in formation."

As he spoke, the Tsurani sounded their battle calls and began to advance. Arutha drew his sword and gave the order for the catapults to fire. Bowmen followed, unleashing a storm of arrows upon the attackers, but still the Tsurani came.

Through the night, wave after wave of brightly armored aliens threw themselves at the west wall of Castle Crydee. Most died on the field before the wall, or at its base, but a few managed to crest the battlements. They, too, died. Still, more came.

Six times the Tsurani wave had broken upon the defenses of Crydee, and now they prepared for a seventh assault. Arutha, covered in dirt and blood, directed the disposition of rested troops along the wall. Gardan looked to the east. "If we hold one more time, the dawn will be here. Then we should have some respite," he said, his voice thick with fatigue.

"We will hold," answered Arutha, his own voice sounding just as tired in his ears as Gardan's.

"Arutha?"

Arutha saw Roland and Amos coming up the stairs, with another man behind. "What now?" asked the Prince.

Roland said, "We can see no activity on the other walls, but there is something here you should see."

Arutha recognized the other man, Lewis, the castle's Rathunter. It was his responsibility to keep vermin from the keep. He tenderly held something in his hands.

Arutha looked closely: it was a ferret, twitching slightly in the firelight. "Highness," said Lewis, his voice thick with emotion, "it's—"

"What, man?" said Arutha impatiently. With attack about to begin, he had little time to mourn a lost pet.

Roland spoke, for Lewis was obviously overcome at the loss of his ferret. "The Rathunter's ferrets didn't return two days ago. This one crawled into the storage room behind the kitchen sometime since. Lewis found it there a few minutes ago."

In choked tones, Lewis said, "They're all well trained, sire. If they didn't come back, it's because something kept them from returnin'. This poor lad's been stepped on. His back's broken. He must've crawled for hours to get back."

Arutha said, "I fail to see the significance of this."

Roland gripped the Prince's arm. "Arutha, he hunts them in the rat tunnels *under the castle.*"

Comprehension dawned upon Arutha. He turned to Gardan and said, "Sappers! The Tsurani must be digging under the east wall."

Gardan said, "That would explain the constant attacks upon the west wall—to draw us away."

Arutha said, "Gardan, take command of the walls. Amos, Roland, come with me."

Arutha ran down the steps and through the courtyard. He shouted for a group of soldiers to follow and bring shovels. They reached the small courtyard behind the keep, and Arutha said, "We've got to find that tunnel and collapse it."

Amos said, "Your walls are slanted outward at the plinth. They'll recognize they can't fire the timbers of the tunnels to bring it down to make a breach. They'll be trying to get a force inside the castle grounds or into the keep."

Roland looked alarmed. "Carline! She and the other ladies are in the cellars."

Arutha said, "Take some men and go to the cellars." Roland ran off. Arutha fell to his knees and placed his ear on the ground. The others followed his example, moving around, listening for sounds of digging from below.

CARLINE SAT NERVOUSLY next to the Lady Marna. The fat former governess made a show of calmly attending to her needlepoint despite the rustling and stirring of the other women in the cellar. The sounds of battle from the walls came to them as faint, distant echoes, muted by the thick walls of the keep. Now there was an equally unnerving quiet.

"Oh! To be sitting here like a caged bird," said Carline.

"The walls are no place for a lady," came the retort from Lady Marna.

Carline stood. As she paced the room, she said, "I can tie bandages and carry water. All of us could."

The other ladies of the court looked at one another as if the Princess had been bereft of her senses. None of them could imagine subjecting herself to such a trial.

"Highness, please," said Lady Marna, "you should wait quietly. There will be much to do when the battle's over. Now you should rest."

Carline began a retort, then stopped. She held up her hand. "Do you hear something?"

The others stopped their movement, and all listened. From the floor came a faint tapping sound. Carline knelt upon the flagstone. "My lady, this is most unseemly," began the Lady Marna.

Carline stopped the complaint with an imperious wave of her hand. "Quiet!" She placed her ear upon the flagstones. "There is something . . ."

Lady Glynis shuddered. "Probably rats scurrying about. There are hundreds of them down here." Her expression showed this revelation was about as unpleasant a fact as imaginable.

"Be quiet!" ordered Carline.

There came a cracking sound from the floor, and Carline leaped to her feet. Her sword came out of its scabbard as a fracture appeared in the stones of the floor. A chisel point broke through the flagstone, and suddenly the upturned stone was pushed up and outward.

Ladies screamed as a hole appeared in the floor. A startled face popped into the light, then a Tsurani warrior, hair filthy from the dirt of the tunnel, tried to scramble upward. Carline's sword took him in the throat as she shouted, "Get out! Call the guards!"

Most of the women sat frozen in terror, refusing to move. Lady Marna heaved her massive bulk from the bench upon which she sat and gave a shrieking town girl a backhanded slap. The girl looked at Lady Marna with wide-eyed fright for an instant, then broke toward the steps. As if at a signal, the others ran after, screaming for help.

Carline watched as the Tsurani slowly fell back, blocking the hole in the floor. Other cracks appeared around the hole, and hands pulled pieces of flagstone downward into the ever-widening entrance. Lady Marna was halfway to the steps when she saw Carline standing her ground. "Princess!" she shrieked.

Another man came scrambling upward, and Carline delivered a death blow to him. She was then forced back as the stones near her feet collapsed. The Tsurani had terminated their tunnel in a wide hole and were now broadening the entrance, pulling down stones so that they could swarm out, overwhelming any defenders.

A man fought upward, pushing Carline to one side, allowing another to start his climb upward. Lady Marna ran back to her former ward and grabbed up a large piece of loose stone, which she brought crashing down on the unhelmeted skull of the second man. Grunts and strange-sounding words came from the tunnel mouth as the man fell back upon those behind.

Carline ran the other man through and kicked another in the face. "Princess!" cried Lady Marna. "We must flee!"

Carline didn't answer. She dodged a blow at her feet delivered by a Tsurani who then sprang nimbly out of the hole. Carline thrust and the man dodged. Another came scrambling out of the hole, and the Lady Marna shrieked.

The first man turned reflexively at the sound, and Carline drove her sword into his side. The second man raised a serrated sword to strike Lady Marna, and Carline sprang for him, thrusting her sword point into his neck. The man shuddered and fell, his fingers releasing their grip on the sword. Carline grabbed Lady Marna's arm and propelled her toward the steps.

Tsurani came swarming out of the hole, and Carline turned at the bottom of the stairs. Lady Marna stood behind her beloved Princess, not willing to leave. The Tsurani approached warily. The girl had killed enough of their companions to warrant their respect and caution.

Suddenly a body crashed past the girl as Roland charged into the Tsurani, soldiers of the keep hurrying behind. The young Squire was in a frenzy to protect the Princess, and he bowled over three Tsurani in his rush. They tumbled backward, disappearing into the hole, Roland with them.

As the Squire vanished from view, Carline screamed, "Roland!" Other guards leaped past the Princess to engage the Tsurani who still stood in the cellar, and more jumped boldly into the hole. Grunts and cries, shouts and oaths rang from the tunnel.

A guard took Carline by the arm and began to drag her up the stairs. She followed, helpless in the man's strong grip, crying, "Roland!"

GRUNTS OF EXERTION filled the dark tunnel as the soldiers from Crydee dug furiously. Arutha had found the Tsurani tunnel and had ordered a shaft sunk near it. They were now digging a countertunnel to intercept the Tsurani, near the wall. Amos had agreed with Arutha's judgment that they needed to force the Tsurani back beyond the wall before collapsing the tunnel, denying them any access to the castle.

A shovel broke through, and men began frantically clearing away enough dirt to allow passage into the Tsurani tunnel. Boards were hastily jammed into place, jerry-rigged supports, preventing the earth above from caving in on them.

The men from Crydee surged into the low tunnel and entered a frantic, terrible melee. Tsurani warriors and Roland's squad of soldiers were locked in a desperate hand-to-hand struggle in the dark. Men fought and died in the gloom under the earth. It was impossible to bring order to the fray, with the fighting in such confinement. An overturned lantern flickered faintly, providing little illumination.

Arutha said to a soldier behind, "Get more men!"

"At once, Highness!" answered the soldier, turning toward the shaft.

Arutha entered the Tsurani tunnel. It was only five feet high, so he moved stooped over. It was fairly wide, with enough room for three men to negotiate closely. Arutha stepped on something soft, which groaned in pain. He continued past the dying man, toward the sound of fighting.

It was a scene from his worst nightmare, faintly lit by widely spaced torches. With little room only the first three men could engage the enemy at any one point. Arutha called out, "Knives!" and dropped his rapier. In close quarters the shorter weapons would prove more effective.

He came upon two men struggling in the darkness and grabbed at one. His hand closed on chitinous armor, and he plunged his knife into the man's exposed neck. Jerking the now lifeless body off the other man, he saw a jam of bodies a few feet away, where Crydee and Tsurani soldiers pressed against one another. Curses and cries filled the tunnel, and the damp earth smell was mixed with the odor of blood and excrement.

Arutha fought madly, blindly, lashing out at barely seen foes. His own fear kept threatening to overcome him as primitive awareness cried for him to quit the tunnel and the threatening earth above. He forced his panic down and continued to lead the attack on the sappers.

A familiar voice grunted and cursed at his side, and Arutha knew Amos Trask was near. "Another thirty feet, lad!" he shouted.

Arutha took the man at his word, having lost all sense of distance. The men of Crydee pressed onward, and many died killing the resisting Tsurani. Time became a blur and the fight a dim montage of images.

Abruptly Amos shouted, "Straw!" and bundles of dry straw were passed forward. "Torches!" he cried, and flaming torches were passed up. He piled the straw near a latticework of timbers and drove the torch into the pile. Flames burst upward, and he yelled, "Clear the tunnel!"

The fighting stopped. Every man, whether of Crydee or Tsurani, turned and fled the flames. The sappers knew the tunnel was lost without means to quench the flames and scrambled for their lives.

Choking smoke filled the tunnel, and men began to cough as they cleared the cramped quarters. Arutha followed Amos, and they missed the turn to the countertunnel, coming out in the cellar. Guardsmen, dirty and bloody, were collapsing on the stones of the cellar, gasping for air. A dull rumble sounded, and with a crash, a blast of air and smoke blew out of the hole. Amos grinned, his face streaked with dirt. "The timbers collapsed. The tunnel's sealed."

Arutha nodded dumbly, exhausted and still reeling from the smoke. A cup of water was handed to him, and he drank deeply, soothing his burning throat.

Carline appeared before him. "Are you all right?" she asked, concern on her face. He nodded. She looked around. "Where's Roland?"

Arutha shook his head. "It was impossible to see down there. Was he in the tunnel?"

She bit her lower lip. Tears welled up in her blue eyes as she nodded. Arutha said, "He might have cleared the tunnel and come up in the courtyard. Let us see."

He got to his feet, and Amos and Carline followed him up the stairs. They left the keep, and a soldier informed him the attack on the wall had been repulsed. Arutha acknowledged the report and continued around the keep until they came to the shaft he had ordered dug. Soldiers lay on the grass of the yard, coughing and spitting, trying to clear their lungs of the burning smoke. The air hung heavy with an acrid haze as fumes from the fire continued to billow from the shaft. Another rumble sounded, and Arutha could feel it through the soles of his boots. Near the wall a depression had appeared where the tunnel had fallen below. "Squire Roland!" Arutha shouted.

"Here, Highness," came an answering shout from a soldier.

Carline dashed past Arutha and reached Roland before the Prince. The Squire lay upon the ground, tended by the soldier who answered. His eyes were closed and his skin pale, and blood seeped from his side. The soldier said, "I had to drag him along the last few yards, Highness. He was out on his feet. I thought it might be smoke until I saw the wound."

Carline cradled Roland's head, while Arutha first cut the binding straps of Roland's breastplate, then tore away the undertunic. After a moment Arutha sat back upon his heels. "It's a shallow wound. He'll be all right."

"Oh, Roland," Carline said softly.

Roland's eyes opened and he grinned weakly. His voice was tired, but he forced a cheery note. "What's this? You'd think I'd been killed."

Carline said, "You heartless monster." She gently shook him but didn't release her hold as she smiled down at him. "Playing tricks at a time like this!"

He winced as he tried to move. "Ooh, that hurts." She placed a restraining hand upon his shoulder.

"Don't try to move. We must bind the wound," she said, caught between relief and anger.

Nestling his head into her lap, he smiled. "I'd not move for half your father's Duchy."

She looked at him in irritation. "What were you doing throwing yourself upon the enemy like that?"

Roland looked genuinely embarrassed. "In truth, I tripped coming down the steps and couldn't stop myself."

She placed her cheek against his forehead as Arutha and Amos laughed. "You are a liar. And I do love you," she said softly.

Arutha stood and took Amos in tow, leaving Roland and Carline to each other. Reaching the corner, they encountered the former Tsurani slave, Charles, carrying water for the wounded. Arutha halted the man.

He stood with a yoke across his shoulders holding two large water buckets. He was bleeding from several small wounds and was covered with mire. Arutha said, "What happened to you?"

With a broad smile, Charles said, "Good fight. Jump in hole. Charles good warrior."

The former Tsurani slave was pale and weaved a little as he stood there. Arutha remained speechless, then indicated he should continue his work. Happily Charles hurried along. Arutha said to Amos, "What do you make of that?"

Amos chuckled. "I've had many dealings with rogues and scoundrels, Highness. I know little of these Tsurani, but I think that's a man to count on."

Arutha watched as Charles dispensed water to the other soldiers, ignoring his own wounds and fatigue. "That was no mean thing, jumping into the shaft without orders. I'll have to consider Longbow's offer to put that man in service."

They continued on their way, Arutha supervising the care of the wounded, while Amos was put in charge of the final destruction of the tunnel.

When dawn came, the courtyard was still, and only a patch of raw earth, where the shaft had been filled in, and a long depression running from the keep to the outer wall showed anything unusual had occurred in the night.

FANNON HOBBLED ALONG the wall, favoring his right side. The wound to his back was almost healed, but he was still unable to walk without aid. Father Tully supported the Swordmaster as they came to where the others waited.

Arutha gave the Swordmaster a smile and gently took him by the other arm, helping Tully hold him. Gardan, Amos Trask, Martin Longbow, and a group of soldiers stood nearby.

"What's this?" asked Fannon, his display of gruff anger a welcome sight to those on the wall. "Have you so little wits among you that you must haul me from my rest to take charge?"

Arutha pointed out to sea. On the horizon dozens of small flecks could be seen against the blue of sea and sky, flashes of brilliant white glinting as the morning sun was caught and reflected back to them. "The fleet from Carse and Tulan approaches the south beaches."

He indicated the Tsurani camp in the distance, bustling with activity. "Today we'll drive them out. By this time tomorrow we'll clear this entire area of the aliens. We'll harry them eastward, allowing them no respite. It will be a long time before they'll come in strength again."

Quietly Fannon said, "I trust you are right, Arutha." He stood without speaking for a time, then said, "I have heard reports of your command, Arutha. You've done well. You are a credit to your father, and to Crydee."

Finding himself moved by the Swordmaster's praise, Arutha tried to make light, but Fannon interrupted. "No, you have done all that was needed, and more. You were right. With these people we must not be cautious. We must carry the struggle to them." He sighed. "I am an old man, Arutha. It is time I retired and left warfare to the young."

Tully made a derisive noise. "You're not old. I was already a priest when you were still in swaddling."

Fannon laughed with the others at the obvious untruth of the statement, and Arutha said, "You must know, if I've done well, it is because of your teachings."

Tully gripped Fannon's elbow. "You may not be an old man, but you are a sick one. Back to the keep with you. You've had enough gadding about. You can begin walking regularly tomorrow. In a few weeks you'll be charging about, shouting orders at everyone like your old self."

Fannon managed a slight smile and allowed Tully to lead him back down the stairs. When he was gone, Gardan said, "The Swordmaster's right, Highness. You've done your father proud."

Arutha watched the approaching ships, his angular features fixed in an expression of quiet reflection. Softly he said, "If I have done well, it is because I have had the aid of good men, many no longer with us." He took a deep breath, then continued, "You have played a great part in our withstanding this siege, Gardan, and you, Martin."

Both men smiled and voiced their thanks. "And you, pirate." Arutha grinned. "You've also played a great part. We are deeply in your debt."

Amos Trask tried to look modest and failed. "Well, Highness, I was merely protecting my own skin as well as everyone else's." He then returned Arutha's grin. "It was a rousing good fight."

Arutha looked toward the sea once more. "Let us hope we can soon be done with rousing good fights." He left the walls and started down the stairs. "Give orders to prepare for the attack."

CARLINE STOOD ATOP the south tower of the keep, her arm around Roland's waist. The Squire was pale from his wound, but otherwise in hale spirits. "We'll be done with the siege, now the fleet's arrived," he said, clinging tightly to the Princess.

"It has been a nightmare."

He smiled down at her, gazing into her blue eyes. "Not entirely. There has been some compensation."

Softly she said, "You are a rogue," then kissed him. When they separated, she said, "I wonder if your foolish bravery was nothing more than a ploy to gain my sympathies."

Feigning a wince, he said, "Lady, I am wounded."

She clung to him. "I was so worried about you, not knowing if you lay dead in the tunnel. I . . ." Her voice dropped off as her gaze strayed to the north tower of the keep, opposite the one upon which they stood. She could see the window upon the second floor, the window to Pug's room. The funny little metal chimney, which would constantly belch smoke when he was at his studies, was now only a mute reminder of just how empty the tower stood.

Roland followed her gaze. "I know," he said. "I miss him, too. And Tomas as well."

She sighed. "That seems such a long time ago, Roland. I was a girl then, a girl with a girl's notion of what life and love were about." Softly she said, "Some love comes like a wind off the sea, while others grow slowly from the seeds of friendship and kindness. Someone once told me that."

"Father Tully. He was right." He squeezed her waist. "Either way, as long as you feel, you live."

She watched as the soldiers of the garrison prepared for the coming sortie. "Will this end it?"

"No, they will come again. This war is fated to last a long time."

They stood together, taking comfort in the simple fact of each other's existence.

KASUMI OF THE Shinzawai, Force Leader of the Armies of the Kanazawai Clan, of the Blue Wheel Party, watched the enemy upon the castle wall.

He could barely make out the figures walking along the battlements, but he knew them well. He could not put names to any, but they were each as familiar to him as his own men. The slender youth who commanded, who fought like a demon, who brought order to the fray when needed, he was there. The black giant would not be too far from his side, the one who stood like a bulwark against every attack upon the walls. And the green-clad one, who could race through the woods like an apparition, taunting Kasumi's men by the freedom with which he passed their lines, he would be there as well. No doubt the broad-shouldered one was nearby, the laughing man with the curved sword and maniacal grin. Kasumi quietly saluted them all as valiant foemen, even if only barbarians.

Chingari of the Omechkel, the Senior Strike Leader, came to stand at Kasumi's side. "Force Leader, the barbarian fleet is nearing. They will land their men within the hour."

Kasumi regarded the scroll he held in his hand. It had been read a dozen times since arriving at dawn. He glanced at it one more time, again studying the chop at the bottom, the crest of his father, Kamatsu, Lord of the Shinzawai. Silently accepting his personal fate, Kasumi said, "Order for march. Break camp at once and begin assembling the warriors. We are commanded to return to Kelewan. Send the trailbreakers ahead."

Chingari's voice betrayed his bitterness. "Now the tunnel is destroyed, do we quit so meekly?"

"There is no shame, Chingari. Our clan has withdrawn itself from the Alliance for War, as have the other clans of the Blue Wheel Party. The War Party is once more alone in the conduct of this invasion."

With a sigh Chingari said, "Again politics interferes with conquest. It would have been a glorious victory to take such a fine castle."

Kasumi laughed. "True." He watched the activities of the castle. "They are the best we have ever faced. We already learn much from them. Castle walls slanted outward at the plinth, preventing sappers from collapsing them, this is a new and clever thing. And those beasts they ride. Ayee, how they move, like Thūn racing across the tundras of home. I will somehow gain some of those animals. Yes, these people are more than simple barbarians."

After a moment's more reflection, he said, "Have our scouts and trailbreakers keep alert for signs of the forest devils."

Chingari spat. "The foul ones move in great number northward once more. They're as much a dagger in our side as the barbarians."

Kasumi said, "When this world is conquered, we shall have to see to these creatures. The barbarians make strong slaves. Some may even prove valuable enough to make free vassals who will swear loyalty to our houses, but those foul ones, they must be obliterated." Kasumi fell silent for a while. Then he said, "Let the barbarians think we flee in terror from their fleet. This place is now a matter for the clans remaining in the War Party. Let Tasio of the Minwanabi worry about a garrison at his rear should he move eastward. Until the Kanazawai once more realign themselves in the High Council, we are done with this war. Order the march."

Chingari saluted his commander and left, and Kasumi considered the implications of the message from his father. He knew the withdrawal of all the forces of the Blue Wheel Party would prove a major setback for the Warlord and his party. The repercussions of such a move would be felt throughout the Empire for some years to come. There would be no smashing victories for the Warlord now, for with the departure of those forces loyal to the Kanazawai lords and the other clans of the Blue Wheel, other clans would reconsider before joining in an all-out push.

No, thought Kasumi, it was a bold but dangerous move by his father and the other lords. This war would now be prolonged. The Warlord was robbed of a spectacular conquest; he was now overextended with too few men holding too much land. Without new allies he would remain unable to press forward with the war. His choices were now down to two: withdraw from Midkemia and risk humiliation before the High Council, or sit and wait, hoping for another shift in politics at home.

It was a stunning move on behalf of the Blue Wheel. But the risk was great. And the risk from the next series of moves in the Game of the Council would be even more dangerous. Silently he said: O my father, we are now firmly committed to the Great Game. We risk much: our family, our clan, our honor, and perhaps even the Empire itself.

Crumbling the scroll, he tossed it into a nearby brazier, and when it was totally consumed by flame, he put aside thoughts of risk and walked back toward his tent.

BOOK II

MILAMBER AND THE VALHERU

We were, fair queen,
Two lads that thought there was no more behind
But such a day to-morrow as to-day,
And to be boy eternal.

—SHAKESPEARE, *The Winter's Tale*

19

▼▼

SLAVE

THE DYING SLAVE LAY SCREAMING.

The day was unmercifully hot. The other slaves went about their work, ignoring the sound as much as possible. Life in the work camp was cheap, and it did no good to dwell on the fate that awaited so many. The dying man had been bitten by a relli, a snakelike swamp creature. Its venom was slow-acting and painful; short of magic, there was no cure.

Suddenly there was silence. Pug looked over to see a Tsurani guard wipe off his sword. A hand fell on Pug's shoulder. Laurie's voice whispered in his ear, "Looks like our venerable overseer was disturbed by the sound of Toffston's dying."

Pug tied a coil of rope securely around his waist. "At least it ended quickly." He turned to the tall blond singer from the Kingdom city of Tyr-Sog and said, "Keep a sharp eye out. This one's old and may be rotten." Without another word Pug scampered up the bole of the ngaggi tree, a firlike swamp tree the Tsurani harvested for wood and resins. With few metals, the Tsurani had become clever in finding substitutes. The wood of this tree could be worked like paper, then dried to an incredible hardness, useful in fashioning a hundred things. The resins were used to laminate woods and cure hides. Properly cured hides could produce a suit of leather armor as tough as Midkemian chain mail, and laminated wooden weapons were nearly the match of Midkemian steel.

Four years in the swamp camp had hardened Pug's body. His sinewy muscles strained as he climbed the tree. His skin had been tanned deeply by the harsh sun of the Tsurani homeworld. His face was covered by a slave's beard.

Pug reached the first large branches and looked down at his friend. Laurie stood knee-deep in the murky water, absently swatting at the insects that plagued them while they worked. Pug liked Laurie. The troubadour had no business being here, but then he'd had no business tagging along with a patrol in the hope of seeing Tsurani soldiers, either. He said he had wanted material for ballads that would make him famous throughout the Kingdom. He had seen more than he had hoped for. The patrol had ridden into a major Tsurani offensive, and Laurie had been captured. He had come to this camp over four months ago, and he and Pug had quickly become friends.

Pug continued his climb, keeping one eye always searching for the dangerous tree dwellers of Kelewan. Reaching the most likely place for a topping, Pug froze as he caught a glimpse of movement. He relaxed when he saw it was only a needler, a creature whose protection was its resemblance to a clump of ngaggi needles. It scurried away from the presence of the human and made the short jump to the branch of a neighboring tree. Pug made another survey and started tying his ropes. His job was to cut away the tops of the huge trees, making the fall less dangerous to those below.

Pug took several cuts at the bark, then felt the edge of his wooden ax bite into the softer pulp beneath. A faint pungent odor greeted his careful sniffing. Swearing, he called down to Laurie, "This one's rotten. Tell the overseer."

He waited, looking out over the tops of trees. All around, strange insects and birdlike creatures flew. In the four years he had been a slave on this world, he had not grown used to the appearance of these life-forms. They were not all that different from those on Midkemia, but it was the similarities as much as the differences that kept reminding him this was not his home. Bees should be yellow-and-black-striped, not bright red. Eagles shouldn't have yellow bands on their wings, nor hawks purple. These creatures were not bees, eagles, or hawks, but the resemblance was striking. Pug found it easier to accept the stranger creatures of Kelewan than these. The six-legged needra, the domesticated beast of burden that looked like some sort of bovine with two extra stumpy legs, or the cho-ja, the insectoid creature who served the Tsurani and could speak their language: these he had come to find familiar. But each time he glimpsed a creature from the corner of his eye and turned, expecting it to be Midkemian only to find it was not, then the despair would strike.

Laurie's voice brought him from his reverie. "The overseer comes."

Pug swore. If the overseer had to get himself dirty by wading in the water, then he would be in a foul mood—which could mean beatings, or a reduction in the chronically meager food. He would already be angered by the delay in the cutting. A family of burrowers—beaverlike six-legged creatures—had made themselves at home in the roots of the great trees. They would gnaw the tender roots, and the trees would sicken and die. The soft, pulpy wood would turn sour, then watery, and after a while the tree would collapse from within. Several burrower tunnels had been poisoned, but the damage had already been done to the trees.

A rough voice, swearing mightily while its owner splashed through the swamp, announced the arrival of the overseer, Nogamu. He himself was a slave, but he had attained the highest rank a slave could rise to, and while he could never hope to be free, he had many privileges and could order soldiers or freemen placed under his command. A young soldier came walking behind, a look of mild amusement on his face. He was clean-shaven in the manner of a Tsurani freeman, and as he looked up at Pug, the slave could get a good look at him. He had the high cheekbones and nearly black eyes that so many Tsurani possessed. His dark eyes caught sight of Pug, and he seemed to nod slightly. His blue armor was of a type unknown to Pug, but with the strange Tsurani military organization, that was not surprising. Even family, demesne, area, town, city, and province appeared to have its own army. How they all related one to another within the Empire was beyond Pug's understanding.

The overseer stood at the base of the tree, his short robe held above the water. He growled like the bear he resembled and shouted up at Pug, "What's this about another rotten tree?"

Pug spoke the Tsurani language better than any Midkemian in the camp, for he had been there longer than all but a few old Tsurani slaves. He shouted down, "It smells of rot. We should rerig another and leave this one alone, Slave Master."

The overseer shook his fist. "You are all lazy. There is nothing wrong with this tree. It is fine. You only want to keep from working. Now cut it!"

Pug sighed. There was no arguing with the Bear, as all the Midkemian slaves called Nogamu. He was obviously upset about something, and the slaves would pay the price. Pug started hacking through the upper section, and it soon fell to the ground. The smell of rot was thick, and Pug removed the ropes quickly. Just as the last length was coiled around his waist, a splitting sound came from directly in front of him. "It falls!" he shouted down to the slaves standing in the water below. Without hesitation they all ran. The cry of "falls" was never ignored.

The bole of the tree was splitting down the middle now that the top had been cut away. While this was not common, if a tree was far enough gone for the pulp to have lost its strength, any flaw in the bark could cause it to split under its own weight. The tree's branches would pull the halves away from each other. Had Pug been tied to the bole, the ropes would have cut him in half before they snapped.

Pug gauged the direction of the fall; then as the half he stood upon started to move, he launched himself away from it. He hit the water flat, back first, trying to let the two feet of water break his fall as much as possible. The blow from the water was immediately followed by the harder impact with the ground. The bottom was mostly mud, so there was little damage done. The air in his lungs exploded from his mouth when he struck, and his senses reeled for a moment. He retained enough presence of mind to sit up and gasp a deep lungful of air.

Suddenly a heavy weight hit him across the stomach, knocking the wind from him and pushing his head back underwater. He struggled to move and found a large branch across his stomach. He could barely get his face out of the water to get air. His lungs burned, and he breathed without control. Water came pouring down his windpipe, and he started to choke. Coughing and sputtering, he tried to keep calm but felt panic rise within him. He frantically pushed at the weight across him but couldn't move it.

Abruptly he found his head above water; Laurie said, "Spit, Pug! Get the muck out of your lungs, or you'll get lung fever."

Pug coughed and spit. With Laurie holding his head, he could catch his breath.

Laurie shouted, "Grab this branch. I'll pull him out from under."

Several slaves splashed over, sweat beading their bodies. They reached underwater and seized the branch. Heaving, they managed to move it slightly, but Laurie couldn't drag Pug out.

"Bring axes; we'll have to cut the branch from the tree."

Other slaves were starting to bring axes over when Nogamu shouted, "No. Leave him. We have no time for this. There are trees to cut."

Laurie nearly screamed at him, "We can't leave him! He'll drown!"

The overseer crossed over and struck Laurie across the face with a lash. It cut deep into the singer's cheek, but he didn't let go of his friend's head. "Back to work, slave. You'll be beaten tonight for speaking to me that way. There are others who can top. Now, let him go!" He struck Laurie again. Laurie winced, but held Pug's head above water.

Nogamu raised his lash for a third blow, but was halted by a voice from behind. "Cut the slave from under the branch." Laurie saw the speaker was the young soldier who had accompanied the slave master. The overseer whirled about, unaccustomed to having his orders questioned. When he saw who had spoken, he bit back the words that were on his lips. Bowing his head, he said, "My lord's will."

He signaled for the slaves with the axes to cut Pug loose, and in short order Pug was out from under the branch. Laurie carried him over to where the young soldier stood. Pug coughed the last water from his lungs and gasped, "I thank the master for my life."

The man said nothing, but when the overseer approached, directed his remarks to him. "The slave was right, and you were not. The tree was rotten. It is not proper for you to punish him for your bad judgment and ill temper. I should have you beaten, but will not spare the time for it. The work goes slowly, and my father is displeased."

Nogamu bowed his head. "I lose much face in my lord's sight. May I have his permission to kill myself?"

"No. It is too much honor. Return to work."

The overseer's face grew red in silent shame and rage. Raising his lash, he pointed at Laurie and Pug. "You two, back to work."

Laurie stood, and Pug tried. His knees were wobbly from his near drowning, but he managed to stand after a few attempts.

"These two shall be excused work the rest of the day," the young lord said. "This one"—he pointed to Pug—"is of little use. The other must dress those cuts you gave him, or festering will start." He turned to a guard. "Take them back to camp and see to their needs."

Pug was grateful, not so much for himself as for Laurie. With a little rest, Pug could have returned to work, but an open wound in the swamp was a death warrant as often as not. Infections came quickly in this hot, dirty place, and there were few ways of dealing with them.

They followed the guard. As they left, Pug could see the slave master watching them with naked hatred in his eyes.

THERE WAS A creaking of floorboards, and Pug came instantly awake. His slave-bred wariness told him that the sound didn't belong in the hut during the dead of night.

Through the gloom, footfalls could be heard coming closer, then they stopped at the foot of his pallet. From the next pallet, he could hear Laurie's sharp intake of breath, and he knew the minstrel was awake also. Probably half the slaves had been awakened by the intruder. The stranger hesitated over something, and Pug waited, tense with uncertainty. There was a grunt, and without hesitation Pug rolled off his mat. A weight came crashing down, and Pug could hear a dull thud as a dagger struck where his chest had been only moments before. Suddenly the room exploded with activity. Slaves were shouting and could be heard running for the door.

Pug felt hands reach for him in the dark, and a sharp pain exploded across his chest. He reached blindly for his assailant and grappled with him for the blade. Another slash, and his right hand was cut across the palm. Abruptly the attacker stopped moving, and Pug became aware that a third body was atop the would-be assassin.

Soldiers rushed into the hut, carrying lanterns, and Pug could see Laurie lying across the still body of Nogamu. The Bear was still breathing, but from the way the dagger protruded from his ribs, not for long.

The young soldier who had saved Pug's and Laurie's lives entered, and the others made way for him. He stood over the three combatants and simply asked, "Is he dead?"

The overseer's eyes opened, and in a faint whisper he said, "I live, lord. But I die by the blade." A weak but defiant smile showed on his sweat-drenched face.

The young soldier's expression betrayed no emotion, but his eyes looked as if ablaze. "I think not," he said softly. He turned to two of the soldiers in the room. "Take him outside at once and hang him. There will be no honors for his clan to sing. Leave the body there for the insects. It shall be a warning that I am not to be disobeyed. Go."

The dying man's face paled, and his lips quivered. "No, master. I pray, leave me to die by the blade. A few minutes longer." Bloody foam appeared at the corner of his mouth.

Two husky soldiers reached down for Nogamu and, with little thought for his pain, dragged him outside. He could be heard wailing the entire way. The amount of strength left in his voice was amazing, as if his fear of the rope had awakened some deep reserve.

They stood in frozen tableau until the sound was cut off in a strangled cry. The young officer then turned to Pug and Laurie. Pug sat, blood running from a long, shallow gash across his chest. He held his injured hand in the other. It was deeply cut, and his fingers wouldn't move.

"Bring your wounded friend," the young soldier commanded Laurie.

Laurie helped Pug to his feet, and they followed the officer out of the slave hut. He led them across the compound to his own quarters and ordered them to enter. Once inside, he instructed a guard to send for the camp physician. He had them stand in silence until the physician arrived. He was an old Tsurani, dressed in the robes of one of their gods —which one the Midkemians couldn't tell. He inspected Pug's wounds and judged the chest wound superficial. The hand, he said, would be another matter.

"The cut is deep, and the muscles and tendons have been cut. It will heal, but there will be a loss of movement and little strength for gripping. He most likely will be fit for only light duty."

The soldier nodded, a peculiar expression on his face: a mixture of disgust and impatience. "Very well. Dress the wounds and leave us."

The physician set about cleaning the wounds. He took a score of stitches in the hand, bandaged it, admonished Pug to keep it clean, and left. Pug ignored the pain, easing his mind with an old mental exercise.

After the physician was gone, the soldier studied the two slaves before him. "By law, I should have you hanged for killing the slave master."

They said nothing. They would remain silent until commanded to speak.

"But as I hanged the slave master, I am free to keep you alive, should it suit my purpose. I can simply have you punished for wounding him." He paused. "Consider yourselves punished."

With a wave of his hand he said, "Leave me, but return here at daybreak. I have to decide what to do with you."

They left, feeling fortunate, for under most circumstances they would now be hanging next to the former slave master. As they crossed the compound, Laurie said, "I wonder what that was about."

Pug responded, "I hurt too much to wonder why. I'm just thankful that we will see tomorrow."

Laurie said nothing until they reached the slave hut. "I think the young lord has something up his sleeve."

"Whatever. I have long since given up trying to understand our masters. That's why I've stayed alive so long, Laurie. I just do what I'm told to, and I endure." Pug pointed to the tree where the former overseer's body could be seen in the pale moonlight—only the small moon was out tonight. "It's much too easy to end up like that."

Laurie nodded. "Perhaps you're right. I still think about escape."

Pug laughed, a short, bitter sound. "Where, singer? Where could you run? Toward the rift and ten thousand Tsurani?"

Laurie said nothing. They returned to their pallets and tried to sleep in the humid heat.

▼▼

THE YOUNG OFFICER sat upon a pile of cushions, cross-legged in Tsurani fashion. He sent away the guard who had accompanied Pug and Laurie, then motioned for the two slaves to sit. They did so hesitantly, for a slave was not usually permitted to sit in a master's presence.

"I am Hokanu, of the Shinzawai. My father owns this camp," he said without preamble. "He is deeply dissatisfied with the harvest this year. He has sent me to see what can be done. Now I have no overseer to manage the work, because a foolish man blamed you for his own stupidity. What am I to do?"

They said nothing. He asked, "You have been here, how long?"

Pug and Laurie answered in turn. He considered the answers, then said, "You"—pointing at Laurie—"are nothing unusual, save you speak our tongue better than most barbarians, all things considered. But you" —pointing at Pug—"have stayed alive longer than most of your stiff-necked countrymen and also speak our language well. You might even pass for a peasant from a remote province."

They sat still, unsure of what Hokanu was leading up to. Pug realized with a shock that he was probably older by a year or two than this young lord. He was young for such power. The ways of the Tsurani were very strange. In Crydee he would still be an apprentice, or if noble, continuing his education in statecraft.

"How do you speak so well?" he asked of Pug.

"Master, I was among the first captured and brought here. There were only seven of us among so many Tsurani slaves. We learned to survive. After some time, I was the only one left. The others died of the burning fever or festering wounds, or were killed by the guards. There were none for me to talk with who spoke my own language. No other countryman came to this camp for over a year."

The officer nodded, then to Laurie said, "And you?"

"Master, I am a singer, a minstrel in my own land. It is our custom to travel broadly, and we must learn many tongues. I have also a good ear for music. Your language is what is called a tone language on my world; words with the same sound save for the pitch with which they are spoken have different meanings. We have several such tongues to the south of our Kingdom. I learn quickly."

A glimmering appeared in the eyes of the soldier. "It is good to know these things." He lapsed deep into thought. After a moment he nodded to himself. "There are many considerations that fashion a man's fortune, slaves." He smiled, looking more like a boy than a man. "This camp is a shambles. I am to prepare a report for my father, the Lord of the Shinzawai. I think I know what the problems are." He pointed at

Pug. "I would have your thoughts on the subject. You have been here longer than anyone."

Pug composed himself. It had been a long time since anyone had asked him to venture an opinion on anything. "Master, the first overseer, the one who was here when I was captured, was a shrewd man, who understood that men, even slaves, cannot be made to work well if they are weak from hunger. We had better food and if injured were given time for healing. Nogamu was an ill-tempered man who took every setback as a personal affront. Should burrowers ruin a grove, it was the fault of the slaves. Should a slave die, it was a plot to discredit his oversight of the work force. Each difficulty was rewarded by another cut in food, or in longer work hours. Any good fortune was regarded as his rightful due."

"I suspected as much. Nogamu was at one time a very important man. He was the hadonra—demesne manager—of his father's estates. His family was found to be guilty of plotting against the Empire, and his own clan sold them all into slavery, those that were not hanged. He was never a good slave. It was thought that giving him responsibility for the camp might find some useful channel for his skills. It proved not to be the case.

"Is there a good man among the slaves who could command ably?"

Laurie inclined his head, then said, "Master, Pug here . . ."

"I think not. I have plans for you both."

Pug was surprised and wondered what he meant. He said, "Perhaps Chogana, master. He was a farmer, until his crops failed and he was sold into slavery for taxes. He has a level head."

The soldier clapped his hands once, and a guard was in the room in an instant. "Send for the slave Chogana."

The guard saluted and left. "It is good that he is Tsurani," said the soldier. "You barbarians do not know your place, and I hate to think what would happen should I leave one in charge. He would have my soldiers cutting the trees while the slaves stood guard."

There was a moment of silence, then Laurie laughed. It was a rich, deep sound. Hokanu smiled. Pug watched closely. The young man who had their lives in his hands seemed to be working hard at winning their trust. Laurie appeared to have taken a liking to him, but Pug held his feelings in check. He was further removed from the old Midkemian society, where war made noble and commoner comrades-in-arms, able to share meals and misery without regard for rank. One thing he had learned about the Tsurani early on was that they never for an instant forgot their station. Whatever was occurring in this hut was by this young soldier's design, not by chance. Hokanu seemed to feel Pug's eyes upon him and looked at him. Their eyes locked briefly before Pug dropped his as a slave is expected to do. For an instant a communication passed between them. It was as if the soldier had said: You do not believe that I am a friend. So be it, as long as you act your part.

With a wave of his hand, Hokanu said, "Return to your hut. Rest well, for we will leave after the noon meal."

They rose and bowed, then backed out of the hut. Pug walked in silence, but Laurie said, "I wonder where we are going." When no answer came, he added, "In any event, it will have to be a better place than this."

Pug wondered if it would be.

A HAND SHOOK Pug's shoulder, and he came awake. He had been dozing in the morning heat, taking advantage of the extra rest before he and Laurie left with the young noble after the noon meal. Chogana, the former farmer Pug had recommended, motioned for silence, pointing to where Laurie slept deeply.

Pug followed the old slave out of the hut, to sit in the shade of the building. Speaking slowly, as was his fashion, Chogana said, "My lord Hokanu tells me you were instrumental in my being selected slave master for the camp." His brown, seamed face looked dignified as he bowed his head toward Pug. "I am in your debt."

Pug returned the bow, formal and unusual in this camp. "There is no debt. You will conduct yourself as an overseer should. You will care well for our brothers."

Chogana's old face split in a grin, revealing teeth stained brown by years of chewing tateen nuts. The mildly narcotic nut—easily found in the swamp—did not reduce efficiency but made the work seem less harsh. Pug had avoided the habit, for no reasons he could voice, as had most of the Midkemians. It seemed somehow to signify a final surrender of will.

Chogana stared at the camp, his eyes narrowed to slits by the harsh light. It stood empty, except for the young lord's bodyguard and the cook's crew. In the distance the sounds of the work crew echoed through the trees.

"When I was a boy, on my father's farm in Szetac," began Chogana, "it was discovered I had a talent. I was investigated and found lacking." The meaning of that last statement was lost on Pug, but he didn't interrupt. "So I became a farmer like my father. But my talent was there. Sometimes I see things, Pug, things within men. As I grew, word of my talent spread, and people, mostly poor people, would come and ask for my advice. As a young man I was arrogant and charged much, telling of what I saw. When I was older, I was humble and took whatever was offered, but still I told what I saw. Either way, people left angry. Do you know why?" he asked with a chuckle. Pug shook his head. "Because they didn't come to hear the truth, they came to hear what they wanted to hear."

Pug shared Chogana's laugh. "So I pretended the talent went away, and after a time people stopped coming to my farm. But the talent never went away, Pug, and I still can see things, sometimes. I have seen something in you, and I would tell you before you leave forever. I will die in this camp, but you have a different fate before you. Will you listen?" Pug said he would, and Chogana said, "Within you there is a trapped power. What it is and what it means, I do not know."

Knowing the strange Tsurani attitude toward magicians, Pug felt sudden panic at the possibility someone might have sensed his former calling. To most he was just another slave in the camp, and to a few, a former squire.

Chogana continued, speaking with his eyes closed. "I dreamed about you, Pug. I saw you upon a tower, and you faced a fearsome foe." He opened his eyes. "I do not know what the dream may mean, but this you must know. Before you mount that tower to face your foe, you must seek your *wal*; it is that secret center of your being, the perfect place of peace within. Once you reside there, you are safe from all harm. Your flesh may suffer, even die, but within your *wal* you will endure in peace. Seek hard, Pug, for few men find their *wal*."

Chogana stood. "You will leave soon. Come, we must wake Laurie."

As they walked to the hut entrance, Pug said, "Chogana, thank you. But one thing: you spoke of a foe upon the tower. Could you mark him?"

Chogana laughed and bobbed his head up and down. "Oh yes, I saw him." He continued to chuckle as he climbed the steps to the hut. "He is the foe to be feared most by any man." Narrow eyes regarded Pug. "He was you."

PUG AND LAURIE sat on the steps of the temple, with six Tsurani guards lounging around. The guards had been civil—barely—for the entire journey. The travel had been tiring, if not difficult. With no horses, nor anything to substitute for them, every Tsurani not riding in a needra cart moved by power of shanks' mare, their own or others. Nobles were carried up and down the wide boulevards on litters borne on the backs of puffing, sweating slaves.

Pug and Laurie had been given the short, plain grey robes of slaves. Their loincloths, adequate in the swamps, were deemed unsightly for travel among Tsurani citizens. The Tsurani put some store upon modesty—if not as much as people in the Kingdom did.

They had come up the road along the coast of the great body of water called Battle Bay. Pug had thought that if it was a bay, it was larger than anything so named in Midkemia, for even from the high cliffs overlooking it, the other side could not be seen. After several days' travel they had entered cultivated pastureland and soon after could see the opposite shore closing in rapidly. Another few days on the road, and they had come to the city of Jamar.

Pug and Laurie watched the passing traffic, while Hokanu made an offering at the temple. The Tsurani seemed mad for colors. Here even the lowliest worker was likely to be dressed in a brightly colored short robe. Those with wealth could be seen in more flamboyant dress, covered with intricately executed designs. Only slaves lacked colorful dress.

Everywhere around the city, people thronged: farmers, traders, workers, and travelers. Lines of needras plodded by, pulling wagons filled with produce and goods. The sheer numbers of people overwhelmed Pug and Laurie, for the Tsurani seemed like ants scurrying about as if the commerce of the Empire could not wait upon the comfort of its citizens. Many who passed stopped to stare at the Midkemians, whom they regarded as giant barbarians. Their own height topped out at about five feet six inches, and even Pug was considered tall, having come to his full growth at five feet eight. For their part, the Midkemians had come to refer to the Tsurani as runts.

Pug and Laurie looked about. They waited in the center of the city, where the great temples were. Ten pyramids sat amid a series of parks differing in size. All were richly appointed with murals, both tiled and painted. From where they were, the young men could see three of the parks. Each was terraced, with miniature watercourses winding through, complete with tiny waterfalls. Dwarf trees, as well as large shade trees, dotted the grass-covered grounds of the parks. Strolling musicians played flutes and strange stringed instruments, producing alien, polytonal music, entertaining those who rested in the parks or passed by.

Laurie listened with rapt attention. "Listen to those halftones! And those diminished minors!" He sighed and looked down at the ground, his manner somber. "It's alien, but it's music." He looked at Pug, and the usual humor was missing from his voice. "If I could only play again." He glanced at the distant musicians. "I could even develop a taste for Tsurani music." Pug left him alone with his longings.

Pug glanced around the busy city square, attempting to sort out the impressions that had been coming without cease since entering the outer precinct of the city. Everywhere people hurried about their business. A short distance from the temples, they had passed through a market, not unlike those in Kingdom cities, but larger. The noise of hawkers and buyers, the smells, the heat, all reminded him of home in an odd way.

When Hokanu's party neared, commoners would step out of the way, for the guards at the head of the procession would call out "Shinzawai! Shinzawai!" letting everyone know a noble approached. Only once did the party give way in the city; a group of red-clad men, robed in cloaks of scarlet feathers. The one that Pug took to be a high priest wore a mask of wood fashioned to resemble a red skull, while the others had red painted faces. They blew reed whistles, and people scattered to clear their line of march. One of the soldiers made a sign of protection, and later Pug learned these men were the priests of Turakamu, the eater of hearts, brother to the goddess Sibi, she who was death.

Pug turned to a nearby guard and motioned for permission to speak. The guard nodded once, and Pug said, "Master, what god resides here?" as he pointed to the temple where Hokanu prayed.

"Ignorant barbarian," answered the soldier in a friendly manner, "the gods do not abide in these halls, but in the Upper and Lower Heavens. This temple is for men to make their devotions. Here my lord's son makes an offering and petitions to Chochocan, the good god of the Upper Heaven and his servant, Tomachaca, the god of peace, for good fortune for the Shinzawai."

When Hokanu returned, they started off again. They made their way through the city, Pug still studying the people they passed. The press was incredible, and Pug wondered how they managed to stand it. Like farmers in a city for the first time, Pug and Laurie kept gawking at the wonders of Jamar. Even the supposedly worldly troubadour would exclaim about this sight or that. Soon the guards were chuckling over the barbarians' obvious delight at the most mundane things.

Every building they passed was fashioned from wood and a translucent material, clothlike but rigid. A few, like the temples, were constructed with stone, but what was most remarkable was that every building they passed, from temple to worker's hut, was painted white, except for bordering beams and door frames, which were polished deep brown. Every open surface was decorated with colorful paintings. Animals, landscapes, deities, and battle scenes abounded. Everywhere was a riot of color to confound the eye.

To the north of the temples, across from one of the parks and facing a wide boulevard, stood a single building, set apart by open lawns bordered with hedges. Two guards, dressed in armor and helm similar to those of their own guards, stood watch at the door. They saluted Hokanu when he approached.

Without a word their other guards marched around the side of the house, leaving the slaves with the young officer. He signaled, and one of the door guards slid the large cloth-covered door aside. They entered an open hallway leading back, with doors on each side. Hokanu marched them to a rear door, which a house slave opened for them.

Pug and Laurie then discovered the house was fashioned like a square, with a large garden in the center, accessible from all sides. Near a bubbling pool sat an older man, dressed in a plain but rich-looking dark blue robe. He was consulting a scroll. He looked up when the three entered, and rose to greet Hokanu.

The young man removed his helm and then came to attention. Pug and Laurie stood slightly behind and said nothing. The man nodded, and Hokanu approached. They embraced, and the older man said, "My son, it is good to see you again. How were things at the camp?"

Hokanu made his report on the camp, briefly and to the point, leaving out nothing of importance. He then told of the actions taken to remedy the situation. "So the new overseer will see that the slaves have ample food and rest. He should increase production soon."

His father nodded. "I think you have acted wisely, my son. We shall have to send another in a few months' time to gauge progress, but things could not become any worse than they were. The Warlord demands higher production, and we border on falling into his bad graces."

He seemed to notice the slaves for the first time. "These?" was all he said, pointing at Laurie and Pug.

"They are unusual. I was thinking of our talk on the night before my brother went to the north. They may prove valuable."

"Have you spoken of this to anyone?" Firm lines set around his grey eyes. Even though much shorter, he somehow reminded Pug of Lord Borric.

"No, my father. Only those who took council that night—"

The lord of the house cut him off with a wave of the hand. "Save your remarks for later. 'Trust no secrets to a city.' Inform Septiem. We close the house and leave for our estates in the morning."

Hokanu bowed slightly, then turned to leave. "Hokanu." His father's voice stopped him. "You have done well." Pride plainly showing on his face, the young man left the garden.

The lord of the house sat again upon a bench of carved stone, next to a small fountain, and regarded the two slaves. "What are you called?"

"Pug, master."

"Laurie, master."

He seemed to derive some sort of insight from these simple statements. "Through that door," he said, pointing to the left, "is the way to the cookhouse. My hadonra is called Septiem. He will see to your care. Go now."

They bowed and left the garden. As they made their way through the house, Pug nearly knocked over a young girl coming around a corner. She was dressed in a slave's robe and carried a large bundle of washing. It went flying across the hall.

"Oh!" she cried. "I've just now washed these. Now I'll have to do them over." Pug quickly bent to help her pick them up. She was tall for a Tsurani, nearly Pug's height, and well proportioned. Her brown hair was tied back, and her brown eyes were framed by long, dark lashes. Pug stopped gathering the clothing and stared at her in open admiration. She hesitated under his scrutiny, then quickly picked up the rest of the clothes and hurried off. Laurie watched her trim figure retreat, tan legs shown to good advantage by the short slave's robe.

Laurie slapped Pug's shoulder. "Ha! I told you things would be looking up."

They left the house and approached the cookhouse, where the smell of hot food set their appetites on edge. "I think you've made an impression on that girl, Pug."

Pug had never had much experience with women and felt his ears start to burn. At the slave camp much of the talk was about women, and this, more than anything else, had kept him feeling like a boy. He turned to see if Laurie was having sport with him, then saw the blond singer looking behind him. He followed Laurie's gaze and caught a glimpse of a shyly smiling face pull back from a window in the house.

THE NEXT DAY the household of the Shinzawai Family was in an uproar. Slaves and servants hurried every which way making ready for the journey to the north. Pug and Laurie were left to themselves, as there was no one among the household staff free enough to assign them tasks. They sat in the shade of a large willowlike tree, enjoying the novelty of free time as they observed the furor.

"These people are crazy, Pug. I've seen less preparation for caravans. It looks as if they plan on taking everything with them."

"Maybe they are. These people no longer surprise me." Pug stood, leaning against the bole. "I've seen things that defy logic."

"True enough. But when you've seen as many different lands as I have, you learn that the more things look different, the more they are the same."

"What do you mean?"

Laurie rose and leaned on the other side of the tree. In low tones he said, "I'm not sure, but something is afoot, and we play a part, be sure. If we keep sharp, we may be able to turn it to our advantage. Always remember that. Should a man want something from you, you can always make a bargain, no matter what the apparent differences in your stations."

"Of course. Give him what he wants, and he'll let you live."

"You're too young to be so cynical," Laurie countered, with mirth sparkling in his eyes. "Tell you what. You leave the world-weary pose to old travelers such as myself, and I'll make sure that you don't miss a single opportunity."

Pug snorted. "What opportunity?"

"Well, for one thing," Laurie said, pointing behind Pug, "that little girl you nearly knocked over yesterday is appearing to have some difficulty in lifting those boxes." Pug, glancing back, saw the laundry girl struggling to stack several large crates ready to be loaded into wagons. "I think she might appreciate a little help, don't you think?"

Pug's confusion was evident on his face. "What . . . ?"

Laurie gave him a gentle push. "Off with you, dolt. A little help now, later . . . who knows?"

Pug stumbled. "Later?"

"Gods!" laughed Laurie, fetching Pug a playful kick in the rump.

The troubadour's humor was infectious, and Pug was smiling as he approached the girl. She was trying to lift a large wooden crate atop another. Pug took it from her. "Here, I can do that."

She stepped away, uncertain. "It's not heavy. It's just too high for me." She looked everywhere but at Pug.

Pug lifted the crate easily and placed it on top of the others, favoring his tender hand only a little. "There you are," he said, trying to sound casual.

The girl brushed back a stray wisp of hair that had fallen into her eyes. "You're a barbarian, aren't you?" She spoke hesitantly.

Pug flinched. "You call us that. I like to think I'm as civilized as the next man."

She blushed. "I didn't mean any offense. My people are called barbarians also. Anyone who's not a Tsurani is called that. I meant you're from that other world."

Pug nodded. "What's your name?"

She said, "Katala," then in a rush, "What is your name?"

"Pug."

She smiled. "That's a strange name. Pug." She seemed to like the sound of it.

Just then the hadonra, Septiem, an old but erect man with the bearing of a retired general, came around the house. "You two!" he snapped. "There's work to do! Don't stand there."

Katala ran back into the house, and Pug was left hesitating before the yellow-robed estate manager. "You! What's your name?"

"Pug, sir."

"I see that you and your blond giant friend have been given nothing to do. I'll have to remedy that. Call him over."

Pug sighed. So much for their free time. He waved for Laurie to come over, and they were put to work loading wagons.

20

▾▾

ESTATE

THE WEATHER HAD TURNED COOLER DURING THE LAST THREE WEEKS. Still it hinted at the summer's heat. The winter season in this land, if a season it properly was, lasted a mere six weeks, with brief cold rains out of the north. The trees held most of their bluish green leaves, and there was nothing to mark the passing of fall. In the four years Pug had abided in Tsuranuanni, there were none of the familiar signs that marked the passing seasons: no bird migrations, frost in the mornings, rains that froze, snow, or blooming of wild flowers. This land seemed eternally set in the soft amber of summer.

For the first few days of the journey, they had followed the highway from Jamar, northward to the city of Sulan-qu. The river Gagajin had carried a ceaseless clutter of boats and barges, while the highway was equally jammed with caravans, farmers' carts, and nobles riding in litters.

The Lord of the Shinzawai had departed the first day by boat for the Holy City, to attend the High Council. The household followed at a more leisurely pace. Hokanu paused outside the city of Sulan-qu long enough to pay a social call upon the Lady of the Acoma, and Pug and Laurie found the opportunity to gossip with another Midkemian slave, recently captured. The news of the war was disheartening. No change since the last they had heard; the stalemate continued.

At the Holy City, the Lord of the Shinzawai joined his son and the retinue on its journey to the Shinzawai estates, outside the City of Silmani. From then, the trek northward had been uneventful.

The Shinzawai caravan was approaching the boundaries of the family's northern estates. Pug and Laurie had little to do along the way except occasional chores: dumping the cook pots, cleaning up needra droppings, loading and unloading supplies. Now they were riding on the back of a wagon, feet dangling over the rear. Laurie bit into a ripe jomach fruit, something like a large green pomegranate with the flesh of a watermelon. Spitting out seeds, he said, "How's the hand?"

Pug studied his right hand, examining the red puckered scar that ran across the palm. "It's still stiff. I expect it's as healed as it will ever be."

Laurie took a look. "Don't think you'll ever carry a sword again." He grinned.

Pug laughed. "I doubt you will either. I somehow don't think they'll be finding a place for you in the Imperial Horse Lance."

Laurie spat a burst of seeds, bouncing them off the nose of the needra who pulled the wagon behind them. The six-legged beast snorted, and the driver waved his steering stick angrily at them. "Except for the fact that the Emperor doesn't have any lancers, due to the fact that he also doesn't have any horses, I can't think of a finer choice."

Pug laughed derisively.

"I'll have you know, fella-me-lad," said Laurie in aristocratic tones, "that we troubadours are often beset by a less savory sort of customer, brigands and cutthroats seeking our hard-earned wages—scant though they may be. If one doesn't develop the ability to defend oneself, one doesn't stay in business, if you catch my meaning."

Pug smiled. He knew that a troubadour was nearly sacrosanct in a town, for should he be harmed or robbed, word would spread, and no other would ever come there again. But on the road it was a different matter. He had no doubt of Laurie's ability to take care of himself, but wasn't about to let him use that pompous tone and sit without a rejoinder. As he was about to speak, though, he was cut off by shouts coming from the front of the caravan. Guards came rushing forward, and Laurie turned to his shorter companion. "What do you suppose that is all about?"

Not waiting for an answer, he jumped down and ran forward. Pug followed. As they reached the head of the caravan, behind the Lord of the Shinzawai's litter, they could see shapes advancing up the road toward them. Laurie grabbed Pug's sleeve. "Riders!"

Pug could scarcely believe his eyes, for indeed it appeared that riders were approaching along the road from the Shinzawai manor. As they got closer, he could see that, rather than riders, there was one horseman and three cho-ja, all three a rich dark blue color.

The rider, a young brown-haired Tsurani, taller than most, dismounted. His movement was clumsy, and Laurie observed, "They will never pose any military threat if that's the best seat they can keep. Look, there is no saddle, nor bridle, only a rude hackamore fashioned from leather straps. And the poor horse looks like it hasn't been properly groomed for a month."

The curtain of the litter was pulled back as the rider approached. The slaves put the litter down, and the Lord of the Shinzawai got out. Hokanu had reached his father's side, from his place among the guards at the rear of the caravan, and was embracing the rider, exchanging greetings. The rider then embraced the Lord of the Shinzawai. Pug and Laurie could hear the rider say, "Father! It is good to see you."

The Shinzawai lord said, "Kasumi! It is good to see my firstborn son. When did you return?"

"Less than a week ago. I would have come to Jamar, but I heard that you were due here, so I waited."

"I am glad. Who are these with you?" He indicated the creatures.

"This," he said, pointing to the foremost, "is Strike Leader X'calak, back from fighting the short ones under the mountains on Midkemia."

The creature stepped forward and raised his right hand—very humanlike—in salute, and in a high, piping voice said, "Hail, Kamatsu, Lord of the Shinzawai. Honors to your house."

The Lord of the Shinzawai bowed slightly from the waist. "Greetings, X'calak. Honors to your hive. The cho-ja are always welcome guests."

The creature stepped back and waited. The lord turned to look at the horse. "What is this upon which you sit, my son?"

"A horse, Father. A creature the barbarians ride into battle. I've told you of them before. It is a truly marvelous creature. On its back I can run faster than the swiftest cho-ja runner."

"How do you stay on?"

The older Shinzawai son laughed. "With great difficulty, I'm afraid. The barbarians have tricks to it I have yet to learn."

Hokanu smiled. "Perhaps we can arrange for lessons."

Kasumi slapped him playfully on the back. "I have asked several barbarians, but unfortunately they were all dead."

"I have two here who are not."

Kasumi looked past his brother and saw Laurie, standing a full head taller than the other slaves who had gathered around. "So I see. Well, we must ask him. Father, with your permission, I will ride back to the house and have all made ready for your homecoming."

Kamatsu embraced his son and agreed. The older son grabbed a handful of mane, and with an athletic leap, remounted. With a wave, he rode off.

Pug and Laurie quickly returned to their places on the wagon. Laurie asked, "Have you seen the like of those things before?"

Pug nodded. "Yes. The Tsurani call them the cho-ja. They live in large hive mounds, like ants. The Tsurani slaves I spoke with in the camp tell me they have been around as long as can be remembered. They are loyal to the Empire, though I seem to remember someone saying that each hive has its own queen."

Laurie peered around the front of the wagon, hanging on with one hand. "I wouldn't like to face one on foot. Look at the way they run."

Pug said nothing. The older Shinzawai son's remark about the short ones under the mountain brought back old memories. If Tomas is alive, he thought, he is a man now. If he is alive.

THE SHINZAWAI MANOR was huge. It was easily the biggest single building —short of temples and palaces—that Pug had seen. It sat atop a hill, commanding a view of the countryside for miles. The house was square, like the one in Jamar, but several times the size. The town house could easily have fit inside this one's central garden. Behind it were the outbuildings, cookhouse, and slave quarters.

Pug craned his neck to take in the garden, for they were walking quickly through, and there was little time to absorb all of it. The hadonra, Septiem, scolded him. "Don't tarry."

Pug quickened his step and fell in beside Laurie. Still, on a brief viewing, the garden was impressive. Several shade trees had been planted beside three pools that sat in the midst of miniature trees and flowering plants. Stone benches had been placed for contemplative rest, and paths of fine pebble gravel wandered throughout. Around this tiny park the building rose, three stories tall. The top two stories had balconies, and several staircases rose to connect them. Servants could be seen hurrying along the upper levels, but there appeared to be no one else in the garden, or at least that portion they had crossed.

They reached a sliding door, and Septiem turned to face them. In stern tones he said, "You two barbarians will watch your manners before the lords of this house, or by the gods, I'll have every inch of skin off your backs. Now make sure you do all that I've told you, or you'll wish that Master Hokanu had left you to rot in the swamps."

He slid the door to one side and announced the slaves. The command for them to enter was given, and Septiem shooed them inside.

They found themselves in a colorfully lit room, the light coming through the large translucent door covered with a painting. On the walls hung carvings, tapestries, and paintings, all done in fine style, small and delicate. The floor was covered, in Tsurani fashion, with a thick pile of cushions. Upon a large cushion Kamatsu, Lord of the Shinzawai, sat; across from him were his two sons. All were dressed in the short robes of expensive fabric and cut they used when off duty. Pug and Laurie stood with their eyes downcast until they were spoken to.

Hokanu spoke first. "The blond giant is called Loh-'re, and the more normal-sized one is Poog."

Laurie started to open his mouth, but a quick elbow from Pug silenced him before he could speak.

The older son noticed the exchange, and said, "You would speak?"

Laurie looked up, then quickly down again. The instructions had been clear: not to speak until commanded to. Laurie wasn't sure the question was a command.

The lord of the house said, "Speak."

Laurie looked at Kasumi. "I am Laurie, master. Lor-ee. And my friend is Pug, not Poog."

Hokanu looked taken aback at being corrected, but the older brother nodded and pronounced the names several times over, until he spoke them correctly. He then said, "Have you ridden horses?"

Both slaves nodded. Kasumi said, "Good. Then you can show me the best way."

Pug's gaze wandered as much as was possible with his head down, but something caught his eye. Next to the Lord of the Shinzawai sat a game board and what looked like familiar figures. Kamatsu noticed and said, "You know this game?" He reached over and brought the board forward, so that it lay before him.

Pug said, "Master, I know the game. We call it chess."

Hokanu looked at his brother, who leaned forward. "As several have said, Father, there has been contact with the barbarians before."

His father waved away the comment. "It is a theory." To Pug he said, "Sit here and show me how the pieces move."

Pug sat and tried to remember what Kulgan had taught him. He had been an indifferent student of the game, but knew a few basic openings. He moved a pawn forward and said, "This piece may move forward only one space, except when it is first moved, master. Then it may move two." The lord of the house nodded, motioning that he should continue. "This piece is a knight and moves like so," said Pug.

After he had demonstrated the moves of the various pieces, the Lord of the Shinzawai said, "We call this game shāh. The pieces are called by different names, but it is the same. Come, we will play."

Kamatsu gave the white pieces to Pug. He opened with a conventional king's pawn move, and Kamatsu countered. Pug played badly and was quickly beaten. The others watched the entire game without a sound. When it was over, the lord said, "Do you play well, among your people?"

"No, master. I play poorly."

He smiled, his eyes wrinkling at the edges. "Then I would guess that your people are not as barbarous as is commonly held. We will play again soon."

He nodded to his older son, and Kasumi rose. Bowing to his father, he said to Pug and Laurie, "Come."

They bowed to the lord of the house and followed Kasumi out of the room. He led them through the house, to a smaller room with sleeping pallets and cushions. "You will sleep here. My room is next door. I would have you at hand at all times."

Laurie spoke up boldly. "What does the master want of us?"

Kasumi regarded him for a moment. "You barbarians will never make good slaves. You forget your place too often."

Laurie started to stammer an apology but was cut off. "It is of little matter. You are to teach me things, Laurie. You will teach me to ride, and how to speak your language. Both of you. I would learn what those" —he paused, then made a flat, nasal wa-wa-wa sound—"noises mean when you speak to each other."

Further conversation was cut off by the sound of a single chime that reverberated throughout the house. Kasumi said, "A Great One comes. Stay in your rooms. I must go to welcome him with my father." He hurried off, leaving the two Midkemians to sit in their new quarters wondering at this newest twist in their lives.

TWICE DURING the following two days, Pug and Laurie glimpsed the Shinzawai's important visitor. He was much like the Shinzawai lord in appearance, but thinner, and he wore the black robe of a Tsurani Great One. Pug asked a few questions of the house staff and gained a little information. Pug and Laurie had seen nothing that compared with the awe in which the Great Ones were held by the Tsurani. They seemed a power apart, and with what little understanding of Tsurani social reality Pug had, he couldn't exactly comprehend how they fit into the scheme of things. At first he had thought they were under some social stigma, for all he was ever told was that the Great Ones were "outside the law." He then was made to understand, by an exasperated Tsurani slave who couldn't believe Pug's ignorance of important matters, that the Great Ones had little or no social constraints in exchange for some nameless service to the Empire.

Pug had made a discovery during this time that lightened the alien feeling of his captivity somewhat. Behind the needra pens he had found a kennel full of yapping, tail-wagging dogs. They were the only Midkemian-like animals he had seen on Kelewan, and he felt an unexplained joy at their presence. He had rushed back to their room to fetch Laurie and had brought him to the kennel. Now they sat in one of the runs, amid a group of playful canines.

Laurie laughed at their boisterous play. They were unlike the Duke's hunting hounds, being longer of leg, and more gaunt. Their ears were pointed, and perked at every sound.

"I've seen their like before, in Gulbi. It's a town in the Great Northern Trade Route of Kesh. They are called greyhounds and are used to run down the fast cats and antelope of the grasslands near the Valley of the Sun."

The kennel master, a thin, droopy-eyelidded slave named Rachmad, came over and watched them suspiciously. "What are you doing here?"

Laurie regarded the dour man and playfully pulled the muzzle of a rambunctious puppy. "We haven't seen dogs since we left our homeland, Rachmad. Our master is busy with the Great One, so we thought we would visit your fine kennel."

At mention of his "fine kennel" the gloomy countenance brightened considerably. "I try to keep the dogs healthy. We must keep them locked up, for they try to harry the cho-ja, who like them not at all." For a moment Pug thought perhaps they had been taken from Midkemia as the horse had been. When he asked where they had come from, Rachmad looked at him as if he were crazy. "You speak like you have been too long in the sun. There have always been dogs." With that final pronouncement on the matter, he judged the conversation closed and left.

LATER THAT NIGHT, Pug awoke to find Laurie entering their room. "Where have you been?"

"Shh! You want to wake the whole household? Go back to sleep."

"Where did you go?" Pug asked in hushed tones.

Laurie could be seen grinning in the dim light. "I paid a visit to a certain cook's assistant, for . . . a chat."

"Oh. Almorella?"

"Yes," came the cheerful reply. "She's quite a girl." The young slave who served in the kitchen had been making big eyes at Laurie ever since the caravan had arrived four days ago.

After a moment of silence, Laurie said, "You should cultivate a few friends yourself. Gives a whole new look to things."

"I'll bet," Pug said, disapproval mixed with more than a little envy. Almorella was a bright and cheerful girl, near Pug's age, with merry dark eyes.

"That little Katala, now. She has her eye on you, I'm thinking."

Cheeks burning, Pug threw a cushion at his friend. "Oh, shut up and go to sleep."

Laurie stifled a laugh. He retired to his pallet and left Pug alone in thought.

THERE WAS THE faint promise of rain on the wind, and Pug welcomed the coolness he felt in its touch. Laurie was sitting astride Kasumi's horse, and the young officer stood by and watched. Laurie had directed Tsurani craftsmen as they fashioned a saddle and bridle for the mount and was now demonstrating their use.

"This horse is combat trained," Laurie shouted. "He can be neck reined"—he demonstrated by laying the reins on one side of the horse's neck, then the other—"or he can be turned by using your legs." He raised his hands and showed the older son of the house how this was done.

For three weeks they had been instructing the young noble in riding, and he had shown natural ability. Laurie jumped from the horse, and Kasumi took his place. The Tsurani rode roughly at first, the saddle feeling strange under him. As he bounced by, Pug called out, "Master, grip him firmly with your lower leg!" The horse sensed the pressure and picked up a quick trot. Rather than be troubled by the increase in speed, Kasumi looked enraptured. "Keep your heels down!" shouted Pug. Then, without instructions from either slave, Kasumi kicked the horse hard in the sides and had the animal running over the fields.

Laurie watched him vanish across the meadow and said, "He's either a natural horseman or he's going to kill himself."

Pug nodded. "I think he's got the knack. He's certainly not lacking courage."

Laurie pulled up a long stem of grass from the ground and put it between his teeth. He hunkered down and scratched the ear of a bitch who lay at his feet, as much to distract the dog from running after the horse as to play with her. She rolled over on her back and playfully chewed his hand.

Laurie turned his attention to Pug. "I wonder what game our young friend is playing at."

Pug shrugged. "What do you mean?"

"Remember when we first arrived? I heard Kasumi was about to head out with his cho-ja companions. Well, those three cho-ja soldiers left this morning—which is why Bethel here is out of her pen—and I heard some gossip that the orders of the older son of the Shinzawai were suddenly changed. Put that together with these riding and language lessons and what do you have?"

Pug stretched. "I don't know."

"I don't know either." Laurie sounded disgusted. "But these matters are of high import." He looked across the plain and said lightly, "All I ever wanted to do was to travel and tell my stories, sing my songs, and someday find a widow who owned an inn."

Pug laughed. "I think you would find tavern keeping dull business after all this fine adventure."

"Some fine adventuring. I'm riding along with a bunch of provincial militia and run right smack into the entire Tsurani army. Since then I've been beaten several times, spent over four months mucking about in the swamps, walked over half this world—"

"Ridden in a wagon, as I remember."

"Well, traveled over half this world, and now I'm giving riding lessons to Kasumi Shinzawai, older son of a lord of Tsuranuanni. Not the stuff great ballads are made of."

Pug smiled ruefully. "You could have been four *years* in the swamps. Consider yourself lucky. At least you can count on being here tomorrow. At least as long as Septiem doesn't catch you creeping around the kitchen late at night."

Laurie studied Pug closely. "I know you're joking. About Septiem, I mean. It has occurred to me several times to ask you, Pug. Why do you never speak of your life before you were captured?"

Pug looked away absently. "I guess it's a habit I picked up in the swamp camp. It doesn't pay to remind yourself of what you used to be. I've seen brave men die because they couldn't forget they were born free."

Laurie pulled at the dog's ear. "But things are different here."

"Are they? Remember what you said back in Jamar about a man wanting something from you. I think the more comfortable you become here, the easier it is for them to get whatever it is they want from you.

This Shinzawai lord is no one's fool." Seemingly shifting topics, he said, "Is it better to train a dog or horse with a whip or with kindness?"

Laurie looked up. "What? Why, with kindness, but you have to use discipline also."

Pug nodded. "We are being shown the same consideration as Bethel and her kind, I think. But we still are slaves. Never forget that."

Laurie looked out over the field for a long time and said nothing.

The pair were rousted from their thoughts by the shouts of the older son of the house as he rode back into view. He pulled the horse up before them and jumped down. "He flies," he said, in his broken King's Tongue. Kasumi was an apt student and was picking up the language quickly. He supplemented his language lessons with a constant stream of questions about the lands and people of Midkemia. There was not a single aspect of life in the Kingdom that he seemed uninterested in. He had asked for examples of the most mundane things, such as the manner in which one bargains with tradespeople, and the proper forms of address when speaking to people of different ranks.

Kasumi led the horse back to the shed that had been built for him, and Pug watched for any sign of footsoreness. They had fashioned shoes for him from wood treated with resin, by trial and error, but these seemed to be holding up well enough. As he walked, Kasumi said, "I have been thinking about a thing. I don't understand how your King rules, with all you have said about this Congress of Lords. Please explain this thing."

Laurie looked at Pug with an eyebrow raised. While no more an authority on Kingdom politics than Laurie, he seemed better able to explain what he knew. Pug said, "The congress elects the King, though it is mostly a matter of form."

"Form?"

"A tradition. The heir to the throne is always elected, except when there is no clear successor. It is considered the best way to stem civil war, for the ruling of the congress is final." He explained how the Prince of Krondor had deferred to his nephew, and how the congress had acquiesced to his wishes. "How is it with the Empire?"

Kasumi thought, then said, "Perhaps not so different. Each emperor is the elect of the gods, but from what you have told me he is unlike your King. He rules in the Holy City, but his leadership is spiritual. He protects us from the wrath of the gods."

Laurie asked, "Who then rules?"

They reached the shed, and Kasumi took the saddle and bridle off the horse and began rubbing him down. "Here it is different from your land." He seemed to have difficulty with the language and shifted into Tsurani. "A Ruling Lord of a family is the absolute authority upon his estate. Each family belongs to a clan, and the most influential lord in the clan is Warchief. Within that clan, each other lord of a family holds certain powers depending upon influence. The Shinzawai belong to the Kanazawai Clan. We are the second most powerful family in that clan next to the Keda. My father in his youth was commander of the clan armies, a Warchief, what you would call a general. The position of families shifts from generation to generation, so that it is unlikely I will reach so exalted a position.

"The leading lords of each clan sit in the High Council. They advise the Warlord. He rules in the name of the Emperor, though the Emperor could overrule him."

"Does the Emperor in fact ever overrule the Warlord?" asked Laurie.

"Never."

"How is the Warlord chosen?" asked Pug.

"It is difficult to explain. When the old Warlord dies, the clans meet. It is a large gathering of lords, for not only the council comes, but also the heads of every family. They meet and plot, and sometimes blood feuds develop, but in the end a new Warlord is elected."

Pug brushed back the hair from his eyes. "Then what is to keep the Warlord's clan from claiming the office, if they are the most powerful?"

Kasumi looked troubled. "It is not an easy thing to explain. Perhaps you would have to be Tsurani to understand. There are laws, but more important, there are customs. No matter how powerful a clan becomes, or a family within it, only the lord of one of five families may be elected Warlord. They are the Keda, Tonmargu, Minwanabi, Oaxatucan, and the Xacatecas. So there are only five lords who may be considered. This Warlord is an Oaxatucan, so the light of the Kanazawai clan burns dimly. His clan, the Omechan, is in ascension now. Only the Minwanabi rival them, and for the present they are allied in the war effort. That is the way of it."

Laurie shook his head. "This family and clan business makes our own politics seem simple."

Kasumi laughed. "That is not politics. Politics is the province of the parties."

"Parties?" asked Laurie, obviously getting lost in the conversation.

"There are many parties. The Blue Wheel, the Golden Flower, the Jade Eye, the Party for Progress, the War Party, and others. Families may belong to different parties, each trying to further their own needs. Sometimes families from the same clan will belong to different parties.

Sometimes they switch alliances to suit their needs for the moment. Other times they may support two parties at once, or none."

"It seems a most unstable government," remarked Laurie.

Kasumi laughed. "It has lasted for over two thousand years. We have an old saying: 'In the High Council, there is no brother.' Remember that and you may understand."

Pug weighed his next question carefully. "Master, in all this you have not mentioned the Great Ones. Why is that?"

Kasumi stopped rubbing down the horse and looked at Pug for a moment, then resumed his ministrations. "They have nothing to do with politics. They are outside the law and have no clan." He paused again. "Why do you ask?"

"It is only that they seem to command a great amount of respect, and since one has called here so recently, I thought you could enlighten me."

"They are given respect because the fate of the Empire is at all times in their hands. It is a grave responsibility. They renounce all their ties, and few have personal lives beyond their community of magicians. Those with families live apart, and their children are sent to live with their former families when they come of age. It is a difficult thing. They make many sacrifices."

Pug watched Kasumi closely. He seemed somehow troubled by what he was saying. "The Great One who came to see my father was, when a boy, a member of this family. He was my uncle. It is difficult for us now, for he must observe the formalities and cannot claim kinship. It would be better if he stayed away, I think." The last was spoken softly.

"Why is that, master?" Laurie asked, in hushed tones.

"Because it is hard for Hokanu. Before he became my brother, he was that Great One's son."

They finished caring for the horse and left the shack. Bethel ran ahead, for she knew it was close to feeding time. As they passed the kennel, Rachmad called her over, and she joined the other dogs.

The entire way there was no conversation, and Kasumi entered his room with no further remark for either of the Midkemians. Pug sat on his pallet, waiting for the call for dinner, and thought about what he had learned. For all their strange ways, the Tsurani were much like other men. He found this somehow both comforting and troublesome.

TWO WEEKS LATER, Pug was faced with another problem to mull over. Katala had been making it obvious she was less than pleased with Pug's lack of attention. In little ways at first, then with more blatant signs, she had tried to spark his interest. Finally things had come to a head when he had run into her behind the cook shed earlier that afternoon.

Laurie and Kasumi were trying to build a small lute, with the aid of a Shinzawai woodcrafter. Kasumi had expressed interest in the music of the troubadour and, the last few days, had watched closely while Laurie argued with the artisan over the selection of proper grains, the way to cut the wood, and the manner of fashioning the instrument. He was perplexed about whether or not needra gut would make suitable strings, and a thousand other details. Pug had found all this less than engrossing, and after a few days had found every excuse to wander off. The smell of curing wood reminded him too much of cutting trees in the swamp for him to enjoy being around the resin pots in the woodcarver's shed.

This afternoon he had been lying in the shade of the cook shed when Katala came around the corner. His stomach constricted at the sight of her. He thought her very attractive, but each time he had tried to speak to her, he found he couldn't think of anything to say. He would simply make a few inane remarks, become embarrassed, then hurry off. Lately he had taken to saying nothing. As she had approached this afternoon, he had smiled noncommittally, and she started to walk past. Suddenly she had turned and looked as if near to tears.

"What is the matter with me? Am I so ugly that you can't stand the sight of me?"

Pug had sat speechless, his mouth open. She had stood for a moment, then kicked him in the leg. "Stupid barbarian," she had sniffed, then run off.

Now he sat in his room, feeling confused and uneasy over this afternoon's encounter. Laurie was carving pegs for his lute. Finally he put knife and wood aside and said, "What's troubling you, Pug? You look as if they're promoting you to slave master and sending you back to the swamp."

Pug lay back on his pallet, staring at the ceiling. "It's Katala."

"Oh," Laurie said.

"What do you mean, 'Oh'?"

"Nothing, except that Almorella tells me the girl has been impossible for the last two weeks, and you look about as bright as a poleaxed steer these days. What's the matter?"

"I don't know. She's just . . . she's just . . . She kicked me today."

Laurie threw back his head and laughed. "Why in the name of heaven did she do that?"

"I don't know. She just kicked me."

"What did you do?"

"I didn't do anything."

"Ha!" Laurie exploded with mirth. "That's the trouble, Pug. There is only one thing I know of that a woman hates more than a man she doesn't like paying her too much attention—and that's lack of attention from a man she does like."

Pug looked despondent. "I thought it was something like that."

Surprise registered on Laurie's face. "What is it? Don't you like her?"

Leaning forward, his elbows on his knees, Pug said, "It's not that. I like her. She's very pretty and seems nice enough. It's just that . . ."

"What?"

Pug glanced sharply over at his friend, to see if he was being mocked. Laurie was smiling, but in a friendly, reassuring way. Pug continued. "It's just . . . there's someone else."

Laurie's mouth fell open, then snapped shut. "Who? Except for Almorella, Katala's the prettiest wench I've seen on this gods-forsaken world." He sighed. "In honesty, she's prettier than Almorella, though only a little. Besides, I've not seen you ever speak to another woman, and I'd have noticed you skulking off with anyone."

Pug shook his head and looked down. "No, Laurie. I mean back home."

Laurie's mouth popped open again, then he fell over backward and groaned. " 'Back home!' What am I to do with this child? He's bereft of all wit!" He pulled himself up on an elbow and said, "Can this be Pug speaking? The lad who counsels me to put the past behind? The one who insists that dwelling on how things were at home leads only to a quick death?"

Pug ignored the sting of the questions. "This is different."

"How is it different? By Ruthia—who in her more tender moments protects fools, drunks, and minstrels—how can you tell me this is different? Do you imagine for a moment you have one hope in ten times ten thousand of ever seeing this girl again, whoever she is?"

"I know, but thinking of Carline has kept me from losing my mind more times . . ." He sighed loudly. "We all need one dream, Laurie."

Laurie studied his young friend for a quiet moment. "Yes, Pug, we all need one dream. Still," he added brightly, "a dream is one thing; a living, breathing, warm woman is another." Seeing Pug become irritated at the remark, he switched topics. "Who is Carline, Pug?"

"My lord Borric's daughter."

Laurie's eyes grew round. "Princess Carline?" Pug nodded. Laurie's voice showed amusement. "The most eligible noble daughter in the

Western Realm after the daughter of the Prince of Krondor? There are sides to you I never would have thought possible! Tell me about her."

Pug began to speak slowly at first, telling of his boyhood infatuation for her, then of how their relationship developed. Laurie remained silent, putting aside questions, letting Pug relieve himself of the pent-up emotions of years. Finally Pug said, "Perhaps that's what bothers me so much about Katala. In certain ways Katala's like Carline. They've both got strong wills and make their moods known."

Laurie nodded, not saying anything. Pug lapsed into silence, then after a moment said, "When I was at Crydee, I thought for a time I was in love with Carline. But I don't know. Is that strange?"

Laurie shook his head. "No, Pug. There are many ways to love someone. Sometimes we want love so much, we're not too choosy about who we love. Other times we make love such a pure and noble thing, no poor human can ever meet our vision. But for the most part, love is a recognition, an opportunity to say, 'There is something about you I cherish.' It doesn't entail marriage, or even physical love. There's love of parents, love of city or nation, love of life, and love of people. All different, all love. But tell me, do you find your feelings for Katala much as they were for Carline?"

Pug shrugged and smiled. "No, they're not, not quite the same. With Carline, I felt as if I had to keep her away, you know, at arm's length. Sort of keeping control of what went on, I think."

Laurie probed lightly. "And Katala?"

Pug shrugged again. "I don't know. It's different. I don't feel as if I have to keep her under control. It's more as if there are things I want to tell her, but I don't know how. Like the way I got all jammed up inside when she smiled at me the first time. I could talk to Carline, when she kept quiet and let me. Katala keeps quiet, but I don't know what to say." He paused a moment, then made a sound that was half sigh, half groan. "Just thinking about Katala makes me hurt, Laurie."

Laurie lay back, a friendly chuckle escaping his lips. "Aye, it's well I've known that ache. And I must admit your taste runs to interesting women. From what I can see, Katala's a prize. And the Princess Carline . . ."

A little snappishly, Pug said, "I'll make a point of introducing you when we get back."

Laurie ignored the tone. "I'll hold you to that. Look, all I mean is it seems you've developed an excellent knack for finding worthwhile women." A little sadly, he said, "I wish I could claim as much. My life has been mostly caught up with tavern wenches, farmers' daughters, and common street whores. I don't know what to tell you."

"Laurie," said Pug. Laurie sat up and looked at his friend. "I don't know . . . I don't know what to do."

Laurie studied Pug a moment, then comprehension dawned and he threw back his head, laughing. He could see Pug's anger rising and put his hands up in supplication. "I'm sorry, Pug. I didn't mean to embarrass you. It was just not what I expected to hear."

Somewhat placated, Pug said, "I was young when I was captured, less than sixteen years of age. I was never of a size like the other boys, so the girls didn't pay much attention to me, until Carline, I mean, and after I became a squire, they were afraid to talk to me. After that . . . Damn it all, Laurie. I've been in the swamps for four years. What chance have I had to know a woman?"

Laurie sat quietly for a moment, and the tension left the room. "Pug, I never would have imagined, but as you said, when have you had the time?"

"Laurie, what am I to do?"

"What would you like to do?" Laurie looked at Pug, his expression showing concern.

"I would like to . . . go to her. I think. I don't know."

Laurie rubbed his chin. "Look, Pug, I never thought I'd have this sort of talk with anyone besides a son someday if I ever have one. I wasn't meaning to make sport of you. You just caught me off guard." He looked away, gathering his thoughts, then said, "My father threw me out when I was just shy twelve years old; I was the oldest boy, and he had seven other mouths to feed. And I was never much for farming. A neighbor boy and I walked to Tyr-Sog and spent a year living on the streets. He joined a mercenary band as a cook's monkey and later became a soldier. I hooked up with a traveling troupe of musicians. I apprenticed to a jongleur from whom I learned the songs, sagas, and ballads, and I traveled.

"I came quickly to my growth, a man at thirteen. There was a woman in the troupe, a widow of a singer, traveling with her brothers and cousins. She was just past twenty, but seemed very old to me then. She was the one who introduced me to the games of men and women." He stopped for a moment, reliving memories long forgotten.

Laurie smiled. "It was over fifteen years ago, Pug. But I can still see her face. We were both a little lost. It was never a planned thing. It just happened one afternoon on the road.

"She was . . . kind." He looked at Pug. "She knew I was scared, despite my bravado." He smiled and closed his eyes. "I can still see the sun in the trees behind her face, and the smell of her mingled with the scent of wildflowers." Opening his eyes he said, "We spent the next two years together, while I learned to sing. Then I left the troupe."

"What happened?" Pug asked, for this was a new story to him. Laurie had never spoken of his youth before.

"She married again. He was a good man, an innkeeper on the road from Malac's Cross to Durrony's Vale. His wife had died the year before of fever, leaving him with two small sons. She tried to explain things to me, but I wouldn't listen. What did I know? I was not quite sixteen, and the world was a simple place."

Pug nodded. "I know what you mean."

Laurie said, "Look, what I'm trying to say is that I understand the problem. I can explain how things work. . . ."

Pug said, "I know that. I wasn't raised by monks."

"But you don't know *how* things work."

Pug nodded as they both laughed. "I think you should just go to the girl and make your feelings known," said Laurie.

"Just talk to her?"

"Of course. Love is like a lot of things, it is always best done with the head. Save mindless efforts for mindless things. Now go."

"Now?" Pug looked panic-stricken.

"You can't start any sooner, right?"

Pug nodded and without a word left. He walked down the dark and quiet corridors, outside to the slave quarters, and found his way to her door. He raised his hand to knock on the door frame, then stopped. He stood quietly for a moment trying to make up his mind what to do, when the door slid open. Almorella stood in the doorway, clutching her robe about her, her hair disheveled. "Oh," she whispered, "I thought it was Laurie. Wait a moment." She disappeared into the room, then shortly reappeared with a bundle of things in her arms. She patted Pug's arm and set off in the direction of his and Laurie's room.

Pug stood at the door, then slowly entered. He could see Katala lying under a blanket on her pallet. He stepped over to where she lay and squatted next to her. He touched her shoulder and softly spoke her name. She came awake and sat up suddenly, gathered her blanket around her, and said, "What are you doing here?"

"I . . . I wanted to talk to you." Once started, the words came out in a tumbling rush. "I am sorry if I've done anything to make you angry with me. Or haven't done anything. I mean, Laurie said that if you don't do something when someone expects you to, that's as bad as paying too much attention. I'm not sure, you see." She covered her mouth to hide a giggle, for she could see his distress in spite of the gloom. "What I mean . . . what I mean is I'm sorry. Sorry for what I've done. Or didn't do . . ."

She silenced him by placing her fingertips across his mouth. Her arm snaked out and around his neck, pulling his head downward. She kissed him slowly, then said, "Silly. Go close the door."

THEY LAY TOGETHER, Katala's arm across Pug's chest, while he stared at the ceiling. She made sleepy sounds, and he ran his hands through her thick hair and across her soft shoulder.

"What?" she asked sleepily.

"I was just thinking that I haven't been happier since I was made a member of the Duke's court."

" 'Sgood." She came a bit more awake. "What's a duke?"

Pug thought for a moment. "It's like a lord here, only different. My Duke was cousin to the King, and the third most powerful man in the Kingdom."

She snuggled closer to him. "You must have been important to be part of the court of such a man."

"Not really; I did him a service and was rewarded for it." He didn't think he wanted to bring up Carline's name here. Somehow his boyhood fantasies about the Princess seemed childish in light of this night.

Katala rolled over onto her stomach. She raised her head and rested it on a hand, forming a triangle with her arm. "I wish things could be different."

"How so, love?"

"My father was a farmer in Thuril. We are among the last free people in Kelewan. If we could go there, you could take a position with the Coaldra, the Council of Warriors. They always have need for resourceful men. Then we could be together."

"We're together here, aren't we?"

Katala kissed him lightly. "Yes, dear Pug, we are. But we both remember what it was to be free, don't we?"

Pug sat up. "I try to put that sort of thing out of my mind."

She put her arms around him, holding him as she would a child. "It must have been terrible in the swamps. We hear stories, but no one knows," she said softly.

"It is well that you don't."

She kissed him, and soon they returned to that timeless, safe place shared by two, all thoughts of things terrible and alien forgotten. For the rest of the night they took pleasure in each other, discovering a depth of feeling new to each. Pug couldn't tell if she had known other men before, and didn't ask. It wasn't important to him. The only important thing was being there, with her, now. He was awash in a sea of new delights and emotions. He didn't understand his feelings entirely, but there was little doubt what he felt for Katala was more real, more compelling, than the worshipful, confused longings he had known when with Carline.

WEEKS PASSED, and Pug found his life falling into a reassuring routine. He spent occasional evenings with the Lord of the Shinzawai playing chess—or shāh, as it was called here—and their conversations gave Pug insights into the nature of Tsurani life. He could no longer think of these people as aliens, for he saw their daily life as similar to what he had known as a boy. There were surprising differences, such as the strict adherence to an honor code, but the similarities far outnumbered the differences.

Katala became the centerpiece of his existence. They came together whenever they found time, sharing meals, a quick exchange of words, and every night that they could steal together. Pug was sure the other slaves in the household knew of their nighttime assignations, but the proximity of people in Tsurani life had bred a certain blindness to the personal habits of others, and no one cared a great deal about the comings and goings of two slaves.

Several weeks after his first night with Katala, Pug found himself alone with Kasumi, as Laurie was embroiled in another shouting match with the woodcrafter who was finishing his lute. The man considered Laurie somewhat unreasonable in objecting to the instrument's being finished in bright yellow paint with purple trim. And he saw absolutely no merit in leaving the natural wood tones exposed. Pug and Kasumi left the singer explaining to the woodcrafter the requirements of wood for proper resonance, seemingly intent on convincing by volume as much as by logic.

They walked toward the stable area. Several more captured horses had been purchased by agents of the Lord of the Shinzawai and had been sent to his estate, at what Pug took to be a great deal of expense and some political maneuvering. Whenever alone with the slaves, Kasumi spoke the King's Tongue and insisted they call him by name. He showed a quickness in learning the language that matched his quickness in learning to ride.

"Friend Laurie," said the older son of the house, "will never make a proper slave from a Tsurani point of view. He has no appreciation of our arts."

Pug listened to the argument that still could be heard coming from the wood-carver's building. "I think it more the case of his being concerned over the proper appreciation of his art."

They reached the corral and watched as a spirited grey stallion reared and whinnied at their approach. The horse had been brought in a week ago, securely tied by several leads to a wagon, and had repeatedly tried to attack anyone who came close.

"Why do you think this one is so troublesome, Pug?"

Pug watched the magnificent animal run around the corral, herding the other horses away from the men. When the mares and another, less dominant, stallion were safely away, the grey turned and watched the two men warily.

"I'm not sure. Either he's simply a badly tempered animal, perhaps from mishandling, or he's a specially trained war-horse. Most of our war mounts are trained not to shy in battle, to remain silent when held, to respond to their rider's command in times of stress. A few, mostly ridden by lords, are specially trained to obey only their master, and they are weapons as much as transport, being schooled to attack. He may be one of these."

Kasumi watched him closely as he pawed the ground and tossed his head. "I shall ride him someday," he said. "In any event, he will sire a strong line. We now number five mares, and Father has secured another five. They will arrive in a few weeks, and we are scouring every estate in the Empire to find more." Kasumi got a far-off look and mused, "When I was first upon your world, Pug, I hated the sight of horses. They rode down upon us, and our soldiers died. But then I came to see what magnificent creatures they are. There were other prisoners, when I was still back on your world, who said you have noble families who are known for nothing so much as the fine stock of horses they breed. Someday the finest horses in the Empire shall be Shinzawai horses."

"By the look of these, you have a good start, though from what little I know, I think you need a larger stock for breeding."

"We shall have as many as it takes."

"Kasumi, how can your leaders spare these captured animals from the war effort? You must surely see the need to quickly build mounted units if you are going to advance your conquest."

Kasumi's face took on a rueful expression. "Our leaders, for the most part, are tradition-bound, Pug. They refuse to see any wisdom in training cavalry. They are fools. Your horsemen ride over our warriors, and yet they pretend we cannot learn anything, calling your people barbarians. I once sieged a castle in your homeland, and those who defended taught me much about warcraft. Many would brand me traitor for saying such, but we have held our own only by force of numbers. For the most part, your generals have more skill. Trying to keep one's soldiers alive, rather than sending them to their death, teaches a certain craftiness.

"No, the truth of the matter is we are led by men who—" He stopped, realizing he was speaking dangerously. "The truth is," he said at last, "we are as stiff-necked a people as you."

He studied Pug's face for a moment, then smiled. "We raided for horses during the first year, so that the Warlord's Great Ones could study the beasts, to see if they were intelligent allies, like our cho-ja, or merely animals. It was a fairly comical scene. The Warlord insisted he be the first to try to ride a horse. I suspect he chose one much like this big grey, for no sooner did he approach the animal than the horse attacked, nearly killing him. His honor won't permit any other to ride when he failed. And I think he was fearful of trying again with another animal. Our Warlord, Almecho, is a man of considerable pride and temper, even for a Tsurani."

Pug said, "Then how can your father continue to purchase captured horses? And how can you ride in defiance of his order?"

Kasumi's smile broadened. "My father is a man of considerable influence in the council. Our politics is strangely twisted, and there are ways to bend any command, even from the Warlord or High Council, and any order, save one from the Light of Heaven himself. But most of all it is because these horses are here, and the Warlord is not." He smiled. "The Warlord is supreme only in the field. Upon this estate, none may question my father's will."

Since coming to the estate of the Shinzawai, Pug had been troubled by whatever Kasumi and his father were plotting. That they were embroiled in some Tsurani political intrigue he doubted not, but what it might prove to be he had no idea. A powerful lord like Kamatsu would not spend this much effort satisfying a whim of even a son as favored as Kasumi. Still, Pug knew better than to involve himself any more than he was involved by circumstance. He changed the topic of conversation. "Kasumi, I was wondering something."

"Yes?"

"What is the law regarding the marriage of slaves?"

Kasumi seemed unsurprised by the question. "Slaves may marry with their master's permission. But permission is rarely given. Once married, a man and wife may not be separated, nor can children be sold away so long as the parents live. That is the law. Should a married couple live a long time, an estate could become burdened with three or four generations of slaves, many more than they could economically support. But occasionally permission is granted. Why, do you wish Katala for your wife?"

Pug looked surprised. "You know?"

Without arrogance Kasumi said, "Nothing occurs upon my father's estates that he is ignorant of, and he confides in me. It is a great honor."

Pug nodded thoughtfully. "I don't know yet. I feel much for her, but something holds me back. It's as if . . ." He shrugged, at a loss for words.

Kasumi regarded him closely for a time, then said, "It is by my father's will you live and by his whim how you live." Kasumi stopped for a minute, and Pug became painfully aware of how large a gulf still stood between the two men, one the son of a powerful lord and the other the lowest of his father's property, a slave. The false veneer of friendship was ripped away, and Pug again knew what he had learned in the swamp: here life was cheap, and only this man's pleasure, or his father's, stood between Pug and destruction.

As if reading Pug's mind, Kasumi said, "Remember, Pug, the law is strict. A slave may never be freed. Still, there is the swamp, and there is here. And to us of Tsuranuanni, you of the Kingdom are very impatient."

Pug knew Kasumi was trying to tell him something, something perhaps important. For all his openness at times, Kasumi could easily revert to a Tsurani manner Pug could only call cryptic. There was an unvoiced tension behind Kasumi's words, and Pug thought it best not to press. Changing the topic of conversation again, he asked, "How goes the war, Kasumi?"

Kasumi sighed, "Badly for both sides." He watched the grey stallion. "We fight along stable lines, unchanged in the last three years. Our last two offensives were blunted, but your army also could make no gains. Now weeks pass without fighting. Then your countrymen raid one of our enclaves, and we return the compliment. Little is accomplished except the spilling of blood. It is all very senseless, and there is little honor to be won."

Pug was surprised. Everything he had seen of the Tsurani reinforced Meecham's observation of years ago, that the Tsurani were a very warlike race. Everywhere he had looked when traveling to this estate, he had seen soldiers. Both sons of the house were soldiers, as had been their father in his youth. Hokanu was First Strike Leader of his father's garrison, due to his being the Lord of the Shinzawai's second son, but his dealing with the slave master at the swamp camp showed a ruthless efficiency in Hokanu, and Pug knew it to be no quirk. He was Tsurani, and the Tsurani code was taught at a very early age, and fiercely followed.

Kasumi sensed he was being studied and said, "I fear I am becoming softened by your outlandish ways, Pug." He paused. "Come, tell me more of your people, and what . . ." Kasumi froze. He seized Pug's arm and cocked his head, listening. After a brief instant he said, "No! It can't be!" Suddenly he wheeled and shouted, "Raid! The Thūn!"

Pug listened and in the distance could hear the faint rumbling, as if a herd of horses were galloping over the plains. He climbed upon the rail of the corral and looked into the distance. A large meadow stretched away behind the corral ending at the edge of a lightly wooded area. While the alarm sounded behind him, he could see forms emerging from the tree line.

Pug watched in terrible fascination as the creatures called Thūn came racing toward the estate house. They grew in stature as they ran furiously toward where Pug waited. They were large, centaurlike beings, looking like mounted riders in the distance. Rather than horselike, the lower body was reminiscent of a large deer or an elk, but more heavily muscled. The upper body was completely manlike, but the face resembled nothing so much as an ape with a long snout. The entire body, except the face, was covered by a medium-length fur, mottled grey and white. Each creature carried a club or ax, the head being stone lashed to the wooden haft.

Hokanu and the household guard came running from the soldiers' building and took up positions near the corral. Archers readied their bows, and swordsmen stood in ranks, ready to accept the charge.

Suddenly Laurie was at Pug's side, holding his nearly finished lute. "What?"

"Thūn raid!"

Laurie stood as fascinated by the sight as Pug. Suddenly he put his lute aside, then jumped into the corral. "What do you think you're doing?" yelled Pug.

The troubadour dodged a protective feint by the grey stallion and jumped upon the back of another horse, the dominant mare of the small herd. "Trying to get the animals safely away."

Pug nodded and opened the gate. Laurie rode the horse out, but the grey kept the others from following, herding them back. Pug hesitated for a minute, then said, "Algon, I hope you knew what you taught." He walked calmly toward the stallion, silently trying to convey a sense of command. When the stallion put back his ears and snorted at him, Pug said, "Stand!"

The horse's ears cocked at the command, and it seemed to be deciding. Pug knew timing was critical and did not break the rhythm of his approach. The horse studied him as he came alongside, and Pug said, "Stand!" again. Then before the animal could bolt, he grabbed a handful of mane and was up on its back.

The battle-trained war-horse, whether by design or luck, decided Pug was close enough to his former master to respond. Perhaps it was due to the clamor of battle around, but for whatever reason, the grey leaped forward in response to Pug's leg commands and was out the gate at a run. Pug gripped with his legs for his life. As the horse cleared the gate, Pug shouted, "Laurie, get the others!" as the stallion turned to the left. Pug glanced over his shoulder and saw the other animals following the herd leader as Laurie brought her past the gate.

Pug saw Kasumi running from the tack house, a saddle in his hand, and shouted, "Whoa!" setting as hard a seat as he could manage bareback. The stallion halted and Pug commanded, "Stand!" The grey pawed the ground in anticipation of a fight. Kasumi shouted as he approached, "Keep the horses from fighting. This is a Blood Raid, and the Thūn will not retreat until each has killed at least once." He called for Laurie to stop, and when the small herd was milling about, he quickly saddled a horse and turned it away from the others.

Pug kicked, and the grey and the mare Laurie rode led the remaining four horses to the side of the estate house. They kept the animals closely bunched out of sight of the attacking Thūn.

A soldier came running around the corner of the house, carrying weapons. He reached Pug and Laurie and shouted, "My master Kasumi commands you defend the horses with your lives." He handed the two slaves each a sword and shield, then turned and dashed back toward the fighting.

Pug regarded the strange sword and shield, lighter by half than any he had ever trained with. A shrill cry interrupted his examination as Kasumi came riding around the house, in a running fight with a Thūn warrior. The eldest son of the Shinzawai rode well, and though he had little training in fighting from horseback, he was a skilled swordsman. His inexperience was offset by the Thūn's lack of experience with horses, for while it was not unlike fighting one of his own kind, the horse was also attacking, biting at the creature's chest and face.

Catching wind of the Thūn, Pug's grey reared and nearly threw him. He held fiercely to the mane and gripped tightly with his lower legs.

The other horses neighed, and Pug fought to keep his from charging. Laurie shouted, "They don't like the way those things smell. Look at the way Kasumi's horse is acting."

Another of the creatures came into sight, and Laurie let out a whoop and rode to intercept. They came together in a clash of weapons, and Laurie took the Thūn club blow on his shield. His own sword struck the creature across the chest, and it cried out in a strange, guttural language, staggering for a moment, then falling.

Pug heard a scream from inside the house and turned to see one of the thin sliding doors erupt outward as a body hurled through it. A stunned house slave staggered to his feet, then collapsed, blood welling up from a wound on his head. Other figures came scurrying through the door.

Pug saw Katala and Almorella running from the house with the others, a Thūn warrior in pursuit. The creature bore down upon Katala, club raised high overhead.

Pug shouted her name, and the grey sensed his rider's alarm. Without command the huge war-horse sprang forward, intercepting the Thūn as it closed with the slave girl. The horse was enraged, from the sounds of battle or the Thūn smell. It crashed heavily into the Thūn, biting and lashing out with heavy forelegs, and the Thūn's legs went out from under it. Pug was thrown by the impact and landed heavily. He lay dazed for a moment, then he climbed to his feet. He staggered to where Katala sat huddled and pulled her away from the maddened stallion.

The grey reared above the still Thūn, and hooves came flashing down. Again and again the war-horse struck at the Thūn, until there was no doubt of there being a breath of life left in the fallen creature.

Pug shouted for the horse to halt and stand, and with a contemptuous snort, the animal ceased the attack, but it kept its ears pinned back, and Pug could see it quiver. Pug approached it and stroked its neck, until the animal stopped trembling.

Then it was quiet. Pug looked about and saw Laurie riding after the scattering horses. He left his own mount and returned to Katala. She sat trembling upon the grass, Almorella at her side.

Kneeling before her, he said, "Are you all right?"

She took a deep breath, then gave him a frightened smile. "Yes, but I was sure I was going to be trampled for a minute."

Pug looked at the slave girl who had come to mean so much to him and said, "I thought so, too." Suddenly they were both smiling at each other. Almorella stood and made some comment about seeing to the others. "I was so afraid you'd been hurt," Pug said. "I thought I would lose my mind when I saw you running from that creature."

Katala put her hand upon Pug's cheek, and he realized they were wet with tears, "I was so frightened for you," he said.

"And I for you. I thought you'd be killed the way you came crashing into the Thūn." Then she was weeping. She came slowly into his arms. "I don't know what I would do if you were killed." Pug gripped her with all his strength. They sat that way for a few minutes, until Katala regained her composure. Gently pulling away from Pug, she said, "The estate is a shambles. Septiem will have a thousand things for us to do." She began to stand, and Pug gripped her hand.

Rising before her he said, "I didn't know, before I mean. I love you, Katala."

She smiled at him, touching his cheek. "And I you, Pug."

Their moment of discovery was interrupted by the appearance of the Lord of the Shinzawai and his younger son. Looking around, he surveyed the damage to his house as Kasumi rode around the corner, splattered in blood.

Kasumi saluted his father and said, "They have fled, I have ordered men dispatched to the northern watch forts. They must have overwhelmed one of the garrisons to have broken through."

The Lord of the Shinzawai nodded he understood and turned to enter his house, calling for his First Adviser and his other senior servants to report the damage to him.

Katala whispered to Pug, "We'll talk later," and answered the hoarse shouts of the hadonra, Septiem. Pug joined Laurie, who had ridden up to Kasumi's side.

The minstrel looked at the dead creatures on the ground and said, "What are they?"

Kasumi said, "Thūn. They're nomadic creatures of the northern tundra. We have forts along the foothills of the mountains separating our estates from their lands, at every pass. Once they roamed these ranges until we drove them north. Occasionally they seek to return to the warmer lands of the south." He pointed to a talisman tied in the fur of one of the creatures. "This was a Blood Raid. They are all young males, unproved in their bands, without mates. They failed in the summer rites of combat and were banished from the herd by the stronger males. They had to come south, killing at least one Tsurani before they would be allowed to return to their band. Each would have to return with a Tsurani head, or not come back. It is their custom. Those who escaped will be hunted down, for they will not cross back to their home range."

Laurie shook his head. "Does this happen often?"

"Every year," said Hokanu with a wry smile. "Usually the watch forts turn them back, but it must have been a large herd this year. Many must have already returned to the north with heads taken from our men at the forts."

Kasumi said, "They must have killed two patrols, as well." He shook his head. "We've lost between sixty and a hundred men."

Hokanu seemed to reflect his older brother's unhappiness at the setback. "I will personally lead a patrol to see to the damage."

Kasumi gave him permission, and he left. Kasumi turned toward Laurie. "The horses?" Laurie pointed to where the stallion Pug had ridden stood watch over a small herd.

Suddenly Pug spoke up. "Kasumi, I do wish to ask your father permission to marry Katala."

Kasumi's eyes narrowed. "Listen well, Pug. I tried to instruct you, but you did not seem to catch my meaning. You are not of a subtle people. Now I will put it plainly. You may ask, but it will be refused."

Pug began to object, but Kasumi cut him off. "I have said, you are impatient people. There are reasons. More I cannot say, but there are reasons, Pug."

Anger flared in Pug's eyes, and Kasumi said, in the King's Tongue, "Say a word in anger within earshot of any soldier of this house, especially my brother, and you are a dead slave."

Stiffly Pug said, "Your will, master."

Witnessing the bitterness of Pug's expression, Kasumi softly repeated, "There are reasons, Pug." For a moment he was trying to be other than a Tsurani master, a friend trying to ease pain. He locked gaze with Pug, then a veil dropped over Kasumi's eyes, and once more they were slave and master.

Pug lowered his eyes as was expected of a slave, and Kasumi said, "See to the horses." He strode away, leaving Pug alone.

PUG NEVER SPOKE of his request to Katala. She sensed that something troubled him deeply, something that seemed to add a bitter note to their otherwise joyful time together. He learned the depth of his love for her and began to explore her complex nature. Besides being strong-willed, she was quick-minded. He only had to explain something to her once, and she understood. He learned to love her dry wit, a quality native to her people, the Thuril, and sharpened to a razor's edge by her captivity. She was an observant student of everything around her and commented unmercifully upon the foibles of everyone in the household, to their detriment and Pug's amusement. She insisted upon learning some of Pug's language, so he began teaching her the King's Tongue. She proved an apt student.

Two months went by uneventfully; then one night Pug and Laurie were called to the dining room of the master of the house. Laurie had completed work upon his lute and, though dissatisfied in a hundred little ways, judged it passable for playing. Tonight he was to play for the Lord of the Shinzawai.

They entered the room and saw that the lord was entertaining a guest, a black-robed man, the Great One whom they had glimpsed months ago. Pug stood by the door while Laurie took a place at the foot of the low dining table. Adjusting the cushion he sat upon, he began to play.

As the first notes hung in the air, he started singing: an old tune that Pug knew well. It sang of the joys of harvest and the riches of the land, and was a favorite in farm villages throughout the Kingdom. Besides Pug, only Kasumi understood the words, though his father could pick out a few that he had learned during his chess matches with Pug.

Pug had never heard Laurie sing before, and he was genuinely impressed. For all the troubadour's braggadocio, he was better than any Pug had heard. His voice was a clear, true instrument, expressive in both words and music of what he sang. When he was finished, the diners politely struck the table with eating knives, in what Pug assumed was the Tsurani equivalent of applause.

Laurie began another tune, a merry air played at festivals throughout the Kingdom. Pug remembered when he had last heard it, at the Festival of Banapis the year before he had left Crydee for Rillanon. He could almost see once more the familiar sights of home. For the first time in years, Pug felt a deep sadness and longing that nearly overwhelmed him.

Pug swallowed hard, easing the tightness in his throat. Homesickness and hopeless frustration warred within him, and he could feel his hard-learned self-control slipping away. He quickly invoked one of the calming exercises he had been taught by Kulgan. A sense of well-being swept over him, and he relaxed. While Laurie performed, Pug used all his concentration to fend off the haunting memories of home. All his skills created an aura of calm he could stand within, a refuge from useless rage, the only legacy of reminiscence.

Several times during the performance, Pug felt the gaze of the Great One upon him. The man seemed to study him with some question in his eyes. When Laurie was finished, the magician leaned over and spoke to his host.

The Lord of the Shinzawai beckoned Pug to the table. When he was seated, the Great One spoke. "I must ask you something." His voice was clear and strong, and his tone reminded Pug of Kulgan when he was preparing Pug for lessons. "Who are you?"

The direct, simple question caught everyone at the table by surprise. The lord of the house seemed uncertain as to the magician's question and started to reply. "He is a slave—"

He was interrupted by the Great One's upraised hand. Pug said, "I am called Pug, master."

Again the man's dark eyes studied him. "Who are you?"

Pug felt flustered. He had never liked being the center of attention, and this time it was focused upon him as never before in his life.

"I am Pug, once of the Duke of Crydee's court."

"Who are you, to stand here radiating the power?" At this all three men of the Shinzawai household started, and Laurie looked at Pug in confusion.

"I am a slave, master."

"Give me your hand."

Pug reached out, and his hand was taken by the Great One. The man's lips moved, and his eyes clouded over. Pug felt a warmth flow through his hand and over him. The room seemed to glow with a soft white haze. Soon all he could see was the magician's eyes. His mind fogged over, and time was suspended. He felt a pressure inside his head as if something were trying to intrude. He fought against it, and the pressure withdrew.

His vision cleared, and the two dark eyes seemed to withdraw from his face until he could see the entire room again. The magician let go of his hand. "Who are you?" A brief flicker in his eyes was the only sign of his deep concern.

"I am Pug, apprentice to the magician Kulgan."

At this the Lord of the Shinzawai blanched, confusion registering on his face. "How . . ."

The black-robed Great One rose and announced, "This slave is no longer property of this house. He is now the province of the Assembly."

The room fell silent. Pug couldn't understand what was happening and felt afraid.

The magician drew forth a device from his robe. Pug remembered that he had seen one before, during the raid on the Tsurani camp, and his fear mounted. The magician activated it, and it buzzed as the other one had. He placed his hand on Pug's shoulder, and the room disappeared in a grey haze.

21

▾▾

CHANGELING

THE ELF PRINCE SAT QUIETLY.

Calin awaited his mother. There was much on his mind, and he needed to speak with her this night. There had been little chance for that of late, for as the war had grown in scope, he found less time to abide in the bowers of Elvandar. As Warleader of the elves, he had been in the field nearly every day since the last time the outworlders had tried to forge across the river.

Since the siege of Castle Crydee three years before, the outworlders had come each spring, swarming across the river like ants, a dozen for each elf. Each year elven magic had defeated them. Hundreds would enter the sleeping glades to fall into the endless sleep, their bodies being consumed by the soil, to nourish the magic trees. Others would answer the dryads' call, following the enchanted sprites' songs until in their passion for the elemental beings they would die of thirst while still in their inhuman lovers' embrace feeding the dryads with their lives. Others would fall to the creatures of the forests, the giant wolves, bears, and lions who answered the call of the elven war horns. The very branches and roots of the trees of the elven forests would resist the invaders until they turned and fled.

But this year, for the first time, the Black Robes had come. Much of the elven magic had been blunted. The elves had prevailed, but Calin wondered how they would fare when the outworlders returned.

This year the dwarves of the Grey Towers had again aided the elves. With the moredhel gone from the Green Heart, the dwarves had made swift passage from their wintering in the mountains, adding their numbers to the defense of Elvandar. For the third year since the siege at Crydee, the dwarves had proved the difference in holding the outworlders across the river. And again with the dwarves came the man called Tomas.

Calin looked up, then rose as his mother approached. Queen Aglaranna seated herself upon her throne and said, "My son, it is good to see you again."

"Mother, it is good to see you also." He sat at her feet and waited for the words he needed to come. His mother sat patiently, sensing his dark mood.

Finally he spoke. "I am troubled by Tomas."

"As am I," said the Queen, her expression clouded and pensive.

"Is that why you absent yourself when he comes to court?"

"For that . . . and other reasons."

"How can it be the Old Ones' magic still holds so strong after all these ages?"

A voice came from behind the throne. "So that's it, then?"

They turned, surprised, and Dolgan stepped from the gloom, lighting his pipe. Aglaranna looked incensed. "Are the dwarves of the Grey Towers known for eavesdropping, Dolgan?"

The dwarven chief ignored the bite of the question. "Usually not, my lady. But I was out for a walk—those little tree rooms fill with smoke right quickly—and I happened to overhear. I did not wish to interrupt."

Calin said, "You can move with stealth when you choose, friend Dolgan."

Dolgan shrugged and blew a cloud of smoke. "Elvenfolk are not the only ones with the knack of treading lightly. But we were speaking of the lad. If what you say is true, then it is a serious matter indeed. Had I known, I would never have allowed him to take the gift."

The Queen smiled at him. "It is not your fault, Dolgan. You could not have known. I have feared this since Tomas came among us in the mantle of the Old Ones. At first I thought the magic of the Valheru would not work for him, being a mortal, but now I can see he is less mortal each year.

"It was an unfortunate series of events brought this to pass. Our Spellweavers would have discovered that treasure ages ago, but for the dragon's magic. We spent centuries seeking out and destroying such relics, preventing their use by the moredhel. Now it is too late, for Tomas would never willingly let the armor be destroyed."

Dolgan puffed at his pipe. "Each winter he broods in the long halls, awaiting the coming of spring, and the coming of battle. There is little else for him. He sits and drinks, or stands at the door staring out into the snow, seeing what no other can see. He keeps the armor locked away in his room during such times, and when campaigning, he never removes it, even to sleep. He has changed, and it is not a natural changing. No, he would never willingly give up the armor."

"We could try to force him," said the Queen, "but that could prove unwise. There is something coming into being in him, something that may save my people, and I would risk much for them."

Dolgan said, "I do not understand, my lady."

"I am not sure I do either, Dolgan, but I am Queen of a people at war. A terrible foe savages our lands and each year grows bolder. The outworld magic is strong, perhaps stronger than any since the Old Ones vanished. It may be the magic in the dragon's gift will save my people."

Dolgan shook his head. "It seems strange such power could still reside in metal armor."

Aglaranna smiled at the dwarf. "Does it? What of the Hammer of Tholin you carry? Is it not vested with powers from ages past? Powers that mark you once more heir to the throne of the dwarves of the West?"

Dolgan looked hard at the Queen. "You know much of our ways, lady. I must never forget your girlish countenance masks ages of knowledge." He then brushed away her comment. "We have been done with kings for many years in the West, since Tholin vanished in the Mac Mordain Cadal. We do as well as those who obey old King Halfdan in Dorgin. But should my people wish the throne restored, we shall meet in moot, though not until this war is over. Now, what of the lad?"

Aglaranna looked troubled. "He is becoming what he is becoming. We can aid that transformation. Our Spellweavers work to this end already. Should the full power of the Valheru rise up in Tomas untempered, he would be able to brush aside our protective magic much as you would a bothersome twig barring your way upon the trail. But he is not an Old One born. His nature is as alien to the Valheru as their nature was to all others. Aided by our Spellweavers, his human ability to love, to know compassion, to understand, may temper the unchecked power of the Valheru. If so, he may . . . he may prove a boon to us all." Dolgan was visited by the certainty the Queen had been about to say something else, but remained silent as she continued. "Should that Valheru power become coupled with a human's capacity for blind hatred, savagery, and cruelty, then he would become something to fear. Only time will tell us what such a blending will produce."

"The Dragon Lords . . . ," said Dolgan. "We have some mention of the Valheru in our lore, but only scraps here and there. I would understand more, if you'll permit."

The Queen looked off into the distance. "Our lore, eldest of all in the world today, tells of the Valheru, Dolgan. There is much of which I am forbidden to speak, names of power, fearful to invoke, things terrible to recall, but I may tell you this much. Long before man or dwarf came to this world, the Valheru ruled. They were part of this world, fashioned from the very fabric of its creation, nearly godlike in power and unfathomable in purpose. Their nature was chaotic and unpredictable. They were more powerful than any others. Upon the backs of the great dragons they flew, no place in the universe beyond their reach. To other worlds they roamed, bringing back that which pleased them, treasure and knowledge plundered from other beings. They were subject to no law but their own will and whim. They fought among themselves as often as not, and only death resolved conflicts. This world was their dominion. And we were their creatures.

"We and the moredhel were of one race then, and the Valheru bred us as you would cattle. Some were taken, from both races, for . . . personal pets, bred for beauty . . . and other qualities. Others were bred to tend the forests and fields. Those who lived in the wild became the forerunners of the elves, while those who remained with the Valheru were the forerunners of the moredhel.

"But then came a time of changing. Our masters ceased their internecine struggles and banded together. Why they did so is forgotten, though some among the moredhel may still know, for they were closer to our masters than we elves. We may have known their reasons then, but this was the time of the Chaos Wars, and much was lost. Only this we know: all the servants of the Valheru were given freedom, and the Old Ones were never again seen by elf or moredhel. When the Chaos Wars raged, great rifts in time and space were opened, and it was through these that goblins, men, and dwarves came to this world. Few of our people or of the moredhel survived, but those that did rebuilt our homes. The moredhel longed to inherit the might of their lost masters, rather than seek their own destiny as the elves did, and used their cunning to find tokens of the Valheru, taking to the Dark Path. It is the reason we are so unalike, who once were brothers.

"The old magic is still powerful. In strength and bravery Tomas matches any. He took the magic unwittingly, and that may prove the difference. The old magic changed the moredhel into the Brotherhood of the Dark Path because they sought the power out of dark longings. Tomas was a boy of good and noble heart, with no taint of evil in his soul. Perchance he will grow to master the dark side of the magic."

Dolgan scratched his head. " 'Tis a grave risk, then, from what you say. I was concerned for the lad, true, and gave little thought to the larger scheme of things. You know the way of it better than I, but I hope we'll not live to regret letting him keep the armor."

The Queen stepped down from her throne. "I also hope there will be no regrets, Dolgan. Here in Elvandar the old magic is softened, and Tomas is of lighter heart. Perhaps that is a sign we do the right thing, tempering the change rather than opposing it."

Dolgan made a courtly bow. "I yield to your wisdom, my lady. And I pray you are right."

The Queen bade them good night and left. Calin said, "I also pray my Mother-Queen speaks from wisdom, and not from some other feeling."

"I don't take your meaning, Elf Prince."

Calin looked down upon the short figure. "Don't play the fool with me, Dolgan. Your wisdom is widely known and highly respected. You see it as well as I. Between my mother and Tomas there is something growing."

Dolgan sighed, the freshening breeze carrying away his pipe's smoke. "Aye, Calin, I've seen it as well. A look, little more, but enough."

"She looks upon Tomas as she once looked upon my Father-King, though she still denies it within herself."

"And there is something within Tomas," said the dwarf, watching the Elf Prince closely, "though it is less tender than what your lady feels. Still, he holds it well in check."

"Look to your friend, Dolgan. Should he try to press his suit for the Queen, there will be trouble."

"So much do you dislike him, Calin?"

Calin looked thoughtfully at Dolgan. "No, Dolgan. I do not dislike Tomas. I fear him. That is enough." Calin was silent for a while, then said, "We will never again bend knee before another master, we who live in Elvandar. Should my mother's hopes of how Tomas will change prove false, we shall have a reckoning."

Dolgan shook his head slowly. "That would prove a sorry day, Calin."

"That it would, Dolgan." Calin walked from the council ring, past his mother's throne, and left the dwarf alone. Dolgan looked out at the fairy lights of Elvandar, praying the Elf Queen's hopes would not prove unfounded.

▼▼

WINDS HOWLED across the plains. Ashen-Shugar sat astride the broad shoulders of Shuruga. The great golden dragon's thoughts reached his master. *Do we hunt?* There was hunger in the dragon's mind.

"No. We wait."

The Ruler of the Eagles' Reaches waited as the streaming moredhel made their way toward the rising city. Hundreds pulled great blocks of stone mined in quarries half a world away, dragging them toward the city on the plains. Many had died and many more would die, but that was unimportant. *Or was it?* Ashen-Shugar was troubled by this new and strange thought.

A roar from above sounded as another great dragon came spiraling down, a magnificent black bellowing challenge. Shuruga raised his head and trumpeted his reply. To his master he said, *Do we fight?*

"No."

Ashen-Shugar sensed disappointment in his mount, but chose to ignore it. He watched as the other dragon settled gracefully to the ground a short distance away, folding its mighty wings across its back. Black scales reflected the hazy sunlight like polished ebony. The dragon's rider raised his hand in salute.

Ashen-Shugar returned the greeting, and the other's dragon approached cautiously. Shuruga hissed, and Ashen-Shugar absently struck the beast with his fist. Shuruga lapsed into silence.

"Has the Ruler of the Eagles' Reaches finally come to join us?" asked the newcomer, Draken-Korin, the Lord of Tigers. His black-and-orange-striped armor sparkled as he dismounted from his dragon.

Out of courtesy Ashen-Shugar dismounted as well. His hand never strayed far from his white-hilted sword of gold, for though times were changing, trust was unknown among the Valheru. In times past they would have fought as likely as not, but now the need for information was more pressing. Ashen-Shugar said, "No. I simply watch."

Draken-Korin regarded the Ruler of the Eagles' Reaches, his pale blue eyes revealing no emotion. "You alone have not agreed, Ashen-Shugar."

"Joining to plunder across the cosmos is one thing, Draken-Korin. This . . . this plan of yours is madness."

"What is this madness? I know not of what you speak. We are. We do. What more is there?"

"This is not our way."

"It is not our way to let others stand against our will. These new beings, they contest with us."

Ashen-Shugar raised his eyes skyward. "Yes, that is so. But they are not like others. They also are formed from the very stuff of this world, as are we."

"What does that matter? How many of our kin have you killed? How much blood has passed your lips? Whoever stands against you must be killed, or kill you. That is all."

"What of those left behind, the moredhel and the elves?"

"What of them? They are nothing."

"They are ours."

"You have grown strange under your mountains, Ashen-Shugar. They are our servants. It is not as if they possessed true power. They exist for our pleasure, nothing more. What concerns you?"

"I do not know. There is something. . . ."

"TOMAS."

For an instant Tomas existed in two places. He shook his head and the visions vanished. He turned his head and saw Galain lying in the brush next to him. A force of elves and dwarves waited some distance behind. The young cousin of Prince Calin pointed toward the Tsurani camp across the river. Tomas followed his companion's gesture and saw the outworld soldiers sitting near their campfires, and smiled. "They hug their camps," he whispered.

Galain nodded. "We have stung them enough that they seek the warmth of their campfires."

The late spring evening mist shrouded the area, mantling the Tsurani camp in haze. Even the campfires seemed to burn less brightly. Tomas again studied the camp. "I mark thirty, with thirty more in each camp east and west."

Galain said nothing, waiting for Tomas's next command. Though Calin was Warleader of Elvandar, Tomas had assumed command of the forces of elves and dwarves. It was never clear when captaincy had passed to him, but slowly, as he had grown in stature, he had grown in leadership. In battle he would simply shout for something to be done, and elves and dwarves would rush to obey. At first it had been because the commands were logical and obvious. But the pattern had become accepted, and now they obeyed because it was Tomas who commanded.

Tomas motioned for Galain to follow and moved away from the riverbank, until they were safely out of sight of the Tsurani camp, among those who waited deep within the trees. Dolgan looked at the young man who once had been the boy he saved from the mines of Mac Mordain Cadal.

Tomas stood six inches past six feet in height, as tall as any elf. He walked with a powerful self-assurance, a warrior born. In the six years he had been with the dwarves, he had become a man . . . and more.

Dolgan watched him, as Tomas surveyed the warriors gathered before him, and knew Tomas could now walk the dark mines of the Grey Towers without fear or danger.

"Have the other scouts turned?"

Dolgan nodded, signaling for them to come forward. Three elves and three dwarves approached. "Any sign of the Black Robes?"

When the scouts indicated no, the man in white and gold frowned. "We would do well to capture one of them and carry him to Elvandar. Their last attack was the deepest yet. I would give much to know the limits of their power."

Dolgan took out his pipe, gauging they were far enough from the river for it not to be seen. As he lit it, he said, "The Tsurani guard the Black Robes like a dragon guards its treasure."

Tomas laughed at that, and Dolgan caught a glimpse of the boy he had known. "Aye, and it's a brave dwarf who loots a dragon's lair."

Galain said, "If they follow the pattern of the last three years, they most likely are done with us for the season. It is possible we shall not see another Black Robe until next spring."

Tomas looked thoughtful, his pale eyes seemingly aglow with a light of their own. "Their pattern . . . their pattern is to take, to hold, then to take more. We have been willing to let them do as they wish, so long as they do not cross the river. It is time to change that pattern. And if we trouble them enough, we may have the opportunity to seize one of these Black Robes."

Dolgan shook his head at the risk implicit in what Tomas proposed. Then, with a smile, Tomas added, "Besides, if we can't loosen their hold along the river for a time, the dwarves and I will be forced to winter here, for the outworlders are now deep into the Green Heart."

Galain looked at his tall friend. Tomas grew more elf-like each year, and Galain could appreciate the obscure humor that often marked his words. He knew Tomas would welcome staying near the Queen. But in spite of his worries over Tomas's magic, he had come to like the man. "How?"

"Send bowmen to the camps on the right and the left and beyond. When I call with the honk of a greylag, have them volley across the river, but from beyond those positions as if the main attack were coming from east and west." He smiled, and there was no humor in his expression. "That should isolate this camp long enough for us to do some bloody work."

Galain nodded, and sent ten bowmen to each camp. The others made ready for the attack, and after sufficient time Tomas raised his hands to his mouth. Cupping them, he made the sound of a wild goose.

A moment later he could hear shouting coming from east and west of the position across the river. The soldiers in the Tsurani camp stood and looked both ways, with several coming to the edge of the water, peering into the dark forest. Tomas raised his hand and dropped it with a chopping motion.

Suddenly it was raining elven arrows on the camp across the river, and Tsurani soldiers were diving for their shields. Before they could fully recover, Tomas led a charge of dwarves across the shallow sandbar ford. Another flight of arrows passed overhead, then the elves shouldered bows, drew swords, and charged after the dwarves, all save a dozen who would stay to offer covering fire should it be needed.

Tomas was first ashore and struck down a Tsurani guard who met him at the river's edge. Quickly he was among them, wreaking mayhem. Tsurani blood exploded off his golden blade, and the screams of wounded and dying men filled the damp night.

Dolgan slew a guard and found none to stand against him. He turned and saw Galain standing over another dead Tsurani, but staring at something beyond. The dwarf followed his gaze to where Tomas was standing over a wounded Tsurani soldier who lay with blood running down his face from a scalp wound, an arm upraised in a plea for mercy. Over him stood Tomas, his face an alien mask of rage. With a strange and terrible cry, in a voice cruel and harsh, he brought down his golden sword and ended the Tsurani's life. He turned quickly, seeking more foes. When none presented themselves, he seemed to go blank for a moment, then his eyes refocused.

Galain heard a dwarf call, "They come." Shouts came from the other Tsurani camps as they discovered the ruse and quickly approached the true battle site.

Without a word Tomas's party hurried across the water. They reached the other side as Tsurani bowmen fired upon them, to be answered by elves on the opposite shore. The attacking group quickly fell back deeply into the trees, until they were a safe distance away.

When they stopped, the elves and dwarves sat down to catch their wind, and to rest from the battle surge still in their blood. Galain looked to Tomas and said, "We did well. No one lost, and only a few slightly wounded, and thirty outworlders slain."

Tomas didn't smile, but looked thoughtfully for a moment, as if hearing something. He turned to look at Galain, as if the elf's words were finally registering. "Aye, we did well, but we must strike again, tomorrow and the next day and the next, until they act."

Night after night they crossed the river. They would attack a camp, and the next night strike miles away. A night would pass without attack, then the same camp would be raided three nights running. Sometimes a single arrow would take a guard from the opposite shore, then nothing, while his companions stood waiting for an attack that never came. Once they struck through the lines at dawn, after the defenders had decided that no attack was coming. They overran a camp, ranging miles into the south forest, and took a baggage train, even slaughtering the strange six-legged beasts who pulled the wagons. Five separate fights were fought as they turned from that raid, and two dwarves and three elves were lost.

Now Tomas and his band, numbering over three hundred elves and dwarves, sat awaiting word from other camps. They were eating a stew of venison, seasoned with mosses, roots, and tubers.

A runner came up to Tomas and Galain. "Word from the King's army." Behind him a figure in grey approached the campfire.

Tomas and Galain stood. "Hail, Long Leon of Natal," said the elf.

"Hail, Galain," answered the tall, black-skinned ranger.

An elf brought over bread and a bowl of steaming stew to the two newcomers, and as they sat, Tomas said, "What news from the Duke?"

Between mouthfuls of food, the ranger said, "Lord Borric sends greetings. Things stand poorly. Like moss on a tree, the Tsurani slowly advance in the east. They take a few yards, then sit. They seem to be in no hurry. The Duke's best guess is they seek to reach the coast by next year, isolating the Free Cities from the north. Then perhaps an attack toward Zūn or LaMut. Who can say?"

Tomas asked, "Any news from Crydee?"

"Pigeons arrived just before I left. Prince Arutha holds fast against the Tsurani. They have luck as poor there as here. But they move southward through the Green Heart." He surveyed the dwarves and Tomas. "I am surprised that you could reach Elvandar."

Dolgan puffed his pipe. "It was a long trek. We had to move swiftly and with stealth. It is unlikely we will be able to return to the mountains now the invaders are aroused. Once in place, they are loath to yield what they have gained."

Tomas paced before the fire. "How did you elude their sentries?"

"Your raids are causing much confusion in their ranks. Men who faced the Armies of the West were pulled out of the line to rush to the river. I simply followed one such group. They never thought to look behind. I had only to slip past their lines when they withdrew and then again across the river."

Calin said, "How many do they bring against us?"

Leon shrugged. "I saw six companies, there must be others." They had estimated a Tsurani company at twenty squads each of thirty men.

Tomas slapped his gloved hands together. "They would bring three thousand men back only if they were planning another crossing. They must seek to drive us deep into the forest again, to keep us from harrying their positions." He crossed to stand over the ranger. "Do any of the black-robed ones come?"

"From time to time I saw one with the company I followed."

Tomas again slapped his hands. "This time they come in force. Send word to the other camps. In two days' time all the host of Elvandar is to meet at the Queen's court, save scouts and runners who will watch the outworlders."

Silently runners sprang up from the fire and hurried off to carry word to the other elven bands strung out along the banks of the river Crydee.

ASHEN-SHUGAR SAT upon his throne, oblivious to the dancers. The moredhel females had been chosen for their beauty and grace, but he was untouched by their allure. His mind's eye was far away, seeking the coming battle. Inside, a strangeness, a hollow feeling without name, came into being.

It is called sadness, said the voice within.

Ashen-Shugar thought: Who are you to visit me in my solitude?

I am that which you are becoming. This is but a dream, a memory.

Ashen-Shugar drew forth his sword and rose from his throne, bellowing his rage. Instantly the musicians stopped their playing. The dancers, servants, and musicians fell to the floor, prostrating themselves before their master. "I am! There is no dream!"

You are but a remembrance of the past, said the voice. *We are becoming one.*

Ashen-Shugar raised his sword, then lashed down. The head of a cowering servant rolled upon the floor. Ashen-Shugar knelt and placed his hand in the fountain of blood. Raising fingers to his lips, he tasted the salty flavor and cried, "Is this not the taste of life!"

It is illusion. All has passed.

"I feel a strangeness, an unease that makes me . . . it makes me . . . there is no word."

It is fear.

Ashen-Shugar again lashed out with his sword, and a young dancer died. "These things, they know fear. What has fear to do with me?"

You are afraid. All creatures fear change, even the gods.

Who are you? asked the Valheru silently.

I am you. I am what you will become. I am what you were. I am Tomas.

▼▼

A SHOUT from below brought Tomas from his reverie. He rose and left his small room, crossing a tree-branch bridge to the level of the Queen's court. At a rail he could make out the dim figures of hundreds of dwarves camped below the heights of Elvandar. He stood for a time watching the campfires below. Each hour hundreds more elven and dwarven warriors made their way to join this army he marshaled. Tomorrow he would sit in council with Calin, Tathar, Dolgan, and others and make known his plan to meet the coming assault.

Six years of fighting had given Tomas a strange counterpoint to the dreams that still troubled his sleep. When the battle rage took him, he existed in another's dreams. When he was away from the elven forest, the call to enter those dreams became ever more difficult to stem. He felt no fear of these visitations, as he had at first. He was more than human because of some long-dead being's dreams. There were powers within him, powers that he could use, and they were now part of him, as they had been part of the wearer of the white and gold. He knew that he would never be Tomas of Crydee again, but what was he becoming . . . ?

The slightest hint of a footfall sounded behind him. Without turning, he said, "Good eve, my lady."

The Elf Queen came to stand next to him, a studied expression on her face. "Your senses are elven now," she said in her own language.

"So it seems, Shining Moon," he answered in the same language, using the ancient translation of her name.

He turned to face her and saw wonder in her eyes. She reached out and gently touched his face. "Is this the boy who stood so flustered in the Duke's council chamber at the thought of speaking before the Elf Queen, who now speaks the true tongue as if born to it?"

He pushed away her hand, gently. "I am what I am, what you see." His voice was firm, commanding.

She studied his face, holding back a shudder as she recognized something fearful within his countenance. "But what do I see, Tomas?"

Ignoring her question, he said, "Why do you avoid me, lady?"

Gently she spoke. "There is this thing growing between us that may not be. It sprang into existence the moment you first came to us, Tomas."

Almost with a note of amusement, Tomas said, "Before that, lady, from the first I gazed upon you." He stood tall over her. "And why may this thing not be? Who better to sit at your side?"

She moved away from him, her control lost for a brief moment. In that instant he saw what few had ever seen: the Elf Queen confused and unsure, doubting her own ancient wisdom. "Whatever else, you are man. Despite what powers are granted you, it is a man's span allotted to you. I will reign until my spirit travels to the Blessed Isles to be with my lord, who has already made the journey. Then Calin rules, as son of a king, as King. Thus it is with my people."

Tomas reached for her and turned her to face him. "It was not always so."

Her eyes showed a spark of fear. "No, we were not always a free people."

She sensed impatience within him, but she also saw him struggle with it as he forced his voice to calmness. "Do you then feel nothing?"

She took a step away. "I would lie if I said not. But it is a strange pulling, and something that fills me with uncertainty and with no small dread. If you become more the Valheru, more than the man can master, then we could not welcome you here. We would not allow the return of the Old Ones."

Tomas laughed, with a strange mixture of humor and bitterness. "As a boy I beheld you and was filled with a boy's longing. Now I am a man and behold you with a man's longing. Is the power that makes me bold enough to seek you out, the power that gives me the means to do so, that which will also keep us apart?"

Aglaranna put her hand to her cheek. "I know not. It has never been with the royal family to be other than what we are. Others may seek alliance with humans. I would not have that sadness when you are old and grey and I am still as you see me."

Tomas's eyes flashed, and his voice gained a harsh edge. "That will never happen, lady. I shall live a thousand years in this glade. Of that I have no doubt. But I shall trouble you no more . . . until other matters are settled. This thing is willed by fate to be, Aglaranna. You will come to know that."

She stood with her hand raised to her mouth, and her eyes moist with emotion. He walked away, leaving her alone in her court to consider what he had said. For the first time since her Lord-King had passed over, Aglaranna knew two conflicting emotions: fear and longing.

TOMAS TURNED at a shout from the edge of the clearing. An elf was walking from the trees followed by a simply dressed man. He stopped his conversation with Calin and Dolgan, and the three hurried to follow the stranger as he was guided up to the Queen's court. Aglaranna sat on her throne, her elders arranged on benches to either side. Tathar stood next to the Queen.

The stranger approached the throne and made a slight bow. Tathar threw a quick glance at the sentry who had escorted the man, but the elf looked bemused. The man in brown said, "Greetings, lady," in perfect elvish.

Aglaranna answered in the King's Tongue. "You come boldly among us, stranger."

The man smiled, leaning on his staff. "Still, I did seek a guide, for I would not enter Elvandar unbidden."

Tathar said, "I think yon guide had little choice."

The man said, "There is always a choice, though it is not always apparent."

Tomas stepped forward. "What is your purpose here?"

Turning at the voice, the man smiled. "Ah! The wearer of the dragon's gift. Well met, Tomas of Crydee."

Tomas stepped back. The man's eyes radiated power, and his easy manner veiled strength that Tomas could feel. "Who are you?"

The man said, "I have many names, but here I am called Macros the Black." He pointed with his staff and swept it around the gathered watchers. "I have come, for you have embarked upon a bold plan." At the last, he pointed his staff at Tomas. He dropped the tip and leaned on the staff again. "But the plan to capture a Black Robe will bring naught but destruction to Elvandar should you not have my aid." He smiled slightly. "A Black Robe you shall have in time, but not yet." There was a hint of irony in his voice.

Aglaranna arose. Her shoulders were back, and her eyes looked straight into his. "You know much."

Macros inclined his head slightly. "Aye, I know much, more than is sometimes comforting." He stepped past her and placed a hand upon Tomas's shoulder. Guiding Tomas to a seat near where the Queen stood, Macros forced him to sit with a gentle pressure on his shoulder. He took a seat next to him and laid the staff against the crook of his neck and shoulder. Looking at the Queen, he said, "The Tsurani come at first light, and they will drive straight through to Elvandar."

Tathar stepped before Macros and said, "How do you know this?"

Macros smiled again. "Do you not remember me in council with your father?"

Tathar stepped back, his eyes widening. "You . . ."

"I am he, though I am no longer called as I was then."

Tathar looked troubled. "So long ago. I would not have thought it possible."

Macros said, "Much is possible." He looked pointedly from the Queen to Tomas.

Aglaranna slowly sat down, masking her discomfort. "Are you the sorcerer?"

Macros nodded. "So I am called, though there is more in the tale than can be told now. Will you heed me?"

Tathar nodded to the Queen. "Long ago, this one came to our aid. I do not understand how it can be the same man, but he was then a true friend to your father and mine. He can be trusted."

"What, then, is your counsel?" asked the Queen.

"The Tsurani magicians have marked your sentries, knowing where they hide. At first light they will come, breaking across the river in two waves, like the horns of a bull. As you meet them, a wave of the creatures called cho-ja will come through the center, where your strength is weak. They have not thrown them against you yet, but the dwarves can tell you of their skill in warfare."

Dolgan stepped forward. "Aye, lady. They are fearsome creatures and fight in the dark as well as do my people. I had thought them confined to the mines."

Macros said, "And so they were, until the raids. They have brought up a host of them, which ready themselves across the river, beyond the sight of your scouts. They will come in numbers. The Tsurani tire of your raids and would put an end to the warring across the river. Their magicians have worked hard to learn the secrets of Elvandar, and now they know that should the sacred heart of the elven forests fall, the elves will be a force no longer."

Tomas said, "Then we shall hold back, and defend against the center."

Macros sat quietly for a moment, as if remembering something. "That is a start, but they bring their magicians with them, anxious as they are for an ending. Their magic will let their warriors pass through your forests unchecked by the power of your Spellweavers, and here they will come."

Aglaranna said, "Then we shall meet them here and stand until the end."

Macros nodded. "Bravely said, lady, but you will need my aid."

Dolgan studied the sorcerer. "What can one man do?"

Macros stood. "Much. Upon the morrow, you shall see. Fear not, dwarf, the battle will be harsh, and many will travel to the Blessed Isles, but with firm resolve, we shall prevail."

Tomas said, "You speak like one who has already seen these things happen."

Macros smiled, and his eyes said a thousand things, and nothing. "I do, Tomas of Crydee, do I not?" He turned to the others and with a sweep of his staff said, "Ready yourselves. I shall be with you." To the Queen he said, "I would rest; if you have a place for me?"

The Queen turned to the elf who had brought Macros to the council. "Take him to a room, bring him whatever he requires."

The sorcerer bowed and followed the guide. The others stood in silence, until Tomas said, "Let us make ready."

AS NIGHT GAVE way to dawn, the Queen stood alone near her throne. In all the years of her rule, she had never known a time like this. Her thoughts ran with hundreds of images, from times as long ago as her youth, and as recently as two nights ago.

"Seeking answers in the past, lady?"

She turned to see the sorcerer standing behind her, leaning on his staff. He approached and stood next to her.

"Can you read my mind, sorcerer?"

With a smile and a wave of his hand, Macros said, "No, my lady. But there is much I do know and can see. Your heart is heavy, and your mind burdened."

"Do you understand why?"

Macros laughed softly. "Without question. Still, I would speak to you of these things."

"Why, sorcerer? What part do you play?"

Macros looked out over the lights of Elvandar. "A part, much as any man plays."

"But you know yours well."

"True. It is given to some to understand what is obscure to others. Such is my fate."

"Why have you come?"

"Because there is need. Without me Elvandar may fall, and that must not be. It is so ordained, and I can only do my part."

"Will you stay if the battle is won?"

"No. I have other tasks. But I will come once more, when the need is again great."

"When?"

"That I may not tell you."

"Will it be soon?"

"Soon enough, though not soon enough."

"You speak in riddles."

Macros smiled, a crooked, sad smile. "Life is a riddle. It is in the hands of the gods. Their will shall prevail, and many mortals will find their lives changed."

"Tomas?" Aglaranna looked deep into the sorcerer's dark eyes.

"He most visibly, but all who live through these times."

"What is he?"

"What would you have him be?"

The Elf Queen found herself unable to answer. Macros placed his hand lightly on her shoulder. She felt calm flow from his fingers and heard herself say, "I would wish nothing of trouble upon my people, but the sight of him fills me with longing. I long for a man . . . a man with his . . . might. Tomas is more like my lost lord than he will ever know. And I fear him, for once I make the pledge, once I place him above me, I lose the power to rule. Do you think the elders would allow this? My people would never willingly place the yoke of the Valheru upon their necks again."

The sorcerer was silent for a time, then said, "For all my arts, there are things hidden from me, but understand this: there is a magic here fey beyond imagining. I cannot explain save to say it reaches across time, more than is apparent. For while the Valheru is present within Tomas now, so is Tomas present within the Valheru in ages past.

"Tomas wears the garb of Ashen-Shugar, last of the Dragon Lords. When the Chaos Wars raged, he alone remained upon this world, for he felt things alien to his kind."

"Tomas?"

Macros smiled. "Think not upon this overly long, lady. These sorts of paradox can send the mind reeling. What Ashen-Shugar felt was an obligation to protect this world."

Aglaranna studied Macros's face in the twinkling lights of Elvandar. "You know more of the ancient lore than any other man, sorcerer."

"I have been . . . given much, lady." He looked over the elven forests and spoke more to himself than to the Queen: "Soon will come a time of testing for Tomas. I cannot be sure what will occur, but this much I do know. Somehow the boy from Crydee, in his love for you and yours, in his simple human caring, has so far withstood the most powerful member of the most powerful mortal race ever to have lived upon this world. And he is well served in withstanding the terrible pain of that conflict of two natures by the soft arts of your Spellweavers."

She looked hard at Macros. "You know of this?"

He laughed with genuine amusement. "Lady, I am not without some vanity. I'm stung you'd think you could fashion so fine a spellweaving without my observing. Little magic in this world escapes my notice. What you have done is wise and may tip the balance in Tomas's favor."

"That is the thought I plead to myself," said Aglaranna quietly, "when I see in Tomas a lord to match the King of my youth, the husband taken too soon from my side. Can it be true?"

"Should he survive the time of testing, yes. It may be the conflict will prove the end of both Tomas and Ashen-Shugar. But should Tomas survive, he may become what you most secretly long for.

"Now I shall tell you something only the gods and I know. I can judge many things yet to come, but much is still unknown to me. One thing I know is this: at your side Tomas may grow to rule wisely and well and, as his youth is replaced by wisdom, grow to be the lord of your wishes, if his power can somehow be tempered by his human heart. Should he be sent away, a terrible fate may await both the Kingdom and the free peoples of the West."

Her eyes asked the question, and he continued. "I cannot see into that dark future, lady; I can only surmise. Should he come into his powers with the dark side in preeminence, he will be a terrible force, one that must be destroyed. Those who see the battle madness come upon him see but a shadow of the true darkness bound up within him. Even if a balance is struck and Tomas's humanity survives, but still you send him away, then humanity's capacity for anger, pain, and hate may come forth. I ask you: should Tomas be driven away and someday raise the dragon standard in the north, what would occur?"

The Queen became frightened and openly showed it, her mask of control lost completely. "The moredhel would gather."

"Aye, my lady. Not as bands of troublesome bandits, but as a host. Twenty thousand Dark Brothers, and with them a hundred thousand goblins, and companies of men whose dark nature would seek profit in the destruction and savagery to follow. A mighty army under the steel glove of a warrior born, a general whom even your own people follow without question."

"Do you advise me to keep him here?"

"I can only point out the alternatives. You must decide."

The Elf Queen threw back her head, her red-gold locks flying and her eyes moist, looking out over Elvandar. The first light of day was breaking. Rosy light lanced through the trees, casting shadows of deep blue. The morning songs of birds could be heard around the glades. She turned to Macros, wishing to thank him for his counsel, and found him gone.

▾▾

THE TSURANI ADVANCED as Macros had foretold. The cho-ja attacked across the river, after the two human waves had carried the flanks. Tomas had set skirmishers, lines of bowmen with a few shield guards, who retreated and fired into the advancing army, giving the impression of resistance.

Tomas stood before the assembled army of Elvandar and the dwarves of the Grey Towers, only fifteen hundred arrayed against the six thousand invaders and their magicians. In silence they waited. As the enemy approached, the shouts of Tsurani warriors and the cries of those who fell to elvish arrows could be heard through the forest. Tomas looked up at the Queen, standing on a balcony overlooking the scene of the coming battle, next to the sorcerer.

Suddenly elves were running toward them, and the first flashes of brightly colored Tsurani armor could be seen through the trees. When the skirmishers had rejoined the main force, Tomas raised his sword.

"Wait," a voice cried out from above, and the sorcerer pointed across the open clearing, where the first elements of the Tsurani forces were running into the clearing. Confronted by the waiting elven army, the vanguard halted and waited as their comrades joined them. Their officers ordered ranks formed, for here was fighting they could understand, two armies meeting on an open plain, and the advantage was theirs.

The cho-ja also stood in ordered ranks, heeding the officers' shouted commands. Tomas was fascinated, for he still knew little of these creatures and counted them animals as much as intelligent allies of the Tsurani.

Macros shouted, "Wait!" again, and waved his staff above his head, inscribing broad circles in the air. A stillness descended upon the glade.

Suddenly an owl flew past Tomas's head, straight for the Tsurani lines. It circled above the aliens for a moment, then swooped and struck a soldier in the face. The man screamed in pain as its talons clawed his eyes.

A hawk sped past and duplicated the owl's attack. Then a large black rook descended from the sky. A flight of sparrows erupted from the trees behind the Tsurani and pecked at faces and unprotected arms. Birds came flying from every part of the forest and attacked the invaders. Soon the air was filled with the sound of flapping wings as every manner of bird in the forest descended upon the Tsurani. Thousands of them, from the smallest hummingbird to the mighty eagle, attacked the outworld host. Men cried out, and a few broke formation and ran, trying to avoid the wicked beaks and talons that tried to scratch at eyes, pull at cloaks, and tear flesh. The cho-ja reared, for though their armored hide was immune to the pecking and clawing, their large, jewellike eyes were easy targets for the feathered attackers.

A shout went up from the elves as the Tsurani lines dissolved in disorder. Tomas gave the order, and elven bowmen added feathered arrows to the fray. Tsurani soldiers were struck and fell before they could come to grips with the enemy. Their own bowmen could not return the fire, for they were harried by a hundred tiny foes.

The elves watched as the Tsurani tried to hold position, while the birds continued their bloody work in their midst. The Tsurani fought back as best they could, striking down many birds in midflight, but for each one killed, three took its place.

Suddenly a hissing, tearing sound cut through the din. There was an instant of silence as everything moving on the Tsurani side of the clearing seemed to pause. Then the birds exploded upward, accompanied by a sizzling crackle of energy, as if thrown back by some unseen force. As the birds cleared the area, Tomas could see the black robes of the Tsurani magicians as they moved through their forces, restoring order. Hundreds of wounded Tsurani lay upon the ground, but the battle-tempered aliens quickly re-formed their lines, ignoring the injured.

The enormous flight of birds gathered again above the invaders and started to dive. Instantly a glowing red shield of energy formed around the Tsurani. As the birds struck, they stiffened and fell, their feathers smoldering and filling the air with a pungent burning stench. Elven arrows that struck the barrier were halted in midflight and burst into flame, falling harmlessly to the ground.

Tomas gave the order to stop the bow fire and turned to look at Macros. Again the sorcerer shouted, "Wait!"

Macros waved his staff and the birds dispersed, hearing his silent command. The staff extended toward the Tsurani, as Macros aimed it at the red barrier. A golden bolt of energy shot forth. It sped across the clearing and pierced the red barrier, to strike a black-robed magician in the chest. The magician crumpled to the ground, and a shout of horror and outrage went up from the assembled Tsurani. The other magicians turned their attention to the platform above the elven army, and blue globes of fire shot toward Macros. Tomas shouted, "Aglaranna!" in rage as the tiny blue stars struck the platform, obliterating all sight of her in a blinding display of exploding light. Then he could see again.

The sorcerer stood upon the platform unharmed, as did the Queen. Tathar pulled her away, and Macros pointed with his staff again. Another black-robed magician fell. The four remaining magicians looked upon Macros's survival and counterattack with expressions of mixed awe and anger, clearly seen across the glade. They redoubled their assault upon the sorcerer, wave after wave of blue light and fire striking Macros's protective barrier. All upon the ground were forced to turn away from the sight, lest they become blinded by the terrible energies being unleashed. After this magical onslaught was ended, Tomas looked upward, and again the sorcerer was unharmed.

One magician gave out with a cry of pure anguish and pulled a device from his robe. Activating it, he vanished from the clearing, followed moments later by his three companions. Macros looked down at Tomas, pointed his staff at the Tsurani host, and called, "Now!"

Tomas raised his sword and gave the signal to attack. A hail of arrows passed overhead as he led the charge across the clearing. The Tsurani were demoralized, their attack blunted by the birds and the sight of their magicians being killed and driven off. Yet they stood their ground and took the charge. Hundreds had died from the claws and beaks of the birds, and more from the flights of arrows, but still they numbered three to one of the elves and dwarves.

The battle was joined, and Tomas was caught up in the red haze that washed away any thought but to kill. Hacking right and left, he carved a path through the Tsurani, confounding their every attempt to strike him down. Tsurani and cho-ja both fell to his blade, as he delivered death with an even hand to all who stood before him.

Back and forth across the clearing the battle moved, as man and cho-ja, elf and dwarf fell. The sun moved higher in the sky, and there was no respite from the fray. The sounds of death filled the air, and high overhead the kites and vultures gathered.

Slowly the Tsurani press forced the elves and dwarves back. Slowly they moved toward the heart of Elvandar. There was a brief pause, as if both sides had struck a balance, when the adversaries moved away from each other, leaving an open space between. Tomas heard the voice of the sorcerer ringing clear above the sounds of battle. "Back!" it cried, and to a man, the forces of Elvandar retreated.

The Tsurani paused a moment, then, sensing the hesitation of the elves and dwarves to continue, started to press forward. Abruptly there came a rumbling sound, and the earth trembled. All stopped moving, and the Tsurani looked fearful.

Tomas could see the trees shake, more and more violently, as the trembling increased. Suddenly there came a crescendo of noise, as if the grandfather of all thunderclaps pealed overhead. With the booming sound, a huge piece of earth erupted upward, as if heaved by some invisible giant's hand. The Tsurani who were standing on it shot upward, to fall hard to the ground, and those nearby were knocked aside.

Another piece of the ground erupted, then a third. Suddenly the air was full of giant pieces of earth that flew upward, then fell upon the Tsurani. Screams of terror filled the air, and the Tsurani turned and fled. There was no order to their retreat, for they flew from a place where the very earth attacked them. Tomas watched as the clearing was emptied of all but the dead and dying.

In a matter of minutes, the clearing was quiet, as the earth subsided and the shocked onlookers stood mute. The sounds of the Tsurani army retreating through the woods could be heard. Their cries told of other horrors being visited upon them as they fled.

Tomas felt weak and weary, and looked down to find his arms covered with blood. His tabard and shield and his golden sword were clean as they always were, but for the first time he could feel human life splattered upon himself. In Elvandar the battle madness did not stay with him, and he felt sick to his inner being.

He turned and said softly, "It is over." There was a faint cheer from the elves and dwarves, but it was halfhearted, for none felt like victors. They had seen a mighty host felled by primeval forces, elemental powers that defied description.

Tomas walked slowly past Calin and Dolgan and mounted the stairs. The Elf Prince sent soldiers to follow the retreating invaders, to care for the allied wounded, and to give the dying Tsurani quick mercy.

Tomas made his way to the small room where he abided, and pulled aside the curtain. He sat heavily upon his pallet, tossing aside his sword and shield. A dull throbbing in his head caused him to close his eyes. Memories came flooding in.

THE HEAVENS WERE torn with mad vortices of energy crashing from horizon to horizon. Ashen-Shugar sat upon mighty Shuruga's back, watching the very fabric of time and space rent.

A clarion rang, the heralding note heard by dint of his magic. The moment he awaited had come. Urging Shuruga upward, Ashen-Shugar's eyes searched the heavens, seeking what must come against the mad display in the skies. A sudden stiffening of Shuruga under him coincided with his sighting of his prey. The figure of Draken-Korin grew recognizable as he sat upon his black dragon. There was a strangeness in his eyes, and for the first time in his long memory Ashen-Shugar began to understand the meaning of horror. He could not put a name to it, could not describe it, but in the tortured eyes of Draken-Korin he saw it.

Ashen-Shugar ordered Shuruga forward. The mighty golden dragon roared his challenge, answered by Draken-Korin's equally mighty black. The two clashed in the sky, and their riders worked their arts upon each other.

Ashen-Shugar's golden blade arched overhead and struck, cleaving the black shield with the grinning tiger's head in twain. It was almost too easy, as Ashen-Shugar had known it would be. Draken-Korin had given up too much of his essence to that which was forming. Before the might of the last Valheru, he was little more than a mortal. Once, twice, three times more Ashen-Shugar struck, and the last of his brothers fell from the back of his black dragon. Downward he tumbled to strike the ground. By force of will, Ashen-Shugar left Shuruga's back and floated to stand beside the helpless body of Draken-Korin, leaving Shuruga to finish his contest with the near-dead black dragon.

A spark of life still persisted within the broken form, life ages past remembering. A pleading look entered Draken-Korin's eyes as Ashen-Shugar approached. He whispered, "Why?"

Pointing heavenward with his golden blade, Ashen-Shugar said, "This obscenity should never have been allowed. You bring an end to all we knew."

Draken-Korin looked skyward to where Ashen-Shugar pointed. He watched the tumbling, raging display of energies, twisted, screaming rainbows of light jagged across the vault of the sky. He witnessed the new horror being formed from the twisted life force of his brothers and sisters, a raging, mindless thing of hate and anger.

In a croaking voice, Draken-Korin said, "They were so strong. We could never have dreamed." His face contorted in terror and hate as Ashen-Shugar raised his golden blade. "But I had the right!" he screamed.

Ashen-Shugar brought down his blade, cleanly severing the head of Draken-Korin from his body. At once both head and body were engulfed with a glimmering light, and the air hissed around Ashen-Shugar. Then the fallen Valheru vanished without trace, his essence returning to that mindless monster raging against the new gods. With bitterness Ashen-Shugar said, "There is no right. There is only power."

Is that how it was?

"Yes, that is how I slew the last of my brethren."

The others?

"They are now part of that." He indicated the terrible sky.

Together, never apart, they watched the madness above as the Chaos Wars raged. After a time Ashen-Shugar said, "Come, this is an ending. Let us be done with it."

They began to walk toward the waiting Shuruga. Then a voice came.

▼▼

"YOU ARE QUIET."

Tomas opened his eyes. Before him knelt Aglaranna, a basin of herb-sweetened water and a cloth in her hand. She removed his tabard and helped him pull off the golden chain. While he sat near exhaustion, she began washing the blood from his face and arms, saying nothing as he watched her.

When he was clean, she took a dry cloth to his face and said, "You look tired, my lord."

"I see many things, Aglaranna, things not meant for a man to see. I bear the weight of ages upon my soul, and I am tired."

"Is there no comfort to be sought?"

He looked at her, their eyes locking. The commanding gaze was tempered by a hint of gentleness, but still she was forced to drop her eyes.

"Do you mock me, lady?"

She shook her head. "No, Tomas. I . . . came to comfort you, if you have need."

He reached out and took her hand, and drew her toward him, hunger in his eyes. When she was encircled by his embrace, feeling the rising passion in his body, she heard him say, "My need is great, lady."

Looking into his pale eyes, she dropped the final barriers between them. "As is mine, my lord."

22

▾▾

TRAINING

HE AROSE IN THE DARKNESS.

He donned a simple white robe, a mark of his station, and left his cell. He waited outside the small and simple room, which contained a sleeping mat, a single candle, and a shelf for scrolls: all that was deemed necessary for his education. Down the corridor he could see the others, all years younger than he, standing quietly before the doors of their cells. The first black-clad master came along the corridor and stopped before one of the others. Without a word the man nodded, the boy fell in behind him, and they marched away into the gloom. The dawn sent soft grey light through the high narrow windows in the hallway. He, like the others, extinguished the torch on the wall opposite his door, at the first hint of day. Another man in black came down the corridor, and another waiting youth left behind him. Soon a third. Then a fourth. After a time he found himself alone. The hallway was silent.

A figure emerged from the darkness, his robes conspiring to mask his coming until the last few feet. He stood before the young man in white and nodded, pointing down the corridor. The youth fell in behind his black-robed guide, and they made their way down a series of torchlit passages, into the heart of the great building that had been the young man's home as long as he could remember. Soon they were traveling through a series of low tunnels, rank with the smell of age, and wet, as if deep below the lake that surrounded the building on all sides.

The man in black paused at a wooden door, slid a bolt aside, and opened it. The younger man entered behind the older and came to stand before a series of wooden troughs. Each was half the length of a man's height, and half that wide. One stood on the floor, and the others were arrayed above it, suspended by wooden supports in steps, one above the next, until the highest stood near the height of a man's head. All of those above had single holes in the end that overhung the trough below. In the bottom trough, water could be heard sloshing, as it responded to the vibrations of their footfalls on the stone floor.

The man in black pointed to a bucket and turned and left the young man in white alone.

The young man picked up the bucket and set about his task. All commands to those in white were given without words, and, as he had quickly learned when he had first become aware, those in white were not allowed to speak. He knew he could speak, for he understood the concept and had quietly tried to form a few words while lying on his mat in the dark. As with so many other things, he understood the fact, without being aware of how he understood. He knew that he existed before his first awakening in his cell, but was not in the least alarmed by his lack of memory. It seemed somehow proper.

He started his task. Like so many other things he was commanded to do, it seemed an impossible undertaking. He took the bucket and filled the topmost trough from the bottom one. As it had on days before, the water spilled from the top down into each successive trough, until the contents of the bucket rested again at the bottom. Doggedly he pursued his work, letting his mind go vacant, while his body undertook the mindless task.

As it did so many other times when left to its own devices, his mind danced from image to image, bright flashes of shapes and colors the eluded his grasp as he sought to close mental fingers around them. First came a brief glimpse of a beach, with crashing waves on rocks, black and weathered. Fighting. A strange-looking cold white substance lying on the ground—a word, snow, that fled as quickly as it came. A muddy camp. A great kitchen with boys hurrying about many tasks. A room in a high tower. Each passed with blinding quickness, leaving only an after-image in its passing.

Daily a voice would sound in his head, and his mind's voice would respond with an answer, while he labored at his endless task. The voice would ask a simple question, and his mind's voice would answer. Should the answer be incorrect, the question would be repeated. If several wrong answers were made, the voice would cease its questioning, sometimes returning later in the day, sometimes not.

The white-clad worker felt the familiar pressure against the fabric of his thoughts.

—*What is the law*—the voice asked.

—*The law is the structure that surrounds our lives, and gives them meaning*—he answered.

—*What is the highest embodiment of the law?*—

—*The Empire is the highest embodiment of the law*—

—*What are you?*—came the next question.

—*I am a servant of the Empire*—

The thought contact flickered for a moment, then returned, as if the other were considering the following question carefully.

—*In what manner are you allowed to serve?*—

The question had been asked several times before, and always his answer had been met with the blank inner silence that told him he had answered incorrectly. This time he carefully considered, eliminating all the answers he had made previously, as well as those that were combinations of extrapolations of the previously incorrect ones.

Finally he answered—*As I see fit*—

There was a surge of feeling from without, a feeling of approval. Quickly another question followed.

—*Where is your allotted place?*—

He thought about this, knowing that the obvious answer was likely to be the incorrect one, but still one that needed to be tested. He answered.

—*My place is here*—

The mind contact was broken, as he suspected it would be. He knew that he was being trained, though the purpose of the training was masked from his mind. Now he could ponder the last question in light of his previous answers and perhaps ascertain the correct response.

THAT NIGHT he dreamed.

A strange man in a brown robe, tied with a whipcord belt, walked along the roadway. The man in brown turned and said, "Hurry up. We don't have much time, and you can't fall behind."

He tried to move faster but found his feet were lead and his arms tied to his sides. The man in brown halted his brisk walk and said, "Very well, then. One thing at a time."

He tried to speak and found his mouth refused to move. The man in brown stroked his beard thoughtfully, then said, "Consider this: you are the architect of your own imprisonment."

He looked down and saw that his bare feet were upon a dusty road.

He looked up, and the man in brown was again walking briskly away. He tried to follow and again couldn't move.

He awoke in a cold sweat.

AGAIN HE HAD been asked where his place was, and again his answer,—*Where I am needed*—was unsatisfactory. He toiled over another pointless task, driving nails into a thick sheet of wool, which let them fall through to the floor, where he picked them up and drove them through again.

His reconsideration of the last question he had been asked was interrupted when the door behind him opened, and his guide motioned for him to follow. They moved through long passages, winding their way up to the level where they would eat the scant morning meal.

When they entered the hall, the guide took a place by the door, while others in black robes similarly escorted the white-clad ones into the hall. This was the day that the young man's guide would stand and watch the boys in white, who, along with the young man, were bound to eat in silence. Each day a different wearer of the black robe filled this function.

The young man ate and considered the last question of the morning. He weighed each possible answer, seeking out possible flaws, and as they were discovered, discarding them. Abruptly one answer came unbidden to his mind, an intuitive leap, as his subconscious provided him with a solution to the question. *I am the architect of my own imprisonment.* Several times in the past, when particularly knotty problems had stopped his progress, this had occurred, which accounted for his rapid advancement in his lessons. He weighed the possible flaws in this answer, and when he was certain he was correct, he stood. Other eyes regarded him furtively, for this was a violation of the rules.

He went over to stand before his guide, who regarded his approach with a controlled expression, his only sign of curiosity being a slight arching of his brows.

Without preamble the young man in white said, "This is no longer my place."

The man in black showed no emotion, but placed a hand on the young man's shoulder and nodded slightly. He reached inside his robe and removed a small bell, which he rang once. Another black-robed individual appeared moments later. Without word the newcomer took the place at the door, as the guide motioned for the young man to follow him.

They walked in silence as they had done many times before, until they came to a room. The man in black turned to the young man and said, "Open the door."

The young man started to reach for the door, then with a flash of insight pulled his hand away. Knitting his brow in concentration, he opened the door by the power of his mind. Slowly it swung inward. The man in black turned and smiled. "Good," he said, in a soft, pleasant voice.

They entered a room with many white, grey, and black robes hanging upon hooks. The man in black said, "Change to a grey robe."

The young man did so quickly and faced the other man. The man in black studied the new wearer of the grey. "You are no longer bound to silence. Any question you may have will be answered, as well as is possible, though there are still things that will be waited upon, until you don the black. Then you will fully understand. Come."

The young man in grey followed his guide to another room, where cushions surrounded a low table, upon which rested a pot of hot chocha, a pungent, bittersweet drink. The man in black poured two cups and handed one to the young man, indicating he should sit. They both sat, and the young man said, "Who am I?"

The man in black shrugged. "You will have to decide that, for only you can glean your true name. It is a name that must never be spoken to others, lest they gain power over you. Henceforward you will be called Milamber."

The newly named Milamber thought for a moment, then said, "It will serve. What are you called?"

"I am called Shimone."

"Who are you?"

"Your guide, your teacher. Now you will have others, but it was given to me to be responsible for the first part of your training, the longest part."

"How long have I been here?"

"Nearly four years."

Milamber was surprised by this, for his memory stretched back only a little, several months at best. "When will my memories be returned to me?"

Shimone smiled, for he was pleased that Milamber had not asked if they would be returned, and said as much. "Your mind will call up your past life as you progress in the balance of your training, slowly at first, with more rapidity later. There is a reason for this. You must be able to withstand the lure of former ties, of family and nations, of friends and home. In your case that is particularly vital."

"Why is that?"

"When your past returns to you, you will understand," was all Shimone said, a smile on his face. His hawkish features and dark eyes were set in an expression that communicated the feeling this was the end of that topic.

Milamber thought of several questions, quickly discarding them as of less immediate consequence. Finally he asked, "What would have happened if I had opened the door by hand?"

"You would have died." Shimone said this flatly, without emotion.

Milamber was not surprised or shocked, he simply accepted it. "To what end?"

Shimone was a little surprised by the question and showed it. "We cannot rule each other, all we can do is ensure that each new magician is able to discharge the responsibility attendant upon his actions. You made the judgment that your place was no longer with those who wore the white, the novices. If that was not your place, then you would have to demonstrate your ability to deal with the responsibilities of this change. The bright but foolish ones often die at this stage."

Milamber considered this and acknowledged the propriety of such a test. "How long will my training continue?"

Shimone made a noncommittal gesture. "As long as it takes. You rise rapidly, however, so I think it will not be too much longer in your case. You have certain natural gifts, and—you will understand this when your memory returns—a certain advantage over the other, younger, students who started with you."

Milamber studied the contents of his cup. In the thin, dark fluid he seemed to glimpse a single word, as if seen from the corner of the eye, that vanished when he tried to focus upon it. He couldn't hang on to it, but it had been a short name, a simple name.

THAT NIGHT he dreamed again.

The man in brown walked along the road, and this time Milamber could follow. "You see, there are few objective limits. What they teach you is useful, but never accept the proposition that just because a solution satisfies a problem, that it must be the *only* solution."

The man in brown stopped. "Look at this," he said, pointing to a flower beside the road. Milamber leaned down to see what the man was pointing at. A small spider spun a web between two leaves. "That creature," said the man in brown, "toils oblivious to our passing. Either of us could crush out its existence at whim. Consider this, then: if that creature could somehow apprehend our existence, our threat to its life, would the spider worship us?"

"I don't know," Milamber answered. "I don't know how a spider thinks."

The man in brown leaned upon his staff. "Considering how little humans think alike, it might be that this spider would react with fear, defiance, indifference, fatalism, or incredulity. Anything's possible." He reached out with his staff and gently caught a piece of spider silk on the wooden pole. Lifting the tiny arachnid, he transported it over to the opposite side of the road. "Do you think the creature knows that this is a different flower?"

"I don't know."

The man in brown smiled. "That is perhaps the wisest of all answers."

Returning to his walk, he said, "You will be seeing many things soon, some of which will make little sense to you. When you do, remember one thing."

"What is that?" asked Milamber.

"Things are not always what they seem. Remember the spider, who at this very moment may be offering prayers to me in thanks for its sudden bounty." Pointing back with the staff at the plant, he said, "There are a great many more bugs on that one than the other." Scratching at his beard he added, "I wonder: is the flower also offering prayers of thanks?"

HE SPENT WEEKS in the company of Shimone and a few others. He knew more of his life, though only a fragment of what was missing. He had been a slave, and he had been discovered to have the power. He remembered a woman, and felt a faint tugging at the thought of her vaguely remembered image.

He was quick to learn. Each lesson was accomplished in a single day, or at most two. He would quickly dissect each problem given, and when it was time to discuss it with his teachers, his questions were to the point, well thought out, and proper.

One day he arose, in a newer but still simple cell, and emerged to find Shimone waiting for him. The black-robed magician said, "From this point on, you may not speak until you have finished the task set for you."

Milamber nodded his understanding and followed his guide down the hall. The older magician led him through a series of long tunnels to a place in the building he had never been before. They mounted a long staircase, rising many stories above where they had started. Upward they climbed, until Shimone opened a door for him. Milamber preceded

Shimone through the door and found himself upon an open flat roof, atop a high tower. From the center of the roof a single spire of stone rose. Skyward it shot, a needle of fashioned rock. Winding upward around it was a narrow stairway, carved into the side of the needle. Milamber's eyes followed it until the top was lost in the clouds. He found the sight fascinating, for it seemed to violate several canons of physical law that he had studied. Still, it stood before him, and what was more, his guide was indicating that he should mount the steps.

He started upward. As he completed his first circumnavigation, he noted that Shimone had disappeared through the wooden door. Relieved of his presence, Milamber turned his gaze outward from the roof, drinking in the vista around him.

He was atop the highest tower of an immense city of towers. Everywhere he looked, hundreds of stone fingers pointed upward, strong structures with windows turning blind eyes outward. Some were open to the sky, as this one was; others were roofed in stone, or in shimmering lights. But of them all, this one alone was topped by a thin spire. Below the hundreds of towers, bridges arched through the sky, connecting them, and farther down could be seen the bulk of the single, incredible building that supported all he saw. It was a monster of construction. Sprawling below him, it stretched away for miles in every direction. He had known it would be a large place, from his travels within, but this knowledge did nothing to lessen his awe at the sight.

Still farther down, in the dim extreme of his vision, he could see the faint green of grass, a thin border edging the dark bulk of the building. On all sides he saw water, the once-glimpsed lake. In the distance he could make out the hazy suggestion of mountains, but unless he strained to see them, it was as if the entire world were arrayed below.

Plodding upward, he turned around the spire as he climbed. Each circle brought him a new detail of the vista. A single bird wheeled high above all else, ignorant of the affairs of men, its scarlet wings spread to catch the air as it watched with keen eye the lake below. Seeing a telltale flicker on the water, it folded back its wings and stooped, hitting the surface for the briefest moment before it climbed aloft once more, a flopping prize clutched in its talons. With a cry of victory it circled once, then sped westward.

A turn. A play of winds. Each carried suggestions of far and alien lands. From the south a gust with a hint of hot jungles where slaves toiled to reclaim farmlands from deadly, water-shrouded marshes. From the east a breeze carried the victory chant of a dozen warriors of the Thuril Confederation, after defeating an equal number of Empire soldiers in a border clash. In counterpoint there was a faint echo of a dying Tsurani soldier, crying for his family. From the north came the smell of ice and the sound of the hooves of thousands of Thūn pounding over the frozen tundra, heading south for warmer lands. From the west, the laughter of the young wife of a powerful noble teasing a half-terrified, half-aroused household guard into betraying her husband, away conducting business with a merchant in Tusan to the south. From the east, the smell of spices as merchants haggled in the market square in far Yankora. Again south, and the smell of salt from the Sea of Blood. North, and windswept ice fields that had never known the tread of human feet, but over which beings old and wise in ways unknown to men walked, seeking a sign in the heavens—one that never came. Each breeze brought a note and tone, a color and hue, a taste and fragrance. The texture of the world blew by, and he breathed deeply, savoring it.

A turn. From the steps below came a pulsing as the world beat with a life of its own. Upward through the island, through the building, through the tower, the spire, and his very body came the urgent yet eternal beating of the planet's heart. He cast his eyes downward and saw deep caverns, the upper ones worked by slaves who harvested the few rare metals to be found, along with coal for heat and stone for building. Below these were other caverns, some natural, others the remnants of a lost city, overblown by dust that became soil as the ages passed. Here once dwelled creatures beyond his ability to imagine. Deeper still his vision plunged him, to a region of heat and light, where primeval forces contested. Liquid rock, inflamed and glowing, pushed against its solid cousin, seeking a passage upward, mindlessly driven by nature. Deeper still, to a world of pure force, where lines of energy ran through the heart of the world.

A turn, and he stepped upon a small platform atop the spire. It was less than his own height in size on each side, an impossibly precarious perch. He stepped to the middle, overcoming a vertigo that tried to send him screaming over the edge. He employed every part of his ability and training to stand there, for he understood without being told that to fail here was to die.

He cleared his mind of fear and looked around at the scene before him, awed by the expanse of emptiness. Never before had he felt so truly isolated, so truly alone. Here he stood with nothing between him and whatever fate was allotted to him.

Below him stretched the world and above him an empty sky. The wind held a hint of moisture, and he saw dark clouds racing up from the south. The tower, or the needle upon it, swayed slightly, and he unconsciously shifted his weight to compensate.

Lightning flashed as the storm clouds rushed toward him, and thunder broke around his head. The very sound was enough to dislodge him from the small platform, and he was forced to delve deeper into his inner well of power, into that silent place known only as *wal,* and there he found the strength to resist the onslaught of the storm.

Winds buffeted him, slamming him toward the platform's edge. He reeled and recovered, the darkling abyss below beckoning to him, inviting his fall. With a surge of will, he brushed aside the vertigo once again and set his mind to the task ahead.

In his mind a voice cried, *—Now is the time of testing. Upon this tower you must stand, and should your will falter, from it you will fall—*

There was a momentary pause, then the voice cried once more, *—Behold! Witness and understand how it was—*

Blackness swept upward, and he was consumed.

FOR A TIME he floats, nameless and lost. A pinpoint of flickering consciousness, an unknown swimmer through a black and empty sea. Then a single note invades the void. It reverberates, a soundless sound, a sense-lacking intruder on the senses. *—Without senses, how is there perception?—* his mind asks. His mind! *—I am!—* he cries, and a million philosophies cry out in wonder. *—If I am, then what is not me?* —he wonders.

An echo replies, *—You are that which you are, and not that which you are not—*

—An unsatisfactory answer— he muses.

—Good— replies the echo.

—What is that note?— he asks.

—It is the touch of an old man's sleep the moment before death—

—What is that note?—

—It is the color of winter—

—What is that note?—

—It is the sound of hope—

—What is that note?—

—It is the taste of love—

—What is that note?—

—It is an alarm to wake you—

HE FLOATS. Around him swim a billion billion stars. Great clusters drift by, ablaze with energy. In riots of color they spin, giant reds and blues, the smaller oranges and yellows, and the tiny reds and whites. The colorless and angry black ones drink in the storm of light around them, while others pulse out energies in an unknown spectrum, and a few twist the fabric of space and time, sending his vision swimming as he tries to fathom their passing. From each to each a line of force stretches, binding them all in a net of power. Back and forth along the strands of this web energy flows, pulsing with a life that is not life. The stars know as they fly by. They are aware of his presence, but acknowledge it not. He is too small for them to be concerned with. Around him stretches away the whole of the universe.

At various points in the web, creatures of power rest or work, each different from the others, but all somehow the same. Some he can see are gods, for they are familiar to him, and others are less or more. Each plays a role. Some regard him, for his passing is not without notice; some are beyond him, too great to comprehend him, and so being, are less than he. Others study him closely, weighing his power and abilities against their own. He studies them in return. All are silent.

He speeds among the stars and the beings of power, until he espies a star, one among the multitude, but one that calls to him. From the star twenty lines of energy lead away, and near each is a being of power. Without knowing why, he understands that here are the ancient gods of Kelewan. Each plays on the nearest line of power influencing the structure of space and time nearby. Some contest among themselves, others work oblivious to the strife, and still others do nothing that is discernible.

He moves closer. A single planet swings about the star, a blue-and-green sphere shrouded in white clouds. Kelewan.

Down the lines of force he plunges, until he is on the surface. Here he sees a world untouched by the footprint of man. Great beasts with six legs stride the land, and hiding from them are a young race of quick-thinking beings.

The cho-ja, a few bands of scurrying creatures, little more than the large insects that spawned them, speed through the trees of the great forests, fearing the large predators who hunt them, as they in turn hunt smaller game. They have begun to reason, and their queens now design each for a specific purpose, so strong and well-armed soldiers protect the foragers. More food is brought to the hive, and the race begins to prosper.

Over the plains the young Thūn males race, fighting among themselves with rocks and sticks, fists and fang. They clash knowing only there is a nameless urge driving them on, demanding that one or another from their band drive off the others and sire the next generation of young. It will be ages before they become reasoning beings, able to work together against the two-legged creatures who have yet to appear upon this world.

Near the sea, not yet named for the blood of thousands killed upon it, the Sunn huddle on the shore, newly emerged from the sea, discomforted upon the land, but no longer able to abide in the deep. Fearing all, they plot in their sea-caves, seeking security and building an attitude toward outsiders that will set the stage for their genocide generations later.

Above the mountains, the Thrillillil soar, their culture formative and crude, only little more than a loose association of breeding pairs and young. Their large but delicate wings cast shadows that hide the Nummongnum, who creep along the edge of the rocks, hidden from sight by their mottled fur, which resembles the stones behind which they scurry, seeking Thrillillil eggs, beginning a war that will last a thousand years and end in the annihilation of both races.

This is a harsh world, abundant with life, but contentious life, with no mercy for the weak. Of those races he sees, only two will endure, the Thūn and the cho-ja. He sees darkness approaching like a sudden storm, and it sweeps over him.

LIKE THE CALM after the storm, light comes.

He stands on a cliff looking down upon a great plain of grass separated from the sea by a small beach. A shimmering in the air begins, and the sea beyond the plain is distorted. Like the agitation of the air by the heat of the day, the scene ripples. Scintillating colors appear in the air. Then, as if by two giant hands, the very fabric of space and time is torn, an ever-widening gap through which he can see. Beyond this fracture in the air, a vision of chaos is revealed, a mad display of energy, as if all the lines of power in that universe are torn asunder. Bolts of energy sufficient to destroy suns explode in displays of color beyond the ability of mortal eyes to describe, leaving them dazzled with lesser lights. From deep within this giant rift, a wide bridge of golden light extends downward, until it touches the grass of the plain. Upon the bridge thousands of figures are moving, escaping the madness beyond the rift to the serenity of the plain.

Downward they hurry, some carrying all they own on their backs, others with animals pulling wagons and sleds heaped with valuables. All press forward, fleeing a nameless horror behind.

He studies the figures, and though much is alien, he can see much that is also familiar. Many wear short robes of plain fashion, and he knows he is looking upon the seeds of the Tsurani race. Their faces are more basic, showing less of the blending with others that would take place in years to come. Most are fair, with brown or blond hair. At their feet run barking dogs, sleek and swift greyhounds and whippets.

Next to them stride proud warriors, with slanted eyes and bronze skin. These are fighting men, but not organized soldiers, for they wear robes of different cut and color one from the other. Each steps down off the bridge, some showing wounds, all hiding terror behind implacable expressions. Over their shoulders they carry long swords of fine steel, fashioned with great care. The tops of their heads are shaved, with the hair around pulled back into a knot. These bear the proud look of men unsure if they are better off for having survived the battle. Mixed among them are others, all strangers.

A race of short people carry nets that proclaim them fishers, though of what sea only they know. They have dark hair, sallow skin, and grey-green eyes. Men, women, and children all wear simple fur trousers, leaving upper bodies bare.

Behind them come a nation of tall, noble, black-skinned people. Their robes are richly fashioned of soft and subtle colors. Many have gems adorning their foreheads, and gold bands on their arms. All are weeping for a homeland never to be seen again.

Then come riders upon impossible beasts that look like flying serpents with feathered birds' heads. Upon the riders' faces are masks of animals and birds, brightly painted and plumed. They are covered in paint alone, for their homeworld was a hot place. They wear their nakedness like a cloak, for there is beauty in their form, as if each had been fashioned by a master sculptor, and they bear weapons of black glass. Women and children ride behind the men unmasked, revealing expressions made harsh by the cruel world they flee. The Serpent Riders turn their creatures eastward and fly away. The great flying snakes will die out in the cold highlands of the east, but will remain forever in the legends of the proud Thuril.

Thousands more come, all walking down the golden ramp to set foot upon Kelewan. When they reach the plain, some move off, traveling to other parts of the planet, but many stay and watch as thousands more come across the bridge. Time passes, night follows day, then gives way to day once more, while the hosts enter from the insane storm of chaos.

With them come twenty beings of power, also fleeing the utter destruction of a universe. The multitudes upon the plain cannot see them passing, but he can. He knows they will become the twenty gods of Kelewan, the Ten Higher and Ten Lower Beings. They fly upward, to wrest the lines of power from the ancient, feeble beings who hold station around this world. There is no struggle as the new gods take their stations, for the old beings of power know a newer order is coming into the world.

After days of watching, he sees that the stream of humanity is thinning. Hundreds of men and women pull huge boats made from some metal, shining in the sun, mounted on wheels of a black substance. They reach the plain and see the ocean beyond the narrow beach. They give a shout and pull their boats to the water and launch them. Fifty boats raise sail and set out across the ocean, heading southward, for the land that will become Tsubar, the lost nation.

The last group is composed of thousands of men in robes of many designs and colors. He knows that these are the priests and magicians of many nations. Together they stand, holding back the raging madness beyond. As he watches, many fall, their lives burning out like spent candles. At some prearranged signal, many of them, but less than one for each hundred standing at the top of the golden bridge, turn and flee downward. All are holding books, scrolls, and other tomes of knowledge. When they reach the bottom of the bridge, they turn and watch the unfolding drama at the top.

Those above, looking not at those who have fled but at what they hold back, give forth a shout, incanting a mighty spell, wielding magic of enormous power. Those below echo their cries, and all who can hear them quail in dread at the sound. The bridge begins to dissolve, from the ground up. A flood of terror and hate comes pouring through the rift, and those who stand atop the bridge begin to crumple before its onslaught. As the bridge and the opening above disappear from sight, a single blast of fury comes through that stuns many who stand upon the plain below, felling them as if with a blow.

For some time those who escaped the nameless terror behind the rift stand mute. Then slowly they start to disperse. Groups break away and move off. He knows that, in years to come, these ragged refugees will conquer this world, for they are the seeds of the nations that populate Kelewan.

He knows he has seen the beginning of the nations, and their flight from the Enemy, the nameless terror that destroyed the homes of the races of mankind, dispersing them to other universes.

Again the cloak of time is drawn over him, creating darkness.

FOLLOWED BY LIGHT.

On the plain that had been empty, a great city stands. Its white towers ascend to the skies. Its people are industrious, and the city prospers. Caravans of trade goods come overland, and great ships call from across the sea. Years speed by, bringing war and famine, peace and bounty.

One day a ship pulls into the harbor, as scarred and ill as its crew. A great battle has been fought, and this ship is one of the few to survive. Those across the water will come soon, and the City of the Plains will fall if help is not forthcoming. Runners are sent north to the cities along the great river, for should the white city fall, nothing will prevent the invaders from striking northward. Runners return, carrying the news. The armies of the other cities will come. He watches as they gather and meet the invaders near the sea. The invaders are repulsed, but the cost is great, for the battle rages twelve days. A hundred thousand men die, and the sands are red for months. A thousand ships burn, and the sky is filled with black smoke, and for days it falls upon the land, covering miles about with a fine, powdery ash. The city of white becomes the city of grey. The sea is called Blood from that day forward, and the great bay is called Battle. But out of the battle an alliance is formed, and the seeds of the great Empire are planted, the world-spanning Empire of Tsuranuanni.

Like silence descending, darkness comes.

AS A CLARION sounding, light returns.

He stands atop a temple, in the heart of the central city of the Empire. Below, thousands of people stand. Shoulder to shoulder they fill the streets, chanting while thousands of upraised hands pass along great wooden platforms overhead. Upon the platforms stand the nobles of the Empire, Lords of the Five Great Families. Upon the last platform, largest of all, rests a golden throne, fashioned from the rarest of metals of this mineral-poor world. Upon this throne sits a young boy. When the platform reaches the Great Square of the Twenty Higher and Lower Gods, it is placed upon the ground, and the throne is carried on the backs of the citizens to the top of the highest temple.

The throne is lowered, facing southeast, from where the nations had come in the beginning. From deep within the temple, a dozen black-clad priestesses rush forth, red-clad priests at their side. The Priestesses of Sibi, the Death Goddess, point out one or another citizen in the crowd, and the red-clad Priests of the Killing God grab them. They seize men, women, and occasionally children. All are dragged to the top of the temple, where waiting priests of the Red God cut their hearts from their bodies, while the priests and priestesses of the other eighteen orders look on silently. When hundreds have been sacrificed, and the temple steps are bathed in blood, the Chief Priestess of the Death

Goddess judges the gods satisfied. They place a silver ring upon the boy's hand, and a golden circlet upon his brow, and proclaim him the Light of Heaven, Minjochka, eleven times Emperor. The boy plays with a wooden toy given to him at the start of the day, for he grows bored easily, while the throng presses forward to dip their hands in the blood of their countrymen, counting it lucky to do so.

In the east, the sky darkens as night approaches.

As the sun rises, he stands near a magician who has worked the night through. The man grows alarmed at what his calculations have shown, and he incants a spell that takes him to another place. The watcher follows. In a small hall, several more magicians react with expressions of dread to the news the first magician brings. A messenger is dispatched to the Warlord, ruler of the Empire in the Emperor's name. The Warlord summons the magicians. The watcher follows. The magicians explain the news. The signs in the stars, along with ancient writings, herald the coming of a great disaster. A star, a wanderer in the heavens sighted where none has been seen before, stands motionless but grows brighter. It will bring destruction to the nations. The Warlord is skeptical, but of late more and more nobles have come to heed the words of magicians. There have always been legends of magicians saving the nations from the Enemy, but few think them likely. Still, there is now this new convocation of magicians, who have formed something called the Assembly, toward what ends only the magicians know. So, with the changing times in mind, the Warlord agrees to take the news to the Emperor. After a time an order is sent to the Assembly by the Emperor. His demand: bring proof. The magicians shake their heads and return to their modest halls.

Decades pass, and the magicians conduct a campaign of propaganda, seeking to influence any noble of the Empire who will listen. The day arrives when the news is proclaimed that the Emperor is dead and his son now reigns. The magicians gather with all who can travel to the Holy City for the coronation of the new Emperor.

Thousands of people line the streets, while slaves bear the nobles of the land in litters to the great temples. The new Emperor rides the ancient golden throne, born by a hundred husky slaves. He is crowned, while a slave is sacrificed deep within the halls of the temple of the Death God, Turakamu, as a petition to the gods to allow the old Emperor's soul to rest in heaven.

The crowd cheers, for Sudkahanchoza, thirty-four times Emperor, is well loved, and this will be the last time they will ever look upon him.

He will now retire to the Holy Palace, where his soul will stand forever vigilant on behalf of his subjects, while the Warlord and the High Council conduct the business of governing the Empire. The new Emperor will live a contemplative life, reading, painting, studying the great books of the temples, seeking to purify his soul for this arduous life.

This Emperor is unlike his father and, after hearing the grave news from the Assembly, orders the building of a great castle upon an island in the center of the giant lake in the midst of the mountains of Ambolina.

Time . . .

. . . PASSES.

Hundreds of black-clad magicians stand atop towers that rise from the city of the island, not yet the magnificent single entity of the future. Two hundred years have passed, and now two suns burn in the sky, one warm and yellow-green, the other small, white, and angry. The watcher sees the men work their magic, the greatest spell cast in the history of the nations. Even the legendary bridge from the outside, the beginning of time, was not so great a feat, for then they had only moved between worlds, now they would move a star. Below he can feel the presence of hundreds of other magicians, adding their power to those above. The spell has been wrought over the last few years, each step taken with the greatest care, as the Stranger approaches. Though powerful beyond compare, this enchantment is also delicate in the extreme. Any misstep and its work will be undone. He looks up and sees the Stranger, its course marked toward the path of this world. It will not strike Kelewan, but there is little doubt that its heat added to Kelewan's already hot star will render the planet lifeless. Kelewan will hang for over a year between its own primary and the Stranger, in constant daylight, and all magicians agree that only a few might survive in deep caves, to emerge to a burned-out planet. Now they must act, before it is too late to try again should the enchantment fail.

Now they do act, all in concert, incanting the last piece of the great arcane work. The world seems to stand still for a moment, reverberating with the final word of the spell. Slowly that reverberation grows louder, picking up resonance, developing new harmonies, new overtones, a character of its own. Soon it is loud enough to deafen those in the towers, who cover their ears. Below, those on the ground stand in mute wonder, looking to the sky where a blaze of color begins to form. Ragged bolts of energy flash, and the light from the two stars is dimmed in momentarily blinding displays that will leave some who viewed them sightless for the rest of their lives. He is not affected by the sound or light, as if some agency has taken care to protect him from their effects. A great rift appears in the sky, much like the one the golden bridge came through ages ago. He watches without emotion, his strongest feeling being detached fascination. It grows in the sky, between the Stranger and Kelewan, and begins to move away from the planet, toward the invading star.

But something else occurs. From the heart of the rift, more violent than at the time of the golden bridge, an unprecedented display of erupting energies comes forth. The chaotic scene is matched with an overwhelming wave of hatred. The Enemy, the evil power that drove the nations to Kelewan, still abides in the other universe, and it has not forgotten those who escaped it ages ago. It cannot pierce the barrier of the rift, for it needs more time to move between universes than the life span of the rift, but it reaches forth and warps it, sending it away from the Stranger. The rift grows larger, and those on the ground see it is going to engulf Kelewan, bringing the planet back into the dominion of the Enemy.

The watcher looks on impassively, unlike those around him, for he knows that this is not the end of the world. The rift rushes toward the planet, and one magician comes forth.

He is somehow familiar to the one who watches. The man, unlike those around him, wears a brown robe, fastened round with a whipcord belt, and holds a staff of wood. He raises the staff above his head and incants. The rift changes, from colors impossible to describe to inky black, and it strikes the planet.

The heavens explode for a moment, then all around is black. When the darkness lifts, the sun, Kelewan's own, is dropping below the horizon.

The magicians who are not dead or mad stare upward in horror. Above them the sky is a void, without stars.

And the man in brown turns to him and says, "Remember, things are not always what they seem."

Blackness . . .

. . . HERALDS THE passing of time again. He is standing in the halls of the Assembly. Magicians are appearing regularly, using the pattern on the floor as a focal point for their transit. Each remembers the pattern like an address, and wills himself there. A message arrives from the Emperor. He begs the Assembly to solve the problem, promising them whatever aid they require.

The watcher moves forward through generations to find the magicians again upon the towers. Now, instead of the invading Stranger, they regard a starless sky. Another spell, years in the fashioning, is being incanted. When it is finished, the earth reverberates with violent energies. Suddenly the sky is ablaze with stars, and Kelewan is again in its normal place.

"Things are not always what they seem," says a voice.

The Emperor sends a command that the full Assembly should come to the Holy City at once. By ones and twos they use the patterns to travel to Kentosani. The watcher follows. There they are taken to the inner chamber of the Emperor's palace, something unheard of in the history of the Empire.

Of the seven thousand magicians who gathered a century before to thwart the Stranger, only two hundred survived. Even now that number has increased but slightly, so that not even one magician for each twenty who stood upon towers against the Stranger answers the Emperor's call. They advance to stand before Tukamaco, forty times Emperor, descendant of Sudkahanchoza, and Light of Heaven. The Emperor asks if the Assembly will accept the charge to stand ever vigilant over the Empire, protecting it until the end of time. The magicians confer and agree. The Emperor then leaves his throne and abases himself before the assembled magicians, something never done before. He sits back and, still on his knees before them, throws wide his arms and proclaims that from this day forth the magicians are the Great Ones, free from all obligations, save the charge just accepted. They are outside the law, and none may command them, including the Warlord, who stands to one side, a frown upon his face. Whatever they desire is theirs to ask, for their words will be as law.

And a magician smiles knowingly at another nearby.

Darkness . . .

. . . AND TIME passes.

The watcher stands before the Warlord's throne. A delegation of magicians stand before the Warlord. They present him with proof of what they have claimed. A controllable rift, free from the Enemy's influence, has been opened, and another world has been found. This is unsuitable for life—but a second has been discovered, a rich, ripe world. They show him a lifetime's worth of wealth in metals, all found lying about, discarded. He who watches smiles to himself over the Warlord's eagerness at the sight of a broken breastplate, a rusted sword, and a handful of bent nails. To further prove this is an alien world, they present him with a strange but beautiful flower. The Warlord smells it and is pleased with its rich fragrance. The watcher nods, for he, too, knows the richness of a Midkemian rose.

The black wing of passing time covers him again.

ONCE MORE HE stood upon the platform. He looked around and saw that the full fury of the storm was breaking around him. Only by his unconscious will had he been able to stand upon this platform, while his conscious mind was occupied by the unfolding history of Kelewan. He now understood the nature of the test, for he found himself exhausted from the energy he had expended during the ordeal. While being instilled with the final instruction in his place in this society, he had been tested with the raw fury of nature.

He took a last look around, finding the grim view of the storm-tossed lake and the shuttered windows of the towers somehow satisfying. He strove to capture this image, as if to ensure that he would forever remember the moment he came to his full awakening as a Great One, for there were no more blocks on his memory, or his emotions. He exulted in his power: no longer Pug the keep boy, but now a magician of power to dwarf the imagination of his former master, Kulgan. And never again would either of these worlds, Midkemia or Kelewan, seem the same to him.

By force of will he descended to the roof, floating gently through the raging wind. The door opened in anticipation of his coming. He entered, and it closed behind him. Shimone was waiting for him, a smile upon his face. As they moved down the long halls of the Assembly building-city, the skies outside exploded with clashes of thunder, as if heralding his arrival.

HOCHOPEPA SAT upon his mat, awaiting the arrival of his guest. The heavy, bald magician was interested in gauging the mettle of the newest member of the Assembly, come into his estate as a wearer of the black robe the previous day.

A chime sounded, announcing his guest's arrival. Hochopepa stood and crossed his richly furnished apartment. He pulled aside the sliding door. "Welcome, Milamber. I am pleased you saw fit to accept my invitation."

"I am honored," was all Milamber said as he entered and regarded the room. Of all the quarters in the Assembly building he had seen, this was by far the most opulent. The hangings on the walls were rich cloth, enhanced with the finest threadwork, and there were several valuable metal objects adorning various shelves.

Milamber made a study of his host as well. The heavyset magician showed Milamber to a cushion before a low table and then poured cups of chocha. His plump hands moved with controlled ease, precisely and efficiently. His dark, nearly black, eyes shone from under the thick brows that accented an otherwise deceptively bland face. He was the stockiest magician Milamber had seen yet, as most who wore the black robe tended to be thin and ascetic looking. Milamber sensed this was largely by design, as if someone occupied with the pleasures of the flesh couldn't be too concerned with matters of deep thought.

After the first sip of chocha had been taken, Hochopepa said, "You pose something of a problem for me, Milamber."

When Milamber made no comment, Hochopepa said, "You make no remark." Milamber inclined his head in agreement. "Perhaps your background accounts for a bit more wariness than is the rule here."

Milamber said, "A slave become magician is something to ponder."

Hochopepa waved his hand. "It is a rarity for a slave to don the black robe, but not unheard of. Occasionally the power is not recognized until adulthood. But the laws are explicit, and no matter how late the power is revealed, nor how mean the station of the man manifesting it, from that instant on he is subject only to the Assembly. Once a soldier was ordered hanged by his lord. He floated, suspended in space, a scant hair's breadth from hanging, by sheer power of will. His power finally manifested itself at the moment of his greatest need. He was given over to the Assembly, where he survived training, but proved to be a magician of indifferent power and overall poor outlook.

"But that is not for this discussion. Your particular situation, the one that makes you somewhat of a problem for me, is that you are a barbarian—excuse me, were a barbarian."

Milamber smiled again. He had left the Tower of Testing with all his memories of his life, though much about his training was still sketchy. He understood the processes that had been used to bring him into control of his magic. They had singled him out as one among a hundred thousand, a Great One. Of the two hundred million people of the Empire, he was one of two thousand magicians of the black robe. His slave-bred wariness, as Hochopepa pointed out, combined with his intelligence to keep him silent. Hochopepa was trying to make a point, and Milamber would wait to hear what it was, no matter how roundabout the stout magician insisted on being.

When Milamber said nothing, Hochopepa continued. "Your position is strange for several reasons. The obvious one is that you are the first to wear the black who is not of this world. The second is that you were the apprentice of a Lesser Magician."

Milamber raised an eyebrow. "Kulgan? You know of my training?"

Hochopepa laughed, a genuine belly laugh, which made Milamber relax his guard a little and regard the other man with a little less distrust. "Of course. There was not one aspect of your background that was not closely examined, for you provided a wealth of information about your world." Hochopepa looked closely at his guest. "The Warlord might choose to launch an invasion into a world we know little about—over the objections of some of his magician advisers, I might add—but we of the Assembly prefer to study our adversaries. We were most relieved to learn magic is restricted to the province of priests and followers of the Lesser Path on your world."

"Again you mention a Lesser Magic. What is your meaning?"

It was Hochopepa's turn to look slightly surprised. "I assumed you knew." Milamber shook his head. "The Path of Lesser Magic is walked by some who can operate certain forces by power of will, though of a different order than we of the black robe."

"Then you know of my previous failure."

Hochopepa laughed again. "Yes. Had you been less suited to the Greater Path, you might have learned his ways. As it is, you had too much ability to have succeeded as a Lesser Path magician. It is a talent rather than an art, the Lesser Path. The Greater Path is for scholars."

Milamber nodded. Each time Hochopepa explained a concept, it was as if Milamber had known it all his life. He remarked on this.

"It is easy enough to understand. During your training many facts and concepts were taught you. The basic concepts of magic were taught early, your responsibility to the Empire later. Part of the process of bringing all your abilities to maturity requires that all these facts be there when you need them. But much of what you were taught was also masked, to be revealed when you needed it, when you could fully understand what was in your mind. There will be a period when thoughts will come unbidden from time to time. As you frame a question, the answer will appear in your mind. And sometimes an answer will come as you read it or hear it. It serves to keep you from reeling under the impact of years of learning coming upon you in an instant.

"It is not unlike the spells used to grant you the visions on the Tower of Testing. Obviously, we have no means to 'see' what occurred before the time of the bridge, or at any other time in history, but we can plant suggestions, create illusion—"

Things are not what they seem. Milamber barely hid his surprise at this unexpected voice in his mind.

"—and provide a construct around which you may add the images most significant to you. Personally, I find the entire presentation upon the Tower reeks of Grand Dō Opera. You may avail yourself of the libraries should you seek history rather than theater." Seeing Milamber's attentions were elsewhere, Hochopepa said, "In any event, we were speaking of other things."

Milamber said, "I would hear of your problem."

Hochopepa adjusted his robe, smoothing the creases. "Indulge me a moment longer for a brief digression. It all has bearing on why I asked you here." Milamber signified that Hochopepa should continue.

"Little is known of our peoples before the Escape. We know that the nations came from many different worlds. There is also some speculation that others fled the Enemy to different worlds, your former homeworld among them perhaps. There are a few shreds of evidence to support that hypothesis, but it is only conjecture at this point." Milamber thought about the games of shāh he had played with the Lord of the Shinzawai and considered the possibility.

"We came as refugees. Of millions, only thousands survived to plant seeds here. We found this world old and used up. Great civilizations once flourished here, and all that is left of them are worn, smooth stones where once cities stood. Who these creatures were, no one knows. This world has few metals, and what was brought with us in the Escape wore away over the ages. Our animals, like your horses and cattle, died out, all save for dogs. We had to adjust to our new homeworld, and to each other.

"We fought many wars between the time of the Escape and the advent of the Stranger. We were little more than city-states until the Battle of a Thousand Ships. Then the humblest of the races, the Tsurani, rose to conquer all others, uniting most of this world in a single Empire.

"We of the Assembly support the Empire because on this world it is the single most powerful force for order—not because it is noble, or fair, or beautiful, or just. But because of it the majority of humanity can live and work without war in their homelands, can live without famine, plagues, and the other disasters of older times. And with this order around us, we of the Assembly can work unhindered.

"It was the attempt to dispel the Stranger that first made it apparent that we must be able to work unhindered by anyone, including the Emperor, with whatever resources are necessary. We were robbed of precious time for action by the Emperor's lack of cooperation when we first learned of the Stranger. Had we been given support at once, we might have been able to deal with the Enemy when it acted to warp the rift. That is why we accepted the charge to defend and serve the Empire, in exchange for total freedom."

Milamber said, "This is all apparent as you speak of it. I am still waiting to hear of your problem regarding me."

Hochopepa sighed. "In good time, my friend. I must finish one last thought. You must understand why the Assembly functions as it does to have any hope of surviving more than a few weeks."

Milamber looked openly surprised at this remark. "Survive?"

"Yes, Milamber, survive, for there are many here who would have seen you at the bottom of the lake during your training."

"Why?"

"We work to restore the Greater Art. When we fled the Enemy, at the dawn of history, only one magician in a thousand who battled the Enemy survived. They, for the most part, were the Lesser Magicians and apprentices. They banded together in small groups to protect the knowledge they brought with them from their homeworlds. At first countryman would seek out countryman, then, later, larger associations grew, as desire grew to restore the lost arts. After centuries had passed, the Assembly was founded, and magicians from all parts of the world came, until today all who walk the Greater Path are members of the Assembly. Most of those who practice the Lesser Art serve here as well, though they are afforded a different level of respect and freedom. They tend to be better at building devices and understanding the forces of nature than we of the black robes—they build the orbs we use to transport ourselves from place to place, for one example. While not outside the law, the Lesser Magicians are protected from interference from others by the Assembly. All magicians are the province of the Assembly."

Milamber said, "So we gain freedom to act as we see fit, as long as we act in the best interest of the Empire."

Hochopepa nodded. "It does not matter what we do, or even that two magicians may find themselves at odds over some action or another, as long as both are working in what they believe is the best interest of the Empire."

"From my somewhat 'barbaric' point of view, a strange law."

"Not a law, but a tradition. On this world, my barbaric friend, tradition and custom can be a much stronger constraint than law. Laws are changed, but tradition endures."

"I think I see what your problem is, my civilized friend. You are not sure if I will act in the best interest of the Empire, being an outlander."

Hochopepa nodded. "Were we certain that you were capable of acting against the Empire, you would have been killed. As it is, we are uncertain, though we tend to believe it unlikely you are capable of such action."

For the first time Milamber was completely unsure of what he was hearing. "I was under the assumption that you had ways of ensuring that all who are trained are loyal to the Empire, as the first duty."

"Normally, yes. In your case we faced problems new to us. As far as we can tell, you are submerged in the underlying cause of the brotherhood of magicians, the order of the Empire. Usually we are certain. We simply read the apprentice's mind. With you we couldn't. We had to rely on truth drugs, long interrogations, and training drills designed to show any duplicity."

"Why?"

"Not for any reason we understand. The spells of thought masking are known. It was nothing of that sort. It was as if your mind held some property we had never encountered before. Perhaps a natural talent unknown to us, but common to your world; or the result of some training at the hands of your Lesser Path master protected you against our mind-reading arts.

"In any event, it created something of a stir in these halls, you may be sure. Several times during your training, the question of your continuing was raised, and each time our inability to read your mind was given as reason for your termination. Each time more were willing to see you continue than not. On the whole you present a possible wealth of new knowledge and, as such, deserve every benefit of the doubt—to ensure we do not lose such a valuable addition to our storehouse of talents, of course."

"Of course," Milamber said dryly.

"Yesterday the question of your continuation became critical. When the time came for your final acceptance into the Assembly, the issue was put to the vote and ended in a tie. There was one abstention, myself. As long as I remain unallied with one side or the other, the question of your survival is moot. You are free to act as a full member of the Assembly until I recast my vote to ratify your selection into the Assembly, or not. Our tradition does not allow a change of vote, once cast, except abstentions. As no one absent during the voting may add their vote later, I am the only one who can break the tie. So the result of the voting, no matter how long delayed, is mine to decide."

Milamber looked long and hard at the older magician. "I see."

Hochopepa shook his head slowly. "I wonder if you do. To put it in its simplest form, the question of the moment is, what am I to do with you? Without meaning to, I find your life is now in my hands. What I have to decide is whether or not you should be killed. That is why I wished to see you, to see if I might have erred in judgment."

Suddenly Milamber threw back his head and laughed, long and hard. In a moment tears were running down his cheeks. When he quieted, Hochopepa said, "I fail to see the humor."

Milamber raised his hand in a placating gesture. "No offense was intended, my civilized friend. But surely you must see the irony of the situation. I was a slave, my life subject to the whim of others. For all my training, and advancement in station, I find that this fact has not been altered." He paused for a moment, and his smile was friendly. "Still, I would rather have you hold my life in your hands than my former overseer. That is what I find so funny."

Hochopepa was startled by the answer, then he, too, started to laugh. "Many of our brothers pay little heed to the ancient teachings, but if you are familiar with our older philosophers, you will understand my meaning. You seem to be a man who has found his *wal*. I think we have an understanding, my barbaric friend. I think we have started well."

Milamber studied Hochopepa. Without knowing the unconscious process whereby he reached the conclusion, he judged he had found an ally, and perhaps a friend. "I think so, as well. And I think you also a man who has found his *wal*."

Feigning modesty, Hochopepa said, "I am but a simple man, too much a slave to pleasures of the flesh to have reached such a state of perfect centering." With a sigh he leaned forward and began to speak intently. "Listen to me well, Milamber. For all the reasons enumerated before, you are as much a weapon to be feared as a possible source of knowledge.

"Tsurani are slaves to politics, as any student of the Game of the Council can attest; while we of the Assembly are reputed to be above such things, we have our own factions and infighting, not always settled in a peaceful, bloodless manner.

"Many of our brothers are little more than superstitious peasants, distrusting that which is alien and unknown. From this day forward, you must bend yourself to one task. Stay peacefully hidden within your *wal*, and become Tsurani. To all outward appearances, you must become more Tsurani than anyone else in the Assembly. Is that understood?"

"It is," Milamber said simply.

Hochopepa poured another cup of hot chocha each. "Be especially wary of the Warlord's pets, Elgahar and Ergoran, and a reckless youngster named Tapek. Their master rankles at the progress of the war upon your former homeworld and is suspicious of the Assembly. Now that two of our brothers died in the last major campaign, fewer of our brothers are willing to lend further aid to that undertaking. The few magicians left within his faction are overtaxed, and it is rumored he will be unable to subdue any more of your world without a miracle. It would take a united High Council—which should happen when the Thūn raiders become agriculturalists and poets, and not before—or a large number of Black Robes agreeing to do his bidding. The latter should occur about a year after the former, so you can see he is in a somewhat poor political situation. Warlords who fail in conducting war tend to fall from grace quickly." With a smile he added, "Of course, we of the Assembly are far above matters political." His tone turned serious once more. "You must face one thing: he may view you as a potential threat, either influencing others not to aid him, or openly opposing him from some deep-rooted sympathy for your former homeland. You are protected from his direct actions, but you still might run afoul of his pets. Some still blindly follow his lead."

" 'The path of power is a path of turns within turns,' " Milamber quoted.

Hochopepa nodded, a satisfied expression upon his face. His eyes seemed to glint. "That is Tsurani. You learn quickly."

IN THE FOLLOWING weeks Milamber grew into the fullness of his new position, learning the responsibilities of his office. It was remarked on more than once, and occasionally with distrust, that there had been few who had demonstrated so much ability so soon after donning the black robe.

For all the changes in his existence, Milamber discovered many things were unchanged. With practice he discovered he still had untapped wells of power within, which could be called up only in times of stress. He studied to bring this wild augmentation of power under control, but with little success. He also discovered he was able to put aside the mental conditions placed upon him during training. He chose not to reveal this fact to anyone, not even Hochopepa. His reordering of these mental conditionings also regained him something else, a nearly overwhelming desire to be with Katala once again. He put aside that desire, to go to her at once and demand her release from the Lord of the Shinzawai, well within his ability now he was a Great One. He hesitated for fear of the reaction of the other magicians, and for fear her feelings might have changed toward him. Instead he plunged into his studies.

His time in the Assembly brought forth his true identity, as he had been told it would. This identity proved the key to his unusual mastery of the Greater Path. He was a being of both worlds, worlds bound together by the great rift. And for as long as those worlds stayed bound together, he drew power from both, twice the power available to others of the black robe. This knowledge revealed his true name, that name which could not be spoken lest it let another gain power over him. In the ancient Tsurani language, unused since the time of the Escape, it meant, "One who stands between worlds."

23

▾▾

VOYAGE

MARTIN WATCHED.

Motioning silently to his companions, they slipped through the wood line, just out of sight of those in the meadow. They could easily hear the shouts in the Tsurani camp as orders were given. Martin crouched low, so no hint of movement would betray their presence. Behind him scurried Garret and the former Tsurani slave, Charles. In the six years since the siege of Crydee, Charles had met Martin's expectations, proving his loyalty and worth a dozen times. He had also become a passable woodsman, though he would never have Garret or Martin's natural ease.

Whispering, Charles said, "Huntmaster, I mark many new banners."

"Where?"

Charles pointed to a spot near the farthest edge of the Tsurani camp. With the aid of the dwarves remaining in the high villages, Martin and his two companions had made the dangerous climb over the Grey Towers, easily passing the few Tsurani sentries left along the western edge of the valley, the flank thought least in need of vigilance. Now they were within a few hundred feet of the main Tsurani camp.

Garret let forth a nearly silent whistle. "The man has eyes like a falcon. I can barely see those banners."

Charles said, "I only know what to look for."

"What do the new banners mean?" asked Longbow.

"Ill news, Huntmaster. Those are the house banners of families that were loyal to the Blue Wheel Party. At least when I was captured. They have been absent since the siege of Crydee. This can mean only another major shift in the High Council." He studied the Huntmaster's face. "It tells us the Alliance for War is again restored. And next spring we can expect a major offensive."

Martin motioned for them to move back into the woods. The trees were fully covered in fall colors, riots of red, gold, and brown. Moving quietly through fallen leaves, they found a sheltering stand of brush skirting an ancient oak and knelt behind it. Martin took out a small piece of dried beef and chewed it. The climb over the Grey Towers, even with the dwarves' help, had taken its toll: they all were hungry, tired, and dirty. "Where are the new companies of soldiers?" Martin asked.

"They won't bring them through this winter. They can stage outside the City of the Plains on Kelewan, at ease in a milder climate. They'll move through the rift just before the spring thaw. By the time flowers are blooming in Princess Carline's garden again, they'll be marching."

A high-pitched keening sound came from the north. Charles's expression changed to one of controlled alarm. "Cho-ja!" He glanced around, then pointed upward.

Martin nodded and made a stirrup with his hands. He boosted first Charles, then Garret, into the oak tree. Then he jumped, and they caught his hands and pulled him up.

Moving into the higher branches, they were motionless and had weapons ready when the cho-ja patrol came into view, passing beneath the tree. Six of the antlike creatures moved at steady pace; then the leader, marked by a crested helm of Tsurani make, motioned them to halt. He turned one way then another, then made commands in their high-pitched language. The other five spread out, and for nearly ten minutes the three men in the tree could hear them searching the area.

When they returned, they quickly formed up and moved off. When Martin was certain they were out of hearing range, he whispered, "What was that?"

"They smelled us. My scent will have changed from all the Midkemian food I have eaten. They knew we were not Tsurani."

Climbing down from the tree, Charles said, "Cho-ja cannot look easily upward, so they rarely do."

Garret asked, "What if some of your former countrymen had been along?"

Charles shrugged. "The cho-ja would have been speaking Tsurani. Their language is almost impossible to learn, so no one tries."

Martin said, "Will they be able to mark our trail?"

Charles said, "I don't think so, but—" He stopped as loud barking came from the Tsurani camp. "Dogs!"

Martin said, "They can track us. Come." He set out at a controlled run, back toward an ancient trail into the mountains, one almost completely overgrown and undiscovered by the Tsurani but used by Martin's band to enter the valley.

For a few moments the three men loped through the woods, listening to the barking behind. Then the sound of the dogs changed, and barks became howls and baying. "They've gotten the scent," said Garret.

Martin only nodded and picked up the pace. They ran for another minute, the sound of the dogs steadily gaining on them, when Martin halted and grabbed at Garret's arm to keep him from running past. With a signal, he changed directions away from the trail and led the others to a small stream. Entering the water, he said, "I remembered hearing this when we passed by before."

The other two entered the water, and Martin said, "We gain only minutes. They'll search up- and downstream."

Garret said, "Which way?"

Martin said, "Downstream. They'll search upstream first, as that's the way out."

Charles said, "Huntmaster, there's another way." He quickly unshouldered his backpack and removed a large pouch. He began sprinkling black powder up and down the shore of the stream where they had entered.

Garret felt his eyes tearing and blew hard through his nose to keep from sneezing. "Pepper!"

Charles said, "Mastercook Megar will be angry, but I thought we might need it. The cho-ja and the dogs will smell nothing for hours when they sniff around here."

Martin nodded. "Upstream!"

The three men splashed through the water, then got into a quieter, steady rhythm. They were out of sight of the place where they entered when the baying of the dogs was interrupted by sneezes. Angry voices shouted commands, and frustrated replies were heard. Charles indulged himself in a faint smile as they continued to move through the water.

Finding a branch low enough over the stream, Martin boosted his companions out and climbed up after them. They moved along the tree until they found another branch of a nearby oak close enough to jump to.

They touched the ground again a dozen yards from the stream bank. Martin glanced around to ensure they were not seen and motioned for the others to follow as he led them back toward the Grey Towers.

▾▾

SEA BREEZES SWEPT the walls. Arutha looked out at the town of Crydee and the sea beyond, his brown hair ruffled by the wind. Patches of light and dark flashed across the landscape as high, fluffy clouds raced overhead. Arutha watched the distant horizon, taking in the vista of the Endless Sea whipped to a froth of whitecaps, as the noise of workmen restoring another building in the town blew by on the wind.

Another autumn visited Crydee, the eighth since the start of the war. Arutha considered it fortunate another spring and summer had passed without a major Tsurani offensive; still, he felt little cause for comfort. He was no longer a boy fresh to command, but a seasoned soldier. At twenty-seven years he had seen more conflict, and had made more decisions, than most men of the Kingdom knew in their lives. In his best judgment, he knew the Tsurani were slowly winning the war.

He let his mind drift a little, then shook himself out of his brooding. While no longer a moody boy, he still tended to let introspection overtake him. He found it best to keep busy and avoid such wasteful pastimes.

"It is a short autumn."

Arutha looked to his left and found Roland standing nearby. The Squire had caught the Prince lost in thought and had made his approach without detection. Arutha found himself irritated. He shrugged it off and said, "And a short winter will follow, Roland. And in the spring . . ."

"What news of Longbow?"

Arutha balled a gloved fist and gently struck the stones of the wall, the slow, controlled gesture, a clear sign of his frustration. "I've regretted the need for his going a hundred times. Of the three, only Garret shows any sense of caution. That Charles is a Tsurani madman, consumed by honor, and Longbow is . . ."

"Longbow," finished Roland.

"I've never met a man who reveals so little of himself, Roland. If I live as long as an elf, I don't think I'll ever understand what makes him the way he is."

Roland leaned against the cool stones of the wall and said, "Do you think they're safe?"

Arutha returned his attention to the sea. "If any man in Crydee can crest the mountains into the Tsurani-held valley and get back, it is Martin. Still, I worry."

Roland found the admission surprising. Like Martin, Arutha was not a man to reveal what he felt. Sensing the Prince's deep trouble, Roland changed the topic. "I've a message from my father, Arutha."

"I was told there was a personal message among the dispatches from Tulan."

"Then you know Father's calling me home."

"Yes. I'm sorry about the broken leg."

"Father was never much of a rider. It's the second time he's fallen from his horse and broken something. Last time, when I was little, it was his arm."

"It's been a long time since you were home."

Roland shrugged. "With the war, I felt little need to return. Most of the fighting's been around here. And," he added with a grin, "there are other reasons to stay."

Sharing the smile, Arutha said, "Have you told Carline yet?"

Roland lost his grin. "Not yet. I thought I'd wait until I'd arranged for a ship south." With the Brotherhood's abandonment of the Green Heart, travel by land to the south was nearly impossible, for the Tsurani had cut off the roads to Carse and Tulan.

A shout from the tower caused them to turn. "Trackers approaching!"

Arutha squinted against the glare reflecting off the distant sea and could make out three figures trotting easily along the road. When they were close enough to be seen clearly, Arutha said, "Longbow." There was a note of relief in his voice.

Leaving the wall, Arutha descended the steps to the courtyard to wait for the Huntmaster and his men. Roland stood by his side as the three dusty men entered the gates of the castle. Both Garret and Charles remained silent as Martin said, "Greetings, Highness."

"Greetings, Martin. What news?" asked the Prince.

Martin began to recount the facts unearthed at the Tsurani camp, and after a moment Arutha cut him off. "Better save your wind for the council, Martin. Roland, go gather Father Tully, Swordmaster Fannon, and Amos Trask, and bring them to the council hall."

Roland hurried off, and Arutha said, "Charles and Garret are to come as well, Martin."

Garret glanced at the former Tsurani slave, who shrugged. Both knew the long-anticipated hot meal would have to wait a little longer upon the Prince's convenience.

MARTIN TOOK the seat next to Amos Trask, while Charles and Garret remained standing. The former sea captain nodded a greeting to Martin, as Arutha pulled out his own chair, as was his habit, ignoring most formalities when with his councillors. Amos had become an unofficial member of Arutha's staff since the siege of the castle; he was an enterprising man of many unexpected skills.

Fannon sat to Arutha's right. Since his wound, he had been content to accept Arutha as commander in Crydee and had sent a personal note to Lord Borric advising him so. The Duke had sent a reply ratifying the transfer of command, and Fannon had returned to his former role as adjutant. The Swordmaster seemed pleased with the situation.

Arutha said, "Martin has just returned from a mission of special importance. Martin, tell us what you've seen."

Martin said, "We climbed the Grey Towers and entered the valley where the Tsurani have their headquarters."

Fannon and Tully looked at the Huntmaster with surprise, while Amos Trask guffawed. "You toss aside a small saga in one sentence," said the seaman.

Martin ignored the comment and said, "I think it best to let Charles tell you what we saw."

The former Tsurani slave's voice held a note of concern. "From all signs, the Warlord will launch another major offensive next spring."

Everyone in the room sat speechless, save Fannon. "How can you be sure? Are there new armies in his camp?"

Charles shook his head. "No, the new soldiers will not arrive until just before the first spring thaw. My former countrymen have little liking for your cold climate. They will stage during the winter months on my former homeworld. They'll move through the rift just before the offensive."

Even after five years, Fannon still had lingering doubts about Charles's loyalty, though Longbow held none. "How, then," said the Swordmaster, "can you be certain there is to be an offensive? We've had none since the assault on Elvandar three years ago."

"There are new banners in the Warlord's camp, Swordmaster, the banners of the houses who belong to the Blue Wheel Party. They have been absent for six years. It can mean only another major change within the High Council. The Alliance for War is again formed."

Of those in the room, only Tully seemed to grasp what Charles was saying. He had made a study of the Tsurani, learning all he could from the captured slaves. He said, "You had better explain, Charles."

Charles took a moment to organize his remarks and said, "You must understand one thing of my former homeland. Above everything except honor and obedience to the Emperor, there is the High Council. To gain in the High Council is worth much, even the risk of life itself.

More than one family has been destroyed by plots and intrigues within the council. We of the Empire refer to this as the 'Game of the Council.'

"My family was well placed within the Hunzan Clan, neither great enough to warrant notice by our clan's rivals, nor small enough to be relegated to only minor roles. We had the benefit of knowing much of the matters before the High Council without having to worry overly much about what decisions were made. Our clan was active in the Party for Progress, for we numbered many scholars, teachers, healers, priests, and artists in our families.

"Then for a time the Hunzan Clan left the Party for Progress, for reasons not clear to any but the highest family leaders, reasons I can only speculate on. My clan joined with the clans of the Blue Wheel Party, one of the oldest in the High Council. While not so powerful as the Warlord's War Party, or the traditionalists of the Imperial Party, it still has much honor and influence.

"Six years ago, when I first came here, the Blue Wheel Party had joined with the War Party to form the Alliance for War. Those of us in the lesser families were not told why such a radical change in alignment had come about, but there was no doubt it was a matter of the Game of the Council.

"My personal fall from grace and my enslavement was certainly necessary to ensure that those of my clan would stay above suspicion until the time was right for whatever move was being planned. It is now clear what that move was.

"Since the siege of this castle, I have seen no sign of any soldier who's a member of the Blue Wheel families. I took it to mean the Alliance for War had been ended."

Fannon interrupted. "Are you then saying the conduct of this war is but an aspect of some political game in this High Council?"

Charles said, "Swordmaster, I know it is difficult for a man as steadfast in his loyalty to his nation as you are to understand such a thing. But that is exactly what I am saying.

"There are reasons, Tsurani reasons, for such a war. Your world is rich in metals, metals we treasure on Kelewan. Also, ours is a bloody history, and all who are not of Tsuranuanni are to be feared and subjugated. If we could find your world, then might you not someday find ours?

"But more, it is a way for the Warlord to gain great influence in the High Council. For centuries we have fought the Thuril Confederation, and when we at last were forced to the treaty table, the War Party lost a great deal of power within the council. This war is a way for that lost power to be regained. The Emperor rarely commands, leaving the Warlord supreme, but the Warlord is still the Lord of a family, the Warchief of a clan, and as such is constantly seeking to gain advantage for his own people in the Game of the Council."

Tully looked fascinated. "So the Blue Wheel Party joining with the Warlord's party, then suddenly withdrawing, was but a ploy in this political game, a maneuver to gain some advantage?"

Charles smiled. "It is very Tsurani, good Father. The Warlord planned his first campaign with great care, then three years into it finds himself with only half an army. He is overextended, unable to bring news of smashing victories to the High Council and the Emperor. He loses position and prestige in the game."

Fannon said, "Unbelievable! Hundreds of men dying for such a thing."

"Such is the way of the Game of the Council, Swordmaster. The Warlord Almecho is an ambitious man. To be Warlord one must be. He must rely on other ambitious men, many who would seek to take his mantle should he falter. To keep these men as allies rather than foemen, he must occasionally look the other way.

"In the first year of the war, the Warlord's subcommander, a man called Tasio of the Minwanabi, ordered an attack upon one of the LaMutian garrisons. Besides being second-in-command in the campaign on this world, Tasio is also the cousin of Lord Jingu of the Minwanabi. The order to attack was given to Lord Sezu of the Acoma, sworn enemy of Jingu. The Acoma soldiers were almost destroyed to a man, including Lord Sezu and his son. Tasio arrived moments too late to save the Acoma, but in time to seize the battle and bring the Warlord a victory."

Fannon's eyes were round with disbelief. "That's the blackest duplicity I have ever heard of."

Arutha said, "It's also brilliant, by these people's standards."

Charles nodded in agreement with the Prince's remark. "The Warlord would forgive Tasio getting one of his better commanders slaughtered and losing the entire Acoma army, in exchange for a victory and strengthened support by the Minwanabi.

"Any Ruling Lord who had no direct stake in the game would applaud the move as a masterstroke, even those who admired Lord Sezu. It gained Almecho and Lord Jingu many allies in the council. So the Warlord's political opponents, needing to devise a way to counter his growing power, created the situation I described, overextending the Warlord and leaving him unable to prosecute this war. Many families hovering near the edge of the War Party would then be drawn to the Blue Wheel and their allies for delivering such a stunning blow."

Arutha said, "But the important fact for us is that this Blue Wheel is once more allied with the Warlord, and their soldiers will be rejoining the war come spring."

Charles looked at those in the council hall. "I cannot begin to guess why there has once again been a realignment in the council. I am too removed from the game. But as His Highness has said, what is important for those of us here in Crydee to know is that as many as ten thousand fresh soldiers may come against one of the fronts in the spring."

Amos scowled. "That's a backbreaker, for certain."

Arutha unfolded a half-dozen parchments. "Over the last few months, most of you have read these messages." He looked at Tully and Fannon. "You've seen the pattern begin to emerge." He picked up one parchment. "From Father: 'Constant Tsurani sorties and raids keep our men in a state of unease. Our inability to close with the enemy has lent a dark aspect to all we do. I fear we shall never see an end to this business. . . .' From Baron Bellamy: '. . . increased Tsurani activity near the Jonril garrison. I deem it advisable to increase our commitment there this winter, while the Tsurani are normally inactive, lest we lose that position next spring.' Squire Roland will be supervising a joint reinforcement from Carse and Tulan at Jonril this winter."

Several in the room glanced at Roland, who stood near Arutha's shoulder. The Prince continued. "From Lord Dulanic, Knight-Marshal of Krondor: 'While His Highness shares your concern, there is little to indicate the need for alarm. Unless some intelligence can be produced to give credence to your fears of possible future Tsurani offensives, I have advised the Prince of Krondor to refuse your request for elements of the Krondorian garrison to be sent to the Far Coast. . . .' " Arutha looked around the room. "Now the pattern is clear."

Setting aside the parchments, Arutha pointed at the map affixed to the tabletop. "We have committed every available soldier. We dare not pull men from the south for fear of the Tsurani moving against Jonril. With the garrison strengthened, we will have a stable situation down there for a while. Should the enemy attack the garrison, it can be reinforced from Carse and Tulan. Should the enemy move against either castle, they leave Jonril at their back. But all that will fail should we strip those garrisons.

"And Father is committed to a long front and has no men to spare." He looked at Charles. "Where would you expect the attack to come?"

The former Tsurani slave looked over the map, then shrugged. "It's difficult to say, Highness. Should the situation be decided solely upon military merits, the Warlord should attack against the weaker front, either toward the elves, or here. But little done in the Empire is free of political considerations." He studied troop dispositions on the map, then said, "Were I the Warlord, in need of a simple victory to bolster my position in the High Council, I would attack Crydee once more. But were I the Warlord and my position in the High Council precarious, in need of a bold stroke to regain lost prestige, I might risk an all-out offensive against the main force of the Kingdom, those armies under Duke Borric's command. To crush the main strength of the Kingdom would give him dominance within the council for years to come."

Fannon leaned back in his chair and sighed. "Then we are faced with the possibility of another assault upon Crydee this spring without recourse to reinforcements for fear of attack elsewhere." He indicated the map with a sweep of his hand. "Now we face the same problem as the Duke. All our forces are committed along the Tsurani front. The only men we have available are those in the towns on leave, only a small part of the whole.

"We can't maintain the army in the field indefinitely; even Lords Borric and Brucal winter in LaMut with the Earl, leaving small companies to guard the Tsurani." Waving his hand in the air, he said, "I digress. What is important is to notify your father at once, Arutha, of the possibility of attack. Then should the Tsurani hit his lines, he'll be back from LaMut early, in position and ready. Even should the Tsurani bring ten thousand fresh troops, he can call up more soldiers from the outlying garrisons in Yabon, fully another two thousand."

Amos said, "Two thousand against ten thousand sounds poor odds, Swordmaster."

Fannon was inclined to agree. "We do all we can. There are no guarantees it will be enough."

Charles said, "At least they will be horse soldiers, Swordmaster. My former comrades still have little liking for horses."

Fannon nodded agreement. "But even so, it is a bleak picture."

"There is one thing," said Arutha, holding up a parchment. "The message from Lord Dulanic stated the need for intelligence to give credence to our request for aid. We now have enough intelligence to satisfy him, I think."

Fannon said, "Even a small portion of the Krondorian garrison here would give us the strength to resist an offensive. Still, it is late in the season, and a message would have to be dispatched at once."

"That's the gods' truth," said Amos. "If you left this afternoon, you'd barely clear the Straits of Darkness before winter shuts them off. In another two weeks it'd be a close thing."

Arutha said, "I have given the matter some thought. I think there is enough need to risk my going to Krondor."

Fannon sat up straight in his chair. "But you're the commander of the Duchy's army, Arutha. You can't abandon that responsibility."

Arutha smiled. "I can and I will. I know you have no wish to resume command here once more, but resume command you will. If we are to win support from Erland, I must convince him myself. When Father first carried word of the Tsurani to Erland and the King, I learned the advantage of speaking in person. Erland's a cautious man. I will need every persuasion I can bring to bear."

Amos snorted. "And how do you plan on reaching Krondor, begging Your Highness's pardon? There's the better part of three Tsurani armies between here and the Free Cities should you go overland. And there are only a few luggers fit for coasting in the harbor, and you'd need a deep-water ship for a sea journey."

"There's one deep-water ship, Amos. The *Wind of Dawn* is still in port."

Amos's mouth dropped open. "The *Wind of Dawn?*" he cried in disbelief. "Beside the fact she's little better than a lugger herself, she's laid up for the winter. I heard her captain crying over her broken keelson when the muddleheaded fool came limping into harbor a month ago. She needs to be hauled out, have the keel inspected and the keelson replaced. Without repair her keel's too weak to take the pounding she'll get from the winter storms. You might as well stick your head in a rain barrel, begging Your Highness's pardon. You'd still drown, but you'd save a lot of other people a great deal of trouble."

Fannon looked incensed at the seaman's remarks, but Tully, Martin, Roland, and Arutha only looked amused. "When I sent Martin out," said Arutha, "I considered the possibility I might need a ship for Krondor. I ordered her repaired two weeks ago. There's a swarm of shipwrights aboard her now." He fixed Amos with a questioning look. "Of course I've been told it won't be as good a job as if they'd hauled her out, but it will serve."

"Aye, for potting up and down the coast in the light winds of spring, perhaps. But you're talking about winter storms, and you're talking about running the Straits of Darkness."

Arutha said, "Well, she will have to do. I'm leaving in a few days' time. Someone must convince Erland we need aid, and I have to be the one."

Amos refused to let the subject drop. "And has Oscar Danteen agreed to captain his ship through the straits for you?"

Arutha said, "I've not told him our destination as yet."

Amos shook his head. "As I thought. That man's got the heart of a shark, which is to say none, and the courage of a jellyfish, which is also to say none. Soon as you give the order, he'll cut your throat, drop you over the side, winter with the pirates of the Sunset Islands, then head straight for the Free Cities come spring. He'll then have some Natalese scribe pen a most grieving and flowery message to your father, describing your valor just before you were lost overboard in high seas while fighting pirates. Then he'll spend a year drinking up the gold you gave him for passage."

Arutha said, "But I purchased his ship. I'm ship's master now."

Amos said, "Owner or not, Prince or not, aboard ship there is but one master, the captain. He is King and High Priest, and no man tells him what to do, save when a harbor pilot's aboard, and then only with respect. No, Highness, you'll not survive this journey with Oscar Danteen on the quarterdeck."

Faint lines of mirth began to crinkle at the corners of Arutha's eyes. "Have you another suggestion, Captain?"

Amos sighed as he sank back into his chair. "I've been hooked; I might as well be gutted and cleaned. Send word to Danteen to clear out the captain's cabin and discharge the crew. I'll see to getting a replacement crew for that band of cutthroats, though there's mostly drunkards and boys left in port this time of year. And for the love of the gods, don't mention to anyone where we're bound. If so much as one of those drink-besotted scoundrels learns you mean to risk the Straits of Darkness this late in the season, you'll have to turn out the garrison to comb the woods for deserters."

Arutha said, "Very well. I'll leave all preparations to you. We depart as soon as you judge the ship ready." He said to Longbow, "I'll want you to come as well, Huntmaster."

Longbow looked a little surprised. "Me, Highness?"

"I'll want an eyewitness for Lord Dulanic and the Prince."

Martin frowned, but after a moment said, "I've never been to Krondor, Highness." He smiled his crooked smile. "I may never have the chance again."

AMOS TRASK'S VOICE cut through the shriek of the wind. Gusts from the sea carried his words to a confused-looking lad aloft. "No, you warped-brained landlubber, don't pull the sheets so damn tight. They'll be humming like a lute string. They don't pull the ship, the mast does.

The lines help when the wind changes quarter." He watched as the boy adjusted the sheets. "Yes, that's it; no, that's too loose." He swore loudly. "Now; there you have it!"

He looked disgusted as Arutha came up the gangway. "Fishing boys who want to be sailors. And drunkards. And a few of Danteen's rogues I had to rehire. This is some crew, Highness."

"Will they serve?"

"They bloody well better, or they'll answer to me." He watched with a critical eye as the sailors crawled over the spars aloft, checking every knot and splice, every line and sheet. "We need thirty good men. I can count on eight. The rest? I mean to put into Carse as well as Tulan on the way down. Maybe then we can replace the boys and less dependable men with experienced seamen."

"What of the delay clearing the straits?"

"If we were there today, we would manage. By the time we get there, a dependable crew will prove more important than arriving a week earlier. The season will be full upon us." He studied Arutha. "Do you know why the passage is called the Straits of Darkness?"

Arutha shrugged. Amos said, "It's no simple sailor's superstition. It's a description of what you find there." He got a far-off look as he said, "Now, I can tell you about the different currents from the Endless Sea and Bitter Sea that come together there, or about the changing, crazy tides of winter when the moons are all in the worst possible aspect in the heavens, or how winds come sweeping down from the north, blowing snow so thick you can't see the decks from the yards. But then . . . There are no words to describe the straits in winter. It is one, two, three days traveling blind. And if the prevailing wind's not blowing you back into the Endless Sea, then it's blowing you to the southern rocks. Or there's no wind, and fog blots out everything as the currents turn you around."

"You paint a bleak picture, Captain," said Arutha with a grim smile.

"Only the truth. You're a young man of uncommonly practical wits and cold nerve, Highness. I've seen you stand when many men of greater experience would have broken and run. I'm not trying to put any scare upon you. I simply wish you to understand what you propose to do. If any can clear the straits in winter in this bucket, it is Amos Trask, and that's no idle boast. I've cut the season so fine before, there's little to tell between autumn and winter, winter and spring. But I would also tell you this: before leaving Crydee, say tender good-byes to your sister, write your father and brother, and leave any testaments and legacies in order."

Without changing expression, Arutha said, "The letters and legacies are written, and Carline and I dine alone tonight."

Amos nodded. "We'll leave on the morning tide. This ship's a slab-sided, wattle-bottomed, water-rotted coaster, Highness, but she'll make it through if I have to pick her up and carry her."

Arutha took his leave, and when he was out of sight, Amos turned his attention heavenward. "Astalon," he invoked the god of justice, "I'm a sinner, it's true. But if you had to measure out justice, did it have to be this?" Now at peace with his fate, Amos returned to the business of seeing everything in order.

CARLINE WALKED IN the garden, the withering blooms reflecting her own sad mood. Roland watched her from a short way off, trying to find words of comfort. Finally he said, "I will be Baron of Tulan someday. It is over nine years since I've been home. I must go down the coast with Arutha."

Softly she said, "I know."

He saw the resignation on her face and crossed to hold her. "You will be Baroness there someday, also."

She hugged him tightly, then stepped away, forcing herself to speak lightly. "Still, you'd think after all these years your father would have learned to do without you."

He smiled. "He was to have wintered in Jonril with Baron Bellamy, overseeing the enlargement of the garrison. I will go in his stead. My brothers are all too young. With the Tsurani dug in for the winter, it is our only chance to expand the fort."

With forced levity she said, "At least I won't have to worry about your breaking the hearts of the ladies of your father's court."

He laughed. "Little chance of that. Supplies and men are already assembling and the barges ready to travel up the river Wyndermeer. After Amos puts me ashore in Tulan, I'll spend one or two days at home, no more, then off I go. It will be a long winter in Jonril with no one for company but soldiers and a few farmers in that gods-forsaken fort."

Carline covered her mouth as she giggled. "I hope your father doesn't discover you've gambled away his barony to the soldiers come spring."

Roland smiled at her. "I'll miss you."

Carline took his hands in hers. "And I you."

They stood in tableau for a time, then suddenly Carline's facade of bravery cracked, and she was in his arms. "Don't let anything happen. I couldn't bear losing you."

"I know," he said gently. "But you must continue to put on a brave face for others. Fannon will need your help in conducting court, and you will have the responsibility for the entire household. You are mistress of Crydee, and many people will depend upon your guidance."

They watched the banners on the walls snapping in the late-afternoon wind. The air was harsh, and he drew his cloak about them. Trembling, she said, "Come back to me, Roland."

Softly he said, "I'll come back, Carline." He tried to shake a cold, icy feeling that had risen within, but could not.

THEY STOOD ON the dock, in the darkness of morning before the sunrise. Arutha and Roland waited by the gangway. Arutha said, "Take care of everything, Swordmaster."

Fannon stood with his hand upon his sword, still proud and erect despite advancing years. "I will, Highness."

With a slight smile Arutha said, "And when Gardan and Algon return from patrol, instruct them to take care of you."

Fannon's eyes blazed as he shot back. "Insolent pup! I can best any man of the castle, save your father. Step down from the gangway and draw your sword, and I'll show you why I still wear the badge of Swordmaster."

Arutha held his hands up in mock supplication. "Fannon, it is good to see such sparks again. Crydee is well protected by her Swordmaster."

Fannon stepped forward and placed his hand upon Arutha's shoulder. "Take care, Arutha. You were always my best student. I should hate to lose you."

Arutha smiled fondly at his old teacher. "My thanks, Fannon." Then his manner turned wry. "I would hate to lose me, also. I'll be back. And I'll have Erland's soldiers with me."

Arutha and Roland sprang up the gangway, while those on the dock waved good-bye. Martin Longbow waited at the rail, watching as the gangway was removed and the men upon the quay cast off lines. Amos Trask shouted orders, and sails were lowered from the yards. Slowly the ship moved away from the quayside into the harbor. Arutha watched silently, with Roland and Martin beside, as the docks fell behind.

Roland said, "I was glad the Princess chose not to come. One more good-bye would be more than I could manage."

"I understand," said Arutha. "She cares for you greatly, Squire, though I can't see why." Roland looked to see if the Prince was joking and found Arutha smiling faintly. "I've not spoken of it," the Prince continued. "But since we may not see each other for some time after you leave us in Tulan, you should know that when the opportunity comes for you to speak to Father, you'll have my word on your behalf."

"Thank you, Arutha."

The town slipped by in darkness, replaced by the causeway to the lighthouse. The false dawn pierced the gloom slightly, casting everything into greys and blacks. Then after some time the large upthrust form of the Guardian Rocks appeared off the starboard quarter.

Amos ordered the helm put over, and they turned southwestward, more sails set to bring them full before the wind. The ship picked up speed, and Arutha could hear gulls crying overhead. Suddenly he was struck with the knowledge they were now out of Crydee. He felt chilled and gathered his cloak tightly around him.

ARUTHA STOOD ON the quarterdeck, sword held ready, Martin to one side notching an arrow to his bowstring. Amos Trask and his first mate, Vasco, also had weapons drawn. Six angry-looking seamen were assembled upon the deck below, while the rest of the crew watched the confrontation.

One sailor shouted from the deck, "You've lied to us, Captain. You've not put back north for Crydee as you said in Tulan. Unless you mean for us to sail on to Keshian Elarial, there's nothing south save the straits. Do you mean to pass the Straits of Darkness?"

Amos roared, "Damn you, man. Do you question my orders?"

"Aye, Captain. Tradition holds there's no valid compact between captain and crew to sail the straits in winter, save by agreement. You lied to us, and we're not obliged to sail with you."

Arutha heard Amos mutter, "A bloody sea-lawyer." To the sailor he said, "Very well," and handed his cutlass to Vasco. Descending the ladder to the main deck, he approached the seaman with a friendly smile upon his face.

"Look, lads," he began as he reached the six recalcitrant sailors, all holding belaying pins or marlinespikes. "I'll be honest with you. The Prince must reach Krondor, or there'll be hell to pay come spring. The Tsurani gather a large force, which may come against Crydee." He placed his hand upon the shoulder of the sailors' spokesman and said, "So what it comes down to is this: we must sail to Krondor." With a sudden motion Amos had his arm around the man's neck. He ran to the side of the ship and heaved the helpless sailor over. "If you don't wish to come along," he shouted, "you can swim back to Tulan!"

Another sailor started to move toward Amos when an arrow struck the deck at his feet. He looked up and saw Martin taking a bead upon him. The Huntmaster said, "I wouldn't."

The man dropped his marlinespike and stepped back. Amos turned to face the sailors. "By the time I reach the quarterdeck, you had better be in the rigging—or over the side, it makes no difference to me. Any man not working will be hanged for the mutinous dog he is."

The faint cries for help of the man in the water could be heard as Amos returned to the quarterdeck. To Vasco he said, "Toss that fool a rope, and if he doesn't relent, pitch him overboard again." Amos shouted, "Set all sails! Make for the Straits of Darkness."

ARUTHA BLINKED SEAWATER out of his eyes and held on to the guide rope with all the strength he possessed. Another wave crashed over the side of the ship, and he was blinded once more. Strong hands grabbed him from behind, and in the darkness he heard Martin's voice. "Are you all right?"

Spitting water, he shouted, "Yes," and continued to make his way toward the quarterdeck, Martin close behind. The *Wind of Dawn* pitched and rolled beneath his feet, and he slipped twice before he reached the ladder. The entire ship had been rigged with safety lines, for in the rough sea it was impossible to keep a footing without something to hang on to.

Arutha pulled himself up the ladder to the quarterdeck and stumbled as much as walked to Amos Trask. The captain waited beside the helmsman, lending his weight to the large tiller when needed. He stood as if rooted to the wood of the deck, feet wide apart, weight shifting with each move of the ship, his eyes peering into the gloom above. He watched, listened, each sense tuned to the ship's rhythm. Arutha knew he had not slept for two days and a night, and most of this night as well.

"How much longer?" Arutha shouted.

"One, two days, who can say?" A snap from above sounded like cracking spring ice upon the river Crydee. "Hard aport!" Amos shouted, leaning heavily into the tiller. When the ship heeled, he shouted to Arutha, "Another day of these gods-cursed winds buffeting this ship, and we'll be lucky if we can turn and run back to Tulan."

They were nine days out of Tulan, the last three spent in the storm. The ship had been relentlessly pounded by waves and wind, and Amos had been in the hold three times, inspecting the repairs to the keelson. Amos judged them due west of the straits, but couldn't be sure until the storm passed. Another wave struck the ship, and it shuddered.

"Weather break!" came the shout from above.

"Where away?" cried Amos.

"Dead starboard!"

"Come about!" ordered Amos, and the helmsman leaned against the tiller.

Arutha strained his eyes against the stinging salt spray and saw a faint glow seem to swing about until it stood off the bow. Then it grew larger as they drove for the thinning weather. As if walking out of a dark room, they moved from gloom to light. The heavens seemed to open above them, and they could see grey skies. The waves still ran high, but Arutha sensed the weather had turned at last. He looked over his shoulder and saw the black mass of the storm as it moved away from them.

Moment by moment the combers subsided, and after the raging clamor of the storm, the sea seemed suddenly silent. The sky was quickly brightening, and Amos said, "It's morning. I must have lost track of time. I thought it still night."

Arutha watched the receding storm and could see it clearly outlined, a churning mass of darkness against the lighter grey of the sky above. The grey quickly turned to slate, then blue-grey as the morning sun broke through the storm. For the better part of an hour Arutha watched the spectacle, while Amos ordered his men about their tasks, sending the night watch below and the day watch above.

The storm raced eastward, leaving a choppy sea behind. Time seemed frozen as Arutha stood in awe of the scene on the horizon. A portion of the storm seemed to have stopped, between distant fingers of land. Great spouts of water spun between the boundaries of the narrow passage in the distance. It looked as if a mass of dark, boiling clouds had been trapped within that area by a supernatural force.

"The Straits of Darkness," said Amos Trask at his shoulder.

"When do we put through them?" Arutha asked quietly.

"Now," answered Amos. The captain turned and shouted, "Day watch aloft! Midwatch turn to and stand ready! Helmsman, set course due east!"

Men scrambled into the rigging, while others came from below, still haggard and showing little benefit from the few hours' sleep since they last stood watch. Arutha pulled back the hood of his cloak and felt the cold sting of the wind against his wet scalp. Amos gripped him by the arm and said, "We could wait for weeks and not have the wind favorable again. That storm was a blessing in disguise, for it will give us a bold start through."

Arutha watched in fascination as they headed for the straits. Some freak of weather and current had created the conditions that held the straits in water-shrouded gloom all winter. In fair weather the straits were a difficult passage, for though they appeared wide at most points, dangerous rocks were hidden just below the water in many critical places. In foul weather they were considered impossible for most captains to negotiate. Sheets of water or flurries of snow blown down from the southernmost peaks of the Grey Towers tried to fall, only to be caught by blasts of wind and tossed back upward again, to try to fall once more. Waterspouts suddenly erupted upward to spin madly for minutes, then dissolve into blinding cascades. Ragged bolts of lightning cracked and were followed by booming thunder as all the fury of colliding weather fronts was unleashed.

"The sea's running high," yelled Amos. "That's good. We'll have more room to clear the rocks, and we'll be through or dashed to pieces in short order. If the wind holds, we'll be through before the day is done."

"What if the winds change?"

"That is not something to dwell on!"

They raced forward, attacking the edge of the swirling weather inside the straits. The ship shuddered as if reluctant once again to face foul weather. Arutha gripped the rail tightly as the ship began to buck and lurch. Amos picked his way along, avoiding the sudden wayward gusts, keeping the ship in the westerly trail of the passed storm.

All light disappeared. The ship was illuminated only by the dancing light of the storm lanterns, casting flickering yellow darts into murk. The distant booming of waves upon rocks reverberated from all quarters, confusing the senses. Amos shouted to Arutha, "We'll keep to the center of the passage; if we slip to one side or the other, or get turned, we'll stave in the hull on rocks." Arutha nodded, as the captain shouted instructions to his crew.

Arutha fought his way to the forward rail of the quarterdeck and shouted Martin's name. The Huntmaster answered from the main deck below that he was well, though waterlogged. Arutha held tight to the rail as the ship dipped low into a trough and then started to rise as it met a crest. For what seemed minutes the ship strained upward, climbing and climbing, then suddenly water swept over the bow and they were heading downward again. The rail became his only contact with a solid world amid a cold, wet chaos. Arutha's hands ached from the effort of hanging on.

Hours passed in cacophonous fury, while Amos commanded his crew to answer every challenge of wind and tide. Occasionally the darkness was punctuated by a blinding flash of lightning, bringing every detail into sharp focus, leaving dazzling afterimages in the darkness.

In a sudden lurch, the ship seemed to slip sideways, and Arutha felt his feet go out from under him as the ship heeled over. He held to the rail with all his strength, his ears deafened by a monstrous grinding. The ship righted itself, and Arutha pulled himself around to see, in the flickering glow of the storm lanterns, the tiller swinging wildly back and forth and the helmsman slumped down upon the deck, his face darkened by blood flowing from his open mouth. Amos was desperately scrambling upright, reaching for the lashing tiller. Risking broken ribs as he seized it, he fought desperately to hang on and bring the ship back under control.

Arutha half stumbled to the tiller and threw his weight against it. A long, low grinding sound came from the starboard side, and the ship shuddered.

"Turn, you motherless bitch!" cried Amos as he heaved against the tiller, marshaling what strength he had left. Arutha felt his muscles protesting in pain as he strained against the seemingly immobile tiller. Slowly it moved, first an inch, then another. The grinding rose in volume, until Arutha's ears rang from the sound of it.

Suddenly the tiller swung free once more. Arutha overbalanced and went flying across the deck. He struck the hard wood and slid along the wet surface until he crashed into the bulwark, gasping as wind exploded from his lungs. A wave drenched him and he spluttered, spitting out a lungful of seawater. Groggily he pulled himself up and staggered back to the tiller.

In the faint light Amos's face was white from exertion, but it was set in a wide-eyed, manic expression as he laughed. "Thought you'd gone over the side for a moment."

Arutha leaned into the tiller, and together they forced it to move once more. Amos's mad laughter rang out, and Arutha said, "What's so damn funny?"

"Look!"

Panting, Arutha looked where Amos indicated. In the darkness he saw huge forms rearing up alongside the ship, blacker shapes against the blackness. Amos yelled, "We're clearing the Great South Rocks. Pull, Prince of Crydee! Pull if you wish to ever see dry land again!"

Arutha hauled upon the tiller, forcing the balky ship away from the terrible stone embrace mere yards away. Again they felt the ship shudder as another low grinding sound came from below. Amos whooped. "If this barge has a bottom when we're through, I'll be amazed."

Arutha felt a gut-wrenching stab of panic, followed immediately by a strange exultation. He found himself seized by a nameless, almost joyous feeling as he struggled to hold the ship on course. He heard a strange sound amid the cacophony and discovered he was laughing with

Amos, laughing at the fury erupting around him. There was nothing left to fear. He would endure or he wouldn't. It didn't matter now. All he could do was give himself over to one task, keeping the ship heading past the jagged rocks. Every fiber of his being laughed in terror, in joy at being reduced to this lower level of existence, this primal state of being. Nothing existed save the need to do this one thing, upon which all was wagered.

Arutha entered a new state of awareness. Seconds, minutes, hours lost all meaning. He struggled, with Amos, to keep the ship under control, but his senses recorded everything around him in minute detail. He could feel the grain of the wood through the wet leather of his gloves. The fabric of his stockings was gathered between his toes in his water-soaked boots. The wind smelled of salt and pitch, wet wool caps, and rain-drenched canvas. Every groan of timber, smack of rope against wood, and shout of men above could be clearly heard. Upon his face he felt the wind and cold touch of melting snow and seawater, and he laughed. Never had he felt so close to death, and never had he felt more alive. Muscles bunched, and he pitted himself against forces primeval and formidable. On and on they plunged, deeper and deeper into the madness of the Straits of Darkness.

Arutha heard Amos as he shouted orders, orchestrating every man's move by the second. He played his ship as a master musician played a lute, sensing each vibration and sound, striving for that harmony of motion that kept the *Wind of Dawn* moving safely through perilous seas. The crew answered his every demand instantly, risking death in the treacherous rigging, for they knew their safe passage rested solely upon his skill.

Then it was over. One moment they were fighting with mad strength to clear the rocks and pass through the fury of the straits, the next they were running before a stiff breeze with the darkness behind.

Ahead the sky was overcast, but the storm that had held them for days was a distant gloom upon the eastern horizon. Arutha looked at his hands, as if at things apart, and willed them to release their hold upon the tiller.

Sailors caught him as he collapsed, and lowered him to the deck. For a time his senses reeled, then he saw Amos sitting a short way off as Vasco took the tiller. Amos's face was still mirthful as he said, "We did it, boy. We're in the Bitter Sea."

Arutha looked about. "Why is it still so dark?"

Amos laughed. "It's nearly sundown. We were on that tiller for hours."

Arutha began to laugh too. Never had he felt such triumph. He laughed until tears of exhaustion ran down his face, until his sides hurt. Amos half crawled to his side. "You know what it is to laugh at death, Arutha. You'll never be the same man again."

Arutha caught his breath. "I thought you mad there for a time."

Amos took a wineskin a sailor handed him and drew a deep drink. He passed it to Arutha and said, "Aye, as you were. It is something only a few know in their lives. It is a vision of something so clear, so true, it can only be a madness. You see what life is worth, and you know what death means."

Arutha looked up at the sailor standing by them, and saw it was the man Amos had pitched over the rail to head off the mutiny. Vasco threw the man a frown as he watched, but the man didn't move. Amos looked up at him, and the seaman said, "Captain, I just wanted to say . . . I was wrong. Thirteen years a sailor, and I'd have wagered my soul to Lims-Kragma no master could pilot a ship such as this through the straits." Lowering his eyes, he said, "I'd willingly stand for flogging for what I done, Captain. But after, I'd sail to the Seven Lower Hells with you, and so would any man here."

Arutha looked about and saw other sailors gathering upon the quarterdeck or looking down from the rigging. Shouts of "Aye, Captain," and "He has the truth of it" could be heard.

Amos pulled himself up, gripping the rail of the ship, his legs wobbling a little. He surveyed the men gathered around, then shouted, "Night watch above! Midwatch and day watch stand down." He turned to Vasco. "Check below for damage to the hull, then open the galley. Set course for Krondor."

ARUTHA CAME AWAKE in his cabin. Martin Longbow was sitting by his side. "Here." The Huntmaster held out a steaming mug of broth.

Arutha levered himself up on his elbow, his bruised and tired body protesting. He sipped at the hot broth. "How long was I asleep?"

"You fell asleep on deck last night, just after sundown. Or passed out, if you want the truth. It's three hours after sunrise."

"The weather?"

"Fair, or at least not storming. Amos is back on deck. He thinks it might hold most of the way. The damage below is not too bad; we'll be all right if we don't have to withstand another gale. Even so, Amos says there are a few fair anchorages to be found along the Keshian coast should the need arise."

Arutha pulled himself out of his bunk, put on his cloak, and went up on deck. Martin followed. Amos stood by the tiller, his eyes studying the way the sail held the wind. He lowered his gaze to watch as Arutha and Martin climbed the ladder to the quarterdeck. For a moment he studied the pair, as if struck by some thought or another, then smiled as Arutha asked, "How do we fare?"

Amos said, "We've a broad reach to the winds; had it since we cleared the straits. If it holds from the northwest, we should reach Krondor quickly enough. But winds rarely do hold, so we may take a bit longer."

A lookout shouted, "Sail ho!"

"Where away?" shouted Amos.

"Two points abaft port!"

Amos studied the horizon, and soon three tiny white specks appeared. To the lookout he shouted, "What ships?"

"Galleys, Captain!"

Amos mused aloud. "Quegan. This is a bit south for their usual patrols if they're warships, and I don't think it likely they're merchantmen." He ordered more canvas on the yards. "If the wind holds, we'll be past before they can close. They're fat-bottomed tubs under sail, and their rowers can't maintain speed over this distance."

Arutha watched in fascination as the ships grew on the horizon. The closest galley turned to cut them off, and after a while he could make out the hulking outline of the galley, its majestic sails above a high fore and aft deck. Arutha could see the sweep of oars, three banks per side, as the captain attempted a short burst of speed. But Amos was right, and soon the galley was falling away behind. As the distance between the *Wind of Dawn* and the galleys slowly increased, Arutha said, "They were flying the Royal Quegan standard. What would Quegan war galleys be doing this far south?"

"The gods only know," said Amos. "Could be they're out looking for pirates, or they could be keeping an eye out for Keshian ships straying north. It's hard to guess. Queg treats the whole of the Bitter Sea as her pond. I'd as soon avoid finding out what they're up to as not."

The rest of the day passed uneventfully, and Arutha enjoyed a sense of respite after the dangers of the last few days. The night brought a clear display of stars; he spent several hours on deck studying the bright array in the heavens. Martin came on deck and found him looking upward. Arutha heard the arrival of the Huntmaster and said, "Kulgan and Tully say the stars are suns much like our own, made small by vast distances."

Martin said, "An incredible thought, but I think they are right."

"Have you wondered if one of those is where the Tsurani homeworld lies?"

Martin leaned upon the rail. "Many times, Highness. In the hills you can see the stars like this, after the campfires are out. Undimmed by lights from town or keep, they blaze across the sky. I also have wondered if one of them might be where our enemies live. Charles has told me their sun is brighter than ours, and their world hotter."

"It seems impossible. To make war across such a void defies all logic."

They stood quietly together watching the glory of the night, ignoring the bite of the crisp wind that carried them to Krondor. Footfalls behind caused them to turn as one, and Amos Trask appeared. He hesitated a moment, studying the two faces before him, then joined them at the rail. "Stargazing, is it?"

The others said nothing, and Trask watched the wake of the ship, then the sky. "There is no place like the sea, gentlemen. Those who live on land all their lives can never truly understand. The sea is basic, sometimes cruel, sometimes gentle, and never predictable. But it is nights like this that make me thankful the gods allowed me to be a sailor."

Arutha said, "And something of a philosopher as well."

Amos chuckled. "Take any deep-water sailor who's faced death at sea as many times as I have, and scratch him lightly. Underneath you'll find a philosopher, Highness. No fancy words, I'll warrant you, but a deep abiding sense of his place in the world. The oldest known sailor's prayer is to Ishap. 'Ishap, thy sea is great and my boat is small; have mercy on me.' That sums it up."

Martin spoke quietly, almost to himself. "When I was a boy, among the great trees, I knew such feelings. To stand by a bole so ancient it is older than the oldest living memory of man gives such a sense of place in the world."

Arutha stretched. "It is late. I shall bid you both a good night." As he started to leave, he seemed taken by some thought. "I am not given to your philosophies, but . . . I am pleased to have shared this voyage with you both."

After he was gone, Martin watched the stars for a time, then became aware Amos was studying him. He faced the seaman and said, "You seem taken by some thought, Amos."

"Aye, Master Longbow." Leaning against the rail, he said, "Nearly seven full years have passed since I came to Crydee. Something has tickled my mind since first meeting you."

"What is that, Amos?"

"You're a man of mysteries, Martin. There're many things in my own life I'd not wish recounted now, but with you it's something else."

Martin appeared indifferent to the course of conversation, but his eyes narrowed slightly. "There's little about me not well known in Crydee."

"True, but it is that little which troubles me."

"Put your mind at ease, Amos. I am the Duke's Huntmaster, nothing more."

Quietly Amos said, "I think more, Martin. In my travels through the town, overseeing the rebuilding, I've met a lot of people, and in seven years I've heard a lot of gossip about you. Some time back I put the pieces together and came up with an answer. It explains why I see your manner change—only a little, but enough to notice—when you're around Arutha, and especially when you're around the Princess."

Martin laughed. "You spin an old and tired bard's tale, Amos. You think I am the poor hunter desperate for love of a young Princess? You think me in love with Carline?"

Amos said, "No, though I have no doubt you love her. As much as any brother loves his sister."

Martin had his belt knife half out when Amos's hand caught his wrist. The thickset seaman held the hunter's wrist in a viselike grip, and Martin could not move his arm. "Stay your anger, Martin. I'd not like to have to pitch you over the side to cool you off."

Martin ceased his struggling against Amos and released his knife, letting it slide back into its sheath. Amos held the hunter's wrist a moment longer, then let go. After a moment Martin said, "She has no knowledge, nor do her brothers. Until this time I thought only the Duke and one or two others might know. How did you learn of it?"

Amos said, "It was not hard. People most often don't see what is right before them." Amos turned and watched the sails above, absently checking each detail of the ship's crew as he spoke. "I've seen the Duke's likeness in the great hall. Should you grow a beard like his, the resemblance would shout for the world to see. Everyone in the castle remarks how Arutha grows to resemble his mother less and father more each passing year, and I've been nagged since we first met why no one else noticed he resembles you as well. I expect they don't notice because they choose not to. It explains so much: why you were granted special favor by the Duke in placing you with the old Huntmaster, and why you were chosen Huntmaster when a new one was needed. For some time now I've suspected, but tonight I was certain. When I came up from the lower deck and you both turned in the darkness, for a moment I couldn't tell which of you was which."

Martin spoke with no emotion, just a statement of fact. "It's your life should you breathe a word of it to anyone."

Amos settled himself against the rail. "I'm a bad man to threaten, Martin Longbow."

"It is a matter of honor."

Amos crossed his arms over his chest. "Lord Borric is not the first noble to father a bastard, nor will he be the last. Many are even given offices and rank. How is the Duke of Crydee's honor endangered?"

Martin gripped the rail, standing like a statue in the night. His words seemed to come from a great distance. "Not his honor, Captain. Mine." He faced Amos, and in the night his eyes seemed alive with inner light as they reflected the lantern hung behind the seaman. "The Duke knows of my birth, and for his own reasons chose to bring me to Crydee when I was still little more than a boy. I am sure Father Tully has been told, for he stands highest in the Duke's trust, and possibly Kulgan as well. But none of them suspect I know. They think me ignorant of my heritage."

Amos stroked his beard. "A knotty problem, Martin. Secrets within secrets, and such. Well, you have my word—from friendship, not from threat—I'll not speak to anyone of this, save by your leave. Still, if I judge Arutha right, he would sooner know as not."

"That is for me to decide, Amos, no one else. Someday perhaps I'll tell him, or I may not."

Amos pushed himself from the rail. "I've much to do before I turn in, Martin, but I'll say one more thing. You've plotted a lonely course. I do not envy you your journey upon it. Good night."

"Good night." After Amos had returned to the quarterdeck, Martin watched the familiar stars in the sky. All the companions of his solitary travels through the hills of Crydee looked down upon him. The constellations shone in the night, the Beasthunter and the Beasthound, the Dragon, the Kraken, and the Five Jewels. He turned his attention to the sea, staring down into the blackness, lost in thoughts he had once imagined buried forever.

"LAND HO!" shouted the lookout.

"Where away?" answered Amos.

"Dead ahead, Captain."

Arutha, Martin, and Amos left the quarterdeck and quickly made their way to the bow. As they stood waiting for land to heave into sight, Amos said, "Can you feel that trembling each time we breast a trough? It's that keelson, if I know how a ship's made, and I do. We'll need to put in at a shipyard for refitting in Krondor."

Arutha watched as the thin strip of land in the distance grew clearer in the afternoon light. While not bright, the day was relatively fair, only slightly overcast. "We should have time. I'll want to return to Crydee as soon as Erland's convinced of the risk, but even if he agrees at once, it will take some time to gather the men and ships."

Martin said, dryly, "And I for one would not care to pass the Straits of Darkness again until the weather is a bit more agreeable."

Amos said, "Man of faint heart. You've already done it the hard way. Going to the Far Coast in the dead of winter is only slightly suicidal."

Arutha waited in silence as the distant landfall began to resolve in detail. In less than an hour they could clearly make out the sights of Krondor's towers rising into the air, and ships at anchor in the harbor.

"Well," said Amos, "if you wish a state welcome, I'd better have your banner broken out and run up the mast."

Arutha held him back, saying, "Wait, Amos. Do you mark that ship by the harbor's mouth?"

As they closed upon the harbor, Amos studied the ship in question. "She's a beastly bitch. Look at the size of her. The Prince's building them a damn sight bigger than when I was last in Krondor. Three-masted, and rigged for thirty or better sail from flying jib to spanker. From the lines of her hull, she's a greyhound, no doubt. I'd not want to run up against her with less than three Quegan galleys. You'd need the rowers, for those oversized crossbows she mounts fore and aft would quickly make a hash of your rigging.

"Now we know why those Quegan galleys were so far from home. If the Kingdom's bringing warships like this to the Bitter Sea, Queg's—"

"Mark the banner at her masthead, Amos," said Arutha.

Entering the harbor, they passed near the ship. On her bow was painted her name, *Royal Griffin.* Amos said, "A Kingdom warship, no doubt, but I've never seen one under any banner but Krondor's." Atop the ship's highest mast a black banner emblazoned with a golden eagle snapped in the breeze. "I thought I knew every banner seen on the Bitter Sea, but that one is new to me."

"The same banner lies above the docks, Arutha," said Martin, pointing toward the distant city.

Quietly Arutha said, "That banner has never been seen on the Bitter Sea before." His expression turned grim as he said, "Unless I say otherwise, we are Natalese traders, nothing more."

"Whose banner is that?" asked Amos.

Gripping the rail, Arutha replied, "It is the banner of the second-oldest house in the Kingdom. It announces that my distant cousin, Guy, the Duke of Bas-Tyra, is in Krondor."

24

▾▾

KRONDOR

THE INN WAS CROWDED.

Amos led Arutha and Martin through the common room to an empty table near the fireplace. Snatches of conversation reached Arutha's ears as they took their seats. On close inspection the mood in the room was more restrained than it had first appeared.

Arutha's thoughts raced. His plans for securing Erland's help had been crushed within minutes of reaching the harbor. Everywhere in the city were signs that Guy du Bas-Tyra was not simply guesting in Krondor, but was now fully in control. Men of the city watch followed officers wearing the black and gold of Bas-Tyra, and Guy's banner flew over every tower in the city.

When a dowdy serving wench came, Amos ordered three mugs of ale, and the men waited in silence until they were brought. When the servingwoman was gone, Amos said, "We'll have to pick our way carefully now."

Arutha's expression remained fixed. "How long before we can sail?"

"Weeks, at least three. We've got to get the hull repaired, and the keelson replaced correctly. How long will depend on the shipwrights. Winter's a bad time: the fair-weather traders haul out their ships, so they'll be fit come spring. I'll begin inquiries first thing tomorrow."

"That may take too long. If needs be, buy another."

Amos raised an eyebrow. "You've funds?"

"In my chest aboard ship." With a grim smile he said, "The Tsurani aren't the only ones who play politics with war. To many of the nobles in Krondor and the East, the war is a distant thing, hardly imaginable. It has gone on for nearly nine years, and all they ever see is dispatches.

"And our loyal Kingdom merchants don't donate supplies and ships out of love for King Rodric. My gold is a hedge against underwriting the cost of bringing Krondorian soldiers to Crydee, both in expenses and bribes."

"Well then," said Amos, "even so it will be a week or two. You don't usually stroll into a ship's brokerage and pay gold for the first ship offered, not if you wish to avoid notice. And most of the ships sold are fairly worthless. It will take time."

"And," put in Martin, "there're the straits."

"That's true," agreed Amos, "though we could take a leisurely turn up the coast to Sarth and wait to time our run through the straits."

"No," said Arutha. "Sarth is still in the Principality. If Guy's in control of Krondor, he'll have agents and soldiers there. We won't be safe until we're out of the Bitter Sea. We'll attract less attention in Krondor than in Sarth: strangers are not uncommon here."

Amos looked long at Arutha, then said, "Now, I don't claim to know you as well as some men I've met, but I don't think you're as concerned for your own skin as something else."

Arutha glanced about the room. "We'd better find a less public place to talk."

With a sound between a sigh and a groan, Amos heaved himself out of his chair. "The Sailor's Ease is not where I'd prefer to stay, but for our purposes it will serve." He made his way to the long bar and spoke at length to the innkeeper. The heavyset owner of the inn pointed up the stairs, and Amos nodded. He signed for his companions to accompany him and led them through the press of the common room, up the stairs, and down a long hall to the last door. Pushing it aside, he motioned for them to enter.

Inside they found a room with little to recommend itself by way of comforts. Four straw-stuffed pallets rested on the floor. A large box in the corner served as a common closet. A crude lamp, a simple wick floating in a bowl of oil, sat upon a rude table; it burned with a pungent odor when Longbow struck a spark to it.

Amos closed the door as Arutha said, "I can see what you meant about choices in rooms."

"I've slept in far worse," answered Amos, settling down on one of the pallets. "If we're to keep our liberty, we'd best establish believable identities. For the time being, we'll call you Arthur. It's close enough to your own to afford a passable explanation should someone call out your real name and cause you to turn or answer. Also, it will be easy to remember."

Arutha and Martin sat down, and Amos continued. "Arthur—get used to that name—of navigating cities you know less than a thimbleful, which is twice as much as Martin knows. You'll do well to play the role of some minor noble's son, from some out-of-the-way place. Martin, you are a hunter from the hills of Natal."

"I can speak the language passing well."

Arutha gave a half-smile. "Get him a grey cloak and he'd make a fair ranger. I don't speak the language of Natal, or the Keshian tongue, so I'll be the son of a minor eastern noble, visiting for recreation. Few in Krondor could know half the barons of the East."

"Just so long as it's not too close to Bas-Tyra. With all those black tabards about, it would be a pretty thing to run into a supposed cousin among Guy's officers."

Arutha's expression turned dark. "You were correct about my concerns, Amos. I'll not leave Krondor until I've discovered exactly what Guy is doing here and what it means for the war."

"Even should I find us a ship tomorrow," said Amos, "which is unlikely, you should have plenty of time to snoop about. Probably find out more than you'll want to know. The city's a lousy place for secrets. The rumormongers will be plying their trade in the market, and every commoner in the city will know enough to give you a fair picture of what's taken place. Just remember to keep your mouth shut and ears open. Rumormongers'll sell you what you want to know, then turn around and sell news of your asking to the city guard so fast it'd make you spin to watch." Amos stretched, then said, "It's still early, but I think we should have a hot meal, then to bed. We've a lot of prowling about to accomplish." With that he rose and opened the door, and the three men returned to the common room.

ARUTHA MUNCHED upon a nearly cold meat pie. Lowering his head, he forced himself to continue consuming the pieman's greasy ware. He refused to consider what was contained within the soggy crust in addition to the beef and pork the seller claimed.

Casting a sidelong glance across the busy square, Arutha studied the gates to Prince Erland's palace. Finishing the pie, he quickly crossed to an ale stand and ordered a large mug to wash away the aftertaste. For the last hour he had moved, seemingly without purpose, from seller's cart to seller's cart, purchasing this and that, posing as a minor noble's son. And in that hour he had learned a great deal.

Martin and Amos came into sight, nearly an hour before the appointed time. Both wore grim expressions and kept glancing nervously about. Without comment Amos motioned for Arutha to follow as they walked by. They pushed through the midday throng and passed quickly away from the great-square district. Reaching a less hospitable-looking though no less busy area, they continued until Amos indicated they should enter a particular building.

Once through the door, Arutha was met by a hot, steamy atmosphere as an attendant came to greet them. "A bathhouse?" said Arutha.

Without humor Amos said, "You need to get rid of some road dirt, Arthur." To the attendant he said, "A steam for us all."

The man led them to a changing room and handed each a rough towel and a canvas bag for belongings. They undressed, wrapped the towels about them, and carried their clothing and weapons in the bags into the steam room.

The large room was completely tiled, though the walls and floors were stained and showed patches of green. The air was close and fetid. A small half-naked boy squatted in the center of the room, before the bed of rocks that supplied the steam. He alternately fed wood to the huge brazier below the stones and poured water upon them, generating giant clouds of steam.

When they were seated upon a bench, in the farthest corner of the room, Arutha said, "Why a bathhouse?"

Amos whispered, "Our inn has *very* thin walls. And a great deal of business is conducted in places such as these, so three men whispering in the corner won't draw undue attention." He shouted to the boy, "You, lad, run and fetch some chilled wine." Amos tossed a silver coin at the boy, who caught it in midair. When he didn't move, Amos tossed him another, and the boy scampered off. With a sigh Amos said, "The price of chilled wine has doubled since I was last here. He'll be gone for a while, but not too long."

"What is this?" asked Arutha, not taking pains to hide his ill humor. The towel itched and the room stank, and he doubted if he'd be any cleaner for the time spent here than if he'd stayed in the square.

"Martin and I both have troublesome news."

"As do I. I already know Guy is Viceroy in Krondor. What else have you learned?"

Martin said, "I overheard some conversation that makes me believe Guy has imprisoned Erland and his family in the palace."

Arutha's eyes narrowed, and his voice was low and angry. "Even Guy wouldn't dare harm the Prince of Krondor."

Martin said, "He would should the King give his leave. I know little of this trouble between the King and the Prince, but it is clear Guy is now the power in Krondor and acts with the King's permission, if not his blessing. You told me of Caldric's warning when you were last in Rillanon. Perhaps the King's sickness has grown worse."

"Madness, if you mean to speak clearly," snapped Arutha.

"To further cloud things in Krondor," said Amos, "it seems we are at war with Great Kesh."

"What!" said Arutha.

"A rumor, nothing more." Amos spoke quietly and quickly. "Before finding Martin, I was nosing around a local joy house, not too far from the garrison barracks. I overheard some soldiers at their ease saying they were to leave at first light for a campaign. When the object of one soldier's momentary ardor asked when she would see him again, he said, 'As long as it takes to march to the vale and back, should luck be with us,' at which point he invoked Ruthia's name, so that the Lady of Luck would not view his discussion of her province disfavorably."

"The vale?" said Arutha. "That can only mean a campaign down into the Vale of Dreams. Kesh must have hit the garrison at Shamata with an expeditionary force of dog-soldiers. Guy's no fool. He'll know the only answer's a quick, unhesitating strike from Krondor, to show Great Kesh's Empress we can still defend our borders. Once the dog soldiers have been driven south of the vale, we'll have another round of useless treaty talks over who has the right to it. That means even should Guy wish to aid Crydee, which I doubt, he could not. There's no time to deal with Kesh, return, and reach Crydee by spring, or even early summer." Arutha swore. "This is bitter news, Amos."

"There is still more. Earlier today I took the trouble to visit the ship, just to ensure Vasco had everything in hand, and that the men weren't chafing too much at being kept aboard. Our ship is being watched."

"Are you sure?"

"Certain. There's a couple of boys who stand around, playing at net mending, but they do no real work. They watched closely as I rowed out and back."

"Who do you think they are?"

"I can't begin to guess. They could be Guy's men, or men still loyal to Erland. They could be agents of Great Kesh, smugglers, even Mockers."

"Mockers?" asked Martin.

"The Guild of Thieves," said Arutha. "Little goes on in Krondor without notice by their leader, the Upright Man."

Amos said, "That mysterious personage runs the Mockers with tighter control than a captain has over his crew. There are places in the city where even the Prince cannot reach, but no place in Krondor is beyond the Upright Man. If he's taken an interest in us, for whatever reason, we have much to fear."

The conversation was interrupted by the serving boy's return. He set down a chilled pewter pitcher of wine and three cups. Amos said, "Fetch yourself to the nearest incense vendor, boy. This place stinks. Buy something sweet to toss upon the fire."

The boy regarded them a little warily, then shrugged as Amos tossed him another coin. He ran from the room, and Amos said, "He'll be back soon, and I've run out of reasons to send him away. In any event this place will soon be thick with merchants taking an afternoon steam.

"When the boy comes back, sip some wine, try to relax, and don't leave too soon. Now, in all this bleak mess, there is one small glimmer of light."

"Then I would hear what it is," said Arutha.

"Guy will soon be gone from the city."

Arutha's eyes narrowed. "Still, his men will be left in charge. But what you say does have some aspect of comfort. There are few in Krondor likely to mark me by sight, for it's nearly nine years since I was last here, and most of those have likely disappeared with the Prince. Also, there is a plan I've been considering. With Guy out of Krondor, I would have an even better chance of success."

"What plan?" asked Amos.

"I'll tell you when I've had more time to dwell upon it. Where could we safely meet?"

Amos considered. "Brothels, drug houses, and gambling halls are all as bad as inns. Either the Mockers control them and note everyone coming and going, or there are others about looking for information to sell. If someone overheard you speaking the wrong phrase, the Mockers or the city guards could be down on you in minutes." He was quiet for a moment. Then he smiled. "I have the very place! When the town watch rings the hour bell, two hours after sunset, meet me at the east end of Temple Square."

The boy returned and tossed a small bundle of incense upon the fire, cutting off conversation. Arutha settled back and drank the chilled wine, rapidly warming in the heat of the steam room. He closed his eyes, but was not relaxing, as he considered the situation. After a while he began to feel his plan might work if he could reach Dulanic. Running out of patience, he was the first to rise, rinse off, dress, and leave.

▼▼

ARUTHA WAITED as Martin and Amos approached from different parts of the city, crossing Temple Square. On all sides the temples of the greater and lesser gods rose up. Several were busy with pilgrims and worshipers entering and leaving, while others were nearly deserted.

Reaching the Prince, Amos said, "How fared you this afternoon?"

Arutha spoke softly. "I occupied my time in a tavern, keeping to myself. I did overhear some conversation about Erland, but when I tried to get closer, the speakers moved off. Otherwise I considered the plan I spoke of."

Martin glanced about, then said, "An ill-omened place you picked, Amos. Gathered at this end of the square are all the gods and goddesses of darkness and chaos."

Amos shrugged. "Which means few travelers nearby after night fall. And a clear view of anyone approaching." To Arutha he said, "Now, what is this plan?"

Quietly and quickly, Arutha said, "I noticed two things this morning: Erland's personal guards still patrol the palace grounds, so there must be limits to Guy's control. Second, several of Erland's courtiers entered and left freely enough, so some large portion of the daily business of governing the Western Realm must remain unchanged."

Amos stroked his chin, thinking. "That would seem logical. Guy brought his army with him, not his administrators. They're still back running Bas-Tyra."

"Which means Lord Dulanic and others not entirely sympathetic to Guy might still be able to aid us. If Dulanic will help, I can still succeed with my mission."

"How?" asked Amos.

"As Erland's Knight-Marshal, Dulanic has control of vassal garrisons to Krondor. Upon his signature alone he could call up the garrisons at Durrony's Vale and Malac's Cross. If he ordered them to march to Sarth, they could join the garrison there and take ship for Crydee. It would be a hard march, but we could still bring them to Crydee by spring."

"And no hardship to your father, either. I was going to tell you: I have heard Guy has sent soldiers from the Krondorian garrison to your father."

Arutha said, "That seems strange. I can't imagine Guy wishing to aid Father."

Amos shook his head. "Not so strange. To your father it will seem as if Guy has been sent by the King only to aid Erland, for I suspect the rumors of Erland's being a prisoner in his own palace are not as yet widespread. Also, it is a fine pretext to rid the city of officers and men loyal to the Prince.

"Still, it is no small boon to your father. From all accounts nearly four thousand men have left or are leaving for the north. That might be enough to deal with the Tsurani should they come against the Duke."

Martin said, "But should they come against Crydee?"

"For that we must seek aid. We must get inside the palace and find Dulanic."

"How?" Amos asked.

"It was my hope you might have a suggestion."

Amos looked down, then said, "Is there anyone in the palace you know to be trustworthy?"

"Before, I could have named a dozen, but this business makes me doubt everyone. Who stands with the Viceroy and who with the Prince I can't begin to guess."

"Then we'll have to nose about some more. And we'll have to listen for news of likely ships for transport. Once we've hired a few, we'll slip them out of Krondor one or two at a time, every few days. We'll need at least a score to carry the men of three garrisons. Assuming you get Dulanic's support, which brings us back to gaining entrance to the palace." Amos swore softly. "Are you sure you wouldn't care to chuck this business and become a privateer?" Arutha's expression clearly showed he was unamused. Amos sighed. "I thought not."

Arutha said, "You seem to know the underside of the city well, Amos. Use your experience to find us a way into the palace, even if through the sewer. I'll keep my eyes open for any of Erland's men who might wander through the great square. Martin, you'll have to simply keep your ears open."

With a long sigh of resignation, Amos said, "Getting into the palace is a risky plan, and I don't mind telling you I don't care for the odds." He hiked his thumb at a nearby temple. "I may even bounce into Ruthia's temple and ask the Lady of Luck to smile upon us."

Arutha dug a gold coin from his purse and tossed it to Amos. "Say a prayer to the Lady for me as well. I'll see you back at the tavern later."

Arutha strode off into the gloom, and Amos inclined his head toward the temple of the Goddess of Luck. "Care to make a votive offering, Martin?"

THE NIGHT'S SILENCE was ruptured by trumpets calling men to arms. Arutha was the first to the window, thrusting aside the wooden shutters and peering through. With most of the city asleep, there were few lights to mask the glow in the east. Amos reached Arutha's side, Martin a step behind.

Martin said, "Campfires, hundreds of them." The Huntmaster glanced heavenward, marking the stars' positions in the clear sky, and said, "Two hours to dawn."

"Guy's readying his army for the march," said Arutha quietly.

Amos leaned far out the window. By craning his neck, he could catch a glimpse of the harbor. In the distance men were calling aboard ships. "Sounds like they're readying ships as well."

Arutha leaned with both hands upon the table by the window. "Guy will send his foot soldiers by ship down the coast, into the Sea of Dreams, to Shamata, while his cavalry rides to the south. His foot will reach the city fresh enough to help bolster the defense, and when his horses arrive, they aren't sick from traveling by ship. And they'll arrive within days of one another."

As if to prove his words, from the east came the sounds of marching men. Then a few minutes later the first company of Bas-Tyra's foot soldiers came into view. Arutha and his companions watched them march past the open gate of the inn's courtyard. Lanterns gave the soldiers a strange, otherworld appearance as they marched in columns down the street. They stepped in cadence, their golden-eagle banners snapping above their heads. Martin said, "They are well-schooled troops."

Arutha said, "Guy is many things, most of them unpleasant, but one thing cannot be argued: he is the finest general in the Kingdom. Even Father is forced to admit that, though he'll say nothing else good about the man. Were I the King, I would send the Armies of the East under his command to fight the Tsurani. Three times Guy has marched against Kesh, and three times he has thrashed them. If the Keshians do not know he's come west, the very sight of his banner in the field may drive them to the peace table, for they fear and respect him." Arutha's voice became thoughtful in tone. "There is one thing. When Guy first came to be Duke of Bas-Tyra, he suffered some sort of personal dishonor—Father never told what that shame was—and took to wearing only black as a badge of sorts, earning him the name Black Guy. That type of thing takes a strange brand of personal courage. Whatever else can be said of Black Guy du Bas-Tyra, none will call him craven."

While the soldiers continued to pass below, Arutha and his companions watched in silence. Then, with the sun rising in the east, the last soldiers disappeared along the streets to the harbor.

▼▼

THE MORNING after Guy's army had marched, it was announced the city was sealed, the gates closed to all travelers and the harbor blockaded. Arutha judged it a normal practice, to prevent Keshian agents from leaving the city by fast sloop or fast horse to carry word of Guy's march. Amos used a visit to the *Wind of Dawn* to view the harbor blockade and discovered it was a light one, for Guy had ordered most of the fleet to stand off the coast at sea ambush, watching for any Keshian flotillas should Kesh learn the city was stripped of her garrison. The city was now policed by city guards in Guy's livery, as the last Krondorian soldiers departed for the north. Rumor had it Guy would also send the garrison at Shamata to the front once the fighting with Kesh had been settled, leaving every garrison in the Principality manned by soldiers loyal to Bas-Tyra.

Arutha spent most of his time in taverns, places of business, and the open markets most likely to be frequented by those from the palace. Amos prowled near the docks or in the city's seedier sections, especially the infamous Poor Quarter, and began making discreet inquiries about the availability of ships. Martin used his guise as a simple woodsman to blunder into any place that looked promising.

Nearly a week went by this way, with little new information being unearthed. Then, late the sixth day after Guy had quit the city, Arutha found himself being hailed in the middle of the busy square by Martin.

"Arthur!" shouted the hunter as he ran up to Arutha. "Best come quickly." He set off toward the waterfront and the Sailor's Ease.

Back at the inn they found Amos already in the room, resting upon his pallet before his nightly sojourn into the Poor Quarter. Once the door was closed, Martin said, "I think they may know Arutha's in Krondor."

Amos bolted upright as Arutha said, "What? How . . . ?"

"I wandered into a tavern near the barracks, just before the midday meal. With the army gone from the city, there was little business. One man did enter, just as I was readying to leave. A scribe with the city's Quartermaster, he was fit to burst with a rumor and in need of someone to tell it to. So, with the aid of some wine, I obliged him by playing the simple woodsy, and by showing respect for so important a personage.

"Three things this man told me. Lord Dulanic has disappeared from Krondor, gone the night Guy left. There's some business of his having retired to nameless estates to the north, now that Guy's Viceroy, but the scribe thought that unlikely. The second thing was news of Lord Barry's death."

Arutha's face showed shock. "The Prince's Lord-Admiral dead?"

"This man told me Barry had died under mysterious circumstances, though there's no official announcement planned. Some eastern lord, Jessup, has been given command of the Krondorian fleet."

"Jessup is Guy's man," said Arutha. "He commanded the Bas-Tyra squadrons of the King's fleet."

"And lastly, the man made a display of knowing some secret concerning a search for someone he only called 'the Viceroy's royal cousin.' "

Amos swore. "I don't know how, but someone's marked you. With Erland and his family virtual captives in the palace, there's hardly a chance another royal cousin's come wandering into Krondor in the last few days, unless you've a few out and about you've not told us of."

Arutha ignored Amos's feeble humor. In the span of time it took for Longbow to tell his tale, all his plans for aiding Crydee were dashed. The city was firmly in control of those either loyal to Guy or indifferent to who ruled in the King's name. There was no one in the city he could turn to for help, and his failure in bringing aid home was a bitter thing. Quietly he said, "Then there's no other course but to return to Crydee as soon as possible."

"That may not be so easy," said Amos. "There's more strange things occurring. I've been in places where a man can usually make contact with those needed for a dishonest task or two, but everywhere I've made inquiries—discreet, have no doubt—I come up against only hard silence. If I didn't know better, I'd swear the Upright Man's closed up shop and all the Mockers are now serving in Guy's army. I've never seen such a collection of dumb barmen, ignorant whores, uninformed beggars, and tongueless gamblers. You don't need to be a genius to see the word's gone out. No one is to talk to strangers, no matter how promising a transaction's being offered. So we can look for no aid in getting free of the city, and if Guy's agents know you're in Krondor, there'll be no lifting of the blockade or opening of the gates until you've been found, no matter how loudly the merchants scream."

"We're deep in the snare," agreed Martin.

"But if Guy's men only suspect I'm in Krondor, they may tire of the search."

"True," agreed Amos, "and after a while, the Mockers may open up as well. Should they agree to help—for a significant price, you can be certain—we'll have powerful help in leaving the city."

Arutha balled his fist and struck the pallet upon which he sat. "Damn Bas-Tyra. I'd gladly murder him this instant. Not only does he imperil the west, he risks a greater schism between the two realms by taking the

Principality under his own banner. Should anything happen to Erland and his family, it's almost certainly civil war."

Amos slowly shook his head. "A bollixed mission this, and through no fault of yours, Arutha." He sighed. "Still, we can't be startled into panic. Friend Martin may have misunderstood the scribe's last remark, or the man may have been speaking simply to hear himself talk. We'll have to be cautious, but we can't bolt and run. Should you vanish from sight completely, someone might take notice. Best if you stay close to the inn, but act as you have been, for the time being. I'll continue to make attempts at reaching someone who may have ways to get us clear of the city—smugglers, if not the Mockers."

Arutha rose from the pallet and said, "I've no appetite, but we've eaten together in the common room every night. I expect we'd best go down for supper soon."

Amos waved him back to his bed. "Stay awhile longer. I'm going to run down to the docks and visit the ship. If Martin's scribe was not just breaking wind, they'll certainly search the ships in the harbor. I'd better warn Vasco and the crew to be ready to go over the side if necessary and find someplace to store your chest. We aren't due to be hauled out for refitting for another week, so we must act with care. I've run blockades before. I wouldn't want to risk it in a hulk as leaky as the *Wind of Dawn*, but if I can't find another ship . . ." At the door he turned back to face Arutha and Martin. "It's a black storm, boys, but we've weathered worse."

ARUTHA AND MARTIN sat quietly as Amos entered the common room. The seaman pulled out a chair and called for ale and a meal. Once he was served, he said, "Everything is taken care of. Your chest is safe as long as the ship is left moored."

"Where did you hide it?"

"It's snugly wrapped in oilcloth and tied securely to the anchor."

Arutha looked impressed. "Underwater?"

"You can buy new clothes, and gold and gems don't rust."

Martin said, "How are the men?"

"Grumbling over being in port another week and still aboard ship, but they're good lads."

The door to the inn opened and six men entered. Five took chairs near the door while one stood surveying the room. Amos hissed, "See that rat-faced fellow who just sat down? He's one of the boys who've been watching the docks for the last week. Look's like I've been followed."

The man who remained standing spotted Amos and approached the table. He was a plain-looking man, of open countenance. His reddish-blond hair was flyaway around his head, and he wore a common sailor's clothing. He clutched a wool cap in hand as he smiled at them.

Amos nodded, and the man said, "If you're the master of the *Wind of Dawn*, I'd have words with you."

Amos raised an eyebrow, but said nothing. He indicated the free chair and the man sat. "Name's Radburn. I'm looking for a berth, Captain."

Amos looked about, seeing Radburn's companions were pretending not to notice what was transpiring at the table. "Why my ship?"

"I've tried others. They're all full up. Just thought I'd ask you."

"Who was your last master, and why did you leave his service?"

Radburn laughed, a friendly sound. "Well, I last sailed with a company of barge ferrymen, taking cargo from ship to shore in the harbor. Been stuck doing that for a year." He fell silent as the serving wench approached. Amos ordered another round of ale, and when one was set before Radburn, he said, "Thank you, Captain." He took a long pull and wiped his mouth with the back of his hand. "Before I came to be beached, I sailed with Captain John Avery, aboard the *Bantamina*."

"I know the Little Rooster, and John Avery, though I haven't seen him since I was last in Durbin, five or six years back."

"Well, I got a little drunk, and the captain told me he'd have none who drank aboard his ship. I drink no more than the next man, Captain, but you know Master Avery's reputation, being an abstentious follower of Sung the White."

Amos looked at Martin and Arutha, but said nothing. Radburn said, "These your officers, Captain?"

"No, business partners." When it was clear Amos was going to say nothing more, Radburn let the topic of identities drop. Amos finally said, "We've been in the city little more than a week, and I've been busy with personal matters. What news?"

Radburn shrugged. "The war goes on. Good for the merchants, bad for the rest. Now we've the business with Kesh. Before the troubles was along the Far Coast, but now . . . Krondor might not prove such a healthy spot if the Viceroy doesn't chase the dogs of Kesh back home. Otherwise, there's the usual gossip . . ." He glanced around, as looking for anyone who might overhear. ". . . and some not so usual."

Amos lifted his mug to his lips saying nothing. "Since the Viceroy's come," said Radburn quietly, "things haven't been the same in Krondor. An honest man isn't safe on the streets anymore, what with Durbin slavers running about and the press gangs almost as bad. That's why I need a ship, Captain."

"Press gangs!" Amos exploded. "There hasn't been a press gang in a Kingdom city in thirty years."

"Once was, but now things have changed again. You get a little drunk and don't find a safe berth for the night, the press gang comes along and slaps you into the dungeon. It just isn't right, no sir. Just because a man's between ships doesn't give anyone the right to ship him out with Lord Jessup's fleet for seven years. Seven years of chasing pirates and fighting Quegan war galleys!"

Amos's eyes narrowed. "How is it that Guy rules in Krondor? We've heard stories, but they seem confused."

Radburn nodded. "Right you are, Captain. For it is confusing. A month ago, Lord Guy rides in with his army behind, flags a'waving, drums beating, and the rest. The Prince, so they say, welcomes him and treats him real friendly, even though du Bas-Tyra is carrying the King's writ naming him Viceroy. The Prince even helps him, they say, until this business of the press gangs and such comes to his ears." Lowering his voice more, he said, "I heard that when he complained, Guy locks him up in his rooms. Nice rooms, I expect, but same as a cell if you can't leave. So I hear."

Arutha was so outraged by the story, he was on the verge of speaking. Amos gripped his arm quickly, warning silence, then said, "Well, Radburn, I can always use a good man who's sailed with John Avery. I'll tell you what. I've one more trip to the ship to make tonight, and there're some personal belongings in my room I'll want aboard. Come along and carry them."

Amos rose and, giving the man no time to object, gripped him by the arm and propelled him toward the stairs. Arutha shot a glance at the group who entered with Radburn. They seemed unaware for the moment of what was transpiring across the crowded common room as Amos took Radburn up the stairs, Arutha and Martin following behind.

Amos hustled Radburn down the hall and, once through the door to their room, spun and delivered a staggering blow to Radburn's stomach, doubling him over. A brutal knee to the face, and Radburn lay stunned upon the floor.

"What is this all about?" said Arutha.

"That man's a liar. John Avery's a marked man in Kesh. He betrayed the Durbin captains to a Quegan raiding fleet twenty years ago. Yet Radburn didn't bat an eye when I said I saw Avery in Durbin six years ago. And he's too free in showing disrespect to the Viceroy. His story stinks like a week-dead fish. We go out the door with him, and inside of two blocks a dozen men or more will be upon us."

"What shall we do?" said Arutha.

"We leave. His friends will be up those stairs in a minute." He pointed to the window. Martin stood by the door as Arutha ripped aside a dirty canvas shade and pushed open the wooden shutters. Amos said, "Now you see why I chose this room." Less than a yard below the window's ledge was the roof of the stable.

Arutha stepped out, Amos and Martin following. They hurried carefully down the steeply sloping roof until they reached the edge. Arutha leaped down, landing quietly, followed a moment later by Martin. Amos landed more heavily, but suffered only a minor bruise to his dignity.

They heard a cough and an oath, and looked up to see a bloodied face at the window. Radburn shouted, "They're in the courtyard!" as the three fugitives started for the gate.

Amos swore. "I should have cut his throat."

They ran to the gate, and as they entered the street, Amos grabbed at Arutha. A group of men were running down the street toward them. Arutha and his companions fled the opposite way, ducking into a dark alley.

Hurrying along between the blank walls of two buildings, they cut across a busy street, overturning several pushcarts, and ducked into another alley, the cart owners' curses following. They continued to run, the sounds of pursuit never far behind, following a twisting maze of back alleys and side streets through darkened Krondor.

Turning a corner, they found themselves intersecting a long narrow street, little more than an alley, flanked on both sides by tall buildings. Amos rounded the corner first and motioned for Arutha and Martin to halt. In low tones, he said, "Martin, hurry down to the corner and take a look around. Arutha, go the other way." He pointed toward a spot where dim light could be seen. "I'll stand watch here. If we become separated, make for the ship. It'll be a desperate chance, breaking the blockade, but should you win free, have Vasco make for Durbin. Your gold will buy you enough protection there to get the ship refitted and you back to Crydee. Now go."

Arutha and Martin ran down the street in opposite directions, and Amos stood watch behind. Abruptly shouts came down the narrow street, and Arutha looked back. At the other end of the street he could see the dim figure of Martin struggling with several men. He started back, but Amos shouted, "Go on. I'll help him. Get away!"

Arutha hesitated, then resumed his run toward the distant light. He was panting when he reached the corner and nearly skidded to a halt as he entered a well-traveled, brightly lit avenue. From carts decorated with lanterns, hawkers sold their wares to passing citizens out for a stroll after supper. The weather was mild—there looked to be little chance of snow this winter—and large numbers of people were about. From the condition of the buildings and the fashions of those in the area, Arutha knew he was in a more prosperous section of the city.

Arutha stepped into the street and forced himself to walk at a leisurely pace. He turned and made a display of examining a garment seller's wares as several men appeared from the street he had just fled. He tugged a garish red cloak from among the goods and swirled it about his shoulder, pulling the hood over his head. "Here now, what do you think you're doing?" asked a dried-faced old man in a reedy whisper.

Affecting a nasal voice, Arutha said, "My good man, you don't expect me to purchase a garment without seeing if it fits?"

Suddenly confronted by a buyer, the man became unctuously friendly. "Oh no, certainly, sir." Looking at Arutha in the ill-tailored cloak, he said, "It's a perfect fit, sir, and the color suits you well, if I may say."

Arutha chanced a glance at his pursuers. The man called Radburn stood at the corner, blood dried upon his face and his nose swollen, but still able to direct his men's search. Arutha adjusted the cloak, a great, cumbersome thing that hung nearly to the ground. In a display of fussiness, he said, "You think so? I wouldn't care to appear at court looking like a vagabond."

"Oh, court is it, sir? Well, it's just the thing, mark me. It adds a certain elegance to your appearance."

"How much is it?" Arutha saw Radburn's men walking through the busy crowd, some looking into each tavern and storefront as they passed, others hurrying on to other destinations. More followed from the smaller street, and Radburn spoke quickly to them. He set some to watching those in the street, then turned and led the rest back the way they had come.

"It's the finest cloth made in Ran, sir," said the seller. "It was brought at great expense from the shore of the Kingdom Sea. I couldn't let it go for less than twenty golden sovereigns."

Arutha blanched, and for a moment was so struck by the outrageous price he nearly forgot himself. "Twenty!" He lowered his voice as a passing member of Radburn's company threw him a quick glance. "My dear man," he said, returning to character, "I seek to purchase a cloak, not establish an annuity for your grandchildren." Radburn's man turned away and disappeared into the press of the crowd. "It is rather a plain wrap, after all. I should think two sovereigns more than sufficient."

The man looked stricken. "Sir, you seek to beggar me. I couldn't think of parting with it for a sum of less than eighteen sovereigns."

They haggled for another ten minutes, and Arutha finally departed with the cloak for the price of eight sovereigns and two silver royals. It was double the price he should have paid, but the searchers had ignored a man haggling with a street seller, and escaping detection was worth the price a hundred times over.

Arutha kept alert for signs he was being watched as he made his way along the street. Unfortunately he knew little of Krondor and had no idea where he was after the flight. He kept to the busier part of the street, staying close to larger groups, seeking to blend in.

Arutha saw a man standing at the corner, seemingly idling the night away, but clearly watching those who passed. Arutha looked around and saw a tavern on the other side of the street, marked by a brightly painted sign of a white dove. He quickly crossed the street, keeping his face turned away from the man at the corner, and approached the doorway of the tavern. As he reached for the door, a hand gripped his cloak, and Arutha spun, his sword halfway out of its scabbard. A boy of about thirteen stood there, wearing a simple, oft-patched tunic and men's trousers cut off at the knees. He had dark hair and eyes, and his smudged face was set in a grin. "Not there, sir," he said with a merry note in his voice.

Arutha slipped his sword back into the scabbard and fell into character. "Begone, boy. I've no time for beggars or panderers, even those of limited stature."

The boy's grin broadened. "If you insist, but there are two of them in there."

Arutha dropped his nasal accent. "Who?"

"The men who chased you from the side street."

Arutha glanced about. The boy appeared alone. He looked into the boy's eyes and said, "What are you talking about?"

"I saw how you acted. Quick on your feet, sir. But they've blanketed the area, and you'll not be slipping by them yourself."

Arutha leaned forward. "Who are you, boy?"

With a toss of his ragged hair he said, "Name's Jimmy. I work hereabouts. I can get you out. For a fee, of course."

"And what makes you think I wish to get out?"

"Don't play the fool with me, like you did with the merchant, sir. You need to get clear of somebody who's likely to pay me to show him where you are. I've run afoul of Radburn and his men before, so you have more of my sympathy than he's likely to get. As long as you can bid more for your freedom than he will for your capture."

"You know Radburn?"

Jimmy grinned. "Not so as I'd care to admit, but yes, we've had dealings before."

Arutha was struck by the boy's cool manner, not what he would have expected from the boys he knew back home. Here stood an old hand at negotiating the treacherous byways of the city. "How much?"

"Radburn will pay me twenty-five gold to find you, fifty if he especially wants your skin."

Arutha took out his coin pouch and handed it to the boy. "Over a hundred sovereigns in there, boy. Get me out of here and to the docks, and I'll double it."

The boy's eyes flickered wide a moment, but he never lost his grin. "You must have offended someone with a lot of influence. Come along."

He darted away so quickly, Arutha almost lost him in the heavy crowd. The boy moved with the ease of experience through the press, while Arutha had to struggle to keep from jostling people in the street.

Jimmy led him into an alley, several blocks away. When they were a short way down the alley, Jimmy stopped. "Better toss that cloak. Red's not my favorite color for looking inconspicuous." When Arutha had pitched the cloak into an empty barrel, Jimmy said, "You'll be pointed at the docks in a moment. If someone tumbles onto us, you're on your own. But for that other hundred gold, I'll try to see you all the way."

They worked their way to the end of the alley, apparently seldom used from the heavy accumulation of trash and discarded objects, packing crates, broken furniture, and nameless goods against the walls around them. Jimmy pulled aside a crate, revealing a hole. "This should put us outside Radburn's net, at least I hope so," said Jimmy.

Arutha found he had to crouch to follow the boy through the small passage. From the rank odor in the tunnel, it was clear something had crawled in here to die fairly recently. As if reading his mind, Jimmy said, "We toss a dead cat in here every few days. Keeps others from sticking their noses too far in."

"We?" said Arutha.

Jimmy ignored the question and kept moving. Soon they exited into another alley overburdened with trash. At the mouth of the alley, Jimmy motioned for Arutha to stop and wait. He hurried along the dark street, then returned at a run. "Radburn's men. They must have known you'd head for the harbor."

"Can we slip past them?"

"No chance. They're as thick as lice on a beggar." The boy took off in the opposite direction down the street they had entered from the alley. Arutha followed as Jimmy turned up another small byway. Arutha hoped he hadn't bargained wrongly in trusting the street boy. After a few minutes of traveling, Jimmy stopped. "I know a place you can hole up awhile, until I can find some others to help get you to your ship. But it'll cost you more than a hundred."

"Get me to my ship before dawn, and I'll give you whatever you ask."

Jimmy grinned. "I can ask a lot." He regarded Arutha for a moment longer, then with a curt nod of his head led off. Arutha followed, and they wound their way deeper into the city. The sounds of people in the streets fell off, and Arutha judged they were moving into an area less well traveled at night. The buildings around them showed they were heading into another poor area of the city, though not close to the docks as far as Arutha could tell.

Several sharp turns through dark, narrow alleys, and Arutha was completely lost. Abruptly Jimmy turned and said, "We're there." He pulled open a door in an otherwise blank wall and stepped through. Arutha climbed a long flight of stairs after him.

Jimmy led him down a long hall at the top of the stairs, to a door. The boy opened it and indicated Arutha should enter. Arutha took a single step, then halted as he discovered three sword points leveled at his stomach.

25

▼▼

ESCAPE

A MAN MOTIONED FOR ARUTHA TO ENTER.

He sat behind a small table facing the door. Leaning forward into the light of the small lamp on the table, he said, "Please come in." The light revealed his face was covered with pockmarks and he possessed a large hooked nose. His eyes never strayed from Arutha as the three swordsmen stepped back, allowing the Prince entrance. Arutha hesitated as he saw the bound and unconscious forms of Amos and Martin slumped against the wall. Amos groaned and stirred, but Martin remained motionless.

Arutha measured the distance between himself and the three swordsmen, his hand hovering near the hilt of his rapier. Any notion of leaping back and drawing his sword vanished when he felt a dagger point pressed against the small of his back. A hand snaked around from behind and relieved him of his sword.

Jimmy then stepped around the Prince, examining the rapier as he carefully hid his dagger in the folds of his loose tunic. He grinned broadly. "I've seen a few of these about. It's light enough I could use it."

Dryly Arutha said, "Under the circumstances, it might not be inappropriate to make it my legacy to you. Use it in good health."

The pock-faced man said, "You keep your wits about you," as Arutha was ushered farther into the room by a swordsman. Another put away his weapon and tied Arutha's arms behind him. He was then roughly thrust into a chair, opposite the man who had spoken, who continued, "My name is Aaron Cook, and you've already met Jimmy the Hand." He indicated the boy. "These others prefer to remain anonymous at present."

Arutha looked at the boy. "Jimmy the Hand?"

The boy executed a fair imitation of a courtly bow, and Cook said, "The finest pickpocket in Krondor and well on his way to becoming the finest thief as well, should you be inclined to believe his self-appraisal.

"Now, to matters of business. Who are you?"

Arutha related the story of being Amos's business partner, calling himself Arthur, and Cook studied him stoically. With a sigh, he nodded, and one of the silent men stepped forward and struck Arutha across the mouth. Arutha's head snapped back from the force of the blow, and his eyes watered. "Friend Arthur," said Aaron Cook, shaking his head, "we can go about this interview two ways. I'd advise you not to make the choice of the difficult way. It will prove most unpleasant, and we shall know what we want in the end in any event. So please consider your answer carefully." He stood and came around the table. "Who are you?"

Arutha began to repeat his story, and the man who struck him stepped forward again, ending his answer with another ringing blow. The man called Cook leaned down so his face was level with Arutha's. Arutha blinked to clear the tears from his eyes, and Cook said, "Friend, tell us what we ask. Now, so as not to waste time"—he pointed at Amos—"that he is the captain of your ship we concede, but you his business partner . . . I think not. That other fellow played the part of a hunter from the mountains in several taverns about town, and I think it no mummery; he has the look of one who knows mountains better than city streets, a look hard to forge." He studied Arutha. "But you . . . you are a soldier at least, and your rich boots and fine sword mark you a gentleman. But I think there is more." Looking into Arutha's eyes, he said, "Now, why is Jocko Radburn so intent upon finding you?"

Arutha looked Aaron Cook squarely in the eyes. "I don't know."

The man who had struck Arutha began to step forward again, but Cook held up his hand. "That may be true. You've been something of a fool, the way you've been popping up here and there, hanging around the gates of the palace, playing the innocent. You are either poor spies, or poor fools, but there is no doubt you've aroused the interest of the Viceroy's men, and therefore ours."

"Who are you?"

Cook ignored the question. "Jocko Radburn's the senior officer in the

Viceroy's secret police. Despite that open, honest face on him, Radburn's one of the most steel-nerved, unmovable bastards the gods ever graced this world with. He'd happily cut his grandmother's heart out if he thought the old girl was making free with state secrets. The fact he put in a personal appearance shows he, at the very least, judges you potentially important.

"We first learned three men were nosing about town a day or two after you arrived, and when our people heard some of Radburn's men were keeping an eye upon you, we decided to do likewise. When they began offering small bribes for information about you three, we became especially interested. We were content to simply keep watching you, waiting until you showed your hand.

"But when Jocko and his men showed at the Sailor's Ease, we were forced to act. We snatched those two from under Jocko's nose, but Jocko and his bully boys came down the alley between you and us, so we hurried them away. Jimmy's finding you was a bit of luck, for he didn't know we were ready to bring you in." He nodded approval to the boy. "You did right bringing him here."

Jimmy laughed. "I was on the rooftops, watching the whole thing. I knew you wanted him in as soon as you grabbed the other two."

One of the men swore. "You'd better not have been trying for a boost without writ from the Nightmaster, boy."

Cook raised his hand, and the man fell silent. "It will not hurt for you to know that some here are Mockers, others are not, but we are all united in an undertaking of great importance. Mark me well, Arthur. Your only hope of leaving here alive rests upon our being satisfied you do not endanger that undertaking I spoke of. It may be Radburn's interest in you is only coincidental to his interest in other matters. Or there may be a weaving of threads here, some pattern as yet unseen. In any event, we shall have the truth, and when we are satisfied with what you have told us, we shall set you free—perhaps even aid you and your companions—or we shall kill you. Now start at the beginning. Why did you come to Krondor?"

Arutha considered. There was little but pain to be gained by lying, yet he was not willing to tell the entire truth. That these men were not working with Guy's men wasn't proved. This could be a ploy, with Radburn in the next room listening to every word. He decided what part of the truth to tell. "I'm an agent for Crydee. I came to speak to Prince Erland and Lord Dulanic in person, to ask for aid against a coming Tsurani offensive. When we learned Guy du Bas-Tyra was in possession of the city, we decided to gauge the temper of things before committing ourselves to a course of action."

Cook listened closely, then said, "Why should an emissary of Crydee slip into the city? Why not come in with banners flying and receive a state welcome?"

"Because Black Guy'd just as soon toss him into a cell as not, you stupid bastard."

Cook's head snapped around: Amos was sitting up against the wall, groggily shaking his head. "I think you busted my skull, Cook."

Aaron Cook looked hard at Amos. "You know me?"

"Aye, you wooden-headed sea rat, I know you. I know you well enough to know we're not speaking another word until you go fetch Trevor Hull."

Aaron Cook rose from the table, an uncertain expression on his face. He motioned to one of the men by the door, who also looked discomforted by Amos's words. The man nodded to Cook and left the room. Minutes later he returned, followed by another man, tall, with a shock of grey hair, but still powerful looking. A ragged scar ran from his forehead through his right eye, which was milky white, and down his cheek. He took a long look at Amos, then laughed aloud and pointed at the captives. "Untie them."

Amos was lifted by two men, then untied. As his ropes were loosened, he said, "I thought they'd hung you years ago, Trevor."

The man clapped Amos on the back. "And I you, Amos."

Cook looked questioningly at the new arrival, while Arutha was untied and Martin revived with a cup of water thrown in his face. The man called Trevor Hull looked at Cook and said, "Have your wits fled, man? He's grown a beard and cut his famous flowing locks—lost some on top and put on a few pounds as well—but he's still Amos Trask."

Cook studied Amos a moment longer, then his eyes widened. "Captain Trenchard?"

Amos nodded, and Arutha looked on in astonishment. Even in far Crydee they had heard of Trenchard the Pirate, the Dagger of the Sea. He'd had a short career, but a famous one. It was reputed even Quegan war galleys had turned and fled at sight of Trenchard's fleet, and there wasn't a town along the coasts of the Bitter Sea that did not fear his marauders.

Aaron Cook extended his hand. "Sorry, Captain. It's been so many years since we last met. We couldn't be certain you weren't part of some plot of Radburn's to locate us."

"Who are you?" asked Arutha.

"All in good time," answered Hull. "Come."

One of the men helped the still-groggy Martin to his feet, and Cook and Hull led them to a more comfortable room, with chairs enough for all. When all were sitting, Amos said, "This old rogue is Trevor Hull, Captain White-eye, master of the *Red Raven.*"

Hull shook his head sadly. "No longer, Amos. Burned off of Elarial she was, three years ago, by imperial Keshian cutters. My mate Cook here and a few of my boys got to shore with me, but most of the crew went down with the *Red Raven.* We made our way back to Durbin, but things are changing, what with the wars and all. Came to Krondor a year ago and have been working here since."

"Working? You, Trevor?"

The man smiled, his scar wrinkling, as he said, "Smuggling, in fact. That's what brought us together with the Mockers. Not much can happen in Krondor along those lines without the Upright Man's permission.

"When the Viceroy first came to Krondor, we started running up against Jocko Radburn and his secret police. He's been a thorn in our side from the first. This business of guards sneaking about dressed as common folk, there's just no honor in it."

Amos muttered, "I knew I should have cut his throat when I had the chance. Next time I won't be so damned civilized."

"Slowing down a bit, Amos? Well, a week ago we got word from the Upright Man he had a precious cargo to leave the city. We've had to bide our time until the right ship was ready. Radburn's very anxious to find that cargo before it leaves Krondor. So, you see, it's a most delicate situation, for we can't ship it until the blockade's lifted, or we find a blockade captain we can bribe. When we first caught wind you three were asking questions, we thought it might be some grand plot of Jocko's to find that cargo. Now we've cleared the air, I'd like to hear the answer to Cook's question explained. Why should an emissary from Crydee fear discovery by the Viceroy's men?"

"Listening in, were you?" Amos turned to Arutha, who nodded. "This is no simple emissary, Trevor. Our young friend is Prince Arutha, son of Duke Borric."

Aaron Cook's eyes went wide, and the man who struck Arutha paled. Trevor Hull nodded understanding. "The Viceroy'd pay handsomely to get his hands upon the son of his old enemy, especially when it came time to press his claim in the Congress of Lords."

"What claim?" said Arutha.

Hull leaned forward, resting his elbows on his knees. "You'd not know, of course. We only heard the news a few days ago ourselves, and it's not common knowledge. Still, I'm not free to speak plainly without permission."

He rose and left the room. Arutha and Amos exchanged questioning glances, then Arutha looked toward Martin. "Are you all right?"

Martin carefully touched his head. "I'll recover, though they must have hit me with a tree."

One of the men grinned in a friendly, almost apologetic way. Patting a wooden billy in his belt sash, he said, "He's a hard one to bring down, that's for certain."

Hull returned to the room, followed by another. The men in the room rose, and Arutha, Amos, and Martin slowly followed suit. Behind Hull came a young girl no more than sixteen years of age. Arutha was instantly struck by the promise of beauty in her features: large sea-green eyes, straight and delicate nose, and slightly full mouth. A faint hint of freckles dusted her otherwise fair skin. She was tall and slender and walked with poise. She came across the room to Arutha, rose up on tiptoes, and kissed him lightly upon the cheek. Arutha looked surprised at this gesture and watched as she stepped back with a smile upon her lips. She wore a simple dress of dark blue, and her red-brown hair hung loosely to her shoulders. After a second she said, "Of course, how silly I am. You'd not know me. I saw you when you were last in Krondor, but we never met. I'm your cousin Anita, Erland's daughter."

Arutha stood thunderstruck. Besides the girl's disquieting effect upon his composure, with her winning smile and clear gaze, he was doubly surprised to find her in this company of brigands. He sat down slowly, and she took a chair. So used to the informality of his father's court, he was somewhat surprised when she gave the others permission to sit.

"How . . . ?" Arutha began.

Amos interrupted. "The Upright Man's precious cargo?"

Hull nodded, and the Princess spoke. Her pretty face clouded with emotion. "When the Duke of Bas-Tyra came with orders from the King, Father greeted him warmly and offered no resistance. At first Father did all he could to aid him in taking command of the army, but when he heard of the things Guy was doing with his secret police and press gangs, Father protested. Then when Lord Barry died and Guy put Lord Jessup in command of the fleet over Father's objections, and Lord Dulanic disappeared so mysteriously, Father sent a letter to the King, demanding Guy's recall. Guy intercepted the message and ordered us kept under guard in a wing of the palace. Then Guy came to my room one night."

She shuddered. Arutha nearly spat when he said, "You don't have to speak of such things." The sudden rage startled the girl.

"No," she said, "it was nothing like that. He was very proper, nearly formal. He simply informed me we were to be wed, and that King Rodric was to name him heir to the throne of Krondor. If anything, he seemed irritated by the bother of having to take such a course."

Arutha slammed his fist against the wall behind. "That tears it! Guy means to have Erland's crown and Rodric's after. He means to be King."

Anita looked at Arutha shyly. "So it seems. Father's not well and couldn't resist, though he refused to sign the proclamation of betrothal. Guy had him taken to the dungeon until he would sign." Her eyes teared as she said, "Father cannot live long in such cold and damp quarters. I fear he will die before agreeing to Guy's wishes." She continued to speak, her face a mask of control, though tears ran down her cheeks as she talked of her mother and father's imprisonment. "Then one of my ladies told me a maid knew some people in the city who might be willing to help."

Trevor Hull said, "With your permission, Highness. One of the girls in the palace is sister to a Mocker. With everything up in the wind, the Upright Man decided it might be to his advantage to take a hand. He arranged to smuggle the Princess out of the palace the night of Guy's departure, and she's been here since."

Amos said, "Then the rumor we overheard before we fled the Sailor's Ease about there being a hunt on for a 'royal cousin' was about Anita, not Arutha."

Hull pointed at the Prince. "It may be Radburn and his boys still have no idea who you are. Most likely, they jumped on you in the hope you'd turn out to be party to the Princess's escape. We're almost certain the Viceroy has no idea she's gone from the palace, for she fled after he rode out. I expect Radburn is desperate to get her back before his master returns from the war with Kesh."

Arutha studied the Princess, feeling a strong desire to do something on her behalf, a desire beyond the consideration of foiling Guy. He shunted aside the strange tug of emotions. He asked Trevor Hull, "Why does the Upright Man wish to contend with Guy? Why isn't he turning her in for a reward?"

Trevor Hull looked to Jimmy the Hand, who answered with a grin. "My master, a most perceptive man, saw at once his own interests were best served by aiding the Princess. Since Erland has been Prince of Krondor, the business of the city runs smoothly, an environment conducive to the success of my master's many undertakings. Stability profits us all, you see. With Guy here, we've his secret police about, upsetting the normal commerce of our guild. And whatever else, we are most loyal subjects of His Highness the Prince of Krondor. If he does not wish his daughter to marry the Viceroy, we do not wish it as well." With a laugh, Jimmy added, "Besides, the Princess has agreed to pay twenty-five thousand gold sovereigns to our master should the guild get her free of

Krondor, to be delivered when her father returns to power, or some other fate places her upon the throne."

Arutha took Anita's hand and said, "Well, cousin, there is nothing else to be done. We must take you to Crydee at the first chance."

Anita smiled, and Arutha found himself smiling back. Trevor Hull said, "As I said before, we were waiting for the right opportunity to smuggle her from the city." He turned to Amos. "You're the man for this, Amos. There's no better blockade runner on the Bitter Sea—excepting myself, of course, but I've other matters to take care of here."

Trask said, "We can't leave for a few weeks yet. Even if the blockade was lifted, my ship's in desperate need of refitting. And if we left now, we'd have to sail about until the weather in the straits breaks. With Jessup's fleet at sea ambush, that would be risky. I'd rather hide here awhile, then a quick run west, through the straits, and up the Far Coast with no delay."

Hull slapped him on the shoulder. "Good, that will give us time. I've heard of your ship; the boys tell me it's little better than a barge. We'll find you another. I'll send word to your men when the time is right. Radburn'll most likely leave your crew alone, hoping you'll turn up. We'll slip them aboard the new ship a few at a time at night and replace them with my own boys, so Radburn's men won't notice anything unusual aboard."

He turned to Arutha. "You'll be safe enough here, Highness. This building is one of many owned by the Mockers, and none will get close without our having ample warning. When the time is right, we'll get you all free of the city. Now we'll take you to your room, so you may rest."

Arutha, Martin, and Amos were shown to a room down the hall from the one where they had met Anita, while the Princess returned to her own quarters. The room they entered was a simple affair, but clean. All three men were tired. Martin fell heavily on one pallet and was quickly asleep. Amos lowered himself slowly, and Arutha watched him for a moment. With a slight smile he said, "When you first came to Crydee, I thought you a pirate."

Struggling to remove a boot, Amos said, "In truth, I tried to leave that behind me, Highness." He laughed. "Perhaps it was the gods working their revenge upon me, but you know, for fifteen years, man and boy, I was a corsair and a captain, then when I try my hand at honest trading for the first time, my ship is captured and burned, my crew slaughtered, and I find myself beached as far from the heart of the Kingdom as you can get and still be in it."

Arutha lay down upon his pallet. "You've been a good counselor,

Amos Trask, and a brave companion. Your help over the years has earned you a good deal of forgiveness for past wrongdoings, but"—he shook his head—"Trenchard the Pirate! Gods, man, there's so much to forgive."

Amos yawned and stretched. "When we return to Crydee, you can hang me, Arutha, but for now please have the good grace to keep silent and put out the light. I am getting too old for this foolishness. I need some sleep."

Arutha reached over and covered the wick of the lamp with a snuff. He lay back in the darkness, images and thoughts crowding his mind. He thought of his father and what he would do were he here, then wondered how his brother and sister were. Thoughts of Carline caused him to think of Roland, and to speculate how the fortifications of Jonril were progressing. He forced aside the buzzing thoughts and let his mind drift. Then before sleep took him, he remembered Anita, as she rose up on tiptoes to kiss his cheek, and felt again a not entirely comfortable churning within. A faint smile crossed his lips as he fell asleep.

ANITA CLAPPED APPRECIATIVELY as Arutha turned aside the point of Jimmy's sword. The boy thief blushed at his awkwardness, but Arutha said, "That was better."

He and Jimmy were practicing basic swordwork, Jimmy using a rapier purchased with some of the gold Arutha had given him. For a month they had passed the time this way, and Anita had taken to watching. Whenever the Princess was around, the usually brash Jimmy the Hand became subdued, and he blushed furiously whenever she spoke to him. Arutha was now certain the boy thief was afflicted by the worst sort of infatuation for the Princess, only three years older than himself. Arutha appreciated Jimmy's distress, for he also found the girl's presence a distraction. Still in the first years of womanhood, she nevertheless carried herself with court-bred grace, had wit and education and showed the promise of mature beauty. Arutha found it easier to turn his thoughts to other topics than the Princess.

The basement where they worked on their swordplay was damp and poorly ventilated, so it soon became close and humid. Arutha said, "That's enough for today, Jimmy. You're still impatient to close, and that can be fatal. You've plenty of speed, and it's good you learn young, but you lack arm strength to bash about as many older men do; with the rapier, that can also prove fatal. Remember, the edge is for cutting—"

"—and the point is for killing," finished Jimmy, with a self-conscious grin. "I can see how you'd have to be cautious against a man with a broadsword. He could break your blade if you tried to block instead of parry, but what do you do if one of those alien warriors comes at you with that greatsword you described?"

Arutha laughed. "You find out who can run faster." Anita's laughter joined with Arutha's and Jimmy's. Arutha said, "Seriously, you must stay to the off-hand side. With the big swords, your opponent gets *one* swing, then you've got an opening—"

The door opened, and Amos walked in with Martin and Trevor Hull. Amos said, "The worse damn luck—begging the Princess's pardon. Arutha, the worst has occurred."

Arutha wiped the perspiration off his brow with a towel and said, "Don't stand there waiting for me to guess. What?"

"News came this morning," said Hull. "Guy is returning to Krondor."

"Why?" asked Anita.

Amos said, "It seems our Lord of Bas-Tyra rode into Shamata and ran his banner up above the walls. The Keshian commander had the good grace to mount one more attack, for the sake of form, then nearly gave himself a ruptured gut racing back home. He left a handful of minor nobles haggling with Guy's lieutenants over the conditions of armistice until a formal treaty can be drawn up between the King and the Keshian Empress. There's only one reason Guy can be hurrying back here."

Quietly Anita said, "He knows I've escaped."

Trevor Hull said, "Yes, Highness. This Black Guy's a wily one. He must have a spy in Radburn's company. It appears he doesn't even trust his own secret police overmuch. Luckily we still have people inside the palace loyal to your father, or we would never have learned of this turn."

Arutha sat down near the Princess. "Well, then we must soon be gone. It's either sail for home or toward Ylith to reach Father."

Amos said, "Looking at the choices, it seems there is little to recommend one course over the other. Both have dangers and advantages."

Martin looked at the girl, then said, "Though I don't think the Duke's war camp any place for a young woman."

Amos sat down by Arutha. "Your presence in Crydee is not vital, at least not for now. Fannon and Gardan are able men, and should the need arise, I think your sister would prove no mean commander. They should be able to keep things under control as well as you."

Martin said, "But you must ask yourself this: what will your father do when he learns Guy does not simply rule in Krondor as Erland's aide but holds the city completely in his power, that he's sending no aid to the Far Coast, and that he means to have the throne?"

Arutha nodded vigorously. "You are right, Martin. You know Father well. It will mean civil war." There was sorrow on his face. "He'll withdraw half the Armies of the West and march down the coast to Krondor and not stop until Guy's head is on a pole before the city's gates. Then the course will be set. He'll have to turn east and march against Rodric. He'd never wish the crown for himself, but once begun, he cannot stop short of total victory or defeat. But we'd lose the West to the Tsurani in time. Brucal couldn't hold them long with only half an army."

Jimmy said, "This civil war sounds a nasty sort of business."

Arutha sat forward. Wiping his forehead, he looked up from under damp locks. "We've not had one in two hundred fifty years, since the first Borric slew his half brother, Jon the Pretender. Compared to what this would be, with all the East marshaled against the West, that was only a skirmish."

Amos looked at Arutha with concern upon his face. "History's not my strong suit, but it seems to me you'd do best by your father keeping him in ignorance of this turn of events until the Tsurani spring offensive is finished."

Arutha exhaled a long, low breath. "There's nothing else for it. We know no aid will be forthcoming for Crydee. I can best decide what to do when I return. Perhaps in council with Fannon and the others we can work out some defense for when the Tsurani come." His tone was one of near-resignation. "Father will learn of Guy's plotting in due time. This sort of news is too hard to keep. The best we can hope for is he'll not hear of it until after the Tsurani offensive. Perhaps by then the situation will have changed." It was obvious from his tone he didn't think that likely.

Martin said, "It may be the Tsurani will choose to march against Elvandar, or carry the battle to your father. Who can say?"

Arutha leaned back and became aware of Anita's hand resting gently upon his arm. "What a choice we have," he said quietly. "To face the possible loss of Crydee and the Far Coast to the Tsurani or to plunge the Kingdom into civil war. Truly the gods must hate the Kingdom."

Amos stood. "Trevor tells me he has a ship. We can sail in a few days. With luck, the straits will be clearing when we arrive."

Lost in the gloom of his own personal defeat, Arutha barely heard him. He had come to Krondor in such confidence. He would win Erland's support for his cause, and Crydee would be rescued from the Tsurani. Now he faced an even more desperate situation than had he stayed home. Everyone left him alone, save for Anita, who spent silent minutes just sitting at his side.

▼▼

DARK FIGURES moved quietly toward the waterfront. Trevor Hull led a dozen men with Arutha and his companions down the silent street. They hugged the walls of the buildings, and every few yards Arutha would cast a backward glance to see how Anita fared. She returned his concern with brave smiles, faintly perceived in the predawn darkness.

Arutha knew that over a hundred men moved down adjacent streets, sweeping the area of the city watch and Radburn's agents. The Mockers had turned out in force so Arutha and the others could safely quit the city. Hull had carried word the night before that for a considerable cost the Upright Man had arranged for one of the blockade ships to "drift" off station. Since learning the true situation, including Guy's plan to become Prince of Krondor, the Upright Man had given over his not inconsiderable resources to aid the Prince's and Anita's escape. Anita wondered if anyone outside the Guild of Thieves would ever learn the mysterious leader's true identity. From what chance remarks Arutha had overheard, it seemed only a few within the Mockers knew who he was.

With Guy on his way back to the city, Jocko Radburn's men had increased their searching to a near-frenzied pitch. Curfew had been instituted and homes randomly entered and searched in the middle of the night. Every known informant in the city, and many of the beggars and rumormongers as well, had been dragged off to the dungeons and questioned, but whatever else Radburn's men accomplished, they did not learn where the Princess was hidden. No matter how much the denizens of the street feared Radburn, they feared the Upright Man more.

Anita heard Hull speaking quietly to Amos. "She's a blockade runner, called the *Sea Swift,* and she's well named. There's no faster ship left in the harbor, with all the big warships out with Jessup's fleet. You should make good time westward. The prevailing winds are northerly, so you'll have a broad reach most of the way."

Amos said, "Trevor, I've sailed the Bitter Sea a bit. I know how the winds blow this time of year as well as any man."

Hull snorted. "Well then, as you say. Your men and the Prince's gold are all safely aboard, and Radburn's watchdogs don't seem to have a notion. They still watch the *Wind of Dawn* like a mouser a rathole, but the *Sea Swift* is left alone. We've arranged for false papers to be posted with a broker, announcing she's for sale, so even if there was no blockade, they'd not imagine she'd be leaving harbor for some time."

They reached the docks and hurried along to a waiting longboat. There were muffled noises, and Arutha knew the Mockers and Trevor's smugglers were disposing of Radburn's watchmen.

Then to the rear, shouts erupted. The clamor of steel broke the still of the morning, and Arutha heard Hull shout, "To the boat!"

The pounding of boots upon the wood of the docks set up a racket as Mockers came swarming out of nearby streets, intercepting whoever sought to cut off the escape.

They reached the end of the dock and hurried down the ladder to the longboat. Arutha waited at the top of the ladder until Anita was safely down, then turned. As he stepped upon the top rung, he heard the sound of hoofbeats approaching and saw horses crashing through the press of Mockers, who fell before the onslaught. Riders in the black and gold of Bas-Tyra hacked down with swords, to break free of those seeking to slow them.

Martin shouted from the boat, and Arutha hurried down the ladder. As he reached the boat, a voice from above shouted, "Farewell!"

Anita looked up and saw Jimmy the Hand hanging over the edge of the dock, a nervous grin on his face. How the boy had managed to join them when everyone thought him safely back at the hiding place, Arutha couldn't guess. Seeing the unarmed boy gave the Prince a momentary start. He unbuckled his rapier and tossed it high. "Here, use it in good health!" As quick as a striking serpent, Jimmy caught the scabbard, then vanished.

Sailors pulled hard against the oars, and the boat sped away from the docks. Lanterns appeared upon the wharves as the sound of battle became louder. Even in the predawn hour, many cries of "What passes?" and "Who goes there?" came from those set to guard ships and cargo in the harbor. Anita watched over his shoulder, trying to see what was occurring behind. More lanterns were being brought, and a fire erupted on the docks. Large bales of something, stored under canvas, exploded into flames.

Those in the boat could now clearly see the fight. Many of the thieves were escaping down city streets, or leaping into the icy water of the harbor. Arutha couldn't see the grey-haired figure of Trevor Hull anywhere, or the small one of Jimmy the Hand. Then clearly he saw Jocko Radburn, dressed in a simple tunic, as before. Radburn came to the edge of the dock and watched the retreating boat. He pointed at the fleeing longboat with his sword and shouted something lost in the clamor.

Arutha turned and saw Anita sitting opposite him, her hood thrown back, her face clearly visible in the blaze of light from the wharf. Her gaze was caught by the spectacle on shore, and she seemed unaware of her discovery. Arutha quickly pulled her cloak hood about her face, snapping her from her glamour, but he knew the damage was done. He looked back again and saw Radburn ordering his men after the fleeing Mockers, retreating down the docks. He stood there alone, then turned away, vanishing in the gloom by the time the longboat reached the *Sea Swift*.

As soon as they were all aboard, Amos's crew cast mooring lines and scrambled aloft to set sails. The *Sea Swift* began to move from the harbor.

The promised gap in the harbor blockade appeared, and Amos set course for it. He was through before any attempt to cut them off could materialize, and suddenly they were outside the harbor, in the open sea.

Arutha felt a strange elation as it struck him they were free of Krondor. Then he heard Amos swear. "Look!"

In the faint light of the false dawn, Arutha saw the dim shape where Amos pointed. The *Royal Griffin*, the three-masted warship they had seen when coming into the harbor, was at anchor beyond the breakwater, hidden from the view of any in the city. Amos said, "I thought her out with Jessup's fleet. Damn that Radburn for a crafty swine. She'll be on our wake as soon as he can get aboard." He shouted for all sails to be set and then watched the retreating ship behind. "I'd say a prayer to Ruthia, Highness. If we can steal enough time before she gets under way, we still may be free. But we'll need all the good fortune the Lady of Luck can spare."

The morning was clear and cold. Amos and Vasco watched the crew work with approval. The less experienced men had been replaced by men handpicked by Trevor Hull. They did their work quickly and well, and the *Sea Swift* raced westward.

Anita had been shown to a cabin below, and Arutha and Martin stood on deck with Amos. The lookout reported the horizon clear.

Amos said, "It's a close thing, Highness. If they've gotten that brute of a ship underway as quickly as possible, we've only stole an hour or two on them. Their captain may choose the wrong course, but seeing as we're trying to stay free of Jessup's sea ambush, they're a good bet to follow close to the Keshian coast, and risk running into a Keshian warship, rather than losing us. I'll not feel comfortable until we're two days free of pursuit.

"But even if they started at once, they'll only make up a small distance each hour. So until we know for certain they have us in sight, we'd all do with a bit of rest. Go below, and I'll call you should anything occur."

Arutha nodded and left. Martin followed. He bid Martin a good rest and watched as the Huntmaster entered the cabin he shared with Vasco. Arutha entered his own cabin and stopped when he saw Anita sitting on his bunk. Slowly he closed the door and said, "I thought you were asleep in your own cabin."

She shook her head slightly, then suddenly she was across the short space separating them, her head buried against his chest. Sobs shook her as she said, "I've tried to be brave, Arutha, but I've been so frightened."

He stood there awkwardly for a moment, then gently placed his arms around her. The self-reliant pose had crumbled, and Arutha now realized how young she was. Her court training and manners had served her well in maintaining poise among the rough company of the Mockers over the month, but her mask could no longer withstand the pressure. He stroked her hair and said, "You'll be fine."

He made other reassuring sounds, not aware of what he was saying, finding her closeness disturbing. She was young enough to make him judge her still a girl, but old enough to make him doubt that judgment. He had never been able to banter lightly with the young women of the court like Roland, preferring a straightforward conversation, which seemed to leave the ladies cold. And he had never commanded their attention the way Lyam had, with his blond good looks and his laughing, easy manner. On the whole women made him uncomfortable, and this woman—or girl, he couldn't decide which—more than usual.

When the tears subsided, he ushered her to the single chair in the cramped cabin and sat upon the bunk. She sniffed once, then said, "I'm sorry, this is so unseemly."

Suddenly Arutha laughed. "What a girl you are!" he said with genuine affection. "Were I in your place, smuggling myself from the palace, hiding amid cutthroats and thieves, dodging Radburn's weasels and all, I'd have fallen apart long since."

She drew a small handkerchief from her sleeve and delicately wiped her nose. Then she smiled at him. "Thank you for saying that, but I think you'd have done better. Martin has told me a lot about you over the last few weeks, and you are a rather brave man by his accounts."

Arutha felt embarrassed by the attention. "The Huntmaster has a tendency to overboast," he said, knowing it to be untrue, and changed the subject. "Amos tells me if we don't sight that ship for two days, we'll have won free."

She lowered her eyes. "That's good."

He leaned forward and brushed a tear from her cheek, then, feeling self-conscious, pulled his hand away. "You will be safe with us in Crydee, free from Guy's plottings. My sister will make you a welcome guest in our house."

She smiled faintly. "Still, I am worried about Father and Mother."

Arutha tried his best to lay her fears to rest. "With you safely gone from Krondor, Guy cannot gain by causing your parents harm. He may still force a consent to marry from your father, but Erland could do no harm by giving it now. With you out of reach, it's a hollow betrothal. Before this is all done, we shall have an accounting with dear cousin Guy."

She sighed, and her smile broadened. "Thank you, Arutha. You've made me feel better."

He rose and said, "Try to sleep. I'll use your cabin for the time being." She smiled as she went to his bunk. He closed the door behind him. All at once he felt little need for rest and returned to the deck. Amos stood by the helmsman, eyes fixed astern. Arutha came to stand at his side. Amos said, "There, on the horizon, can you see it?"

Arutha squinted and made out a faint white speck against the blue of the sky. "Radburn?"

Amos spat over the transom. "My guess. Whatever start we've had is being slowly eaten away. But a stern chase is a long chase, as the saying goes. If we can keep far enough ahead for the rest of the day, we might slip them at night—if there's enough cloud cover so the moons don't mark our passage."

Arutha said nothing, watching the faint speck in the distance.

THROUGHOUT THE DAY they had watched the pursuing ship grow slowly in size. At first the tiny speck grew with maddening slowness, but now with alarming speed. Arutha could see the sails clearly defined, no longer a simple blur of white, and he could see a hint of a black speck at the masthead, undoubtedly Guy's banner.

Amos regarded the setting sun, directly ahead of the fleeing *Sea Swift*, then watched the following ship. He shouted to the watch aloft, "Can you mark her?"

The lookout cried down, "Three-masted warship, Captain."

Amos looked at Arutha. "It's the *Royal Griffin*. She'll overtake us at sundown. If we had but ten more minutes, or some weather to hide in, or she was just a trifle slower . . ."

"What can you do?"

"Little. In a broad reach she's faster, fast enough that we can't shake her with any sort of fancy sailing. If I tried to turn to a beam reach just as she came near, I could put a bit of space between us, for we'd both lose speed, but she'd fall off faster for a time. Then as soon as they trimmed sails, they'd overhaul us. But that'd send us southward, and there're some fairly nasty shoals and reefs along this stretch of coast, not far from here. It'd be chancy. No, she'll come in somewhat to the windward. When she's alongside, her taller masts will cut our wind, and we'll slow enough for them to board without so much as a by-your-leave."

Arutha watched the closing ship for another half hour. Martin came on deck and watched as the distance between the two ships shrank by a few feet each minute. Amos held the ship tight to the wind, driving her to the limit of her speed, but still the other closed.

"Damn!" said Amos, nearly spitting from frustration. "If we were running east, we'd lose them in the dark, but westward we'll be outlined against the evening sky for some time after the sun sets. They'll still be able to see us when we'll be blind to them."

The sun sank and the chase continued. As the sun neared the horizon, an angry red ball above the black-green sea, the warship followed by less than a thousand yards.

Amos said, "They might try to foul the rigging or sweep the decks clear with those oversized crossbows, but with the girl aboard, Radburn might not risk it for fear of injuring her."

Nine hundred, eight hundred yards, the *Royal Griffin* came on, rolling inexorably toward them. Arutha could see figures, small silhouettes in the rigging, black against sails turned blood-red by the setting sun.

When the pursuing ship was five hundred yards behind, the lookout shouted, "Fog!"

Amos looked up. "Where away?"

"South by west. A mile or more."

Amos sped for the bow and Arutha followed. In the distance they could see the sun setting, while off to the left a hazy white band stretched across the top of the black sea. "Gods!" shouted Amos. "We have a chance."

Amos shouted for the helmsman to come to a southwest heading, then sprinted for the stern, Arutha behind him by a step. When they reached the stern, they saw the turn had halved the distance between the ships. Amos said, "Martin, can you mark their helmsman?"

Martin squinted, then said, "It's a bit gloomy, but he's not a difficult mark."

Amos said, "See if you can take his mind off holding course."

Martin uncovered his ever-present bow and strung it. He drew out a cloth-yard shaft and sighted on the pursuing ship. He waited, shifting weight to compensate for the rolling of the ship, then let fly. Like an angry bird, the arrow arched over the water, clearing the stern of the following ship.

Martin watched the shaft's flight, then quietly hummed an "Ah" to himself. In a single fluid motion he drew out another arrow, fitted it to the bowstring, pulled, and released. It followed the path of the first, but instead of clearing the rear of the other ship, struck in the transom, quivering mere inches from the helmsman's head.

From the *Sea Swift* they could see the *Royal Griffin*'s helmsman dive for the deck, releasing the tiller. The warship swung over and began to fall away. Martin said, "A little gusty for fine shooting," and sent another arrow to strike within inches of the first, keeping the tiller unmanned.

Slowly the distance between the ships began to widen, and Amos turned to his crew. "Pass the word. When I give the order for silence, any man who drops so much as a whisper is fish bait."

The warship wobbled behind a minute, then swung back on course. Martin said, "Looks like they'll keep a little less broad to us, Amos. I can't shoot through sails."

"No, but if you'd oblige me by keeping those lads in the bow away from their ballista, I'd be thankful. I think you irritated Radburn."

Martin and Arutha saw the ballista crew readying their weapons. The Huntmaster sent a flurry of arrows at the pursuing ship's bow, one arrow following the last before it was halfway to the target. The first struck a man in the leg, felling him, and the other men dove for cover.

"Fog dead ahead, Captain!" came the shout from above.

Amos turned to the helmsman. "Hard to port."

The *Sea Swift* angled to the south. The *Royal Griffin* came hard after, now less than four hundred yards behind. As they changed course, the wind died. Approaching the fog bank, Amos said to Arutha, "The winds fall off to less than a bilious fart in there; I'm reefing sails, so the sound of flapping canvas doesn't give us away."

Abruptly they entered a wall of grey, murky fog, quickly becoming black as the sun sank over the horizon. As soon as the warship vanished from sight, Amos said, "Reef sails!"

The crew hauled in sails, quickly slowing the ship. Then Amos said, "Hard to starboard, and pass the word for silence."

Suddenly the ship became graveyard quiet. Amos turned to Arutha and whispered, "There's currents here running to the west. We'll let them carry us away from here and hope Radburn's captain is a Kingdom Sea man.

"Tiller to midships," he whispered to the helmsman. To Vasco, he said, "Pass the word to lash down the yards. And those aloft are to remain motionless."

Suddenly Arutha became aware of the quiet. After the clamor of the chase, with the fresh north wind blowing, the ropes and sheets singing in the yards, the canvas snapping constantly, this muffled fogbank was unnaturally silent. An occasional groan of a yard moving, or the snap of a rope, were the only sounds in the murk. Fear dragged the minutes out in the seemingly endless vigil.

Then, like an alarm ringing out, they heard voices and the sounds of a ship. Creeking yards and the snap of canvas as it moved in the faint wind echoed from all quarters. Arutha couldn't see anything for minutes, until a faint glow pierced through the murk to the rear, passing from northeast to southwest, lanterns from the pursuing *Royal Griffin*. Every man aboard the *Sea Swift*, on deck and above, stayed at his station, afraid to move for the noise that would carry over the water like a clarion. In the distance they could hear a shout from the other ship, "Quiet, damn it! We can't hear them for our own noise!" Then it was suddenly still, save for the rippling of canvas and ropes from the *Royal Griffin*.

Time passed without measure as they waited in the blackness. Then came a hideous grinding sound, ringing like a thunder peal, a tearing, cracking shriek of wood being crushed. Instantly the cries of men could be heard, shouts of panic.

Amos turned to the others, half-seen in the darkness. "They've shoaled out. From the sound, they've torn the hull right out from under. They're dead men." He ordered the helm put over to the northwest, away from the shoals and reefs, as sailors hurriedly set sail.

"A bad way to die," said Arutha.

Martin shrugged, half-lit by the lanterns being brought up on deck. "Is there a good way? I've seen worse."

Arutha left the quarterdeck, the faint, pitiful cries of the drowning men still carrying across the water, a grisly counterpoint to Vasco's more mundane shout to open the galley. He closed the door to the companionway and shut out those unhappy sounds. He quietly opened the door to his cabin and saw Anita lying asleep in the faint light of a shuttered candle. Her red-brown hair looked nearly black as it lay spread about her head. He started to close the door, when he heard her say, "Arutha?"

He stepped in, finding her watching him in the dim light. He sat on the edge of the berth. "Are you well?" he asked.

She stretched and nodded. "I've been sleeping soundly." Her eyes widened. "Is everything all right?" She sat up, bringing her face close to his.

He reached out and put his arms around her, holding her close. "Everything is fine. We're safe now."

She sighed as she rested her head on his shoulder. "Thank you for everything, Arutha."

He said nothing, suddenly caught up in strong emotion, a protective feeling, a need to keep Anita from harm's way, to care for her. For long moments they sat this way, then Arutha regained control over his surging feelings. Pulling away a little, he said, "You'd be hungry, I'd think."

She laughed, an honestly merry sound. "Why yes, as a matter of fact I'm famished."

He said, "I'll have something sent down, though it will be plain fare, I'm afraid, even compared to what you were given by the Mockers."

"Anything."

He went on deck and ordered a seaman to the galley to fetch something for the Princess, then returned to find her combing her hair. "I must look a mess," she said.

Arutha suddenly found himself fighting the urge to grin. He didn't know why, but he was inexplicably happy. "Not at all," he said. "You look quite nice, actually."

She stopped her combing, and Arutha marveled at how she looked so young one minute, so womanly the next. She smiled at him. "I remember sneaking a peek at you during Father's court dinner, when you were last in Krondor."

"At me? What in heaven's name for?"

She seemed to ignore the question. "I thought you looked nice then as well, though a bit stern. There was a boy there who held me up to see. He was with your father's party. I've forgotten his name, but he said he was apprentice to a magician."

Arutha's smile faded. "That was Pug."

"What ever happened to him?"

"He was lost in the first year of the war."

She put aside her comb. "I'm sorry. He was kind to a bothersome child."

"He was a kind lad, given to doing brave things, and he was very special to my sister. She grieved for a long time when he was lost." Fighting back a gloomy mood, he said, "Now, why did a Princess of Krondor want to sneak a look at a distant and rural cousin?"

Anita watched Arutha for a long moment, then said, "I wanted to see you because our fathers thought it likely we would marry."

Arutha was stunned. It took all his control to retain his composure. He pulled over the single chair and sat. Anita said, "Didn't your father ever mention it to you?"

For want of anything clever to say, Arutha merely shook his head.

Anita nodded. "I know, the war and all. Things did get quite frantic soon after you left for Rillanon."

Arutha swallowed hard, finding his mouth suddenly dry. "Now, what is this about our fathers' plans for . . . our marriage?"

Arutha looked at Anita, her green eyes flickering with reflected candlelight, and something else. "Matters of state, I'm afraid. Father wanted my claim to the throne bolstered, and Lyam's too dangerous a match, being the older. You'd be ideal, for the King would not likely object . . . or wouldn't have then, I guess. Now, with Guy set upon having me, I suppose the King is in agreement."

Arutha became suddenly irritated, though he wasn't certain why. "And I suppose we're not to be consulted in the matter!" His voice rose.

"Please, it's not my doing."

"I'm sorry. I didn't mean to offend you. It's only I'd never given much thought to marriage, and certainly not for reasons of state." The wry grin reappeared. "That is usually the province of eldest sons. We second-born as a rule are left to get by as best we can, an old widowed countess, or a rich merchant's daughter." He tried to make light of it. "A rich merchant's beautiful daughter, if we're lucky, which we usually are not." He couldn't manage a light tone and sat back. Finally he said, "Anita, you will stay at Crydee as long as need be. It may prove dangerous because of the Tsurani for a time, but we'll see that through, somehow; send you down to Carse, perhaps. When this war is over, you'll go home in safety; I promise you. And never, never shall anyone force you to do anything against your will."

The conversation was interrupted by a knock on the door, and a seaman entered with a steaming bowl of chowder, hard bread, and salted pork on a platter. As the seaman placed the food on the table and poured a cup of wine, Arutha watched Anita. When the sailor was gone, Anita began to eat.

Arutha spoke of little things with Anita, finding himself once more captivated by the girl's open, appealing manner. When he finally bade her good night and closed the door, he was abruptly aware the idea of a state marriage was causing him only a little discomfort. He went up on deck; the fog had lifted, and once more they were running before a light breeze. He watched the stars above and, for the first time in years, whistled a happy air.

Near the helm Martin and Amos shared a wineskin and spoke low. "The Prince seems unusually cheerful tonight," said Amos.

Martin blew a puff of smoke from a pipe, which was quickly carried away on the wind. "And it's a good bet he's not even aware why he feels so cheerful. Anita's young, but not so young he'll be able to ignore her attentions for very long. If she's made up her mind, and I think she has, she'll have him snared within the year. And he'll be glad to be caught."

Amos laughed. "Though it will be some time before he owns up to it. I'm willing to wager young Roland is hauled up before the altar sooner than Anita."

Martin shook his head. "That's no wager. Roland's been caught for years. Anita has some work to do yet."

"You've never been in love, then, Martin?"

Martin said, "No, Amos. Foresters, like sailors, make poor husbands. Never at home long and spending days, even weeks, alone. Tends to make them a brooding, solitary lot. You?"

"Not so you'd notice." Amos sighed. "The older I get, the more I wonder what I've missed."

"But would you change anything?"

With a chuckle Amos said, "Probably not, Martin, probably not."

AS THE SHIP put in at the quayside, Fannon and Gardan dismounted. Arutha led Anita down the gangway and introduced her to the Swordmaster of Crydee.

"We've no carriages in Crydee, Highness," Fannon said to her, "but I'll have a cart sent for at once. It's a long walk to the castle."

Anita smiled. "I can ride, Master Fannon. Any horse that's not too spirited will do."

Fannon ordered two of his men to ride to the stable and bring one of Carline's palfreys with a proper sidesaddle. Arutha asked, "What news?"

Fannon led the Prince off a short distance and said, "A late thaw in the mountains, Highness, so there has been no major Tsurani movement as yet. A few of the smaller garrisons have been raided, but there is nothing to indicate a spring offensive here. Perhaps they'll move against your father."

"I hope you're right, for Father's received most of the Krondorian garrison." He quickly outlined what had occurred in Krondor, and Fannon listened closely.

"You did well not sailing for your father's camp. I think you judged things correctly. Nothing could prove more disastrous than a major Tsurani offensive against Duke Borric's position as he was marshaling to march against Guy. Let us keep this to ourselves for a time. Your father will learn what has occurred soon enough, but the more time it takes for him to discover Guy's treachery, the more chance we have of keeping the Tsurani at bay another year."

Arutha looked troubled. "This cannot continue much longer, Fannon. We must soon see an end to this war." He turned for a moment and saw townspeople begin to gawk at the Princess. "Still, we at least have a little time to come up with something to counter the Tsurani, if we can but think of it."

Fannon thought a moment, started to speak, then stopped. His expression became grim, almost painful. Arutha said, "What is it, Swordmaster?"

"I have grave and sorry news to greet you with, Highness. Squire Roland is dead."

Arutha was rocked by the news. For a brief moment he wondered if Fannon made some tasteless joke, for his mind would not accept what he had heard. Finally he said, "What . . . how?"

"News came three days ago from Baron Tolburt, who is most sorely grieved. The Squire was killed in a Tsurani raid."

Arutha looked at the castle upon the hill. "Carline?"

"As you would expect. She weeps, but she also bears up well."

Arutha fought back a choking sensation. His face was a grim mask as he moved back to Anita, Amos, and Martin. Word had spread that the Princess of Krondor was upon the wharf. The soldiers who had ridden with Fannon and Gardan formed a quiet ring around her, keeping the townsfolk at a respectful distance, while Arutha shared the sad news with Amos and Martin.

Soon the horses arrived and they were in the saddle, riding toward the castle. Arutha spurred his horse on and was dismounted before the others had entered the courtyard. Most of the household staff awaited him, and with little ceremony he shouted to Housecarl Samuel, "The Princess of Krondor is guesting with us. See rooms are made ready. Escort her to the great hall and tell her I will join her shortly."

He hurried through the entrance of the keep, past guards who snapped to attention as their Prince strode by. He reached Carline's suite and knocked upon the door.

"Who is it?" came the soft voice from within.

"Arutha."

The door flew open, and Carline rushed into her brother's arms, holding him tightly. "Oh, I'm so glad you are back. You don't know how glad." She stepped back and looked at him. "I'm sorry. I was going to ride down to meet you, but I just couldn't seem to gather myself together."

"Fannon just told me. I'm so very sorry."

She regarded him calmly, her face set in an expression of acceptance. She took him by the hand and led him to her chambers. Sitting upon a divan, she said, "I always knew it might happen. It was the silliest thing, you know. Baron Tolburt wrote a very long letter, the poor man. He saw so little of his son and was stricken." Tears began to come, and she swallowed hard, looking away from Arutha. "Roland died . . ."

"You don't have to tell me."

She shook her head. "It's all right. It hurts. . . ." Again tears came, but she spoke through them. "Oh, it hurts, but I'll get over the pain. Roland taught me that, Arutha. He knew there were going to be risks, and should he die, I'd have to keep living my own life. He taught me well. I think because I finally learned how much I loved him, and told him so, I gained the strength to cope with this loss.

"Roland died trying to save some farmer's cows." Through the tears, she smiled. "Isn't that like him? He spent the entire winter building up the fort, and then the first time there's trouble, it's some hungry Tsurani trying to steal some skinny cows. Roland went riding out with his men to chase them away, but got shot by an arrow. He was the only one hurt, and he died before they could get him back to the fort." She sighed long. "He was such a jester at times, I almost think he did it on purpose."

She began to weep, and Arutha watched in silence. Quickly she regained control over herself and said, "No good comes from this, you know." She rose and looked out a window and said, quietly, "Damn this stupid war."

Arutha came over to her, holding her tightly for a moment. "Damn all wars," he said.

For a few more minutes they were quiet, then she said, "Now tell me, what news from Krondor?"

Arutha gave her a brief account of his experiences in Krondor, half his attention on her. She seemed much more accepting of Roland's loss than she had when grieving for Pug. Arutha shared her pain, but also felt certain she would be all right. He was pleased to discover just how much Carline had matured over the last few years. When he finished telling of Anita's rescue, Carline interrupted. "Anita, the Princess of Krondor, is here?"

Arutha nodded, and Carline said, "I must look a fright, and you bring the Princess of Krondor here. Arutha, you are a monster." She rushed to a polished metal mirror and fussed with her face, daubing at it with a damp cloth.

Arutha smiled. Under the mantle of mourning, his sister still showed a spark of her natural spirit.

Combing her hair out, Carline turned to face her brother. "Is she pretty, Arutha?"

Arutha's wry smile was replaced by a grin. "Yes, I'd say she is pretty."

Carline studied Arutha's face. "I can see I'll have to get to know her well." She put down her comb and straightened her gown. Extending her hand to him, she said, "Come, we can't keep your young lady waiting."

Hand in hand they left the room and walked down the stairs to the main hallway, to welcome Anita to Crydee.

26

▾▾

GREAT ONE

AN ABANDONED HOUSE OVERLOOKED THE CITY.

The site upon which the house had been constructed had once seen the lights of a great family manse. On top of the highest of many rolling hills surrounding the city of Ontoset, it was considered the choicest view of the city and the sea beyond. The family had come to low estate, the result of being on the losing side in one of the Empire's many subtle but lethal political struggles. The house had fallen into disrepair and the property been ignored, for while it was as fine a building site as any found in the area, the association of ill fortune with the property was too real for the superstitious Tsurani.

One day news reached the city that some kula herders had awakened to the sight of a single black-robed figure walking up the hill toward the old house. They all acted with haste to avoid him, in the socially correct fashion for their station. They stayed within the area, tending their animals—the source of their meager income: kula wool—when, near midday, they heard a great noise, as if the heavens above them had erupted with the grandfather of all thunder peals. The herd scattered in terror, some running up the hill. The herders were no less terrified, but true to their trade, they put aside their fears and chased after the animals.

One herder, a man named Xanothis, came to the top of the once-famous hill to be greeted by the sight of the black-robed magician he had seen earlier, standing upon the crest. Where the run-down great house had stood moments before, a large patch of smoking land was laid bare, several feet below the level of the grass that surrounded it. Fearing he had intruded upon some business of a Great One, Xanothis started to back away, hoping to avoid detection, for the Great One's back was to the herder and his cowl was drawn over his head. As he took the first step backward, the magician turned to face him, fixing him with a pair of unsettlingly deep brown deep eyes.

The herder lowered himself as custom demanded, on his knees, eyes cast downward. He did not fully abase himself, for he was a freeman, and while not a noble, he was head of his family.

"Stand up," the magician ordered.

Slightly confused, Xanothis rose, eyes still cast downward.

"Look at me."

He looked up and found the face in the cowl regarding him closely. A beard as dark as the eyes framed a fair face, a fact that added to Xanothis's discomfort, as only slaves wore beards. The magician smiled at this obvious confusion and walked around the herder, inspecting him.

The magician saw a man tall for a Tsurani, an inch or two taller than his own five feet eight. His skin was dark, like unclouded chocha or coffee. His eyes were black, and his hair was black as well, save where it was shot with white. The herder's short green robe revealed the powerful build of a former soldier, a fact the magician gleaned from the man's erect posture and several scars. Past fifty he looked, but still capable of the strenuous life of a herder. Though shorter, this man resembled Gardan of Crydee slightly.

"Your name?" asked the magician, as he came round to stand before the herder. Xanothis answered, his voice betraying his unease. The magician then startled him by asking, "Would you agree that this is a good place for a home, herdsman?"

Confused, Xanothis stammered, "If . . . if it . . . is your will, Great One."

The magician snapped, "Ask not what I think! I ask *your* thoughts!"

Xanothis could barely hide his anger at his own shame. Great Ones were sacrosanct, and to be false with one was to do a dishonor. "Forgive me, Great One. It is said this spot is ill favored by the gods."

"And who is it that says so?"

The sharpness in the magician's voice caused the older man's head to snap up as if he had been struck. His eyes hid little of his anger, but his voice remained calm as he said, "Those who live in the city, Great One, and others about the countryside." The herdsman met the magician's gaze and held it.

The corners of the magician's eyes wrinkled in mirth, and his mouth turned up a little, but his voice still rang out. "But not you, herder?"

"I was fifteen years a soldier, Great One. I have found it often the case that the gods favor those who take care of their own welfare."

The magician smiled at this, though it was not an entirely warm expression. "A man of self-reliance. Good. I am glad we are of a like mind, for I plan to build my estate here, as I have a taste for the view of the sea."

A certain stiffness of posture in the herder's stance at this remark caught the magician's notice, and he said, "Have I your approval, Xanothis of Ontoset?"

Xanothis shifted his weight from one foot to the other, then said, "The Great One jests with me. My approval or disapproval is of no consequence, I am certain."

"True, but you still avoid my question. Have I your approval?"

Xanothis's shoulders sagged a little as he said, "I will have to move my herds, Great One. That is all. I mean no disrespect."

"Tell me of this house, Xanothis, that stood here before this day."

"It was the home of the Lord of the Almach, Great One. He backed the wrong cousin against Almecho when the office of Warlord was contested." He shrugged. "I was once a Patrol Leader of that house. I was a prideful man, which limited my advancement as a soldier. My lord gave me permission to leave his service and marry, so I took over my wife's father's herds. Had I stayed a soldier, I would now be a slave, dead, or a grey warrior." He glanced out toward the sea. "What more would you know, Great One?"

The magician said, "You may keep your herds upon this hill, Xanothis. The grazers keep the grass neat, and I have no liking for unkempt grounds. Just keep them away from the main house where I will be working, else I cook one for my supper now and again."

Without another word, the magician pulled a device from within his robe and activated it. A strange hum was emitted for a moment; then the black-robed figure disappeared with a small popping sound. Xanothis stood quietly for a few minutes, then resumed his search of his lost animals.

Later that night, around a campfire, he told his family and the other herders of his meeting with the Great One. None doubted his word, for whatever his other faults might be, Xanothis was not one to expand upon the truth, but they were amazed. And they never quite got used to one other thing: over the following months while a new great house was being built, one or another of the herdsmen would occasionally catch sight of Xanothis engaged in conversation with a Great One, atop the hill while kula grazed below them.

NOW A NEW and strange house stood atop the hill. It was the source of both some speculation and a little envy. The speculation was about its owner, the strange Great One. The envy was over its design and construction, something of a revolution in Tsurani architecture. Gone was the traditional three-story, open-center building. In its place was a long, single-story building, with several smaller ones attached to it by covered walkways. It was a rambling affair, with many small gardens and waterways winding between the structures. Its construction was as much a sensation as its design, for it consisted mainly of stone, with fired brick tiles upon the roof. Some speculated that it offered cool protection during the heat of summer.

Two other facts added to the fascination evidenced over the house and its owner. First was the manner in which the project had been commissioned. The magician had first appeared in Ontoset one day, at the home of Tumacel, the richest moneylender in the city. He appropriated over thirty thousand imperials in funds and left the moneylender stricken over his loss of liquidity. This was Milamber's method of dealing with the Tsurani passion for bureaucracy. Any merchant or tradesman commanded to render service to a Great One was forced to petition the imperial treasury for repayment. This resulted in slow delivery of ordered materials, less than enthusiastic service, and resentment. Milamber simply paid in advance and left it to the moneylender—who was better able to account for his losses than most other merchants, by nature of his bookkeeping—to recover from the treasury. The second fact was the style of decoration. Instead of the garishly bold wall paintings, the building was left mostly unpainted, except for an occasional landscape in muted, natural colors. Many fine young artists were employed on this project, and when it was done, the demand for their services was phenomenal. Within a month a new wave in Tsurani art was in progress.

Fifty slaves now worked the outlying fields, all free to come and go as they wished, dressed in the garb of their homeworld, Midkemia. All had been taken from the slave market one day, without payment, by the Great One.

Many travelers to Ontoset would make an afternoon of climbing the hills nearby to see the house. From a respectable distance, of course. The herder, Xanothis, was questioned many times about the strange

Great One who lived in that house, but the former soldier said nothing, only smiling a great deal.

"THE BELIEF that the current great rift to Midkemia is controllable is only partially correct." Milamber paused, allowing his scribe to finish copying the dictation. "It can be stated that rifts may be established without the release of destructive energies associated with their accidental creation, either through poorly effected magic spells or by the proximity of too many unstable magic devices."

Milamber's research into the special aspects of rift energies would be added to the Assembly's archives when completed. Like other projects he had read of in the archives, research into rifts had shown what Milamber took to be a grievous flaw in most of his brother magicians' work. In general, projects were not carried through to completion, showing a lack of thoroughness. Once the procedure to establish rifts safely had been developed, further research into their nature had been halted.

Continuing, he dictated: "What is lacking in the concept of control is the ability to select the terminus of contact, the ability to 'target' the rift. It has been shown by the appearance of the ship carrying Fanatha on the shores of Crydee, on the world of Midkemia, that a certain affinity between a newly forming rift and an existing one is probable. However, as shown by further testing, this affinity is limited, such limits being as yet not fully understood. While there is increased probability of a second rift appearing within a regional proximity to the first, it is by no means a certainty."

When the scribe was caught up, Milamber added, "Also, there is a question of why rifts show certain inconsistencies. Size appears relative to the energy employed in their formation, but other characteristics seem without pattern. Some rifts are single direction"—Milamber had lost several valuable devices discovering this fact—"while others allow movement in two directions. And then there are 'bonded pairs,' two single-direction rifts that appear simultaneously, both allowing one-way travel between origin and terminus. Though they may appear miles apart, they are related—"

Milamber's narration was interrupted by the sound of the chimes announcing the arrival of someone from the Assembly. He dismissed his scribe and made his way to the pattern room. As he walked, he mused on the real reason for his submersion in research over the last two months. He was avoiding the decision he must soon make, whether or not to return to the Shinzawai estate for Katala.

Milamber knew there was a chance she had become the wife of another, for their separation had been nearly five years, and she would have no reason to think he'd ever be returning. But time and training had done nothing to dull his feelings toward her. As he reached the transporting room with its tiled pattern, he made his decision: tomorrow he would go to see her.

As he entered the room, he saw Hochopepa step off the pattern in the tile floor. "Ah," said the plump magician, "there you are. Since it has been two weeks since I last saw you, I decided to pay a visit."

"I am glad to see you. I have been deeply involved in study and could do with a short respite."

They walked from the room into one of the several gardens nearby. Hochopepa said, "I have been meaning to ask you: what is the significance of the pattern you chose? I don't recognize it."

Milamber said, "It is a stylized recreation of a pattern I once saw in a fountain. Three dolphins."

"Dolphins?"

Milamber explained about the Midkemian sea mammals, while they seated themselves upon cushions between a pair of dwarf fruit trees.

"Why the dolphins from that fountain?"

"I don't know. A compulsion, perhaps. Also, when I underwent my final testing on the tower, I saw something that didn't register for a month or two after."

"What does one have to do with the other?"

"In the representation of the final challenge to the Stranger, do you remember a single brown-robed magician, who bent the rift to keep Kelewan from entering the Enemy's universe?"

Hochopepa looked thoughtful. "I can't say as I do, Milamber. But then the spell used to create that image affects each of us differently. If you compare visions with others, you'll discover a great deal of variation. But at the time of the Stranger, we were all black robes. Who could this odd brown-robed magician be?"

Milamber said, "A man I have met, years ago."

"Impossible. That scene took place centuries ago."

Milamber smiled and said, "Nevertheless, I have met him. I made my pattern of three dolphins as something of a commemorative to our meeting."

"How very strange. There has been some speculation on time travel, which would have to be the answer in this case, unless your barbaric mind played false with you upon the tower." He said the last with a smile.

Milamber clapped his hands, and a servant arrived with a platter of refreshments. The servant, Netoha, at one time had been hadonra for the family that resided there previously. Milamber had found him while securing someone to plant the varieties of vegetation he wanted in his gardens. The man was bold enough to approach, something that singled him out from the common Tsurani. Unable to find the work he was trained for since the demise of his employer's estate, Netoha had scratched out a meager living over the years. Milamber had taken him on as much out of sympathy as out of any real need. He had quickly made himself useful in a hundred ways the young magician had never dreamed of, and the relationship was mutually satisfactory.

Hochopepa took the offered sweets and drink. "I have come to tell you some news. There is to be an Imperial Festival in two months' time, with games. Will you come?"

Milamber found his curiosity piqued. With a wave he dismissed Netoha. "And what makes this festival so special? I can't remember having seen you so animated before."

"This festival is being given by the Warlord in honor of his nephew, the Emperor. He has plans for a new major offensive the week before the games, and it is hoped he will announce the success of the campaign." He lowered his voice. "It is no secret to those with access to court gossip he is under a great deal of pressure to justify his conduct of the war before the High Council. Rumor has it he has been forced to offer major concessions to the Blue Wheel Party to regain their support in the war.

"But what will make the games unusual is that the Light of Heaven will leave his Palace of Contemplation, breaking with ancient tradition. It would be a proper occasion for you to make some sort of entrance into court society."

"I'm sorry, Hocho," Milamber said, "I have little desire to attend any festivals. I have been to one earlier this month, in Ontoset, as part of my studies. The dances are boring, the food tends toward the awful, and the wine is as flat as the speeches. The games are of less interest still. If this is the court society you speak of, then I'll be fine without it."

"Milamber, there are many holes left in your education. Gaining the black robe did not mean instant mastery of our craft. There is quite a bit more involved in protecting the Empire than sitting about dreaming up new ways of tossing energy around, or creating economic chaos with the local moneylenders." He took another sweet and returned to his chiding. "There are several reasons you must come with me to the festivities, Milamber. First, you are something of a celebrity to the nobles of the realm, for news of your wondrous house has spread from one corner of the Empire to the other, mostly by aid of those young bandits you paid so well to execute the delicate paintings you love so much. It is now considered the mark of some distinction to have the same sort of work done.

"And this place"—his hand inscribed an arc before them, mock wonder upon his face—"anyone who could be so clever to design such an edifice must surely be worthy of attention." His mocking tone vanished as he added, "By the way, this entire bit of nonsense has not been diminished one whit by your mysterious isolation here in the hinterlands. If anything, it has added to your reputation.

"Now to more important reasons than social ones. As you no doubt know, there is growing concern that the news from the war is somehow being downplayed. In all these years there has been little gain, and some talk is going about that the Emperor may take a stand against the Warlord's policies. If so . . ." He let the thought go unfinished.

Milamber was silent for a time. "Hocho, I think it is time that I told you something, and if you feel it's sufficient to warrant my life, then you may return to the Assembly and bring charges."

Hochopepa was raptly attentive, all quips and sharp remarks put aside.

"You who trained me did your work well, for I am filled with a need to do what is best for the Empire. I hold only a little feeling for the land of my birth anymore, and you will never know what that signifies. But in the process of making me what I am, you could never create the love of home within my being that I once felt for my own Crydee. What you have created is a man with a strong sense of duty, untempered by any love for that thing he feels duty toward." Hochopepa remained silent as the impact of what Milamber had said penetrated, then he nodded as Milamber continued.

"I may be the greatest threat to the Empire since the Stranger invaded your skies, for if I become involved with its politics, I will be justice without mercy.

"I have known of the factions within the parties, the crossover of families from one party to another, and the consequences of those acts. Do you think because I sit atop my hill in the eastlands, I am unaware of the shifts and stirrings of the political animals in the capital? Of course not. If the Blue Wheel Party collapses and its members realign with the War Party or the Imperials, every street merchant in Ontoset is speculating on the news the next day in the marketplace. I know what is taking place as well as any other who is not directly involved. And in the months since I came to live here, I have come to one conclusion: the Empire is slowly killing itself."

The older magician said nothing for a moment, then asked, "Have you wondered at all why our system is such that we are killing ourselves?"

Milamber stood and paced a little. "Of course. I am studying it, and have chosen to wait before I act. I need more time to understand the history you taught me so well. But I do have some speculations of sorts on what's wrong, and they will give me a starting point." He inclined his head, asking if he should go on. Hochopepa nodded that he should. "It seems to me there are several major problems here, problems I can only guess at in terms of impact upon the Empire.

"First"—he held up his index finger—"those in power are more concerned with their own grandeur than with the well-being of the Empire. And as they are those who appear to the casual eye to be the Empire, it is an easy thing not to notice."

"What do you mean?" the older magician asked.

"When you think of the Empire, what comes to mind? A history of armies warring across the lands? Or the rise of the Assembly? Perhaps you think of a chronicle of rulers? Whatever it is, most likely the single most obvious truth is overlooked. The Empire is all those who live within its borders, from the nobles to the lowest servant, even the slaves who work the fields. It must be seen as a whole, not as being embodied by some small but visible part, such as the Warlord or the High Council. Do you understand that?"

Hochopepa looked troubled. "I'm not sure, but I think . . . Go on."

"If that is true, then consider the rest. Second, there must never be a time when the need for stability overrules the need for growth."

"But we have always grown!" objected Hochopepa.

"Not true," countered Milamber. "You have always expanded, and that seems like growth if you don't investigate closely. But while your armies have been bringing new lands into your borders, what has happened to your art, your music, your literature, your research? Even the vaunted Assembly does little more than refine that which is already known. You implied earlier that I was wasting my time finding new ways to 'toss energy around.' Well, what is wrong with that? Nothing. But there is something wrong with the type of society that looks upon the new as suspect.

"Look around you, Hocho. Your artists are in shock because I described what I had seen in paintings in my youth, and a few young artists became excited. Your musicians spend all their time learning the old songs, perfectly, to the note, and no one composes new ones, just clever variations on melodies that are centuries old. No one creates new epics, they only retell old ones. Hocho, you are a people stagnating. This war is but one example. It is unjustified, fought from habit, to keep certain groups in power, to reap wealth for those already wealthy, and to play the Game of the Council. And the cost! Thousands of lives are wasted each year, the lives of those who are the Empire, its own citizens. The Empire is a cannibal, devouring its own people."

The older magician was disturbed by what he heard, in total contradiction with what he believed he saw: a vibrant, energetic, alive culture.

"Third," said Milamber, "if my duty is to serve the Empire, and the social order of the Empire is responsible for its own stagnation, then it is my duty to change that social order, even if I must destroy it."

Now Hochopepa was shocked. Milamber's logic was without fault, but the suggested solution was potentially fraught with danger to everything Hochopepa knew and revered. "I understand what you say, Milamber, but what you speak of is too difficult to contemplate all at once."

Milamber's voice took on reassuring tones. "I do not mean to imply that the destruction of the present social order is the only solution, Hocho. I used that to shock and to drive home a point. That is what much of my research is about, not only the visible mastery of energy, but also investigations into the nature of the Tsurani people and the Empire. Believe me, I am more than willing to spend as much time on the question as I need. I plan on spending some time in the archives."

Hochopepa's brows furrowed, and he studied his younger friend's face. "Be warned, you may find some unsettling things in those archives. As I said, your education is not complete."

Milamber let his voice drop. "I have already found some unsettling things, Hocho. Much of what is held to be common truth by the nations is based upon falsehoods."

Hochopepa became concerned. "There are things that are forbidden for any but members of the Assembly to know, Milamber, and even then it is unwise to speak about them to even one of your brethren." He glanced away, thinking, then said, "Still, when you have finished prowling around in those musty old vaults, if you need to discuss your findings, I'll be a willing ear." He looked back at his friend. "I like you and think you're a refreshing change of pace for us, Milamber, but there are many who would rather see you dead as not. Don't go chattering on to anyone but Shimone or myself about this social research you're doing."

"Agreed. But when I reach a judgment as to what must be done, I shall act."

Hochopepa stood, an expression of concern on his face. "It is not that I disagree with you, my friend, it is simply that I must have time to assimilate what you have said."

"I could only speak the truth to you, Hocho, no matter how disturbing."

Hochopepa smiled. "A fact I appreciate, Milamber. I must spend some time considering the proposition." Some of his usual humor crept back into his voice. "Perhaps you will accompany me to the Assembly? You have been absent much of the time with this house building and all; you would do well to put in an appearance now and again."

Milamber smiled at his friend. "Of course." He indicated that Hochopepa should lead the way to the pattern. As they walked, Hochopepa said, "If you wish to study our culture, Milamber, I still suggest you come to the Imperial Festival. There will be more political activity in the seats of the arena in that one day than could be observed in a month in the High Council."

Milamber turned toward Hochopepa. "Perhaps you're right. I shall think about it."

WHEN THEY APPEARED on the pattern of the Assembly, Shimone was standing close by. He bowed slightly in greeting and said, "Welcome. I was about to go looking for you two."

Hochopepa said with mild amusement, "Are we so vital to the business of the Assembly that you must be sent to fetch us back?"

Shimone inclined his head a little. "Perhaps, but not today. I merely thought you would find the business at hand interesting."

Milamber asked, "What is happening?"

"The Warlord has sent messages to the Assembly, and Hodiku raises questions about them. We best hurry, for they are nearly ready to begin."

They walked quickly to the central hall of the Assembly and entered. Arrayed about a large open area was an amphitheater of open benches; they took seats in a lower row. Already several hundred black-robed Great Ones were in place. In the center of the floor they could see Fumita, the one-time brother of the Shinzawai lord, standing alone; he would be presiding over the business of the day. The presidency was allotted by chance to one of those in attendance. Milamber had seen Fumita in the Assembly only twice since being brought here.

Shimone said, "It has been nearly three weeks since I saw you in the Assembly, Milamber."

"I must apologize, but I have been busy getting my home in order."

"So I hear. You're something of a source of gossip in the imperial court. I hear the Warlord himself is anxious to meet you."

"Perhaps someday."

Hochopepa said to Shimone, "Who can understand such a man? Taking to building such a strange home." He turned to Milamber. "Next you'll be telling me that you're taking a wife."

Milamber laughed. "Why, Hocho, how did you guess?"

Hochopepa's eyes grew wide. "You're not!"

"And why shouldn't I?"

"Milamber, it is not a wise course, believe me. To this day I have regretted my own marriage."

"Hocho, I didn't know you were a married man."

"I choose not to speak of it much. My wife is a fine woman, though given to an overly sharp tongue and scathing wit. In my own home I'm not much more than another servant to be ordered about. That is why I see her only on prescribed holidays; it would be bad for my nerves to see her more often."

Shimone said, "Who is your intended, Milamber? A noble daughter?"

"No. She was a slave with me at the Shinzawai estate."

Hochopepa mused, "A slave girl . . . hmm. That might work out."

Milamber laughed, and Shimone chuckled. Several other magicians regarded them with curiosity, for the Assembly was not a regular forum for mirth.

Fumita held up his hand, and the Assembly became quiet. "Today there is a matter being brought before the Assembly by Hodiku."

A thin Great One, with shaved head and hooked nose, walked from his seat in front of Milamber and Hochopepa to the center of the floor.

He surveyed the magicians in the hall, then spoke. "I come today so that I may speak about the Empire." It was the formal opening of any business brought before the Assembly. "I speak for the good of the Empire," he added, completing the ritual. "I am concerned about the demand made today by the Warlord for aid so he may broaden the war against the Midkemian world."

A chorus of jeers and cries of "Politics" and "Sit down!" erupted from around the room. Soon Shimone and Hochopepa were on their feet with others crying, "Let him speak!"

Fumita held up a hand for silence, and soon the room quieted. Hodiku continued. "We are precedented. Fifteen years ago the Assembly sent an order to the Warlord to end the war against the Thuril Confederation."

Another magician jumped to his feet. "If the Thuril conquest had continued, there would have been too few in the north to repulse the

Thūn migration that year. It was a clear case of the salvation of Szetac Province and the Holy City. Now our borders in the north are secure. The situation is not the same."

Arguments erupted over the entire hall, and it took several minutes for Fumita to restore order. Hochopepa rose and said, "I would like to hear Hodiku's reasons for considering this request vital to the security of the Empire. Any magician who is willing is free to work on behalf of the conquest."

"That is the point," responded Hodiku. "There is no reason for any magician who feels this war into another space-time is right and proper for the Empire not to work in support of the conquest. Without the Black Robes who already serve the Warlord, the rift would never have been prepared for such an undertaking. It is that he now makes demands of the Assembly itself I find objectionable. If five or six magicians choose to serve in the field, even to traveling to this other world to risk their lives in the battle, then it is their own concern. But if one magician responds to this demand without considering the issues, it will appear the Assembly is now subject to the will of the Warlord."

Several magicians applauded this sentiment, and others seemed to weigh its merits. Only a few booed and jeered. Hochopepa stood again. "I would like to offer a proposal. I will undertake on behalf of the Assembly to send a message to the Warlord expressing our regret that the Assembly as a body may not order any magician to perform as requested, but that he is free to seek the services of any magician willing to work on his behalf."

A general murmur of approval ran through the room, and Fumita asked, "Hochopepa offers a proposition to send a statement of policy to the Warlord on behalf of the Assembly. Does anyone find this objectionable?" When no objections were forthcoming, he said, "The Assembly thanks Hochopepa for his wisdom."

He paused for a moment, then said, "Another matter needs our attention: the novice Shiro has been found lacking in the moral qualities necessary for the Greater Art. The mind probes reveal that he harbors anti-Imperial feelings, learned as a youth from his maternal grandmother, a Thuril woman. Is the Assembly agreed?"

Hands were raised, and each bore a nimbus of light as the magicians voted. Green for life, red for death, and blue for abstention. Milamber abstained, but the vote was otherwise unanimous for death. One Black Robe rose, and Milamber knew that within minutes the novice would be stunned senseless, then teleported to the bottom of the lake, where his lifeless body would remain, too cold to rise to the surface.

After the meeting broke up, Shimone said, "You should make a point of coming more often, Milamber. We hardly see you anymore. And you spend too much time alone."

Milamber smiled. "That is true, but I plan to remedy the situation tomorrow."

THE CHIME SOUNDED throughout the house, and servants jumped to make ready for the Great One's visit. Kamatsu, Lord of the Shinzawai, knew that a Great One had struck a chime in the halls of the Assembly, willing the sound to come here, to announce his imminent appearance.

In Kasumi's room, Laurie and the elder son of the house sat engrossed in a game of pashawa, played with painted pieces of stiff paper. It was common to alehouses and inns in Midkemia and was one more detail in the young Tsurani's drive to master every facet of Midkemian life.

Kasumi stood. "It is most likely he who once was my uncle; I had best go."

Laurie smiled. "Or could it be that you wish to stem your losses?"

The Tsurani shook his head. "I fear I have created a problem in my own house. You were never a good slave, Laurie, and if anything, you have grown more intractable. It is a good thing I like you."

They both laughed, and the elder son of the house left. A few minutes later a house slave came running to Laurie and informed him that the lord of the house commanded him to come at once. Laurie jumped up, more from the slave's obvious agitation than from any inbred obedience. He hurried to the lord's room and knocked on the doorjamb. The door slid to one side, and Kasumi held it. Laurie stepped through and saw the Shinzawai lord and his guest, and then confusion overtook him.

The guest was wearing the black robe of the Tsurani Great Ones, but the face was Pug's. He started to speak, stopped, and started again. "Pug?"

The lord of the house looked outraged at this forward behavior by the slave, but his nearly voiced command was stopped by the Great One. "May I have the use of this room for a few minutes, lord? I wish to speak to this slave in private."

Kamatsu, Lord of the Shinzawai, bowed stiffly. "Your will, Great One." He left the room with his son behind; he was still in shock over the appearance of the former slave and confused at the conflicts within himself. The Great One he was, there could be no thought of fraud: his manner of arrival proved it. But Kamatsu couldn't help feeling that his arrival heralded disaster for the plan he and his son had so carefully nurtured for the last nine years.

Milamber spoke. "Shut the door, Laurie."

Laurie shut it, then studied his former friend. He looked fit, but vastly changed. His bearing was nearly regal, as if the mantle of power he now wore reflected some inner strength he had lacked before.

"I . . . ," Laurie began, then lapsed into silence, confused about what to say. Finally he said, "Are you well?"

Milamber nodded. "I am well, old friend."

Laurie smiled and crossed the room and embraced his friend, then pushed himself away. "Let me look at you."

Milamber smiled. "I am called Milamber, Laurie. The boy you knew as Pug is as dead as last year's flowers. Come, sit and we will talk."

They sat at the table and poured two cups of chocha. Laurie sipped at the bitter brew and said, "We heard nothing about you. After the first year I gave you up for lost. I'm sorry."

Milamber nodded. "It is the way of the Assembly. As a magician I am expected to forgo all my former ties, except for those that can be maintained in a socially acceptable manner. Being without clan or family, I had nothing to forgo. And you were always a poor slave who never knew his place. What better friend for a renegade, barbarian magician?"

Laurie nodded. "I am glad you have returned. Will you stay?"

Milamber shook his head no. "I have no place here. Besides, there is work I must be about. I now have an estate of my own, near the city of Ontoset. I have come for you. And Katala, if . . ." His voice trailed off, as if he were fearful of asking about her.

Sensing his distress, Laurie said, "She is still here and has not taken a husband. She would not forget you." He broke into a grin. "Gods of Midkemia! It completely slipped my mind. You would have no way of knowing."

"What?"

"You have a son."

Milamber sat dumbstruck. "A son?"

Laurie laughed. "He was born eight months after you were taken. He is a fine boy, and Katala is a fine mother."

Milamber felt overwhelmed at the news and said, "Please. Would you bring her here?"

Laurie jumped to his feet. "At once."

He rushed from the room. Milamber sat fighting down the upsurge of emotion. He composed himself, using his magician's skills to relax his mind.

The door slid open, and Katala was revealed, uncertainty on her face. Laurie stood behind, a boy of about four in his arms.

Milamber rose and spread his arms to her. Katala rushed to him, and he nearly cried in his joy. They clung quietly for a moment, then she murmured, "I thought you gone. I hoped . . . but I thought you gone."

They stood for several minutes, each lost in the pure pleasure of the other's presence, until she pushed herself away. "You must meet your son, Pug."

Laurie brought the boy forward. He regarded Milamber with large brown eyes. He was a well-formed boy, with a stronger likeness to his mother, but something in the way he tilted his head made him resemble the boy from Crydee keep. Katala took him from Laurie and passed him to Milamber. "William, this is your father."

The boy seemed to take this in with some skepticism. He ventured a shy smile, but leaned back, keeping his distance. "I want down," he said abruptly. Milamber laughed and put the boy down. He looked at his father, then immediately lost interest in the stranger in black. "Ooh!" he cried, and rushed over to play with the Lord of the Shinzawai's shāh pieces.

Milamber watched him for a moment, then said, "William?"

Katala stood next to him with her arm around his waist, hugging him as if afraid he would disappear again. Laurie said, "She wanted a Midkemian name for him, Milamber."

Katala started. "Milamber?"

"It is my new name, love. You must get used to calling me that." She frowned, not entirely pleased with the thought. "Milamber," she repeated, testing the sound. She then shrugged. "It is a good name."

"How did he become William?"

Laurie went over to the boy, who was trying to stand the pieces one atop the other, and gently took them away. The boy threw him a black look. "I want to play," he said indignantly.

Laurie picked him up and said, "I gave her a bunch of names, and she picked that one."

"I liked its sound," she said; "William."

At the sound of his name the boy looked at his mother. "I'm hungry."

"I favored James or Owen, but she insisted," Laurie said, while the boy tried to wriggle out of his arms.

Katala took him. "I must feed him. I'll take him to the kitchen." She kissed Milamber and left the room.

The magician stood quietly for a moment. "It is all more than I had hoped for. I was afraid she'd have found another."

"Not that one, P—Milamber. She would have nothing to do with any of the men who paid court to her, and there were a few. She's a good woman. You need never doubt her."

"I never will, Laurie."

They seated themselves; a discreet cough at the door made them turn. Kamatsu stood at the door. "May I enter, Great One?"

Milamber and Laurie started to rise, and the lord of the house waved them back into place. "Please, stay seated." Kasumi entered behind his father and closed the door. Milamber noticed for the first time that the son of the house was wearing garments that were Midkemian in fashion. He raised an eyebrow, but said nothing.

The head of the Shinzawai family looked deeply troubled and tried to collect his thoughts. After a few moments he said, "Great One, may I be frank with you? Your arrival today is something unexpected and the source of some possible difficulty."

"Please," said Milamber. "I do not intend to cause disruption in your household, lord. I want only my wife and son. And I will require this slave also." He indicated Laurie.

"Your will, Great One. The woman and the boy should, of course, go with you. But if I may beg of you, please allow the slave to remain."

Milamber looked from face to face. The two Shinzawai maintained control, but by the way they glanced from one to the other and at Laurie, their distress was poorly hidden. Something had changed here in the last five years. The relationship between the men in the room was not what it should have been between masters and slave.

"Laurie?" Milamber looked at his friend. "What is this?"

Laurie looked at the other two men, then at Milamber. "I will have to ask you to promise me something."

Kamatsu's shock was signaled by a sharp intake of breath. "Laurie! You dare too much. One does not bargain with a Great One. His words are as law."

Milamber held up a hand. "No. Let him speak."

In imploring tones Laurie said to his friend, "I know little of these matters, Milamber. You know I have no sense about protocol. I may be violating custom, but I ask you for the sake of our former friendship, will you keep a trust and vow to keep what you hear in this room to yourself?"

The magician pondered the matter. He could command the Shinzawai lord to tell all, and the man would, as automatically as a soldier following orders, but his friendship with the troubadour was important to him. "I give you my word that I will not repeat what you tell me."

Laurie gave a sigh and smile, and the Shinzawai seemed to lose some of their tension. Laurie said, "I have struck a bargain with my lord here. When we have completed certain tasks, I am to be given my freedom."

Milamber shook his head. "That is not possible. The law does not permit a slave to be freed. Even the Warlord cannot free a slave."

Laurie smiled. "And yourself?"

Milamber looked stern. "I am outside the law. None may command me. Are you claiming to be a magician?"

"No, Milamber, nothing like that. It is true that I can only be a slave here. But I won't be here. I will return to Midkemia."

Milamber looked puzzled. "How is that possible? There is only one rift into Midkemia, and that is controlled by the Warlord's pet magicians. There are no others, or I would know of them."

"We have a plan. It is involved and will take much explaining, but simply put, it is this: I will accompany Kasumi, disguised as a priest of Turakamu the Red. He will be leading soldiers replacing troops at the front. No one is likely to notice my height, for the Red One's priests are given wide berth. The troops are all loyal to the Shinzawai. Once in Midkemia, we will slip through the lines and find our way to the Kingdom forces."

Milamber nodded. "Now I understand the language lessons and the clothes. But tell me, Laurie. Are you willing to spy for the Tsurani in exchange for your freedom?" There was no disapproval in his voice, it was a simple question.

Laurie flushed. "I am not going as a spy. I am going as a guide. I am to take Kasumi to Rillanon, for an audience with the King."

"Why?" Milamber was surprised.

Kasumi interrupted. "I go to meet the King and bring him an offer of peace."

MILAMBER RAISED an argument. "How can you possibly expect to end the war with the War Party still in control of the High Council?"

"There is one thing in our favor," responded Kamatsu. "This war has lasted for nine years, and the end is nowhere in sight. Great One, I don't presume to instruct you, but if I may explain some things?"

Milamber nodded that he should continue. Kamatsu sipped his drink and went on. "Since the end of the war with the Thuril Confederation, the War Party has been pressed to maintain its dominance over the High Council. Each border clash with Thuril brought the call for a renewal of the conflict. Between the fighting on the border, and the constant attempts by the Thūn to break through the passes in the north and regain their former southern range, the War Party managed barely to maintain a majority. A coalition led by the Blue Wheel Party was on the verge of dislodging them ten years ago, when the Assembly discovered the rift into your former homeland. The call for war rang out in the council as soon as the rich metals of your homeland were known to exist. All the progress we had made over the years was lost in that instant.

"So we began at once to counter this madness. The metals being mined on your former world are, from what Laurie has told us, the leavings of abandoned mines, not considered worth the bother by those you call dwarves. There is nothing in this for Tsuranuanni but an excuse to raise the War Banner again and shed blood.

"You know our history. You know how difficult it is for us to settle our differences in a peaceful manner. I have been a soldier and know the glories of war. I also know its waste. Laurie has convinced me that my suspicions about those who live in the Kingdom were correct. You are not a very warlike people, in spite of your nobles and their armies. You would have been willing to trade."

Milamber interrupted. "This is all true. But I am not sure that it has any bearing on things as they stand now. My former nation had not fought a major war in nearly fifty years, except for skirmishes with the goblins of the north and along the Keshian border. But now the battle drums sound in the West. The Armies of the Kingdom have been blooded. The nation has been invaded without cause. They would not, I think, be willing simply to stop and forgive. There would be demands for retribution, or at least reparation. Would the High Council be willing to surrender the honor of Tsuranuanni and make restitution for the wrong done at the hands of its soldiers?"

The Shinzawai lord looked troubled. "The council would not, I am sure. But the Emperor would."

"The Emperor?" Milamber said, surprised. "What has he to do with this?"

"Ichindar, may heaven bless him, feels the war is bleeding the Empire of its resources. When we campaigned against the Thuril, we learned that some frontiers are simply too vast and far from the Empire to control, save at costs far greater than the victories are worth. The Light of Heaven understands that nowhere could there be a frontier as vast or far as that we have found on Midkemia. He is taking a hand in the Game of the Council. It is perhaps the greatest game ever played in the history of Tsuranuanni. The Light of Heaven is willing to command the Warlord to peace, to have him removed from office if need be. But he will not take the risk of so great a break with tradition unless he is guaranteed the willingness of King Rodric to come to terms. He must go before the High Council with peace a fait accompli; otherwise he risks too much.

"Regicide has been committed only once in the history of the Empire, Great One. The High Council hailed the killer and named him Emperor. He was the son of the man he slew. His father had tried to order taxes imposed upon the temples, the last time an Emperor played in the Game of the Council. We can be a hard people, Great One, even with ourselves, and never has an Emperor sought to do what Ichindar seeks, what others, many others, will see as laying down the honor of the Empire, an unthinkable act.

"But if he can deliver peace to the council, then it will clearly show the gods give their blessing to such an undertaking, and none will dare challenge him."

"You risk much, Lord of the Shinzawai."

"I love my nation and the Empire, Great One. I would willingly die in the field for her, and I risked that often when I was younger, during the Thuril campaigns. I would also risk my life, my sons, the honor of my house, family, and clan to bring the Empire to sanity. As would the Emperor. We are a patient people. This plan is years in preparation. The Blue Wheel Party has long been secretly allied with the Party for Peace. We withdrew in the third year of the war to embarrass the Warlord and set the stage for Kasumi's training for the coming journey. Over a year was spent in traveling to various lords within the Blue Wheel and Peace parties, ensuring cooperation, that every member would play his part in the Game of the Council, before you and Laurie were brought here to be his tutors.

"We are Tsurani, and the Light of Heaven would not allow an overture to be made until he had a ready messenger. We have made Kasumi that messenger, seeking to give him the best possible chance of reaching your former King safely. It must be this way, for should any outside our faction learn of the attempt if it fails, many heads, including my own, would fall, the price of losing the game. If you take Laurie away, Kasumi has little chance of reaching your former King, and the peace effort will be postponed until we can find another trustworthy guide, a delay almost certain to last one or two more years. The situation is now critical. The Blue Wheel Party is again part of the Alliance for War, after years of negotiation with the War Party, and thousands of men are being sent to fight so that Kasumi may slip through Kingdom lines into your former homeland. The time will soon be ripe. You must consider what even another year of war would mean. With the conquest of your former homeland, the Warlord could become invulnerable to any move we may make."

Milamber considered, then to Kasumi said, "How soon?"

Kasumi said, "Soon, Great One, a matter of weeks. The Warlord has spies everywhere and has some hint of our plans. He has little trust of the Blue Wheel's sudden shift in the council, but he cannot refuse the aid. He feels the need to strike a great victory. He plans the major spring offensive against the forces of Lords Borric and Brucal, the Kingdom's main strength. It will be timed to occur just before the Imperial Festival, orchestrated so he can announce the victory at the Imperial Games, for his own personal glory."

Kamatsu said, "It is much like an end-game gambit in shāh, Great One.

"A smashing victory will gain the Warlord all he needs to take control of the High Council, but we risk this to play for our final move. The front will be in confusion as preparations are being made for the offensive. Kasumi and Laurie will have their best opportunity to slip through the lines. Should King Rodric agree, then the Light of Heaven can appear in the High Council with an announcement of peace, and all that the Warlord's power and influence is based upon will crumble. In terms of shāh, we expose our last piece to capture so that our Emperor may checkmate a Warlord."

Milamber was thoughtful for a time. "I think you have embarked on a bold plan, Lord of the Shinzawai. I will honor my pledge to say nothing. Laurie may continue here." He looked at Laurie. "May the gods of our forefathers protect you and bring you success. I pray this war may end soon." He stood up. "If you don't mind, I will take my leave. I would have my wife and child home now."

Kasumi rose and bowed. "I should like to say one thing more, Great One."

Milamber indicated he should proceed. "Years ago, when you asked for Katala for your wife, and I told you the request would be refused, I also told you there was a reason. It was our plan you would also return to your homeworld. I trust you understand that now. We are a hard people, Great One, but not cruel."

"It was apparent as soon as the plan was revealed." He looked at Laurie. "For what I am now, this is my homeland, but there is still a part of me unchanged within, and for that reason I envy you your homecoming. You will be well remembered, old friend."

So saying, Milamber left the room. Outside the great house he found Katala waiting in a garden, watching their son at play. She came to him and they embraced, savoring sweet reunion. After a long moment he said, "Come, beloved, let us take our son home."

27

▾▾

FUSION

LONGBOW WEPT IN SILENCE.

Alone in a glade near the edge of the elven forests, the Huntmaster of Crydee stood over three fallen elves. Their lifeless bodies lay sprawled upon the ground with arms and legs bent at impossible angles, their fair faces covered in blood. Martin knew what death meant to the elves, where one or two children to a family in a century was the norm. One face he knew well, Algavins, Galain's companion since boyhood, less than thirty years of age, still a child by the elven folk's measure.

Footsteps from behind caused Martin to wipe away the tears and resume his usually impassive expression. From behind he heard Garret say, "There's another bunch down the trail, Huntmaster. The Tsurani went through this part of the forest like a bad wind."

Martin nodded, then set out without comment. Garret followed. For all his youth, Garret was Longbow's best tracker, and they both moved lightly along the trail toward Elvandar.

After traveling for hours, they crossed the river west of a Tsurani enclave, and when they were safely into the elven forests, a voice hailed them from the trees. "Well met, Martin Longbow."

Martin and Garret halted and waited as three elves appeared from among the trees, seemingly forming out of the air. Galain and his two companions approached the Huntmaster and Garret. Martin inclined his head slightly back toward the river, and Galain nodded. It was all the communication they needed to exchange the fact both knew of Algavins's death, along with the others. Garret noticed the exchange, though he was far from conversant with the subtleties of elvish ways.

"Tomas? Calin?" asked Martin.

"In council with the Queen. Do you bring news?"

"Messages from Prince Arutha. Are you bound for council?"

Galain smiled the elvish half-smile that indicated ironic humor. "It has fallen to us to guard the way. We must remain for a time. We will come as soon as the dwarves cross the river. They are due anytime now."

The comment was not lost on Martin as he bade them good-bye and continued toward Elvandar. Approaching the clearing surrounding the elvish tree-city, he wondered at the exclusion of Galain and the other young elves from council. They were all constant companions of Tomas since he came to take up permanent residency in Elvandar. Martin had not been there since just before the siege of Crydee, but in those years he had spoken to some of the Natalese Rangers who ran messages from the Duke to Elvandar to Crydee. On several occasions he had spent hours talking with Long Leon and Grimsworth of Natal. While close-mouthed when not among their own kind, they were less guarded with Longbow, for in the Huntmaster of Crydee they sensed a kindred spirit. He was the only man not a Ranger of Natal who could enter Elvandar unbidden. The two Natalese Rangers had indicated great changes in the Elf Queen's court, and Martin felt a strange sort of silent disquiet.

As they approached Elvandar in an easy, loping run, Garret said, "Huntmaster, will they not send someone to fetch the fallen?"

Martin stopped and leaned upon his bow. "Garret, it is not their way. They will let the forest reclaim them, for they believe their true spirits are now abiding in the Blessed Isles." He thought a moment, then said, "Among my trackers, you are perhaps the best I've known." The still young man blushed at the compliment, but Longbow said, "No flattery, but simply fact. I mention it because you are the one most likely to replace me should anything happen."

Garret's usual hangdog expression gave way to one of close attention to what Martin was saying. Martin continued, "If something should occur that takes me from this life, I would hope that someone would continue to keep Elvandar and the human world from drifting apart."

Garret nodded. "I think I understand."

"You must, for it would be a sad thing for the two races to grow away from one another." He spoke softly. "About their beliefs you must learn as you can, but a few things you should know, especially in this time of war. Do you remember how it is claimed that certain priests can recall the dead, if they are no more than an hour departed?"

Garret said, "I have heard the story, but I have never met anyone who claims to have seen it done, or even claims to know someone who has seen it."

"It is true. Father Tully says so, and he's not the sort to be less than forthright on matters of faith." Martin looked down at the soil. "There is a story: an important priest—of which order I do not know—found himself grown away from the gods and caught up in the human world. He cast off his fine robes and golden ornaments and donned the simple homespun of an itinerant monk. He wandered the wilderness, seeking humility. Time and chance brought him to Elvandar, where he came upon a newly fallen elf, dead by accident but a few minutes before the priest arrived. He began to recall the elf from death, for he was a priest of great powers, and sought to share his abilities with all in need. He was halted by the elf's wife, and when he asked her why, she said, 'It is not our way. He is now in a far better place, and should you recall him, he will not return but against his will and to our sorrow. That is why we will not speak his name, lest he hear longing in our voices and return to comfort us at cost of his own.' From what I know, no elf has ever been recalled from death.

"I have been told by some that no elf can be revived by human arts. Others have said that elves have no true souls, which is why they do not return. I think both are false, and they have a finer sense of where they live in the world."

Garret was quiet for a moment while he digested this information. "It is a strange tale, Huntmaster. What brought it to mind?"

"The death of those elves and your question. It is to show you how they differ from us, and how you must work to learn their ways. You will spend time among them."

"Is the tale of the dead elf true?"

"Yes. The newly fallen elf was the late Elf King, Queen Aglaranna's husband. I was but a boy then, thirty years ago, but I remember it. I was with the hunting party when the accident happened, and I met the priest."

Garret said nothing, and Martin picked up his weapon and resumed his journey.

They soon came to the edge of Elvandar. Martin stopped while Garret stood enraptured by the sight of the great trees. The late-afternoon sun cast long shadows through the forest, but the high boughs were already glimmering with their own fairy light.

Martin took Garret by the elbow and gently guided the gawking tracker along to the Queen's court. He reached the council ring and entered, saluting the Queen.

Aglaranna smiled at sight of him. "Welcome, Martin Longbow. It has been too long since you last came to us."

Martin introduced Garret, who bowed awkwardly before the Queen. Then another figure entered the court, from where he had stood in the shadows.

Martin had grown alongside elven children and was as able as any man in hiding his emotions when need be, but the sight of Tomas rocked him to the point of nearly exclaiming. Biting back a comment, he forced himself not to stare and heard Garret's indrawn breath of amazement. They had heard of the changes in Tomas, but nothing had prepared either Martin or Garret for the sight of the towering man before him. Alien eyes regarded them. There was little remaining of the happy, grinning boy who had once followed Martin through the woods begging for tales of the elves, or played barrel ball with Garret. Without cordiality Tomas stepped forward and said, "What word from Crydee?"

Martin leaned upon his bow. "Prince Arutha sends his greetings," he said to the Queen, "and his affections, as well as his hope for your good health." Turning to Tomas, who had obviously usurped some position of command within the Queen's council, he said, "Arutha sends the following news: Black Guy, Duke of Bas-Tyra, now rules in Krondor, so no help will be forthcoming to the Far Coast. Also, the Prince has good cause to believe the outworlders plan to mount a major offensive soon, whether against Crydee, Elvandar, or the Duke's army he cannot tell. However, the southern enclaves are not being reinforced through the dwarven mines, though they are strongly dug in. My trackers have had some signs of northward movement, but nothing on a large scale. It is Arutha's guess the most likely offensive will be against his father and Brucal's army." Then he said, "And I bring word that Arutha's Squire has been slain." He observed the elven avoidance of naming the dead.

Tomas's eyes betrayed a glint of emotion at the news of Roland's death, but all he said was, "In war men die."

Calin realized the exchange was something of a personal matter between Longbow and Tomas. No one else in the court had known Roland well, though Calin remembered him from the dinner that night so many years ago in Crydee. Martin was troubled by Tomas's reaction to the news of his boyhood friend's death. Returning to the business of the war, the Elf Prince said, "It is a logical thing. Should the Kingdom army in the West be broken, the outworlders could then turn their full attention on the other fronts, gaining the Free Cities and Crydee quickly.

Within a year, two at the most, all of what once was Keshian Bosania would be under their banners. Then they could march easily upon Yabon. In time they could march to the gates of Krondor."

Tomas faced Calin, as if to speak, his eyes narrow. A flash of communication passed between the Queen and Tomas, and he stepped back into his place in the council circle. Calin continued, "If the outworlders are not staging to the west of the mountains, then we should be joined by the dwarves soon. We've had sorties across the river from the outworlders, but no sign of major attacks to come. I think Arutha is correct in his surmise, and should the dukes call, we should try to aid them."

Tomas turned upon the Elf Prince. "Leave Elvandar unprotected!" His face showed outrage. Martin was startled by the ferocity of Tomas's barely checked anger. "Without stripping the elven forests of defenders, we could not mount enough numbers to matter in such a battle."

Calin's face remained impassive, but his eyes mirrored Tomas's anger. His words came forth quietly. "I am Warleader of Elvandar. I would not leave our forests unprotected. But should the outworlders mount a major offensive against the dukes, they will not leave sufficient soldiers along the river to menace our forests. They have not come against us since we defeated them with the sorcerer's aid and their Black Robes were killed. But should they battle Lords Borric and Brucal, and should the battle be a close thing, our numbers might tip the balance, especially as we can strike against their weaker flank."

Tomas maintained his self-control, standing rigidly for a moment; then in icy tones he said, "The dwarves follow Dolgan, and Dolgan follows my lead. They will not come unless I call them to battle." Without another word he left the council circle.

Martin watched Tomas leave. His skin crawled as he felt for the first time the power contained within this strange blend of man and whatever else lived inside the boy from Crydee. He had caught only a glimpse of what was within Tomas, but it had been enough. Tomas was a being to be feared.

Martin then saw a flicker of expression on Aglaranna's face. She rose and said, "I had better have words with Tomas. He has been overwrought of late."

As she left, Martin was struck by a certainty. Whatever else he had seen, he had witnessed a conflict between the Elf Queen's son and her lover, and a deep conflict within herself, as well. Aglaranna had worn the expression of one caught in a hopeless fate.

When the Queen had left, Calin said, "You have come at a propitious time, Martin. We have need of your wisdom."

Martin nodded. He sent Garret away to get something to eat, and when he was gone, Martin studied the Elf Prince, then the others in the council. Tathar stood at his usual place, to the right of the Queen's throne. Others he knew, all old and trusted advisers of the Queen. Many were ancient Spellweavers.

Martin sat down, patiently waiting for Calin to speak. The Elf Prince remained silent for a time. Martin studied Calin, for he knew him and could sense his disquiet. As a boy, Martin had thought the Elf Prince the finest embodiment of all elven virtues. While his boyish hero worship had passed, he still regarded Calin with undiminished respect.

Calin said, "Martin, of all here you are the only one to have known Tomas before this change. What can you say of the transformation you've seen?"

Martin spent time considering his reply. "I have only glimpsed these changes over the years, until this day. That they are great is obvious. But as to what they herald, I cannot begin to guess. He was a good enough boy; one not overly given to mischief, though with enough curiosity to find it. He had a tender side and did not hold back in his affections. His temper was moderate, though he could lose control when a friend was threatened or struck. In all, he was much like other boys, a dreamer."

"And now?"

Martin was troubled and took no pains to hide this. "He is something beyond my understanding."

Tathar said, "Your words are clear to us, Martin, and true, for he has also gone beyond our understanding."

Calin spoke softly. "Of men, you know our history more than any. You know of our hatred for the ages spent in bondage to the Valheru. You know we reject the Dark Path they trod. We fear the return of that power as much as we do this invasion of outworlders and their Black Robes. You have seen Tomas. You must know what we are forced to consider."

Martin nodded. "Yes. You weigh his life."

"Many of the younger elves follow him blindly," said Tathar. "They lack the maturity and wisdom to withstand the subtle influence of the Valheru magic with him. And while the dwarves do not follow blindly, still they follow, for they have none of our heritage of fear, and they put great faith in his leadership. He has proved the means of their survival for eight years now, saving many of them from death repeatedly.

"But while Tomas has been a boon to us in this struggle against the invaders, we may have to put aside all other considerations save one: will this half man, half Valheru attempt to become our master?" Tathar frowned. "If so, he must be destroyed."

Martin felt cold inside. Of all the boys he had known at Crydee, he had held special affection for three, Garret, Tomas, and Pug. He had mourned silently when Pug had been taken by the Tsurani, and had often wondered if it had been to his death or captivity. Now he mourned for Tomas, for whatever else might occur, Tomas would never again be as he once was.

Martin said to Calin. "Can nothing be done?"

Calin indicated Tathar should answer the question. The old Spellweaver looked around the circle, gaining silent agreement from the other Spellweavers. To Martin he said, "We do what we can to bring this to a good ending. But should the Valheru come forth in his might, we would not withstand, so we are fearful. We harbor no hatred for Tomas. But even as you pity a rabid wolf, you must kill it."

Martin looked grimly out at the lights of Elvandar, as darkness deepened. As long as he remembered, it had been a comforting sight. Now he felt only cold bitterness. "When shall you decide?"

Tathar said, "You understand our ways. We shall decide when we must decide."

Martin rose slowly to his feet. "My counsel to you then is this: until the change has clearly shown itself to be toward the Dark Path, do not mistakenly give too much weight to ancient fears. I have long been taught that those who now rule in Elvandar are of heartier nature and more independent mind than those who were first set free by the Valheru. Stay your hand until the last. Something good may come of this yet, or if not that, something that is not entirely ill."

Tathar nodded. "Your counsel is given well. It is well received."

Martin looked heavily burdened. "I will do what I can. Once I was able to influence Tomas, perhaps I may yet again. I will go meditate upon the matter, then seek him out and speak with him." None in the circle around the Queen's court spoke as he left. They knew his heart was as troubled as their own.

THE THROBBING had become worse, not quite a pain, but a discomfort that grew unnervingly more persistent. Tomas sat in the cool glade, near the quiet pool, struggling within himself. Since coming to live in Elvandar, he had found his dreams little more than vague shadowy images, with half-remembered phrases and names to grasp. They were less troublesome, less fearful, less a presence in his daily life, but the pressure within his head, the dull near-ache had grown. When he was in battle, he became lost in red rage, and there was no sense of the ache, but when the battle lust subsided, especially when he was slow to return to Elvandar, the throbbing returned.

Footsteps sounded lightly behind, and without turning, he said, "I wish to be alone."

Aglaranna said, "The pain, Tomas?"

A faint stirring of some strange feeling rose briefly within, and he cocked his head as if listening for something. Then he answered curtly, "Yes. I will return to our rooms soon. Leave now and prepare for me to join you later."

Aglaranna stepped back, her proud features showing pain at being addressed in such a tone. She turned quickly and left.

As she walked through the woods, her emotions churned within. Since surrendering to Tomas's desire, and her own, she had lost the ability to command him, or to resist his commands. He was now lord over her, and she felt shame. It was a joyless union, not the return of lost happiness she had hoped for. But there was a will-sapping compulsion, a need to be with him, to belong to him, that stripped away her defenses. Tomas was dynamic, powerful, and sometimes cruel. She corrected herself: not cruel, just so removed from any other being, no comparison could be made. He was not indifferent to her needs; he simply was unaware she had any. As she approached Elvandar, the soft fairy lights reflected in the shimmering tears that touched her cheeks.

Tomas was only partially aware of her departure. Under the dull ache within his head, a voice faintly called to him. He strained to listen, knowing its timbre, its color, knowing who called. . . .

"Tomas?"

Yes.

Ashen-Shugar looked across the desolation of the plains, dry cracked lands devoid of moisture save for bubbling alkali pots that spewed foul odors into the air. Aloud, to his unseen companion, he said, "It has been some time since we last spoke."

Tathar and the others seek to keep us apart. You are often forgotten.

The fetid winds blew from the north, cold but cloying. The smell of decay was everywhere, and in the residue of the mighty madness that had gripped the universe around, only faint stirrings of life reasserting itself were felt.

"No matter. We are together again."

What is this place?

"The Desolation of the Chaos Wars. Draken-Korin's monument, the lifeless tundra that was once great grasslands. Few living things abide here. Most creatures flee to the south, and more hospitable climes."

Who are you?

Ashen-Shugar laughed. "I am what you are becoming. We are one. So you have said many times."

I had forgotten.

Ashen-Shugar called, and Shuruga sped toward him over a grey landscape, while black clouds thundered overhead. The mighty dragon landed, and his master climbed upon his back. Casting a glance at the spot marked by ash, the only reminder of Draken-Korin's existence, the Valheru said, "Come, let us see what fate has wrought."

Shuruga leaped into the heavens, and above the desolation they flew. Ashen-Shugar was silent as he rode upon Shuruga's broad back, feeling the wind blowing across his face. They flew, and time passed them by, as they shared the death of one age and the birth of another. High in the blue sky they soared, free of the horror of the Chaos Wars.

It is worthy of sorrow.

"I think not. There is a lesson, though I cannot bring myself to know it. Yet I sense you do." Ashen-Shugar closed his eyes as the throbbing returned.

Yes, I remember.

"TOMAS?"

Tomas's eyes snapped open. He found Galain standing a short way off, near the edge of the clearing. "Shall I return later?"

Tomas rose slowly from where he had sat dreaming. His voice was rough and tired. "No, what is it?"

"Dolgan's dwarven band has reached the outer forest and waits for you near the winding brook. The dwarves struck an outworld enclave as they crossed the river." There was a merry smile upon the young elf's face. "They have finally captured prisoners."

A strange look of mixed delight and fury passed over Tomas's face. Galain felt strange emotions as he regarded the reaction of the warrior in white and gold to this news. As if listening to a distant call, Tomas spoke distractedly. "Go to the dwarven camp. I will join you there presently."

Galain withdrew, and Tomas listened. A distant voice grew louder.

"HAVE I ERRED?"

The hall echoed with the words, for now it was vacant, the servants having slipped away. Ashen-Shugar brooded upon his throne. He spoke to shadows. "Have I erred?"

Now you know doubt, answered the ever-present voice.

"This strange quietness within, what is it?"

It is death approaching.

Ashen-Shugar closed his eyes. "I thought as much. So few of my kind lived beyond battle. It was a rare thing. I am the last. Still, I would like to fly Shuruga once more."

He is gone. Dead, ages past.

"But I flew him this morning."

It was a dream. As is this.

"Am I then also mad?"

You are but a memory. This is but a dream.

"Then I will do what is planned. I accept the inevitable. Another will come to take my place."

So it has happened already, for I am the one who came, and I have taken up your sword and put upon your mantle; your cause is now mine. I stand against those who would plunder this world.

"Then am I content to die."

Opening his eyes, he took one last look at his hall now cloaked in ancient dust. Closing them for the last time, the Ruler of the Eagles' Reaches cast his final spell. His waning powers, still unmatched upon this world by any save the new gods, flowed from his tired body, infusing his armor. Smoky wisps wafted upward from where his body had rested, and soon only the golden armor, white tabard, shield, and sword of white and gold remained.

I am Ashen-Shugar; I am Tomas.

TOMAS'S EYES OPENED, and for a moment he was confused to find himself in the glade. A strange passion grew within as he felt a new strength flowing throughout his being. In his mind rang a clarion call: I am Ashen-Shugar, the Valheru. I will destroy all who seek to plunder my world.

With a terrible resolve he left the glade, to find the place the dwarves had brought his enemies.

"IT IS GOOD to see you again, friend Longbow," said Dolgan, puffing away on his pipe. They had not seen each other since a chance meeting several years before when the dwarves passed through the forest east of Crydee on their way to Elvandar.

Martin, Calin, and a few elves had come to see the dwarves' prisoners, who were still bound. They waited in a group in a corner of the clearing, glaring at their captors. Galain entered the clearing and said, "Tomas is coming soon."

Martin said, "How is it, Dolgan, after all these years, you managed to capture prisoners, and an entire enclave at that?"

Behind the eight bound warriors stood a fearful group of Tsurani slaves, unbound but huddled together, uncertain of their fate. Dolgan gave an offhanded wave. "Usually we're raiding across the river, and prisoners tend to slow things down during a withdrawal, being either unconscious or uncooperative. This time we had little choice in the matter, as we needed to cross the river Crydee. In past years we'd wait to sneak across in darkness, but this year they're as close as nettles in a thicket everywhere along the river.

"We found this band in a relatively isolated spot, with only these eight to guard the slaves. They were repairing an earthwork, one that I judge was overrun a short while ago during an elven sortie. We slipped around them, then a few of the lads climbed into the trees—though they liked it little. We dropped down upon the three outer guards, silencing them before they could shout the alert. The other five were napping, the lazy louts. We slipped into camp, and after a few well-placed strokes with our hammers, we bound them. These others"—he indicated the slaves—"were too timid to make a sound. When it was clear we had not alarmed the nearby enclaves, we thought to bring them along. Seemed a waste to leave them behind. Thought we might learn something useful." Dolgan tried to keep an impassive expression, but pride over his company's work shone through like a beacon in the night.

Martin smiled his approval and said to Calin, "I hope we may learn what is coming, if the feared offensive is really to be mounted and where. I've learned a few phrases of their tongue, but not enough to make any sense of what they might tell us. Only Father Tully and Charles, my Tsurani tracker, can speak to them fluently. Perhaps we should attempt to move them to Crydee?"

Calin said, "We have the means to learn their tongue, given time. I doubt they would lend much cooperation in their transport. Most likely they would try to raise the alarm every step of the way."

Martin conceded the point. Then a disturbance caused him to turn.

Tomas came striding into the clearing. Dolgan began to greet him, but something in the young warrior's manner and expression silenced him. There was madness in Tomas's eyes, something the dwarf had glimpsed before as a glimmer, but which now shone forth brightly.

Tomas regarded the bound prisoners, then pulled his sword slowly and pointed at them. The words he spoke were alien to both Martin and the dwarves, but the elves were rocked by what they heard. Several of the older elves dropped to their knees in supplication, and the younger ones drew away in reflexive fear. Only Calin stood his ground, though he appeared shaken. Then slowly the Elf Prince turned to Martin, his face drained of color. In terrified tones he said, "At last the Valheru is truly among us."

Ignoring all others in the clearing, Tomas walked up to the first Tsurani prisoner. The bound soldier looked up with a mixture of fear and defiance. Suddenly the golden sword was raised high and arced down, severing the man's head from his shoulders. Blood splattered the white tabard, then flowed off, leaving it spotless. A low moan of fear came from the huddled slaves, and the remaining soldiers' eyes were wide in terror. Slowly Tomas turned to face the next prisoner, and again his sword took a life.

Martin freed himself from shocked paralysis, forcing his eyes away from the butchery. He felt terrible dread, but it appeared as nothing to what the elves revealed in their abasement before Tomas. Calin's face showed a struggle within as he tried to overcome a nearly instinctive obedience to the words spoken in the ancient language of the Valheru, masters of all, ages past. The younger elves, less studied in the old wisdom, simply had no understanding of the overwhelming need to obey this man in white and gold. The language of the Valheru was still the language of power.

Tomas turned away from his slaughter, and Martin felt struck by the strength of his gaze. Gone was any vestige of the boy from Crydee. Now an alien presence suffused his being. Tomas's arm drew back, and Martin tensed to dodge the blow. Any human was a potential victim, and even the dwarves drew back at the awesome menace Tomas projected. Then a faint spark of recognition entered Tomas's eyes, and he said, in a distant voice, "Martin, by the love I once bore you, be gone or your life is forfeit."

Mustering courage against the most consuming fear he had ever felt, Martin shouted, "I'll not stand and watch you slaughter helpless men!"

Again a distant voice answered, steeped in ancient majesty and lost grandeur regained. "These come into my world, Martin. None may seek that which is my domain, my preserve, mine alone! Shall you, too, come into my world, Martin?" With inhuman speed Tomas wheeled, and two Tsurani died.

Martin charged, crossing the gap between them in a bound, and knocked Tomas away from the prisoners. They went down in a heap, and Martin grabbed at the wrist that held the golden sword.

A strong man capable of carrying a freshly killed buck for miles, Martin was no match for Tomas. As easily as picking up a bothersome infant, Tomas pushed Martin aside and came lightly to his feet. Martin sprang at Tomas again, but this time Tomas stood ready. He simply seized Martin by the tunic and said, "None may interfere with my will." He tossed Martin across the clearing as if he weighed less than a tenth his weight. Martin's arms flailed the air as he arced high over the ground, striving to control his fall. He landed hard, and all around could hear the breath explode from his lungs as he struck.

Dolgan rushed to his side, for the elves were still held in thrall by what they had witnessed. The dwarven chief poured water from a skin at his side upon Martin's face and shook him awake. The strangled cries of terror from the Tsurani slaves watching soldiers being butchered greeted Martin as he regained his wits.

Martin struggled to focus his vision, the scene before him swimming and shifting. When he could see, he drew a hissing breath in horror.

Tomas struck down the last Tsurani soldier and began to advance upon the cringing slaves. They appeared unable to move, watching with wide eyes the bringer of their destruction, looking like nothing so much to Martin as a band of deer startled by a sudden light in the night.

A ragged cry came from Martin's lips as Tomas killed the first Tsurani slave, a pitiful-looking willow of a man. Longbow struggled to rise, senses reeling, and Dolgan helped him to his feet.

Tomas raised his sword and another died. Again the golden blade was raised, and he looked into the face of his victim. Eyes round with fear, a young boy, no more than twelve years old, stood waiting for the blow that would end his life.

Suddenly time expanded for Tomas, the moment frozen in his mind. He studied the shock of dark hair and the large brown eyes of the boy. The child crouched awaiting the death he saw over him, his head shaking no, as his lips formed a single phrase over and over.

In the faint light of the clearing, Tomas saw an old ghost, the specter of a friend long forgotten. A remembered bond, from his earliest memories as a child, reassociated itself with his consciousness. Images blurred, past and present confused, and he said, "Pug?"

Within his mind, pain exploded, and another will sought to overwhelm him.

Pug! it shrieked.

Kill him! came a raging answer, and within him two wills battled.

No! screamed the other.

To everyone in the glade, Tomas stood frozen, shaking with some inner struggle, his sword still held high, waiting for release.

These are the enemy! Slay them.

He is a boy! Only a boy!

He is the enemy!

A boy!

Tomas's face became a mask of pain; his teeth clenched, and every muscle drew taut, stretching skin tightly over skull. His eyes grew round, and perspiration began to flow from under his helm, down his brows and cheeks.

Martin stumbled to his feet. He moved slowly, every gesture bringing pain from the battering he had taken.

Tomas's hand slowly moved downward, each inch a shaking, trembling passage as he warred within. The boy was transfixed, unable to move, his eyes following the movement of the blade.

I am Ashen-Shugar! I am Valheru! sang a voice within, in a torrent of anger, battle madness, and bloodlust.

Against this sea of rage stood a single rock, a calm, small voice within that said, simply, *I am Tomas.*

Again and again the sea of hate crashed over the rock of calm, each time engulfing it, then sliding back, to come again. But each time the tide diminished and the rock stood clear, rising above the mad surf. A shattering of something, the thundering of ages lost and passing, rocked Tomas's mind. He reeled, then swam within an alien landscape, seeking a pinpoint of light he knew was his way to freedom. Tides swept him along, and he battled, struggling to keep his head above the strangling black sea. A shrieking, evil wind blew overhead, and to his ears it sang a song of woeful meter. He struck out, and again he saw a pinpoint of light. Again the tide engulfed him, forcing him away from his goal, but this time it was weaker. Once more he struggled toward the light. Then came a surge, a last, terrifying assault culminating in a total attack upon him. I am *Ashen-Shugar!* There came a breaking of the will, something snapping like the dead branch of a tree under the weight of newly fallen snow, like the sound of old winter ice breaking at spring's touch, as if the last assault took too great a toll.

The black sea lost its fury and subsided, and he was again standing upon firm ground, a single rock. *I am Tomas.* In the distance the pinpoint of light began to expand before his eyes, racing forward to engulf him.

I am Tomas.

"Tomas!"

He blinked and saw he was again in the glade. Before him crouched the boy, waiting to die. He turned his head and saw Martin, sighting along a cloth-yard arrow, drawn hard against his cheek. The Huntmaster of Crydee said, "Put down your sword, or by the gods, I'll kill you where you stand."

Tomas's gaze wandered about the glade, and he saw the dwarves with weapons drawn, as had some of the older elves. Calin, still shaking, had his sword out and was slowly advancing upon him.

Martin watched Tomas closely, not fearing him, but respectful of his awesome strength and speed. He waited and saw the flicker of madness still in Tomas's eyes, then, as if a veil were lifted, saw them clear. Abruptly the golden sword fell from his hand, and the pale, nearly colorless eyes filled with tears. Tomas dropped to his knees, and a moan of terrible anguish was torn from his lips, and Tomas cried out, "Oh, Martin, what have I become?"

Martin lowered his bow, watching as Tomas gathered his arms about himself. Into the glade came Tathar and the other Spellweavers. They approached Tomas and then surveyed the others in the glade. So terrible were Tomas's sobs of anguish, so filled with sorrow and remorse, that many of the elves discovered they also wept.

Tathar said to Martin Longbow, "We felt the fabric of our spells torn asunder a short while ago, and came at once. We feared the Valheru had come, rightly it seems."

Martin said, "Now?"

"The other side of the balance. That the Valheru is at last displaced by the boy there can be no doubt, but the boy now must feel the weight of ages of slaughter, and the guilt over joy felt when taking other lives. The burdens felt by mortals are again his, and we shall now see if he can withstand them. This agony may prove his end."

Martin left the ancient elf and crossed to Tomas. In the dim light he was the first to perceive the change. Gone were the alien cast to his features, the gleaming eyes, the haughty brow. Again he was Tomas, a man, though there were still legacies of his experience that would forever proclaim him something more than a man: the elven ears, the pale eyes. Gone was the Lord of Power, the Old One, the Valheru. Where before a Dragon Lord had stood now crouched a troubled, sick man in torment over what he had done.

Tomas raised his head as Martin touched him upon the shoulder. Red-rimmed eyes, nearly mad from grief, regarded Martin for a brief moment, then closed as if seeking oblivion to all around. For some time the elves and dwarves watched, and the Tsurani slaves were silent, aware that some miracle had occurred, not understanding, but suddenly sure they were spared. For some time they watched, as Martin Longbow cradled the sobbing man in white and gold, who cried in anguish so terrible to hear.

▾▾

AGLARANNA SAT upon her sleeping pallet, brushing her long red-gold hair. As before, she waited for Tomas, half hoping, half fearing he would come.

A shout from outside caused her to rise. She gathered her robes around her and left her quarters. Standing upon a platform, she watched as a group of elves and dwarves came toward Elvandar's heart. With them came Martin Longbow and some humans, clearly outworlders from their dress.

Her hands went to her mouth as she gasped. In the center of the group walked Tomas, at his side a young boy with eyes wide at the splendor of Elvandar.

Aglaranna was unable to move, fearful that what she witnessed was the product of delusion born of hope. Time sped past as she waited, then Tomas stood before her. Leaving the boy, he stepped forward. Martin took the boy by the hand and led him away, the others following, giving the Elf Queen and Tomas the solitude they needed.

Tomas reached out slowly and touched her face, and he drank in the sight of her, as if seeing her as he had first at Crydee. Then, without words, he slowly, gently enfolded her in his arms. He held her in silence, letting her feel the warmth of the love that filled him at sight of her.

After a time he whispered in her ear, "For each moment of sorrow I have visited upon you, O my lady, I pray the gods grant me a year to gift you with joy. I am again your adoring subject."

Too filled with happiness to speak, the Elf Queen simply clung to him, her sorrow only a dim memory.

28

▾▾

EMISSARY

THE TROOPS STOOD QUIETLY.

Long columns of men awaited their turn at passing through the rift into Midkemia. Officers walked by, their presence ensuring discipline in the lines. Laurie, in the mask and robe of a Red Priest, was impressed at the level of control these officers had over their men. He judged the Tsurani code of honor, where orders were followed without question, a very alien thing.

He and Kasumi moved quickly down the line, heading for the first detachment behind the one now entering the rift. Laurie bent his knees and stooped, to detract from his noticeable height. As they had hoped, more soldiers than not looked away as the bogus Red Priest passed.

When they reached the head of the column, Kasumi fell in. His younger brother, who had been promoted to Strike Leader for this offensive, seemed to pay no attention to his commander's late arrival, or to the priest of Turakamu who arrived with him.

After a seemingly interminable delay, the command came, and they stepped forward into the shimmering glow of "nothingness" that marked the rift between the two worlds. There was a brief flash of lights, a momentary dizziness, and they found themselves walking forward into a light Midkemian rain. Sheets of wetness, little more than a heavy mist, fell around them. The Tsurani soldiers, hot-weather-bred, wrapped cloaks about themselves.

A staging officer briefly conferred with Kasumi, and the troops were ordered to move off to the northeast a specified distance and erect a camp. Kasumi and Hokanu were then to report to the Warlord's tent for briefings. The Warlord himself was back in Kentosani, the Holy City, preparing for the Imperial Games, but his subcommander was to instruct them in their duties and areas of responsibility until his return.

They quickly moved up toward the front and set up camp. Once the commander's tent was up, Laurie and the Shinzawai brothers ducked inside. While bundles containing Midkemian clothing and weapons were unpacked, Kasumi said, "As soon as we return from our meeting with the subcommander, we will eat. Tonight we will lead a patrol of our area and try to slip through the lines." Kasumi looked at his brother. "After we have gone, brother, it will be your responsibility to hide our departure for as long as possible. Once there has been fighting reported, you may claim we have been lost to the enemy."

Hokanu agreed. "We had best report now."

Kasumi looked at Laurie. "Stay inside. We want no risk. You are the tallest damned priest I have ever seen."

Laurie nodded. He sat upon some cushions and waited.

THE PATROL MOVED silently through the trees. The rain had stopped, but the weather had turned colder, and Laurie suppressed a shiver. Years in the hot climes of Kelewan had driven away his ability to ignore the chill. He wondered about the new troops from Tsuranuanni and how they would react when the first snowfalls came. Most likely with studied indifference, regardless of what they felt inside. A Tsurani soldier would never let himself appear upset by something as trivial as solid water falling from the sky.

They elected the North Pass, for it led to the largest front, and they were less likely to be noticed passing through the lines. They reached the head of the pass, and a station guard passed them along. Once outside the valley they struck slightly more eastward than their patrol called for.

Beyond the rolling hills and light woods was the road from LaMut to Zūn. Once the two travelers had left their patrol and reached the road, they would head for Zūn, buy horses, and ride south. With luck they would reach Krondor in two weeks. There they would change mounts and head for Salador, where they would find passage on a ship for Rillanon.

The only obstacle between them and the road was a large portion of the Kingdom's Army. If they were discovered by a Kingdom patrol, they would try to pass themselves off as travelers who had been captured by the Tsurani and escaped. There could be no question of Laurie being Tsurani, and Kasumi's command of the King's Tongue was so complete that he could easily pass for a Kingdom citizen from the Vale of Dreams; several languages were spoken in that border area with Great Kesh, so Kasumi's slight accent would be reasonable.

The patrol moved at a dogtrot that ate up miles. Laurie ran beside Kasumi, marveling at the soldiers' stamina. They might not be showing fatigue, but he was feeling it. Hokanu signaled for the patrol to stop at the head of a large, flat area near the woods. "Here we will start our swing back to our patrol area. We should not see any Tsurani soldiers from here. Let us hope, for your sake, we don't meet with Kingdom troops either."

He gave a signal, and they moved out. Laurie and Kasumi were handed backpacks and clothing. They quickly changed, then followed the route taken by the patrol. They would follow for a short distance, using the patrol for cover should any Kingdom troops be nearby.

They moved into a small vale and found the patrol held up by something ahead. The last man in line motioned them for quiet. They moved to the head of the line, and Laurie looked around for a quick exit route should there be any trouble. Hokanu said softly, "I thought I heard something, but there has been no sound for several minutes."

Kasumi nodded. "Then move forward. We will wait until you have crossed that open area ahead, then follow to the woods." He indicated a stand of trees, on the other side of the clearing.

When the patrol had reached the center of the open area, the clouds parted and shafts of moonlight lit up the area. "Damn!" Kasumi swore under his breath. "They might as well light torches now."

Suddenly the trees erupted with motion and sound. The ground trembled as riders came charging forward, out from the trees that hid them. Each wore heavy chain mail and a full helm. Long lances were leveled at the surprised Tsurani soldiers.

The Tsurani had barely enough time to ready a rude line for defense before the riders were upon them. Cries of horses and men filled the air, and the Tsurani fell before the charge. The riders rode over the Tsurani and re-formed at the end of the vale where the two fugitives hid. They wheeled about and charged again. The Tsurani survivors of the last charge, less than half the men, moved quickly up the west side of the vale, where the trees and incline of the hillside would counter the horsemen's ability to charge.

Laurie touched Kasumi's arm and motioned to the right. It was evident the Tsurani officer was barely holding himself in check from joining his men. Suddenly Kasumi was off, hugging the edge of the trees as he ran low. Laurie followed and spotted what appeared to be a rough path heading eastward. He grabbed Kasumi's sleeve and pointed. They turned their backs to the fighting and moved off.

THE NEXT DAY found two travelers moving down the road to Zūn. Both wore woolen shirts, trousers, and cloaks. Closer examination by a trained eye would have revealed that the material was not really wool, but something like it. Their belts and boots were made from needra hide dyed to resemble leather. The fashion was Midkemian, as were the swords they wore on their belts.

One was obviously a minstrel, for he wore a lute slung over his backpack. The other looked to be a freebooter mercenary. Any casual observer would have been unlikely to guess their origins, or the riches carried in those backpacks, for each had a small fortune in gems tucked away in the bottom of his pack.

A northbound troop of light cavalry passed them on the road, and Laurie said, "Things have changed since I was last here. Those men in the forest were Royal Krondorian Lancers, and those who just passed wore the colors of Quester's View. All the forces of the Armies of the West must be marshaling here. Something seems to be in the air. Perhaps they have somehow gleaned your Warlord's plan for a major offensive?"

"I don't know. Whatever is happening does not seem to indicate that things are as stable as we have been led to believe back home. Alliances are very uneasy since the death of the Lord of the Minwanabi and the emergence of new forces in the Great Game. The Warlord may be more desperate than my father judged. And the concentration of troops here makes me think the Warlord's victory may not be easily won." Kasumi was quiet for a moment as they walked along the road. "I hope that Hokanu was among those who reached the trees." It was the first time he had mentioned his brother, and Laurie could think of nothing to say.

TWO DAYS LATER, Laurie, a minstrel late of Tyr-Sog, and Kenneth, a mercenary from the Vale of Dreams, sat in the Green Cat Inn in the city of Zūn. Both ate with hearty appetite, for they had lived on soldiers' rations—cakes of grain and dried fruit—for two days.

Laurie had spent over an hour negotiating with a less than reputable gem broker for several smaller stones' value. He had settled for one third their actual worth, stating, "If he thinks they are stolen, he will not be too quick to ask questions."

Kasumi asked, "Why didn't you sell him all the stones?"

"Your father has given us enough to retire on for the rest of our days. I doubt if all the brokers in Zūn could raise the gold to pay for them. We will sell a few as we travel; besides, they weigh less than gold."

Finishing their meal, the two men paid and left. Kasumi could only just refrain from staring at all the metal he could see everywhere, a lifetime's riches on Kelewan. Just the cost of the meal in silver could support a Tsurani family for a year.

They hurried along one of the city's business streets, heading to the south gate. Near there, they had been informed, a reputable trader in horses would sell them mounts and tack for a fair price. They found the man, a thin, hawk-beaked fellow by the name of Brin. Laurie spent the better part of an hour haggling with the horse trader for two of his better mounts. They left him expressing concern over their ability to sleep nights after cheating an honest businessman out of the money he needed to feed his starving children.

As they rode through the gate that put them on the road to Ylith, Kasumi said, "Much of this land of yours seems odd, but as you haggled with that merchant, I was reminded of home. Our traders are much more polite and would never think of raising their voices in such a manner, but it is still the same thing. They all have starving children."

Laurie laughed and spurred his mount forward. Soon they were out of sight of the city.

SOUTH OF QUESTER'S View they passed more troops on the road, this time Kingdom regulars and auxiliaries trudging along on foot while their officers rode. Laurie and Kasumi had stopped to untack and graze their horses while the column moved past. The fighter watched the soldiers passing with an expert's eye. Red-uniformed soldiers marched in tight formation, while the more ragged auxiliaries still managed a look of organization. The baggage train moved in good order, experienced cart drivers keeping the animals in proper intervals. When they passed, Kasumi said, "Those soldiers are better than any I've seen so far on your world, Laurie. Those in red look like professionals. They march well. And those others seem experienced, despite their motley look."

Laurie nodded. "I recognize the standard. That's the garrison of Shamata, in the Vale of Dreams. They have had their fair share of fighting Kesh's dog-soldiers and are a veteran outfit. Those others are auxiliaries, Valemen mercenaries; a less tender band of lads you'd be hard pressed to find." Laurie started to resaddle his horse. "They're as seasoned a force of men as your countrymen will have faced, in truth."

When the horses were tacked up, Laurie and Kasumi remounted and rode on. Soon they could see the Bitter Sea, as the road rounded the hills of Quester's View.

Laurie pulled up his horse and stared out to sea. "What is it?" asked Kasumi.

Laurie shaded his eyes. "Ships! A whole fleet of them sailing north." He sat for a moment watching, and at last Kasumi could see dots of white upon the blue of the sea.

"Where are they bound?" Kasumi asked.

"Ylith is the only major point north of here. They must be carrying supplies for the war."

They resumed their ride. A sense of urgency descended upon them both, as everything they saw pointed to an intensification of the war, and the longer they tarried, the less likely the success of their mission.

FOURTEEN DAYS LATER, they reached the northern gate of Krondor. As they rode through, they were regarded suspiciously by several guards dressed in black and gold. Once beyond earshot of the gate guards, Laurie said, "Those are not the Prince's tabards. The banner of Bas-Tyra flies over Krondor."

They rode slowly for a minute, then Kasumi said, "What does it mean?"

"I don't know. But I think I know a place we can find out." They rode through a series of streets bounded on each side by warehouses and commercial enterprises. Sounds from the docks, several streets away, could be heard. Otherwise the district was quiet. "Strange," remarked Laurie, as they rode on. "This part of the city is usually busiest at this time of day."

Kasumi looked around, not sure of what he expected to see. The Midkemian cities, compared to those of the Empire, seemed small and dirty. Still, there was something strange about the lack of activity here. Both Zūn and Ylith had been teeming with soldiers, traders, and citizens at midday, even though they were smaller cities than Krondor. As they rode, a feeling of disquiet visited Kasumi.

They entered a section of the city even more run-down than the warehouse district. Here the streets were narrow, with four- and five-story buildings hugging closely to either side. Dark shadows abounded, even at noon. Those in the street, a few traders and women going to market, moved quietly and with speed. Everywhere the riders looked, they could see expressions of caution and distrust.

Laurie led Kasumi to a gate, behind which the upper part of a three-story building could be seen. Laurie leaned over in the saddle and pulled on a bell rope. When there was no answer after a few minutes, he pulled again.

A moment later a peek window in the door slid aside, two eyes could be seen, and a voice said, "What's your business?"

Laurie's tone was sharp. "Lucas, is that you? What is happening when travelers can't gain entrance?"

The eyes widened, and the peek window slid shut. The gate swung open with a creaking protest, and a man stepped out to push it wide. "Laurie, you scoundrel!" he said as he admitted the riders. "It's been five—no, six years."

They rode in, and Laurie was shocked by the condition of the inn. Off to one side was a dilapidated stable. Opposite the gate a sign hung over the main entrance, depicting in faded hues a parrot of many colors with wings spread. They could hear the gate close behind them.

The man called Lucas, tall and gaunt, with grey hair, said, "You'll have to stable the animals yourself. I am alone here and must return to the common room before my guests steal everything there. I'll see you and your friend inside and we can talk." He turned away, and the two riders were left to tend to their mounts.

As they removed the saddles from the horses, Laurie said, "There is a lot happening here that I don't understand. The Rainbow Parrot was never a showplace, but it was always one of the better taverns in the Poor Quarter." He quietly rubbed down his animal. "If there is any place we can find out what is truly going on in Krondor, this is it. And one thing I have learned over my years of traveling through the Kingdom is when gate guards are watching travelers closely, it is time to stay somewhere they are not likely to visit. You can get your throat cut quickly in the Poor Quarter, but you'll rarely see a guardsman about. And if they do come, the man who was trying to cut your throat will more than likely hide you until they are gone."

"And then try to cut your throat."

Laurie laughed. "You learn quickly."

When the horses were cared for, the two travelers carried their saddles and packs into the inn. Inside they were greeted by the sight of a dimly lit common room, with a long bar along the rear wall. On the left stood a large fireplace, and on the right a stairway leading upward. There were a number of empty tables in the room, and two with customers. The newcomers were given a quick look by the guests, who then returned to their drinks and quiet conversation.

Laurie and Kasumi crossed over to the bar, where Lucas stood cleaning some wine cups with a less than clean rag. They dropped their packs at their feet, and Laurie said, "Any Keshian wine?"

Lucas said, "A little, but it is expensive. There has been little trade with Kesh since the trouble started."

Laurie looked at Lucas, as if weighing the cost. "Then two ales."

Lucas drew two large tankards of ale and said, "It is good to see you, Laurie. I've missed that tender voice of yours."

Laurie said, "That's not what you said the last time. As I recall, you likened it to the screeching of a cat looking for a fight."

They chuckled over that, and Lucas said, "With things so bleak, I have mellowed toward those who were true friends. There are few of us left." He threw a pointed look at Kasumi.

Laurie said, "This is Kenneth, a true friend of mine, Lucas."

Lucas continued to regard the Tsurani for a moment, then smiled. "Laurie's recommendation counts heavily. Welcome." He extended his hand, and Kasumi shook with him, Kingdom fashion.

"I am pleased at your welcome."

Lucas frowned at the sound of his accent. "An outlander?"

"From the Vale of Dreams," said Kasumi.

"The Kingdom side," added Laurie.

Lucas studied the fighter. After a moment he shrugged. "Whatever. It matters not a whit to me, but be wary. These are suspicious times, and there is little love wasted on strangers. Take care who you speak with, for there are rumors that Kesh's dog-soldiers are ready to move north again, and you are not far from being Keshian."

Before Kasumi could say anything, Laurie said, "Is there to be trouble with Kesh, then?"

Lucas shook his head. "I can't say. The market has more rumors than a beggar has boils." His voice lowered. "Two weeks back, traders arrived with word the Empire of Great Kesh was again fighting far to the south, seeking to subdue their former vassals in the Confederacy once more. So things should stay quiet for a while. They learned the folly of a two-front war over a hundred years back when they managed to lose all of Bosania and still not beat the Confederacy."

Laurie said, "We have been traveling for a very long time and have heard little news. Why is Bas-Tyra's banner over Krondor?"

Lucas quickly looked around the room. The drinkers seemed oblivious to the conversation at the bar, but Lucas motioned for silence. "I will show you a room," he said loudly. Both Laurie and Kasumi were a little surprised, but picked up their belongings and followed Lucas upstairs without comment.

He led them to a small room, with two beds and a nightstand. When the door was closed behind, he said, "I trust you, Laurie, so I'll ask no questions, but know things have changed greatly since last you were here. Even in the Poor Quarter there are ears that belong to the Viceroy. Bas-Tyra has the city under his boot-heel, and it is a foolish man who speaks without seeing who is listening."

Lucas sat down on one of the beds, and Laurie and Kasumi sat across from him. Lucas continued, "When Bas-Tyra came to Krondor he carried the King's warrant naming him ruler of Krondor, with full viceregal powers. Prince Erland and his family were locked up in the palace, though Guy calls it 'protective custody.' Then Guy came down hard on the city. Press-gangs roamed the waterfront, and many a man now sails in Lord Jessup's fleet without his wife or children knowing what became of their old pa. Since then, any who speak against the Viceroy or King simply vanish, 'cause Guy's got a secret police listening at every door in the city.

"Taxes increase each year to pay for the war, and trade's drying up, except for those selling to the army for the war, and they're getting paid in worthless vouchers. These are hard times, and the Viceroy's doing nothing to make them easier. Food is scarce, and there is little money to pay for what there is. Many farmers have lost their farms for taxes, and now the land lies fallow for want of someone to till it. So the farmers wander into the city, swelling the population. Most of the young men have been drafted into the army or the fleet. Be careful you aren't picked up by the guards, for whatever reason, and be wary of the press-gangs.

"Still," Lucas said with a chuckle, "things got lively around here for a time when Prince Arutha came to Krondor."

"Borric's son? He's in the city?" asked Laurie.

A twinkle of pleasure showed in Lucas's eyes. "No longer." He chuckled again. "Last winter, as bold as bright brass, the Prince comes sailing into Krondor. He must have taken the Straits of Darkness during the winter, or he never would have reached the city when he did." He quickly told them of Arutha and Anita's escape.

Laurie said, "Did they return to Crydee?"

Lucas nodded. "A trader in from Carse a week ago was full of news of this and that. One thing he heard was some Tsurani were acting up around Jonril, and the Prince of Crydee was ready to come down to help if needed. So Arutha must have made it back."

Laurie said, "Guy must have been fit to burst at the news."

Lucas's smile vanished. "Well, he was, Laurie. He'd tossed Prince Erland into the dungeon to get his permission to marry Anita. He kept him there after he heard of Anita's escape. I guess he thought the girl would come back rather than let her father stay in a damp cell, but he was wrong. Now the word's on the street the Prince is near death from the chill. That's why the city's in such a state. No one knows what will happen if Erland dies. He's well liked, and there might be trouble." Laurie looked at Lucas with an unspoken question. "Nothing like rebellion," Lucas answered. "We're too dispirited. But a few of Guy's guards may turn up missing at muster, and there'll be many inconveniences getting supplies to the garrison and palace and the like. And I wouldn't wish to be the Viceroy's taxman when he's next sent into the Poor Quarter."

Laurie considered what he had heard. "We are headed east. What about conditions on the road?"

Lucas slowly shook his head. "There is still some traveling done. Once past Darkmoor, you should have scant trouble, I'm thinking. We hear that things in the East are more as they used to be. Still, I'd move carefully."

Kasumi asked, "Will we be troubled leaving the city?"

"The north gate is still the best way. It is undermanned, as usual. For a small fee, the Mockers can see you safely through."

"Mockers?" asked the fighter.

Lucas raised his brows in surprise. "You are from a long way off. The Guild of Thieves. They remain in control of the Poor Quarter, and the Upright Man still has influence with the merchants and traders, especially along the docks. The warehouse district is their second home, after the Poor Quarter. They can get you out, if you have any trouble at the gate."

Laurie said, "We will keep that in mind, Lucas. What of your family? I have not seen them around."

Lucas seemed to shrink into himself, "My wife is dead, Laurie, of the fever, a year ago. My sons are both in the army. I have heard little of them in a year. Last time I received a message, they were in the north with Lords Borric and Brucal.

"The city is full of veterans of the war. You can see them everywhere. They are the ones with missing limbs, or blind eyes. But they always wear their old tabards. And a pathetic sight they are, too." He got a faraway look in his eyes. "I just hope my boys don't end up like that."

Laurie and Kasumi said nothing. Lucas came out of his reverie. "I must return downstairs. Supper will be ready in four hours, though nothing like I used to serve." As the innkeeper turned to go, he said, "If you need to contact the Mockers, let me know."

After he had left, Kasumi said, "It is a hard thing to know your country, Laurie, and still look upon the war as glorious."

Laurie nodded.

THE WAREHOUSE was dark and musty. Except for Laurie and Kasumi and two fresh horses, it was empty. They had stayed at the Rainbow Parrot the night before and had purchased new mounts at great expense, then had tried to leave the city. When they had reached the city gates, they had been stopped by a detachment of Bas-Tyra's guards. When it was obvious that the guards were not likely to let them leave without trouble, Laurie and Kasumi had broken away from them, and a mad dash through the city had followed. They had lost their pursuers in the Poor Quarter and had returned to the Rainbow Parrot. Lucas had sent word to the Upright Man, and now they waited for a thief to guide them out of the city.

A whistle broke the silence, and Laurie and Kasumi had their swords in hand in an instant. A high-pitched chuckle greeted them, and a small figure dropped from above. In the dark it was difficult to see where the figure sprang from, but Laurie suspected their visitor had been hiding in the rafters for some time.

The figure stepped forward, and in the dim light they could see it was a boy, no older than thirteen. "There's a party at Mother's," the newcomer said.

"And a good time will be had by all," Laurie answered.

"You're the travelers, then."

"You're the guide?" asked Kasumi, taking no effort to hide the surprise in his voice.

The boy's voice was filled with bravado. "Aye. Jimmy the Hand is your guide. And a better one in all Krondor you'll not find."

Laurie said, "What's to be done?"

"First there's the matter of payment. It's a hundred sovereigns each."

Without comment Laurie dug out several small gems and handed them over. "Will these do?"

The boy turned to the warehouse door and cracked it slightly, admitting a shaft of moonlight. He inspected the gems with an expert's eye and returned to stand before the two fugitives. "These'll do. For another hundred, you can have this." He offered a piece of parchment.

Laurie took it, but couldn't make out what was written on it in the dim light. "What is it?"

Jimmy chuckled. "A royal warrant, allowing the bearer to travel the King's Highway."

"Is it genuine?" asked the minstrel.

"My word. I nicked it myself from a trader from Ludland this morning. It's valid for another month."

"Done," said Laurie, and the minstrel gave the boy another gem.

When the gems were safely in the thief's pouch, he said, "Soon we'll be hearing a brouhaha at the gate. A few of the boys will put on some mummery for the guards. When everything's up in the wind, we'll slip through."

He returned to the door and looked out without further comment. While they waited, Kasumi whispered, "Can he be trusted?"

"No, but we have no choice. If the Upright Man could show a larger profit by turning us in, he might. But the Mockers have little love for the guards, and now less than usual, according to Lucas, so it is unlikely. Still, keep your wits about you."

Time stretched on interminably, then suddenly shouts could be heard. Jimmy signaled with a sharp whistle, which was answered by another from outside. "It's time," he said, and was out the door.

Laurie and Kasumi led their horses out after him. "Follow closely and quickly," their small guide said as he set off.

They rounded the corner of a building and could see the north gate. A group of men were involved in a brawl, many appearing to be sailors from the docks. The guards were doing their best to restore order, but each time one pushed a combatant away from the fray, another would appear from the shadows around the gate and join in. In a few minutes every guard was involved in breaking up the fight, and Jimmy said, "Now!"

He broke from the building, with the travelers close behind, and dashed to the wall next to the gatehouse. They edged their way along in the shadows, the horses' clatter covered by the noise of the brawl. When they were near the gate, a single guard could be seen, on the other side, whom they hadn't been able to see from their previous location.

Laurie gripped Jimmy's shoulder. "We'll have to take him quickly."

Jimmy said, "No. If weapons are drawn, the guards will leave that little bit of fun like a burning whorehouse. Leave him to me."

Jimmy sprang forward and ran to the guard. As the guard brought his spear forward across his chest and shouted, "Halt!" Jimmy kicked him hard in the leg, above the boot. The man let out a howl, then looked at his small assailant with fury on his face. "Why you little—"

Jimmy stuck out his tongue and started to run toward the docks. The guard set out in hot pursuit, and the two travelers slipped through the gate. Once outside the city, they mounted quickly and rode off. As they rode away from Krondor, they could hear the sounds of the brawl.

THEY RESTED a day at Darkmoor, in an inn in the town below the castle. They had been two days in the hills and needed to rest their mounts before journeying over the grasslands to Malac's Cross. The town was quiet, and little of interest occurred until the inn door opened and a man in dirty brown robes entered. The man was old and bent with years, and thin to the point of gauntness. The innkeeper looked up from cleaning ale cups and said, "What do you wish?"

Softly the old man said, "Please, sir, a little food."

"Can you pay?"

"I can fashion spells to rid your inn of vermin, should you be plagued by rats, sir. Perhaps—"

"Begone! I have no food for beggars or magicians. Get out! And if I find my milk clabbered, I'll set my dogs upon you!"

The magician looked around. Laurie reached across the table and touched Kasumi upon the arm. His Tsurani heritage was betraying him, as he was showing open astonishment at what he saw. Before him stood a magician, being treated as shabbily as his clothes. Laurie's touch caused him to regain his composure. The magician slowly turned and left the inn.

Laurie sprang up and crossed to the innkeeper. Slapping some coins on the table, he said, "Quick. A joint of cold meat, a loaf of bread, and a skin of wine."

The innkeeper looked surprised, but the coins on the bar convinced him to do as ordered. When the items ordered were upon the bar, Laurie scooped them up. He paused a moment to grab a wedge of cheese off a platter and rushed out the door. Kasumi was as amazed as the innkeeper appeared to be.

Laurie looked down the road and saw the old man, his posture erect as he moved along with a staff in one hand, using it as a walking stick. He ran after the man and, when he had overtaken him, said, "Excuse me, but I was in the tavern a moment ago, and . . ." He held out the food and wineskin.

He saw pride diminish in the old man's eyes. "Why are you doing this, minstrel?"

Laurie said, "I have a friend who is a magician, a special friend. He did me a great kindness once, and I . . . it's something of a repayment."

The magician accepted this explanation and took the food. While he struggled with the burden, Laurie slipped a pair of gems into the magician's empty belt pouch. There would be enough there to insure the magician never had to go hungry again if he lived modestly. "What is this magician's name; perhaps I know him?"

"Milamber."

The old man shook his head. "I have not heard of him. Where does he abide?"

Laurie looked to the west, where the sun set behind the hills. With strong emotions in his voice, he said, "Far from here, my friend. Very far from here."

THE SHIP beat against the waves, while the crew reefed the sails. Laurie and Kasumi stood on deck watching the spires and towers of Rillanon as the ship put into harbor. "A fabulous city," said the former Tsurani officer. "Not as large as the cities of home, but so different. All those tiny fingers of stone and the colors of the banners make it look like a city of legend."

"Strange," said Laurie, "Pug and I felt the same when we first saw Jamar. I suppose it is simply that they're so different from each other."

They stood on the open deck, cool in the breezes, but still able to feel the warmth of the sun. Both were dressed in the finest clothing they could buy in Salador, for they wished to be presentable at court and knew they had little chance of being admitted to see the King should they look like simple vagabonds.

The ship's captain ordered the last sails taken in, and the ship slid into place alongside the docks a few moments later. Ropes were thrown to men waiting on the quay, and the vessel was quickly made fast.

As soon as they were able, the two travelers were down the gangway and making their way through the city. Rillanon, the fabled and ancient capital of the Kingdom of the Isles, stood bedecked in colors, flashing brightly in the sunlight, but there was an undercurrent of tension in the atmosphere of the streets and markets. Everywhere they passed, people spoke in hushed tones, as if they feared someone might overhear them, and even the hawkers in the street stalls seemed to offer their wares halfheartedly.

It was nearly the noon hour, and without seeking rooms, they headed straight for the palace. When they reached the main gate, an officer in the purple and gold of the Royal Household Guard inquired their business.

Laurie said, "We bring messages of the greatest importance to the King, regarding the war."

The officer considered. They were dressed well enough and didn't appear to be the usual madmen with predictions of doom, or prophets of some nameless truth, but they were not officials of the court or army either. He decided on the course of action followed most often in the armies of all nations in all times: passing them along to a higher authority.

A guard escorted them to the office of an assistant to the Royal Chancellor. Here they were made to wait for a half hour before the assistant would see them. They entered the man's office and were confronted by the Steward of the Royal Household, a self-important little man with a potbelly and a chronic wheeze when he spoke. "What business do you gentlemen have?" he inquired, making it clear that his estimation of them was provisional.

"We carry word to the King regarding the war," Laurie answered.

"Oh?" he sniffed, "and why aren't these documents or messages or whatever they are being delivered by the proper military pouch?"

Kasumi, obviously frustrated with the wait now that they were in the palace, said, "Let us speak with someone who can take us to the King."

The Steward of the Royal Household looked outraged. "I am Baron Gray. I am the one to whom you will speak, man! And I have a good mind to have the guards toss you into the street. His Majesty cannot be bothered with every charlatan who tries to seek an audience. I am the one you must satisfy, and you have not."

Kasumi stepped forward and gripped the man by the front of his tunic. "And I am Kasumi of the Shinzawai. My father is Kamatsu, Lord of the Shinzawai, and Warchief of the Kanazawai Clan. I will see your King!"

Lord Gray paled visibly. He frantically pulled at Kasumi's hand and tried to speak. His shock at what he had just heard and what he felt at being handled this way raced within him. It all proved to be too much for him to speak. He nodded frantically until Kasumi released him.

Brushing at his tunic front, the man said, "The Royal Chancellor will be informed—at once."

He walked to a door, and Laurie watched him in case he called for guards, thinking them madmen. Whatever else the man thought, Kasumi's manner convinced him he was something quite different from anything heretofore seen. A messenger was sent, and in a few minutes an elderly man entered the room.

He simply said, "What is it?"

"Your Grace," said the Steward, "I think you had best talk to these men and consider if His Majesty should see them."

The man turned to study the two other men in the office. "I am Duke Caldric, the Royal Chancellor. What reason do you have to see His Majesty?"

Kasumi said, "I bring a message from the Emperor of Tsuranuanni."

THE KING SAT in a pavilion on a balcony overlooking the harbor. Below, a mountain river passed directly before the palace, part of the original defense design though no longer needed as a moat. Graceful bridges could be seen arching above it, carrying people from one side of the river to the other.

King Rodric sat, seemingly attentive to what Kasumi was saying. He toyed absently with a golden ball in his right hand, while Kasumi outlined in detail the Emperor's message of peace.

Rodric was silent for a while after Kasumi finished, as if weighing what he had heard. Kasumi handed a sheaf of documents to Duke Caldric, then waited for the King's answer. After another moment of silence Kasumi added, "The Emperor's proposals are outlined in these parchments in detail, Your Majesty, should you wish to study them at your leisure. I will wait upon your convenience to carry your reply."

Still Rodric was silent, and the courtiers gathered nearby looked at one another nervously. Kasumi was about to speak again when the King said, "I am always amused when watching my little subjects hurrying about the city, like so many ants. I often wonder what they think, living out their simple little lives." He turned to look at the two emissaries. "You know, I could order any one of them put to death. Just pick one out, from this very balcony, should I choose. I could just say to my guards, 'See that fellow in the blue cap? Go hack his head off,' and they would, you know. That's because I'm King."

Laurie felt a chill run up his back. This was worse than anything he had imagined. The King seemed not to have heard a single word spoken. Kasumi said very quietly in the Tsurani language, "If we should fail, one of us must carry word back to my father."

At this, the King's head snapped up. His eyes grew wide, and he spoke with a tremble in his voice. "What is this?" His voice rose in pitch. "I will have no one whispering!" His face took on a feral appearance. "You know they are always whispering about me, the disloyal ones. But I know who they are, and I will see them on their knees before me; yes I will. That traitor Kerus was on his knees before I had him hanged. I would have hanged his family had they not fled to Kesh." He then studied Kasumi. "You think to trick me with your strange story and these so-called documents. Any fool could see through your guise. You are spies!"

Duke Caldric looked pained and tried to calm the King. Several guards stood nearby, shifting their weight from foot to foot, uncomfortable at what they were hearing.

The King pushed the solicitous Duke away. His voice took on a near-hysterical tone. "You are agents of that traitor Borric. He and my uncle were plotting to take my throne. But I stopped that. My uncle Erland is dead. . . ." He paused for a moment, as if confused. "No, I mean he is ill. That is why my loyal Duke Guy was sent from Bas-Tyra to rule Krondor until my beloved uncle was well. . . ." His eyes seemed to clear for a moment, then he said, "I am not feeling well. Please excuse me. I will speak to you again tomorrow." He rose from his chair. After he had taken a step, he turned back to look at Laurie and Kasumi. "What was it you wanted to see me about? Oh yes, peace. Yes, that is good. This war is a terrible thing. We must end it so that I can go back to my building. We must begin the building again."

A page took the King's arm and led him away. The Royal Chancellor said, "Follow me, and say nothing."

He hurried them through the palace and led them to a room with two guards before the door. One guard opened the door for them, and they entered. Inside they found a bedroom with two large beds and a table with chairs in the corner. The Chancellor said, "Your arrival is poorly timed. Our King is, as you no doubt can see, a sick man, and I fear that he will not recover. I hope he will be better able to understand your message tomorrow. Please stay here until you are sent for. A meal will be brought to you."

He crossed over to the door, and before he left said, "Until tomorrow."

A SHOUT AWOKE them in the night. Laurie rose quickly and went to the window. Peering through the curtains, he could see a figure on the balcony below. In his nightshirt, King Rodric stood sword in hand, poking into the bushes. Laurie opened the window as Kasumi joined him. From below they could hear the King's cries: "Assassins! They have come!" Guards ran out and searched the bushes, while court pages led the shrieking monarch back to his room.

Kasumi said, "In truth, the gods have touched him. They must surely hate your nation."

Laurie said, "I am afraid, friend Kasumi, that the gods have little to do with this. Right now I think we had best see to finding a way out of here. I have a feeling that His Royal Majesty is ill suited for the finer points of negotiating a peace. I think we had best make our way west and speak with Duke Borric."

"Will he be able to stop the war, this Duke?"

Laurie crossed over to the chair upon which his clothing was draped. Picking up his tunic, he said, "I hope so. If the lords here can watch the King behave in such a manner and do nothing, then we will have civil war soon. Better to settle one war before beginning another."

They dressed quickly. Laurie said, "Let us hope we can find a ship putting out on the morning tide. If the King orders the port closed, we are trapped. It is a long swim."

As they gathered up their belongings, the door opened and the Royal Chancellor entered. He stopped and saw them standing there, fully dressed. "Good," he said, quickly closing the door. "You have as much sense as I had hoped you would. The King has ordered the spies put to death."

Laurie was incredulous. "He thinks us spies?"

Duke Caldric sat in one of the chairs by the table, fatigue clearly showing on his face. "Who knows what His Majesty is thinking, these days? There are a few of us who try to stay his more terrible impulses, but it becomes more and more difficult each day. There is a sickness in him that is terrible to watch. Years ago he was an impetuous man, it is true, but there was also a vision to his plans, a certain mad brilliance that could have made this the greatest nation in Midkemia.

"There are many in the court now who take advantage of him, using his fears to further their own designs. I am afraid that soon I will be branded traitor and join the others in death."

Kasumi buckled on his sword. "Why stay, Your Grace? If this is true, why not come with us to Duke Borric?"

The Duke looked at the older son of the Shinzawai. "I am a noble of the Kingdom, and he is my King. I must do whatever I can to keep him from harming the Kingdom, even if the price is my life, but I cannot raise arms against him, nor aid those who do. I don't know how things are with your world, Tsurani, but here I must stay. He is my King."

Kasumi nodded. "I understand. In your place, I would do the same. You are a brave man, Duke Caldric."

The Duke stood. "I am a tired man. The King has taken strong drink, from my hand. He will drink from no other, for he fears poison. I had the chirurgeon give him something for sleep. You should be out to sea when he awakens. I don't know if he will remember your visit, but rest assured that someone will remind him within a day, or two at the outside. So do not linger. Make straight for Lord Borric and tell him what has happened."

Laurie said, "Is Prince Erland truly dead?"

"Yes. Word reached us a week ago. His failing health could not withstand the cold dungeon. Borric is now heir to the throne. Rodric has never wed: his fear of others is too deep. The fate of the Kingdom rests with Borric. Tell him so."

They crossed to the door. Before the Duke opened it, he said, "Also tell him that it is likely I will be dead should he come to Rillanon. It will be a good thing, for I would have to stand against any who raised arms against the Royal Standard."

Before Laurie or Kasumi could say anything, he opened the door. Two guards stood outside, and the Duke ordered them to escort Laurie and Kasumi to the docks. "The *Royal Swallow* is anchored in the harbor. Give this to the captain." He held out a piece of paper to Laurie. "It is a royal warrant, commanding him to carry you to Salador." He held out a second paper. "This is another, commanding any of the Armies of the Kingdom to aid your travel."

They grasped each other by the hand, then the two emissaries followed the guards down the corridor. Laurie looked over his shoulder at Caldric as they left. The old Duke waited, stoop-shouldered and tired, his face lined by worry and sorrow, as well as fear. As they turned a corner, losing sight of the Duke, Laurie thought no price in the world would make him exchange places with that old man.

THE HORSES were lathered. The riders whipped them up the hill. They were on the last leg of their journey to Lord Borric, begun over a month before, and the end was in sight. The *Royal Swallow* had sped them to Salador, where they had left at once for the West. They had slept little along the way, trading for fresh mounts or commandeering them, whenever possible, from horse patrols with the royal warrant given them by Caldric. Laurie wasn't sure, but he suspected they had covered the distance faster than it had ever been traveled before.

Several times since leaving Zūn, they had been challenged by soldiers. Each time they had presented the Chancellor's warrant and were passed through. Now they approached the Duke's camp.

The Tsurani Warlord had unleashed his major offensive. The Kingdom forces had held for a week, then collapsed, when ten thousand fresh Tsurani soldiers had come pouring through their lines, tipping the balance. The fighting had been bitter then, a raging, running battle lasting three days, before the Kingdom army was finally routed. When it was over, a large portion of the front had fallen, and the Tsurani had thrown up a salient out of the North Pass.

Now the elves and dwarves, as well as the castles of the Far Coast, were cut off from the main force of the Kingdom army. There was no communication of any sort, for the pigeons used to carry messages had been destroyed when the old camp had been overrun. The fate of the other fronts was unknown.

The Armies of the West were regrouping, and it took Laurie and Kasumi some time to find the headquarters camp. As they rode up to the command pavilion, they saw signs of bitter defeat on every side. It was the worst setback of the war for the Kingdom. Everywhere they looked they saw wounded or sick men, and those who showed no wounds had the look of despair.

A guard sergeant inspected their warrant and sent a guard with them to show them where the Duke's tent stood. They reached the large command tent, and a lackey took their mounts from them as the guard went inside. A moment later a tall young man, blond-bearded and wearing the tabard of Crydee, came out. Behind him appeared a stout man with a grey beard—a magician by his garb—and another man, large, with a ragged scar down his face. Laurie wondered if they might be old friends Pug had spoken of, but quickly focused his attention on the young officer, who stopped before him. "I bring a message to Lord Borric."

The young man smiled a bitter smile, then said, "You may give me the message, sir. I am Lyam, his son."

Laurie said, "I mean no disrespect, Highness, but I must speak with the Duke in person. So I was instructed by Duke Caldric."

At mention of the Royal Chancellor's name, Lyam exchanged glances with his companions, then held aside the tent flap. Laurie and Kasumi entered, the others following. Inside, there was a small brazier burning and a large table with maps upon it. Lyam led them to another section of the huge tent, curtained off from the rest. He pulled back the hanging, and they saw a man lying upon a sleeping pallet.

He was a tall man, with dark hair streaked with grey. His face was drawn, drained of blood, his lips nearly blue. His breathing was ragged, each breath rattling loudly as he slept. He wore clean bed clothing, but heavy bandages could be seen beneath his loose collar.

Lyam put back the hanging as another man entered the tent. Old, with a near-white mane of hair, he was still erect and broad-shouldered. Softly he said, "What is this?"

Lyam answered, "These men bring messages for Father from Caldric."

The old warrior stuck out his hand. "Give them to me."

When Laurie hesitated, the man nearly barked, "Damn it, fellow, I'm Brucal. With Borric wounded, I'm commander of the Armies of the West."

Laurie said, "I've no written message, Your Grace. Duke Caldric says to introduce my companion. This is Kasumi of the Shinzawai, emissary of the Emperor of Tsuranuanni, who carries an offering of peace to the King."

Lyam said, "Is there to be peace at last?"

Laurie shook his head. "Sadly, no. The Duke also said to say this: the King is mad, and the Duke of Bas-Tyra has slain Prince Erland. He fears only Lord Borric can save the Kingdom."

Brucal was visibly shaken by the news. To Lyam he quietly said, "Now we know the rumors to be true. Erland *was* Guy's prisoner. Erland dead. I can scarcely believe it." Shaking off his shock, he said, "Lyam, I know your mind is upon your father now, but you must bend thought to this: your father is near death; you will soon be Duke of Crydee. And with Erland dead, you will also be heir to the throne by right of birth."

Brucal sat heavily upon a stool near the map table. "This is a heavy burden thrust upon you, Lyam, but others in the West will look to you for leadership as they once looked to your father. If there was ever any love between the two realms, it is now strained to the breaking point, with Guy upon the throne in Krondor. It is now clear for all to see, Bas-Tyra means to be King, for a mad Rodric cannot be allowed his throne much longer." He fixed Lyam with a steady gaze. "You will soon have to decide what we in the West shall do. Upon your word, we have civil war."

29

▾▾

DECISION

THE HOLY CITY WAS FESTIVE.

Banners flew from every tall building. People lined the streets, throwing flowers before the nobles who were carried on their litters to the stadium. It was a day of high celebration, and who could feel troubled on such a day?

One who did feel troubled arrived in the pattern room of the stadium, the final reverberations of a chime signaling the appearance of a Great One of Tsuranuanni. Milamber shrugged off his preoccupation for a moment as he left the pattern room, near the central gallery of the Grand Imperial Stadium. The crowd of Tsurani nobles, idling away the time before the games began, parted to allow Milamber to pass through the archway leading to the magicians' seats. Glancing around the small sea of black robes, he noticed Shimone and Hochopepa, who were keeping a place for him.

They signaled greetings as he left the aisle between the magicians' section and the Imperial Party's and joined them. Below, on the arena floor, some of the dwarf-like folk from Tsubar—the so-called Lost Land across the Sea of Blood—were fighting large insect creatures, like cho-ja but without intelligence. Soft wooden swords and essentially harmless bites from mandibles provided a conflict more comic than dangerous. The commoners and lesser nobles already in their seats laughed in appreciation. These contests kept them amused while the great and near-great were waiting to enter the stadium. Tardiness in Tsuranuanni became a virtue when one reached a certain social level.

Shimone said, "It is a shame you took so long getting here, Milamber. There was a singularly fine match a short while ago."

"I was under the impression the killing wasn't to begin just yet."

Hochopepa, munching nuts cooked in sweet oils, said, "True, but our friend Shimone is something of an aficionado of the games."

Shimone said, "Earlier young officers of noble family fought with training weapons to first blood, to better display their skills and win honors for their clans—"

"Not to mention the fruits of some rather heavy wagering," interjected Hochopepa.

Ignoring the remark, Shimone continued. "There was a spirited match between sons of the Oronalmar and the Keda. I've not seen a better display in years."

While Shimone described the match, Milamber let his gaze wander. He could see the small standards of the Keda, Minwanabi, Oaxatucan, Xacatecas, Anasati, and other great families of the Empire. He noticed that the banner of the Shinzawai was absent, and wondered at it. Hochopepa said, "You seem much preoccupied, Milamber."

Milamber nodded agreement. "Before leaving for today's festival, I received word that a motion to reform land taxes and abolish debt slavery had been introduced in the High Council yesterday. The message came from the Lord of the Tuclamekla, and I couldn't for the life of me understand why he sent it until, near the end, he thanked me for providing the concepts of social reform the motion was intended to enact. I was appalled at such an action."

Shimone laughed. "Had you been so thick-witted a student, you'd still be wearing the white robe."

Milamber looked back blankly, and Hochopepa said, "You go about causing all sorts of rumblings with your speeches before the Assembly, constantly harping on all manner of social ills, and then sit dumbfounded because someone out there listened?"

"What I said to our brother magicians was not intended for discussion outside the Assembly halls."

"How unreasonable," said Hochopepa. "Someone in the Assembly spoke to a friend who wasn't a magician!"

"What I'd like to know," said Shimone, "is how this potful of reforms placed before the High Council by the Hunzan Clan has your name appended to it?"

Milamber looked uncomfortable, to the delight of his friends. "One of the young artists who worked on the murals at my estate is a son of the Tuclamekla. We did discuss differences between Tsurani and Kingdom cultures and social values, but only as an outgrowth of our discussions of the differences in styles of art."

Hochopepa looked skyward, as if seeking divine guidance. "When I heard the Party for Progress—which is dominated by the Hunzan Clan, which is dominated by the Tuclamekla Family—cited you as inspiration, I could scarcely believe my hearing, but now I can see your hand is in every problem plaguing the Empire." He looked at his friend with a mock-serious expression. "Tell me, is it true the Party for Progress is going to change its name to the Party of Milamber?"

Shimone laughed while Milamber fixed Hochopepa with a baleful look. "Katala thinks it amusing when I get upset by this sort of thing, Hocho. And you might think it funny as well, but I want it publicly known I did not intend for this to happen. I simply offered some observations and opinions, and what the Hunzan Clan and the Party for Progress does with them is not my doing."

Hochopepa said in chiding tones, "I fear that if so famous a personage as yourself wishes not to have such things occur, then such a personage should have his mouth sewn shut."

Shimone laughed, and Milamber felt his own mirth rise. "Very well, Hocho," answered Milamber. "I will take the blame. Still, I don't know if the Empire is yet ready for the changes I think needed."

Shimone said, "We have heard your arguments before, Milamber, but today is not the time, nor is this the place for social debate. Let us attend to the matters at hand. Remember, many of the Assembly are offended by your concerns over matters they judge political. And while I tend to support your notions as refreshing and progressive, keep in mind you are making enemies."

Trumpets and drums sounded, signaling the approach of the Imperial Party and cutting off further conversation. The Tsubar folk and the insectoids were chased from the arena, handlers herding them away. When the field was cleared, grounds keepers hurried out with rakes and drags to smooth the sand. The sound of the trumpets could be heard again, and the first members of the imperial procession, heralds in the imperial white, entered. They carried long, curved trumpets, fashioned from the horns of some large beast, which curled around their shoulders to end above their heads. They were followed by drummers who beat a steady tattoo.

When they were in position in the front of the imperial box, the Warlord's honor guard entered. Each wore armor and helm finished in needra hide bleached free of all color. Around the breastplate and helm of each, precious gold trim gleamed in the sun. Milamber heard Hochopepa mutter at the waste of this rare metal.

When they were stationed, a senior herald shouted, "Almecho, Warlord!" and the crowd rose, cheering. He was accompanied by his retinue including several in black robes—the Warlord's pet magicians, as the others of the Assembly referred to them. Chief among these were the two brothers, Elgahar and Ergoran.

Then the herald cried, "Ichindar! Ninety-one times Emperor!" The crowd roared its approval as the young Light of Heaven made his entrance. He was attended by priests of each of the twenty orders. The crowd stood thundering. On and on it went, and Milamber wondered if the love of the Tsurani people would sustain the Light of Heaven should a confrontation between Warlord and Emperor take place. In spite of the Tsurani reverence for tradition, he did not think the Warlord a man to step down meekly from his office—a thing unheard of in history—should the Emperor so order.

As the noise died down, Shimone said, "It seems, friend Milamber, that the contemplative life doesn't suit the Light of Heaven. Can't say that I blame him, sitting around all day with no one for company but a lot a priests and silly girls chosen for their beauty instead of conversational ability. Must become frightfully boring."

Milamber laughed. "I doubt most men would agree."

Shimone shrugged. "I constantly forget you were quite old when you were trained, and you have a wife also."

At mention of wives, Hochopepa looked pained. He interrupted. "The Warlord is going to make an announcement."

Almecho rose and held his hands aloft for silence. When the stadium fell quiet, his voice rang out. "The gods smile upon Tsuranuanni! I bring news of a great victory over the otherworld barbarians! We have crushed their greatest army, and our warriors celebrate! Soon all the lands called the Kingdom will be laid at the Light of Heaven's feet." He turned and bowed deferentially to the Emperor.

Milamber felt a stab at the news. Without being aware, he began to stand, only to have Hochopepa grip his arm and hiss, "You are Tsurani!"

Milamber shook himself free of the unexpected shock and composed himself. "Thank you, Hocho. I nearly forgot myself."

"Hush!" said Hochopepa.

They returned their attention to the Warlord. ". . . and as a sign of our devotion to the Light of Heaven, we dedicate these games to his honor." A cheer rang through the arena, and the Warlord sat down.

Milamber spoke quietly to his friends. "It seems the Emperor is less than ecstatic at the news." Hochopepa and Shimone turned to watch the Emperor, who was sitting with a stoic expression upon his face.

Hochopepa said, "He hides it well, but I think you are right, Milamber. Something in all this disturbs him."

Milamber said nothing, knowing well enough the cause: this victory would blunt the Blue Wheel peace initiative, and would gain the Warlord more power at the Emperor's expense.

Shimone tapped Milamber upon the shoulder. "The games begin."

As the doors on the arena floor opened to admit the combatants, Milamber studied the Emperor. He was young, in his early twenties, and possessed a look of intelligence. His brow was high, and his reddish-brown hair was allowed to grow to his shoulders. He turned in Milamber's direction, to speak with a priest at his side, and Milamber could see his clear green eyes glint in the sun. Their eyes made contact for a moment, and there was a brief flicker of recognition, and Milamber thought: So you have been told of my part in your plan. The Emperor continued his conversation, without missing a beat, and no one else saw the exchange.

Hochopepa said, "This is a clemency spectacle. They will all fight until only one stands. He will be pardoned for his crimes."

"What are their crimes?" Milamber asked.

Shimone answered. "The usual. Petty theft, begging without temple authority, bearing false witness, avoiding taxes, disobeying lawful orders, and the like."

"What about capital crimes?"

"Murder, treason, blasphemy, striking one's master, all are unpardonable crimes." His voice rose to carry over the crowd noises. "They are put in with war prisoners who will not serve as slaves. They are sentenced to fight over and over until they are killed."

A guard of soldiers left the floor, abandoning the sand to the prisoners. Hochopepa said, "Common criminals. There will be little sport."

There seemed to be accuracy in the remark, for the prisoners were a sad-looking lot. Naked but for loincloths, they stood with weapons and shields that were foreign to them. Many were old and sick, seemingly lost and confused, holding their axes, swords, and spears loosely at their sides.

The trumpet sounded the start of combat, and the old and sick ones were quickly killed. Several had never even raised their weapons in defense, being too confused to try to stay alive. Within minutes nearly half the prisoners lay dead or dying on the sand. Shortly the action slackened, as combatants came to face opponents of more equal skill and cunning. Slowly the numbers diminished, and the free-flowing riotous nature of the contest changed. Occasionally when an opponent fell, a combatant was left standing next to another fighting pair. Often this resulted in three-way combat, which the mob approved with loud cheering, as the awkward combat would result in an excess of bloodshed and pain.

At the end three fighters remained. Two of them had not managed to resolve their conflict. Both were on the verge of exhaustion. The third man approached cautiously, keeping equal distance between himself and both men, looking for an advantage.

He had it a few seconds later. Using knife and sword, he jumped forward and dealt one of the combatants a blow to the side of the head that felled him. Shimone said, "The idiot! Couldn't he see the other man is the stronger fighter? He should have waited until one man was clearly at an advantage, then struck at him, leaving the weaker opponent to fight."

Milamber felt shaky. Shimone, his former teacher, was his closest friend after Hochopepa. Yet for all his education, all his wisdom, he was howling after the blood of others as if he were the most ignorant commoner in the least expensive seat. No matter how he tried, Milamber could not master the Tsurani enthusiasm for the death of others. He turned to Shimone and said, "I'm sure he was a little too busy to trouble himself over the finer points of tactics." His sarcasm was lost on Shimone, closely watching the combat.

Milamber noticed Hochopepa was ignoring the contest. The wily magician was taking note of every conversation in the stands: to him the games were only another opportunity to study the subtle aspects of the Game of the Council. Milamber found this blindness to the death and suffering below as disturbing as Shimone's enthusiasm.

The fight was quickly over, the man with the knife winning. The crowd greeted the victory with enthusiasm. Coins were thrown on the sand, so that the victor would return to society with a small amount of capital.

While the arena was being cleared, Shimone called over a herald and inquired about the balance of the day's activities. He turned to the others, obviously pleased at the news. "There are only a few matched pairs, then two special matches, a team of prisoners against a starving harulth, and a match between some soldiers from Midkemia and captured Thuril warriors. That should prove most interesting."

Milamber's expression indicated that he didn't agree. Judging the time right for the question, he said, "Hocho, have you noticed any of the Shinzawai Family in attendance?"

He glanced around the stadium, looking for the family banners of the more prominent houses of the Empire. "Minwanabi, Anasati, Keda, Tonmargu, Xacatecas, Acoma . . . No, Milamber. I can't say if any of your former, ah, benefactors are to be seen about. Not that I would expect them to be."

"Why?"

"They find themselves in the Warlord's bad graces of late. Something to do with failing some task or another he gave them. And I have heard that they are considered suspect, despite their clan's suddenly rejoining the war effort. The Kanazawai Clan is lost in its past glories, and the Shinzawai are the most old-fashioned of the lot."

Through the afternoon the matches wore on, each more artful than the previous as the skill level of the opponents increased. Soon the last pairs were done. Now the crowd waited in hushed anticipation, even the nobles quieted, for the next event was unusual. A team of twenty fighters, Midkemian from their size, marched out into the center of the arena. They carried ropes, weighted nets, spears, and long curved knives. They wore only loincloths, their bodies oiled and gleaming in the late afternoon light. They stood around looking relaxed, but the soldiers in the crowd recognized the subtle signs of tension common to fighters before a battle. After a minute the large double doors at the opposite end of the stadium opened, and a six-legged horror came shambling into the arena.

The harulth was all long teeth and sharp claws, complete with a belligerent attitude and a hidelike armor, and close to the size of a Midkemian elephant. It hesitated only long enough to blink at the light, then charged straight at the party of men before it.

They scattered before the creature, seeking to confuse it. The harulth, through simple- or single-mindedness, pursued one hapless fellow. In three enormous strides he ground the man underfoot, then gobbled him down in two bites. The others regrouped behind the animal and quickly deployed the nets. The hexapod spun about, faster than looked possible for a creature of such bulk, and charged again. This time the men waited until the last moment, tossed the nets, then dived away. The nets were edged with hooks to catch in the thick hide of the beast. It stepped into them and soon was busily tearing apart the mesh. While it was momentarily occupied, the spearmen ran in to strike. The harulth reacted in confusion, not being sure from which quarter its torment originated. The spears were proving ineffectual, for they could not penetrate the hide of the beast. Quickly realizing the futility of this approach, one fighter grabbed another and pointed to the rear of the creature. They dashed back toward the tail, which was sweeping back and forth along the ground with the force of a battering ram.

They conferred momentarily, then dropped their spears as the creature decided upon a target. It lashed forward and had another man in its maw. For a moment it was still as it swallowed its prey. The two men at the rear ran forward, leaping high up onto the tail of the animal. It seemed not to notice for a moment, then reacted by swinging around violently, throwing the second man off. Having come completely about, it stopped to devour the stunned man. The other somehow contrived to hang on and employed the few moments the harulth used to eat his comrade to pull himself higher on the creature's tail, where it joined the animal's haunches. With an overhand stroke he plunged his long-bladed knife between two vertebrae where they were outlined by loose-hanging skin. It was a desperate gamble, and the stadium crowd screamed approval. The knife penetrated the tough cartilage between the bone segments and pierced the spinal column. The creature bellowed with rage and started to spin, threatening to toss the unwelcome rider, but in a moment the rearmost pair of legs collapsed. The harulth stood baffled for a moment, its two forward pairs of legs pulling against the dead weight of its hind quarters. Twice it tried vainly to snap at its small tormentor, but its thick neck was insufficient for the task. The man pulled the blade loose and crawled forward along the spine while the surviving spearmen darted in and out, distracting the creature. Three times he was nearly tossed off the animal's back, but somehow he managed to retain his position. When he found himself slightly forward of the middle pair of legs, he drove his blade between vertebrae. The central legs collapsed an instant later, and the man was thrown clear of the animal's back. The harulth screamed its rage and pain, but was effectively immobilized. The fighters backed away and waited. Two spinal cuts proved to be enough, for minutes later the harulth fell over in shock, thrashed its forelegs for a time, and lay still.

The crowd shouted its enthusiastic approval of the contest, for never had a group of fighters bested a harulth without losing at least five times as many men. In this contest only three had died. The fighters stood around, exhaustion causing weapons to fall from limp fingers. The battle had lasted less than ten minutes, but the expenditure in energy, concentration, sweat, and fear had worn each man to near-prostration. Numbly oblivious to the crowds cheering, they stumbled toward the exit. Only the man who had actually driven in the knife showed any expression, and he was openly weeping as he moved across the sand.

"Why do you think that man is so distraught?" asked Shimone. "It was a grand triumph."

Milamber said in a voice forced to calmness, "Because he is exhausted and afraid, and sick from it." He then added softly, "And he is very far from home." He swallowed hard, struggling against outrage, then said, "He knows it is for nothing. Again and again he will march into this arena, to fight other creatures, other men, even friends from his homeland, and sooner or later he will die." Hochopepa stared at Milamber, and Shimone looked confused. "But for chance, I might have been with those below," added Milamber. "Those who fought are men. They had families and homes, they loved and laughed. Now they wait to die."

Hochopepa waved a hand absently. "Milamber, you have a disturbing habit of taking things personally."

Milamber felt sickened and angered by the bloody spectacle, but forced those emotions down within himself. He was determined to stay. He would be Tsurani.

The sand was cleared and trumpets blew again, signaling the final match of the afternoon. A dozen proud-looking warriors dressed in leather battle harnesses, wristbands set with studs, and headdresses plumed in many colors came striding out of one end of the arena. Milamber had never seen their like in person, but recognized their dress from his vision on the tower. These were the descendants of the proud Serpent Riders, the Thuril. Each wore a hard-eyed expression of grim determination.

From the other end, twelve warriors in color-splashed imitations of Midkemian armor marched out. Their own metal armor had been deemed both too valuable and too dull for the contest, and Tsurani artisans had provided stylized imitations.

The Thuril stood watching the newcomers with implacable contempt. Of all the races of humanity, only the Thuril had been able to withstand the Empire. The Thuril were uncontestedly the finest mountain fighters in Kelewan, and their mountain holds and high farm pastures were impossible to conquer. They had held the Empire at bay for years until peace had been declared. They were a tall people, the result of their lack of interbreeding with the shorter races of Kelewan, whom they considered inferior.

The trumpets blew again, and a hush fell over the crowd. A herald shouted in a clear voice, "As these soldiers of the Thuril Confederacy have violated the treaty between their own nations and the Empire, by making war upon the soldiers of the Emperor, they have been cast out by their own people, who have named them outlaws and bound them over for punishment. They will fight the captives from the world of Midkemia. All will strive until one is left standing." The crowd cheered.

The trumpet sounded, and the fighters squared off. The Midkemians crouched, weapons at the ready, but the Thuril stood tall, defiant looks upon their faces. One of the Thuril strode forward, halting before the nearest Midkemian. With contemptuous tones he spoke rapidly and made a sweeping motion around the arena.

Milamber felt a hot flush of anger begin to grow inside, coupled with shame at what he was seeing. There were games in Midkemia—he had heard of them—but they were nothing like this. The men who fought in Krondor and other places throughout the Kingdom were professionals who made a living by fighting to first blood. Occasionally a duel to the death would be fought, but it was always a personal matter, after all other means of settling the dispute had been exhausted. This was a mindless waste of human life for the titillation of the bored and idle, the satiated in search of more and more vivid reminders that their own lives were worth something. Milamber looked around and felt disgust at the expressions on the faces of those nearby.

The Thuril warrior continued his ranting, while the Midkemian watched, with something in their manner suggesting a shift of mood. Before, they were tensed, battle-ready; now they seemed almost relaxed. The Thuril continued pointing up at the assembled throng.

Then a Midkemian, tall and broad-shouldered, stepped forward as if to speak. The Thuril came on guard, his sword high, ready to strike. A voice rang out from behind, as another warrior said something that carried a note of reassurance. The first Thuril visibly relaxed.

The Midkemian slowly removed his helm, revealing a tired, haggard face, framed by damp, stringy black hair. He looked about the arena while the crowd began to whisper and grumble at the unexpected behavior of the warriors, and then gave a curt nod. He dropped his sword and shield and said something to his companions. Quickly the other fighters in the arena followed suit, and soon all weapons were lying upon the ground.

Milamber wondered at this strange behavior, and Shimone said, "This will end a shambles. The Thuril will not fight their own kind, and it seems they won't fight the barbarians either. I once saw six Thuril kill everyone sent against them, then refuse to fight one another. When the guards came to kill them, they fought, driving them back. Finally bowmen on the wall had to shoot them down. It was a disgrace. The crowd rioted, and the games director was torn to bits. Over a hundred citizens died."

Milamber felt relief: at least he would be spared the spectacle of Katala's people and his own killing one another. Then the crowd began to shout their disapproval, jeering the reluctant combatants.

Hochopepa nudged Milamber and said, "The Warlord appears less than amused by this."

Milamber saw the Warlord's livid expression as he watched his presentation to the Emperor turned into a farce. Almecho slowly rose from his place near the Light of Heaven and bellowed, "Let the fighting begin!"

Burly handlers, guards who worked on behalf of the games director, ran into the arena, wielding whips. They circled the motionless fighters and began lashing out at them. Milamber felt his gorge rise as the handlers laid about, tearing the exposed skin from the arms and legs of the Thuril and Midkemian soldiers. No stranger to the whip when in the swamp, he knew its terrible touch. He felt each stroke as it fell upon those on the sand below.

The crowd began to grow restive, for watching motionless men being whipped was not what they had come to see. Jeers and catcalls rang down upon those in the imperial box, and a few bolder souls threw litter and small coins into the arena, showing what they thought of such sport. Finally one of the handlers grew impatient, stepped up to a Thuril warrior, and struck him across the face with a whip handle. Before the handler could react, the Thuril sprang forward and tore the whip from the startled man's hands. In an instant he had it firmly wrapped about the man's throat, choking him.

The other handlers turned their attention to the warrior attacking their companion and began to flail wildly at him. After a dozen or so blows the Thuril began to wobble, and fell to his knees. But he held tightly to the whip, strangling the gasping handler. Again and again blows rained down upon the Thuril, until all his armor ran red with blood from the lashing. Still he held on to his victim.

When the handler died, eyes protruding from a blue face, whatever strength left to the Thuril seemed to die as well. As the handler's limp body came to rest on the sand, the Thuril warrior fell beside him.

It was a Midkemian soldier who reacted first. With cold detachment he simply picked up a sword and ran one of the handlers through. Then, as one, the Thuril and Midkemian soldiers had weapons in hand, and within a minute all the handlers were dead. Then, again as one, the prisoners threw their weapons to the ground.

Milamber battled to stay calm in the face of such display. He felt nothing but admiration for those men. They accepted death rather than slay one another. Possibly some of those men had ridden through the valley with him on the raid to discover the rift machine so many years before. Outwardly he appeared calm, a Tsurani, but inwardly he seethed.

Hochopepa whispered, "I have a bad feeling here. Whatever gain Almecho sought from this day to bolster his position with the Emperor is badly shaken. I fear he is not taking well your former countrymen's reluctance to die for the entertainment of the Light of Heaven."

Milamber nearly spit when he said, "Damn such entertainment." He looked at Hochopepa with a burning expression, one never seen by the fat magician before. Milamber half stood as he added, "And damn all those who find pleasure in such bloody sport."

Hochopepa seized him by the arm and tried to pull him firmly into his seat, saying, "Milamber, remember yourself!"

Milamber pulled himself free, ignoring the command.

Milamber and his companions looked to the imperial box, where a guard captain conferred with the Warlord. Milamber felt a strange hot flush inside and for a moment battled a sudden impulse to use his powers to put the Warlord amid those below, to see how he fared against those who refused to die gracefully at his command.

Then Almecho's voice rang out, silencing all those nearby. "No, no bowmen. Those animals will not die a warrior's death." He turned to one of his pet magicians and issued instructions. The black-robed man nodded and began to incant. Milamber felt his neck hairs rise as the presence of magic made itself known.

A hushed sound of awe swept about the stadium as those on the sand below fell senseless, to roll about in a daze.

The Warlord shouted, "Now go bind them, build a platform, and hang them for all to see."

Stunned silence greeted his words, then shouts of "No!"—"They are warriors!"—and—"This is without honor!" rang throughout the crowd.

Hochopepa closed his eyes and sighed audibly. He spoke to himself much as his companions. "The Warlord lets his famous temper get the best of him once more, and now we have a debacle before us. This will not help his position in the High Council or the stability of the Empire." Like an enraged beast at bay, the Warlord turned, and all nearby fell silent, but those at greater distances picked up the cries. By Tsurani standards this was too much of an indignity to be visited on any save those without honor. While balking the mob's sport, the prisoners had shown they were still fighting men, and as such deserved an honorable death.

Hochopepa turned to speak to Milamber, then stopped himself as he saw the expression on his friend's face. Milamber's anger was now fully revealed, his rage a match for the Warlord's. Sensing something terrible was about to occur, Hochopepa sought Shimone's attention, only to find he was also silently watching Milamber's fearsome countenance. All Hochopepa could manage to say was a quiet "Milamber, no!" Then the slave-become-magician was moving.

He swept past the shocked Hochopepa, saying only, "See to the Emperor's safety." Milamber was reeling with the impact of sudden emotion bottled up for years, now surging free. A strange and powerful certainty struck him. I am not Tsurani! he acknowledged to himself. I could not be a party to this. For the first time since donning the black robe, his two natures were in harmony. This was a dishonor by the standards of both cultures, something that filled him with a dread purpose free of any doubt.

Save those near the imperial box, the entire crowd was chanting, "The sword, the sword, the sword," demanding a warrior's death for each man below. The rhythm became a pounding pulse beat for Milamber, heightening his nearly unchecked fury.

Reaching a point between the magicians and the imperial box, Milamber regarded the soldiers and carpenters rushing onto the arena floor. The stunned Midkemians and Thuril were being bound like animals for slaughter, and the crowd's anger was reaching a dangerous level. Some of the younger officers of noble families in the lower levels of the stadium seemed ready to take swords and jump onto the sand, to contest personally for the prisoners' right to die as warriors. These had been valiant foemen, and many of those watching had fought against both Thuril and Kingdom soldiers. They would willingly kill these men on the field of battle, but would not watch this humiliation visited on brave enemies.

A black flood of anger, loathing, and sorrow poured through Milamber. His mind screamed in outrage, despite his attempts to control it. His head tilted back, and his eyes rolled up into his head, and as had happened twice before in his life, letters of fire appeared in his mind's eye. But never before had he had the strength to seize the moment, and with a nearly animal joy he dived into the newly opening well of power within. His right arm shot forward, and energy exploded from his hand. A bolt of blue flame, scintillating even in the sunlight, hurled downward, to strike the sand amid the Warlord's guards. Living men were swept in all directions, like leaves before the wind. Those just entering with the materials for the scaffolding were knocked to their knees by the blast, and those in the lower seats were stunned by its fury. All noise in the arena stopped as the crowd fell into mute shock.

All eyes turned to the source of that bolt, while those near him reflexively drew back. He was red-faced with anger, and the whites of his eyes showed around dark irises as he scanned the arena. With a short chopping motion of one hand, the magician said, "No more!"

No one moved save Hochopepa and Shimone. They had no idea what Milamber's intentions were, but in the face of this act they took his command seriously. They hurried to where a half-stunned, half-fascinated young Emperor sat watching with everyone else in the stadium. They quickly conferred with Ichindar, and a moment later the Emperor's seat was empty.

Milamber looked to his left as a bellow of outrage sounded. "Who dares this!"

Milamber was confronted by the sight of the Warlord, standing like an enraged demigod in his white armor. The Warlord's expression matched Milamber's.

"I dare this!" Milamber shouted back. "This cannot be; will not be! No more will men die for the sport of others!"

Barely holding himself in check, Almecho, Warlord of the Nations of Tsuranuanni, screamed, "By what right do you do this thing!" The cords on his neck stood out clearly, and every muscle of his body quivered as sweat beaded his brow.

Milamber's voice lowered, and his words came carefully measured with controlled, defiant rage. "By my right to do as I see fit." He then spoke to a nearby guard. "Those on the arena floor are to be released. They are free!"

The guard hesitated for a moment, then his Tsurani training came to the fore. "Your will, Great One."

The Warlord shouted, "You will stay!"

The crowd hissed with intaken breath. In the history of the Empire such a confrontation between Great One and Warlord had never occurred. The guard stopped, and Milamber spoke through a snarl. "My words are as law. Go!"

Suddenly the guard was moving, and the Warlord screamed his rage. "You break the law! No one may free a slave!"

His anger boiling back up again, Milamber shouted back, "I can! I am outside the law!"

The Warlord fell back, as if struck an invisible blow. In his life no one had dared to thwart his will in this manner. No Warlord in history had ever been forced to endure such public shame. He was dazed.

Near the Warlord another magician leaped to his feet. "I call you traitor and false Great One. You seek to undermine the Warlord's rule and bring chaos to the order of the Empire. You will recant this effrontery!"

Instantly there was frantic activity as all within earshot scrambled to get clear of the two magicians. Milamber regarded the Warlord's pet. "Do you think to match your powers against mine?"

The Warlord looked at Milamber with naked hatred on his face. He never took his eyes from the young magician's face as he said to his pet, "Destroy him!"

Milamber's arms shot upward, crossing at the wrists. Instantly a soft golden nimbus of light surrounded him. The other magician hurled a bolt of energy, and the blue ball of fire struck harmlessly against the gold shield.

Milamber tensed, suffused with anger. Twice before in his life, when attacked by the trolls and when fighting with Roland, he had reached into hidden reservoirs of power and drawn upon them. Now he tore aside the last barriers between his conscious mind and those hidden reserves. They were no longer a mystery to him but the wellspring from which all his power stemmed. For the first time in his experience, Milamber came to understand fully what he was, who he was: not a Black Robe, limited by the ancient teachings of one world, but an adept of the Greater Art, a master in full possession of all the energy provided by two worlds.

The Warlord's magician regarded him in fear. Here was more than a curiosity, a barbarian magician. Here stood a figure to awe, arms stretched upward, body trembling with rage, eyes seemingly aglow with strength.

Milamber clapped his hands above his head, and thunder pealed, rocking those around him. Energy exploded upward from his hands, held high above his head. A vortex of coruscating forces spun above him, rising like a bowshot. The fountain continued until it was high overhead. It began to flatten, covering the stadium like a great canopy. The dazzling display continued briefly, then the skies seemed to explode, blinding many who were looking upward. The sky turned dark, and the sun faded as if grey veils were slowly being drawn before it.

Milamber's voice carried to the farthest corner of the stadium as he said, "That you have lived as you have lived for centuries is no license for this cruelty. All here are now judged, and all are found wanting."

More magicians departed, disappearing from their seats, but many yet remained. More judicious commoners fled by nearby exits, but still many waited, thinking this but another contest for their amusement. Many were too drunk or excited by the spectacle for the magician's warning to reach them.

Milamber's arm swept an arc around him. "You who would take pleasure from the death and dishonor of others, see then how well you face destruction!" A gasp from the crowd answered his pronouncement.

Milamber raised one hand high overhead, and all became silent. Even the light summer breeze ceased. Then with a terrible strength, he spoke. They paled at his words, for it was as if death had become incarnate and had spoken. Echoing throughout the stadium were the words of Milamber: "Tremble and despair, for I am Power!"

A shrill keening sound began, with Milamber at its source. The very air shuddered as mighty magic was forged. "Wind!" Milamber cried.

A bitter breeze reeking of carrion, foul and loathsome in its touch, blew through the stadium. A low moan of sorrow and fear was carried away by the wind. It blew stronger and, each moment it grew, carried more menace, more despair. It turned colder, until it was stinging to those who had rarely known cold. Men wept at its biting caress, and high above the stadium, clouds formed in the murk.

The winds howled, drowning out the cries of the multitude in the arena. Nobles tried to flee, now too terrified to do anything but claw past their own families, trampling the old and slow underfoot. Many were buffeted to their knees, or knocked from the seats to the sands of the arena floor.

Great thunderheads, black and grey, raced overhead, seeming to swirl around a point directly over Milamber's head. The magician was engulfed in an eerie light, pulsating with energy. He stood at the center of the storm, a terrible figure in the dark. The wind shrieked its fury, but Milamber's voice cut through the sound like a knife.

"Rain!"

A cold rain fell, blown hard before the gale. Quickly it grew in tempo, becoming a pounding torrent, then a deluge. The cascade pelted those below, painfully driving them down, beating them senseless with a frightening strength clearly unnatural. A few managed to flee to the tunnels, while others clutched at one another in terror.

Other magicians tried to counter the spells but could not, and fainted from the exertion. Never had there been such a display of raw power. Here was a true master of magic, one who could control the very elements, come into his own. The magician who had challenged Milamber lay back across his seat, stunned, his eyes blinking as he struggled to sort some semblance of order out of the chaos around. The Warlord tried to withstand the storm, struggling to remain upright and refusing to submit to the terror of those around him.

Milamber dropped his arm, then raised one hand before him, stretching outward. "Fire!" he shouted, and again all could hear him.

The clouds seemed to burn. The heavens erupted as sheets of terrible colors, flames of every hue, ran riot through the darkness. Jagged bolts of lightning flashed across the sky, as if the gods were announcing the final judgment of mankind. People screamed in primitive terror at the element gone mad.

Then the rain of fire began. Drops struck arms and clothing, faces and cloaks, and began to burn. Shrieks of pain came from all sides, and people tried vainly to swat out the fires that burned their flesh. More magicians disappeared from the arena, taking their unconscious comrades. Milamber stood alone in the magicians' section. The stink of burned flesh filled the air, mixed with the acrid odor of fear.

Milamber crossed his arms before him. He turned his gaze downward.

"Earth!"

From below a deep rumbling commenced. The ground under the stadium began to tremble slightly. The vibrations grew in intensity, and the air was filled with an angry buzzing, as if a swarm of giant insects had surrounded the arena. Then a low rumbling added its harmony to the buzzing, and the ground began to move.

The vibrations became a shaking, then a violent rolling, surging, motion. Milamber stood calmly, as if on an island. It was as if the soil, the earth, had become fluid. People were thrown down onto the arena floor. The huge stadium throbbed from forces primeval. Statues tumbled from their pedestals, and the huge gates were ripped from their hinges, in a crackling splintering of ancient wood. They moved from before the tunnels in a staggering, drunken walk, then fell to the sand, crushing those who lay before them. Many of the beasts below the arena were driven mad by the earthquake and thrashed in their cages, smashing locks and opening doors. They fled the tunnels and raced over the fallen gates; they bellowed, howled, and roared at the fire rain. Enraged by terror, they fell upon the stunned spectators lying on the sand, killing at random. A man would sit dazed, absently slapping at the burning drops from the skies, while another a few feet away was being gutted by some horror from the distant forests.

Now the arena itself began to wail as the ancient stones moved, slipping across one another. Mortar a millennium old turned to dust in an instant as the very stadium crumbled. Cries for mercy were swept away by the winds or drowned in the cacophony of destruction. The fury mounted, and the world seemed ready to be torn asunder. Milamber raised his hands above his head again. He brought his palms together, and the mightiest thunder peal of all sounded. Then, abruptly, the chaos ceased.

Above, the sky was clear and sunny, a light breeze once more blowing from the east. The ground stood as it should, motionless and solid, and the rain of fire was a memory.

The silence that followed was deafening. Then the groans of the injured and the sobs of the terrified could be heard. The Warlord remained standing, his face drained of all color, small burns scarring his features and arms. In place of the mighty leader of the Empire stood a man bereft of any emotion save terror. His eyes were wide enough to show whites. His mouth moved, as if he were trying to speak, but no words were forthcoming.

Milamber raised his hands overhead again, and the Warlord fell back with a sob of fear. The magician clapped his hands and was gone.

THE AFTERNOON BREEZE carried the scent of summer flowers. In the garden Katala was playing a word game with William; she had insisted they should both learn the language of her husband's homeland.

It was almost evening, for they were farther east than the Holy City. The sun was low in the west, and the shadows in the garden were long. Without the chime announcing Milamber's arrival, Katala was startled when her husband appeared in the doorway of their home. She rose slowly from her seat, for she sensed at once something was wrong. "Husband, what is it?"

William ran up to his father, while Milamber said, "I will tell you everything later. We must take William and flee."

William tugged on his father's black robe. "Papa!" he cried, demanding attention. Milamber picked up his son and hugged him tightly, then said, "William, we are going on a journey to my homeland. You must be a brave boy and not cry."

William stuck out his lower lip, for if his father was asking him not to cry, then there must be a very good reason to do so, but he nodded and held back the tears.

"Netoha! Almorella!" Milamber called, and in a moment the two servants entered the garden. Netoha bowed, but Almorella rushed to Katala's side. Katala had insisted she accompany them to Milamber's new home when he brought his family from the Shinzawai estate. She was more sister to Katala and aunt to William than a slave. She could see at once that something was wrong, and tears came unbidden to her eyes.

"You're leaving," she said, a statement more than a question.

Netoha looked at his master. "Your will, Great One?"

Milamber said, "We are leaving. We must. I am sorry." Netoha took the news stoically, in the proper Tsurani fashion, but Almorella embraced Katala, openly weeping.

Milamber said, "I wish to ensure that you are both provided for. I have prepared documents against this day. When we have gone, you will find all my work cataloged in my study. Above my study table, on the top shelf, you will find a parchment with a black seal upon it. I am giving the estate to you, Netoha." He said to Almorella, "I know you two care for each other. The document giving Netoha the estate also contains a provision granting you your freedom, Almorella. He will make you a good husband. Even the Emperor cannot set aside a document bearing a Great One's seal, so do not worry."

Almorella's expression was a mixture of complete disbelief, happiness, and sorrow. She nodded slowly that she understood, thanks clearly showing in her eyes.

Milamber returned his attention to Netoha. "I am deeding the lower pasture land to Xanothis the herdsman. Provide well for the others of this household, Netoha.

"Now, in my study you will also find several parchments sealed with red wax. These must be burned at once. Whatever you do, do not break the seals before you burn them. All other works are to be sent to Hochopepa of the Assembly, with my deepest affection and the wish that he find them useful. He will know what to do with them."

Almorella again embraced Katala, then kissed William. Netoha said, "Quickly, girl. You're not mistress of this estate yet, and there is important work to do." The hadonra started to bow, then said, haltingly, "Great One, I . . . I wish you well." He quickly bowed and started for the study. Milamber could see a hint of moisture in his eyes.

Almorella, tears running down her cheeks, followed Netoha into the house. Katala turned to Milamber. "Now?"

"Now." As he took them to the pattern room, he said, "There is one thing I must find out before we attempt the rift." He held his wife, with their son between them, and willed himself to another pattern.

They were shrouded in a white haze for an instant, then were in a different room. They hurried through the door, and Katala saw they went into the home of the Shinzawai lord.

They hurried to Kamatsu's study and opened the door without ceremony. Kamatsu looked up, annoyed at the interruption. His expression changed immediately when he saw who was at his door. "Great One, what is it?" he asked, as he arose.

Milamber quickly conveyed the events of the day, and Katala paled at the recounting. The Lord of the Shinzawai shook his head. "You may have set processes in motion that will forever change the internal order of the Empire, Great One. I hope it is not a death blow. In any event, it will take years to gauge their effects. Already the Party for Progress is making overtures to the Party for Peace for alliance. In a short time you have had great effect upon my homeland."

Kamatsu continued, preventing Milamber from speaking. "That is not a thing of the moment, though. You who were once my slave have learned greatly, but you are still not Tsurani. You must understand the Warlord cannot allow such a setback and save face. He most likely will take his life in shame, but those who follow his lead—his family, his clan, his subordinates—will all mark you for death. Already there may be assassins hired, or magicians who are ready to act against you. You have no choice but to flee to your homeland with your family."

William decided it was appropriate now to cry, for in spite of his attempts at bravery his mother was frightened, and the boy felt it. Milamber turned away from Kamatsu and incanted a spell, and William was immediately asleep. "He will sleep until we are safe." Katala nodded and knew it was for the best, but still she disliked the necessity.

"I have no fear of any magician, Kamatsu," Milamber said, "but I fear for the Empire. I know now that, no matter how hard my teachers in the Assembly tried, I can never be Tsurani. But I do serve the Empire. In my disgust over what I witnessed in the arena, I became sure of what I've suspected for some time now. The Empire must change its course, or it is doomed to fall. The rotten, weak heart of this culture cannot support its own weight much longer, and like a ngaggi tree with a rotten core, it will collapse under its own weight. There are other things, things of which I may not speak, that I have learned in my time here, that tell me great change must come.

"I must leave, for should I stay, the Assembly, the High Council, all the Empire will be divided. I would have difficulty leaving the Empire were it not in the best interest of Tsuranuanni for me to depart. That is my training. But before I leave, I must know, has there been word from Laurie and your son of the Emperor's overture of peace?"

"No. We know they disappeared during a skirmish the first night. Hokanu's men searched the area after the fight and found no signs of them, so it is assumed they were safely away. My younger son is certain they reached a road behind Kingdom lines. Since then we have had no further word. Other members of our faction wait with as much trepidation as I."

Milamber considered. "Then the Emperor is still not ready to act. I had hoped it might be soon, so we could safely leave under the truce, before opposition to me becomes organized. Now, with the Warlord's announcement of victory over Duke Borric's army, we may never see peace."

Kamatsu said, "It is clear you are not Tsurani, Great One. With the Warlord in disgrace from your destruction of games he dedicated to the Light of Heaven, the War Party will be in disorder. Now the Kanazawai Clan will once more remove itself from the Alliance for War. Our allies in the Blue Wheel will work doubly hard to press for a truce in the High Council. The War Party is without an effective leader. Even should the Warlord prove shameless and not kill himself, he will be quickly removed, for the War Party needs a strong leader, and the Minwanabi are ambitious; for three generations they have sought the white and gold. But others in the High Council will press the claims as well. The War Party will be in disarray, and we shall gain time to strengthen our position, as the Game of the Council continues."

Kamatsu looked long at Milamber. "As I have said, there are those who are already plotting to take your life. Make for your homeworld now. Do not delay, and you should likely win safely through. It might not occur to any but a few that you will strike for the rift at once. Any other Great One would take a week putting his house in order." He smiled at Milamber. "Great One, you were a fresh breeze in a stale room while you were with us. I am sorry to see you leave our land, but you must go at once."

"I hope the day will come when we may meet again as friends, Lord of the Shinzawai, for there is much that our two people could learn from one another."

The Shinzawai lord placed his hand upon Milamber's shoulder. "I hope also for that day, Great One. I will send prayers with you. One thing more. If you should perchance see Kasumi in your homeworld, tell him his father thinks of him. Now go, and good-bye."

"Good-bye," said Milamber. He took his wife by the arm and hurried back toward the pattern room. When they reached it, a chime sounded, and Milamber pushed his wife and son behind him. A brief haze of white appeared over the pattern in the floor, and Fumita stood there, startled.

"Milamber!" he said, stepping forward.

"Stop, Fumita!"

The older magician stood still. "I mean you no harm. Word of what occurred has reached those of the Assembly not attending the games. The Assembly is in turmoil. Tapek and the other Warlord's pets demand your life. Hochopepa and Shimone argue on your behalf. Never has such discord been seen. In the High Council, the War Party demands an end to the independence of the Assembly during times of war, and the Party for Progress and the Party for Peace are in open alliance with the Blue Wheel Party. The Empire is upside down."

The older magician seemed to droop visibly as he related this. He looked years older than Milamber had ever remembered seeing him. "I think you may have been right in many of your beliefs, Milamber. We must have changes in the Empire if we are not to decay, but so many changes so quickly? I don't know."

There was a moment of silence between them; Milamber said, "What I did was for the Empire, Fumita. You must believe that."

The older magician nodded slowly. "I believe you, Milamber, or at least I wish to." He seemed to stand more erect. "Whatever the outcome there will be much for the Assembly to do when things have settled. Perhaps we can steer the Empire to a healthier course.

"But you must go quickly. No soldier will try to stop you, for only a few outside the Holy City know of your actions, but the Warlord's pets may already be seeking you out. You caught our brothers by surprise at the games, and none singly could stand against you, but if they coordinate against you, even your vaunted powers will avail you little. You would have to kill another magician, or be killed in turn."

"Yes, Fumita, I know. I must go. I have no desire to kill another magician, but I shall if I must."

Fumita looked pained at hearing this. "How are you to reach the rift? You haven't been to the staging area, have you?"

"No, but I go to the City of the Plains, and from there I can command litter."

"It is too slow. The litter will take over an hour to reach the staging area." He reached into his robe and pulled out a transfer device. He held it out to Milamber. "The third setting will take you directly to the rift machine."

Milamber took it. "Fumita, I mean to try to close the rift."

Fumita shook his head. "Milamber, even with your powers I don't think you can. Scores of magicians worked to create the great rift, and the controlling spells were established only on the Kelewan side. The Midkemian machine is only to stabilize the rift's location."

"I know, Fumita. You'll soon know, for I've sent my works to Hocho. My 'mysterious' research has been an intensive study of rift energies.

"I may now know more about them than any other magician in the Assembly. I know it would be a desperate, possibly destructive, action from the Midkemian side, but this war must end."

"Then get free to your homeworld and wait. The Emperor will act soon, I am sure. The Warlord could not have been handed a bigger blow by losing the war than the one you handed him in the arena. If the Light of Heaven orders peace, then perhaps we can deal with the question of the rift. Stay your hand until you've learned what the King's reaction to the peace offer is."

"Then you also play the Great Game?"

Fumita smiled. "I am not the only magician to descend into playing politics, Milamber. Hochopepa and I have been a part of this from the onset. Go now, and may the gods be with you. I wish you a safe journey and a long, prosperous life on your homeworld."

He then walked past Milamber and his family. Once he was out of sight, Milamber activated the device.

THE SOLDIER JUMPED. One moment he had been sitting under a tree, shaded from the setting sun's heat, then the next moment a magician with a woman and child suddenly appeared before him. By the time he was on his feet, they were moving toward the rift machine, several hundred yards away. When they reached the machine, a platform with tall poles rising up on either side of it, between which a glimmering "nothingness" could be seen, an officer who was in charge of the troops moving through snapped to attention.

"Get these men back from the platform."

"Your will, Great One." He barked orders, and the men fell back. Milamber took Katala by the hand and led her through the rift.

One step, a moment of disorientation, and they were standing in the middle of the Tsurani camp in the valley in the Grey Towers. It was night, and campfires burned brightly. Several officers were startled at the unusual arrival, but stepped out of their way.

Milamber said, "Have you captured horses?"

One of the officers nodded dumbly.

"Bring two, at once. Saddled."

"Your will, Great One," said the man, and rushed off.

Soon a soldier brought two horses toward him. When the soldier came close, Milamber could see it was Hokanu. The younger Shinzawai son looked quickly about as he handed the reins to Milamber. "Great One, we have just received word something terrible has occurred at the Imperial Games, though the reports are vague. I suspect your sudden appearance here has something to do with those reports. You must be away quickly, for these are the Warlord's men in camp, and should they arrive at the same conclusion, there is no telling what they might risk."

Milamber held William while Katala mounted with Hokanu's aid. He handed their son up to her and mounted his own steed. "Hokanu, I have just seen your father. Go to him; he has need of you."

"I will return to my father's estate, Great One." The young Tsurani hesitated, then added, "Should you see my brother, tell him I live, for he does not know."

Milamber said he would, then turned to Katala and took the reins of her horse. "Hold to the saddle horn, beloved. I will carry William."

Without another word they rode out of camp. Several times guards started to challenge them, but the sight of the black robe stopped them. They rode for hours in the moonlight. Milamber could hear the shouts of soldiers as he led his family to safety.

Katala bore up under it all like the warriors she was descended from, and Milamber marveled at her. She had never sat a horse before, but she made no complaint. To be taken from her home and whisked away to a strange, dark world, where she knew no one, must be a frightening experience. She revealed a tough fiber to her character he had only guessed at before.

After the seemingly endless ride, a voice sounded from out of the darkness. Dim shadowy figures could be seen moving among the trees. "Halt! Who rides this night?" The voice was speaking the King's Tongue. The three riders halted, and the man in front, with relief in his voice, shouted, "Pug of Crydee!"

30

▾▾

UPHEAVAL

KULGAN SAT QUIETLY.

It was a reunion tempered with sadness. Pug stood near Lord Borric's bed, openly showing his grief as the dying Duke smiled wanly up at him. Lyam, Brucal, and Meecham waited a short way off, speaking softly, and Katala distracted William while the Duke and Pug spoke.

Borric's voice came softly, weak from his illness, and his face contorted with pain as he struggled for breath. "I am glad to see you . . . returned to us, Pug. And doubly glad to see your wife and child." He coughed, and a foam appeared at the corner of his mouth, flecked with blood.

Katala's eyes were tearing, for the open affection her husband held for this man touched her. Borric motioned toward Kulgan, and the stout magician came to stand next to his former pupil. "Yes, Your Grace."

Borric whispered, and Kulgan turned to Meecham. "Will you see Katala and the boy to our tent? Laurie and Kasumi are waiting there."

Katala threw Pug a questioning look, and he nodded. Meecham had already picked up the boy, who regarded him with some skepticism. When they had left, Borric struggled to sit higher, and Kulgan helped him, placing pillows behind his back. The Duke coughed loudly and long, his eyes clenched tightly shut from pain.

When at last he could breathe again, he sighed, then spoke slowly. "Pug, do you remember when I rewarded you for saving Carline from the trolls?" Pug nodded, afraid to speak for the emotions he felt. Borric continued, "Do you remember my promise of another gift?" Again Pug nodded. "Would that Tully were here to give it to you now, but I will tell you in brief. I have long thought the Kingdom wastes one of its greatest resources by regarding magicians as outcasts and beggars. Kulgan's faithful service over the years has shown me I was right. Now you return, and though I understand only a little of what you've told, I can see you have become a master of your arts. It was my hope you would, for I have had a vision.

"I had left a sum of gold in trust for you, against the day you became a master magician. With it, I would like you and Kulgan, and other magicians, to establish a center for learning, where all may come and share. Tully will give you the documents with my instructions, explaining in detail my design. But for now I can only ask: Will you accept this charge? Will you build an academy for the study of magic and other knowledge?"

Pug nodded, tears in his eyes. Kulgan stood agape, not trusting what he had heard. His fondest wish, his life's ambition, shared with the Duke in the idle hours of speaking of dreams over cups of wine, was now granted.

Borric began to cough again, then when the fit passed, said, "I hold title to an island, in the heart of the Great Star Lake, near Shamata. When this war is at last done, go there and build your academy. Perhaps someday it will be the greatest center for learning in the Kingdom."

Again the Duke was racked by coughing, the sound more terrible than before. He gasped after the attack, barely able to talk. He motioned for Lyam to come close, pointed to Pug, and said, "Tell him," then fell back upon his pillows.

Lyam swallowed hard, fighting back the tears, and spoke to Pug. "When you were taken by the Tsurani, Father wished for some memorial in remembrance. He considered what would be proper, for you had shown bravery on three occasions, twice saving Kulgan's life in addition to my sister's. He judged the only thing you lacked was a name, for none knew your parentage. So he ordered a document drawn up and sent to the Royal Archives, inscribing your name on the rolls of the family conDoin, adopting you into our house." Lyam forced a smile. "I only wish times were gladder to share such news with you."

Overcome with emotion, Pug sank to his knees at the Duke's side. He took the Duke's hand and kissed his signet, unable to speak. Softly Borric said, "I could be no more proud of you than were you my own son." He gasped for breath. "Bear our name with honor."

Pug squeezed the once powerful hand, now weak and limp. Borric's eyes began to close, and he struggled for breath. Pug released his hand, and the Duke motioned for all to come closer. Even old Brucal was red-eyed as they waited for the Duke's life to slip away.

To Brucal he whispered, "You are witness, old companion."

The Duke of Yabon raised an eyebrow and looked questioningly toward Kulgan. "What does he mean?"

Kulgan said, "He wishes you to witness his dying declaration. It is his right."

Borric looked at Kulgan and said, "Care for all my sons, old friend. Let the truth be known."

Lyam said to Kulgan, "Why does he say 'all my sons'? What truth?"

Kulgan stared at Borric, who nodded weakly. The magician's words came quietly. "Your father acknowledges his eldest son, Martin."

Lyam's eyes grew wide. "Martin?"

Borric's arm shot out in a sudden surge of strength, catching at Lyam's sleeve. He pulled Lyam to him and whispered, "Martin is your brother. I have wronged him, Lyam. He is a good man, and well do I love him." To Brucal he croaked a single word, "Witness!"

Brucal nodded. With tears streaming down into his white moustache, he swore, "So do I, Brucal, Duke of Yabon, bear witness."

Suddenly Borric's eyes went blank. His death rattle sounded deep in his chest, and he lay still.

Lyam fell to his knees and wept, and the others also let their grief come unrestrained. Never to Pug had a moment been so bittersweet.

THAT NIGHT it was a quiet group in the tent that Meecham had commandeered for Pug and his family. The news of Borric's death had cast a pall over the camp, and much of Kulgan's joy at seeing his apprentice returned safely had been blunted. The day slowly passed, with everyone becoming reacquainted, though they spoke softly and felt little joy. Occasionally one would leave the tent, wandering off to be alone with his thoughts for a while. Nine years of history had been exchanged slowly, and now Pug spoke of his flight from the Empire.

Katala kept one eye on William, who lay curled up on a bed with one arm thrown over Fantus. The firedrake and the boy had taken one look at each other and decided they were friends. Meecham sat by the cook fire, watching the others carefully. Laurie and Kasumi sat on the floor, Tsurani fashion, while Pug finished his narrative.

Kasumi was the first to speak. "Great One, how is it that you could leave the Empire now, and not before?"

Kulgan raised one eyebrow. He was still absorbing the changes in his former apprentice. This talk of Greater Path and Lesser Path was still difficult to understand, and he couldn't believe the Tsurani attitude toward the boy. He amended that, the young man.

"After my confrontation with the Warlord, it became clear to me that I would serve the Empire by leaving, for my continued presence could only bring divisiveness at a time the Empire needs to heal itself. The war must be ended, and peace established, for the Empire is being drained."

"Aye," added Meecham, "as is the Kingdom. Nine years of war are bleeding us dry."

Kasumi was equally discomforted by the casual tone these people took toward Pug. "Great One, what if the Emperor cannot stop the new Warlord? The council will surely be quick to elect one."

"I don't know, Kasumi. I will then have to try to close the rift."

Kulgan pulled long on his pipe, then blew a thick cloud. "I am still not clear on everything you have said, Pug. From what you have said, I can see nothing that will prevent them from opening another rift."

"There is nothing, except that rifts are unstable things. There is no way to control where a rift will go; it was mere chance that caused the one between this world and Kelewan. Once that one was established, others could follow, as if the path between the two worlds acted to other rifts like a lodestone to metal.

"The Tsurani could attempt to reestablish the rift, but each attempt would probably take them to other, new worlds. If they returned here, it would be by the merest chance, one in thousands. If the rift is closed, it would be years before they returned, if ever."

"From what you said about the Warlord's taking his own life," said Kulgan, "can we expect a respite in the fighting?"

It was Kasumi who answered. "I fear not, friend Kulgan, for I know this Warlord's Subcommander. He is Minwanabi, a proud family from a powerful clan, and it would serve his cause well when the High Council meets for his clan to bring word of a great victory. Most likely he will attack in force within days."

Kulgan shook his head. "Meecham, you had best ask Lord Lyam to join us; he must hear this." The tall franklin rose and left the tent.

Kasumi frowned. "I have come to know this world a little, and I agree with the Great One. Peace would surely profit us both, but I do not see it coming."

The young Duke followed Meecham into the tent a few minutes later, and Kasumi repeated his warning. "We had best be ready, then, for the attack," said Lyam.

Kasumi looked uncomfortable. "Lord, I must beg your pardon, but should fighting come, I cannot stand against my own people. May I have your permission to return to my own lines?"

The Duke considered this, and Pug noticed that his face was becoming lined with the strain of command. Gone were the laughing eyes and ever present smile. Now he resembled his father more than ever. "I understand. I will order you passed through the lines, if I have your parole that you will repeat nothing you have heard here."

Kasumi agreed and rose to leave. Pug stood also and said, "I will issue one last order to you, Kasumi, as a magician of Tsuranuanni. Return to your father, for he has need of you. One more soldier dying will aid your nation little."

Kasumi bowed his head. "Your will, Great One."

Kasumi embraced Laurie and left with Lyam.

Kulgan said, "You have told me so much that is difficult to absorb. I think for now we had best retire, for I feel the need of resting."

As the old magician rose, Pug said to him, "There is one thing I have been waiting to ask. What of Tomas?"

"Your childhood friend is well and with the elves of Elvandar. He is a warrior of great renown, as he had wished to be."

Pug smiled. "I am glad to hear that. Thank you."

Kulgan, Laurie, and Meecham bade them good night and left. Katala said, "Husband, you are tired. Come rest."

Pug crossed over to the bed she sat upon. "You amaze me. You have been through so much tonight, and yet you fret about me."

She took his hand. "When I am with you, everything is as it should be. But you look as if the weight of the world sits upon you."

"The weight of two worlds, I fear, love."

THEY WERE AWAKENED by the sound of trumpets. As they rose from the bed, Pug and Katala were startled by Laurie rushing into the tent. From the light behind him as he tossed aside the tent flap, it was evident that they had slept late. "The King comes!" He held out some clothing to Pug. "Put these on."

Seeing the wisdom of not walking the camp in the black robe, Pug complied. Katala pulled her robe on over her head, while Laurie turned his back. She went over to William, who was sitting up in his bed, looking frightened. He quickly calmed down and started to pull on Fantus's tail, causing the drake to snort a protest over such indignities.

Pug and Laurie left the tent and walked to the commander's pavilion, overlooking the camp of the Kingdom armies. Away to the southeastern end of the camp they could see the royal party quickly approaching, and could hear the cheers of the soldiers as they saw the royal banner pass. Thousands of soldiers took up the cheer, for they had never seen the King before, and his presence served to lift their spirits, badly sagging since the rout by the Tsurani.

Laurie and Pug stood off to one side of the command tent, but close enough to ensure they could hear what transpired. Duke Brucal kept his eyes on the King, but Lyam noticed the two and nodded his approval of their presence.

The two lines of Royal Household Guard rode up to the front of the tent, then parted so the King might ride to the fore. Rodric, King of the Realm, rode on a huge black war-horse, who pawed at the ground as he came to a halt before the two dukes. Rodric was dressed in a gaudy array of gold-trimmed battle armor, with many flutings and reliefs fashioned into the breastplate. His helm was golden, with a circlet crown. A royal purple plume flew from the crest, blown by the morning wind.

When he had been sitting for a moment, he removed his helm and handed it to a page. He stayed atop his horse and studied the two commanders, looking down at them with a crooked smile. "What, have you no greeting for your liege lord?"

The dukes bowed. Brucal said, "Your Majesty. We were just surprised. We had no word."

Rodric laughed, and the sound was tinged with madness. "That is because I sent no word. I wanted to surprise you." He looked at Lyam. "Who is this in the tabard of Crydee?"

"Lyam, Your Majesty," answered Brucal. "The Duke of Crydee."

The King shouted, "He is Duke only if I say he is Duke." With a sudden change of mood, he said, in solicitous tones, "I am sorry to hear of your father's death." He then giggled. "But he was a traitor, you know. I was going to hang him." Lyam tensed at Rodric's words, and Brucal gripped his arm.

The King saw and screamed, "You would attack your King? Traitor! You are one with your father and the others. Guards, seize him!" He pointed at the young man.

Royal guards dismounted, and the soldiers of the West who stood nearby moved to stop them. "Stop!" commanded Brucal, and the western soldiers stopped. He turned to Lyam. "On your word, we have civil war," he hissed.

Lyam said, "I submit, Your Majesty." The western soldiers grumbled.

The King said coldly, "I shall have to hang you, you know. Take him to his tent and keep him there." The guards complied. The King turned his attention to Brucal. "Are you loyal to me, my lord Brucal, or shall there be a new Duke in Yabon as well as Crydee?"

"I am ever loyal to the crown, Your Majesty," came the answer.

The King dismounted. "Yes, I believe that." He giggled again. "You knew my father thought highly of you, didn't you?" He took the Duke's arm, and they entered the command tent.

Laurie touched Pug's shoulder and said, "We had best stay in our tents. If one of those courtiers recognizes me, I may join the Duke on the gibbet."

Pug nodded. "Get Kulgan and Meecham, and have them meet us in my tent."

Laurie hurried off, and Pug returned to his tent. Katala was feeding William from a bowl of stew from the night before. "I fear we have found another pot of trouble, love," Pug said. "The King is in camp, and he is madder than I dreamed possible. We must leave soon, for he has ordered Lyam imprisoned."

Katala looked shocked. "Where will we go?"

"I can manage to take us to Crydee, to Prince Arutha. I know the court of Castle Crydee as well as if there were a pattern there. I should have no trouble transporting us."

Laurie, Meecham, and Kulgan joined them a few minutes later, and Pug outlined his plan for escape. Kulgan shook his head. "You take the boy and Katala, Pug, but I must stay."

Meecham added, "And I."

Pug looked incredulous. "Why?"

"I served Lyam's father, and now I serve him. If the King tries to execute Lyam, there will be fighting. The Armies of the West will not stand idly by and watch Lyam hanged. The King has only the Royal Guard, and they will be easily defeated. Once that happens, it is civil war. Bas-Tyra will lead the Armies of the East. Lyam will need my aid."

Meecham said, "The issue won't be quickly decided. The Armies of the West are veteran, but they're tired. There's little spirit left in them. The Armies of the East are fresh, and Black Guy is the best general in the Kingdom. Lyam's unproved. It'll be a long struggle."

Pug understood what they were saying. "It may not reach that point, though. Brucal seems ready to follow Lyam's lead, but if he changes his mind? Who knows if Ylith, Tyr-Sog, and the others will follow Lyam without Yabon's lead?"

Kulgan sighed. "Brucal will not waver. He hates Bas-Tyra as much as Borric did, though for less personal reasons. He sees Guy's hand in every move to break the West. I think the Duke of Yabon would happily take Rodric's head, but even so, Lyam may submit rather than risk a civil war and lose the West to the Tsurani. We shall have to see what passes.

"Which is all the more reason you must go to Crydee, Pug. If Lyam dies, then Arutha is heir to the crown. Once begun, the King cannot stop the killing until Arutha is dead. Even Martin—whose claim would be blemished by his illegitimacy—and Carline would be hunted down and killed. Perhaps Anita as well. Rodric would not risk a western heir to the throne. Upon Lyam's death, the bloodletting will not end until either Rodric or Arutha sits the throne of the Kingdom uncontested. You are the most powerful magician in the Kingdom." Pug started to protest. "I know enough of the arts to know your skills from the events you related to us. And I remember your promise as a boy. You are capable of feats unmatched by any in our world. Arutha will have grave need of your aid, for he would not let his brother's death go unpunished. Crydee, Carse, and Tulan will march once the Tsurani have been dealt with. Others, especially Brucal, would join them. Then we would have civil war."

Meecham spat out of the tent. He froze, holding aside the tent flap for a moment, then said, "I think the argument is over. Look."

They joined him at the opening. None had the franklin's sharp eyesight, and at first they couldn't see what he was pointing out. Then slowly they recognized the cloud of dust hanging in the air, far to the southeast. It spread across the horizon for miles, a dirty brown ribbon that ran below the blue of the sky.

The franklin turned to look at the others. "The Armies of the East."

THEY STOOD near the command pavilion, among a group of LaMutian soldiers. With Laurie, Kulgan, Pug, and Meecham was Earl Vandros of LaMut, the former cavalry officer who had commanded the raid through the valley years ago, when they had first seen the rift. He had gained the title upon his father's death, less than a year after Pug's capture, and had proven to be one of the Kingdom's most able field commanders.

A company of nobles was riding up the hill toward the pavilion. The King and Brucal stood waiting for them. Next to each lord rode a standard-bearer, who held the banner of that noble. Vandros announced the name of each army represented. "Rodez, Timons, Sadara, Ran, Cibon, they're all here." He turned to Kulgan. "I doubt there are a thousand soldiers left between here and Rillanon."

Laurie said, "There is one whose banner I don't see. Bas-Tyra."

Vandros looked. "Salador, Deep Taunton, Pointer's Head . . . no, you are right. The golden eagle on black is not among the standards."

Meecham said, "Black Guy is no fool. He is already upon the throne of Krondor. Should Lyam be hanged, and Rodric fall in battle, it would be only a short step to the throne in Rillanon."

Vandros looked back at the gathering nobles. "Nearly the entire Congress of Lords is present. Should they return to Krondor without the King, then Guy would be King in short order. Many of these are his men."

Pug said, "Who is that under the banner of Salador? It is not Lord Kerus."

Vandros spat upon the ground. "It is Richard, formerly Baron of Dolth, now Duke of Salador. The King hung Kerus, and his family fled to Kesh. Now Richard rules the third most powerful duchy in the East. He is one of Guy's favorites."

When the nobles were assembled before the King, Richard of Salador, a red-faced bear of a man, said, "My liege, we are assembled. Where are we to camp?"

"Camp? We make no camp, my lord Duke. We ride!" He turned to Lord Brucal. "Marshal the Armies of the West, Brucal." The Duke gave the signal, and heralds ran through the camp, shouting the order to muster. The battle drums and war trumpets were shortly sounding throughout the western camp.

Vandros left to join his soldiers, and soon there were few observers nearby. Kulgan, Pug, and the others moved off to one side, keeping clear of the King's gaze.

The King said to the assembled nobles, "We have had nine years of the western commander's tender ways. I shall lead the attack that will drive the foe from out of our lands." He turned to Brucal. "In deference to your advancing years, my lord Duke, I am giving command of the infantry to Duke Richard. You will stay here."

The old Duke of Yabon, who was in the process of donning his armor, looked stung. He said nothing save, "Your Majesty," his tone cold and strained. He stiffly turned and entered the command tent.

The King's horse was brought, and Rodric mounted. A page handed up his crowned helm, and the King placed it upon his head. "The infantry shall follow as quickly as possible. Now we ride!"

The King spurred his horse down the hill, followed by the Royal Guard and the assembled nobles. When he was out of sight, Kulgan turned to the others and said, "Now we wait."

THE DAY GREW long. Every hour that passed was like a slowly unfolding day. They sat in Pug's tent, wondering what was occurring to the west.

The army had marched forward, under the King's banner, with drums and trumpets sounding. Over ten thousand horsemen and twenty thousand foot soldiers had advanced upon the Tsurani. There were only a few soldiers left in camp, the wounded and an orderly company. The quiet outside was unnerving after the almost constant camp noise of the previous day.

William had grown restless, and Katala had taken him outside to play. Fantus welcomed the opportunity to rest untroubled by his tireless playmate.

Kulgan sat quietly, puffing on his pipe. He and Pug passed the time by occasionally speaking of matters magical, but mostly were silent.

Laurie was the first to break the tension. He stood and said, "I can't take this waiting anymore. I think we should go to Lord Lyam and help decide what is to be done once the King returns."

Kulgan waved him back into his seat. "Lyam will do nothing, for he is his father's son and would not start a civil war, not here."

Pug sat absently toying with a dagger. "With the Armies of the East in camp, Lyam knows that an outbreak of fighting would hand the West to the Tsurani and crown to Bas-Tyra. He'll walk to the gibbet and put the rope around his own neck rather than see that."

"It's the worst kind of foolishness," countered Laurie.

"No," answered Kulgan, "not foolishness, minstrel, but a matter of honor. Lyam, like his father before him, believes that the nobility have a responsibility to give their lives' work, and their lives if need be, for the Kingdom. With Borric and Erland dead, Lyam is next in line for the throne. But the succession is unclear, for Rodric has not named an heir. Lyam could not bear to wear the crown if he would be thought a usurper. Arutha is another matter, for he would simply do what was expedient, take the throne—though he would not wish to—and worry about what was said of him when it was said."

Pug nodded. "I think that Kulgan has the right of things. I do not know the brothers as well as he, but I think it might have been a better thing had the order of their birthing been reversed. Lyam would make a good king, but Arutha would make a great one. Men would follow Lyam to their deaths, but the younger brother would use his shrewdness to keep them alive."

"A fair assessment," conceded Kulgan. "If there is anyone who could find a way out of this mess, it is Arutha. He has his father's courage, but he also has a mind as quick as Bas-Tyra's. He could weather the intrigues of court, though he hates them." Kulgan smiled. "When they were boys, we called Arutha the 'little storm cloud,' for when he got angry, he would turn to black looks and rumbles, while Lyam would be quick to anger, quick to fight, and quick to forget."

Kulgan's reminiscences were interrupted by the sound of shouting from outside. They jumped up and rushed out of the tent.

A blood-covered rider, in the tabard of LaMut, sped past them, and they ran to follow. They reached the command tent as Lord Brucal came out. The old Duke of Yabon said, "What news?"

"The Earl Vandros sends word. Victory!" Other riders could be heard approaching the camp. "We rode through them like the wind. The line on their east is breached, and the salient is rent. We broke them, isolating those in the salient, then wheeled to the west and rolled back those who sought to aid them. The infantry now holds fast, and the cavalry drives the Tsurani back into the North Pass. They flee in confusion! The day is ours!"

A wineskin was handed to the rider, who sounded as if his voice would fail. He tilted it over his face and let the wine pour into his mouth. It ran down his chin, joining the deeper red splattered over his tabard. He threw aside the wineskin. "There is more. Richard of Salador has fallen, as has the Earl of Silden. And the King has been wounded."

Concern showed on Brucal's face. "How does he fare?"

"Badly, I fear," said the rider, holding his nervous horse as it pranced around. "It is a grievous wound. His helm was cleaved by a broadsword after his horse was killed beneath him. A hundred died to protect him, for his royal tabard was a beacon to the Tsurani. He comes now." The rider pointed back the way he had come.

Pug and the others turned to see a troop of riders approaching. In the van rode a royal guardsman with the King held before him. The monarch's face was covered in blood, and he held to the saddle horn with his right hand, his other arm dangling limply at his side. They stopped before the tent, and soldiers helped the King from the horse. They started to carry him inside, but he said, in a weak and slurred voice, "No. Do not take me from the sun. Bring a chair so I may sit."

Nobles were riding up even as a chair was placed for the King. He was lowered into it and leaned back, his head lolling to the left. His face was covered with blood, and white bone could be seen showing through his scalp wound.

Kulgan moved to Rodric's side. "My King, may I attend?"

The King struggled to see who was speaking. His eyes seemed to lose focus for a moment, then became clear. "Who is speaking? The magician? Yes, Borric's magician. Please, I am in pain."

Kulgan closed his eyes, willing his powers to ease the King's suffering. He placed his hand upon Rodric's shoulder, and those nearby could see the ruler of the Kingdom visibly relax. "Thank you, magician. I feel more at ease." Rodric struggled to turn his head slightly. "My lord Brucal, please bring Lyam to me."

Lyam was in his tent, under guard, and a soldier was sent to bring him out. Moments later the young man knelt before his cousin. "My liege, your wound?"

Kulgan was joined by a Priest of Dala, who agreed with his assessment of the wound. He looked at Brucal and shook his head slowly. Herbs and bandages were brought, and the King was cared for. Kulgan left the priest to his ministrations and returned to stand where the others looked on. Katala had joined them, holding William in her arms. Kulgan said, "I fear it is a mortal wound. The skull is broken, and fluids seep through the crack."

In silence they watched. The priest stood to one side and began praying for Rodric. All the nobles, save those commanding the infantry, were now arrayed before the King. More horsemen could be heard riding into camp. They joined the others who stood watching and were told what had happened. A hush fell over the assembly as the King spoke.

"Lyam," he said in a faint voice. "I have been ill, haven't I?" Lyam said nothing, his face betraying conflicting emotions. He had little love for his cousin, but he was still the King.

Rodric ventured a weak smile. One side of his face moved only slightly, as if he could not control the muscles well. Rodric reached out with his good right hand, and Lyam took it. "I do not know what I have been thinking of late. So much of what has happened seems like a dream, dark and frightening. I have been trapped within that dream, but now I am free of it." Sweat appeared upon his brow, and his face was nearly white. "A demon has been driven from me, Lyam, and I can see much of what I have done was wrong, even evil."

Lyam knelt before his King. "No, my King, not evil."

The King coughed violently, then gasped as the attack subsided. "Lyam, my time grows short." His voice rose a little, and he said, "Brucal, bear witness." The old Duke looked on, his face an implacable mask. He stepped over next to Lyam and said, "I am here, Your Majesty."

The King gripped Lyam's hand, pulling himself a little more upright. His voice rose as he said, "We, Rodric, fourth of that name, hereditary ruler of the Kingdom of the Isles, do hereby proclaim that Lyam conDoin, our blood cousin, is of the royal blood. As oldest conDoin male, he is named Heir to the throne of our Kingdom."

Lyam shot Brucal an alarmed look, but the old Duke gave him a curt shake of his head, commanding silence. Lyam bowed his head, and his sorrow was heartfelt. He tightly gripped the King's hand. Brucal said, "So do I, Brucal, Duke of Yabon, bear witness."

Rodric's voice sounded faint. "Lyam, one boon do I ask. Your cousin Guy has done what he has done at my command. I grieve for the madness that drove me to have Erland deposed. I knew his going to the dungeon was his death warrant, and I did nothing to halt it. Have mercy on Guy. He is an ambitious man, but not an evil one."

The King then spoke of his plans for the Kingdom, asking that they be continued, though with more regard for the populace. He spoke of many other things: of his boyhood, and his sorrow that he had never married. After a time his speech became too slurred to understand, and his head fell forward upon his chest.

Brucal ordered guards to attend the King. They gently raised him and carried him inside. Brucal and Lyam entered the tent, while the other nobles waited outside. More new arrivals were gathering, and they were told the news. Nearly a third of the Armies of the Kingdom stood before the commander's pavilion, a sea of upturned faces extending down the hill. Each stood without speaking, waiting out the death watch.

Brucal closed the tent flap behind and shut out the red glow of the sunset. The Priest of Dala examined the King, then looked at the two dukes. "He will not regain consciousness, my lords. It is only a matter of time."

Brucal took Lyam by the arm and led him to one side. In a hushed whisper he said, "You must say nothing when I proclaim you Heir, Lyam."

Lyam pulled his arm from Brucal's grasp, fixing his gaze upon the old warrior. "You bore witness, Brucal," he whispered back. "You heard my father acknowledge Martin as my brother, legitimizing him. He is the oldest conDoin male. Rodric's proclamation of succession is invalid. It presumed I was the oldest!"

Brucal spoke quietly, but his words were ungentle. "You have a war to end, Lyam. Then, if you should accomplish that small feat, you have to take your father and Rodric back to Rillanon, to bury them in the tomb of your ancestors. From the day Rodric is interred, there will be twelve days of mourning, then on noon of the thirteenth, all the claimants for the crown will present themselves before the priests of Ishap, and the entire, bloody damn Congress of Lords. Between now and then you'll have plenty of time to decide what to do. But for now, you needs must be Heir. There is no other way.

"Have you forgotten Bas-Tyra? Should you dither, he'll be in Rillanon with his army a month before you. Then you'll have bitter civil war, boy. As soon as you agree to keep your mouth shut, I'm ordering my own trusted troops to Krondor, under royal seal, to arrest Black Guy. They'll toss Bas-Tyra into the dungeon before his own men can stop them—there'll be enough loyal Krondorians around to ensure that. You can have him held until you reach Krondor, then cart him off to Rillanon for the coronation, either your own or Martin's. But you must act, or by the gods, we'll have Guy's lackeys brewing civil war within a day of your naming Martin the true Heir. Do you understand?"

Lyam nodded silently. With a sigh he said, "But will Guy's men let him be taken?"

"Even the captain of his own guard will not stand against a royal warrant, especially countersigned by the representatives of the Congress of Lords. I shall guarantee signatures on the warrant," he said, clenching his gloved fist before his face.

Lyam was quiet for some time, then said, "You are right. I have no wish to visit trouble upon the Kingdom. I will do as you say."

The two men returned to the King's side and waited. Nearly another two hours passed before the priest listened at the King's chest and said, "The King is dead."

Brucal and Lyam joined the priest in a silent prayer for Rodric. Then the Duke of Yabon took a ring from Rodric's hand and turned to Lyam. "Come, it is time."

He held aside the tent flap, and Lyam looked out. The sun had set, and the night sky glittered with stars. Fires had been lit and torches brought, so that now the multitude appeared to be an ocean of firelight. Not one man in twenty had left, though they were all tired and hungry after the victory.

Brucal and Lyam appeared before the tent, and the old Duke said, "The King is dead." His face was stony, but his eyes were red-rimmed. Lyam looked pale but stood erect, his head high.

Brucal held something above his head. A glint of deep red fire reflected off the small object as it caught the torchlight. The nobles who stood close nodded in understanding, for it was the royal signet, worn by all the conDoin kings since Delong the Great had crossed the water from Rillanon to plant the banner of the Kingdom of the Isles upon the mainland shore.

Brucal took Lyam's hand and placed the ring upon his finger. Lyam studied the old and worn ring, with its device cut into the ruby, still undimmed by age. As he raised his eyes to behold the crowd, a noble stepped forward. It was the Duke of Rodez, and he knelt before Lyam. "Your Highness," he said. One by one the others before the tent, nobles of both East and West, knelt in homage, and like a wave rippling, all those assembled knelt, until Lyam alone was standing.

Lyam looked at those before him, overcome with emotion and unable to speak. He placed his hand upon Brucal's shoulder and motioned for them all to stand.

Suddenly the multitude was upon its feet, and the cheer went up, "Hail, Lyam! Long live the Heir!" The soldiers of the Kingdom roared their approval, doubly so, for many knew that hours ago the threat of civil war had hung over their heads. Men of both East and West embraced and celebrated, for a terrible future had been avoided.

Lyam raised his hands, and soon all were silent. His voice rang out over their heads, and all could hear him say, "Let no man rejoice this night. Let the drums be muffled and the trumpets blown low, for tonight we mourn a King."

BRUCAL POINTED at the map. "The salient is surrounded, and each attempt to break through to the main body has been turned back. We have isolated nearly four thousand of their soldiers there." It was late night. Rodric had been buried with what honor could be afforded in the camp.

There had been none of the trappings common to a royal funeral, but the business of war made it necessary. He had been quickly embalmed and buried in his armor next to Borric, on a hillside overlooking the camp. When the war was over, they would be returned to the tombs of their ancestors in Rillanon.

Now the young Heir looked over the map, gauging the situation in light of the latest communiqué from the front. The Tsurani held in the North Pass, at the entrance to the valley. The infantry had dug in before them, bottling up those in the valley, and isolating both the forces along the river Crydee and what was left of the salient.

"We have broken their offensive," said Lyam, "but it is a two-edged sword. We cannot attempt to fight on two fronts. We must also be ready should the Tsurani try to move against us from the south. I see no quick ending yet, in spite of our gains."

Brucal said, "But surely those in the salient will surrender soon. They are cut off, with little food or water, and cannot expect to be resupplied. In a matter of days they will be starving."

Pug interrupted. "Forgive me, Lord Brucal, but they will not."

"What can they gain by resisting? Their position is hopeless."

"They tie up your forces that would otherwise be attacking the main camp. Soon the situation in Tsuranuanni will be resolved enough for magicians to return from the Assembly. Then food and water can be transported in without interference. And each day they hold strengthens the Tsurani as reinforcements arrive from Kelewan. They are Tsurani and will gladly die rather than be taken captive."

Lyam asked, "Are they so honor bound to die, then?"

"Yes. On Kelewan they know only that captives become slaves. The idea of a prisoner exchange is unknown to them."

"Then we must bring all our weight to bear upon the salient at once," said Brucal. "We must crush them and free our soldiers to deal with other threats."

"It will prove costly," Lyam observed. "This time there will be no element of surprise, and they are dug in like moles. We could lose two men for each of theirs."

Kulgan had been sitting off to one side with Laurie and Meecham. "It is a tragedy that we have gained only a broadening of the fighting. And so soon after the Emperor's offer of peace."

Pug said, "Perhaps it is still not too late."

Lyam looked at Pug. "What do you mean? Kasumi must have already sent word that the peace was refused."

"Yes, but there may still be time to send word that there will be a new king who is willing to talk peace."

"Who will carry the message?" asked Kulgan. "Your life might be forfeit if you return to the Empire."

"We may be able to solve two problems at once. Your Highness, may I have your leave to promise the Tsurani in the salient safe passage to their lines?"

Lyam considered this. "I will, if I have their parole not to return for a year's time."

"I will go to them, then," said Pug. "Perhaps we can still end this war in spite of the calamities that have befallen us."

THE TSURANI GUARDS, nervous and alert, tensed at the sound of an approaching rider. "They come!" one shouted, and men seized weapons and hurried to the barricades. The southern earthworks were still intact, but here at the western edge of the former salient the pickets had thrown up a hasty barrier of felled trees and shallow trenches.

Bowmen stood ready, arrows notched, but the expected charge did not come. A single figure on horseback came into view. His hands were raised overhead, palms together in the sign for parley. And more, he wore the black robe.

The rider walked his horse to the edge of the barricade and asked, in perfect Tsurani, "Who commands here?"

A startled officer said, "Commander Wataun."

The rider snapped, "You forget your manners, Strike Leader." He took note of the colors and devices on the man's breastplate and helm. "Are the Chilapaningo so lacking in civility?"

The officer came to attention. "Your pardon, Great One," the man stammered. "It is only that you were unexpected."

"Bring Commander Wataun here."

"Your will, Great One."

The commander of the Tsurani salient came a short time later. He was a bandy-legged, barrel-chested old fighter, and Great One or not, his first concern was for the welfare of his troops. He looked at the magician suspiciously. "I am here, Great One."

"I have come to order you and your soldiers back to the valley."

Commander Wataun smiled ruefully and shook his head. "I regret, Great One, that I may not. Word of your exploits has been carried to us here, and that the Assembly has called your status into question. You may be no longer outside the law by now. If you had not come under a sign of parley, I would have you taken, though it would cost us dearly."

Pug felt a hot flush come to his cheeks. He had known it was likely the Assembly would cast him out, but to hear this still caused him pain. Ruefully, he knew that because of the training he had undergone, he would still feel a sense of loyalty to that alien place and would never fully feel at home in his native land.

With a sigh Pug said, "What then will you do?"

The Force Commander shrugged. "Hold our position. Die if we must."

"Then I will make you an offer, Commander. You must decide if it is a trick or not. Kasumi of the Shinzawai carried an offer from the Light of Heaven to the Midkemian King. It was an offer of peace. The King rejected it, but now there is to be a new king who is willing to make peace. I would ask you to carry word to the Holy City, to the Emperor, that Prince Lyam will accept peace. Will you do so?"

The commander considered. "If what you say is true, then I would be a fool to waste my men. What guarantees are you willing to make?"

"I give you my word, as a Great One—if that means anything still—that what I say is true. I also promise that your men will be given safe conduct back to the valley, on promise they return to the Empire for a year's time. And I will ride to the valley entrance, to your lines, as hostage. Is that enough?"

The commander thought it over for a moment as he surveyed his tired, thirsty troops. "I will agree, Great One. If it is the Light of Heaven's will that the war end, who am I to prolong it?"

"The Oaxatucan have long been known for their bravery. Let it be said they are also worthy of honor for their wisdom."

The commander bowed, then turned to his soldiers. "Pass the word. We march . . . home."

WORD THAT THE Emperor would agree to peace reached the camp four days later. Pug had given a message to Wataun to be carried through the rift. It bore the black seal of the Assembly, and no one would impede its swift delivery. It had been addressed to Fumita, asking him to carry word to the Holy City that the new King of the Realm would not require retribution but would accept peace.

Lyam had shown visible emotion when Pug had read the message. The Emperor himself would come through the rift in a month's time and would sign formal treaties with the Kingdom. Pug had felt close to tears when he read the news, which soon spread through the camp that the war was over. A great cheering could be heard.

Pug and Kulgan sat in the older magician's tent. For the first time in years they had been feeling something like their old relationship. Pug was finishing up a long explanation of the Tsurani system of instructing novices.

"Pug," said Kulgan around a long pull on his pipe. "It seems that now the war is over, we can return to the business of magicians. Only now it is you who are master, and I who would be student."

"There is much we may learn from each other, Kulgan. But I fear old habits die hard. I don't think I could ever get used to the idea of your being a student. And there are many things you are capable of that I still cannot do."

Kulgan seemed surprised. "Really? I would have thought my simple arts beneath your greatness."

Pug felt the old embarrassment from when he had been Kulgan's student. "You make sport of me yet."

Kulgan laughed. "Only a little, boy. And you are still a boy to one of my advancing years. It is not easy for me to see an indifferent apprentice become the most powerful magician of another world."

"Indifferent was the proper word for it. At first I only wanted to be a soldier. I think you knew that. Then when I had finally decided to devote myself to study, the invasion began." Pug smiled. "I think you felt sorry for me that day when I stood alone before the Duke's court, the only boy not called."

"That is partly true, though I was the first to sense the power in you.

And the judgment was borne out, no matter the amazing events required to bring your ability to fruition."

Pug sighed. "Well, the Assembly is nothing if not complete in its training. Once the power is detected, there are but two options, success or death. With all other thoughts banished, there is little to concern the student but the study of magic. Without that, I doubt I would ever have amounted to much."

Kulgan said, "I think not. Had the Tsurani never come, there would still have been a path to greatness for you to follow."

They sat and talked and were comforted by each other's presence. After a while they lit fires, for darkness was falling. Katala came to the tent to see if her husband was to join her and the boy at the celebration feast being given by King Lyam. She looked inside and saw the two of them lost in conversation.

She backed out and, with a faint smile on her lips, returned to her son.

31

▾▾

DECEPTIONS

TOMAS AWOKE WITH A START.

In the predawn darkness something strange called to him. He sat up, every sense extended, trying to recapture what had awakened him.

Aglaranna stirred next to him. Since his return from the confrontation with Martin over the Tsurani prisoners, he had been free of the alien dreams and the blind rages. He was no longer the boy from Crydee or the ancient Dragon Lord, but a new being possessing qualities of both.

She came awake and slowly reached out to touch his shoulder. The muscles were relaxed, free of the tension that marked his grappling with an ancient dream. She breathed a long sigh, then said, "Tomas, what is it?"

He reached up to cover her hand with his own. "I don't know. Something odd occurred a moment ago." He sat with his head slightly turned, as if listening to something distant. "A change . . . a shift in the pattern of things, perhaps."

The Elf Queen said nothing. Since becoming his lover she had grown used to his uncanny ability to sense events elsewhere, an ability unmatched by even the most gifted of the ancient Spellweavers. A remnant of his Valheru heritage, this awareness had come fully into bloom since he recovered his humanity. She thought it strange, yet reassuring, that his Valheru powers had become more pronounced and acute only since regaining his humanity. It was as if some force had conspired to keep them blunted until he possessed the wisdom to use them.

Tomas stopped listening. "It is something to the east, a mixture of rejoicing and a great sadness." His voice sounded thick with emotion. "An age is dying."

He rolled off the sleeping pallet and stood, powerful muscles revealed to Aglaranna's elven eyes in the dim light. He stood at the door of their sleeping chamber, looking out over Elvandar, listening to the sounds of the night. Everything appeared calm.

The scent of the forest, thick, sweet, and heady, was overlaid with the faint hints of aromas from last night's supper, and the smell of bread fresh from the oven for this morning's meal. Night birds sang, while day birds began their predawn warbling, and the sun prepared to rise in the east. The touch of cool air upon his naked skin was a caress to Tomas, and he felt more complete and at peace than he had ever been in his young life.

Aglaranna's arms went around his waist, and he felt her press tight against him. He could feel the beat of her heart as she held him close. "My lord, my love," she said, "return to our bed."

He turned within the circle of her arms and felt the warmth of her body against his. "There is something . . ." He gripped her close, but gently. "There is a feeling of hope."

She could feel his heat as his desire answered hers. "Hope. Would that it is true."

He looked down at her face, his senses as acute in the gloom as hers, drinking in the sight of her. "Never lose hope, my Queen."

He kissed her deeply, and whatever awakened him was quickly forgotten.

LYAM SAT QUIETLY in his tent. He was composing the message he would send to Crydee when a guard entered and announced the arrival of Pug and Kulgan. Lyam rose and greeted them, and when the guards left, indicated they should sit. "I am sorely in need of your wisdom." He sat back and waved at the parchments before him. "If Arutha is to reach us in time for the peace conference, these must leave today. But I have never been much for letters, and I also confess to great difficulty in sharing the events of the last week."

Kulgan said, "May I?" pointing to the letter.

Lyam waved consent, and the magician picked up the parchment and began to read. " 'To my beloved brother and sister: It is with the deepest sorrow I must tell you of our father's death. He was injured mortally in the great Tsurani offensive, leading a counterattack to rescue surrounded soldiers, mainly Hadati hillmen, auxiliaries to the garrison of Yabon. The Hadati sing his name and make sagas in his honor, such was his bravery. He passed thinking of his children, and his love for us all was undiminished.

" 'The King has also passed, and it has fallen to me to lead our armies. Arutha, I would have you here, for we now are at the war's end. The Emperor is willing to make peace. We shall meet in the north valley of the Grey Towers in twenty-nine days' time, at noon. Carline, I would have you take ship to Krondor with Anita, for there is much to be done there, and Princess Alicia will have need of her daughter. I will join you with Arutha once peace has been made. With love, and sharing in your sorrow, I am, your most loving brother, Lyam.' "

Kulgan was quiet for a moment, and Lyam said, "I thought you might be able to add something or other, to lend elegance to it."

Kulgan said, "I think you announced your father's passing with simplicity and gentleness. It is a fine message."

Lyam shifted uncomfortably in his chair. "There is so much yet to write. I have said nothing about Martin."

Kulgan took up a quill. "I will copy this again, for your pen is a bit strangled, Lyam." With a warm smile he added, "You were always one to prefer the sword to the quill. I'll add some instructions to the end, asking that Martin go to Krondor with your sister. Gardan and Fannon should also make the journey. And an honor company of the castle garrison. It will make it seem you mean to honor those who served so well in Crydee. Then you will have ample time to decide how to tell Martin what you must."

Pug shook his head sadly. "I only wish you could add Roland's name to that list." Since coming to the camp, he had learned of the Squire of Tulan's death. Kulgan had told him of what he knew of events in Crydee and elsewhere concerning his old friends over the last few years.

Lyam said, "Curse me for a fool! Carline has no idea you are back, Pug. You must add that, Kulgan."

Pug said, "I hope it will not come as too much of a shock."

Kulgan chuckled. "Not so much of a shock as discovering you've a wife and child."

Memories of his boyhood and his tempestuous relationship with the Princess returned, and Pug said, "I hope also she has outgrown some of the notions she held nine years ago."

Lyam laughed for the first time since his father's death, genuinely entertained by Pug's discomfort. "Rest assured, Pug. I've had many long communications with my brother and sister over the years, and I judge

Carline a greatly changed young woman from the girl you once knew. She was fifteen years old when last you saw her. Think of your own changes in the last nine years."

Pug nodded.

Kulgan finished his copy work and handed the document to Lyam. He read it and said, "Thank you, Kulgan. You've added just the right note of gentleness."

The tent flap opened and Brucal entered, his old, lined face animated with glee. "Bas-Tyra's fled!"

"How?" asked Lyam. "Our soldiers must still be a week from Krondor, maybe more."

The old Duke sat heavily in a chair. "We found a hidden cage of messenger pigeons, belonging to the late Richard of Salador. One of his men sent word to Guy of Rodric's death, and your being named Heir. We've questioned the fellow, a valet of Richard's. He's admitted to being one of Bas-Tyra's spies in Richard's court. Guy's fled the city, knowing one of your first acts as King will be to have him hung. My guess is he will make straight for Rillanon."

"I would have thought that would be the last place on Midkemia he would wish to be," remarked Kulgan.

"Black Guy is no man's fool, whatever else may be said of him. He'll be underground, no doubt, but you'll see his handiwork again before we are through. Until the crown is resting upon Lyam's head, Guy is still a power in the Kingdom."

Lyam looked troubled at the last remark, thinking of his father's dying declaration. Since Brucal's admonition to say nothing of Martin, everyone had spoken only of Lyam's coronation, nothing of Martin's possible claim to the crown.

Lyam let these disturbing thoughts pass by as Brucal continued speaking: "Still, with Bas-Tyra on the sly, most of our troubles are now behind. And with the war near an end, we can get back to the business of rebuilding the Kingdom. And I for one am glad. I am getting too old for much more of this nonsense of war and politics. I only regret I am without a son, so I could announce in his favor and retire."

Lyam studied Brucal with affectionate disbelief. "You'll never bow down gracefully, old war dog. You'll go to your deathbed scratching and clawing every inch of the way, and that day is years off."

"Who's talking of dying?" snorted Brucal. "I mean to hunt my hounds and fly my falcons, and do some fishing as well. Who knows? I may find some comely wench hearty enough to keep up with me, say about seventeen or eighteen years of age, and remarry and father a son yet. If that young fool Vandros ever gathers his wits about him and marries my Felinah, you just see how fast he'll become Duke of Yabon when I retire.

"Why she still waits for him is anybody's guess." He heaved himself up from his chair. "I am for a hot bath and some sleep before supper. By your leave?"

Lyam motioned he might leave and, when he was gone, said, "I will never get used to this business of people needing my permission to come and go."

Pug and Kulgan rose from their chairs. Kulgan said, "You had better, for everyone will ask it of you from now on. With your permission . . . ?"

Feigning disgust, Lyam motioned they might go.

THE COUNCIL SAT in assembly as Aglaranna took her place upon the throne. Besides the normal council, Martin Longbow was present, standing beside Tomas. When all were in place, Aglaranna said, "You have asked for council, Tathar. Now tell us what cause you bring before us."

Tathar bowed slightly to the Queen. "We of the council felt it time for an understanding."

"Of what, Tathar?" asked the Elf Queen.

Tathar said, "We have labored long to bring a peaceful, secure ending to this business of Tomas. It is known by all here that our arts were turned to calming the rage within, softening the might of the Valheru, so the young man who was transformed would not be overwhelmed in the course of time."

He paused, and Martin leaned close to Tomas. "Trouble."

Tomas startled him with a slight smile and a wink. Once more Martin was reassured that the mirthful boy he had known in Crydee was as much present in this young man as the Dragon Lord. "Everything will be fine," said Tomas in a whisper.

"We have," said Tathar, "come to judge this business done, for Tomas is no longer to be feared as an Old One."

Aglaranna said, "That is happy news indeed. But is this then cause for a council?"

"No, lady. Something else must also be laid to rest. For while we no longer fear Tomas, still we will not place ourselves under his rule."

Aglaranna stood, outrage clear upon her face. "Who dares to presume this? Has there been a single word from any to suggest that Tomas seeks to rule?"

Tathar stood firm before his Queen's displeasure. "My lady, you see with a lover's eyes." Before she could answer, he held up his hand. "Speak not sharp words with me, daughter of my oldest friend; I make no accusations. That he shares your bed is no one's concern save yourself. We begrudge you nothing. But he now has the means of a claim, and we would have the matter settled now."

Aglaranna paled, and Tomas stepped forward. "What means?" he said, his voice commanding.

Tathar looked slightly surprised. "She carries your child. Did you not know?"

Tomas was bereft of words. Conflicting feelings ran through him. A child! Yet he had not been told. He looked at Tathar. "How do you know?"

Tathar smiled, and there was no mockery in it. "I am old, Tomas. I can see the signs."

Tomas looked to Aglaranna. "It is true?"

She nodded. "I would not tell you until it was no longer possible to hide the truth."

He felt a stab of uncertainty. "Why?"

"To spare you any worry. Until the war is through, you must put your mind to nothing else. I would not burden you with other thoughts."

Tomas stood quietly for a moment, then threw back his head and laughed, a clear, joyous sound. "A child. Praise the gods!"

Tathar looked thoughtfully at Tomas. "Do you claim the throne?"

"Aye, I do, Tathar," Tomas said, a smile upon his face.

Calin spoke for the first time. "It is my inheritance, Tomas. You will have to contest with me for it."

Tomas smiled at Calin. "I will not cross swords with you, son of my beloved."

"If you seek to be King among us, then you must."

Tomas walked over to Calin. There had never been any affection between them, for more than the others, Calin had feared Tomas's potential threat to his people and now stood ready to fight if need be.

Tomas placed his hand upon Calin's shoulder and looked deeply into his eyes. "You are Heir. I speak not of being your King." He stepped away and addressed the council. "I am what you see before you, a being of two heritages. I possess the power of the Valheru, though I was not born to it, and my mind remembers ages long gone to dust. But I can remember a boy's memories and can again feel the joy in laughter and a lover's touch." He looked at the Elf Queen. "I claim only the right to sit beside my Queen, with your blessings, as her consort. I will take only what rule she and you give, nothing more. Should you give none, still I will remain at her side." Then, with firmness, he added, "But I will not stand down from this: our child shall have a heritage unblemished by a sinister birth."

There was a general murmur of approval, and Tomas faced Aglaranna. "If you will take me as husband?" he said in the ancient elven language.

Aglaranna sat with eyes gleaming. She looked to Tathar. "I will. Is there any who denies me the right?"

Tathar looked around at the other councillors. Seeing no dissension, Tathar said, "It is permitted, my lady."

Abruptly there was a shout of approval from the gathered elves, and soon others were coming to investigate the unusual display of activity in the council. They in turn joined in the celebration, for all knew of the Queen's love for the warrior in white and gold, and they judged him a fit consort.

Calin said, "You are wise in our ways, Tomas. Had you done otherwise, there would have been strife, or lingering doubt. I thank you for your prudence."

Tomas took his hand in a firm grip. "It is only just, Calin. Your claim is without question. When your Queen and I have journeyed to the Blessed Isles, then our child will be your loyal subject."

Aglaranna came to Tomas's side, and Martin joined them, to say, "Joy in all things." Tomas embraced his friend, as did the Queen.

Calin shouted for silence. When the noise had died, he said, "It is time for clear speaking. Let all know that what has been fact for years is now openly acknowledged. Tomas is Warleader of Elvandar, and Prince Consort to the Queen. His words are to be obeyed by all save the Queen. I, Calin, have spoken."

"And I, too, say this is true," echoed Tathar. Then the council bowed before the Queen and her husband-to-be.

Martin said, "It is well I shall leave Elvandar as happiness returns."

Aglaranna said, "You are leaving?"

"I fear I must. There is still a war, and I am still Huntmaster of Crydee. Besides," he said with a grin, "I fear young Garret is growing overly content to rest and partake of your largess. I must harry him along the trail before he gets fat."

"You'll stay for the wedding?" asked Tomas.

As Martin began to apologize, Aglaranna said, "The ceremony can be tomorrow."

Martin conceded. "One more day? I will be pleased."

Another shout went up, and Tomas could see Dolgan pushing through the crowd. When the dwarf chief stood before them, he said,

"We were not invited to the council, but when we heard the shouts, we came." Behind him Tomas and Aglaranna could see the other dwarves approaching.

Tomas placed his hand upon Dolgan's shoulder. "Old companion, you are welcome. You have come to a celebration. There is to be a wedding."

Dolgan fixed them both with a knowing smile. "Aye, and high time."

THE RIDER SPURRED his horse past the lines of Tsurani soldiers. He was still discomforted by the sight of so many of them passing to the east, and the recent enemy watched him ride by with guarded expressions as he headed toward Elvandar.

Laurie pulled in his horse near a large outcropping of rock where a Tsurani officer in black-and-orange armor supervised the passing soldiers. From his officer's plume and insignia, he was a Force Leader, surrounded by his cadre of Strike Leaders and Patrol Leaders. To the Force Leader he said, "Where lies the closest ford across the river?"

The other officers regarded Laurie with suspicion, but if the Force Leader felt any surprise at the barbarian's nearly perfect Tsurani, he did not show it. He inclined his head back the way his men marched from and said, "A short way from here. Less than an hour's march. Faster on your beast, I'm sure. It is marked by two large trees on either side of a clearing, above a place where the river falls a short way."

Laurie had no difficulty identifying the house colors the man wore, as it was one of the Five Great Families, and said, "Thank you, Force Leader. Honor to your house, son of the Minwanabi."

The Force Leader stood erect. He did not know who this rider was, but he was courteous, and that courtesy must be returned. "Honor to your house, stranger."

Laurie rode forward past the dispirited Tsurani soldiers plodding along the banks of the river. He found the clearing above the small falls and rode into the water. The river ran swiftly here, but the horse managed to cross without incident. Laurie could feel the spray from the falls as the wind blew it back in his direction. It felt cool and refreshing after the hot ride. He had been in the saddle since before daybreak and would not finish his ride until after night had fallen. By then he would be close enough to Elvandar to be intercepted by elven sentries. They would certainly be watching the Tsurani withdrawal with interest, and one could guide him to their Queen.

Laurie had volunteered to carry the message, for it was felt that the messenger would be less likely to encounter trouble if he could speak

Tsurani. He had been challenged three times during his ride, and each time he had explained his way past suspicious Tsurani officers. There might be a truce, but there was little trust yet.

When he was clear of the river, Laurie dismounted, for his horse was tired. He walked the animal to cool it off. He pulled the saddle from the mount's back and was rubbing him down with a brush carried in his saddlebags when a figure stepped out from among the trees. Laurie was startled, for the figure was not an elf. He was a dark-haired man with grey at the temples, dressed in a brown robe, and holding a staff. He approached the minstrel, without hurry and seemingly at ease. He stopped a few feet away and leaned on his staff. "Well met, Laurie of Tyr-Sog."

The man possessed a strange manner, and Laurie did not remember having met him before. "Do I know you?"

"No, but I have knowledge of you, troubadour."

Laurie edged closer to his saddle, where his sword lay. The man smiled and waved his hand in the air. Abruptly Laurie was filled with calm, and he stopped moving for his sword. Whoever this man was, he was obviously harmless, he thought.

"What brings you to the elven forest, Laurie?"

Without knowing why, Laurie answered. "I bring messages to the Elf Queen."

"What are you to say?"

"That Lyam is now Heir, and peace has been restored. He invites the elves and the dwarves to the valley in three weeks' time, for there will they seal the peace."

The man nodded. "I see. I am on my way to see the Elf Queen. I will carry word. You must have better things you can do with your time."

Laurie started to protest, but stopped. Why should he travel to Elvandar when this man was bound there anyway? It was a waste of time.

Laurie nodded. The man chuckled. "Why don't you rest here for the night? The sound of water is soothing, and there is little chance of rain. Tomorrow return to the Prince and tell him that you carried the message to Elvandar. You spoke with the Queen and Tomas, and they were agreed to the Prince's wishes. The dwarves of Stone Mountain will hear also. Then tell Lyam that the elves and the dwarves will come. He may rest assured, they will come."

Laurie nodded. What the man was saying made a great deal of sense. The stranger turned to leave, then said, "By the way, I think you'd best not mention our meeting."

Laurie said nothing, but accepted what the stranger said without question. After the man was gone, he felt a great sense of relief that he was on his way back from Elvandar and that his message had been received.

THE CEREMONY TOOK place in a quiet glade, with Aglaranna and Tomas exchanging vows before Tathar. No one else was there, as was the elven way, while they pledged their love. Tathar invoked the blessings of the gods and instructed them on their duty, one to the other.

When the ceremony was complete, Tathar said, "Now return to Elvandar, for it is time for feasting and celebration. You have brought joy to your people, my Queen and my Prince."

They rose from their kneeling positions and embraced. Tomas stepped back and said, "I would have this day remembered, beloved." He turned and cupped his hands around his mouth. In the ancient language of the elves he cried, "Belegroch! Belegroch! Attend us."

The sound of hooves pounding the earth could be heard. Then a small band of white horses raced into the glade, ran toward them, and reared in salute to the Elf Queen and her consort. Tomas leaped upon the back of one. The elf steed stood quietly, and Tathar said, "By no other way could you have shown so well that you are now one with us."

Aglaranna and Tathar mounted, and they rode back to Elvandar. When they came into sight of the tree-city, a great shout went up from the assembled elves. The sight of the Queen and her Prince Consort riding the elf steeds was, as Tathar said, a confirmation of Tomas's place in Elvandar.

The feasting went on for hours, and Tomas observed that the joy he felt was shared by everyone. Aglaranna sat next to him, for a second throne had been placed in the council hall, acknowledging Tomas's rank. Every elf who was not keeping watch over the outworlders came to stand before them, pledging loyalty and offering blessings on the union. The dwarves also offered their congratulations and joined in the festivities wholeheartedly, filling the glades of Elvandar with their boisterous singing.

Long into the night the celebration wore on. Suddenly Tomas stiffened. A chilled wind seemed to pass through him. Aglaranna gripped his arm, sensing something amiss. "Husband, what is it?"

Tomas stared into space. "Something . . . strange . . . like the other night: hopeful, but sad."

Abruptly there was a shout from the edge of the clearing below Elvandar. It cut through the sound of the celebration, but what was being said was unclear. Tomas rose, with Aglaranna at his side, and crossed to the edge of the huge platform. Looking down, he could see an elven scout below, clearly out of breath. "What is afoot?" Tomas shouted.

"My lord," came the reply, "the outworlders—they withdraw."

Tomas was rooted in place. Those simple words struck him like a blow. His mind couldn't comprehend the Tsurani's leaving after all these years of fighting. He shook off the feeling. "To what ends? Do they marshal?"

The scout shook his head. "No, my lord, they are not staging. They move slowly, without alarm. Their soldiers look dispirited. They break camp along every mile of the Crydee and turn east." The guard's upturned face showed an expression of stunned but joyful understanding. He looked at those nearby, then with a smile said simply, "They are leaving."

A shout of incredible joy went up, and many openly wept, for it seemed that at last the war was ended. Tomas turned and saw tears on the face of his wife. She embraced him, and they stood quietly for a moment. After a time the new Prince Consort of Elvandar said to Calin, who stood nearby, "Send runners to follow, for it may be a trick."

Aglaranna said, "Do you truly think so, Tomas?"

He shook his head. "I only wish to make sure, but something inside tells me this is truly the end. It was the hope of peace with the sadness of defeat mingled together that I felt."

She touched his cheek, and he said, "I will send runners to the Kingdom camp and inquire of Lord Borric what is happening."

She said, "If it is peace, he will send word."

Tomas looked at her. "True. We shall wait, then." He studied her face, centuries old, but still filled with the beauty of a woman in her first bloom. "This day will doubly be remembered as a day to celebrate."

NEITHER TOMAS NOR Aglaranna was surprised when Macros arrived in Elvandar, for they had ceased being amazed at the sorcerer after his first visit. Without ceremony he stepped forward from the trees surrounding the clearing and crossed toward the tree-city.

The entire court was assembled, including Longbow, when Macros came to stand before the Queen and Tomas. He bowed and said, "Greetings, lady, and to your consort."

"Welcome, Macros the Black," said the Queen. "Have you come to unravel the mystery of the outworlders' withdrawal?"

Macros leaned upon his staff and nodded. "I bring news." He seemed to consider his words carefully. "You should know that both the King and the Lord of Crydee are dead. Lyam is now Heir."

Tomas noticed Martin. The Huntmaster's face was drained of blood. His features remained impassive, but it was clear to Tomas that Martin was rocked by the news. Tomas turned toward Macros. "I knew not the King, but the Duke was a fine man. I am sorry for such news."

Macros went over to Martin. Martin watched the sorcerer, for while he had never met him, he knew him by reputation, having been told by Arutha of the meeting upon his island and by Tomas of his intervention during the Tsurani invasion of Elvandar. "You, Martin Longbow, are to go at once to Crydee. There you will sail with the Princesses Carline and Anita for Krondor." Martin was about to speak when Macros raised his hand; those of the court paused as if taking a breath. In a near-whisper Macros said, "At the last, your father spoke your name in love." Then his hand dropped, and all was as it had been.

Martin felt no alarm, but rather a sense of comfort from the sorcerer's words; he knew no one else had been aware of the brief remark.

Macros said, "Now hear more glad tidings. The war is over. Lyam and Ichindar meet in twenty days' time to sign a peace treaty."

A cheer went up in the court, and those above shouted the news to those below. Soon all of the elven forests echoed with the sound of rejoicing. Dolgan again entered the council, wiping his eyes. "What's this? Another celebration without us while I nap? You'll make me think we're no longer welcome."

Tomas laughed. "Nothing of the kind, Dolgan. Fetch your brethren and have them join our celebration. The war is over."

Dolgan took out his pipe and knocked the dottle from it, kicking the burned-out tabac over the edge of the platform. "Finally," he said as he opened his pouch. He turned away, as if intent upon filling his pipe, and Tomas pretended not to notice the wetness upon the dwarven chief's face.

ARUTHA SAT upon his father's throne, alone in the great hall. He held the message from his brother, which he had read several times, trying to understand that their father was truly gone. Grief sat heavy upon him.

Carline had taken the news well. She had gone to the quiet garden beside the keep, to be alone with her thoughts.

Thoughts ran riot through Arutha's mind. He remembered the first time his father had taken him hunting, then another time when he had come back from hunting with Martin Longbow and how proudly he had listened to his father exclaim over the large buck he had taken. He vaguely recalled the ache when he had learned of his mother's death, but it was a distant thing, dulled by time. The image of his father enraged in the King's palace suddenly came to him, and Arutha let out a slow sigh. "At least," he said to himself, "most of what you had wished has come to pass, Father. Rodric is gone and Guy is in disgrace."

"Arutha?" said a voice from the other side of the hall.

Arutha looked up: stepping from the shadows of the doorway came Anita, her satin-slippered feet making no sound as she crossed the stone floor of the hall.

Lost in his thoughts, he hadn't noticed her enter. She carried a small lamp, for evening had cast the hall into deep gloom. "The pages were reluctant to disturb you, but I couldn't see you sitting alone in the darkness," she said. Arutha felt pleasure at the sight of her and relief she had come. A young woman of uncommon sense and tender ways, Anita was the first person Arutha had known to see beneath his surface calm and dry humor. More than those who had known him since boyhood, she understood his moods and could lighten them, knowing the right words to comfort him.

Without waiting for him to answer, she said, "I have heard the news, Arutha. I am so terribly sorry."

Arutha smiled at her. "Not yet over your own grief at your father's passing, and you share mine. You are kind."

Word of Erland's death had come a week before on a ship from Krondor. Anita shook her head, her soft red hair moving in a rippling wave around her face. "Father was very ill for many years. He prepared us well for his death. It was a near-certainty when he was put into the dungeon. I knew that when we left Krondor."

"Still, you show strength. I hope I am able to bear up as well. There is so much to be done."

She spoke quietly. "I think you will rule wisely, Lyam in Rillanon, you in Krondor."

"I? In Krondor? I've avoided thinking about that."

She sat at his side, taking the throne Carline sat in when at her father's side in court. She reached over and placed her hand upon Arutha's, resting on the arm of the throne. "You must. After Lyam, you are Heir to the crown. The Prince of Krondor is the Heir's office. There is no one to rule there but you."

Arutha looked uncomfortable. "Anita, I have always assumed I would someday become Earl of some minor keep, or perhaps seek a career as an officer in one of the Border Barons' armies. But I had never thought to rule. I am not sure I welcome being Duke of Crydee, let alone Prince of Krondor. Besides, Lyam will marry, I am sure—he always caught the girls' eyes, and as King he'll certainly have his pick. When he has a son, the boy can be Prince of Krondor."

Anita shook her head firmly. "No, Arutha. There is too much work to be done now. The Western Realm needs a strong hand, your hand. Another Viceroy is not likely to win trust, for each lord will suspect any other who is named. It must be you."

Arutha studied the young woman. In the five months she had been at Crydee, he had come to care dearly for her, though he had been unable to express his feelings, finding words lacking when they were together. She was each day more a beautiful woman, less a girl. She was still young, which made him uncomfortable. With the war in progress, he had kept his thoughts away from their respective fathers' plans for a possible marriage, revealed to him that night aboard the *Sea Swift*. Now, with peace at hand, Arutha was suddenly confronted with that question.

"Anita, what you say is possibly true, but you also have a claim to the throne. Didn't you say your father's plan for our marriage was designed to bolster your claim to Krondor?"

She looked at him with large green eyes. "That was a plan to foil Guy's ambitions. It was to strengthen your father's or brother's claim to the crown should Rodric die heirless. Now you need not feel bound to those plans."

"Should I take Krondor, what will you do?"

"Mother and I have other estates. We can live quite well upon the revenues, I am sure."

Struggling with emotions within himself, Arutha spoke slowly. "I have not had time to weigh this in my mind. When I was last in Krondor, I learned how little I know of cities, and I know less than that of governing.

"You were raised for such undertakings. I . . . I was only a second son. My education is lacking."

"There are many able men, here and in Krondor, who will advise you. You have a good head for things, Arutha, the ability to see what must be done, and the courage to act. You will do well as Prince of Krondor."

She rose and leaned over to kiss his cheek. "There is time for you to decide how best to serve your brother, Arutha. Try not to let this new responsibility weigh too heavily upon you."

"I will try. Still, I would feel better knowing you were close by—you and your mother," he added with a rush.

She smiled warmly. "We will be close at hand should you have need of our advice, Arutha. We will likely stay upon our estate in the hills near Krondor, just a few hours' ride from the palace. Krondor is the only home I've known, and Mother has lived nowhere else since she was a girl. Should you wish to see us, you have but to command, and we will happily come to court. And should you wish to find respite from the burdens of office, you will be a welcome guest."

Arutha smiled at the girl. "I suspect I will be visiting with regularity, and I hope I do not wear out my welcome."

"Never, Arutha."

TOMAS STOOD ALONE on the platform, watching the stars through the branches above. His elven senses informed him someone had come up behind. With a nod he greeted the sorcerer. "I am but twenty-five years in this life, Macros, though I bear memories of ages. All my adult life I have been waging war. It seems a dream."

"Let us not turn this dream into a nightmare."

Tomas studied the sorcerer. "What do you mean?"

Macros said nothing for a time, and Tomas awaited his words with patience. At last the sorcerer spoke. "There is this thing which must be done, Tomas, and it has fallen to you to finish this war."

"I like little the tone of your words. I thought you said the war was finished."

"On the day of the meeting between Lyam and the Emperor, you must marshal the elves and dwarves to the west of the field. When the monarchs meet in the center of the field, then will there be treachery."

"What treachery?" Tomas's face showed his anger.

"I may say little more, save that when Ichindar and Lyam are seated, you must attack the Tsurani with all your forces. Only this way can Midkemia be saved from utter destruction."

A look of suspicion crossed Tomas's face. "You ask much for one unwilling to give more."

Macros stood tall, holding his staff to one side, like a ruler his scepter. His dark eyes narrowed, and his brows met over his hooked nose. His voice stayed soft, but his words were hot with anger. Even Tomas felt something akin to awe in his presence.

"More!" he said, biting off the word. "I gave you all, Valheru! You are here by dint of my actions over many years. More of my life than you will know has been given to preparing for your coming. Had I not bested, then befriended Rhuagh, you would never have survived in the mines of Mac Mordain Cadal. It was I who prepared the armor and sword of Ashen-Shugar, leaving them with the Hammer of Tholin and my gift to the dragon, so that centuries later you would discover them. It was I who set your feet upon the path, Tomas. Had I not come to aid you, years past, Elvandar would now be ashes. Do you think Tathar and the other Spellweavers of Elvandar were the only ones to work on your behalf? Without my aid over these last nine years, you would have been destroyed utterly by the dragon's gifts. No mere human could have withstood such ancient and powerful magic without the intervention only I could make. When you were swept along upon your dream quests to the past, it was I who guided you back to the present, I who returned you to sanity." The sorcerer's voice rose. "It was I who gave you the power to influence Ashen-Shugar! You were my tool!" Tomas stepped back before the controlled fury of the sorcerer's words. "No, Tomas, I have not given you much. I have given you everything!"

For the first time since donning the armor in Mac Mordain Cadal, Tomas felt fear. In the most basic fiber of his being he suddenly was aware of how much power the sorcerer possessed, and that should Macros choose, he could brush him aside like a nettlesome insect. "Who are you?" he asked quietly, controlled fear in his voice.

Macros's anger vanished. He leaned once again upon his staff, and Tomas's fears fled and with them all memory of his fears. With a chuckle, Macros said, "I tend to forget myself upon occasion. My apologies." Then he grew serious once again. "I do not ask this thing from any demand of gratitude. What I have done is done, and you owe me nothing. But know this: both the creature called Ashen-Shugar and the boy called Tomas shared an abiding love of this world, each in his own way, incomprehensible to each other as that love was. You possess both aspects of the love of land: the desire of the Valheru to protect and control, and the desire of the keep boy to nurture and nourish. But should you fail in this task I set before you, should you stint in resolve when the moment is nigh, then know with dread certainty, this world upon which we stand shall be lost, lost beyond recalling. This on my most holy oath is the truth."

"Then I shall do as you instruct."

Macros smiled. "Go then to your wife, Prince Consort of Elvandar, but when it is time, marshal your army. I go to Stone Mountain, for Harthorn and his soldiers will join you. Every sword and war hammer is needed."

"Will they know you?"

Macros gazed at Tomas. "Indeed they will know me, Tomas of Elvandar, never doubt."

"I shall gather all the might of Elvandar, Macros." A grim note entered his voice. "And for all time, we will put an end to this war."

Macros waved his staff and vanished. Tomas waited alone for a time, struggling with a newfound fear, that this war would last forever.

32

▾▾

BETRAYAL

THE ARMIES STOOD FACING ONE ANOTHER.

Seasoned veterans eyed each other across the open valley floor, not quite ready to feel at ease in the presence of an enemy they had fought for nine years and longer. Each side was composed of honor companies, representing the nobles of the Kingdom and clans of the Empire. Each numbered in excess of a thousand men. The last of the Tsurani invasion army was now entering the rift, returning home to Kelewan, leaving only the Emperor's honor detachment behind. The Kingdom army was still camped at the mouths of the two passes into the valley and would not leave the area until the treaty was finalized. There was still a cautious aspect to the newfound trust.

On the Kingdom side of the valley, Lyam sat astride a white warhorse, awaiting the Emperor's arrival. Nearby the nobles of the Kingdom, their armor cleaned and polished, sat their horses. With them were the leaders of the Free Cities militia and a detachment of Natalese Rangers.

Trumpets sounded from across the field, and the Emperor's party could be seen emerging from the rift. Imperial banners fluttered in the breeze as the procession moved to the head of the Tsurani contingent.

Awaiting the Tsurani herald, who was walking across the several hundred yards that separated the opposing monarchs, Prince Lyam turned to regard those who sat on horseback nearby. Pug, Kulgan, Meecham, and Laurie were accorded their position of honor by dint of their service to the Kingdom. Earl Vandros and several other officers who had distinguished themselves were also close by. Next to Lyam sat Arutha, astride a chestnut war-horse, who pranced in place out of high spirits.

Pug looked around, feeling a giddy sensation at the sight of all the symbols of two mighty nations with whose fates he had been so closely tied. Across the open field he could see the banners of the powerful families of the Empire, all familiar to him: the Keda, the Oaxatucan, the Minwanabi, and the rest. Behind him were the fluttering banners of the Kingdom, all the duchies from Crydee in the west to Ran in the east.

Kulgan noticed his former student's far-off gaze and tapped him on the shoulder with the long staff he was holding. "Are you all right?"

Pug turned. "I'm fine. I was just a little overwhelmed for a moment, engulfed in memories. It seems strange to see this day, in a way. Both sides of the war were bitter enemies, and yet I have ties with both lands. I find I have feelings I've yet to explore."

Kulgan smiled. "There will be much time for introspection later. Perhaps Tully and I can offer some aid." The old cleric had accompanied Arutha on his brutal ride, not wishing to miss the peace meeting. The fourteen days in the saddle had taken a toll, however, and now he lay ill in Lyam's tent. It had taken a command from Lyam to keep him there, for he had been determined to accompany the royal party.

The Tsurani herald reached a place before Lyam. He bowed low, then said something in Tsurani. Pug rode forward to translate. "He says, 'His Most Imperial Majesty, Ichindar, ninety-one times Emperor, Light of Heaven, and ruler of all the nations of Tsuranuanni, sends greetings to his brother monarch, His most Royal Highness, Prince Lyam, ruler of the lands known as the Kingdom. Will the Prince accept his invitation to join with him at the center of the valley?' "

Lyam said, "Tell him that I return his greetings and will be pleased to meet with him at the appointed place." Pug translated, with the appropriate Tsurani formality, and the herald bowed low and returned to his own lines.

They could see the imperial litter being carried forward. Lyam signaled that his escort should accompany him, and they rode out to meet the Emperor in the center of the valley floor. Pug, Kulgan, and Laurie rode with the honor escort; Meecham waited with the soldiers.

The Kingdom horsemen reached the designated place first and waited while the imperial retinue approached. The litter was born on the backs of twenty slaves, chosen for their uniformity in height and appearance. Their thick muscles bunched under the strain of carrying the heavy, gold-encrusted litter. Gauzy white curtains hung from gold-inlaid wooden supports, decorated with gems of great value and beauty. The rare metal and gems caught the sun's rays and glittered brightly.

Behind the litter marched representatives of the most powerful families in the Empire, clan Warchiefs. There were five of them, one for each family eligible to elect a new Warlord.

The litter was lowered, and Ichindar, Emperor of the nations of Tsuranuanni, stepped out. He was dressed in golden armor, its value immeasurable by Tsurani standards. Upon his head was a crested helm covered in the same metal. He walked over to Lyam, who had dismounted to meet him. Pug, who was to translate, dismounted and walked to stand to one side of the two rulers. The Emperor nodded curtly to him.

Lyam and Ichindar studied one another, and both seemed surprised at the other's youthfulness. Ichindar was only three years older than the new Heir.

Lyam began by welcoming the Emperor with friendship and the hope of peace. Ichindar responded in kind. Then the Light of Heaven stepped forward and extended his right hand. "I understand this is your custom?"

Lyam took the hand of the Emperor of Tsuranuanni. Suddenly the tension broke, and cheers went up from both sides of the valley. The two young monarchs were smiling, and the handshake was vigorous and firm.

Lyam said, "May this be the beginning of a lasting peace for our two nations."

Ichindar answered, "Peace is a new thing to Tsuranuanni, but I trust we will learn quickly. My High Council is divided over my actions. I hope the fruits of trade and the prosperity gained by learning from one another will unify attitudes."

"That is my wish also," said Lyam. "To mark the truce, I have ordered a gift prepared for you." He signaled, and a soldier trotted out from the Kingdom lines, leading a beautiful black war-horse behind. A black saddle set with gold was upon its back, and from the saddle horn hung a broadsword, with a jeweled scabbard and hilt.

Ichindar regarded the horse with a little skepticism, but was awed by the workmanship of the sword. He hefted the great blade and said, "You honor me, Prince Lyam."

Ichindar turned to one of his escorts, who ordered a chest carried forward. Two slaves set it before the Emperor. It was carved ngaggi wood, finished to a deep and beautiful shine. Scrollwork surrounded bas-relief carvings of Tsurani animals and plants. Each had been cleverly stained in lighter and darker tones, in nearly lifelike detail. In itself it was a fine gift, but when the lid was thrown back, a pile of the finest cut stones, all larger than a man's thumb, glistened in the sun.

The Emperor said, "I would have difficulty justifying reparation to the High Council, and my position with them is not the best at present, but a gift to mark the occasion they cannot fault. I hope this will repair some of the destruction my nation has caused."

Lyam bowed slightly. "You are generous and I thank you. Will you join me for refreshments?" The Emperor nodded, and Lyam gave a command for a pavilion to be erected. A dozen soldiers galloped forward and dismounted. Several carried poles and bolts of material. In short order a large, open-sided pavilion was erected. Chairs and a table were set up under the covering. Other soldiers brought wine and food and placed them upon the table.

Pug pulled out a large cushioned chair for the Emperor, as Arutha did for his brother. The two rulers sat, and Ichindar said, "This is quite a bit more comfortable than my throne. I must have a cushion made."

Wine was poured, and Lyam and the Emperor toasted each other. Then a toast to peace was offered. Everyone present drank it.

Ichindar turned to Pug. "Great One, it seems that this meeting will prove more salubrious to those around than our last."

Pug bowed. "I trust so, Your Imperial Majesty. I hope I am forgiven my disruption of the Imperial Games."

The Emperor frowned. "Disruption? It was closer to destruction."

Pug translated for the others while Ichindar smiled ruefully in appreciation. "This Great One has done many innovative things in my Empire. I fear we will not see the end of his handiwork long after his name is forgotten. Still, that is a thing of the past. Let us concern ourselves with the future."

The honored guests from both camps stood in the pavilion as the two monarchs began their discussion of the best way to establish relationships between the two worlds.

TOMAS WATCHED the pavilion. Calin and Dolgan waited on either side. Behind them more than two thousand elves and dwarves stood ready. They had entered the valley through the North Pass, moving by the Kingdom forces that were gathered. They had circled around the clearing, gathering in the woods to the west, where they were accorded a clear view of the proceeding.

Tomas said to both his comrades, "I see little to indicate trickery."

A second dwarf, Harthom of Stone Mountain, walked over to them. "Aye, elfling. All looks peaceful enough, in spite of the sorcerer's warning."

Abruptly there was a heat shimmer across the field, as if their vision swam and flickered; then Tomas and the others could see Tsurani soldiers drawing weapons.

Tomas turned to those behind and said, "Be ready!"

A KINGDOM SOLDIER rode up to the pavilion. The Tsurani lords looked at him with distrust, for so far the only soldiers who neared the pavilion were those serving refreshments.

"Your Highness!" he shouted. "Something strange is occurring."

"What?" said Lyam, disturbed at the man's excitement.

"From our position we can see figures moving through the woods to the west."

Lyam rose and saw figures near the edge of the trees. After a moment, while Pug translated the exchange for the Emperor, Lyam said, "That would be the dwarves and elves." He turned to Ichindar. "I sent word to the Elf Queen and the dwarven Warleaders of the peace. They must be now approaching."

The Emperor came over to Lyam and studied the woods. "Why are they remaining in the trees? Why do they stay hidden?"

Lyam turned to the horseman. "Ride and bid those in the trees join us."

The guard obeyed. When he was halfway to the woods, a shout went up from the trees, and green-clad elves and armored dwarves came running forward. Battle chants and cries filled the air. Ichindar looked at the onrushing figures in confusion. Several of his companions drew weapons. A soldier from the Tsurani lines dashed to the pavilion and cried, "Majesty, we are undone. It is a trap!"

Every Tsurani backed away, swords drawn. Ichindar shouted, "Is this how you treat for peace? Mouthing pledges while you plot treachery?"

Lyam didn't understand his words, but the tone made the meaning clear. He gripped Pug's arm and said, "Tell him I know nothing of this!"

Pug tried to raise his voice over the commotion in the pavilion, but the Tsurani nobles were backing away, surrounding the Light of Heaven, while soldiers were rushing forward from the Tsurani lines to join in protecting Ichindar.

Lyam shouted, "Back! Back to our own lines!" as the Tsurani soldiers approached. The Midkemians quickly mounted.

Pug heard Ichindar's voice carrying over the noise: "Treacherous one, you show your true nature. Never will Tsuranuanni deal with those without honor. We will grind your Kingdom into dust!"

Sounds of fighting erupted as the elves and dwarves clashed with the Tsurani soldiers. Lyam and the others raced back to their own soldiers, who sat waiting to join the fight. As Lyam reined up, Lord Brucal said, "Shall we advance, Highness?"

Lyam shook his head. "I will not be a party to treachery."

He regarded the scene before him. The elves and dwarves were pushing the Tsurani back toward the rift machine. The Emperor and his guards were circling, avoiding the fighting, keeping the thousand honor guards between the attackers and themselves. Runners could be seen disappearing into the rift.

A moment later Tsurani soldiers erupted from the rift. They rushed forward to engage the attackers. The collapsing Tsurani line held, then started to push the elves and dwarves back.

Arutha moved his horse next to Lyam's. "Lyam! We must attack. Soon the elves and the dwarves will be overwhelmed. There are ten thousand more Tsurani on the other side of that rift, only a step away. If you ever hope to end this bloody war, we must capture and hold that machine."

Pug forced his own horse to the other side of Lyam's mount. "Lyam!" he shouted. "You must do as Arutha says."

Doubt still held the young Heir. Pug raised his voice even louder. "Understand this: for nine years you've faced only a part of the might within the Empire, only those soldiers belonging to the clans of the War Party. Until now you had many hidden allies, blocking a major effort against the Kingdom. But now this betrayal has inflamed the one man who can command unquestioned obedience from all the clans of the Empire. Ichindar can order every clan of Tsuranuanni to marshal!

"You've never faced more than thirty thousand warriors along all fronts. By tomorrow those thirty thousand can be back in this valley. In a week double again that number. Lyam, you have no idea how vast his powers are. Within a year he can send a million men and a thousand magicians against us! You must act!"

Lyam sat stiffly, the bitterness of the moment clearly showing in his expression. "Can you aid us?"

"I may, should you open a path for me to reach the machine, but I don't know if I have the ability to shut off the rift. Other powers I have, but even if I overcame my conditioning and could oppose the Empire and I killed every man on this field, it would avail little, for a greater host would still be but a step away."

Lyam gave a curt nod. Slowly he faced Arutha. "Send gallopers to the North and South passes. Call all the Armies of the Kingdom to arms." Arutha wheeled and shouted the order, and riders sped away toward both passes.

Lyam looked back toward Pug. "If you can help, do so, but not until the way is safe. You are the only master of your arts upon this world." Indicating Laurie, Meecham, and Kulgan, he said, "Keep them from the fighting as well, for they have no part in it. Stay back, and should we fail, use your arts to go to Krondor. Carline and Anita must be taken to the east, to their grand-uncle Caldric, for the West will surely be Tsurani." He drew his sword and gave the order to advance.

The thousand horsemen lumbered forward, a moving wall of steel gaining momentum as officers shouted orders, keeping the columns orderly. Then Lyam signaled the charge, and the lines became ragged as horsemen rushed across the clearing toward the Tsurani. The Tsurani heard the rumbling of cavalry, and many fell back from the elves and dwarves to form a shield wall. Pug, Laurie, Meecham, and Kulgan watched while the Kingdom horsemen collided with it. Horses and men screamed as long spears bent and broke. The shield wall wavered as men died, but others leaped forward to take their places, and the Kingdom host was turned back. Lyam re-formed his troops and charged again, this time breaking through the shields.

Pug could see the right side of the Tsurani forces rolled back before the horsemen, but the Emperor himself rallied the balance of his soldiers, and the center of the line held. Even at this distance Pug could see the Tsurani nobles entreating the Emperor to flee.

THE EMPEROR STOOD with sword drawn, shouting orders. He refused to leave the field. He was forming his men into a tight circle protecting the rift machine, so others could return to this valley from Kelewan. He looked and saw that soldiers were now rushing forth from the rift in greater numbers. Soon there would be enough of them to destroy the King's small force.

A faint trembling could be felt beneath his feet, then one of the Tsurani lords pointed behind the Emperor. Ichindar saw hundreds of horsemen erupting from the trees to the north. The northern cavalry units were the first to answer Lyam's call. The Emperor directed newly arriving soldiers to the north line to meet the new threat.

A shout from the left caused him to turn. A tall warrior, clad in white and gold, was cutting a swath through the Tsurani guards, heading straight for the Light of Heaven. All the Tsurani lords rushed to cut him off. A clan Force Leader stood nearby. He raced to the Emperor and shouted, "Your Majesty, you must leave. We can hold only a short while. If you are lost, the Empire is without a heart, and the gods will turn their faces from us."

The Emperor tried to push past him, as the gold-and-white giant cut down another Tsurani lord. The officer said, "May heaven understand," and struck Ichindar across the back of the head with the flat of his sword. The Emperor crumpled to the ground, and the Force Leader shouted for soldiers to carry him through the rift. "The Emperor is overcome! Take him to safety!" Without question the soldiers picked up the supreme ruler and conveyed him to the machine.

A Strike Leader rushed to the Force Leader's side, shouting, "Sir, all our lords have been killed!" The Force Leader saw that the tall warrior was being forced back by the sheer number of Tsurani soldiers intercepting him, but not until after he had butchered every senior Warchief who had accompanied the Emperor. A quick glance informed the Force Leader the Emperor was near safety, as the guards carrying Ichindar disappeared from view at the far side of the rift. More soldiers came streaming through from the near side of the rift. Seeing no more time to waste, the Force Leader said, "I will act as Force Commander! You are acting Subcommander. More men to the north!" The man rushed off to place more men along the north line as the cavalry from the North Pass bore down in a mad gallop.

The attackers from the north hit the Tsurani position with a thunderous crash. The hastily erected shield wall wavered, but finally held. The Force Commander looked about and prayed they could hold until sufficient reinforcements arrived.

PUG AND HIS three companions could see the northern elements of the Kingdom army hit the shield wall. Spears shattered and horses fell, while screaming men were trampled underfoot. The wall still held, and the Kingdom forces withdrew to re-form for another charge. Lyam's command was being pushed back, and he ordered a withdrawal, so that he could coordinate his attack with the one from the north. The elves and dwarves under Tomas were among the Tsurani, to the west, and were causing them the most difficulty, though they also were being slowly repulsed.

As the horsemen pulled back, the Tsurani's attention was turned to the elves and dwarves. Those behind the north and south shield positions left their posts to lend support to their comrades on the west flank.

Seeing this, Meecham observed, "If the elves don't withdraw, the Tsurani will overwhelm them." As if he had been heard, the four observers could see the western confrontation broken off. Elves and dwarves retreated under cover of elven bowmen.

Kulgan said to Pug, "This respite serves to strengthen the Tsurani." They could see the flood of Tsurani soldiers coming through the rift. "If Lyam does not reach the machine after the next charge, the Tsurani will gain in strength as we weaken."

Pug said, "He can bottle them up only if he can station bowmen at the entrance to the rift. A steady stream of bowfire through it should keep them back long enough to erect some sort of barrier. Then we might be able to render it inoperative."

Laurie said, "Can't it be destroyed? The other way is fraught with risk."

Pug sat quietly for a moment. "I don't know if my powers are sufficient to destroy the rift. But I think it is time to try."

As he started to spur his horse, a voice behind rang out: "No!"

They all turned and saw a brown-clad figure standing, staff in hand, where no one had been a moment earlier. "Even your powers are not equal to the task, Great One."

"Macros!" Kulgan exclaimed.

Macros smiled a bitter smile. "As I foretold, I am here when the need is greatest, the hour most grave."

Pug said, "What is to be done?"

"I will close the rift, but I have need of your aid." He returned his attention to Kulgan. "I see you still have the staff I gave you. Good. Dismount."

Pug and Kulgan got down from their mounts. Pug had forgotten that Kulgan's ever present staff had been the one Macros had given him.

Macros went over to stand before Kulgan. "Plant the end of the staff firmly in the ground." He turned and handed the staff he carried to Pug. "This staff is twin to that one. Hold it tightly, and never for an instant release your hold, if you have any hope of surviving our task." He regarded the conflict a short distance away. "It is almost the appointed hour, but not quite. Listen carefully, for time grows short." He looked at Pug, then Kulgan. "When this is all over, if the rift is destroyed, then return to my island. There you will find explanations for everything that has occurred, though perhaps not to your full satisfaction." Again there was a bitter smile. "Kulgan, if you have any hope of seeing your former pupil again, hold to that staff with all the strength you possess. Keep Pug in your mind, and never let the staff break contact with Midkemian soil. Is that understood?"

Kulgan said, "But what of yourself?"

Macros's tone was harsh. "My safety is my own concern. Trouble not yourself about me. My place in this drama was as foreordained as your own. Now watch."

They returned their attention to the battle. The northern elements of the Kingdom army charged, and Lyam and Tomas gave orders for their own units to join in the attack. The horsemen hit the shield walls again, and the Tsurani lines broke. For a moment the Kingdom cavalry was in command of the field, and the Tsurani collapsed inward. Then, as the advantage of the charge was offset by the milling swarm of foot soldiers who cut horses out from under riders, or conspired to pull horsemen to the ground, the balance returned. A sea of battling figures could be seen around the rift machine. There was no organization, and little discipline. Men fought to survive, not for any gain in position. The sounds of metal clashing against hardened wood and hides rang through the valley. Everywhere the onlookers turned their attention, blood flowed, and the sound of death was terrible.

Macros looked at Pug and said, "Now is the time. Walk with me."

Pug walked behind the brown-robed sorcerer. He held tightly to Macros's staff, for he believed the sorcerer's warning that it was his only hope of surviving what lay before them. They walked through the battle, as if some agent were protecting them. Several times a soldier turned to strike, only to be intercepted by one from the other side. Horses would be ready to trample them only to wheel away at the last instant. It was as if a path opened before them and closed behind.

They approached what was left of the Tsurani line. A shield holder fell to a horseman's lance. They stepped over the fallen body and entered the small, relatively calm circle around the rift. Soldiers were still pouring forth from the rift, and the circle was widening. Macros and Pug mounted the platform to the far side of the rift, while soldiers rushed out of the near side. The soldiers seemed oblivious to the two magicians.

Macros stepped into the void of the rift. Pug entered behind. Instead of the expected emergence into Kelewan, they hung in a colorless place. There was little sensation of direction. The place was without light, but not dark, only various shades of grey. Pug found himself alone, with only the sound of his heart beating in his ear to reassure him that existence had not ceased. Softly he said, "Macros?"

Macros's voice came to him: "Here, Pug."

"I cannot see you."

A chuckle was heard. "No, for there is no light. What you see is a faint illusion granted by my arts so you might have some point of reference here. Without ample preparation, even your vaunted powers would avail you little in keeping your sanity, Pug. Simply accept that the human mind is poorly equipped to deal with this place."

"What is this place?"

"This is the place between. Here the gods struggled during the Chaos Wars, and here we shall do our work."

"Men are dying, Macros. We should hurry."

"Here there is no time, Pug. Relative to those who battle, we are frozen in an instant. We could grow old and die, and not a full second would pass upon the battlefield.

"But we must still be quickly about our task. Even I could not do this without spending a bit of energy to keep us alive, energy we'll need to finish this business. We dare not tarry long, but there are a few things I would say to you. I have waited a long while for you to fulfill your promise. I could not close the rift without your aid."

Pug spoke, though his senses rebelled at the grey landscape on all sides and the disembodied voice that seemed a short distance away from him. "It was you who turned the rift aside, when the Stranger came and the Enemy sought to reclaim the nations of Tsuranuanni. Surely that took awesome power."

He could hear the sorcerer chuckle. "You remember that detail? Well, I was younger then." As if he knew it was an unsatisfactory answer, Macros added, "Then the rift was a wild thing, created by the wills of those who stood atop the towers of the Assembly. I only turned it to another place, balking the Enemy's design, and that at great risk. Now this rift is a controlled thing, firmly anchored in Kelewan, managed by a machine. That which controls it, many intricate spells, keeping it in harmony with Midkemia, keeps me from manipulating it. All I may do is end it, but for that I need help.

"Before we end this particular drama, I would say this to you: you will understand most things after you reach my island. But one thing above all I ask of you to bear in mind as you hear my message. Please remember I did what I did because it was my fate. I would ask you to think of me kindly."

While he could not see the sorcerer, Pug felt his presence close by. He started to speak, but was interrupted by Macros's voice. "When I am done, use whatever shred of energy you have left to will yourself to Kulgan. The staff will aid you, but you must bend all your efforts to that task. If you fail, you will perish."

It was Macros's second warning, and Pug felt dread for the first time in years. "What of yourself?"

"Take care of yourself, Pug. I have other concerns."

There came a sensation of change, as if the fabric of nothingness around them was subtly altering. Macros said, "At my command, you must unleash the full fury of your power. All that you did at the Imperial Games was but a shadow of what you must do now."

"You know of that?"

Again there was a chuckle. "I was there, though my seat was poor compared to your own. I must admit it was quite impressive. Even I would have been hard-pressed to provide as spectacular a show. Now, there is no more time. Await my command, then let your power flow toward me."

Pug said nothing. He could feel the sorcerer's presence before him, as if it were being defined for him by Macros. Again he felt the sensation of twisting change around him. Suddenly there was a blinding light, then darkness. An instant later all around him erupted in mad displays of energy, much like those he witnessed in the rift of the Golden Bridge. On every side blinding colors exploded, primal forces he did not recognize.

"Now, Pug!" came Macros's cry.

Pug bent his will to the task. He reached down into the deepest recesses of his being. From there he brought forth all he could of the magic power he had gained from two worlds. Forces sufficient to destroy mountains, move rivers from their courses, and level cities to rubble, all these he focused. Then, like casting away something painful to hold, he directed all this energy toward where he sensed the sorcerer to be. There came an unimaginable, insane explosion of those forces, and the primal matter of time and space screamed in protest at its presence. Pug could feel it writhe and twist around him, as if the fundamental universe were trying to cast the invaders out. Then there came a sudden release, and they were expelled.

Pug found himself floating in total blackness. He drifted, numb and without coherent thought. His mind was unable to accept what he had sensed, and he was close to losing consciousness. He felt his fingers go lax, and the staff began to slip from his hand. He clutched spasmodically at it from blind instinct. He then felt a faint tugging. His mind resisted the cool blackness that was trying to overtake him, and he tried to remember something. It was growing cold around him, and he could feel his lungs burning for lack of air. He tried to remember something once more, but it would not come to him. Then he felt the tug again, and a faint but familiar voice seemed to sound close by.

"Kulgan?" he said weakly, and let the darkness take him.

▾▾

THE TSURANI FORCE Commander was alive. He wondered at that miracle as he saw those around him who lay dead before the rift machine. The explosion a minute before had killed hundreds, and others lay dazed a little way beyond.

He rose and took stock of what was occurring. The terrible destruction of the rift had not served to aid the Kingdom forces, either. Riders frantically tried to control near-hysterical horses, and other mounts could be seen running madly away, their riders thrown from their backs. All about, confusion reigned. But those at the edge of the conflict were less dazed than the others, and the fighting was resuming.

There was little hope, now that Kelewan was cut off to them, either of aid or of a safe return. Still, they numbered only slightly less than the enemy, and there was a chance that the field could yet be theirs. There might be time to worry about the rift later.

Abruptly the sounds of fighting stopped as the Kingdom forces withdrew. The Force Commander looked about and, still seeing no officer of greater rank, started shouting orders to ready the shield wall for another assault.

The Kingdom forces were slowly regrouping. They did not attack, but took up position opposite the Tsurani. The Force Commander waited, while his soldiers made ready the lines. On all sides Kingdom horsemen stood ready, but still they did not come.

Slowly the tension grew. The Force Commander ordered a platform raised. Four Tsurani grabbed a shield, he stood upon it, and they lifted him up. His eyes widened. "They have reinforcements." Far to the south he could see the advancing columns of the South Pass Kingdom forces. They had been farther removed from the parley site and were only now reaching the battlefield.

A shout from the opposite direction caused him to look to the north: lines of the Kingdom infantry were advancing from the trees. Again he turned his attention southward and strained his eyes. In the distant haze he could see the signs of a large force of infantry following behind the cavalry. The officer ordered the shield lowered, and his Subcommander said, "What is it?"

"Their entire army is in the field." He swallowed hard, the usual Tsurani impassivity broken. "Mother of gods! There must be thirty thousand of them."

"Then we shall give them a battle worthy of a ballad before we die," said the Subcommander.

The Force Commander looked about him. On all sides stood bleeding, wounded, and dazed soldiers. Of the Kingdom armies arrayed against them, only a third had fought. Fully twenty thousand rested soldiers approached four thousand Tsurani, half of them unable to fight at their normal efficiency.

The Force Commander shook his head. "There will be no fighting. We are cut off from home, perhaps for all time. There is no purpose."

He stepped past his startled Subcommander and walked beyond the shield wall. Raising both hands above his head in the sign of parley, he walked toward Lyam, slowly, dreading the moment when he would be the first Tsurani officer in living memory to surrender his forces. It took only a matter of minutes to reach the Prince. He removed his helm and knelt.

He looked up at the tall, golden-haired Prince of the Kingdom and said, "Lord Lyam. Into your care I give my men. Will you accept surrender?"

Lyam nodded. "Yes, Kasumi. I will accept surrender."

DARKNESS. THEN a gathering greyness. Pug forced his heavy eyelids open. Above him was the familiar face of Kulgan.

The face of his old teacher split into a wide smile. "It is good to see you are with us again. We did not know if you were really alive. Your body was so cold to the touch. Can you sit up?"

Pug took the offered arm and found that Meecham knelt next to him, aiding him to sit up. He could feel the cold leave his limbs as the bright sunlight warmed his body. He sat still for a moment, then said, "I think I will live." As he said it, he could feel strength returning to him. After a moment he felt able to stand and did so.

Around him he could see the assembled armies of the Kingdom. "What has happened?"

Laurie said, "The rift is destroyed, and the Tsurani who remain have surrendered. The war is over."

Pug felt too weak for emotion. He looked at the faces of those around him and could see deep relief in their eyes. Suddenly Kulgan engulfed him in a hug. "You risked your life to end this madness. It is your victory as much as any man's."

Pug stood quietly, then stepped away from his former master. "It is Macros who ended the war. Did he return?"

"No. Only you, and as soon as you were here, both of the staffs disappeared. There is no sign of him."

Pug shook his head, clearing away the fogginess. "What now?"

Meecham looked over his shoulder. "It might be wise if you joined Lyam. There seems to be some commotion taking place."

Laurie and Kulgan assisted Pug, for he was still weak from his ordeal within the rift. They walked to where Lyam, Arutha, Kasumi, and the assembled Kingdom nobles stood waiting. Across the field they could see the elves and dwarves approaching, with the northern Kingdom forces behind.

Pug was surprised to see the older son of the Shinzawai present, for he had thought him back on Kelewan. He looked a figure of dejection, standing without weapon or helm, and with head downcast, so he didn't see Pug and the others arrive.

Pug turned his attention to the elves and dwarves. Four figures walked at their head. Two he recognized, Dolgan and Calin. There was another dwarf with them who was unknown to the magician. As the four reached a place before the Prince, Pug realized that the tall warrior in white and gold was his boyhood friend. He stood speechless, amazed at the change in Tomas, for his old friend was now a towering figure who resembled an elf as much as a human.

Lyam was too exhausted for outrage. He looked at the Warleader of Elvandar and said quietly, "What cause did you have to attack, Tomas?"

The Prince Consort of the elves said, "The Tsurani drew weapons, Lyam. They were ready to attack the pavilion. Could you not see?"

In spite of his fatigue, Lyam's voice rose. "I saw only your host attack a conference of peace. I saw nothing in the Tsurani camp that was untoward."

Kasumi raised his head. "Your Highness, on my word, we drew weapons only when we were set upon by those." He pointed at Tomas's forces.

Lyam turned his attention back to Tomas. "Did I not send word that there was to be a truce, and a peace?"

"Aye," answered Dolgan, "I was there when the sorcerer brought word."

"Sorcerer?" said Lyam. He turned and shouted, "Laurie! I would have words with you."

Laurie stepped forward and said, "Highness?"

"Did you carry word to the Elf Queen as I bid?"

"On my honor. I spoke with the Elf Queen herself."

Tomas looked Lyam in the eye, head tilted back, an expression of defiance upon his face. "And I swear that I have never seen that man before this moment. Word of the planned Tsurani treachery was carried to us by Macros."

Kulgan and Pug came forward. "Your Highness," said Kulgan, "if the sorcerer's hand is in this—and it has been in everything else, it seems—then it may be best to unravel this mystery at leisure."

Lyam still fumed, but Arutha said, "Let it lie. We can sort out this mess back at the camp."

Lyam gave a curt nod. "We return to camp." The Heir turned to Brucal and said, "Form a proper escort for the prisoners and bring them along." He then looked at Tomas. "You I would also have in my tent when we return. There is much we must explain." Tomas agreed, though he did not look happy at the prospect. Lyam shouted, "We return to camp at once. Give the order."

Kingdom officers rode toward their companies, and the order was given. Tomas turned away and found a stranger standing next to him. He looked at the smiling face, then Dolgan said, "Are you blind, boy? Can't you recognize your own boyhood companion?"

Tomas looked at Pug as the exhausted magician moved close. "Pug?" he said softly. Then he reached out and embraced his once-lost foster brother. "Pug!"

They stood together quietly, amid the clamor of armies on the move, both with tears upon their faces. Kulgan placed his hands upon both men's shoulders. "Come, we must return. There is much to speak of, and thank the gods, there is now ample time to do so."

The camp was in full celebration. After more than nine years, the soldiers of the Kingdom knew they would not have to risk death or injury tomorrow. Songs rang out from around campfires, and laughter came from all quarters. It mattered little to most that others lay wounded in tents, tended by the priests, and that some would not live to see the first day of peace, or taste the fruits of victory. All the celebrants knew was that they were among the living, and they reveled in the fact. Later there would be time for mourning lost comrades. Now they drank in life.

Within Lyam's tent, things were more subdued. Kulgan had given a great deal of thought to the day's occurrences as they had ridden back. By the time they had reached the tent, the magician from Crydee had pieced together a rough picture of what had occurred. He had presented his opinion to those assembled there, and was now finishing.

"It would seem, then," said Kulgan, "that Macros intended for the rift to be closed. Everything points to the terrible duplicity as having been used for that purpose."

Lyam sat with Arutha and Tully by his side. "I still can't understand what would possess him to undertake such grave measures. Today's conflict cost over two thousand lives."

Pug spoke up. "I suspect we may find the answer to that and other questions when we reach his island. Until then I don't think we can begin to guess."

Lyam sighed. He said to Tomas, "At least I am convinced that you acted in good faith. I am pleased. It would have been a hard thing to imagine you responsible for all the carnage today."

Tomas held a wine cup, from which he sipped. "I also am pleased that we have no cause for contention. But I feel ill-used in this matter."

"As were we all," echoed Harthom and Dolgan.

Calin said, "It is likely that we have all played a part in some scheme of the Black One's. Perhaps it is as Pug has said, and we shall learn the truth at Sorcerer's Isle, but I for one resent this bloody business."

Lyam looked to where Kasumi sat stiffly, eyes forward, seemingly oblivious to what was being said around him. "Kasumi," Lyam said, "what am I to do with you and your men?"

Kasumi's eyes came into focus at mention of his name. He said, "Your Highness, I know something of your ways, for Laurie has taught me much. But I am still Tsurani. In our land the officers would be put to death, and the men enslaved. I may not advise you in this matter. I do not know what is the usual method of dealing with war prisoners in your world."

His tone was flat, without emotion. Lyam was about to say something, but a signal from Pug silenced him. There was something the magician wanted to say. "Kasumi?"

"Yes, Great One?" Tomas looked surprised at the honorific, but said nothing. There had been time only for the most superficial exchange of histories between the two boyhood friends as they had returned to the camp.

"What would you have done if you had not surrendered to the Prince's custody?"

"We would have fought to the death, Great One."

Pug nodded. "I understand. Then you are responsible for preserving the lives of nearly four thousand of your men? And thousands more Kingdom soldiers?"

Kasumi's expression softened, revealing his shame. "I have been among your people, Great One. I may have forgotten my Tsurani training. I have brought dishonor upon my house. When the Prince has disposed of my men, I will ask permission to take my own life, though it may be too much of an honor for him to grant."

Brucal and others looked shocked at this. Lyam showed no expression, but simply said, "You have earned no dishonor. You would have aided no cause in dying. There ceased to be one when the rift was destroyed."

Kasumi said, "It is our way."

Lyam said, "No longer. This is now your homeland, for you have no other. What Kulgan and Pug have said about rifts makes it unlikely you shall ever return to Tsuranuanni. Here you will remain, and it is my intention to see that prospect turned to good advantage for us all."

A faint flicker of hope entered Kasumi's eyes. The Heir turned toward Lord Brucal and said, "My lord Duke of Yabon. How do you judge the Tsurani soldiers?"

The old Duke smiled. "Among the finest I have ever beheld." Kasumi showed a little pride at the remark. "They match the Dark Brotherhood for ferocity and are of nobler nature; they are as disciplined as Keshian dog-soldiers and have the stamina of Natalese Rangers. On the whole they are without question superior soldiers."

"Would an army of such provide additional security for our troubled northern borders?"

Brucal smiled. "The LaMutian garrison was among the hardest hit during the war. They would be a valuable addition there."

The Earl of LaMut echoed his Duke's comment. Lyam turned to Kasumi. "Would you still take your life if your men could remain freemen and soldiers?"

The Shinzawai son said, "How is that possible, Your Highness?"

"If you and your men will swear loyalty to the crown, I will place you under the command of the Earl of LaMut. You will be both freemen and citizens and will be given the charge to defend our northern border against the enemies of humanity who abide in the Northlands."

Kasumi sat silently, unsure of what to say. Laurie stepped over to Kasumi and said, "There is no dishonor."

Kasumi's face broke into an expression of open relief. "I accept, as I am sure my men will." He paused, then added, "We came as an honor guard for the Emperor. From what I have heard said here, we have been used by this sorcerer as much as anyone. I would not have any more blood spilled on his account. I thank Your Highness."

Lord Vandros said, "I think a Knight-Captaincy would be proper for the leader of nearly four thousand. Do you agree, my lord Duke?" Brucal nodded in agreement, and Vandros said, "Come, Captain, we should speak with your new command."

Kasumi rose, bowed to Lyam, and left with the Earl of LaMut. Arutha touched his brother on the shoulder. Lyam turned his head, and the Prince said, "Enough of matters of state. It is time to celebrate the ending of the war."

Lyam smiled. "True." He turned to Pug. "Magician, run and fetch your lovely wife and fine son. I would have things that smack of home and family about."

Tomas looked at Pug. "Wife? Son? What is this?"

Pug laughed. "There is much to talk about. We can catch up with each other after I bring my family."

He made his way to his own tent, where Katala was telling William a story. They both jumped up and ran to him, for they had not seen him since his return. He had sent a soldier with the news that he was well but busy with the Prince.

"Katala, Lyam would like you to join us for dinner."

William tugged at his father's robe. "I want to come too, Papa."

Pug picked up his son. "You too, William."

THE CELEBRATION within the tent was of a quieter sort than the one taking place outside. Still, they had been entertained by Laurie's ballads and had enjoyed the exhilaration of knowing that peace had finally come. The food was the same camp fare as before, but somehow it tasted better. A great deal of wine had also added to the festive mood.

Lyam sat with a cup of wine in his hand. Around the tent the others were engaged in quiet conversation. The Heir was a little drunk, and none grudged him that relief, for he had endured much in the last month. Kulgan, Tully, and Arutha, who knew him best, understood that Lyam was thinking of his father, who but for a Tsurani arrow would now be sitting here with them. With the responsibility of first the war, then the succession thrust upon him, Lyam had not found time for mourning as his brother had. Now he was fully feeling the loss.

Tully stood. In a loud voice he said, "I am tired, Your Highness. Have I your leave to withdraw?"

Lyam smiled at his old teacher. "Of course. Good night, Tully."

The others in the tent quickly followed suit and took leave of the Heir. Outside the pavilion the guests bade each other good night. Laurie, Kulgan, Meecham, and the dwarves also left, leaving Pug and his family standing with Calin and Tomas.

The childhood friends had spent the evening exchanging histories of the last nine years. Each was equally amazed at the other's story. Pug had expressed interest in the Dragon Lords' magic, as had Kulgan. They expressed an interest in visiting the Dragon's Hall someday. Dolgan allowed he would be willing to guide them should they wish to make the journey.

Now the reawakened friendship glowed within the two young men, though they understood it was not what it had once been, for there had been many and great changes in both. As much as by the dragon armor and the black robe, this point was dramatized by the presence of William and Katala.

Katala had found the dwarves and elves fascinating—William had found everything fascinating, especially the dwarves, and now lay asleep in his mother's arms. Of Tomas she didn't know what to make. He resembled Calin in many ways, but still looked a great deal like the other men in camp.

Tomas regarded the sleeping boy. "He has his mother's looks, but there is enough devil in him to put me in mind of another boy I knew."

Pug smiled at that. "His life will be far calmer, I hope."

Arutha left his brother's tent and came to join them. He stood beside the two boys who had ridden with him to the mines of Mac Mordain Cadal so many years ago. "I should probably not say this, but years ago —when you first came to visit my father, Calin—two boys were overheard in conversation while they tussled in a hay wagon."

Tomas and Pug both looked at the Prince uncomprehendingly. "You don't remember, do you?" Arutha asked. "A blond thin-ribbed lad was sitting atop a shorter boy promising he would someday be a great warrior who would be welcomed in Elvandar."

Pug and Tomas both laughed at that. "I remember," said Pug.

"And the other promised to become the greatest magician in the Kingdom."

Katala said, "Perhaps William will also grow up to realize his dream."

Arutha smiled with a wicked light in his eyes. "Then watch him closely. We had a long chat before he went to sleep, and he told me he wanted to grow up to be a dwarf." All of them laughed, except Katala, who looked at her son for a moment with worry upon her face, but then she, too, joined in the merriment.

Arutha and Calin bade the others good night, and Tomas said, "I, too, will be to bed."

Pug said, "Will you come to Rillanon with us?"

"No, I may not. I would be with my lady. But when the child is born, you must guest with us, for there will be a great celebration." They promised they would come. Tomas said, "We are for home in the morning. The dwarves will return to their villages, for there is much work to be done there. They have been overlong from their families. And with the return of Tholin's hammer, there is talk of a moot, to name Dolgan King in the West." Lowering his voice, he added, "Though my old friend will most likely use that hammer on the first dwarf to openly suggest it in his presence." Placing his hand upon Pug's shoulder, he said, "It is well we both came through this; even in the depths of my strange madness, I never forgot about you."

Pug said, "I never forgot you either, Tomas."

"When you unravel this mystery on Sorcerer's Isle, I trust you will send word?"

Pug said he would. They embraced, saying good-bye, and Tomas walked away, but stopped and looked back, a boyish glint in his eyes. "Still, I would love to be there when you meet Carline again with a wife and son in tow."

Pug flushed, for he viewed that coming reunion with mixed feelings. He waved to Tomas as he walked from sight, then found Katala regarding him with a determined look upon her face. In even, measured tones she said, "Who is Carline?"

LYAM LOOKED UP as Arutha entered the command tent. The younger brother said, "I thought you would have retired by now. You're exhausted."

"I wanted some time to think, Arutha. I have had little time alone and wanted to put things in order." His voice was tired and troubled.

Arutha sat next to his brother. "What sort of things?"

"This war, Father, you, I"—he thought of Martin—"other things . . . Arutha, I don't know if I can be King."

Arutha raised his eyebrows a little. "It is not as if you had a choice, Lyam. You will be King, so make the best of it."

"I could refuse the crown in favor of my brother," said Lyam slowly, "as Erland renounced it in favor of Rodric."

"And what a fine kettle of soup that became. Should you want a civil war, that would be one way to get it. The Kingdom cannot afford a debate in the Congress of Lords. There are still too many wounds to be healed between East and West. And du Bas-Tyra is still at large."

Lyam sighed. "You would make a better king, Arutha."

Arutha laughed. "Me? I am little pleased at the prospect of being Prince of Krondor. Look, Lyam, when we were boys, I envied you the affection you gained so quickly. People always preferred you to me. As I grew older, I understood it wasn't that I was disliked; it was simply there was something about you that brings out trust and love in people. That is a good quality for a king to possess. I never envied the fact you would follow Father as Duke, nor do I now envy your crown. I once thought I might take some time after the war to travel, but now that will not be possible, for I must rule Krondor. So do not wish this additional burden of the entire Kingdom upon me. I would not take it."

"Still, you would make a better king." Lyam caught Arutha's gaze and held it.

Arutha paused, frowned, then fixed his brother with a skeptical look. "Perhaps, but you are to be King, and I expect you will remain King for quite some time." He stretched as he rose. "I am for bed. It has been a long and hard day." Nearing the entrance to the tent, he said, "Ease your doubts, Lyam. You will be a good ruler. With Caldric to advise you, and the others, Kulgan, Tully, and Pug, you will lead us through this time of rebuilding."

Lyam said, "Arutha, before you go . . ." Arutha waited, as Lyam made a decision. "I wish you to go with Kulgan and Pug to Sorcerer's Isle. You've been there once before, and . . . I'd like your judgment on what is found there." Arutha was displeased and started to object. Lyam cut him off. "I know you wish to go to Krondor, but it will take only a few days. There will be twelve days between the time we reach Rillanon and the coronation, ample time for you to join us."

Arutha again began to object, then with a wry smile, acceded. "Trust in yourself, Lyam. If I won't take the crown, you're left with it." As he departed the tent, he added with a laugh, "There's no other brother to claim it."

Lyam sat alone, absently sipping at his wine. With another long sigh he said to himself, "There is one other, Arutha, and may the gods help me decide what is right to do."

33

▾▾

LEGACY

THE SHIP DROPPED ANCHOR.

The crew secured the sails aloft while the landing party made ready. Meecham watched the preparation of the longboat. The magicians were anxious to reach the castle of Macros, for they had more questions than the others. Arutha was also curious, after resigning himself to the voyage. He found he also had little desire to take part in the long funeral procession that had left from Ylith the day they sailed. He had buried his grief for his father deep inside and would deal with it in his own time. Laurie had stayed with Kasumi to aid the assimilation of the Tsurani soldiers into the LaMutian garrison, and would meet them later in Rillanon.

Lyam and his nobles had shipped for Krondor, escorting the bodies of Borric and Rodric. They would be joined by Anita and Carline, then all would convey the dead in a procession of state to Rillanon, where they would be laid to rest in the tomb of their ancestors. After the traditional period of twelve days' mourning, Lyam would be crowned King. By then all who would attend the coronation would have gathered in Rillanon. Pug and Kulgan's business should be completed in ample time for them to reach the capital.

The boat was readied, and Arutha, Pug, and Kulgan joined Meecham. The longboat was lowered, and six guards bent their backs to the oars.

The sailors had been greatly relieved that they were not required to accompany the landing party, for in spite of the magicians' reassurances, they had no desire to set foot upon Sorcerer's Isle.

The boat was beached, and the passengers stepped out. Arutha looked about. "There seems to have been no change here since we last came."

Kulgan stretched, for the ship's quarters had been cramped, and he enjoyed the sensation of dry land under his feet again. "I would have been surprised to find it otherwise. Macros was one to keep his house in order, I wager."

Arutha turned and said, "You six will stay here. If you hear our call, come quickly." The Prince started toward the path up the hill, and the others fell in without comment. They reached the place where the path forked, and Arutha said, "We come as guests. I thought it best not to appear invaders."

Kulgan said nothing, being occupied with observing the castle they were approaching. The strange blue light that had been so visible when they had last visited the island was absent from the window of the high tower. The castle had the look of a place deserted, without movement or sound. The drawbridge was down and the portcullis raised. Meecham observed, "At least we won't have to storm the place."

When they reached the edge of the drawbridge, they halted. The castle rose above them, its high walls, and taller towers, forbidding. It was built of dark stone, unfamiliar to them. Around the great arch over the bridge, strange carvings of alien creatures regarded them with fixed gazes. Horned and winged beasts sat perched atop ledges, seemingly frozen in an instant, so cleverly were they fashioned.

They stepped on the bridge and crossed the deep ravine that separated the castle from the rest of the island. Meecham looked down, seeing the rock walls of the crevice fall away to the level of the sea, where waves crashed through the passage between. "It serves better than most moats I've seen. You'd think twice before trying to cross this while someone was shooting at you from the walls."

They entered the court and looked about, as if expecting to see someone appear at one of the many doors in the walls at any moment. Nowhere was there sign of any living creature, yet the grounds about the central keep were well tended and in order.

When no one was forthcoming, Pug said, "I imagine we'll find what we're after in the keep." The others moved with him toward the broad stairs that led to the main doors. As they mounted the steps, the large doors began to swing open, until they could all see a figure standing in the darkness beyond. As the doors finished their movement with a loud thump against the keep walls, the figure stepped forward into the sunlight.

Meecham's sword was in his hand without thinking, for the creature before them bore a strong resemblance to a goblin. After a brief examination, Meecham put up his weapon; the creature had made no threatening gesture, but simply stood waiting for them at the top of the stairs.

It was taller than the average goblin, being nearly Meecham's height. Thick ridges dominated its forehead, and a large nose was the focus of its face, but it was nobler in features than a goblin. Two black, twinkling eyes regarded them as they resumed their climb. As they came up to it, the creature gave a toothy grin. Its head was covered with a thick mat of black hair, and its skin was tinged with the faint green of the goblin tribe, but it lacked the hunched-shouldered posture of a goblin, instead standing erect much like a man. It wore a finely fashioned tunic and trousers, both bright green. Upon its feet were a pair of polished black boots, reaching nearly to its knees.

The creature said, grinning, "Welcome, masters, welcome. I am Gathis, and I have the honor of acting as your host in my master's absence." There was a slight hiss to its speech.

Kulgan said, "Your master is Macros the Black?"

"Of course. It has been ever thus. Please enter."

The four men accompanied Gathis into the large entry hall and stopped to look about. Except for the absence of people and of the usual heraldic banners, this hall looked much like the one in Castle Crydee.

"My master has left explicit instructions for your visit, as much as was possible to anticipate, so I have prepared the castle for your arrival. Would you care for some refreshments? There are food and wine ready."

Kulgan shook his head. He was unsure of what this creature was, but he was not overly comfortable with anything that so resembled a servant of the Dark Brotherhood. "Macros said there would be a message. I would see it at once."

Gathis bowed slightly. "As you will. Please come with me."

He led them along a series of corridors to a flight of stairs that spiraled up into the large tower. They mounted the steps and soon came to a locked door. "My master said you would be able to open this door. Should you fail, you are impostors, and I am to deal with you harshly."

Meecham gripped his sword at hearing this, but Pug placed his hand on the big franklin's arm. "Since the rift is closed, half my power is lost, that which I gained from Kelewan, but this should prove no obstacle."

Pug concentrated upon opening the door. Instead of the usual response of the door swinging open, a change occurred in the door itself. The wood seemed to become fluid, flowing and ebbing as it fashioned its surface into a new form. In a few moments a face could be seen, formed in the wood. It looked like a bas-relief, with a slight resemblance to Macros. It was very lifelike in detail and appeared to be asleep. Then its eyelids opened, and they could see that the eyes were alive, black centers showing against white. Its mouth moved, and a voice issued from it, the sound deep and resonant as it spoke in perfect Tsurani. "What is the first duty?"

Without thinking, Pug answered, "To serve the Empire."

The face flowed back into the door, and when there was no trace of it before them, the door swung aside. They entered and found themselves in the study of Macros the Black, a large room occupying the entire top of the tower.

Gathis said, "I take it I have the honor of hosting Masters Kulgan, Pug, and Meecham?" He then studied the fourth member of the party. "And you must be Prince Arutha?" When they nodded, he said, "My master was unsure if Your Highness would attend, though he thought it likely. He was certain the other three gentlemen would be here." He indicated the room with a sweep of his hand. "All that you see is at your disposal. If you will excuse me, I will return with your message and some refreshments."

Gathis left, and all four looked at the contents of the room. Except for one bare wall where it was obvious that a bookcase or cupboard had recently been removed, the entire room was surrounded with tall shelves from floor to ceiling, all heavily laden with books and scrolls. Pug and Kulgan were almost paralyzed by indecision about where to begin their investigation.

Arutha solved that problem by crossing over to a shelf where lay a large parchment bound with a red ribbon. He took it down and laid it upon the round table in the center of the room. A shaft of sunlight from the room's single large window fell across the parchment as he unrolled it.

Kulgan came over to see what he had found. "It is a map of Midkemia!"

Pug and Meecham crossed over to stand behind Kulgan and Arutha. "Such a map!" Prince Arutha exclaimed. "I have never seen its like." His finger stabbed at a spot upon a large landmass in the center. "Look! Here is the Kingdom." Across a small portion of the map were inscribed the words *Kingdom of the Isles*. Below could be seen the larger borders of the Empire of Great Kesh. To the south of the Empire, the states of the Keshian Confederacy were clearly shown.

"To the best of my knowledge," said Kulgan, "few from the Kingdom have ever ventured into the Confederacy. Our only knowledge of its members is through the Empire and a few of our more venturesome captains who've visited some of their ports. We hardly know the names of these nations, and nothing about them."

Pug said, "We learn much about our world in an instant. Look at how small a part of this continent the Kingdom is." He pointed to the great sweep of the Northlands to the north of the Kingdom, and the far-reaching mass of land below the Confederacy. The entire continent bore the inscription *Triagia*.

Kulgan said, "It appears there is a great deal more to our Midkemia than we had dreamed." He indicated additional landmasses across the sea. These were labeled *Wiñet* and *Novindus*. Upon each, cities and states were delineated. Two large chains of islands were also shown, many with cities marked. Kulgan shook his head. "There have been rumors of traders from far distant lands, venturing into the trading ports in the Keshian Confederacy, or treating with the pirates of Sunset Islands, but they are only rumors. It is small wonder we have never heard of these places. It would be a brave captain who set his ship upon a course for so far a port."

They were brought out of their study by the sound of Gathis returning to the room. He carried a tray with a decanter and four wine cups. "My master bade me say that you are to enjoy the hospitality of his home as long as you desire." He placed the tray on the table and poured wine into the cups. He then removed a scroll from within his tunic and handed it to Kulgan. "He bade me give you this. I will retire while you consider my master's message. Should you need me, simply speak my name, and I will return quickly." He bowed slightly and left the room.

Kulgan regarded the scroll. It was sealed with black wax, impressed with the letter *M*. He broke the seal and unrolled the parchment. He started to read to himself, then said, "Let us sit."

Pug rolled up the large map and put it away, then returned to the table where the others were sitting. He pulled out a chair and waited with Meecham and Arutha while Kulgan read. Kulgan shook his head slowly. "Listen," he said, and read aloud:

" 'To the magicians Kulgan and Pug, greetings. I have anticipated some of your questions and have endeavored to answer them as best I can. I fear there are others that must go begging, as much about myself must remain known only to me. I am not what the Tsurani would call a Great One, though I have visited that world, as Pug knows, upon a number of occasions. My magic is peculiar to myself and defies description in your terms of Greater and Lesser Paths. Suffice it to say I am a walker of many paths.

" 'I see myself as a servant of the gods, though that may be only my vanity speaking. Whatever the truth is, I have traveled to many lands and worked for many causes.

" 'Of my early life I will say little. I am not of this world, having been born in a land distant both in space and time. It is not unlike this world, but there are ample reasons to count it strange by your standards.

" 'I am older than I care to remember, old even by the elves' reckoning. For reasons I do not understand, I have lived for ages, though my own people are as mortal as yours. It may be that when I entered into the magic arts, I unwittingly gave this near-immortality to myself, or it may be the gift—or curse—of the gods.

" 'Since becoming a sorcerer, I have been fated to know my own future, as others know their pasts. I have never retreated from what I knew to be before me, though often I wished to. I have served great kings and simple peasants both. I have lived in the greatest cities and the rudest huts. Often I have understood the meaning of my participation, sometimes not, but always I have followed the foreordained path that was set for me.' "

Kulgan stopped for a moment. "This explains how he knew so much." He resumed his reading.

" 'Of all my labors, my role in the rift war was the hardest. Never have I experienced such desire to turn from the path before me. Never have I been responsible for the loss of so many lives, and I mourn for them more than you can know. But even as you consider my "treachery," consider my situation.

" 'I was unable to close the rift without Pug's aid. It was fated for the war to continue while he learned his craft on Kelewan. For the terrible price paid, consider the gain. There now is one upon Midkemia who practices the Greater Art, which was lost in the coming of man during the Chaos Wars. The benefit will be judged only by history, but I think it a valuable one.

" 'As to my closing the rift once peace was at hand, I can only say it was vital. The Tsurani Great Ones had forgotten that rifts are subject to the Enemy's detection.' " Kulgan looked up in surprise. "Enemy? Pug, this refers to something I think you need explain."

Pug told them quickly of what he knew of the legendary Enemy. Arutha said, "Can such a terrible being really exist?" His expression betrayed disbelief.

Pug said, "That it once existed, there is no doubt, and for a being of such power still to endure is not beyond imagining. But of all conceivable reasons for Macros's actions, this is the last I would have thought possible. No one in the Assembly had dreamed of it. It's incredible."

Kulgan resumed reading. " 'It is to him like a beacon, drawing that terrible entity across space and time. It might have been years more before he would have appeared, but once here, all the powers of your world would be hard-pressed, perhaps even insufficient, to dislodge him from Midkemia. The rift had to be closed. The reasons I chose to ensure its closing at the cost of so many lives should be apparent to you.' "

Pug interrupted. "What does he mean, 'should be apparent'?"

Kulgan said, "Macros was nothing, it seems, if not a student of human nature. Could he alone have convinced the King and Emperor to close the rift, with so much to be gained by keeping it open? Perhaps, perhaps not, but in any event there would have been the all-too-human temptation to keep it open 'just a little longer.' I think he knew that and was ensuring there would be no choice." Kulgan returned to reading the scroll. " 'As to what will happen now, I cannot say. My seeing of the future ends with the explosion of the rift. Whether it is, finally, my appointed hour, or simply the beginning of some new era of my existence, I do not know. In the event you have witnessed my death, I have decided upon the following course. All my research, with some exceptions, is contained within this room. It is to be used to further the Greater and Lesser Arts. It is my wish that you take possession of the books, scrolls, and tomes contained here and use them to that end. A new epoch of magic is beginning in the Kingdom, and it is my wish for others to benefit from my works. In your hands I leave this new age.'

"It is signed, 'Macros.' "

Kulgan placed the scroll upon the table. Pug said, "One of the last things he said to me was he wished to be remembered kindly."

They said nothing for a time, then Kulgan called, "Gathis!"

Within seconds the creature appeared at the doorway. "Yes, Master Kulgan?"

"Do you know what is contained within this scroll?"

"Yes, Master Kulgan. My master was most explicit in his instructions. He made sure that we were aware of his requirements."

"We?" said Arutha.

Gathis smiled his toothy grin. "I am but one of my master's servants. The others are instructed to keep from your sight, for it was feared their presence might cause you some discomfort. My master lacked most of the human prejudices and was content to judge each creature he met on its own merits."

"What exactly are you?" asked Pug.

"I am of a race akin to the goblins, as the elves are to the Dark

Brotherhood. We were an old race and perished but for a few, long before humans came to the Bitter Sea. Those that were left were brought here by Macros, and I am the last."

Kulgan regarded the creature. In spite of his appearance, there was something about him that was likable. "What will you do now?"

"I will wait here for my master's return, keeping his home in order."

"You expect him to return?" asked Pug.

"Most likely. In a day, or a year, or a century. It does not matter. Things will be ready for him should he return."

"What if he has perished?" asked Arutha.

"In that event, I shall grow old and die waiting, but I think not. I have served the Black One for a very long time. Between us is . . . an understanding. If he were dead, I think I would know. He is merely . . . absent. Even if he is dead, he may return. Time is not to my master as it is to other men. I am content to wait."

Pug thought about this. "He must truly have been the master of all magic."

Gathis's smile broadened. "He would laugh to hear that, master. He was always complaining of there being so much to learn and so little time to learn it. And that from a man who had lived years beyond numbering."

Kulgan said, as he rose from his chair, "We will have to fetch men to carry all these things back to the ship."

Gathis said, "Worry not, master. Retire to your ship when you are ready. Leave two boats on the beach at the cove. At first light the next day you will find everything placed aboard, packed for shipment."

Kulgan nodded. "Very well; then we should start at once to catalog all these works, before we move them."

Gathis went over to a shelf and returned with a rolled parchment. "In anticipation of your needs, master, I have prepared such a listing of all the works here."

Kulgan unrolled the parchment and began reading the inventory of works. His eyes widened. "Listen," he said, excitedly. "There's a copy of Vitalus's *Expectations of Matter Transformation* here." His eyes grew bigger still. "And Spandric's *Temporal Research.* That work was thought lost a hundred years ago!" He looked at the others, wonder upon his face. "And hundreds of volumes with Macros's name on them. This is a treasure beyond measure."

Gathis said, "I am pleased that you find it so, master."

Kulgan started to ask for those volumes to be brought to him, but Arutha said, "Wait Kulgan. Once you begin, we'll have to tie you up to get you out of here. Let us return to the ship and wait for all this to be brought. We must be off soon."

Kulgan looked like a child whose sweets had been taken from him. Arutha, Pug, and Meecham all chuckled at the stout magician. Pug said, "There is no good reason to stay now. We shall have years to study these after the coronation. Look around, Kulgan. Do you mean to inhale all this in one breath?"

A look of resignation crossed Kulgan's face. "Very well."

Pug surveyed all in the room. "Think of it. An academy for the study of magic, with Macros's library at the heart."

Kulgan's eyes grew luminous. "I had all but forgotten the Duke's bequest. A place to learn. No longer will an apprentice learn from this master or that, but from many. With this legacy and your own teachings, Pug, we have a wonderful start."

Arutha said, "Let us be on our way if we're to have any sort of start. There's a new king to crown, and the longer you tarry, the more likely you'll lose yourself in here."

Kulgan looked as if his good name were impugned. "Well, I will take a few things to study while on the ship—if you have no objections?"

Arutha raised a placating hand. "Whatever you wish," he said with a rueful smile. "But please, no more than we can reasonably lug down to the boat."

Kulgan smiled, his mood lightening. "Agreed." He turned to Gathis. "Would you fetch those two volumes I mentioned."

Gathis held out the two volumes, old and well read. Kulgan looked surprised, while Gathis said, "I thought you might reach such an understanding and removed them from the shelves while you discussed the matter."

Kulgan walked toward the door, shaking his head slowly as he regarded the two books he held. The others followed, and Gathis closed the door behind them. The goblinlike creature guided them to the courtyard and bid them a safe journey at the door of the keep.

When the large doors had closed behind them, Meecham said, "This fellow Macros seems to have raised five questions for each he answered."

Kulgan said, "You have that right, old friend. Perhaps we will gain additional knowledge from his notes, and other works. Perhaps not, and maybe that's the right of it."

34

▼▼

RENAISSANCE

RILLANON WAS IN A FESTIVE MOOD.

Everywhere banners rippled in the breeze, and garlands of summer flowers replaced the black bunting that had marked the period of mourning for the late King and his cousin Borric. Now they would be crowning a new king, and the people rejoiced. The people of Rillanon knew little of Lyam, but he was fair to view, and generous with his smile in public. To the populace it was as if the sun had come out from behind the dark clouds that had been Rodric's reign.

Few among the people were aware of the many royal guards who circulated throughout the city, always alert for signs of Guy du Bas-Tyra's agents and possible assassins. And fewer still noticed the plainly dressed men who were always near when groups gathered to speak of the new King, listening to what was said.

Arutha cantered his horse toward the palace, leaving Pug, Meecham, and Kulgan behind. He cursed the fate that had delayed them nearly a week, becalmed less than three days from Krondor, then the slowness of their journey to Salador. It was midmorning, and already the Priests of Ishap were bearing the King's new crown through the city. In less than three hours they would appear before the throne and Lyam would take the crown.

Arutha reached the palace, and shouts from the guards echoed across the vast courtyard, "Prince Arutha arrives!"

Arutha gave his mount to a page and hurried up the steps to the palace. As he reached the entranceway, Anita came running in his direction, a radiant smile on her face. "Oh," she cried, "it is so good to see you!"

He smiled back at her and said, "It is good to see you, also. I must get ready for the ceremony. Where is Lyam?"

"He has secreted himself in the Royal Tomb. He left word you were to come straight away to him there." Her voice was troubled. "There is something strange taking place here, but no one seems to know what it is. Only Martin Longbow has seen Lyam since supper last night, and when I saw Martin, he had the strangest look upon his face."

Arutha laughed. "Martin is always full of strange looks. Come, let us go to Lyam."

She refused to let him ignore the warning. "No, you go alone; that is what Lyam ordered. Besides, I must dress for the ceremony. But, Arutha, there is something very queer in the wind."

Arutha's manner turned more reflective. Anita was a good judge of such things. "Very well. I'll have to wait for my things to be brought from the ship, anyway. I will see Lyam, then when this mystery is cleared up, join you at the ceremony."

"Good."

"Where is Carline?"

"Fussing over this and that. I'll tell her you've arrived."

She kissed his cheek and hurried off. Arutha hadn't been to the vault of his ancestors since he was a boy, the first time he had come to Rillanon, for Rodric's coronation. He asked a page to lead him there, and the boy guided him through a maze of corridors.

The palace had been through many transformations over the ages, new wings being added on, new constructions over those destroyed by fire, earthquake, or war, but in the center of the vast edifice the ancient first keep remained. The only clue they were entering the ancient halls was the sudden appearance of dark stone walls, worn smooth by time. Two guards stood watch by a door over which was carved a bas-relief crest of the conDoin kings, a crowned lion holding a sword in its claws. The page said, "Prince Arutha," and the guards opened the door. Arutha stepped through into a small anteroom, with a long flight of stairs leading down.

He followed the stairs past rows of brightly burning torches that stained the stones of the walls with black soot. The stairs ended, and Arutha stood before a large, high-arched doorway. On both sides loomed heroic statues of ancient conDoin kings. To the right, with features dulled with age, stood the statue of Dannis, first conDoin King of Rillanon, some seven hundred fifty years past. To the left stood the statue of Delong, the only King called "the Great," the King who first brought the banner of Rillanon to the mainland with the conquest of Bas-Tyra, two hundred fifty years after Dannis.

Arutha passed between his ancestors' likenesses and entered the burial vault. He walked between the ancient forebears of his line, entombed in the walls and upon great catafalques. Kings and queens, princes and princesses, scoundrels and rogues, saints and scholars lined his way. At the far end of the huge chamber he found Lyam sitting next to the catafalque that supported his father's stone coffin. A likeness of Borric had been carved in the coffin's surface, and it looked as if the late Duke of Crydee lay sleeping.

Arutha approached slowly, for Lyam seemed deep in thought. Lyam looked up and said, "I feared you might come late."

"As did I. We had wretched weather and slow progress, but we are all here. Now, what is this strange business? Anita told me you've been here all night, and there is some mystery. What is it?"

"I have given great thought to this matter, Arutha. The whole of the Kingdom will know within a few hours' time, but I wanted you to see what I have done and hear what I must say before any others."

"Anita said Martin was here with you this morning. What is this, Lyam?"

Lyam stepped away from his father's catafalque and pointed. Inscribed upon the stones of the burial place were the words:

HERE LIES BORRIC, THIRD DUKE OF CRYDEE,
HUSBAND OF CATHERINE,
FATHER OF
MARTIN,
LYAM,
ARUTHA,
AND CARLINE

Arutha's lips moved, but no words came forth. He shook his head, then said, "What madness is this?"

Lyam came between Arutha and the likeness of their father. "No madness, Arutha. Father acknowledged Martin on his deathbed. He is our brother. He is the eldest."

Arutha's face became contorted with rage. "Why didn't you tell me?" His voice was tormented. "What right had you to hide this from me?"

Lyam raised his own voice. "All who knew were sworn to secrecy. I could not risk anyone knowing until the peace was made. There was too much to lose."

Arutha shoved past his brother, looking in disbelief at the inscription. "It all makes an evil sense. Martin's exclusion from the Choosing. The way Father always kept an eye on his whereabouts. His freedom to come and go as he pleased." Bitterness rang in Arutha's words. "But why now? Why did Father acknowledge Martin after so many years of denial?"

Lyam tried to comfort Arutha. "I've pieced together what I could from Kulgan and Tully. Besides them, no one knew, not even Fannon. Father was a guest of Brucal's when he was in his first year of office, after Grandfather's death. He tumbled a pretty serving girl and conceived Martin. It was five years before Father knew of him. Father had come to court, met Mother, and married. When he learned of Martin, he had already been abandoned by his mother to the monks of Silban's Abbey. Father chose to let Martin remain in their care.

"When I was born, Father began to feel remorse over having a son unknown to him, and when I was six, Martin was ready for Choosing. Father arranged to have him brought to Crydee. But he wouldn't acknowledge him, for fear of shaming Mother."

"Then why now?"

Lyam looked at the likeness of their father. "Who knows what passes through a man's mind in the moments before death? Perhaps more guilt, or some sense of honor. Whatever the reason, he acknowledged Martin, and Brucal bore witness."

Anger still sounded in Arutha's voice. "Now we must deal with this madness, regardless of Father's reasons for creating it." He fixed Lyam with a harsh stare. "What did he say when you brought him down to see this?"

Lyam looked away, as if pained by what he now said. "He stood silently, then I saw him weep. Finally he said, 'I am pleased he told you.' Arutha, he knew." Lyam gripped his brother's arm. "All those years Father thought him ignorant of his birthright, and he knew. And never once did he seek to turn that knowledge to his own gain."

Arutha's anger subsided. "Did he say anything more?"

"Only 'Thank you, Lyam,' and then he left."

Arutha paced away for a moment, then faced Lyam. "Martin is a good man, as good a man as I've ever known. I'll be the first to say so. But this acknowledgment! My gods, do you know what you've done?"

"I'm aware of my actions."

"You've placed all we've won over the last nine years in the balance, Lyam. Shall we fight ambitious eastern lords who might rally in Martin's name? Do we end one war simply to begin an even more bitter one?"

"There will be no contestation."

Arutha stopped his pacing. His eyes narrowed. "What do you mean? Has Martin promised to voice no claim?"

"No. I have decided not to oppose Martin should he choose the crown."

Arutha was speechless for a moment, in shock as he regarded Lyam. For the first time he understood the terrible doubts his brother had been voicing over being King. "You don't want to be King," he said, his tone accusatory.

Lyam laughed bitterly. "No sane man would. You have said as much yourself, brother. I don't know if I am a match for the burdens of kingship. But the matter is out of my hands now. If Martin speaks for himself as King, I will acknowledge his right."

"His right! The royal signet passed to your hand, before most of the Lords of the Kingdom. You are not sick Erland deferring to his brother's son because of ill health and by reason of no clear succession. You are the named Heir!"

Lyam lowered his head. "The announcement of succession is invalid, Arutha. Rodric named me Heir as 'eldest conDoin male,' which I am not. Martin is."

Arutha confronted his brother. "A pretty point of law, Lyam, but one that may prove the destruction of this Kingdom! Should Martin voice a claim before the congress assembled, the Priests of Ishap will break the crown, and the matter passes to the Congress of Lords for resolution. Even with Guy in hiding, there are dozens of dukes, scores of earls, and a host of barons who would willingly cut their neighbors' throats to convene such a congress. Such bargaining would end with half the estates in the Kingdom switching hands in trade for votes. It would be a carnival!

"If you take the crown, Bas-Tyra cannot act. But if you back Martin, many will refuse to follow. A deadlocked congress is exactly what Guy wishes. I'll bet all I own he is somewhere in the city at this very moment, plotting against such an event. If the eastern lords bolt, Guy will emerge, and many will flock to his banner."

Lyam appeared overwhelmed by his brother's words. "I cannot say what will happen, Arutha. But I know I could not do other than I have done."

Arutha looked on the verge of striking Lyam. "You may have inherited the burden of Father's sense of family honor, but it will fall to the rest of us to deal with the killing! Heaven's mercy, Lyam, what do you think will happen if some heretofore nameless huntsman sits the conDoin throne simply because our father tumbled a pretty maid nearly forty years ago! We shall have civil war!"

Lyam stood firm. "Should our positions have been reversed, would you have robbed Martin of his birthright?"

Arutha's anger vanished. He looked at his brother with open amazement on his face. "Gods! You feel guilt because Father denied Martin all his life, don't you?" He stepped away from Lyam, as if trying to gain perspective on him. "Should our positions have been reversed, I most assuredly would deny Martin his birthright. After thirty-seven years, what matter a few more days? After I was King, firm on my throne, then I would make him a duke, give him an army to command, name him First Adviser, whatever need be to salve my conscience, but not until the Kingdom was secure. I would not wish Martin to play Borric the First to Guy's Jon the Pretender, and I would do whatever must be done to see that would not come to pass."

Lyam sighed with deep regret. "Then you and I are two different sorts of men, Arutha. I told you back at camp I thought you would make a better king than I. Perhaps you are right, but what's done is done."

"Does Brucal know of this?"

"Only we three." He looked directly at Arutha. "Only our father's sons."

Arutha flushed, irritated at the remark. "Don't misunderstand me, Lyam. I hold Martin in no little affection, but there are issues here much larger than any personal consideration." He thought quietly for a moment. "Then it is in Martin's hands. If you had to do this, at least you did right in not making it a public matter. There will be shock enough should Martin come forth at the coronation. At least with advance warning we can prepare."

Arutha moved toward the stairs, then stopped and faced his brother. "What you said cuts both ways, Lyam. Perhaps because you cannot deny Martin, you'll make a better king than I. But as much as I love you, I'll not let the Kingdom be destroyed over the succession."

Lyam seemed unable to contest with his brother any longer. Fatigue, a weary resignation toward what fate would bring, sounded in his words. "What will you do?"

"What must be done. I will ensure that those who are loyal to us are forewarned. If there comes a need to fight, then let us have the advantage of surprise." He paused for a moment. "I have nothing but the greatest affection for Martin, Lyam, you must know that. I hunted with him as a boy, and he was in no small part responsible for my safely getting Anita away from Guy's watchdogs, a debt beyond repaying. In another time and place, I would gladly accept him as my brother. But should it come to bloodshed, Lyam, I'll willingly kill him."

Arutha left the vault of his ancestors. Lyam stood alone, feeling the chill of ages press in upon him.

PUG LOOKED OUT the window, reminiscing. Katala came to his side, and he came out of his reverie. "You look lovely," he said. She was dressed in a brilliant gown of deep red, with golden trim at the bodice and sleeves. "The finest Duchess of the court could not match your beauty."

She smiled at his flattery. "I thank you, husband." She spun, showing off the gown. "Your Duke Caldric is the true magician, I am thinking. How his staff could manage to find all these things and have them ready in two short hours is true magic." She patted at the full skirt. "These heavy gowns will take some practice getting around in. I think I prefer the short robes of home." She stroked the material. "Still, this is a lovely cloth. And in this cold world of yours, I can see the need." The weather had turned cooler, now that summer was waning. In less than two months snow would begin falling.

"Wait until winter, Katala, if you think it's cold now."

William came running into the room, from the bedroom that adjoined their own. "Mama, Papa," he yelled in boyish exuberance. He was dressed in a tunic and trousers befitting a little noble, of fine material and workmanship. He leaped into his father's outstretched arms. "Where are you going?" he asked with a wide-eyed look.

Pug said, "We go to see Lyam made King, William. While we are gone, you mind the nurse and don't tease Fantus."

He said he would and wouldn't, respectively, but his impish grin put his credibility in doubt. The maid who was to act as William's nurse entered and took the boy in tow, leading him back into his own room.

Pug and Katala left the suite Caldric had given them and walked toward the throne room. As they turned a corner, they saw Laurie leaving his room, with Kasumi standing nervously to one side.

Laurie brightened upon seeing them and said, "Ah! There you are. I was hoping we'd see you two before all the ceremonies had begun."

Kasumi bowed to Pug, though the magician now wore a fashionable russet-colored tunic and trousers in place of his black robe. "Great One," he said.

"That is a thing of the past here, Kasumi. Please call me Pug."

"You two look so handsome in your new clothes and uniform," said Katala. Laurie wore bright clothing in the latest fashion, a yellow tunic with a sleeveless overjacket of green, and tight-fitting black trousers tucked into high boots. Kasumi wore the uniform of a Knight-Captain of the LaMutian garrison, deep green tunic and trousers, and the grey wolf's-head tabard of LaMut.

The minstrel smiled at her. "In all the excitement of the last few months, I had forgotten I had a small fortune in gems with me. Since I cannot conspire to return them to the Lord of the Shinzawai, and his son refuses to take them, I suppose they are mine by rights. I will no longer have to worry about finding a widow with an inn."

Pug said, "Kasumi, how goes it with your men?"

"Well enough, though there is still some discomfort between them and the LaMutian soldiers. It should pass in time. We had an encounter with the Brotherhood the week after we left. They can fight, but we routed them. There was much celebrating among all the men in the garrisons, both Tsurani and LaMutian. It was a good beginning."

It had been more than an encounter. Word had reached Rillanon of the battle. The Dark Brothers and their goblin allies had raided into Yabon, overrunning one of the border garrisons, weakened during the war. The Tsurani had turned from their march to Zūn, dashed northward, and relieved the garrison. The Tsurani had fought like madmen to save their former enemies from the larger goblin host, which they had driven back into the mountains north of Yabon.

Laurie winked at Pug. "Having made something of heroes of themselves, our Tsurani friends were given quite a welcome when they arrived here in Rillanon." Being distant from the center of the war, the city's citizens felt little fear or hatred toward their former enemies, giving them a welcome that would have been unimaginable in the Free Cities, in Yabon, or along the Far Coast. "I think Kasumi's men were a little overcome by it all."

"In truth they were," agreed Kasumi. "Such a reception on our homeworld would have been impossible, but here . . ."

"Still," continued Laurie, "they seemed to take it in stride. The men have developed a rapid appreciation for Kingdom wines and ale, and they've even managed to overcome their distaste for tall women."

Kasumi looked away with an embarrassed smile on his face. Laurie said, "Our dashing Knight-Captain was guested a week ago by one of the richer merchant families—one seeking to develop broader trade with the West. He has since been seen often in the company of a certain merchant's daughter."

Katala laughed, and Pug smiled at Kasumi's embarrassment. Pug said, "He was always a quick student."

Kasumi lowered his head, cheeks flushed, but grinning broadly. "Still, it is a hard thing learning that your countrywomen have such freedom.

Now I see why you two were always so strong-willed. You must have learned from your mothers."

Laurie's attention was diverted by someone approaching. Pug noticed a look of open admiration upon the singer's face. The magician turned and was greeted by the sight of a beautiful young woman approaching with a guard escort. Pug's eyes widened as he recognized Carline. She was as lovely a woman as her girlhood had promised. She came up to them and with a wave of her hand dismissed the guard. She looked regal in a fine green gown, with a pearl-studded tiara crowning her dark hair.

"Master magician," she said, "have you no greeting for an old friend?"

Pug bowed before the Princess, and Kasumi and Laurie did also. Katala curtseyed as she had been shown by one of the maids. Pug said, "Princess, you flatter me by remembering a simple keep boy."

Carline smiled, with a gleam in her blue eyes. "Oh, Pug . . . you were never a simple anything." She looked past him to Katala. "Is this your wife?" When he nodded and introduced them, the Princess kissed Katala's cheek and said, "My dear, I had heard you were lovely, but the reports my brother gave did you little justice."

Katala said, "Your Highness is gracious."

Kasumi had returned to his nervous posture, but Laurie stood unable to take his eyes from the young woman in green. Katala had to grip his arm firmly to recapture his attention. "Laurie, will you show Kasumi and me about the palace a little, before the ceremonies begin?"

Laurie smiled broadly, bowed to the Princess, and accompanied Kasumi and Katala down the hallway. Pug and the Princess watched their retreating backs.

Carline said, "Your wife is a most perceptive woman."

Pug smiled. "She is indeed remarkable."

Carline looked genuinely glad to see him. "I understand you also have a son."

"William. He is a little devil, and a treasure."

There was a trace of envy in Carline's expression. "I would like to meet him." She paused, then added, "You've been most fortunate."

"Most fortunate, Highness."

She took his arm and they slowly started to walk. "So formal, Pug? Or should I call you Milamber, as I have heard you were known?"

He saw her smile and returned it. "I sometimes don't know, though here Pug seems more proper." He grinned. "You seem to have learned a great deal about me."

She feigned a small pout. "You were always my favorite magician."

They shared a laugh. Then, lowering his voice, Pug said, "I am so very sorry about your father's death, Carline."

She clouded a little. "Lyam told me you were there at the last. I am glad he saw you safely back before he died. Did you know how much he cared for you?"

Pug felt himself flush with emotion. "He gave me a name; there is little more he could have done to show me. Did you know that?"

She brightened. "Yes, Lyam also told me that. We're cousins of sorts," she said with a laugh. As they walked, she spoke softly. "You were my first love, Pug, but even more, you were always my friend. And I am pleased to see my friend once more home."

He stopped and kissed her lightly upon the cheek. "And your friend is most pleased to be home."

Blushing slightly, she led him to a small garden on a terrace. They walked out into bright sunlight and sat upon a stone bench. Carline let out a long sigh. "I only wish Father and Roland, could be here."

Pug said, "I was also grieved to hear of Roland's death."

She shook her head. "That jester lived as much in his few years as most men do in their entire lives. He hid much behind his raffish ways, but do you know, I think he may have been one of the wisest men I'll ever know. He took every passing minute and squeezed all the life from it he could." Pug studied her face and saw her eyes were bright with memory. "Had he lived, I would have married him. I suspect we would have fought every day, Pug; oh, how he could make me angry. But he could make me laugh as well. He taught me so very much about living. I shall always treasure his memory."

"I am pleased you are at peace with your losses, Carline. So many years a slave, then a magician, in another land have changed me much. It seems you have greatly changed as well."

She tilted her head to look at him. "I don't think you've changed all that much, Pug. There's still some of the boy in you, the one who was so rattled by my attentions."

Pug laughed. "I guess you're right. And in some ways you are also unchanged, or at least you still have the knack of rattling men if friend Laurie's reaction is any measure."

She smiled at him, her face radiant, and Pug knew a faint tugging, an echo of what he had felt when he was a boy. But now there was no discomfort, for he knew he would always love Carline, though not in the way he had imagined as a boy. More than any tumultuous passion, or the deep bond he had with Katala, he knew what he felt was affection and friendship.

She pursued his last comment. "That beautiful blond man who was with you a few minutes ago? Who is he?"

Pug smiled knowingly. "Your most devoted subject, from all appearances. He is Laurie, a troubadour from Tyr-Sog, and a rascal of limitless wit and charm. He has a loving heart and a brave spirit, and is a true friend. I'll tell you sometime of how he saved my life at peril of his own."

Carline again cocked her head to one side. "He sounds a most intriguing fellow." Pug could see that while she was older and more self-possessed and had known sorrow, much about her remained unchanged.

"I once, in jest, promised him an introduction to you. Now I am sure he would be most delighted to make Your Highness's acquaintance."

"Then we must arrange it." She rose. "I fear I must go make ready for the coronation. Any time now the bells will sound and the priests will arrive. We shall speak again, Pug."

Pug came to his feet as well. "I shall enjoy it, Carline."

He presented his arm. A voice from behind said, "Squire Pug, may I speak with you."

They turned around and found Martin Longbow standing some distance away, farther back in the garden. He bowed to the Princess. Carline said, "Master Longbow! There you are. I've not seen you since yesterday."

Martin smiled slightly. "I've had a need to be alone. In Crydee when such a mood strikes, I return to the forest. Here"—he indicated the large terraced garden—"this was the best I could manage."

She looked quizzically at him, but shrugged off the remark. "Well, I expect you will manage to attend the coronation. Now, if you'll excuse me, I must be off." She accepted their polite good-byes and left.

Looking at Pug, Martin said, "It is good to see you once again, Pug."

"And you, Martin. Of all my old friends here, you are the last to greet me. Except for those still in Crydee I've yet to see, you've made my homecoming complete." Pug could see Martin was troubled. "Is something wrong?"

Martin looked out over the garden, toward the city and sea beyond. "Lyam told me, Pug. He told me you know as well."

Pug understood at once. "I was there when your father died, Martin," he said, his voice remaining calm.

In silence Martin began to walk, and when he came to the low stone wall around the garden he gripped it hard. "My father," he said, bitterly. "How many years I waited for him to say, 'Martin, I am your father.' " He swallowed hard. "I never cared for inheritance and such things. I was content to remain Huntmaster of Crydee. If only he had told me himself."

Pug thought over his next words. "Martin, many men do things they regret later. Only a few are granted the opportunity to make amends. Had a Tsurani arrow taken him quickly, had a hundred other things come to pass, he might not have had the chance to do what little he did."

"I know, but still that is cold comfort."

"Did Lyam tell you his last words? He said, 'Martin is your brother. I have wronged him, Lyam. He is a good man, and well do I love him.' "

Martin's knuckles turned white gripping the stone wall. Quietly he replied, "No, he did not."

"Lord Borric was not a simple man, Martin, and I was only a boy when I knew him, but whatever else may be said of him, there was no meanness of spirit in the man. I don't pretend to understand why he acted as he did, but that he loved you is certain."

"It was all such folly. I knew he was my father, and he never knew I had been told by Mother. What difference in our lives had I gone to him and proclaimed myself?"

"Only the gods might know." He reached out and touched Martin's arm. "What matters now is what you will do. That Lyam told you means he will make public your birthright. If he's already told others, the court will be in an uproar. You are the eldest and have the right of first claim. Do you know what you will do?"

Studying Pug, Martin said, "You speak calmly enough of this. Doesn't my claim to the throne disturb you at all?"

Pug shook his head. "You would have no way of knowing, but I was counted among the most powerful men in Tsuranuanni. My word was in some ways more important than any king's command. I think I know what power can do, and what sort of men seek it. I doubt you have much personal ambition as such, unless you've changed a great deal since I lived in Crydee. If you take the crown, it will be for what you believe are good reasons. It may be the only way to prevent civil war, for should you choose the mantle of King, Lyam will be the first to swear fealty. Whatever the reason, you would do your best to act wisely. And if you take the purple, you will do your best to be a good ruler."

Martin looked impressed. "You have changed much, Squire Pug, more than I would have expected. I thank you for your kind judgment of me, but I think you are the only man in the Kingdom who would believe such."

"Whatever the truth may be, you are your father's son and would not bring dishonor upon his house."

Again Martin's words were tinged with bitterness. "There are those who will judge my birth itself a dishonor." He looked out over the city below, then turned to stare at Pug. "If only the choice were simple, but Lyam's seen that it is not. If I take the crown, many will balk. If I renounce in Lyam's favor, some may use me as an excuse to refuse Lyam their allegiance.

"Gods above, Pug. Were the issue between Arutha and myself, I would not hesitate for an instant to stand aside in his favor. But Lyam? I've not seen him for seven years, and those years have changed him. He seems a man beset with doubts. An able field commander, no question, but a king? I am faced with the fearful prospect I would prove a more able king."

Pug spoke softly. "As I have said, should you claim the throne, you will do so for what you judge good reasons, reasons of duty."

Martin's right hand closed into a fist, held before his face. "Where ends duty and begins personal ambition? Where ends justice and begins revenge? There is a part of me, an angry part of me, that says, 'Wring all you can from this moment, Martin.' Why not King Martin? And then another part of me wonders if Father may have placed this upon me knowing someday I must be King. Oh, Pug, what is my duty?"

"That is something each of us must judge for himself alone. I can offer you no counsel."

Martin leaned forward upon the rail, hands covering his face. "I think I would like to be alone for a time, if you do not mind."

Pug left, knowing a troubled man considered his fate. And the fate of the Kingdom.

PUG FOUND KATALA with Laurie and Kasumi, speaking with Duke Brucal and Earl Vandros. As he approached, he could hear the Duke saying, "So we'll finally have a wedding, now that this young slow-wit"—he indicated Vandros—"has asked for my daughter's hand. Maybe I'll have some grandchildren before I die, after all. See what comes of waiting so many years to marry. You're old before your children marry—" He inclined his head when he saw Pug. "Ah, magician, there you are."

Katala smiled when she saw her husband. "Did you and the Princess have a nice reunion?"

"Very nice."

Prodding him in the chest with her forefinger, she said, "And when we're alone, you'll repeat every single word."

The others laughed at Pug's embarrassment, though he could see she was only having fun with him.

Brucal said, "Ah, magician, your wife is so lovely, I wish I were sixty again." He winked at Pug. "Then I'd steal her from you, and damn the scandal." He took Pug by the arm and said to Katala, "If you'll forgive me, lady, instead I'll have to steal a moment of your husband's time."

He steered Pug away from the surprised group and when they were out of earshot said, "I have grave news."

"I know."

"Lyam is a fool, a noble fool." He looked away for a moment, his eyes filming over with memory. "But he is his father's son, and his grandfather's grandson as well, and like both before him has a strong sense of honor." The old eyes came into sharp focus again. "Still, I wish his sense of duty were as clear." Lowering his voice even more, he said, "Keep your wife close about. The guards in the hall wear the purple and will die defending the King, whoever he may be. But it may get messy. Many of the eastern lords are impulsive men, overly used to having their petty demands instantly gratified. A few might open their mouths and find themselves chewing steel.

"My men and Vandros's are positioned throughout the palace, while Kasumi's Tsurani are outside, at Lyam's request. The eastern lords don't like it, but Lyam is Heir, and they cannot say no. With those who will stand with us, we can seize the palace and hold it.

"With du Bas-Tyra hiding, and Richard of Salador dead, the eastern lords have lost their leadership. But there are enough of them on the island, with enough of their 'honor guards' in and around the city, to turn this island into a pretty battleground should they flee the palace before a king is named. No, we'll hold the palace. No traitorous easterner will leave to plot treason with Black Guy. Each one will bend a knee before whichever brother takes the crown."

Pug was surprised by this. "You'll support Martin, then?"

Old Brucal's voice became harsh, though he kept it low. "No one will plunge my Kingdom into civil war, magician. Not while I have a breath left to spend. Arutha and I have spoken. Neither of us likes the choices, but we are clear on our course. Should Martin be King, all will bow before him. Should Lyam take the crown, Martin will swear fealty or not leave the palace alive. Should the crown be broken, we hold this palace, and no lord leaves until a congress has named one brother King, even if we're a year in that bloody damned hall. We've already picked up several of Guy's agents in the city. He's here in Rillanon, there's no doubt. If even a handful of nobles can win free of the palace before a congress is convened, we have civil war." He struck his fist into his open hand. "Damn these traditions. As we speak, the priests walk toward the palace, each step bringing them closer to the moment of choice. If only

Lyam had acted sooner, given us more time, or not acted at all. Or if we could have caged Guy. If we could have spoken to Martin, but he's vanished. . . ."

"I've spoken to Martin."

Brucal's eyes narrowed. "What is his mood? What are his plans?"

"He's a troubled man, as well you might imagine. To have all this put upon him with scant time to adjust. He has always known who his father was, and was resigned to take the secret with him to the grave, I'll wager, but now he is suddenly thrust into the heart of the matter. I don't know what he will do. I don't think he'll know, until the priests put the crown before him."

Brucal stroked his chin. "That he knew and tried not to use that knowledge for his own gain speaks well of him. But there's still no time." He indicated the group by the main door to the hall. "You'd best be back to your wife. Keep your wits sharp, magician, for we may have need of your arts before this day is through."

They returned to the others, and Brucal led Vandros and Kasumi inside, speaking with them in low tones. Before Katala could speak, Laurie said, "What is afoot? When I took Katala and Kasumi outside to a balcony overlooking the courtyard, I saw Kasumi's men everywhere. For a moment I thought the Empire had won the war. I couldn't get a thing from him."

Pug said, "Brucal knows they can be trusted to follow Kasumi's orders without question."

Katala said, "What is this, husband? Trouble?"

"There is little time to explain. There may be more than one claimant to the crown. Stay near Kasumi, Laurie, and keep your sword loose. If there's trouble, follow Arutha's lead."

Laurie nodded, his face set in a grim expression of understanding. He entered the hall, and Katala said, "William?"

"He is safe. If there is trouble it will be in the great hall, not in the guest quarters. It will be afterward the true grief will begin." Her expression showed she didn't understand fully, but she quietly accepted what he said. "Come, we must take our places inside."

They hurried into the great hall, to a place of honor near the front. As they passed by the throng gathered to see the King crowned, they could hear the buzz of voices as rumor swept the room. They came up to Kulgan, and the stout magician nodded greeting. Meecham waited a few paces behind, his back to a wall. His eyes surveyed the room, marking the positions of all within a sword's length of Kulgan. Pug noticed the old, long-bladed hunter's knife was loose in its scabbard. He might not know what the problem was, but he would be instantly ready to protect his old companion.

Kulgan hissed, "What is going on? Everything was calm until a few minutes ago; now the room is abuzz."

Pug leaned his head closer to Kulgan's and said, "Martin may announce for the crown."

Kulgan's eyes widened. "Gods and fishes! That'll set this court on its ear." He looked around and saw most of the Kingdom's nobles had taken their places within the hall. With a sigh of regret he said, "It's too late to do anything now but wait."

AMOS CRASHED THROUGH the garden, swearing furiously. "Why the hell does anyone want all these bloody posies about anyway?"

Martin looked up and barely caught the crystal goblet thrust at him by Amos Trask. "What—" he said, as Amos filled it with wine from a crystal decanter he held.

"Thought you might be in need of a bracer, and a shipmate to share it with."

Martin's eyes narrowed. "What do you mean?"

Amos filled his own goblet and took a long pull. "It's all over the palace now, fellow-me-lad. Lyam's a good enough sort, but he's got rocks for ballast if he thinks he can have a crew of stonecutters put your name on your father's tomb, then hush them up with something as petty as a royal command. Every servant in the palace knew you were the new first mate within an hour after those boys finished work. It's all up in the wind, you can believe me."

Martin drank the wine and said, "Thank you, Amos." He studied the deep red wine in the glass. "Shall I be King?"

Amos laughed, a good-natured, hearty sound. "I have two thoughts on that, Martin. First, it's always better to be captain than deckhand, which is why I'm a captain and not a deckhand. Second, there's some difference between a ship and a kingdom."

Martin laughed. "Pirate, you're no help at all."

Amos looked stung. "Blast me, I got you to laugh, didn't I?" He leaned over, resting an elbow on the garden wall while he poured more wine into his cup. "See here, there's this pretty little three-master in the royal harbor. I've not had much time, but with the King's pardon being declared, there's plenty of good lads fresh from the brig who'd jump to sail with Captain Trenchard. Why don't we cast off from here and go a'roving?"

Martin shook his head. "That sounds fine. I've been on a ship three times in my life, and with you I nearly got killed all three times."

Amos looked injured. "The first two times were Arutha's fault, and the third time wasn't my fault. I didn't send those Ceresian pirates to chase us from Salador to Rillanon. Besides, if you sign aboard with me, we'll do the chasing. The Kingdom Sea's a whole new sea for Trenchard to sail. What do you say?"

Martin's voice turned somber. "No, Amos, though I'd almost as soon sail with you as return to the forest. But what I must decide cannot be run from. For good or ill, I am the eldest son, and I have the first claim to the crown." Martin looked hard at Amos. "Do you think Lyam can be King?"

Amos shook his head. "Of course, but that's not the question, is it? What you want to know is, can Lyam be a good King? I don't know, Martin. But I'll tell you one thing. I've seen many a sailor gone pale with fear in battle, yet fight without hesitation. Sometimes you can't know what a man's capable of until the time comes for him to act." Amos paused for a moment, considering his words. "Lyam's a good enough sort, as I said. He's scared silly of becoming King, and I don't blame him. But once upon the throne . . . I think he could be a good enough King."

"I wish I could know you were right."

A chime sounded, then great bells began to ring. "Well," said Amos, "you don't have much time left to decide. The Priests of Ishap are at the outer gates, and when they reach the throne room, there's no cutting grapples and sailing away. Your course will be set."

Martin turned away from the wall. "Thank you for your company, Amos, and the wine. Shall we go change the fate of the Kingdom?"

Amos drank the last of the wine from the crystal decanter. He tossed it aside and over the sound of shattering glass said, "You go decide the fate of the Kingdom, Martin. I'll come along later, perhaps, if I can't arrange for that little ship I spoke of. Maybe we'll sail together again. If you change your mind about being King, or decide you're in need of quick transportation from Rillanon, fetch yourself down to the docks before sundown. I'll be about somewhere, and you'll always be welcome in my crew."

Martin gripped his hand tightly. "Always fare well, pirate."

Amos left and Martin stood alone, ordering his thoughts as best he could, then, making his decision, he began his journey to the throne room.

▼▼

BY CRANING his neck, Pug could see those entering the great hall. Duke Caldric escorted Erland's widow, Princess Alicia, down the long isle toward the throne. Anita and Carline followed. From Kulgan came the observation, "By those grim expressions and pale complexions, I wager Arutha has told them what may come."

Pug noticed how Anita held tightly to Carline's hand when they reached their appointed places. "What a thing, to discover you've an elder brother in these circumstances."

Kulgan whispered, "They all seem to be taking it well enough."

Gongs announced the Ishapian priests had entered the anteroom, and Arutha and Lyam entered. Both wore the red mantles of Princes of the Realm and walked quickly to the front of the hall. Arutha's eyes darted around the room, as if trying to judge the temper of those on all sides. Lyam looked calm, as if somehow resigned to accept whatever fate brought.

Pug saw Arutha whisper a short word to Fannon, and the old Swordmaster in turn spoke to Sergeant Gardan. Both looked about tensely, hands near sword hilts, watching everyone in the room.

Pug could see no sign of Martin. He whispered to Kulgan, "Perhaps Martin has decided to avoid the issue."

Kulgan looked about. "No, there he is."

Pug saw where Kulgan indicated with a bob of his head. By the far wall, near a corner, a giant column rose. Standing deep within its shadow was Martin. His features were hidden, but his stance was unmistakable.

Bells began to chime, and Pug looked to see the first of the Ishapian priests entering the great hall. Behind, others followed, all walking in unison at the same measured pace. From the side doors came the sound of bolts being driven into place, for the hall traditionally was sealed from the start of the ceremony to its end.

When sixteen priests had entered the room, the great doors were closed behind. The last priest paused before the door, a heavy wooden staff in one hand and a large wax seal in the other. Quickly he affixed the seal to the doors. Pug could see that the seal bore the seven-sided device of Ishap inscribed upon it, and he felt the presence of magic within it. He knew the doors could not be opened save by the one who affixed the seal, or by another of high arts, and then at great risk.

When the doors were sealed, the priest with the staff walked forward between the lines of his brother priests, who waited, incanting soft prayers. One held the new crown, fashioned by the priests, resting upon a cushion of purple velvet. Rodric's crown had been destroyed by the blow that had ended his life, but had it survived, according to custom it would have been interred with him. Should no new King be crowned today, this new crown would be smashed upon the stones of the floor, and no new one made until the Congress of Lords informed the priests they had elected a new king. Pug marveled how much importance could be attached to such a simple circlet of gold.

The priests moved forward, to stand before the throne, where other priests of the lesser orders were already waiting. As was the custom, Lyam had been asked if he wished his family priest to officiate at the investiture, and he had agreed. Father Tully stood at the head of the delegation from the Temple of Astalon. Pug knew the old priest would be quick to take charge of things without question, regardless of which of Borric's sons took the crown, and counted it a wise choice.

The chief Ishapian priest struck his staff upon the floor, sixteen even, measured blows. The sound rang through the hall, and when he was done, the throne room was silent.

"We come to crown the King!" exclaimed the head priest.

"Ishap bless the King!" answered the other priests.

"In the name of Ishap, the one god over all, and in the name of the four greater and twelve lesser gods, let all who have claim to the crown come forth."

Pug found himself holding his breath as he saw Lyam and Arutha come to stand before the priests. A moment later Martin stepped from the shadows and walked forward.

As Martin came into view, there was a hissing of intaken breath, for many in the hall had either not heard the rumor or not believed it.

When all three were before the priest, he struck the floor with the heavy staff. "Now is the hour and here is the place." He then touched Martin upon the shoulder with his staff, resting it there as he said, "By what right do you come before us?"

Martin spoke in a clear, strong voice. "By right of birth." Pug could feel the presence of magic. The priests were not leaving the claims to the throne subject to honor and tradition alone. Touched by the staff, no one could bear false witness.

The same procedure was repeated and the same answer given by Lyam and Arutha.

Again the staff rested upon Martin's shoulder as the priest asked, "State your name and your claim."

Martin's voice rang out. "I am Martin, eldest son of Borric, eldest of the royal blood."

A slight buzzing ran through the hall, silenced by the priest's staff striking the floor. The staff was placed upon Lyam's shoulder, and he answered, "I am Lyam, son of Borric, of the royal blood."

A few voices could be heard saying, "The Heir!"

The priest hesitated, then repeated the question to Arutha, who answered, "I am Arutha, son of Borric, of the royal blood."

The priest looked at the three young men, then to Lyam said, "Are you the acknowledged Heir?"

Lyam answered with the staff resting upon his shoulder. "The right of succession was given to me in ignorance of Martin. It is a false bequest, for Rodric thought me the eldest conDoin male."

The priest removed the staff and conferred with his fellow priests. The hall remained silent as the priests gathered together to discuss the unforeseen turn of events. Time passed torturously, until at last the chief priest turned once more to face them. He surrendered his staff and was handed the golden circle that was the crown of the Kingdom. He uttered a brief prayer: "Ishap, give all before us in this matter guidance and wisdom. Let the appointed one do right." In a strong voice he said, "That the succession is flawed is clear." He placed the crown before Martin. "Martin, as eldest son of the royal blood you have the right of first claim. Will you, Martin, take up this burden, and will you be our King?"

Martin looked at the crown. Silence hung heavy in the room as every eye was fixed upon the tall man in green. Breath was held as the throng in the hall waited upon his answer.

Then Martin slowly reached out and took the crown from the cushion upon which it rested. He raised it up, and every gaze in the room followed it, as it caught a ray of light entering through a high window, scattering glittering glory throughout the hall.

Holding it above his head, he said, "I, Martin, do hereby abdicate my claim to the crown of the Kingdom of the Isles, for now and forever, on my own behalf and on behalf of all my issue from now henceforth to the last generation." He moved suddenly and placed the crown upon Lyam's brow. Martin's voice rang out once more, his words a defiant challenge. "All hail Lyam! True and undoubted King!"

There was a pause, as those in the hall took in what they had seen. Then Arutha faced a stunned, silent crowd, and his voice filled the air. "Hail Lyam! True and undoubted King!"

Lyam stood flanked by his brothers, one to each side, and the hall erupted into shouts and cheers. "Hail Lyam! Hail the King!"

The chief priest let the shouting continue for a time, then recovered his staff and struck the floor, bringing silence. He looked at Lyam and said, "Will you, Lyam, take up this burden and be our King?"

Looking at the priest, Lyam answered, "I will be your King."

Again the room sounded with cheers, and the chief priest let the din go unchecked. Pug looked and saw relief on the faces of many, Brucal, Caldric, Fannon, Vandros, and Gardan, all who had stood ready to face trouble.

Again the head priest silenced the room with the striking of his staff. "Tully of the order of Astalon," he called, and the old family priest stepped forward.

Other priests removed Lyam's red mantle, replacing it with the purple mantle of kingship. The priests stepped away, and Tully came before Lyam. To Martin and Arutha he said, "All in the Kingdom thank you for your forbearance and wisdom." The brothers left Lyam's side and returned to stand with Anita and Carline.

Carline smiled warmly at Martin, took his hand, and whispered, "Thank you, Martin."

Tully faced the crowd and intoned, "Now is the hour and here is the place. We are here to witness the coronation of His Majesty, Lyam, first of that name, as our true King. Is there any here who challenge his right?"

Several eastern lords looked unhappy, but no objection was raised. Tully again faced Lyam, who went on his knees before the priest. Tully placed his hand upon Lyam's head. "Now is the hour and here is the place. It is to you this burden has fallen, Lyam, first of that name, son of Borric, of the conDoin line of kings. Will you take up this burden and will you be our King?"

Lyam answered, "I will be your King."

Tully removed his hand from Lyam's head and reached down to take his hand, gripping the royal signet upon it. "Now is the hour and here is the place. Do you, Lyam conDoin, son of Borric, of the line of kings, swear to defend and protect the Kingdom of the Isles, faithfully serving her people, to provide for their welfare, weal, and prosperity?"

"I, Lyam, do so swear and avow."

Tully began a long liturgy, then when the prayers were done, Lyam rose. Tully removed his ritual miter and handed it to the Head Priest of Ishap, who passed it along to another of Tully's order. Tully knelt before Lyam and kissed his signet. He then rose and escorted Lyam to the throne, while the Ishapian priest incanted, "Ishap bless the King!"

Lyam sat. An ancient sword, once carried by Dannis, the first conDoin King, was brought to him and rested across his knees, a sign he would defend the Kingdom with his life.

Tully turned and nodded to the Chief Priest of Ishap, who struck the floor with his staff. "Now it is past, the hour of our choosing. I hereby proclaim Lyam the First our right, true, and undisputed King."

The crowd responded with a roar. "Hail Lyam! Long live the King!"

The Priests of Ishap chanted low, and the chief priest led them to the door. He struck the wax seal with his staff, and it split with a cracking sound. He struck the door three times more, and the guards outside opened it. Before stepping out, he intoned the last phrase of the ritual of coronation. To those outside the hall, not privileged to watch the ceremony, he announced, "Let the word go forth. Lyam is our King!"

Faster than a bird's flight, the word went out of the hall, through the palace, and into the city. Celebrants in the street toasted the new monarch, and not one in a thousand knew how close disaster had come to visiting the Kingdom this day.

The Ishapian priests left the hall, and all eyes returned to the new ruler of the Kingdom.

Tully motioned to the members of the royal family, and Arutha, Martin, and Carline came before their brother. Lyam extended his hand, and Martin knelt and kissed his brother's signet. Arutha followed, then Carline.

Alicia led Anita to the throne, the first of the long line of nobles who followed, and the lengthy business of accepting the fealty of the peers of the realm began. Lord Caldric bent a trembling knee to his King, and there were tears of relief upon his face as he rose. When Brucal swore his loyalty, he briefly spoke to the King as he stood, and Lyam nodded.

Then in turn came the other nobles of the Kingdom until, hours later, the last of the Border Barons, those guardians of the Northern Marches, vassal to no Lord but the King, rose and returned to stand with the others in the hall.

Handing the sword of Dannis to a waiting page, Lyam stood and said, "It is our wish that a time of celebration be at hand. But there are matters of state that must be attended to at once. Most are of a happy nature, but first there is one sad duty that must be discharged.

"There is one absent today, one who sought to gain the throne upon which we are privileged to sit. That Guy du Bas-Tyra did plot treason cannot be denied. That he did commit foul murder is unquestioned. But it was the late King's wish that mercy be shown in this matter. As it was Rodric's dying request, I shall grant this boon, though it would be our pleasure to see Guy du Bas-Tyra pay in full for his deeds.

"Let the word go from this day that Guy du Bas-Tyra is named outlaw and banished from our Kingdom, his titles and lands forfeit to the crown. Let his name and arms be stricken from the role of Lords of the Kingdom. Let no man offer him shelter, fire, food, or water." To the assembled lords he added, "Some here have been allied with the former

Duke, so we have little doubt he will hear our judgment. Tell him to flee, to go to Kesh, Queg, or Roldem. Tell him to hide in the Northlands if no other will take him, but should he be found inside our borders within a week's time, his life is forfeit."

No one in the hall spoke for a moment, then Lyam said, "It has been a time of great sorrow and suffering in our realms; now let us embark upon a new era, one of peace and prosperity." He indicated that his two brothers should return to his side, and as they approached, Arutha looked at Martin. Suddenly he grinned and, in an unexpected display of emotion, hugged both Martin and Lyam. For a brief instant all in the hall were silent as the three brothers clung closely to one another, then again cheers filled the room.

While the clamor continued, Lyam spoke to his brothers. At first Martin smiled broadly, then suddenly his expression changed. Both Arutha and Lyam nodded vigorously, but Martin's face drained of color. He started to say something, his manner intense and remonstrative. Lyam cut him off and held up his hand for silence.

"There is a new ordering of things in our Kingdom. Let it be known that from this day forward, our beloved brother Arutha is Prince of Krondor, and until such time as there is a son in our house, Heir to the throne." At the last, Arutha seemed less than pleased. Then Lyam said, "And it is our wish that the Duchy of Crydee, home of our father, stay within our family so long as his line remains. To this end I name Martin, our beloved brother, Duke of Crydee, with all lands, titles, and rights pertaining thereunto."

A cheer again rose from the crowd. Martin and Arutha left Lyam's side, and the new King said, "Let the Earl of LaMut and Knight-Captain Kasumi of LaMut approach the throne."

Kasumi and Vandros started. Kasumi had been nervous all day, for Vandros had placed a great trust in him. His Tsurani impassivity asserted itself, and he fell in beside Vandros as he reached the throne.

Both men knelt before Lyam, who said, "My lord Brucal has asked us to make this happy announcement. His vassal the Earl Vandros will wed his daughter, the Lady Felinah."

From the crowd Brucal's voice could be heard clearly saying, "And it's about time." Several of the older courtiers from Rodric's court blanched, but Lyam joined in the general laughter.

"It is also the Duke's wish that he be allowed to retire to his estates, where he may seek the rewards of a long and useful service to his Kingdom. We have given consent. And as he has no son, it is also his wish that his title pass to one able to continue in the service of the

Kingdom, one who has shown uncommon ability in commanding the LaMutian garrison of the Armies of the West during the late conflict. For his many brave actions and his faithful service, we hereby approve his marriage and are pleased to name Vandros Duke of Yabon, with all lands, titles, and rights pertaining thereunto. Rise, Lord Vandros."

Vandros rose, a little shaken, then returned to the side of his father-in-law-to-be. Brucal struck him a friendly blow on the back and gripped his hand. Lyam turned his attention to Kasumi and smiled. "There is one here before us who was recently counted our enemy. He is now counted as our loyal subject. Kasumi of the Shinzawai, for your efforts to bring peace to two warring worlds, and your wisdom and courage in the defense of our lands against the Brotherhood of the Dark Path, we give to you command of the garrison of LaMut, and name you Earl of LaMut, with all lands, titles, and rights pertaining thereunto. Rise, Earl Kasumi."

Kasumi was speechless. He slowly reached out and took the King's hand, as he had seen the other nobles do, and kissed the signet. To the King he said, "My lord King, my life and my honor do I pledge."

Lyam said, "My lord Vandros, do you accept Earl Kasumi as your vassal?"

Vandros grinned. "Happily, Sire."

Kasumi rejoined Vandros, his eyes illuminated by pride. Brucal administered another hearty slap on the back.

Several more offices were given, for there were vacancies from the intrigues of Rodric's court and from deaths in the war. When it seemed all business was over, Lyam said, "Let Squire Pug of Crydee approach the throne."

Pug looked at Katala and Kulgan, surprised at being called. "What . . . ?"

Kulgan pushed him forward. "Go and find out."

Pug came before Lyam and bowed. The King said, "What has been done was a private matter, between our father and this man. Now it is our wish all in our realm know that this man, once called Pug, the orphan of Crydee, has had his name inscribed upon the rolls of our family." He held out his hand, and Pug knelt before him. Lyam presented his signet and then took Pug by the shoulders and bade him rise. "As it was our father's wish, so it is ours. From this day let all in our Kingdom know this man is Pug conDoin, member of the King's family."

Many in the hall were surprised by Pug's adoption and elevation, but those who knew of his exploits cheered lustily as Lyam said, "Behold our cousin Pug, Prince of the Realm."

Katala ignored all propriety and ran forward to embrace her husband. Several of the eastern lords frowned, but Lyam laughed and kissed her upon the cheek.

"Come!" Lyam cried. "It is now time for celebration. Let the dancers, musicians, and tumblers come forth. Let tables be brought and food and wine be placed upon them. Let merriment reign!"

THE FESTIVITIES CONTINUED. Celebration had run unchecked throughout the afternoon. A herald next to the King's table read messages to the King from those unable to attend, many nobles and the King of Queg, as well as monarchs of the small kingdoms of the eastern shores. Important merchants and Guildmasters from the Free Cities also sent congratulations. There were also messages from Aglaranna and Tomas, and from the dwarves of the West at Stone Mountain and the Grey Towers. Old King Halfdan, ruler of the dwarves of the East in Dorgin, sent his best wishes, and even Great Kesh had sent greetings, with a request for more meetings to settle peacefully the issue of the Vale of Dreams. The message was personally signed by the Empress.

Hearing the last message, Lyam said to Arutha, "For Kesh to have sent us a personal message in so short a time, the Empress must boast the most gifted spies in Midkemia. You'll have to keep your wits about you in Krondor."

Arutha sighed, not happy at that prospect. Pug, Laurie, Meecham, Gardan, Kulgan, Fannon, and Kasumi all sat at the royal table. Lyam had insisted they join the royal family. The new Earl of LaMut still seemed in shock at his office, but his happiness was clearly showing, and even in this noisy hall the sound of his warriors outside singing Tsurani songs of celebration could be faintly heard. Pug mused over the discomfort that must be causing the royal porters and pages.

Katala joined her husband, reporting their son napping, and Fantus as well, exhausted from play. Katala said to Kulgan, "I hope your pet will be able to withstand such constant aggravation."

Kulgan laughed. "Fantus thrives on the attention."

Pug said, "With all those rewards being passed out, Kulgan, I'm surprised there was no mention of you. You've given faithful service to the King's family as long as anyone save Tully and Fannon."

Kulgan snorted. "Tully, Fannon, and I all met with Lyam yesterday, before we knew he was going to acknowledge Martin and throw the court into turmoil. He began to mumble something or another about offices and rewards and such, but we all begged off. When he began to protest, I told him I didn't care what he did for Tully and Fannon, but if he tried to haul me up before all those people, I'd straightway turn him into a toad."

Anita, overhearing the exchange, laughed. "So it is true!"

Pug, remembering the conversation he had with Anita in Krondor, so many years ago, joined in the merriment. He looked back on all that had occurred to him in the years since he had first chanced to come to Kulgan's cottage in the forests, and reflected for a moment. After much risk and many conflicts he was safe with family and friends, with a great adventure, the building of the academy, yet to come. He wished that a few others—Hochopepa, Shimone, Kamatsu, Hokanu, as well as Almorella and Netoha—could share in his happiness. And he wished Ichindar and the Lords of the High Council could know the true reason for the betrayal on the day of peace. And most of all, he wished Tomas could have joined them.

"So thoughtful, husband?"

Pug snapped out of his mood and smiled. "Beloved, I was thinking that in all things I am a most fortunate man."

His wife placed her hand upon his and returned his smile. Tully leaned across the table and inclined his head toward the other end, where Laurie sat enraptured by Carline, who was laughing at some witticism he had made. It was obvious she found him as charming as Pug had promised; in fact, she looked captivated. Pug said, "I think I recognize that expression on Carline's face. I think Laurie may be in for some trouble."

Kasumi said, "Knowing friend Laurie, it is a trouble he will welcome."

Tully looked thoughtful. "There is a duchy at Bas-Tyra now in need of a duke, and he does seem a competent enough young man. Hmmm."

Kulgan barked, "Enough! Haven't you had your fill of pomp? Must you go marrying the poor lad off to the King's sister so you can officiate in the palace again? Gods! They just met today!"

Tully and Kulgan seemed about to launch into another of their famous debates when Martin cut them both off. "Let us change the subject. My head is awhirl, and we don't need your bickering."

Tully and Kulgan exchanged startled looks, then both smiled. As one they said, "Yes, my lord."

Martin groaned while those close by joined in the laughter. Martin shook his head. "This seems so strange, after so much fear and worry such a short time back. Why, I nearly chose to go with Amos—" He looked up. "Where is Amos?"

Upon hearing the seaman's name, Arutha also looked up from his conversation with Anita. "Where is that pirate?"

Martin answered. "He said something about arranging for a ship. I thought he was only making light, but I haven't seen him since the coronation."

Arutha said, "Arranging for a ship! The gods weep!" He stood and said, "With Your Majesty's permission."

Lyam said, "Go and fetch him back. From all you have told me, he warrants some reward."

Martin stood and said, "I'll ride with you."

Arutha smiled. "Gladly."

The two brothers hurried from the hall, making quick time to the courtyard. Porters and pages held horses for guests departing early. Arutha and Martin grabbed the first two in line, unceremoniously leaving two minor nobles without mounts. The two noblemen stood with mouths open, caught halfway between anger and amazement. "Your pardon, my lords," shouted Arutha as he galloped his horse toward the gate.

As they rode through the gates of the palace, across the arched bridge over the river Rillanon, Martin said, "He said he would sail at sundown!"

"That gives us scant time!" shouted Arutha. Down winding streets they flew to the harbor.

The city was thick with celebrants, and several times they had to slow to avoid harming those who crowded the streets. They reached the harborside and pulled up their mounts.

A single guard sat as if sleeping before the entrance to the royal docks. Arutha jumped down from his horse and jostled the man. The guard's helm fell from his head as he toppled over, slumping to the ground. Arutha checked him and said, "He's alive, but he'll have a head on him tomorrow."

Arutha remounted and they hurried along Rillanon's long dockside to the last wharf. Shouts from men in the rigging of a ship greeted them as they turned their horses toward the end of a long pier.

A beautiful vessel was slowly moving away from the docks, and as they pulled up, Martin and Arutha could see Amos Trask standing upon the quarterdeck. He waved high above his head, still close enough so they could see his grinning face. "Ha! It seems all ends well!"

Arutha and Martin dismounted as the distance between ship and pier slowly lengthened. "Amos!" shouted Arutha.

Amos pointed at a distant building. "The boys who stood watch here are all in that warehouse. They're a little bruised, but they're alive."

"Amos! That's the King's ship!" yelled Arutha, waving for the ship to put back.

Amos Trask laughed. "I thought the *Royal Swallow* a grand name. Well, tell your brother I'll return it someday."

Martin began to laugh. Then Arutha joined in. "You pirate!" shouted the youngest brother. "I'll have him give it to you."

With a deep cry of despair, Amos said, "Ah, Arutha, you take all the fun out of life!"